Epic of Ahiram

༂༄

Book Two

Wrath of the Urkuun

Books By Michael Joseph Murano

Epic of Ahiram

Book One - Age of the Seer

Book Two - Wrath of the Urkuun

Epic of Ahiram

☙☙

Book Two

Wrath of the Urkuun

Michael Joseph Murano
Candle Bright Books
EpicOfAhiram.com/WrathOfTheUrkuun

Copyright © Wrath of the Urkuun Michael J. Murano.
Published in the United States by Candle Bright Books in Wrath of the Urkuun.
All rights reserved.
This book, or parts thereof may not be reproduced in any form without permission in writing from the publisher, Candle Bright Books, 1451 N. Ivy Street, Suite 201, Escondido, CA 92026. The scanning, uploading and distribution of this book via the Internet or via any other means without the permission of the publisher is illegal and punishable by law.
Please purchase only authorized electronic editions, and do not participate in or encourage electronic privacy of copyrighted materials. Your support of the author's rights is appreciated. The publisher does not have any control over and does not assume any responsibility for author or third-party websites or their contents.
Printed in the United States of America.
Text set in Adobe Jenson.
Book cover by Maria Bowman

Murano, Michael (Michael Joseph) Wrath of the Urkuun/ Michael J. Murano. – 1st American ed.
p. cm. – (The Epic of Ahiram; bk. 2)

ISBN: 978-0-9913200-3-5

0 1 1 2 3 5 8 13 21 34

Wrath of the Urkuun

To Team Ahiram

*To your unwavering generosity
perseverance and dedication*

Thank you

Content

Maps i

Part One: Xarg-Ulum
1. Wings of Light 1
2. Crossing 19
3. Wings of Shame 35
4. Orwutt and Zurwott 52
5. Rescue Mission 73
6. Counceling Council 90
7. Sacrifice to a Béghôm 115
8. Recovery 135
9. Northbound 154

Part Two: Ashod's Choice
10. Southbound 174
11. Tyrulan 193
12. Contact 209
13. Fire-Storm 225
14. Permission To Kill 240
15. Tirkalanzibar 262

Part Three: Middle Road
16. Magdala 283
17. Northern Plains 300
18. Undying Love 314
19. Gaëla Meïr Pen 338
20. Sylveeds Prowling 357
21. Confluence 383
22. Northern Council 401
23. Broken Sheath 418

Part Four: Battle of Hardeen
24. Jaguar Night 434
25. Trapped 457
26. Hardeen 479
27. Revelation 496
28. Guiding Light 514
29. Sylveedian Pool 536
30. God-Crusher 550
31. Come What May 572
32. Departure 593

Glossary 607
About the Author 617

Acknowledgment

I wish to thank, first and foremost, my editors, Melanie Gambrell and Anouk Mouawad for their dedication and love of the written word. Their unwavering and relentless effort has turned my initial manuscript into this published book.

I would like to thank Maria Bowman, our graphic artist, for the eye-catching and professional cover gracing the front of the book, and Rich Evert for so graciously lending his talent and voice for the audible version of *Wrath of the Urkuun*.

I would like to thank the rest of the members of Team Ahiram for their constant dedication, hard work, and determination that saw this book through.

Finally, to the members of our beta-team, to all those who read the book and provided feedback, thank you.

*Twenty-two uncreated Letters of supernal power
To free from the Bottomless Pit the Lords of Darkness.
Their sleepless malice stirs beneath the mighty fallen tower,
Yearning to fill the hearts of men with madness.*

In the raging Pit of Fire and everlasting darkness. Standing before the dawn of the second Age of Blood,

*Facing the terror of the Pit at the final hour,
A Seer alone will rise to stem the raging flood,
Commanding the twenty-two Letters of supernal power. In the raging Pit of Fire and everlasting darkness*

Maps

1. A Brief Overview of the World of Ahiram
2. Finikia, the Land of Ahiram
3. The Kingdom of Tanniin
4. From Bar Tanic to Thermodon
5. From Gordion to Tirkalanzibar

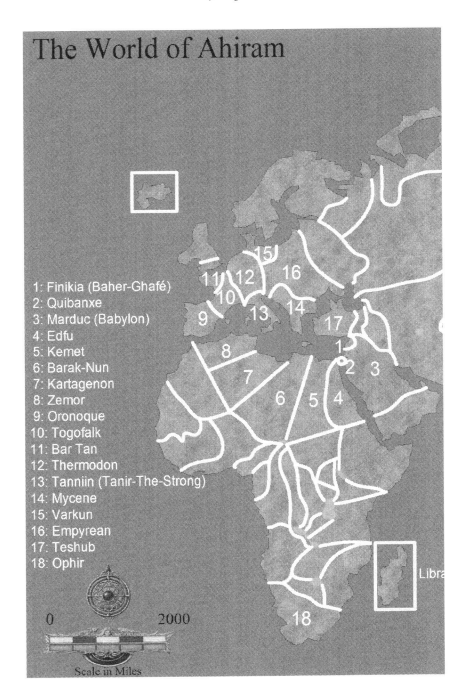

Wrath of the Urkuun – World of Ahiram

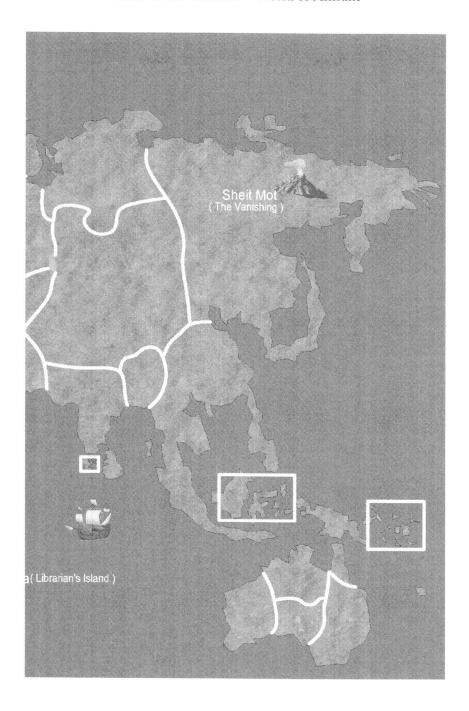

Michael Joseph Murano

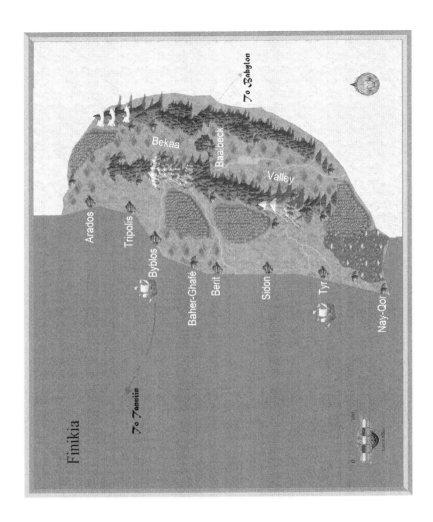

Wrath of the Urkuun – Kingdom of Tanniin

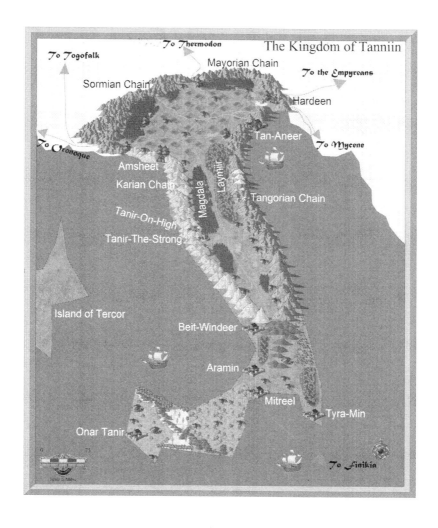

From Bar-Tanic to …

Wrath of the Urkuun – From Bar-Tanic to Thermodon

… Thermodon

Michael Joseph Murano

From Gordion to …

Wrath of the Urkuun – From Gordion to Tirkalanzibar

… the caravan city of Tirkalanzibar

Xarg-Ulum

❧⊰⊱❧

Part One

1. Wings of Light

> "The master blacksmiths of old forged the most powerful swords ever known. Chiefly among these, we mention Terragold, the mighty sword of Muhaijar, twelfth king of Marada; Utal, the swift sword of Shahrab, seventh Lord of the Desert Legions; and Layaleen, the shining sword of El-Windiir."
> –Philology of the Dwarfs, Anonymous.

High above the mines of Tanniin, darkness swallowed the world. An unforgiving wind whipped tormented clouds into a maddening dance like a puppeteer punishing his puppets. They raged and thundered, flailed and lit the heavens with jagged screams of blinding light as if they wanted to scar the skies and leave behind an indelible mark of their suffering. At long last, exhausted and spent like a herd of slayed dragons, they poured out their bloody streams of icy-cold silver water onto the earth below.

The rain slapped the ground the way a master slaps an obstinate slave. Forming rivulets, the water streamed down the back of ancient stones that took the beating with the resignation of orphans who have nowhere else to go. It flowed down into the dirt like a panicked scorpion seeking an escape route and slithered haphazardly as it sought a way down: down to the sea that called its name. It formed puddles and drowned in it. It careened down steep inclines and sniffed the roots of trees like a dog searching for who knows what. One stream, more agile than the others, found a hole that swallowed it hungrily. It gushed into the blackness, and its gurgle became a rallying cry that turned into a rapid stream. Leaving behind the raging storm, the water fell into cracks in the earth, into spaces so deep they had never seen the light of day; and still the stream continued its hellish descent, bouncing, splashing, crashing blindly into rocks that had been smoothed by a millennial wind. Refusing to become a pool of stagnant water, the rain forced its way through the depths of the mountain like a worm whose sole purpose was to burrow. At last, the water broke free from the embrace of the rock and fell into a large, open cave where a young man stood triumphantly holding a sword.

Five days ago, Ahiram the slave, Ahiram the Silent, had disrupted the well-mandated order of the Games of the Mines. Against all odds, he chose to participate alone and unaided. In order to gain back his freedom he needed to win all four Games even as the competing teams had the right and the opportunity to kill him. Amazingly, he managed to win the first three Games and in doing so gained the attention of the powerful Temple of Baal who had ordained his death for political expediency. Hounded by the Temple's High Riders, he had fallen into a subterranean river that carried him into the Eye of Death—a submerged tunnel where he should have drowned and his body would have washed out miles away into the Renlow River.

Unexpectedly, he survived. He followed a narrow passage that led him to the hidden tomb of El-Windiir, founder of the Kingdom of Tanniin. Ahiram discovered El-Windiir's legendary sword—named Layaleen for the hero's wife—as well as his shoes of bronze, belt of silver, mask of gold, and wings of meyroon. These were the magical artifacts that had given flight to El-Windiir hundreds of years ago and helped him liberate the land from the Lords of the Pit. Along the way, Ahiram had taken possession of a small golden tile with a strange inscription on it. He knew to call it "taw," but he did not know what it meant or what it represented.

Ahiram held the sword high and smiled broadly as he imagined the scene when he would land on the third floor of Taniir-the-Strong Castle. He visualized a full moon lighting the majestic castle's marble balcony. Hundreds of couples from all over the world would be strolling the wide esplanade while an orchestra played "O Flag of My Heart". Ahiram envisioned King Jamiir standing to address the crowd: *"My dear friends, we have gathered to bestow on the winner of the Games the golden sword which has so generously been offered by High Priestess Bahiya,"* Ahiram thought. His imagination continued to play out the scene.

Just then, a trembling finger points to the moon.

"Look! Look at the moon!"

They all look and their jaws drop. They are amazed because the moon frames something dark—a giant flying creature that stands over the castle, wings extended like a vengeful bat.

A vengeful bat? That's ridiculous, try something else ... like a vengeful dragon. Much better.

The Queen gasps. Everyone freezes as the creature suddenly descends on the castle.

"It is El-Windiir come back from the dead!" Hiyam screams. She runs to her mother and bumps into a waiter carrying a bowl of soup. Jostled, he flings the bowl, whose contents cover the mother and daughter with chicken soup.

No, make that cod soup.

... covers the mother and daughter with cod soup.

The creature lands with a mighty thud on the balcony, a mighty sword in his left hand.

"It is Ahiram, the slave," exclaims the King. "He holds El-Windiir's sword. I declare him a free man! I make him a prince! All bow down to Prince Ahiram!"

"My adopted son!" exclaims the Queen.

She would never say that.

"My son," exclaims the Queen.

No, no, she won't say any of it.

Anyway, they all bow. Bahiya and Hiyam beg forgiveness for hours and hours. Everyone is so happy, they cry, and Jedarc wails with happiness. Everyone stands for hours in line to shake their hero's hand. It would have lasted three days and three nights, but Jedarc starts singing. Everyone panics and runs. They take the chicken with them, before our hero has a chance to eat …

Snap out of it, Ahiram.

When Ahiram opened his eyes, he became aware of his ridiculous pose. He was standing in front of El-Windiir's sarcophagus with his left hand raising the sword torch-like, his right hand on his heart, and a smug smile stuck on his face.

Cod soup? Begging forgiveness? Jedarc's singing causing a general panic?

Weariness came down upon him like a crashing wave. His muscles ached, and the scrapes and cuts he had received while crawling from the Eye of Death to the secret Temple of Tannin stung like a vengeful beehive. Conflicting thoughts clamored for his attention: *I can still make it to the castle in time to win. What is a taw? The King will free me. I found the tomb of El-Windiir. I will finally go home. What's that golden tile for? I will see Hoda again. What shall I do next? I'm very hungry. I wish Nora were here to see all of this.*

Guilt seized him, sticky and stubborn like a leech. He had not thought of Noraldeen since that fateful evening when she had kissed him before slipping into the night. Even though it had been a mere five days since he had seen her, her absence opened an old festering wound. Noraldeen was to his heart what El-Windiir's sarcophagus was to Tanniin: a perennial source of strength, resplendent in its light, yet regal and mysterious.

I have been busy these five days. I hardly had a minute to myself. Olothe tried to kill me. Twice. I've been accused of murder and relentlessly pursued by Baal. I nearly fell to my death, and now, this, he gestured toward the sarcophagus. *I will soon be free and then …*

Relief washed over him, pushing his guilt away. The six-year-long wait was over now. Soon he would be free. The muted tension that had shadowed him all these years had begun to dissolve. He was relieved and elated like a fisherman who had survived the darkest of storms. He started to smile when guilt rushed at him again like a prowling shark. *I have maimed a man. I have turned him into a cripple for life.* He vividly remembered pounding Prince Olothe with no mercy during the Game of Silver, after the reckless and haughty prince had taunted him beyond his breaking point. His hands could still feel the sickening crunch of the man's crushed bones; broken ribs and limbs twisted beyond repair. He could still hear the screams of pain that quickly turned into a pitiful whimper: "Not the dogs, not the dogs." Ahiram could still hear his voice echo in the caves when he had told Olothe: "You will not be able to make use of your arms or your legs for the rest of your miserable life. A slave will live a better life. If you ever call my father a slave again, wherever you may be, even in the depths of the earth, I will find you and inflict even greater pain upon you than now, then I will leave you to the dogs. Do you understand me? To the dogs!" He knew he would never forget what he had done to the prince for as long as he lived.

You beat the prince senseless.

Ahiram demurred, trying to ignore the mounting guilt, but his remorse hounded him like a feral dog searching for another bone to pick, another failure, another regret to prick Ahiram's conscience. *You forgot about Noraldeen. You did not think about visiting her before leaving.*

"Who cares what I thought or did not think?" he yelled. "What matters is what I do, not what I think."

You've beaten the prince, pounded his guilt, *that's what you did. And you did not think of Noraldeen. You were going to leave her behind, just like your sister left you behind.*

An image from his past flashed before his eyes: a shark tugging a fishing boat away, a young frightened boy aboard, and a voice screaming, "Hoda, Hoda." Feeling his head about to explode, he raised a fist to the heavens to let out a powerful shout of anger, but he stopped abruptly when he glimpsed the wings of El-Windiir floating gently overhead.

"What am I doing? What am I doing? I am going crazy, that's what I am doing." He paced quickly. In this moment of elation and relief, powerful emotions repressed since Kwadil took him away from his family, overwhelmed his will. He felt helpless, unable to contain the emotional rush or ascend to the hope it carried with it. He leaned the sword against the sarcophagus' base, dropped to the ground and pumped out sixty rapid push-ups. He lay on his back, aching and panting. *Go to the castle, win your freedom, say your good-byes to Noraldeen, and go home. Then what? What if the Queen refuses to let me go?*

"She can try," he growled. "I'd like to see her try. I *will* be free. I will go home, and …"

The accumulated weariness mixed with guilt, apprehension, and hope surged like a mighty tide. Then sleep snatched him away.

≻ ◦◦◦ ≺

Of the 288 soldiers of Baal who protected the castle, only 164 had retreated hurriedly to the second level. The rest were not so fortunate. Their leader sat by the barricade they had erected to stop the mob from reaching the Royal Hall. The bloodied bandage around one eye partially covered his mouth and muffled a string of curses against the ragtag horde holed up in the kitchen below.

"Why the kitchen?" This question had tormented him for the past hour. With his good eye, he glanced at his men and saw what he had never seen before: a sense of looming defeat.

Earlier that day, the King had commanded them to protect the castle, and Bahiya, the high priestess of the Temple of Baalbek, had given them stern and unyielding orders: "Protect the King. Impose the law."

In Temple jargon, she had given them complete latitude to deal with intruders as they saw fit, which invariably meant an expeditious end to their foes—swift and bloody.

"Why in Baal's name are they occupying the kitchen? What could they possibly be waiting for in that blasted kitchen?"

"Reinforcements, perhaps?" suggested a soldier.

"Why? As soon as the barracks catch wind of the uprising, our troops will wipe them out. Like I said, it's senseless."

The High Riders of the Temple of Baal had seldom known fear. They were well trained, disciplined, and battle-hardened. Combat was an all-too-familiar pain with its grinding motions, moans of suffering from friends and foes, and its usual victorious outcome. The Adorant conditioned these men to fear nothing, save the Temple, to fight until the end, and to never give up. The unorganized mob outnumbered them ten to one, but it was composed—in the main—of peasants, shepherds, smiths, merchants, and young men who had yet to taste blood. Ordinarily, the High Riders would have mowed down the first ten or fifteen rows, sowing the fear of Baal into the hearts of the wannabe soldiers, which would be enough to break any insurrection. Ordinarily, a light guard consisting of 288 soldiers, would have been sufficient to subdue a force ten times its size. Ordinarily, they would not retreat.

But this brief battle had not been ordinary. The moon still shone behind heavy clouds, and the wind had turned to the northeast signaling an imminent storm. The soldiers who manned the outer wall had gazed longingly at the brightly lit Royal Hall where the King and his retinue celebrated Hiyam's victory. The Games of the Mines had ended with the predictable triumph of Baal's team. Then, a clamor had reached them from the valley below. It started as a faint echo, that became a threatening rumble, and finally as it drew closer, turned into a chanted, full-fledged scream. Their leader had sent one hundred archers to the outer wall.

Nothing like a well-aimed arrow-hail to cool these hot heads, their leader thought. *Once they see a few hundred bodies littering the ground, they will turn tail and run back to the hole from which they came.*

When the archers saw the attackers running up Royal Road, torches in hand, they had shaken their heads in disbelief. This wasn't even an armed mob, rather, a motley crowd of townsfolk who chanted rhythmically.

"What are they saying?" asked one of the soldiers.

"*We took the mitten*," offered another man of Baal.

"No," added a third man with a keener ear. "*We cook the chicken*."

"Huh?"

"Must be a signal of sorts."

"Archers at the ready," called their leader.

Thunder answered and the downpour came. Lightning cut through the night like a lion's claws through fallen prey, and the rain hit the cobblestones like a distracted drummer repeating a beat gone senseless. The night became a wet fluttering sheet, and the torches in the distance became the ragged grins of crazed lunatics.

In one synchronized movement, the archers drew their arrows, fletched, aimed and pulled; but then the attackers stopped well outside of their range.

"Huh, they have more brains than I was willing to give 'em credit for," the lead archer commented, "mayhap they'll turn tail and run." He ordered his men to stand down. A long military career had turned the anxiety of his youth into an indolent discipline that had born many victories which he now summed up in three words: "Wait, break, and clean up." Soon enough the crowd would grow impatient and charge, heedless of danger. The wait would be over, and his men would break the Tanniinites' short-lived enthusiasm. Then would come the grinding, dirty business of breaking bones and skulls, while the survivors spread the fear of Baal like an infectious disease. The populace would submit to the Temple for a few dozen years until the passing of seasons washed away the memory of the bloodshed and another cycle would begin. In the end, he saw his job as a High Rider akin to a cleaning crew taking out the dirt to keep an assigned space tidy.

"Keep 'em arrows notched; I wouldn't want 'em rabbits tak'n us by any sort of surprise."

Across the main road the mob had remained motionless while its tail continued to swell.

The soldiers muttered among themselves.

"What are they waiting for?"

"Who knows?"

"Who cares? Let 'em come and die."

"What's that?" their leader snapped.

The rain had slightly abated. Across the wet road, a flat block of wood was fast approaching.

"Archers at the ready. Aim. Release!"

One hundred arrows flew straight and true. They thudded into the wood plank in a perfect staccato, tac-tac-tac-tac, but if the archers' lead hoped to slow, stop, or pulverize the shield, he had been disappointed. The plank continued its approach, no more hindered by the arrows than a horse by flies. Then, when it was one hundred yards from the castle's gate, the plank sped into a full sprint.

"Who could carry a wood plank this thick and run this fast?"

"Nah, there's a few of 'em behind it. I'll say their shield is sturdy, I'll give 'em as much, but they're stupid dead once they reach the wall. Once they drop that shield, we'll nail 'em like sparrows on a skewer."

The archer who had asked this question saw the logic in his leader's words and relaxed. The walls were thirty-two feet high. No group of men could climb them fast enough and escape Baal's arrows. Further, assuming one or two did succeed in setting foot on the wall, what could they do against one hundred High Riders?

Still, the mysterious wood blank had continued its advance, and being forced to wait, the archers shuffled their feet. When the plank had been within fifteen feet of the wall, it was catapulted toward the far right archers. Grazing the edge of the wall, it smashed into three soldiers and threw them over the side as it fell with them into the inner court.

Reflexively, the archers had followed the fall of the screaming soldiers and failed to notice a man dressed in black sprint up the wall—thanks to the rope which the falling plank pulled. Reaching the top, he had let go of the rope and landed nimbly on his feet. Not waiting, he set his shoulder against a sturdy shield he had with him and screamed "For the chicken!" as he rammed into the closest archer.

Had his strength just been that of a normal man, he might have managed to push two, three, or maybe four archers out of the way, but Frajil's strength was anything but normal. Frajil was the offspring of a giant father and a human mother. Normally, such a union would produce a stillborn child; but not Frajil. He was a fighter from the womb, and though his mother had not survived, he had been born strong and healthy, though dim-witted. His father had brought him to his wife's sister, Soloron's mother, who adopted the cute and cuddly baby and raised him as her own.

As an adult, Frajil had the mental capacity of a young child and required supervision in most circumstances; in most circumstances perhaps, but never in battle. Whatever intelligence Frajil's brain had managed to collect, it had channeled it into the art of survival, and by extension, into the art of fighting. Though a little over nine feet tall and weighing close to four hundred and fifty pounds, Frajil could carry a horse—something he had done once when he confused Soloron's order: "Carry on with the horse." Instead of saddling up, he lifted the steed to the confusion and astonishment of both Soloron and the horse.

Despite his size and weight, Frajil was frighteningly fast. He moved with the speed of a lion after its prey, and there was no stopping him.

Thus, when Frajil's shield had crashed into the first archer, it threw him back like a human projectile, tearing through the line. The giant had pushed his shield into the opening and mowed half of the soldiers down before anyone reacted.

By the time the archers and the soldiers within the castle's precinct focused on him, he had cleared half the wall. Archers from within the walls had their arrows aimed at him, but they hesitated for fear of killing their fellow soldiers.

"I don't care who dies," shouted their leader. "Kill him!"

Just then, the men of Tanniin had launched their attack. With one bellow that filled the valley, they surged forward. Some of the archers had turned their attention to stave off the incoming wave, while the rest tried to stop Frajil, but to no avail. He moved quickly, unpredictably, while he stayed behind his shield. With its remarkably long reach, his blade was precise and deadly. Confusion had reigned on the wall, and then the mob surged like a dragon trampling everything on its path.

The leader of Baal's guard had sounded the retreat and the soldiers reached the second floor expecting to see the mob on their tail. Instead, the devil of a man that led the mob ordered his troop to overtake the kitchen, where they had been holed up for the past hour.

"Why the kitchen?" repeated their leader for the third time.

As if on cue, Frajil's voice boomed, "Tonight, we roast the chicken!"

A roar answered him. His men surrounded him as he sat grinning on a chair, happy as a rooster in a coop, convinced he had done something grand for his brother. What that was, he had not the faintest idea.

One of his followers unclipped his *oudal*, a crossover between a mandolin and a banjo, and improvised a song in honor of their hero:

> "Frajil the mighty, stand undefeated,
> In the royal kitchen where he is now seated.
> Let all gray owls in fear contort:
> Frajil has come with his cohort.

Tonight, tonight we roast the chicken;
Tomorrow morning Baal will be stricken.

Frajil the warrior conquered the wall,
Where he stood proud, strong, and tall.
Let all gray owls fear and tremble:
Frajil's cohorts will now assemble.

Tonight, tonight we roast the chicken.
Tomorrow morning Baal shall be stricken.

Frajil the mighty roars like a lion,
A beast of old, a mighty dragon.
Let all gray owls weep in defeat;
Frajil's cohorts shall never retreat.

Tonight, tonight we roast the chicken.
Tomorrow morning Baal shall be stricken.

Frajil the great has opened the path,
He has unleashed Tannin's fiery wrath.
Let all gray owls cower and tremble.
Frajil's cohorts arise and assemble.

Tonight, tonight we roast the chicken.
Tomorrow morning Baal shall be stricken."

The tune was lively and easy to follow, so when the bard had reached the last verse, the walls of the castle shook with Frajil's name. The giant of a man sat still as a statue, a smile affixed on his face like a crescent moon in the dark night. Normally, Frajil would have hit anyone brandishing a weapon—or a ladle—in his face, but the men around him were content to clap and sing his name. Unsure of what to do next, he remained motionless and hoped Soloron would join him soon.

Obeying the King's command to secure safe passage for Bahiya and her retinue on a vessel sailing for Baalbek, Tanios and his Silent led the high priestess, her daughter Hiyam, and their companions down the path for slaves that ran parallel to Royal Road until it rejoined the road south of Taniir-the-Strong Castle.

Situated at the southern tip of the Karian Chain, the commercial port of Beit-Windeer was one hundred and fifty miles away. Its citizens led an indolent life and had not a care in the world, so long as goods-laden ships flowed in and out of their protected bay. By the master of the Silent's estimate, they would reach Beit-Windeer in five or six days, and with any luck, find a moored ship flying Baal's colors. Otherwise, they would have to cross another seventy-five miles to reach Mitreel, the southernmost port of Tanniin, which housed Baal's main camp. Unfortunately, the main road from Beit-Windeer to Mitreel went through the city of Aramin, and the Araminites were no friends of Baal. It had taken the better part of Jamiir's reign to avoid bloodshed between Aramin and Mitreel. Tanios knew he could not cross this rowdy city with a high priestess in tow. Also, asking Bahiya to wear a disguise was an affront to the Temple. No, if forced to reach Mitreel, he would have to take a detour through the eastern marshes, populated by shady characters, where neither Baal nor any sane person ventured. This was less than ideal but he would have time to prepare.

The rain beat on the group and their beasts like the stubborn tears of Astarte refusing to be consoled after Adonis, her beloved, had passed away. After several hours, the horses had not managed a single canter, let alone a gallop, and were nervous and restless. Tanios waited until they reached the mouth of the Great Pass before stopping. There they took shelter under the trees.

The Silent, an elite royal corps protecting the king and the castle, was his to command. The thirty-five members of the corps were trained diplomats, accomplished guardians, stealth fighters; all ready to take on the most dangerous undercover missions for the kingdom. Their favorite weapon was a furtive dart they threw using specialized crossbows.

"We will give the horses a short rest before proceeding forward."

Immediately, the Silent set up a wide perimeter, and standing still, they blended with their surroundings. Moments later, a vanishing dart streaked the night and smeared a trunk nearby.

"Nobody moves," said Tanios quietly. "Keep the horses quiet."

Hiyam, who happened to be near him, wanted to know why, but seeing him shake his head, she kept her peace. They waited in a tense silence, and after a while, a second vanishing dart hit the same tree. Tanios relaxed his stance. Hiyam was about to speak when a Silent appeared before them. She nearly jumped. Tanios smiled.

"Commander, a large group of men are heading north."

"High Riders?" asked Bahiya who had just joined them.

"No," replied the Silent who kept his eyes fixed on his commander. "Folks from Tanniin. Some of them carry swords."

"Very well," said Tanios. "Let us be on our way."

"When do we reach Mitreel?" asked Bahiya.

"I will not take us to Mitreel if I can spare it," corrected Tanios. "We aim for Beit-Windeer. Weather permitting, we should be there in just about two weeks."

Bahiya nodded.

They cinched the horses and Tanios ordered everyone to walk. "We are about to cross the Great Pass," he explained. "It is encased between two mountainsides and therefore hemmed in by towering walls that are, in some places, over three hundred feet high. Everything is louder in there, especially thunder. Walk slowly and keep your horses calm."

As they rejoined the road, Bahiya gave a start.

"Where is my daughter?"

"Over there," said Jedarc, pointing toward the Great Pass. "She is just a little bit ahead of us."

After the Game of Meyroon, Hiyam heard that Ahiram perished in the mines. she could not accept the role the Temple had played in the fall of the Silent. The young woman was beginning to question her loyalty to Baal. In need of space and solitude, she ventured ahead on the road.

Tanios and Bahiya saw her faint outline vanish inside the pass.

"No!" yelled Bahiya. "She must not be there …" Bahiya regained control. "Not on her own."

A deafening roar filled the air, terrifying the horses.

"Everyone off the road," shouted the commander.

An avalanche of mud carrying rocks and trees slid from the right slope and closed the mouth of the pass. It filled the road with sludge and debris. The rain redoubled and become a torrent.

The pile of mountain rubble was at least sixty feet high. Bahiya groaned. "What is wrong with that girl?" she cried out. "Why can't she do as she's told?"

Tanios was not surprised by Bahiya's apparent lack of concern. He knew the priestess of Baal could summon her magic to protect her daughter. *Hiyam must be safe.*

A freezing gust of wind smashed into the massive landslide and careened inside the pass, howling like a giant wounded beast.

"I must … I cannot leave Hiyam," shouted Bahiya over the din of wind and rain. "I must go to her."

Tanios shook his head.

"The mountain is not stable and more angry men are headed to Taniir-the-Strong. You are not safe here."

"In this storm? Are you serious?"

"The folks of Tanniin are used to downpours. This rain will not keep them in. If they see you, it would complicate our mission. I cannot risk it."

"I will not abandon my daughter."

"That is not my intention. A shadow of Silent will cross over and rescue her. They will bring Hiyam back to you."

One of Hiyam's teammates stepped forward.

"Your Honor, command us to search for her—"

"I will not allow it," said Tanios. "You are a danger to yourselves here. You do not know the terrain, and you are not welcome by the people. No one will help you. You stay with me."

"Why would the Silent risk their lives for my daughter? Why should I trust them?"

"They follow my orders."

Blast that girl, thought the high priestess. *Bringing this avalanche down took all my strength, and I am exhausted. I cannot reach her. Can she not do as she is told?*

High above, lightning struck a giant pine tree that burned brightly despite the downpour. Their eyes locked. Her eyes implored: *This is my daughter*. His eyes were even: *The Silent obey me*.

"If I may say," intervened Master Habael, "the Silent standing behind me would be delighted to rescue your daughter."

Bahiya glanced back and saw Jedarc's honest face.

"Fine," she told the commander. "I will follow your lead, but I will hold you personally responsible for her safety."

Tanios smiled a slow bitter smile, then turned around and signaled to Jedarc. The young man bounded forward.

"Jedarc, form a Shadow, find and retrieve the priestess' daughter, and meet us at the southeastern limit of Magdala."

Jedarc's face brightened instantly. "Yes, Commander."

"Magdala?" asked Bahiya. "That is north. It is the wrong direction."

Tanios shook his head. "We cannot wait here. It is too dangerous. We will head for a northern port from where you will be able to sail to Byblos. It is longer but safer."

She nodded and said nothing.

"If we must press forward to Hardeen," the commander instructed, "I will leave you a sign on a tree by the edge of the road at the southern limit of Magdala. You will then proceed immediately to the fortress."

"Yes, Commander," replied Jedarc.

"Silent, assemble."

Instantly, thirty-four Silent stood before their commander. "We will descend Shepherd's Path into the valley, follow the Renlow to the north, bypass Tanniin-the-Strong, cross the marshes, and then go into the forest until we reach the edge of Magdala. Any questions?"

"Where do we go from there?" Bahiya spoke so softly Habael was the only one who heard her.

"I suspect the commander will want to take us across the hidden river and along the forest until we reach the northeastern port of Hardeen. There you will be able to take a boat that will bring you safely to Baalbek. It is a six day journey and a long detour, but given the circumstances, it is the only safe way out of Tanniin."

"Six only? Then why go down to Beit-Windeer on a three-week journey?" asked the priestess.

"Beit-Windeer is more tolerant of Baal than the north," replied Habael tactfully.

Bahiya nodded.

"And Hardeen is where Lord Orgond resides?"

"Yes."

Good. Things are proceeding as planned. Sharr will be satisfied.

"Silent, to your positions. Onward. Go."

"Please, bring my daughter back to me," said Bahiya.

"We will do our best, ma'am." Jedarc replied, a twinkle in his eyes.

A moment later, the Silent Corps and the priestess disappeared from view. The rain turned suddenly into hail, forcing Jedarc and his three companions to take shelter before the mission even started.

Hiyam woke up in pain. Her head throbbed and she could barely keep her eyes open. She struggled to remember where she was and what happened. She tried to clear her mind and take stock of her situation.

Where am I? What has happened to me?

Drops of water splashed on her face. She jerked her head and felt a warm and furry surface. *Who is taking me away?* Forcing her eyes to open, she lifted her head and saw up ahead two other creatures pulling her dead horse. Droplets of rain fell intermittently and Hiyam wanted to scream. Instead, she only managed a feeble moan.

Best to bide my time and wait for an opening.

The creature carrying her moved into a thick cluster of trees.

Hiyam saw hail fall, glittering in the dark. Lightning flashed like a dagger that tore the night apart. Thunder boomed angrily, and the downpour that followed buried every other sound—as if the world were about to drown under a storm that would last a lifetime.

Wearily, she closed her eyes and slipped out of consciousness.

2. CROSSING

> *"Who needs friends? Who needs help, support, or a comforting word? Kings? Queens and their cohorts of noble men and women entrenched in costly attire and royal jewelry? No, they are too rich for friends; only the poor need friends."*
> —Soliloquy of Zuzu the Hip, Jester of the Royal Court of Tanniin.

"I hope Hiyam found shelter from the hail," muttered Jedarc.

"I hope she's still alive," replied Sondra.

"I'm sure she is," Sheheluth said. They looked at her. "Her mother is the high priestess 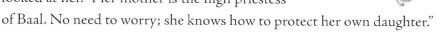 of Baal. No need to worry; she knows how to protect her own daughter."

"You've got a point there," said Sondra.

"So you called the high priestess *ma'am*? Really, Jedarc?" derided Banimelek, "Why, while you're at it, you may just as well call her *Mother*."

Jedarc ignored the jibe.

"What's this all about?" asked Sondra.

"Jedarc is in looove," cooed Banimelek.

"Tinantel? You fell for a gray owl?" Sondra whacked him on the head.

"Stop it. This is serious business."

"Looove is a serious business," chirped Banimelek.

"I mean rescuing her," said Jedarc.

"Why do you call him Tinantel?" asked Sheheluth. Her eyes darted from left to right, and she jumped when she heard something roll down a nearby tree. It was an acorn.

Sondra gave her a wide grin that lit her ordinarily stoic, dark-skinned face. "In my language, Tinantel means *Light Foot*. Most Silent call Jedarc *His Highness* or *Prince Jedarc*, but I call him *Tinantel* because he is quick on his feet."

"Stop giving me this prince title, all right?" He leaned forward and exposed his hand to the hail but retracted it quickly. "That hurts."

"Hail the size of pigeon eggs." said Sondra, "It can seriously hurt you." She placed a protective arm around Sheheluth's shoulders and smiled again. Sheheluth relaxed.

"I know this is your first mission. Tinantel may be as dull as a porcupine when it comes to choosing a mate, but he's not stupid when choosing teammates."

"So, why did he pick two girls to be on the team?"

Sondra raised her left eyebrow but managed to keep her smile in place. She could tell the young girl was nervous and worried. "Well, we're going to rescue Hiyam, and she is the priestess' daughter. How would you like it if a bunch of smelly guys rescued you?"

"Hey, I'm not smelly, okay?" complained Jedarc. "I am as fresh as the breeze. Now Banimelek …"

Banimelek did not reply. He was used to his friend's banter and could immediately tell when the lanky blond Silent was serious or facetious.

Sheheluth pursed her lips and managed a timid grin.

"Smelly guys. That makes sense."

"I was joking," explained Sondra.

"Oh, I see. I noticed the three of you joke a lot. It's childish. That's surprising for an elite corps. I thought you would be more serious."

Sondra chuckled. "That's because you've never been in mortal danger.

'A Silent who cannot make light of his enemy has lost the battle. A somber Silent is a dead Silent.' The *Book of Lamentation*, chapter twelve, verse one," she replied. "The Corps takes humor seriously. It's one of our hidden weapons."

Sheheluth blushed. "Do the boys care as much about cleanliness?"

Sondra chuckled. "Tinantel and Faernor are not too bad."

"Tinantel is Jedarc, so Faernor is Banimelek, right?"

"You catch on quickly. That's right. Faernor means *Wolf-bear.*"

"Suits him well," said Sheheluth. "So tell me Sondra, do they *really* care about cleanliness?"

"They're decent all right. Now, Ahiram, well he's something else. He's a stickler for cleanliness. When he washes a dish, he first scrubs it as if he were sanding it down. Next, he runs his fingers on its surface to make sure there are no particles still stuck to it. If the poor dish passes these two tests, he smells it like a dog hounding a squirrel, and if it smells fresh, he dries it. Then, he runs his fingers again over its surface and it must squeak. Believe it or not, if it does not squeak he goes through the whole operation again."

"Oh, and does he do the dishes often?"

"No!" exclaimed all three Silent.

"Categorically, no," added Jedarc. "When he does the dishes we don't get to eat, the servants don't get to eat, and the slaves don't get to sleep. It takes him ten times longer to do the dishes. We don't let him do it."

"We work around him," Banimelek explained. "If he ends up with the kitchen chore, then we take it away from him."

"Who? The Silent?"

"Yes," confirmed Sondra, "and the servants, and the slaves, and Master Habael. You don't want Ahiram doing the dishes. Everyone in the castle from the King on down will hear about it. It's dreadful."

The three older Silent shared a chuckle at the thought of Ahiram complaining loudly about dirty dishes.

Sheheluth smiled. "You said when he *does* the dishes, not when he *did* the dishes, which means you believe he is still alive."

Sondra nodded.

"He doesn't die easily."

"Still, I'm just a beginner, I don't know much, and—"

"So begin then," said Sondra. "That's a good place as any to start, besides, you've got nothing to fear. Faernor is with us."

"That's … Banimelek, right?"

"That's right. Wolf-bear."

"He is very strong. He scares me."

"You'd do well to feel that way. He's quiet as a reed when the sun shines but quick to anger when darts fly."

Sheheluth smiled. "I like how you speak of them, Sondra. I think I am going to come up with a good name for you." Sondra grinned and shrugged her shoulders. Encouraged, Sheheluth prodded further. "So, do you have a name for Ahiram?"

Sondra stayed silent for a long time, then fixed her big black eyes on Sheheluth. "*Alendiir*," she said finally. "Blazing Fire."

≻ ◦◦◦◦ ≺

Ahiram woke up shivering and confused. He saw high walls that vanished into darkness above, and a pair of glittering wings rotating overhead. *The wings of Tanniin.*

He sat and rubbed his arms. During the preceding commotion and excitement, he had not noticed how cold the cave was. He gave his legs a vigorous rub, got up and stretched, then went over to the sarcophagus just as a bright flash lit the cave. He heard a faint rumble. *Thunder. This room must be closer to the mountainside than I thought. The dwarfs must have designed hidden shafts to allow light into this cave. All right, no more nonsense, no more questions. I've got to reach the surface.*

Resolutely, he climbed back up to the tomb. Quickly, but respectfully, he removed the mask of gold, the belt of silver, and the shoes of bronze, and laid them neatly at the base of the tomb near the sword. His search for a sheath proved to be in vain. Gently, he slid the cover back in place and bowed three times to honor the dead hero. He went back down and began a careful examination of the artifacts when he felt a light touch against his shoulder. He jerked his elbow back and turned around, expecting to see the men of Baal, but there was no one. *Someone touched me.* He stood abruptly, his nerves on edge. *Who just touched me?*

He eyed the sarcophagus' cover, wondering if somehow the hero of legends had managed to come back to life. *Stop it, Ahiram, stop it. The dead do not come back to life.*

Once more, he felt something brush his shoulders lightly and his hand moved swiftly, trying to catch the perpetrator, but caught nothing. He whirled around, and once more, saw no one.

Is it magic? Is someone using a cloak to hide himself from me? He went back to his breathing exercises, forcing himself to calm down and clear his head. *Think Ahiram, review the facts. I felt someone touch me twice in the same spot.* This sounded odd. *Why would someone try to touch my shoulders? This makes no sense.* He smiled wryly. *Well, let's see what they will do now.* Quickly, he backed into the wall. *Unless they can reach through walls, I will be able to see them.*

He did not have long to wait. Something fluttered down from the ceiling, something dark with a brilliant blue halo and rested on his right shoulder. Ahiram laughed, chiding himself. *The wings, how silly of me. I guess removing artifacts from a dead body would make anyone nervous.* He barely touched the strange object when it fell limply on his shoulder. Gently, he held them to the dim light. Each wing was one foot long and made of two impossibly thin, seamless sheets of blue steel that were joined by three golden scarabs.

This is meyroon, then. He ran his hand over their surface. They felt as soft and smooth as velvet and were warm to the touch. And although they were as light as feathers and pliable like reeds, he knew they were harder than Damascus steel.

"No wonder meyroon is prized in all the kingdoms," he whispered. "Now, how do I use these wings?" There were no straps, no threads, nothing to tie or clasp them. Carefully, he returned them to his shoulders where they had landed. Slowly he moved away from the wall and looked up. Instantly, the wings settled between his shoulder blades. He felt a lightning bolt jolt down his spine. The experience was jarring but not painful. Reinvigorated, he willed to go up, but nothing happened.

"Up," he whispered.

Nothing happened.

"Up!" he commanded.

Still, nothing happened.

"Ah, I bet I need the belt and the shoes. Time to try the power of El-Windiir." He grabbed the shoes and felt them, amazed by their suppleness. They resembled leather more so than metal.

"These are no ordinary shoes," he whispered. Their surface was as smooth as bronze beaten by a master smith; and being open-toed, they were more like sandals than boots. *Hum ... they're wide, made for big feet, unless ...* He went back to the sarcophagus, slid the cover open once more, and glanced inside the tomb. *Judging by El-Windiir's skeleton, these bronze shoes were too big for him ... I wonder ...* He closed the sarcophagus, bowed three times, stepped back down, and slid the shoes of bronze over his own leather boots. *They fit snugly. Makes sense.*

He buckled the belt of silver onto his waist and strapped the mask around his head—he did not set it on his face, perhaps because it was hard to see anything in the cave as it was. Ahiram willed to go up. He felt a wave of heat radiate from the shoes and felt a slight tightening of the belt. Suddenly, he was airborne, and moved slowly upward.

"I'm flying!" he shouted.

Elated, he arched his back in an attempt to execute a flip, but only managed to complete three-quarters of a rotation. He ended up flying face down with his arms and legs dangling beneath him.

Not dignified. He still moved upward. He tried to stand in the air but ended up on his back with arms and legs flailing widely.

"Stop!" he said.

He nearly fell to his death.

"Fly, fly!"

He immediately shot back toward the roof of the massive cave.

"Slow down!" he ordered as the artifacts pinned him to the ceiling. Ahiram strained to move away from the cold surface. *This is not easy.*

"Down. Slowly," he commanded, and he began to slide downward, still on his back and suspended in the air. He tried again to stand, but flipped forward and ended up once more in a horizontal position, his arms and legs beneath him. He raised his arms trying to mimic the wings of a bird, but instead, performed another flip and landed once more on his back in the dirt.

"This hurts," he said as he turned around and got up. Splintered wood and chunks of rock littered the ground, and a large pile of debris filled the back of the cave. This was the remnant of the hallway where he had found the tile after having survived the plunge into the Eye of Death at the end of the Game of Meyroon. He shuddered at the thought of landing on the jagged mass. A jolt along his spine told him the wings had separated. They came and rested together on his right shoulder.

"I could have impaled myself. This is not going to be easy."

Seeing the sword he left leaning against the sarcophagus' base, he remembered the part of the story of El-Windiir that had fascinated him the most when he had first heard it. Allegedly, El-Windiir had given his sword the name of his wife, Layaleen. According to the legend of El-Windiir, he had but to extend his hand, call to the sword, and the weapon would answer his command and come to him.

I need to try this, he thought, *and better to try it here where no one can see me. After all, it must look a bit strange, a man extending his hand and calling to a sword.*

Solemnly, he raised his left hand and called out the name of the sword with a loud voice, "Layaleen."

The sword leaped, tip first, and so fast it nearly skewered him. Ahiram managed to jump aside just in time. The sword reached the opposite wall and its blade dove into the rock with a loud thud. It remained there, vibrating. Shocked, Ahiram went over, grabbed the handle and pulled. The blade came free without any difficulty.

"Wow. Amazing." He cut the air with the sword. "This blade is truly incredible. Still," he added, grumbling, "I better learn to use it before I kill myself," he sighed. "All right. I'm being naïve," he said to himself in a chuckle. "I mean, it took me four years to master the throw of a dart, and now I expect to gain mastery over magical artifacts in an instant."

He leaned the blade against the wall, stepped back thirty feet and pictured the sword flying in his direction, pommel first.

"Layaleen."

In the blink of an eye, the sword leaped, pommel first and point down. Ahiram tried to grab the handle but missed. The pommel hit him in the chest and sent him tumbling. The sword swiveled, its blade plunging into the opposite wall like a knife through butter. A cloud of shrapnel ricocheted against the walls and the sarcophagus in a loud staccato.

Ahiram got up and moaned with pain. He rubbed his chest and knew he had another bruise to add to his present collection. "So much for framing the moon like a dragon," he grumbled. "This is one wild sword I must tame." Wearily, he approached the sword and half expected it to leap toward him like a crouching tiger waiting for its victim to come closer. He grabbed the hilt and yanked. The blade came free, as if the stone had been liquefied. He inspected it carefully and saw no dents or scratches. It was as sharp as when El-Windiir first forged it. Forgetting his throbbing bruises, he sliced the air with the weapon; the blade sang a joyful, conquering song, and commanded the enemy—whomever that was—to surrender. The blade was exquisitely balanced and its handle fit perfectly into his hand. Elated, he lifted the sword and danced with it, calling its name until he noticed a ledge high above the opposite end of the vast cave from which a faint light seeped in.

He stood on his toes and arched his head back to see what was beyond the ledge but could see nothing more.

"Let's go take a closer look," he said grinning.

He pointed the sword toward the ledge and said, "Fly."

Instantly, the wings slithered down his back. The jolt was stronger this time. He felt it course down his legs and up his neck and into his ears where it produced a ringing sound. He was about to give the order again when the sword drew him up, nearly yanking his arm from its socket. Ahiram raced toward the ceiling faster than before. He screamed "Slow. Stop!" and came to a screeching halt, midair. He dropped, and unable to control his fall, slammed against the wall on the way down.

"Ouch," he moaned as he got up. *This is much more difficult than I thought. Well, I may have to reach the ledge like everyone else and get to the castle by foot. If I manage to leap from the garden to the third floor without killing myself, it would still be impressive.*

He inspected the wings and wondered if he had broken them, but they were just as supple as when he had found them. He willed for the wings to detach and they ended up on his left shoulder. He felt for the mask, thinking he may have lost it, but it was still on his head.

I can barely feel it. Amazing.

He removed El-Windiir's artifacts, took off his shirt, wrapped the mask, shoes, belt, and wings in it and tied them firmly around his waist. With a piece of rope he made a makeshift sheath able to hold the sword to his side. He went for his crossbow and saw it was broken. He checked the second one and found it intact. He tied his last rope to his last hook dart, nocked and drew his crossbow, aimed at the ceiling over the ledge and released. The dart flew straight and true. He tugged on the rope a few times, then used the special clamps to quickly climb up the wall. The platform formed a small alcove, and in his excitement he saw—or imagined he saw—in the deep shadows, a beautiful young woman holding a torn flag, her eyes fixed on the sarcophagus.

"Layaleen?" he whispered. He had goose bumps. The image faded gently away. He shook his head. *What's wrong with me?*

He looked ahead and saw a round opening from which light was seeping. He peered into the narrow hallway. The left side was dark and the right side illuminated.

Hoda, Noraldeen, Prince Olothe, King Jamiir, freedom, home … Ahiram closed his eyes and regained his focus. *No matter what, I must find a way out. That's all that matters right now.* He opened his eyes and breathed deeply. "Now then, let's find out where this light is coming from."

His heart raced as he descended the corridor. He hoped ardently to make it to the castle in time to be declared the winner.

➤ ◦•◦•◦ ≺

As soon as the hail stopped, the four Silent stepped out from under the trees and rejoined the road. Jedarc went straightaway to the fallen rocks, wanting to cross over them as fast as possible, but Banimelek stood in his way and forced him to rethink his plan.

"I don't care how quickly you think we can climb this mess, Jedarc. These are unstable rocks covered in slippery mud, and more of them could come tumbling down any moment now."

"How do you propose we cross over?"

Banimelek turned to Sondra. "You're the better climber."

"Sheheluth goes first. She's the lightest."

Banimelek nodded and turned to Jedarc who gave Sheheluth a friendly wink. "Go ahead, show us what you can do."

The young Silent was grateful that the twilight hid her crimson blush.

Nimbly, she stepped onto the first rock and placed her right foot on a second, carefully shifting her weight to test its stability. She was halfway up when they all heard a loud snap followed by a mix of rumbles and thuds. The ground began to roll.

"Down, now!" yelled Banimelek. "Jump!"

Sheheluth whirled around and leaped with precision from rock to rock and hit the ground running just as the earth behind them shook violently causing a powerful burst of air that slammed their backs and threw them off the road. Banimelek crashed into a tree, Sheheluth managed to stop herself before she collided against a boulder. Sondra scrapped both knees as she fell into a tumble and landed flat on her face, while Jedarc ended up standing beside a tree.

"I've got mud on my pants," he scoffed. "Scandalous. Hey Banimelek, how's that tree doing?"

"Thanks," grumbled Banimelek. "Sheheluth, are you all right?"

Sheheluth nodded. She ran over to Sondra and examined her exposed knees. "You need to clean those wounds," she said. "They're full of mud."

Sondra smiled, dropped to her knees and walked on them in the grass. "There," she said. "All clean."

"They're bloodied," said Sheheluth.

"They'll dry. Tinantel, look behind you, we've got a looker."

A rock sixty feet high blocked the way. It had flattened the previous pile of rocks and stood like a foreboding door closing the pass along its entire width.

"How did this monster manage to fall so neatly into the pass? You would think it would have hit the other wall and gotten stuck between them, forming a bridge or something."

"Bridge, bridge," grumbled Banimelek, "who cares? It's there and we've got to deal with it."

"I'll go first this time," said Sondra.

"Shouldn't we make certain this rock is stable?" ventured Sheheluth.

"After all, pebbles may be the only thing preventing it from falling more."

"Not this one," explained Sondra. "Just follow the outline of its edges to see that it won't budge. It's snug between the two mountainsides."

"You can see that in the dark?"

"Standard Silent training," offered Sondra. "Nothing special."

"Don't listen to her, Sheheluth," interjected Jedarc. "Sondra has a keen eye. She can see better than most. That's why I wanted her on our little expedition."

"I see," muttered Sheheluth. "So why did you ask me to come?"

"Because you're lithe like a reed and nimble like a monkey," said Jedarc with a wide grin.

Sheheluth stopped in her tracks, Banimelek slapped his forehead and Sondra heaved a deep sigh. "To think I was starting to worry about you getting Hiyam all tangled up with your boyish smile. 'Nimble like a monkey', really?"

"Where I come from, we hold monkeys in high esteem."

"No you don't," Sondra said.

"What do you know about where I come from?"

"They've shipped you here, haven't they?"

"Huh? What do you … hey, are you saying *I'm* a monkey?"

"Lithe like a reed and all that sort of thing," retorted Sondra.

"Fine," grumbled Jedarc. "Back to our problem. How shall we cross?"

"Well, since I'm a monkey," Sheheluth said, "I may as well be the first one to climb."

"Sheheluth, come on, I didn't mean it that way."

"Oh yes, you did," chorused Sondra and Banimelek.

"Sondra, could you shoot a hook dart?" asked Sheheluth.

"Why don't you … oh, that's right, you're a first year recruit, you don't have a dart crossbow yet."

A few moments later, all four Silent stood atop the boulder and overlooked a much larger pile of rocks. Apparently, the boulder had fallen on the edge of the pile, leaving most of it intact.

"Do you want me to go down first?" asked Sheheluth.

Jedarc shook his head. "Not without a rope. These rocks may look sturdy, but cave-ins are still possible and if you step wrong, they're much worse than quicksand; they'll suck you in instantly."

"A three-to-one?" asked Banimelek.

Sondra nodded. "We've got to do it right. No margin for error here."

Jedarc stretched as each of the three older Silent produced a hook dart and rope. Banimelek secured all three ropes to his dart, while Sondra and Jedarc each secured the end of their own rope to their darts. Banimelek tied the other end of his rope to a rock and stepped on it with both feet. He then directed Sondra and Jedarc to stand a few feet away, one to his left and the other to his right. He guided them until they stood precisely where he wanted them to be.

"Ready?" he asked.

They locked their crossbows and aimed at opposite sides of the road.

"Release."

They heard a single twang, which indicated both Silent had discharged their darts at the exact moment. The darts vanished into the surrounding darkness, and they heard a soft thud just as Banimelek's rope became taut.

"Looks like we pulled an Ahiram," hooted Jedarc.

"What did you do?" inquired Sheheluth.

"Jedarc and Sondra anchored their ropes to the opposite sides of the road, and I bridged the two ropes by tying them to my dart. Get it?" explained Banimelek.

"And Banimelek's rope is in the middle of that bridge," continued Jedarc. "He attached it to this rock to make sure he does not lose it. Now we're going to tie it to your waist and we'll follow you down. If you fall we'll pull you right back out."

"Why did you have to time it?" asked the fascinated girl.

"If we overshot, Banimelek's rope would have either snapped, gotten lost, or not be sufficiently taut."

"I see, but what if his rope breaks while I'm falling?"

"Not with your weight, it won't. These ropes are made to carry two fat Silent the size of Banimelek."

They progressed at a snail's pace, careful not to disturb the rocks beneath their feet. On several occasions, they were forced to backtrack when the rocks gave in. Eventually, they made it back down to the road and began in earnest to search for Hiyam.

"It stopped raining," remarked Jedarc.

"It stopped while we were on that boulder," corrected Sondra.

"She's not here," said Jedarc, the slightest quiver in his voice, "do you think she may be under—"

"Over here," called Sheheluth. "Come and see."

They joined her. She was crouching by the roadside. "Here, there is a trail of a horse lying on its side. It's been dragged back onto the road. It must be dead." Pointing to a smaller, fainter puddle, she continued, "Look, the outline of a person. See these footprints? There are at least four people. The footprints over there are a bit heavier, so it looks like they must have carried someone away."

"Well done, Sheheluth," exclaimed Jedarc. He tousled her hair. "I'll be sure to let the commander know. You're a born Silent scout."

"Does this mean I am not a monkey anymore?"

"Sure you are. The best of them," retorted Jedarc. "Once we're in Hardeen, the commander will award you with a banana."

"What's a banana?" she asked with a frown.

"Some fictional fruit Jedarc keeps raving about," grumbled Banimelek while he scanned the ground. "It doesn't exist."

"It does, believe you me, I've had it on several occasions while in—"

"Look here," Sondra said as she rubbed an object between her fingers. "Look what I found."

"A thunderbolt," whispered Jedarc. "The insignia of Baal given to High Riders. Praise the gods, she is still alive."

"Shall we follow the trail?"

Jedarc, Sondra and Banimelek exchanged glances. The mission had suddenly become more complicated, and now possibly dangerous. Jedarc had selected Sheheluth to exonerate himself from the punishment he had brought upon her with his misplaced wit back at the castle, during the Games. He knew her light frame would help them navigate the avalanche. He had assumed they would cross over, find Hiyam and rescue her. They did not expect a third party to have already rescued or to have possibly abducted her. This meant they might have to extract Hiyam from a hostile party and a fight could possibly result. Sheheluth was simply not combat ready.

Sondra sighed. "We have no choice, we continue as planned."

"I can defend myself," objected Sheheluth.

"Sure you can," replied Jedarc grinning. "And for that achievement, you'll get two bananas."

≻ ⋅⋄⋅⋄⋅ ≺

Like the spine of a giant dragon, Royal Road ran the length of the Kingdom of Tanniin from Mitreel in the south to the fortress of Amsheet in the north. Past Taniir-The-Strong Castle on the way to Amsheet, Royal Road separated Royal Forest and Magdala on the right from the Forest of Laymiir on the left.

Despite the prevailing bad weather and downpour of rain, Ibromaliöm strolled up the road like a tourist by the seashore, whistling a toneless tune.

Lightning whipped the road with blinding white strobes that revealed a large group of people swarming within Laymiir. They stood in the shadows eying the lonely traveler with murderous eyes and grins to chill hardened killers.

Ibromaliöm stopped, a crazed smile splitting his face from ear to ear. "So many, of them," he whispered. His eyes darted from one being to another like a famished toad lusting after a swarm of flies.

The attackers crept on the road, and Ibromaliöm saw they were no longer fully human. Their skin was now ashen, their eyes had lost their pupils, and their lips were gone. Their breathing was labored and sounded as if they were constantly repeating the same word: "Sylveeds. Sylveeds. Sylveeds." Ibromaliöm opened his arms wide, as if to welcome them. His laughter was that of a deranged madman.

"Welcome my children," he boomed. "Come to me, all of you, and drink from my light." He grabbed the *Ithyl Shimea* and flipped it open to the first page. The falling rain parted, leaving the book dry. He held it with both hands against his chest and displayed it for all to see.

The creatures crept forward until they were able to see what the man was holding.

Their shrieks of agony rang loudly, echoing like a bad dream along the road. Ibromaliöm's laughter rang louder still.

3. Wings of Shame

> *"The Temple knows no bounds, no borders, no limits. It is not defined by its structure, however magnificent, by its order, however efficient, or by its army, however powerful. It is not held together by its priesthood, or even by its magic. No, the Temple of Baal is defined by a negation, an interdiction, or a rejection: Never the Pit. Everything else, no matter its importance or beauty, is irrelevant before the Pit."*
> —**Sayings of Jehdi, Great Priest of the Temple of Baal.**

"The kitchen? Why the kitchen?" asked King Jamiir, bemused.

"We don't know, sir, but the attackers have holed themselves up in the kitchen. Reinforcements from Baal are on their way, sir."

King Jamiir stood in full armor in Silent Training Area 1, which had been transformed into a central command for the forces of Baal. They had defended the castle while the guests were confined to the Royal Hall. Jamiir could not understand why the attackers had gone to the kitchen rather than storming the upper levels of the castle. "Have you sent for reinforcements?"

"Yes, sir, two contingents of Baal should be joining us soon. With the additional force we will be able to overtake the enemy."

"Enemy, enemy? These are my people, and they remain so even if they have lost their senses. Remember this, Captain."

"Yes, sir."

The King sighed. "Let them have their way inside the kitchen and wait for reinforcements. Hopefully, when they see they are outnumbered, they may come back to their senses and we may avoid bloodshed."

"Yes, Your Majesty."

"Have you been able to locate the Queen?"

"No, Your Highness. As soon as the castle has been pacified we will continue the search."

"You do realize what it would mean for all of us if the slightest misfortune were to have inconvenienced my wife?"

The King had invited him to attend Hiyam's victory that evening, and to keep a low profile, the man of Baal had the good sense to show up in civilian attire. The captain's vague look of concern told King Jamiir that he did not know whom Ramel was related to.

"My wife, the Queen, is the High Priest Sharr's niece …" The King watched with cynical amusement as the captain's expression changed from professional flaccidity, to slight annoyance, to vague disquietude. The name of the priest was familiar, but the captain could not place it.

"The High Priest of the Temple of Babylon," whispered the King.

Instantly, the captain's placid cheeks caved in as if sucked by an interior void. Anguish became distress, and distress wrung his face as it burst into utter despair the way pus, when left untreated, bursts from an infected wound. Sweat trickled down his large forehead, ran around his bulging eyes, and moistened the tip of his well-kept mustache. The King's smile broadened into a sickening rictus. Feeling already guilty, even though he was innocent of the Queen's disappearance, the captain's eyes darted from left to right in search of an unsuspecting victim to lay the blame on, someone who could shield him from the wrath to come. He feared the torture chambers of Baal in the depths of the temples. He feared the *Arayat*, the Spell World, where death never comes as a merciful end to unbearable pain. He gazed at the King as if he were seeing him for the first time, the way a famished toad eyes a nearby fly. Inwardly, the captain pleaded with the gods to use Jamiir as his shield, his scapegoat. As if he were able to read the man's mind, the King's frame shook under a silent chuckle, for he knew that Sharr would have neither the time, nor the patience, to triage the guilty from the innocent. Sharr would send the whole lot of them, everyone still alive in this castle, to the Kerta priest, and once their minds had been turned inside out, once their every thought and feeling had been made known to Baal, they would be condemned to an eternity of suffering in the Spell World.

The King was certain the captain did not know half of what he himself knew about the ways of Baal, but it did not matter. The man had enough knowledge of the Temple to know they were now no better off than a pair of walking dead, unless, and until, they were able to locate Her Majesty and present her safe and sound to her uncle.

"Your Majesty, in this case, there is not a moment to lose. I will give orders to my men to mount a counter-attack and regain control of the castle, then we should—"

"This will not be necessary, my good man," interrupted Hylâz as he entered. "I would rather avoid senseless bloodshed, if we could."

"My dear Hylâz, do you have news of my wife?"

"Your Majesty, *news* is a lofty word a lowly zakiir such as myself does not have the luxury to use. Nevertheless, I would say that any search for Her Majesty within the castle's precinct will, I am afraid, prove futile."

The King's eyes narrowed to a slit. The captain felt what scores of people had felt over the years: the strong urge to pry open a zakiir's mind by any means possible and force him to reveal his secrets. However, he knew the attempt would be futile, resulting in the zakiir's death and the onset of a terrible curse on him. To his knowledge, no one had ever succeeded in forcing a zakiir to reveal his secrets. Those learned in the ways of the Arayat were painfully aware of the curses that would render a zakiir mute and deaf, while his attackers would be quickly found and delivered in the hands of a Kerta priest. Blackmailing a zakiir was suicide.

"Is Her Majesty well?" asked the King.

"I cannot tell," replied Hylâz.

"Should we search for her?"

"I would advise His Majesty to do what is on His Majesty's heart, all else would be in vain at the present moment." Hylâz bowed. "I bid His Majesty goodbye. Duty takes me northward."

The King and the captain watched with jealousy as the zakiir left the Royal Hall completely unconcerned by the crisis at hand.

"So it is true," said the captain at last, "A zakiir's freedom is greater than that of the King's."

"You may return to your task, Captain."

After the captain's departure, the King stood motionless.

"I would advise His Majesty to do what is on His Majesty's heart, all else would be in vain at the present moment." The words of Hylâz rang in his ears like a mental scream. Ramel was twenty years his junior and there was no love lost between them. She was beautiful and haughty, beyond his reach, and their marriage was one of convenience. Had she borne an heir, she would have assumed the reins of power and he would have been a mere figure, until the return of his son or daughter from Babylon.

Still, I was not entirely without resources. Knowledge of medicinal plants can be readily available to a king, and she never suspected that she ingested a slow-acting poison every day that kept her barren.

He had bargained that once Babylon realized she was unable to carry an heir, they would consider her to be cursed by the gods and not even Sharr would be able to protect her. Then, a different poison would have delivered him from her cruelty. All these years, his head had been filled with thoughts of Ramel, but not his heart. He could not stand her pompous, arrogant, impatient attitude filled with an air of Babylonian superiority that nothing seemed to satisfy; just as she could not understand his willingness to bow to Baal and play the diplomatic game. Their union had been one of mutual contempt, and in that, they had been faithful to each other. He had never been unfaithful to her out of fear, and she had never been unfaithful to him out of contempt, for no man in Tanniin could be worthy of her attention. In the end, they were made for one another, so alike, and yet, so different.

"At the very least, my dear Ramel," whispered the King, "I can take consolation in the fact that you will not be able to witness my disgrace this time around."

How long had he been pulling this cart with his bare hands? Rain fell gently through the forest's high canopy and mingled with his tears. Disheveled, haggard, lost and afraid, Garu plowed on, and hauled the peasant's cart he had purchased for one gold coin. It was an open cart cobbled together from rough wood planks, with a left wheel slightly wider than the right, enough to jerk the cart with every rotation and cause Ramel to moan with pain.

He could not recall how he had managed to carry her from the depth of the earth back to the surface. A remnant of reason in his tormented mind told him not to go back to the castle, that it would be her death, and his execution. When a peasant, with his cart and pony, had passed by the entrance to the Mine of Bronze, Garu entreated him, promising him a coin if he would take him and his "sick sister" back north.

They had ridden for most of the evening and into the night, but the peasant, now closer to home, refused to go any further. After Garu had convinced the man to sell him the cart, the elated peasant continued his journey home with his pony and one gold coin to gladden the heart of his wife and children.

Like a muted beast, Garu had plowed forward, pulling the cart through sheer determination, ignoring the pain that racked his body and ignoring his hunger and exhaustion. He kept moving forward, guided by an old memory from that happy time in his life when he did not know Ramel, when he did not love her. He had left the main road and followed a path in the dark, a path that seemed all at once foreign and familiar; one he must have trodden hundreds of times before. As he drew closer to a cluster of giant pine trees, he knew he had reached his destination. His mind cleared and he understood why he had brought Ramel here. He stood beneath a particular tree, and his hands shook as he felt the wide trunk. Garu sighed with relief when his fingers found what he had been looking for: the start of a ladder that had been hammered into the living wood. *Up there you will be safe, my love. No one will harm you again. I will search the forest for medicinal plants and I will heal you.*

Resolutely, Garu grabbed the third rung of the ladder and pulled himself up. Ramel, sensing his disappearance, moaned louder for she could no longer speak.

"I am here, Your Majesty," he said softly. "I am by your side."

He forced himself to ignore her pitiful moans and climbed as quickly as his strength allowed. Panting, he reached a platform that he had built during his youth, a sturdy surface wide enough to hold a small house, and strong enough to perdure as long as the tree stood. Quickly, Garu unlatched the simple lock, pushed the door, and peered inside. The room smelled of resin and dust. He stepped in and rummaged in the dark for the lantern he had stowed away. Quickly, he lit it, hung it on the ceiling, then went back outside and found the loading cart he had used in the past to haul pots and plants; it still hung against one of the walls of his room. Water had rotted the edges of two of the four planks, but for the most part, it was still as sturdy as when he had made it. More importantly, the rough net that had prevented the cart's contents from spilling was intact.

Did I leave the pulley and the rope inside, or did I take them with me the last time I was here? He could not remember. Feverishly, he went back inside and forced himself to calm down. *No sense to panic now, they must be here*. He opened several trunks, rummaged through their dusty contents, and let go a quick shout of victory when he found what he had been looking for. Garu went back outside and hung the pulley on the hook protruding from a nearby branch, nearly falling to his death in the process. He then tied one end of the rope to a ring that held the net together and quickly lowered the cart to the forest floor. Finally, he tied the other end of the rope to a ring located on the outer wall of his small room; his hands worked efficiently, as if he had never left the forest.

He heaved a sigh and wiped the sweat from his forehead. He knew he had to go back down and transfer Ramel from the cart and haul her up to the safety of his treehouse. As he began his descent, he bitterly wished that for once, the Silent were there with him to lend him a hand.

≻⁘⁘≺

Soloron raised his sword in the pouring rain. Lightning, thunder and a great shout answered him. The undergrounders had won a decisive battle. Before them, scattered along Royal Road were the dead bodies of the men of Baal. They were close to two thousand. When he heard Frajil had stormed the castle, Soloron wagered that the soldiers manning the castle would send for reinforcements. He had moved his forces, three thousand strong, from their hideout and managed to reach the last bend in Royal Road, south of the plaza and facing the Mine of Bronze. This bend was at a near right angle with a steep incline. He had positioned his archers on the eastern hills overlooking the bend, while his infantry lay in wait below the road along the western side.

The High Riders processed up, four by four. They marched confidently, in expectation of a swift victory against a ragtag band of ill-equipped peasants. When the first hail of black arrows found their mark, the High Riders did not react as swiftly as usual, and it was only after a second deadly volley that they regrouped into their defensive formation: a series of rectangular blocks covered on all sides by their iron shields.

Under normal circumstances, one or two Kerta priests would have been present among the soldiers to sow fear in the heart of the enemy and provide an additional ring of defense for the men of Baal. But there were no Kerta priests stationed within the barracks of Tanniin-the-Strong—a concession the King had won on behalf of the kingdom. Even if a priest had been on hand, he would not have joined a contingent of soldiers about to invade the royal castle.

Still, a fully formed contingent of High Riders was deadly in action, but Soloron was a former High Rider, and he, therefore, was ready.

He nodded to the archer standing beside him, and a lone fiery arrow streaked the night. Immediately, his infantry went into action. They adopted an identical formation to the men of Baal, but the forward face of their block consisted of a single piece of sturdy wood from which six light-iron rams jutted. These rams were carried by the soldiers, who instead of walking, took to running. Soloron had forced his men to go through this drill hundreds of times until they had perfected their synchronized attack. Their attack was similar to Frajil's, but with more thrust and strength.

The High Riders of the forward block, seeing a dark mass approach, had stood their ground behind a barrage of spears, but the rams had a longer reach than the spears, and when they crashed into the forward shields of Baal, the formation exploded.

The undergrounders backed away and their archers went about their deadly business. Within minutes, the first block of Baal was decimated, leaving the second block exposed. A second fiery arrow streaked the sky and four more fortified blocks of undergrounders, with rams at the ready, rose from the western side and slammed laterally into the High Riders before retreating rapidly to avoid the incoming black arrows. Deprived of a counter-coverage to stem the flow of arrows, and maimed by the iron rams, the High Riders were defeated in short order.

Soloron knew all too well that had the men of Baal been prepared, the battle would have been uncertain at best. But the bad weather, the surprise effect, and the lack of a full contingent of archers to defend them had made the High Riders vulnerable. Still, this was a great victory for his men, for they now knew that the army of Baal was not invincible; it could be defeated.

"Despoil the Baalites. Take their armors, swords, and banners," he shouted. "We will disguise ourselves and overtake the castle. Death to the men of Baal, but the King is mine. Bring him to me alive."

His men shouted in response, and then a great crowd surged from the neighboring hills. Having watched the battle and witnessed its outcome, they were eager to walk under Soloron's banner. He positioned them at the rear, behind his trained men, so that no harm would come to them, and having disguised his troops as High Riders, he marched on the castle after dispatching a dozen scouts southward.

"Spread the word as you go, tell our people the flag of Tanniin flies anew. Let them know the days of Baal are numbered. Then keep watch on the enemy camps at Mitreel and Yaneer, and send news as soon as you see them preparing to move our way."

As he walked at the head of his small army, he looked with great satisfaction at the peasants that swelled his ranks. Soon he would raise a mighty army and march on the main southern encampments of Baal. Once the two southern ports were under his banner, Baal would have effectively lost control over the land. The kingdom would be his to rule.

Frajil had a puzzled look on his face. His men had inspected the kitchen meticulously and did not find a smidgen of roasted chicken anywhere. This was disturbing news to the giant because Soloron had told him, "Tonight we roast the chicken." How can you roast a chicken when there was no chicken? He sat on the kitchen table, trying to unravel the riddle, oblivious of the men who had taken him for their leader, and of the slaves who had joined them alongside some of the kitchen servants.

"Master, what should we do?" asked one of the men.

Frajil took no notice of the question. He was processing the situation. *If Frajil has chicken, Frajil roasts chicken, but no chicken, so …* He grinned, raised himself up and declared triumphantly: "Soloron brings chicken." He looked at the man who had spoken and said, "We wait for chicken here. Soloron brings chicken."

The men around him nodded approvingly. They were convinced that these mysterious sayings had a deep strategic meaning. As far as they were concerned, Frajil was a hero. His fighting skills were matched only by his boldness and courage. Baal had been forced to concede the castle's lower level to the insurrection.

Up one level, the men of Baal were on edge. The reinforcements should have arrived by now. They were beginning to wonder if there had been a change of plans when their sentinels that manned the large balcony cheered. Their forces were finally there.

"Should we press the enemy?" asked a soldier.

Their leader shook his head. "They'll deal with 'em soon enough. You just wait and see."

There were loud shouts outside the castle, then a contingent of High Riders charged the main door. "This is the 6th and 22nd contingent of Baal, open the door by order of the King."

Loud cheers erupted from the second floor while consternation, fear and dismay dissolved the insurgents' courage.

"Open the door, in the name of Baal."

Frajil bolted from his chair and ran to the door. His men, awed by such courage, were determined to fight to the last, but the giant threw the door open, grabbed the captain of the High Riders and … hugged him hard, nearly choking him.

"Look, he's not even using his weapons," whispered some of the men.

"He is smothering the captain of the gray owls."

"He is filled with Tanniin's wrath," answered others.

"Frajil," croaked Soloron, "put me down!"

The giant ignored his brother's command and instead gave him two sonorous kisses, one on each cheek.

"This must be the kiss of death," whispered another of Frajil's followers. "Incredible."

"Frajil happy to see Soloron. Frajil wants chicken."

"Put me down, *now!*"

At last, Frajil relented and let go of his brother. He turned around and was about to loudly proclaim that his brother had come, when Soloron signaled for him to wait.

"Everyone," he said with a hushed voice, "I am Soloron, leader of the undergrounders. My men have ambushed the High Riders and defeated them as you can see by the shields and helmets we bear. Fear not, victory shall soon be ours. To avoid further bloodshed, I will need a few of you to go up ahead of us with your hands over your heads. The men of Baal holed-up on the second floor will think you are defeated and will lower their guard. We will then quickly subdue them."

"High Riders of Baal, do you hear me?"

The call was from the second floor.

"Loud and clear," replied Soloron. "We are nearly done down here. We are rounding up the few survivors and we will be up shortly."

"It's too quiet down there."

"They have all run away. Now shut up and let us do our job."

Soloron looked expectantly at Frajil's men, but they did not seem ready to lower their weapons. *They don't trust me*, he thought.

"Frajil, drop your weapons, put your hands on your head, and walk in front of me." Immediately, Frajil did as his brother asked. He tried to stop himself from laughing but ended-up with his hand on his mouth, his huge frame shaking as if he were about to play a good practical joke. "Do not spoil the surprise," grumbled Soloron. "By the way, what were you doing in the kitchen?"

Frajil became dead serious. The change was disconcerting. "Soloron told Frajil, 'tonight we roast chicken.' Frajil loves chicken."

Soloron's anger flared, but he managed to contain it. His dimwitted brother had stormed the castle because he, Soloron, had used a metaphor that involved a stupid, two-legged bird. This could have ended in utter disaster, but somehow, he had managed to rally these men and storm the castle by himself. Soloron realized this and smiled broadly.

"Frajil, the King is eating the chicken right now."

"Where?" asked the giant, alarmed.

"Upstairs." Soloron addressed Frajil's followers. "Yes, my friends, the chicken of which my brother, Frajil, spoke so poetically is your wealth, your wages, your work, all eaten by that despot who despoils you to fatten Baal. The chicken is your freedom and the freedom of Tanniin. Will you put up with this tyrant?" Before anyone could respond, Soloron placed a finger on his lips. "Are you ready to free the chicken?" They shook their heads vehemently. "Then, let's do this."

The High Riders leaped to their feet when they heard men climb the stairs and relaxed their stance immediately when they saw the prisoners being pushed forward by men of Baal.

"About time," said the man in charge. "What took you so long?"

"It's better to negotiate than to spill blood," replied Soloron evenly. "These are the King's subjects, and it would not go very well with him if we were to kill his people needlessly. A bit of persuasion and here we are."

"How did you manage to subdue this one?" he said, pointing at Frajil.

"He is not all put together, if you follow my meaning. All you had to do was promise him a dish of chicken and that would have been that."

"You mean to say he stormed the castle for—"

"Frajil roast chicken," exclaimed Frajil as if on cue.

"See what I mean?" added Soloron. "You could have saved yourself a a bundle of trouble if you had you paid more attention."

The man was stricken. Negligence was punishable by fifteen lashes, and that meant a bloodied back and a demotion.

"Listen, Captain, why don't we—"

"Why don't you and your men go back to the barracks? This is neither the place nor the time to discuss such things. I'll deal with the King."

Vanquished and dejected, the men of Baal obtemperated. As the last of them left the second floor, Soloron grinned widely. "If you'll hand over your weapons, I'll speak to the Kerta priest," he added for good measure. Soldiers were waiting to collect their weapons at the bottom of the stairs, when their leader suddenly realized what the captain had just said.

"Wait," he yelled. "There are no Kerta priests at the barracks."

A shout of victory answered him as the men of Tanniin streamed into the hallway.

"Drop your weapons!" said one of Soloron's men. The men of Baal understood they had been completely defeated.

≻◦◦◦≺

"Your Majesty, it is over," said the commander of the forces of Baal. "The enemy will be here soon. We must abandon the castle."

"Abandon Taniir-the-Strong? Never!"

"Your Majesty, we must leave or else I cannot guarantee your safety. We will regroup at Mitreel and subdue our enemies. We have no alternative but to abandon the castle, and quickly."

"But what about the Queen? Where is she?"

"Despite our best efforts, she is nowhere to be found. She must have been captured somewhere and forced to leave the castle, Baal be praised. I am certain that by now she is safely away from these savages. I beg Your Majesty to follow me. We have no time to waste."

King Jamiir followed the commander of Baal. He was abandoning his guests, but it could not be helped. He acknowledged his defeat. The remnant of the contingent of Baal went quickly toward the secret stairs by the High Tower. They descended the narrow slippery steps casting off trembling shadows from the uncertain light of the torches. They opened the narrow door that gave way to the inner garden and from there followed the same path that Tanios had taken several hours ago. They opened the hidden gate and walked in the pouring rain toward the stables. They entered quickly to mount their horses, only to find that the stable sheltered no horses. Suddenly the door to the stable was flung open and Abiil, followed by armed men, streamed in. One torch was lit, then another and another. In the progressive light, the King and the men of Baal could see that the stable was full of men in arms. They were outnumbered and more were pouring in.

"Men of Baal," said Abiil, "drop your swords and you shall live."

"Who are you?" asked the King.

Abiil looked at him and spat on the ground. The King knew what that meant: no mercy would be shown to him. He was a dead man. Abiil looked at the men in arms and repeated his call. "You are outnumbered and without hope. We have overtaken the two contingents that came to help you and none of them survived. If you want to avoid their fate, drop your arms and you shall live. You have my word."

Jamiir heard the thud of a sword falling to the ground, followed by another and another. The men of Baal in whom he had trusted deserted him. He was left standing alone with the commander.

"You may go, my friend, they are after me," said the King.

The commander looked at the King, who pushed him gently toward Abiil. The commander laid his sword on the ground.

"Take the traitor to Soloron. He wants to dispose of him personally," said Abiil. He added nonchalantly, "As for the men of Baal, kill them all."

"But you gave your word," shouted the King.

"True," said Abiil with a smile. "I gave my word that they would live, and they did. Now it is time for them to die. I must avenge the blood of my brother. As for you, traitor, your death shall restore to this kingdom its flag and its wings."

"Do not speak of the wings of Tanniin," retorted the King. "Your despicable murder has cast a shadow upon this kingdom, its honor, and its fate. If you must speak of wings, then speak of wings of shame, your shame and mine, for we have failed this great kingdom."

≻ ✦ ✦ ✦ ≺

Soloron smugly sat on the throne as he looked down at the King who stood before him. He felt heady with his new power. Soon he would be crowned king. Soon he would free the kingdom from Baal.

"What a pitiful king you made. You placed your hope in Baal and Baal dropped you like a worthless shoe, a broken bottle. You were a king of illusions, a toy, a thing in the hands of Babylon. You cared more for yourself than you cared for the people or the kingdom. You lived in riches while Baal levied heavy taxes on our people. What have you to say in your own defense?"

The King lifted his head and looked at Soloron. "Would anything I say change my fate?"

"Speak, and I will listen."

"Baal was about to overtake Tanniin. I tried to compromise and give up what was unimportant in order to preserve the crown."

"You have given them open access to the land. The ports of Mitreel and Yaneer are under their control. They have turned them into fortresses. They tax our people heavily and force our men into slavery. Many have disappeared and their parents have not seen them since. Ask the men around you. These were your subjects. Ask them about their firstborn sons, ask them about their daughters."

"I see wisdom in your words," replied Jamiir, contemptibly, "but how will this wisdom stand before the might of Baal? What will you do when their forces come to raze every house, field, and city; when they kill every man and take everyone else into slavery? What will you say to those who will be deported to Babylon to serve as sacrifices to their gods or in their games? Who will stand by them and defend them? You are naïve if you think that a bunch of undisciplined men can withstand the forces of Baal and their magic. They will crush you mercilessly and crucify your men as a lesson for all. Is this fate any better than the one we have? I have tried to weather the storm and preserve the crown of Tannin until better days. I stand before you, guilty, but my heart is at peace. I did what I thought was best for the land."

"You may think of yourself as wise," replied Soloron, "but in your cowardice you confused wisdom with capitulation, courage with subservience, and strength with servile diplomacy. Kingdoms are not forged compromises with a tyrant; they are forged with the steel of hope and the might of beating hearts who know the meaning of freedom. You will be hanged three days hence, and Tanniin will rejoice over your death. Lock the prisoner in the high tower and watch him closely."

The King was taken away and Soloron sat back on the throne, surprised he had stayed the execution by three days. This was unlike him for he favored swift judgments followed by an immediate execution of the sentence. Why he let the man he wanted dead live another day was beyond him. Perhaps the fact that he now assumed responsibility of the kingdom gave him a new appreciation of Jamiir's attempt to negotiate with Baal. Or was it the simple fact that he was now king and wanted to begin his kingdom by a show of generosity? The truth of the matter was that he conceived sympathy for the dethroned king. Under a different set of circumstances, who knows, they might have been friends.

A soldier interrupted his train of thought.

"Sir, what should we do with the dead Baalites in the stable?"

"The Baalites are dead? I thought they had surrendered peacefully."

"Master Abiil ordered them killed to avenge his brother."

"He did what?" Soloron was beyond himself. "Abiil acted rashly, and there is nothing I hate more than men who act rashly. Off with his head!"

"Yes, sir."

The man left and Frajil walked in, looking depressed.

"Frajil, what's the matter?"

"No roasted chicken. Frajil sad."

Soloron sighed. His ambition had been to dethrone the King. Now that it had been satisfied, he realized that he had not given much thought to the daily routine of reigning on a throne. He also knew that his brother's complaint was the first of many he would find difficult to satisfy or assuage.

Suddenly, he noticed that he had never given much attention to an obvious question he should have asked himself at the start of this adventure: *Do I want to be king?*

He was not so sure anymore.

4. Orwutt and Zurwott

"*The Xarg-Ulum is more powerful than the Xarg; it is larger and faster. Like the Xarg, it was created by the Lords of the Deep primarily to help them in their struggle against the dwarfs. Xarg-Ulums pounded at rocks with their fists and dislodged many of the mighty portals that had been erected by the dwarfs to protect their caves. Even though in the end the dwarfs prevailed over these creatures, they did so at a great loss, not the least of which was the destruction of Andaxil, the great cave of the north.*
Since the end of the Wars of Meyroon, the dwarfs never regained the stature they had enjoyed before these wars."
—**Philology of the Dwarfs, Anonymous.**

Resting for a third time, Ahiram sat on a cold slab of rock. He had hoped to stand with El-Windiir's artifacts before the King. *It's already past midnight.* Gloomily, he leaned back and closed his eyes.

Layaleen, EL-Windiir's sword, began to quiver gently against his shoulder. *Strange*, he thought, his senses on alert. *Why is the sword quivering?*

After leaving the tomb of El-Windiir, he had turned right into the narrow passage and had walked for a little over three miles. The light progressively disappeared until he walked in darkness along a steep upward incline that dead-ended abruptly. He bumped into a wall, and to steady his footing, leaned against the stone, only to feel it give way. A hidden door had rotated silently, and he had stepped out in darkness.

That was easy. Outside, his foot hit an obstacle and he fell forward. He crawled on all fours and ended up on the staircase that he had been climbing for the past few hours.

The sword's quivering grew stronger. He shifted his position and rubbed his shoulder, believing it was his sore muscles that tingled.

I climbed 6,674 steps, and each step is about three inches high, so that's close to 1,700 feet. But these steps are four feet long, so as best as I can tell, I must have moved close to five miles eastward.

He sniffed the air. *Fresh. There must be vents, but I can't feel air flowing in.* Ahiram sighed. *If I keep going up, I will soon reach the abode of the gods.*

The sword's vibrations were now jarring.

What's going on?

He touched the blade. *Is this sword going to pummel me?*

An icy shriek cut through the silence like a knife. He sprung to his feet, holding the weapon. How it had landed in his hand, he did not know.

The shriek shattered the silence again just as the wall next to him shook under powerful blows.

Stay, climb down, or climb up?

Having memorized the size and shape of the stairs, he ran up, praying to El he does not bump into a wall or a low ceiling. The shriek sounded repeatedly but it grew distant. *Good, it's not following me. Is it the urkuun?*

His senses on alert, he stopped running and resumed his steady climb until he saw a small point of light ahead. He gripped the sword with both hands and resolutely continued to move forward until he came face-to-face with two identical dwarfs, each holding an odd-looking lantern that cast a soft blue glow.

"Frighteningly frightening is she not?" said one of them.

They were about four and a half feet tall, with braided hair and trimmed beards. They wore sleeveless denim jackets with three large buttons over what looked like thick, collarless burgundy shirts. A five-inch-wide belt cinched baggy, brown leather pants tucked into sturdy work boots. They wore tall, conical-shaped, steel helmets. The base of each helmet was wrapped in a fine silver mesh that was trimmed with a strip of red leather. Diamond-shapes were cut into the leather and strung together with thick silver links.

Ahiram recognized the helmet at once. *Two dwarfs from the southern realm. What are they doing here, thousands of miles from Korridir?*

The dwarf to his left had a gold earring pinned in his left ear, and symmetrically, the dwarf to his right had a gold earring pinned in his right ear. Slowly, Ahiram lowered his blade.

"Who are you? What are you doing here?"

"I am Zurwott," said the leftmost dwarf as he bowed.

"And I, Orwutt," said the other as he bowed in turn.

Ahiram returned their bows.

"We are dwarfs," they said in tandem, "and we are brotherly brothers and brothers of a most brotherly nature," they added, as if it were not obvious that they were twins. "We are enchantingly enchanted to make your quaint acquaintance."

Ahiram cocked his head, canting a smile. He did not expect to meet anyone in this part of the mines, let alone dwarfs. He had so many questions, he did not know where to begin.

"You must be the silently Silent who deftly defied the odious odds by peremptorily participating in the challenging challenge, are you not?"

"I am," replied Ahiram as his smile widened. This was his first conversation with dwarfs. "How did you know?"

"She is not a strangely stranger or a stranger of a strangely stock," explained Zurwott.

"Who is *she*?" wondered Ahiram, confused.

"The Games."

Wrath of the Urkuun – Orwutt and Zurwott

"You call the four Games *she?*"

"Ah," explained Zurwott, "I so happen to be a grammatically inclined grammarian of the dwarfish language. With effusive joy and a joy most effusive, I shall explain plainly and plainly explain, the deeply deep reasons that *she* is the way she is and none other. This shall be done with great alacrity and an alacrity of the first order."

"My brother," translated Orwutt "wants to explain our grammatical rules. He said *she* because in dwarfish, the four Games are one. In the common tongue, we say *one body* to speak of one head, two hands, two feet, and all the rest. The four Games are one challenge, and since *challenge* is feminine, the Games are a *she*, you see?"

"My brotherly brother ought not speak so speedily, and speedily speak in the common tongue, the tongue of the commoners. It behooves him to behave as a dwarfish dwarf, and a dwarf of a dwarfish descending descent, and a descent of the most descending antique antiquity."

"Surely my brotherly brother, and my brother most brotherly has not failingly failed, nor failed failingly to be an observant observer, and an observer of the most observant kind? She is not, at this most present presence, in the best conditioned conditions."

"Who is *she?* The Games?" interjected Ahiram.

"No, your health," observed Orwutt.

Zurwott bowed. "My deeply deepest apologetic apologies, and apologies most apologetically apologizing. I have failed to see that she is presently in need of immediate care and care most immediate. We shall take you right this instant, and instantly to our leading leader, and leader of the greatest leadership, Master Xurgon."

"I would gladly follow you, but I need to get to Taniir-The-Strong as quickly as possible. I thought these stairs would get me there."

"They will bring you to Taniir-On-High," replied Orwutt, who evidently enjoyed the common tongue.

"You may longingly long, and long longingly to know that he is forebodingly forbidden, and forbidden forebodingly," added Zurwott.

"Who is 'he'?" asked Ahiram.

"These stairs," replied Orwutt. "What you are casually calling stairs is in dwarfish *karak stirks*, or wrinkled giant."

"Wrinkled giant?" confirmed Ahiram. "So, if he is forbidden," he continued, a twinkle in his eye, "why are the two of you in it?"

"No, no, not *in* it," said a shocked Zurwott. "*In it—karak stirks kin arix*—this would be dreadfully dreadful, and dreadful beyond any dreadfully descriptive description. *Karak stirks xal kadum. On him*, see?"

"Fine," grumbled Ahiram. "Why are you *on him?*"

"We were conductively conducting a pressingly pressing examination of a strip that abides above our currently current position. A surprise most surprising came to be in existence today and not earlier. We observingly observed, and observed most observingly, that she has been exceedingly extended, and extended most exceedingly."

Ahiram gazed at Orwutt, waiting for a translation.

"A flat strip, two hundred yards above us, is longer than she was yesterday. She grew by seventy feet overnight and broke into these stairs. We were assessing the damage."

"Strips don't extend on their own," noted Ahiram.

Unknowingly, the Silent had just questioned the dwarfs' alibi. Their honor demanded a robust counterargument. A robust dwarfish argument consists of a flourish of repetition—up to seven—all stressing the same point.

"Exact exactitude, and exactitude most exact," began Orwutt who spoke in dwarfish to mollify his brother. "This strip was shorter than she is today, and we are bereft of a tangibly tangible explaining explanation."

"She was not yesterday where she is today," forged ahead Zurwott. "Accidentally, and by an accident of the most accidental nature, we landed in the most inappropriately inappropriate, and coincidentally coincidental manner, here and nowhere else."

Wrath of the Urkuun – Orwutt and Zurwott

"Which is of course inappropriately inappropriate," advanced Orwutt. "Unless, one considers with considerate consideration, that our presence is innocently inadvertent, and inadvertently innocent."

"Even though it is not licitly licit," rejoined Zurwott.

The brothers had begun to warm up for the real argument.

"Neither is our present presence illicitly illicit since there is no voluntary breach of the dwarfish code of conduct," clarified Orwutt.

"Such an illicitly illicit presence must be voluntarily assumed, and assumed most voluntarily. This would be a demeaning misdemeanor, and a misdemeanor most demeaning no respectably respecting dwarf would wittingly commit," stipulated Zurwott.

"As a matter of course," echoed Orwutt.

Zurwott drew closer and said in a hushed voice, "You must understandably understand, and understand most understandably that Master Xurgon will inquire inquiringly about our present presence in this locatable local."

Orwutt took over. "Such an inquiring inquiry will require a tactfully tactful explaining explanation."

Seeing that Ahiram was confused, Zurwott thought to clarify, "The explanation would consider considerately, and considerately consider every factual fact under consideration which has been presently presented before your present presence."

Feeling dizzy, Ahiram leaned against the wall. The two dwarfs drew closer to steady him.

"It would be judiciously judicious to reservedly reserve the remaining remainder of our argumentative argument until later and not before," suggested Zurwott.

"A wise wisdom, and a wisdom most wise," concurred his brother.

"So what brought your colony to the mines of Tanniin?" Ahiram's voice was faint, but the dizziness was starting to fade.

"Our forefathers forged these august mines under Erux the Great."

Orwutt glanced at Zurwott to stave off any further recrimination about the use of the common tongue.

"By this august name, he designated with intentional intent, El-Windiir; a man of happily happy memorable memory amongst the dwarfs. We remember him by many names," added Zurwott, who tried to speak in a dwarfish language that approximated the common tongue. Ordinarily, he would have said, "for we memorably remember and remember most memorably," instead, he shortened it to "we remember him." Dwarfs seldom spoke in the direct mode, as it was considered a threat among them. They preferred to speak with flourish, doubling and tripling the adjectives to defuse any possible tension arising from an unintended—or sometimes intended— misunderstanding.

"A long-standing tradition between Tanniin and our forefathers requires a colony of dwarfs to be present in the upper mines."

"I was not aware of this arrangement," replied Ahiram.

"Which is a great consoling consolation to our earful ears. Had it been differently different, and different most differently, we would be directed directly to conclusively conclude that a desolating desolation had invaded the presently present. Your uttering utterance suggestively suggests, and suggests suggestively, that he is well protectively protected and protected in the most protective manner."

As they continued to climb, Orwutt restated Zurwott's statement. "The arrangement between Tanniin and the dwarfs—that's the 'he' my brother is referring to—is a secret. Since you were not aware of this arrangement, our presence remains a secret."

Ahiram nodded. "Where did that shriek come from?" he asked.

Among dwarfs, abrupt topic change was typical. The dwarfs loved to weave disparate topics into a loosely connected conversation. A dwarfish discussion was a mental promenade meant to forge friendships by a mutual enjoyment of words crafted into sentences like gems lining an elegant crown.

"Ah, we cannot freely speak, nor speak freely of such meaty matters and matters so meaty. They effectively affect, and affect effectively the tempered temper, and temper most tempered of our fearsomely fearless leader and leader most fearlessly fearsome," said Zurwott with an accompaniment of animated hand gestures.

"Master Xurgon would be upset," translated Orwutt.

"Nevertheless, we are required per our sundry sojourn in these remarkably remarkable halls to bring her immediately, and no later than necessary, before Master Xurgon," added Zurwott.

"Who? The conversation?"

"No, the extended strip," clarified Zurwott.

"Fine," sighed Ahiram. "Let's go have a chat with Master Xurgon."

At the word "chat," Zurwott frowned disapprovingly, and Orwutt grinned. Ahiram sheathed his sword and followed the two dwarfs. As they continued up, they heard the shriek again. They felt the ground rumble beneath their feet.

"An earthquake," said Ahiram.

"No, no. No earthquake," replied Orwutt hastily before his brother had the chance to express profusely his vehement disagreement. In Zurwott's eyes, Ahiram had displayed a shocking ignorance of the ways of the rocks—the deep dwarfish knowledge of all that existed beneath the surface of the earth. From childhood, dwarfs were taught the language of the rocks. The twins were in their early twenties and could easily distinguish the sound of a tumbling boulder from that of a rock avalanche, a tremor, a tear, a crack, a cleft, a fissure, a cave-in, and a myriad of other subterranean movements. The display of ignorance that men put forth whenever they ventured into caves was appalling.

"A controlled avalanche," explained Orwutt. "Master Xurgon must have ordered a passage to be closed. Let us hasten."

They heard the shriek again, and it kept them company as they quickly climbed the stairs. They reached the collapsed wall the dwarfs had mentioned and stepped off the staircase. They followed a path that led them to a perfectly aligned set of stairs. The smooth walls were interspersed with regularly spaced alcoves where small torches burned, which Ahiram knew meant they had reached the dwarfs' quarters. Exhausted, he wished he could rest. Progressively, the steps stretched and became a flat passage leading, after several turns, to a comfortable cave where a wood-burning fire crackled brightly. Six dwarfs stood guard by three doors. A delicious smell of chicken soup filled the air and Ahiram could see freshly baked bread.

Orwutt and Zurwott brought him near the hearth while the cook, who happened to be a man and not a dwarf, served him a hearty bowl of chunky soup and a generous piece of bread. Ahiram recognized the cook; he was the butcher that had sliced the meat for the praniti at the start of the Games of Bronze.

"Isn't it past supper time? Why is the kitchen still open?"

"A dwarf's kitchen never closes," replied the cook as he wiped his hands with the towel tied to his side. "They eat day and night."

No one seemed surprised to see the Silent, or if they were, they hid it well. He wanted to ask questions but was too tired and too happy to sit next to the hearth. He bit into the bread and smiled contentedly. After the events of the day, this felt like home.

"More?" asked the cook as he saw him devour his dinner. Ahiram blushed. The cook gave him a second bowl and a larger chunk of bread. "I bet you haven't eaten in a while," he said with a smile.

Just then, another dwarf walked in. Ahiram saw he was dressed in the fashion of the northern dwarfs: black pants over leather sandals, a black flowing shirt, and no helmet.

Orwutt and Zurwott rose to their feet and bowed. Ahiram was about to copy them when the cook placed a hand on his shoulder and shook his head. "Keep eating," he whispered. "Interrupting a guest's meal is rude among dwarfs."

Wrath of the Urkuun – Orwutt and Zurwott

Two southern dwarfs bowing before a member of the northern realm. How interesting, thought the Silent.

Master Xurgon's long, braided silver hair reached down to mid-back. His arms and legs were knots of muscles, and his black eyes shone like obsidian. He starred at the two dwarfs who stood as still as rocks.

"Had I knowingly known where you had been, I would have sent you to the quarry to turn flinted flint into pebbles. You have been imprudent. A danger has been occasioned by your absent absentmindedness. I should punish you in proportion to the rising voice thundering behind these walls. This is a bear to carry, for you are the nephews of the immense Kwadil who forwarded your singular personal personalities to me."

Ahiram gave a start when he heard the name of Kwadil, for this was the dwarf that had sold him into slavery to Commander Tanios. He did not know how to react. *Wait and see*, he thought.

"He is not speaking real dwarfish," he whispered in the cook's ear, mostly to distract himself.

"The northern jargon is less wordy, especially when a northern dwarf is angry, as Master Xurgon is presently. And by the way, he can hear us."

Ahiram busied himself with his soup.

"But Master, we were not consciously conscious, nor conscious in a consciously manner that she even existed. She was not there before, and now she is." Orwutt was visibly agitated.

"I would say more," protested Zurwott, "we were conscientiously conscientious, and conscientious in the most conscientious of ways."

"Hush now, Orwutt and Zurwott. Do not add humdrum to badly bad deeds. You were where you should not have been, and were not where you should have been. Is it not so? Now then, a corridor is a faithfully faithful friend. She does not move and go about like mindless dwarfs. She stays where she was carved."

"Carved she was and carved she remains." replied Orwutt, rather vehemently. "But I dare say that in the day that preceded this day she was shorter than what she is now." He waived his hand to prevent a forthcoming interruption by Xurgon. "I say that she was shorter because of a landslip. There is a scree to assuage your commanding irritation and demonstrate beyond remonstration that it is as I say."

"And we can demonstrate with the assuredness of the rocks that it is as my brother has said," added Zurwott.

"Is this one of your disorderly disordered ordinarily ordinary tricks layered in extraordinarily extraordinary empty utterances?"

"I should like to negatively assert with the most assertive negativity that no tricky tricks, nor tricks of a tricky nature, are hiding behind our most sincerely sincere stand."

"Our stand can be effectively demonstrated and demonstrated with great effectiveness," added Orwutt.

Master Xurgon's gaze bore into the twin brothers as if wanting to extract truth out of them. He grunted, shrugged his shoulders, and looked at Ahiram.

"Well now, my friend, what is your opinion?"

The abrupt change in style surprised Ahiram. He desired to stay outside the verbal joust, so thought it best to tell Xurgon that he had no opinion but recalled a lecture from Commander Tanios, *"If a dwarf directs an intelligible question to you, he wants your opinion. Not to offer one would gravely insult him."*

"The broken wall is real. The shrieks are real," advanced Ahiram prudently. "Orwutt and Zurwott strike me as reasonable dwarfs. I would look into their claim before drawing any conclusions."

A thundering roar answered him, followed by powerful poundings. Ahiram nearly jumped. He thought the roaring monster was standing beside him. Three dwarfs ran in, stopped and bowed respectfully before their master.

"Xern, first ax reporting, sir."

"Brix, second ax reporting, sir."

"Arax, third ax reporting, sir."

"Xern, please provide your truthfully true report now, and not a moment later," replied Xurgon.

Ahiram may have been amused by the greetings had the shriek been less chilling. By asking for their "truthfully true report now, and not a moment later," Master Xurgon had the young man convinced he was minimizing the danger, but this was due to the Silent's lack of experience. Among dwarfs, poor diction and slouched posture were dishonorable. When sojourning among dwarfs, humans quickly learn not to measure danger by the length of a dwarfish conversation; better to measure danger by their feet. Indeed, dwarfs' feet rarely touched—a sign of timidity and punctiliousness tantamount to cowardice—unless they were facing a grave danger. Presently, the left foot of each dwarf hugged his right foot like a newlywed couple.

"Master Xurgon," said Xern, in a booming voice. "It has become impossibly impossible, and impossible in the most impossible manner to contain the uncontainable. She is growingly growing frantically frantic."

"She has reached such a degree of agitated agitation," added Brix in a louder voice, "and an agitation so agitated that it is agitating us to the highest level of agitation."

"It is preventing our cogitated cogitation and our cogitation that is customarily cogitated," interjected Arax, in a voice so soft Xurgon had to strain to hear what he said. Arax's sadness was painted on his face. "It is preventing our preventative strategic stratagem from strategically preventing our stratagem from turning into a preventative retreat."

Xurgon tapped his pipe on the chimney's sill before filling it with fresh tobacco. "I thank you for the confirmation of the factual facts, plainly painful, which have been imposed, with a momentous imposition on our broad shoulders. Do get back to your respectable positions and thrive to protect her from the assaults of the uncontainable one. She must not cross our linear lines."

"Will the beast quietly quiet down, and quiet down quietly, once the happening of the sacrificing sacrifice has happened?" asked Arax.

"Master Arax," interjected Zurwott, "I would give this advising advice to constrict constructively, and constructively constrict peremptory confabulating confabulation until they acquire the solidifying solidity of solids, and not before."

Arax and Zurwott locked eyes—or rather locked brows. Ahiram quickly understood there was no friendship lost between these two.

The dwarfs bowed before leaving the room. Ahiram could tell Master Xurgon was not pleased with Arax's mention of a sacrifice. The Silent wanted to know more, but chose to temporize.

Master Xurgon waited for the three dwarfs to leave before focusing on Ahiram. "Now my young friend, has our food assuaged your hunger?"

"Yes, thank you," replied Ahiram. "How do you know the common tongue so well?"

Master Xurgon chuckled. "I am far older than I seem and have spent many years in the company of Commander Tanios. I hail from the northern realm," he added, with a mischievous glint in his eyes, "and have been with the commander to Alep and back. One of these days you should ask me about Alep."

"The northern realm," said Ahiram, pretending he did not know, "so why are you are commanding a—"

"A southern host? You have an observing eye, my young friend."

"There is a full dwarfish host in these mines?" asked Ahiram, shocked.

A *host* was a military dwarfish unit comprised of seven hundred and fifty dwarfs.

Xurgon chuckled. "I shall forthwith remember that I am speaking to a Silent. Your knowledge of our lore is greater than that of most humans. Technically, it is a minor host, consisting of three companies minus two platoons, but we need not quibble among friends." *Six hundred and fifty dwarfs are living in these mines behind our backs.* Ahiram was amazed.

"Regrettably, I am unable to disclose the reasons that placed a northern dwarf in charge of a southern host. But enough about me, let us talk about you instead. The regrettable news concerning your demise was happily premature."

Ahiram smiled.

"I want to know what you were doing on these stairs. Legends dwell in their realm." He eyed the Silent like a dragon eyes an intruder.

Ahiram relaxed his shoulders and adopted a disaffected stance. "High Riders chased me over a cliff and left me for dead. I managed to escape and accidentally stumbled upon these stairs. I thought they would lead me back to the castle."

"Accidentally, accidentally," grumbled Master Xurgon, "you should learn to choose your words more carefully. You have revealed much more than you intended, but you are hiding more than I thought. No matter, in time all shall be revealed. Tell me now, young Silent, do you really believe it is a coincidence that you showed up here a few days after the *xarg-ulum* manifested her presence?"

"Xarg-Ulum?" asked Ahiram as he tried to understand. "Is this the name of the creature behind the shrieks we have heard?"

"Indeed. What you have heard, friend, is the dreaded xarg-ulum, or a *béghôm* as you commonly say."

"A béghôm?" Ahiram jumped to his feet and his empty bowl tumbled noisily. "It exists?"

"Yes, my friend, *she* exists," explained Xurgon. With an agility that surprised the Silent, he picked up the bowl and handed it to the cook. "To subdue both dwarfs and giants, the Lords of the Deep created the *Annuna-Ki*, strident hordes, as they called them. These creatures were swift with both swords and axe but were no match for the shield-stone of the Marada or the strength of our portals. So the Lords of the Pit, created the béghôms to strengthen the Annuna-Ki and break down our defenses. Despite this reinforcement, the Annuna-Ki failed to conquer

Andaxil, the greatest dwarfish cave. May Kerishal, gentle goddess of healing, preserve us from this plight."

"If I may," interjected Ahiram, "why is Andaxil the greatest of all dwarfish caves?"

Master Xurgon smiled gently. Unlike most dwarfs, interruptions and abrupt change of subject aggravated him, especially when a tale was being told, and most especially when he was the tale-teller. Still, he had to admit the question was pertinent and was well worth an answer.

"Two words, if I may speak in your hasty ways: liquefied meyroon. One ounce of which is worth four kingdoms. Alone, the Malikuun, the Lords of Light, can bring forth the mystical steel that no fire can melt. In Andaxil, our forefathers managed to store a great quantity of meyroon in liquid form. How they did it, no one knows. This treasure is Andaxil's unsurpassed glory and the reason behind the Lord of the Deep's assault."

"So then," Ahiram surmised, "this explains how the dwarfs forged swords of meyroon. But then when El-Windiir was a slave mining the meyroon for the Lords of the Deep in Tanniin, were there dwarfs with him who knew how to melt meyroon?"

Master Xurgon's eyes narrowed. "Why do you ask?"

Ahiram shrugged his shoulders. "I've heard tales. The stuff of legends I suppose, about a sword of meyroon the dwarfs forged for El-Windiir. I don't suppose this sword would have been forged in Andaxil?"

Master Xurgon grunted. "On this point, our tale differs from Tanniin's lore."

"I see." Not wanting to offend his host by asking pointed questions, Ahiram reverted back to the main topic. "So the attack occurred during the Wars of Destruction?"

"We believe it happened after the fall of Harbor Rohanon."

"Almost five thousand years ago?"

"Yes, indeed."

"So then, this béghôm is five thousand years old?"

"If we let the tale be told, answers shall be provided appropriately," stated Master Xurgon somewhat flatly.

Ahiram felt like adding: and shall be appropriately provided. Instead, he bit his tongue.

"As I was saying," continued the old dwarf, "the Lords of the Deep created béghôms at great expense of their powers, and embedded them in the twelve hives of *Annuna-Ki*, each twelve thousand strong. Then the armies of the Pit fell on the combined forces of dwarfs and the Marada like a raging flood. The war raged for three years and six months. In the end, the Annuna-Ki broke through our ranks, and we were defeated. Many dwarfs died, but many more of the Pit's offspring perished. When the remaining hordes reached the great cave, they found its portal open, and in their great haste, rushed inside. The great portal slammed shut, and even the mighty béghôms could not destroy the greatest door built by dwarfish hands. Enraged, the monsters destroyed the cave's foundation, and she crushed them as she died. We lost her in the heart of the mountains."

"Who is 'she'?" asked Ahiram prudently. "Andaxil?"

Xurgon nodded in silence. The Silent understood how the dwarf felt. After a short while, Xurgon continued.

"We lived in peace, and many of us forgot the existence of these beings. Then, Dilandiir I, invited Karak-Dargon, my ancestor of illustrious memory, to come and take possession of these caves."

"Dilandiir the First?" Ahiram asked, "He was the fifty-eighth King of Tanniin and the first monarch who was not of El-Windiir's blood. He led Tanniin two thousand years ago and his reign lasted for twenty-six years."

"You are correct. Our tale recounts a famous battle that Karak-Dargon fought against a xarg-ulum, and we thought our ancestors had defeated the monster. But, two years ago, she showed up again."

"After *two thousand years?*" Ahiram was skeptical. "That does not make any sense."

"Yes, after two thousand years," Xurgon agreed.

Right when I started training for the Games. What a strange coincidence, Ahiram thought.

"We built massive walls to contain her, and then six days ago, she began pounding on these walls with a ferocity we have never seen before."

Master Xurgon grabbed a chair and set it down with its back toward Ahiram. He sat facing the Silent and leaned his powerful arms on the back of the chair.

"As you pointed out, this béghôm is long-lived, far beyond her mortal years. So, the source of her longevity must be found in—"

"Magic!" interrupted Ahiram.

"Magic indeed," retorted Xurgon. "So, there we are, there *you are*, and there *she is*."

Master Xurgon's implied accusation did not go unnoticed by Ahiram. He pondered if he should tell the dwarf that he had found El-Windiir's sarcophagus, but decided against it.

I need stronger evidence that links this monster to El-Windiir's artifacts.

He changed the subject slightly and asked, "Have you ever seen this béghôm? What does she look like?"

"Seen her?" snorted Xurgon. "We fought her. She is twelve or thirteen feet tall, with the head of a large cat, yellowish eyes cast between a bear's snout and bat-like ears. She is covered with white fur, and moves with great alacrity. Her eyesight is keener than an eagle's even in the darkness of the caves, and her olfactory sense is superior to dogs. One of her blows would kill the strongest man. She is a mighty enemy."

"Still, *one* xarg-ulum against a dwarfish host?"

"We have wounded her multiple times, but she always recovers. The magic that sustains her also heals her."

"Can you not break this spell?"

Xurgon snorted derisively. "Magic is the offspring of fools."

"Tonight's report says that you are losing ground."

"She has been pounding on a wall for the last three nights and three days. We fear she will break through, unless we can stop her." The dwarf's eyes bore into Ahiram's. "What is driving her, I wonder?"

"Hmm, I wonder too," replied Ahiram. Master Xurgon's breath was fouled by his constant pipe smoking; and Ahiram coughed from the smoke as well as the stench.

"Something that was not here before the black sun."

"The black sun?" asked Ahiram, surprised. "An eclipse?"

"It happened yesterday. Now the monster is beyond herself with rage and foaming fury."

Ahiram grinned. "Never fear, Master Dwarf. A Silent is always of service. I must go to the castle as quickly as possible and not a moment later. I shall then speak to my commanding commander and will bring him to you to help solve this mysterious urgent urgency."

Masker Xurgon's roaring laughter filled the cave. "I told Tanios to hire a proper dwarfish grammarian to teach his Silent, but being the miser that he is, he preferred to teach you himself. Well, my young one, you should stick to the common tongue until someone teaches you proper dwarfish speech."

"About that sacrifice then ..." asked Ahiram, mortified.

"An unpleasant unpleasantness I would rather not deal with," replied Xurgon behind a cloud of smoke. "A tribe living in the southwestern side of Taniir-On-High worships the béghôm."

"How?" asked Ahiram, confused. "The beast showed up two years ago. Is that when they started worshiping her?"

Xurgon shrugged his shoulders. "Who knows? They may remember her like we do and think their godly god is back. They believe the wrath of the béghôm must be assuaged or their crops will fail and their women of child-bearing age will not bring forth offspring for the next seven years." Xurgon heaved a deep sigh. "To calm her wrathful wrath, they want to present her with a peace offering. We have tried to dissuade them from this unpalatable practice, but they adamantly insist that the god of thunder, as they call her, will not be appeased unless a sacrifice is offered."

"Why does it bother you if they sacrifice to the béghôm?"

Xurgon winced. "They do not offer an animal. They offer a slave." Xurgon fell silent. Orwutt and Zurwott suddenly felt a great urge to inspect their nails, which every self-respecting dwarf must keep clean.

Ahiram sat motionless, then calmly asked, "When is the sacrifice?"

"Seven days from now," answered Orwutt.

"How far is this cave?"

"Why?" asked Xurgon with a worried expression on his face.

"I will rescue this slave."

"You cannot," Xurgon said. "To reach that cave, you must follow a slippery passage close to the béghôm's lair."

"What about reaching it from the outside?"

"Impossible, these people guard it possessively during the sacrificial sacrifice and they will not give us peaceful permission to enter. Our exchange degenerates into impolite recriminations with the tearing of beards and hair. This is undignified," he said, caressing his beard. "She is a difficult tribe to deal with."

Ahiram fell silent for a moment. A plan formed rapidly in his mind. Zurwott and Orwutt followed the conversation with great interest.

"You said the béghôm is trying to break through the great wall, did you not?" asked Ahiram.

"Yes, I did."

"Let her."

"What?" Xurgon almost lost his temper.

"Commander Tanios taught us that sometimes the worst thing we can do to an opponent is to give him what he wants."

"Commander Tanios is wise, but this precept is strange to my ears."

"Well, your béghôm—"

"Not *my* béghôm." Xurgon shot the Silent an accusing glare.

"Fair. The béghôm, *this* béghôm, wants to break the wall and you are determined to stop her. What would happen if you weaken the wall at a specific spot?"

"She would break through and attack."

"Perfect," Ahiram continued, "Then she would not expect to find a large, gaping hole under her feet, would she now? Instead of protecting the wall, lay a trap for her. Dig a hole so deep not even a béghôm can escape. Give her what she wants, only give it your way."

"Commander Tanios taught you well I see," said Xurgon.

"The béghôm will instinctively pound in a repetitive manner against the walls of the pit to the point of annoyance," objected Orwutt. "She will then perseveringly fill the hole with rocks and climb out."

"How long would that take?"

"If we spend four days to dig a pit deep enough and wide enough to contain her," asserted Orwutt, "she would escape in two or three days."

"Thirty feet deep and twenty feet wide," confirmed Xurgon. "We can do no more."

"Fine. Then after her capture, use these two or three days to rebuild the great wall around the hole and strengthen it. In the meantime, we can mount a rescue operation to free the slave," said Ahiram.

"This is a dangerously dangerous operation containing a great operational danger," whispered Zurwott.

"I will attempt to rescue this slave whether you help me or not," Ahiram affirmed.

"Negatively negative, and negative to the extreme point of negativity. We love it lovingly and lovingly love it," replied Zurwott.

"We dwarfs thrive on well thought out dangers." Interjected Orwutt, "and she is most deliciously dangerous."

"Let a counseling council assemble. We will hear what she will have to say," said Xurgon.

"Who?" asked Ahiram, confused, "the béghôm?"

"The council of course," replied Xurgon. He added, "She will not convene before dawn of the morrow when the head of the three companies shall be present."

"Meanwhile, let's find you a place to rest," invited Orwutt.

Ahiram shook his head. "I must go the castle."

It was Master Xurgon's turn to shake his head. "In broad daylight, it would take you a day and a half to reach Taniir-the-Strong Castle. At night, with a powerful storm raging, you will need three days to reach your destination, and in optimal conditions, two days to return. You will have no leeway to deal with unexpected events."

Ahiram bit his lower lip and contained his anger. He had hoped the King could declare him a free man just in time to rescue the slave.

I've got to rescue this slave. I have missed the closing ceremony for the Games. Still, when I do show up with the sword of El-Windiir, the King will set me free. I have waited six years, I can wait a little longer.

The roar of the béghôm followed by savage pounding answered him. He shuddered, wondering if he had not acted irresponsibly.

Leaving the slave with this monster is reckless.

He shrugged his shoulders and decided that the best thing he could do until the council meeting was to rest, form a plan of attack, and train with his newly found weapons. *I have four days to learn how to use them.*

"Fine," he said. "Time to rest."

A little while later, after a long-awaited bath, he donned clean clothes and finally lay on a comfortable mattress.

He yawned and closed his eyes. "Béghôm or not," he muttered, "no one will lay his hand on this slave for as long as I live."

Five days hence, he would bitterly regret these words.

5. Rescue Mission

"To sacrifice is to perform a sacred ritual through which blood is spilled to appease and please the gods. With every sacrifice, with every drop of blood, man is bound ever more tightly to the gods. Across the land, there is one high priest, who alone does not sacrifice flesh and blood, but bread and wine. This is Melkizedek of Salem. In my youth, I despised Melkizedek and his sacrifice. Now that I am nearing the gate of death, I have come to understand the meaning of his offering, and I must say that I take great comfort in it."
—Teaching of Oreg, High Priest of Baal.

While Ahiram was speaking with Master Xurgon, the Shadow of Silent headed by Jedarc had ventured deep into the forest west of Royal Road. They had followed the dead horse's tracks out of the Great Pass and along a dirt path that ran parallel to the road for three miles then abruptly veered west into the forest. Thunder rumbled in the distance threatening more rain. A cold wind blew through the underwood and the growing darkness hampered their progress until they could barely see their own boots. Banimelek called a halt.

"No use continuing. We stop here."

"They may still be close," objected Jedarc.

"We don't know what they want. Sheheluth is not combat-ready. We stop for the night."

"But, Banimelek—"

"Tinantel, Faernor is right," said Sondra.

Jedarc was about to give up. "We don't know what they will do to her."

"Why would they drag her this far into the forest? Much easier to kill her somewhere closer to the road and be done with it. No. They are going somewhere specific."

"Faernor is right, Tinantel. We cannot risk it."

"I can manage in the dark," protested Sheheluth. "You go ahead, I don't want to slow you down."

"They don't know we're following them, so they'll stop for the night too," Sondra reasoned.

"Sheheluth," added Banimelek, "We are the Silent. We stick together. We'll spend the night in those trees."

"You guys climb up," Jedarc said. "I'll … ouch. Sondra, no more whacking me on the head."

Sondra ignored his protest. "Tinantel, a word."

"Sheheluth, show me your climbing skills," prodded Banimelek.

"Faernor, I can climb trees just fine, but I'm no monkey."

"That's not what I mean," replied Banimelek.

Sondra waited until she could no longer hear them move up the tree. Jedarc saw her stare at him sternly and laughed. "Hey, you're not going to pull a grumpy-lumpy on me now, are you?" The Silent had nicknamed Commander Tanios grumpy-lumpy for he was prone to lump the innocent with the guilty when dispensing punishments.

Sondra was not amused. Quick as a snake she whacked him on the head again.

"Ouch! Stop it. That hurts."

"How many Silent rules are you proposing we break? You're no Solitary. We stick together and that's an order."

"Fine," grumbled Jedarc, "but at the first light we—"

"Snap out of your romance or so help me, Tinantel, I'll tie you to this tree and leave you here till we get back."

"Sondra, I—"

"What? You're in love? You're willing to risk your life for a girl who tried to kill Ahiram?" Her voice was now hard, unflinching. "Either you'll act as a Silent of the Silent Corps, or I will take the lead. Understood?"

Jedarc smirked. "You're not in love with *me*, are you? This isn't a case of jealousy is it?"

Sondra threw her hands in the air. "You're impossible. I'm in love with the commander."

"You're what?" Jedarc's expression was comical. "Honestly?"

Sondra sighed and began to climb the tree as she grumbled about gullible youth and romantic fools. "Get up that tree and stay there until daylight. That's an order."

Jedarc heaved a sigh and nimbly climbed the old oak as he muttered something about strong-willed women and the bitter lack of bananas.

Moments later, Sondra leaned her back against the thick trunk and sat cross-legged on a massive branch. Holding her crossbow, she assumed the first watch. Assigned by seniority, Jedarc came second, and Banimelek third. Sheheluth would take her turn at dawn.

"Sondra, a word."

"Yes, Faernor?" The Silent did not flinch, but she had to admit that Banimelek's movements were uncanny. Lithe as a leopard, he settled next to her on the branch.

"You want to know how long I'm willing to search for Hiyam?"

He nodded.

"Three days and three nights, then we seek help."

"Sheheluth's safety over Hiyam's?"

"The Silent take care of their own. She's not ready for this."

"Agreed. Will you deal with Jedarc, or will I have to?"

She nodded. "Tinantel can be stubborn when he wants to, Faernor. You deal with him."

He nodded and scaled back up the tree.

Sondra sighed. *I hate leading missions.*

Among the Silent, mission leaders were never imposed. Instead, team members selected their leaders based on trust and merit, in that order. When on a mission, the Silent must be able to blindly trust their leader, which is why Jedarc, with his quick wit, concern for others, and clear-minded vision, was their best leader. Ahiram was too intense for leadership—he was far more suited for the work of a Solitary. As the highest rank of the Silent Corps, a Solitary takes on dangerous missions unaided and alone. Banimelek was taciturn, while Sondra had a tendency for strict formality. Allelia, Alviad and Corialynn were almost as affective as Jedarc and she wished Alviad—with whom she shared more than a passing friendship—was with her now.

She chided herself for this selfish thought and called to mind one of the teachings on friendship from the *Book of Siril 11:1*. *The Silent shall strive to share his friends with new members and turn new members into friends.* "All right then, time to befriend Sheheluth."

⤠·✦·✦·⬸

"This is amazing," whispered Sheheluth. She stood on the topmost branch of the tall oak, arms wide open, eyes closed, her face wet from the rain. "The wind, the rain, the smells. So amazing."

"I take it you don't have much of this where you come from?" asked Banimelek. He was lying on a sturdy branch just below her.

Quick as a cat, she dropped down, sat beside him and dangled her feet. "Where I come from there's not much of anything," she whispered.

He smiled.

"Faernor, do you like being a Silent?"

"Banimelek is just fine," he said softly.

"I think *Faernor* suits you. So do you like being a Silent?"

"Love it."

"Why?"

"Cause witty young girls like you get to ask me impossible questions in the middle of the night."

"I'm not a young girl."

He snorted. "Young means you're new, that's all. It says nothing about who you are. Remember that. It may sound like a curse, because when you're young, you're no better than a slave, but it'll pass. You've got the mettle; you've got the nerves. You're smart and you can handle yourself. The commander is the greatest leader you could wish for. He's got an eye for what's good for you. If he didn't think you could do this, he would not have let you come."

"I didn't think about that."

He grunted.

After a quiet moment she began to sing in a foreign tongue:

> Halen raho malan rajeen,
> Lama bahro alam lateen.
> Neina meto kenna natreen,
> Sorna shadwoh baraa jayeen.

Her voice was beautiful and carried the strength of proud flags fluttering in the morning breeze. To Banimelek, the song evoked the vastness of the sea, still meadows in the early spring, and dawn by the snow-covered Tangorian peaks. Sheheluth switched to another language but kept the melody.

> Jérimal é réro dal si loronond,
> Enté leux sanmiral avion omond.
> Dukelmage aven tu dal si courou onde,
> Majical serein su leuréte en golonde.

Images filled Banimelek's heart with a deep longing for a city he knew was vast beyond comprehension; a city he had never seen. Images of couples strolling lazily on cobblestone riversides as swift ships flowed silently down clear waters.

> Zamein yadal agar çafa karini,
> Beyi biliy uzak lara gidkin.
> Benor mandagi bendagit delmini,
> Benar seuden uzal algidkin.

Sheheluth changed languages yet again. Now, tired men sat in a hookah parlor surrounded by a cloud of smoke. Across the room, on a small stage, a man danced alone, twirling round and round, eyes closed, smiling contentedly. This image surprised Banimelek and stirred memories he did not know he had.

> Maa manta uyol gan lahaba,
> Manahon araw sa buka dalaba.
> Gusk o pumuun mhon ala sahaba,
> Kunin pu umunta sa pama kagu haba.

Sheheluth sang the last verse twice and then grew silent. A bamboo pyramid stood on a promontory overlooking a raging sea where a giant ship, massive beyond reason, was sailing away. Standing by the pyramid a lonely figure waved goodbye. The viewpoint drew progressively closer until Banimelek clearly saw the person's face. He opened his eyes, inhaled sharply and sat erect.

Sheheluth looked at him wide-eyed. "Did I do something wrong?"

Banimelek laughed and rubbed his head. "No, you didn't. That song was beautiful. What is it about?"

"It's known as *Styrol Piatrov*, Song of Four Friends."

"Sounds like the title of a good story."

"Yes, it's a wonderful tale. A wonderful and terrible tale. It's too long to tell in one night, but as the story goes, a cook, a builder, a warrior, and a teacher came from four different kingdoms to Babylon, seeking their fortune. No one would hire them because they did not understand or speak the common tongue."

"Why did they leave their homes?"

"Like I said, it's a long and complicated tale, filled with the sorrow of those who are forced to leave and those who wished they could go but are forced to stay. Anyway, these four asked Sureï the Sorcerer to teach them how to speak in the common tongue in one week, but he refused and told them to go back home. 'Babylon is not for you,' he told them. 'You will only find misery here.' But they couldn't not return home because they had each made a promise."

"And you won't tell me what that promise is because it is part of the long story?"

Sheheluth nodded.

"I didn't know Sureï spoke so many languages," observed Banimelek.

She gazed at him wide-eyed, and he smiled. Her big blue eyes in her small face gave him the impression that she still carried her childhood on her sleeve, as if she had never stopped being a child.

"Where I'm from, we call him *Sureï Arkama*, Sureï the Arch-mage, master of languages."

"I see," said Banimelek. "Please continue."

"The four friends ignored Sureï's warning, pooled what little money they had, and bought a powerful spell that taught them the common tongue like that." Sheheluth snapped her fingers.

"So what happened?"

"They learned to speak it after only a few hours."

"That's it?"

Sheheluth gazed at Banimelek. "They had to pay a price, of course. They forgot their own language and couldn't remember where they had come from. Before they could forget everything, they composed that song and memorized it even though they could no longer tell which language belonged to whom."

"Sad tale."

"Well that's not the end of the story." She smiled and continued. "That happens somewhere in the middle of the story. The end is beautiful."

"Good. I love stories that end well." Banimelek leaned against the tree and closed his eyes. "You should go to sleep now. We'll have a busy day tomorrow."

Sheheluth nodded, and dropped down a few branches where she curled up and closed her eyes. *Faernor is not that scary after all.*

The next morning was cold and drizzly. Sondra woke up to the smell of rabbit roasting over a slow fire. She sauntered back down to the ground and performed a series of stretches.

"Good morning, princess," greeted Jedarc with his unflappable smile.

She turned around to scold him for calling her *princess* and ended up with a peck on her cheek. "You're a pooch," he said. He went over to Sheheluth who had just finished climbing down and tousled her hair.

"Pooch? Tinantel," she protested. "You're taking this too far."

"Hey monkey," said Jedarc over Sondra's protest, "I picked these for you." He produced a bunch of boysenberries.

"I am not—"

Skillfully, Jedarc threw three berries into the young Silent's open mouth. "Good, aren't they?"

"—a monkey," snapped Sheheluth.

I wonder what kind of an animal a pooch is, Sondra thought.

After breakfast, a quick search put them back on Hiyam's trail. The folks who captured her did not try to be discrete. By midmorning, they reached a small clearing where they found the horse's remains under a cloud of flies. The saddle lay to one side, and a large portion of the animal's hind was missing.

"At least fifteen people were here," said Sheheluth.

"Look at the footprints over here," called Jedarc as he bent down beneath a nearby tree.

Wrath of the Urkuun – Rescue Mission

"High Rider's boots," confirmed Sondra.

"How can you tell?" asked Sheheluth.

"This smudge here," explained Jedarc.

"The one that looks like a thunderbolt?"

"Exactly. Distinctively High Riders."

"It's a perfect footprint," observed Sheheluth.

"Hiyam must have left it, hoping someone would be looking for her," Sondra pointed out. "That's a bit of good news."

"Come see. I know who took her."

They joined Banimelek by the horse's carcass.

"There's a pit fire. They ate the horse!"

"The desert people?" offered Sondra.

Banimelek nodded. Jedarc winced.

Commander Tanios had mentioned the desert people in passing once or twice, but did not explain why they were known as the desert people, for they were forest and cave dwellers. Perhaps they acquired this term because of the color of their skin, which was as pale as the sand, or because they were reclusive and exceptionally hard to track.

"Why take her?" wondered Jedarc. "These folks are reclusive and have very little interaction with the outside world."

"They saw she was hurt and wanted to help her, or they have a different purpose in mind," replied Sondra.

"Do they know who the High Riders are?" wondered Sheheluth.

"Unlikely," offered Banimelek.

"No use speculating," said Jedarc. "Let's go."

As time went on, the tracks became fainter and harder to follow until they were gone completely. Despite their extensive training, Sondra, Jedarc and Banimelek were stumped. Hiyam's captors seemed to have completely vanished.

But not Sheheluth. Her ability to read her surroundings was uncanny: a patch of grass bent a different way, a fallen bunch of leaves, a cracked blade of grass, and she knew where to go. When she could not find any trace to follow, she would climb up a tree, examine the surroundings, and know just where to go. She led them relentlessly, deeper and higher, until, by the third day around noon, they reached a narrow plateau encased between three mountainsides.

"They're here," she whispered as the four of them lay in the tall grass.

"How can you be so sure?"

She shrugged her shoulders. "It's as plain as the day is day."

"Over there," Jedarc pointed at three small, white patches visible far against a dark gray mountainside. How Sheheluth managed to find them, she did not explain, and they did not ask. The origin of each Silent was a respected secret. The Corps attracted candidates the world over for reasons none of the Silent could explain. "Where are you from" was not a question a Silent would ask another. Which kingdom each of them hailed from was anybody's guess. Sondra was dark-skinned, rolled the 'r' sound and snapped her tongue whenever a word ended with a 't' sound. This suggested she hailed from the south, but more than that no one could say with any degree of certainty. Whenever he was upset, Banimelek would drop his voice to a whisper and then stress every word as if he were a foreigner speaking the common tongue for the first time. His thick, curly hair and his olive skin made him a citizen of the world. Jedarc was tall and slender with broad shoulders and hair as blonde as a field of wheat in summer. He was at ease with everyone, implying that he grew up in a royal court or a metropolitan city with a sophisticated social life. He spoke without an accent.

"When you become a Silent, you leave your past at the door," Tanios had told them. "Here no one will ask where you are from, how old you are, or whether the name you carry now is your name of origin. We are the Silent and we do not speak of our past."

Whether the commander knew of the Silent's origins was an altogether different question.

Wrath of the Urkuun — Rescue Mission

"Sheheluth, how did you know there were people here?"

Sheheluth pointed to the mountainside. "See the tiny dark patches in the mountain that look like a beehive? Those are caves; lots of them. If they were attacked from this plateau, they could escape through the caves. Then look, you see that stream of water? Everyone needs water."

Jedarc nodded. "Sheheluth, you're the most amazing ... ouch! Stop pinching my nose."

"I don't like it when you say I'm a monkey."

"But ... fine, what do you want me to call you then?"

"Sheheluth."

"You got it. Sheheluth, you're the most amazing Sheheluth I've ever met. One day I'll bring a banana tree, just for you."

Seeing her pout, he tousled her hair. "Wait for me here," he added. "I'll scout ahead."

Sheheluth rubbed her cheek as she opened her mouth to complain about Jedarc's public show of affection, but instead she squinted at the field ahead of her.

Gently, Banimelek placed a finger under her chin. She closed her mouth, and unable to contain her surprise, she whispered, "I can't see him. He vanished. Does he use magic?"

"That's Tinantel for you."

"How does he do it? How does he disappear like that?" Her keen eyes scanned the plain, but she could not see him anywhere. "I have never seen anyone disappear so quickly."

"A lot of hard work, Sheheluth," replied Banimelek. "Lots and lots of it. Now let's go. We have our part to do."

≻ ·:◦:·:◦:· ≺

Evening came and brought scattered clouds with it. The skies had been clear for the past three days, but now a new storm began to form.

"It won't be long before it rains again," muttered Banimelek.

"Aren't you worried about Jedarc?" asked Sheheluth. "He's been gone for the entire day."

Sondra shook her head. "That's typical. Two hours to cross the field and two to come back, undetected. That'll leave him three hours to locate Hiyam; plenty of time to observe the people's movement and figure out the best route to take for the plan of attack. Hardly long, really."

"You all learned to do this?"

"All the Silent are trained in the art of infiltration and observation."

"I see." Sheheluth heaved a deep sigh when Banimelek handed her a piece of roasted rabbit. "Not again. We've been eating rabbit for four days, morning and evening. Do I have to?"

Banimelek smiled. "It won't be much longer, Sheheluth. We're really close now. I know you're tired of eating rabbit meat and wild berries, but you are a Silent, and 'The Silent rejoices in every trial where he learns to serve a friend.' See?"

"That's from the *Book of Siril?*"

"Yep. Chapter eleven, verse two."

"She is not our friend."

"Hiyam is Jedarc's friend, which makes her our friend."

Sheheluth shrugged her shoulders. She did not want to upset Banimelek, however, she could not help but think that Ahiram would not see it the same way. She changed the topic.

"Why do we memorize these verses?"

They were perched up a tall tree from which they could see the field ahead of them. Toward noon, they had seen folks go about their business, but they were too far away to make anything of it. Since then, the camp looked deserted. Sondra leaned over and peeked at the field, but Jedarc had not come back yet. Distractedly, she answered, "'The Silent shall be united in thought and action,' chapter one, verse one of the *Book of Siril*."

Having finished her frugal meal, Sheheluth took a draft from her water skin. Streams were plentiful in Tanniin and they had no difficulty finding one. Sondra looked affectionately at the young recruit.

"You have done well, Sheheluth," she said smiling. "Good job."

Sheheluth looked up surprised, and flashed a grateful smile. Unwittingly, she had helped Banimelek and Sondra avoid a painful confrontation with Jedarc: They had both agreed to stop looking for Hiyam after three days and knew Jedarc would not relent without an intense confrontation. By finding Hiyam before the end of the third day, Sheheluth rendered the argument moot.

While Jedarc had gone scouting, Banimelek set out to make a dozen torches in anticipation of a rescue mission deep inside the network of caves Sheheluth had shown them. Sondra and Sheheluth gathered dry wood for him. Ordinarily, a torch held an oil lamp with a thick wick that burned slowly, and in the best cases, cleanly. But they did not have that luxury here, and the tall Silent knew how to bundle wooden sticks into a makeshift torch that would burn slowly, though *not* cleanly. "Inside these caves, we can use the smoke to our advantage," he explained. He prepared the last torch, when Sheheluth felt something creep up her right shoulder. She smacked it and the intruder retreated. As she turned around she let out a scream that Sondra muffled instantly.

"Got you," whispered Jedarc grinning widely.

"Tinantel," Sheheluth protested, tearing up, "you scared me."

"Tinantel, eh? Sondra is rubbing off on you, I see. I did scare you," he added settling next to her on the tree branch. "You were so busy complaining, you did not hear me climb up. If I were an enemy, you would be dead by now."

"Most of us have learned this the hard way," concurred Banimelek.

Sondra nodded in agreement.

"Tinantel did that to you too?"

"Yes," sighed Sondra, "he did."

"So who did it to him? Who did it to you?"

"Ahiram," replied Jedarc without a hint of a smile, while Banimelek and Sondra began to chuckle quietly, "And it wasn't funny."

"Oh yes, it was," said Sondra, amused. "But that's a story for another time. What did you find out about Hiyam, Tinantel?"

"She's there all right, in a heavily guarded cave. I couldn't get any closer, but that's the only cave being watched this way."

"What do you think they are planning?"

"I don't know, but from the looks of it, the action will take place in the largest cave, which it seems, is at ground level. They were busy cleaning it up. It is mostly empty, except for a tall pole."

"I have a plan," said Banimelek.

"Let's hear it," replied Jedarc eagerly. When it came to caves and plans, he trusted Banimelek.

"A big cave in a complex of caves seldom has just one way in. So we go with a right-out and left-in."

"Why not left-in, right-out?" inquired Sondra.

Banimelek raised two fingers. "We are closer to the left side than we are to the right, second, the cluster of caves on the left side is denser than the caves on the right."

"And if it's a dead end?"

"I doubt that it would be, because this is a village. These caves are interconnected, and owing to the importance of the main one, I am confident there are at least two interior passages, one from the left and the other from the right, that lead to this main cave."

"What's a right-out, left-in?" asked Sheheluth.

"Simple," explained Sondra, "We create a diversion on the right side of the camp which will draw the people out to it, and while they're distracted, we sneak inside a cave on the left. See? Right-out, left-in."

Sheheluth nodded. "What's the distraction?"

Banimelek pointed to the torches and smiled.

"One more thing," explained Jedarc, "These guys are massive. They're huge with long arms, tall legs, oversized muscles, and jaws like flint, even the women. Their skin is snowy white. When roused they'll be fast. Hit to cripple and we may hurt them. We better make use of our darts."

They waited for nightfall and for the moon to disappear behind thick clouds, then they moved like shadows along the left side of the mountain. The Silent used stealth when on approach. A sentry would be looking for fast-moving intruders, therefore, they creeped slowly, cautiously, pausing between every few steps. As they blended with their environment, they became undetectable.

When they reached the edge of the camp, they looked for a sentinel, but could not find any. Still, they moved forward carefully, trying to get as close as possible to the main cave. Now and then, they heard the whimper of a young child or the heavy breathing of a sleeping adult. A powerful odor of fur, sweat, and something rancid, wafted from the nearby cave and Jedarc—who was in the lead—took a quick peak and signaled for his friends to climb up. Above, they could see two other openings. Fortunately, the jagged wall facilitated their movements. The second cave was also occupied, so they moved on to the third but could not tell if anyone was in it. Jedarc went in first and signaled for them to join him. The cave was empty.

Time for a distraction. Banimelek stood at the ledge of the third cave. Holding a pair of torches, he eyed Sondra beside him, who stood with a dart crossbow in each hand. These weapons, designed by dwarfs, allowed a Silent to fire darts single-handedly. When folded, they were easily concealed within the dart belt, and each Silent carried two of them. Sondra nodded and he threw the two torches in rapid succession. Sondra pulled the trigger of the first dart crossbow, and a fraction of a second later, that of the second. Sheheluth took the two discharged crossbows away, and Jedarc handed Sondra two newly loaded crossbows. Banimelek threw two more torches. Sondra pulled the trigger twice more. The first torch exploded into a ball of fire, then the next three followed suit. The sound boomed between the mountains amplifying the effect.

Pandemonium followed so quickly that it took the Silent by surprise. The desert people streamed out from their caves as if they had not been asleep, but instead of confusion, a quiet order reigned. Some of them pointed at the flying torches, then sniffed the air. In the glow of the dying light, the Silent were dismayed to see a group of women pointing with unnerving precision at their cave, then a dozen men charged them.

Banimelek quickly lit a torch, and simply said, "Run!"

The cave slopped downward for a short distance, then leveled into a tunnel high enough to run in. Bones littered the ground. No one wanted to know where they had come from. Abruptly, the tunnel dead-ended.

"That didn't go as expected," muttered Jedarc.

"We acted without sufficient knowledge," countered Sondra, "and there was no time to study these people. Tinantel, you couldn't have known they do not fear fire or that their sense of smell is this developed."

"What do we do now?" asked Jedarc.

"Up," said Banimelek.

How he knew to look for an opening above his head was anyone's guess. He handed the torch to Sondra, grabbed Sheheluth by the waist and hoisted her up unceremoniously. The young girl adjusted her position and managed to slip through the opening unharmed. Next, Banimelek cupped his hands. Sondra stepped into them and leaned one arm against his shoulder. He tensed his body and jerked up, raising her toward the ceiling. She reached the opening, grabbed the edges and pulled herself up. Not waiting, Jedarc climbed onto Banimelek's shoulders, reached and pulled himself up just as the desert men entered the cave. Sondra dropped a rope. Banimelek grabbed it with one hand and waited until the invaders rounded the corner. He threw his torch and heard it slam into one them. Not waiting, he hauled himself up and Sheheluth pulled the rope before their pursuers could use it.

But the desert people had no need for a rope. With one powerful push, one of them reached the opening and peered through it only to see Jedarc slam him on the head with a rock. He fell back down, more angry than hurt. Sondra threw three smoke pellets down the hole, while Banimelek and Jedarc prevented them from taking a foothold, but it was all in vain. Other members of the desert people streamed into the cave and surrounded them.

They expected their enemies to beat them and take their weapons, but when the Silent offered no resistance, their pursuers immediately quieted. With no sign of aggression, they nudged the Silent forward and led them to another cave. Two brawny men rolled a stone over the opening and the Silent were left to their own device. They were now prisoners of the desert people.

Banimelek was grateful for the darkness as he did not have to see the anguish on Jedarc's face.

6. Counceling Council

> *"The Temple knows how to keep the Pit sealed; a store of knowledge, spanning hundreds of years, guides the priesthood of Baal in protecting the seal of the Pit. Still, there is a power source the Temple does not control, nor fully understand: the Letters of Power."*
> —Sayings of Jehdi, Great Priest of the Temple of Baal.

The four Silent had finished their breakfast in the forest and were following the trail of the dead horse; while a short distance away, north of their camp, Ahiram woke up. Fully rested and hungry, he yawned and stretched. He closed his eyes, wanting to take in the fresh scent of clean linen, and enjoyed the comfortable mattress he slept on. His stomach grumbled, shattering the quiet of the room like an importunate zakiir in the middle of night.

Reluctantly, he pushed off the covers. He realized the nightgown Orwutt had given him reached only to his knees and was striped vertically in red and pink. *I look like a rooster.*

To his relief, someone had left a set of clean clothes on a chair: new leather pants, a deep green shirt with streaks of white and pink, and white and purple wool socks.

Wrath of the Urkuun – Counceling Council

I guess, when you spend most of your life underground, you use color wherever you can.

He got up from bed and inspected the clothes carefully. *Look at these pants. They're worn at the hem, but there are no stains.* He sniffed the garment. *Smells clean. I've got to find out what they do to remove the stains.* Next, he turned the shirt inside out, looked closely at the cuffs, the neckline, and sniffed the armpits. *No sweat stains and smells clean, like traces of lavender, lemon, and something else I don't recognize.*

Reassured that the clothes were clean, he went about his morning exercise routine—in the stripped nightgown. He showered in cold water and got dressed. His new pants were knee-high, the shirt's sleeves barely covered his elbows, and the vestments fit him snuggly.

Dwarfs' garments are certainly colorful but way too short for this Silent.

He slipped into a pair of sturdy sandals, which actually fit, but the helmet was too small, so he left it on the chair. He stepped out feeling awkward in the colorful, clothing, but when several dwarfs greeted him without a hint of irony, he relaxed and went in search of something to eat.

Imagine what Jedarc would say if he saw me now. No, I don't want to imagine. I better grab a Silent uniform from the castle before he sees me.

He sat alone at the main table. The chairs were lower than he would have liked and the kitchen felt cramped and smaller than normal, as if his perception of reality was somehow off. He knew he had missed the King's celebration and the chance of a lifetime, however he was not just a Silent, but a Solitary—the elite of the Corps—trained to serve and defend. And he could not leave another slave at the mercy of a monster. *Besides*, he thought as he gulped down his second serving of hot porridge with honey and roasted almonds, *this is what Hoda would have me do.*

Ahiram served himself a glass of goat's milk, grabbed a chunk of sweet bread and sunk his teeth into a delicious piece of cheese.

He poured a cup of hot tea and realized he could go train with his new weapons now. He went back to his room and fetched his sword and Silent belt. *I can't go walking around with the sword unsheathed like this.* He took his bed sheet, rolled the sword in it, and tied it around his shoulder. *I don't like to dirty such a clean sheet, but I'll wash it before the day is over.* He went back to the dining area, snatched another piece of bread, and feeling like a thief, hurried out of the kitchen He found his way to the lower caves where a group of dwarfs were fixing a steel foundry. He bowed down and addressed the most senior member.

"Is there a secluded area where I could go through my training routine? I don't want to disturb anyone."

Another dwarf got up, wiped his hands with a dirty apron and motioned for the Silent to follow him. They went into an adjoining storehouse filled with torches, shields, swords, helmets, ropes, picks, axes, and a whole host of shovels.

"I have never seen so many different types of shovels before," commented Ahiram. Some of the shovel blades were as wide as a man's shoulders and others as thin as a child's hand.

A roar reverberated in the storeroom, though fainter than before.

These caves must be farther away from the beast's location. Good. I hope I won't have to fight this monster, but if I have to, I want to know how to use the sword well. Something tells me I'm going to need it.

"What is your needy need and need most needy?" asked the dwarf.

"Two torches and something to light them."

The dwarf handed him four torches and a sword.

"Thank you," said Ahiram as he took the torches. "These are all I need. I have my own weapons."

"To light the torching torches, use these," said the dwarf as he handed him a pair of black stones. "Be carefully careful and careful with the utmost care. These are *xirixs sikirril*, lighting stones."

"Are you certain you can give them to me?"

"Master Xurgon's has given instructing instructions."

Ahiram bowed. "Where may I train?"

The dwarf motioned for him to follow, and he led him through a set of spiraling stairs to a large cave below. The dwarf held a torch and walked to a small alcove recessed in the wall. He took two stones similar to the ones he had given Ahiram and struck them together over the wick. From the light of the torch, Ahiram could tell that the cave was vast.

"Will she fittingly fit?" he asked.

"She most certainly will."

"Who?" asked the confused dwarf.

"The cave."

"Ah, her."

"Yes. Did I not say that?" asked Ahiram.

"You said 'she', when you should have said *sheee*, see?"

"There's a difference?"

The dwarf smiled. "More of a different difference than between this cave and a shovel. Dwarfish intoning intonation is critically critical."

"So what did I say?"

"You said 'she' as if you meant your mother-in-law."

"You mean there's a different way to speak of the cave and your mother-in-law?"

"Wider than the dividing divide between the earthly earth and the heavenly heavens. Speaking of your own mother, you say 'sheee' with levitating levity and joyful joy. Speaking of your mother-in-law, you say 'she' with respectful respect and diffident diffidence. When speaking of a cave, you say she with power and awe. No respectable respecting dwarf would confusedly confuse his mother-in-law with a cave."

"I see." Ahiram bowed, carefully avoiding saying "she". "I am mortified beyond any mortification."

The dwarf laughed and patted him on the shoulder. "This, you would say to your wife."

Dwarfish grammar is a lot tougher than the commander taught us. It's enough to leave you dumbstruck.

The dwarf left the cave, and Ahiram grabbed the lit torch and took a second one. He saw a passage at the other end, followed it and entered a second cave similarly equipped with torches. He continued until he found another cave that was not only bare, but wide enough for his exercises and as far from the dwarfs' quarters as security allowed. He wedged his burning torch between two rocks at the foot of a wall, walked thirty feet and secured the second torch in a similar fashion. The lighting rocks were practical. A quick scrape was enough to ignite the wick. He laid his sword on the ground and went back to the wall.

It's time I learned to use this blade the way it's supposed to be used. It can't be much harder than learning a proper dart throw.

"Layaleen!" he commanded raising his hand. The sword shot up and the Silent ducked. The pommel smashed into the wall behind him sending shards everywhere. It fell to the ground in a cloud of dust. Ahiram got up, grabbed the sword and laid it next to the torch; then he went back to the wall and called it again.

A few hours later, Ahiram lay panting on the cold stone ground. The wall behind him—smooth and even at the beginning of his practice—now looked battered like the face of a battle siege.

I can't manage to catch this sword. How did El-Windiir do it? Did he use magic? I don't get it.

He heaved a sigh and got up. During his last attempt, the weapon nearly skewered him. *There must be a way to do this right. I can't give up.*

His belt dangled from his right side, so he adjusted it, but it fell again. Realizing the clip was damaged, he fidgeted with it until it opened.

I can't forget my belt here. Best to set it by the second torch so I won't stumble over it when evading the blade. After pulling the sword from the wall, he dropped his belt by the torch and laid the weapon on the ground. He went back to the wall, took a deep breath and said, "Layaleen."

The sword lifted gracefully and moved toward him. If the sword were a hawk, it would have been gliding now, whereas before, it dove at top speed. With a quick flick of his wrist, he grabbed the handle. The sword was in his hand.

He stood mesmerized, eyeing the blade as if he were seeing it for the first time; unable to believe he was holding it firmly in his hand.

What just happened?

He repeated the experiment with the same success.

What changed? What's different? Is the urkuun behind this?

Uneasiness settled in like a thick blanket in the heat of summer. He moved to another cave and repeated the experiment with the same result: The sword flew at a manageable speed and he caught it.

Maybe it's the dwarfish clothing? Maybe the cleaning product they use has a special property that sets in when someone begins to sweat? He shook his head. *That's stupid. Come on, Ahiram, what's changed? What is diff—*

"Young silently Silent, are you healthily healthy?"

Zurwott's voice surprised him, and out of habit his hand went to his dart belt. *My belt, I left it in the other cave.*

"Yes, I am fine, Zurwott."

There was much clearing of the throat—the preferred way of a proper grammarian to properly express his displeasure.

"The counseling council is in progressive progression, which is why my brotherly brother and I would like to have a comfortably comfortable conversational conversation about cheesy cheese and meaty meat."

"Sure thing, I'll be there in a short while."

More clearing of the throat, and Zurwott left the cave.

My belt.

He ran back to retrieve it, and midway, stopped abruptly. "Why didn't I think of it? The golden tile! The sword's behavior changed when I removed my belt."

Excited, he continued to run and found his belt where he had left it. His torch now sputtered. *No time to waste.* He laid the sword next to the farthest torch and returned to his position in front of the wall.

Again, he called to the sword, and once more, it flew straight and swiftly into his hand. Quickly, he placed the sword back in place by the wall, but this time he grabbed the tile from his belt, held it in his left hand and called to the sword.

"Layaleen."

The sword moved with frightening speed, much faster than before, faster than the fury of a storm or the strongest arrows. The Silent knew he did not have enough time to react. His hand, wrist, and forearm would shatter on impact.

But it did not break his arm. The sword pommel connected firmly with his fingers. He felt a powerful heat wave irradiate from the tile that was still in his hand. Instinctively, he gripped the hilt and gasped. The sword, firmly in his grasp, was submerged in a brilliant blue halo that left a visible trail when he moved it. He opened his hand and inhaled sharply. The grip had become translucent. He could see the tile floating inside of it in a thick, clear liquid filled with sparkling gold specks.

"Wow," he whispered. "That's incredible."

"Silently, Silent? Are you coming?" called out Zurwott once more.

Ahiram whispered the name of the Letter, "Taw." Instantly, the tile appeared back in his hand, the halo snuffed out, and the sword became heavier again. He dropped the tile inside his pocket and ran out to meet Zurwott. *I need to train more. This is incredible.*

Twice the rock had been rolled back to let the desert people bring them food. It was not meat, but a thick soup of greens, carrots, potatoes, and a kind of white flat beans they did not recognize. It was hearty and satisfying. Jedarc had tried to strike up a conversation, but his smile confused their jailers who quickly retreated. Banimelek surprised his friends when he spoke in a guttural tongue and the desert folks reacted positively. Soon after, a tall male walked in and sat cross-legged facing

Banimelek. A halted conversation followed, punctuated by grunts. There were no hand or head movements. The two of them sat still, barely batting an eye, and spoke tonelessly.

"Well, well, well," chuckled Jedarc, after the desert people had gone. "We have now discovered Banimelek's secret. He just had a long heart-to-heart exchange with his father-in-law."

"Sheheluth, could you hold this torch for me?" asked Banimelek.

He struck flint stones and a moment later their strained eyes were relieved when light flooded the cave. Banimelek looked up.

"There's ventilation in here. We won't suffocate."

"Why did you light it now?"

"Because Xendorac said I could."

"Faernor, you speak their language?" said Sondra.

"Their fighting skills reminded me of dwarfish combat style, so I thought this tribe may be linked to the dwarfs and …"

"You speak dwarfish, of course," added Jedarc.

"I paid attention during class," retorted Banimelek. "Anyway, they will sacrifice a slave to receive their god's blessing. Their god will visit the cave tomorrow."

"So, that's why they grabbed Hiyam," whispered Jedarc. Frantically, he got up and inspected the cave.

"It's no use, Jedarc. This cave has no other exit. Besides, they'll catch you before you can move."

"What do they plan on doing with us?" asked Sondra.

"Since we managed to discover the captors, they are afraid someone else may offer a sacrifice before them. They're going to do it tomorrow instead of in two days like originally planned. They want us to sit with them so they can watch us. If we try anything, he'll kill Sheheluth."

"Why me?"

"Because they're convinced we came here to sacrifice you. If we move, he'll take you away from us. Permanently."

"Ah, cheese," sighed Orwutt as he brought a full platter into the main room. "It is like a pearl. It grows best in dark places and must not be awakened before its time."

"A dwarfish proverb?" Famished again, Ahiram stuffed himself with a humongous chunk of cheese and bread.

"Not in the leasting least," replied the dwarf, offended, "Chapter 2, verse 2 of the *Book of Siril*."

Ahiram frowned thinking it through, then burst out in laughter. "That's not what the *Book of Siril* says."

Zurwott leaned over and watched Ahiram closely. "Are you positively positive and certainly certain in the utmost certitude of this negatively negative assertion?"

Orwutt's eyes darted from Ahiram to his twin brother.

"Absolutely," confirmed Ahiram. "Here's the actual saying, 'The Silent's courage is like a pearl. It grows best in dark places and must be awakened at the appropriate time.' See, it's about courage," he added with a grin. "Who told you it was about cheese?"

Orwutt eyed Zurwott, who felt an urge to inspect his buttons. "Then I would sayingly say," lectured Zurwott, "that courage is like cheese. When it is ripe, its aroma is contagious. Let it sit unused and it stinks." Not waiting, he turned to Ahiram. "Are you haltingly halted in your active activities while the counseling counsel and the counsel most counseling reflect reflectively on your propositional proposition and proposition most propositional?"

"Can you talk while the council is meeting?" translated his brother.

"Yes, I do."

"Well then, this is the perfectly perfect moment for friends to fittingly fit and fit most fittingly, a *karak en larx*, in this availably available time."

Orwutt saw the question in Ahiram's eyes and quickly interjected, "A friendly and free exchange of information. You tell us something we want to know, we tell you something in return, and we do it for free."

"Usually, you pay for information?"

"Of course, *larx em korok seynne*. Utilitarian information is worth a few precious stones."

"I see," said Ahiram. "So what do you want to know?"

"No, no, no," complained Zurwott, "this is unbecoming of properly proper dwarfish traditional tradition. We must go through *kin xerk aruk*. The seven steps of politely polite commercially commercial commerce: disgust, distrust, mistrust, adjust, readjust, trust, and entrust. Then, and only then, can an informatively informed exchange of informational information take place."

"What my brotherly brother means to say is that before we can relay what information we are ready to exchange, we first act as if you and we, the two parties in this exchange, are disgusted, really."

"Disgusted? What's the cause of our disgust?"

"No causing causality," explained Zurwott patiently. "Rather a stately state of mind when we engagingly engage in commercial commerce. Disgust is the startling starting point of any fruitfully fruitful commerce."

"Then," chained Orwutt, "after well-intended innuendos about the weathering weather, the beauty of rocks, and the lasting loss of Andaxil, we progress from disgust to mistrust."

"What happened to distrust?" asked Ahiram.

"Ah yes," lectured Zurwott, "We reminisce reminiscently about the weathering weather, our ancestral ancestors, and the beauty of stones, in that order, for a few hourly hours to adjust our impressive impressions of one another. At which point we move from *dis*trust to mere *mis*trust."

"A few hourly hours?" confirmed Ahiram.

"No, no, no," protested Zurwott "Not a 'phewh owerly owers, a feeeewwww haaaouuurly haaours.'"

"But, to test our resolve," interjected Orwutt, "we attempt to insult one another, avoiding any allusive allusion to mother-in-laws or beards."

Ahiram was overwhelmed. *I have never been frightened in a Silent battle, but this dwarfish grammar is downright scary.*

"If both partying parties are not insultingly insulted, we correctly readjust our misconceived misconceptions," continued Zurwott.

"Yes," boomed Orwutt, "We learn to truthfully trust our mutual family lineage. Now that we know who you are, and you know who we are, we can entrust each other with the bit of information we wish to exchange for free."

"I see. So, how long does this ... ahem ... prologue last?"

"Oh, from eight days to three months, give or take a week."

Ahiram gave the two brothers a stern look. "You want me to sit here with you for *at least* eight days before we can say anything useful?"

"Dwarfs live by the quietly quiet heartbeat of the rocks," reproached Zurwott. "Eight days is a momentary moment's breath."

Ahiram stared at them as if they had turned into two donkeys wearing iron helmets. *No wonder Sureï turned two dwarfs into statues.*

"Goat's milk?" Ahiram offered, with a twinkle in his eye.

They accepted. He served each of them a full glass. "There, you see? I offered you a glass of milk and you gladly accepted. We made it past *disgust, distrust, mistrust,* and went straight to *entrust.* Next, I handed you the glass of milk and you took it from my hand, which means we are now past *adjust, trust, and entrust.* In short and in fine, I say sayingly let us exchangingly exchange some informational information."

Orwutt guffawed, and Zurwott rubbed both ears. "Your dwarfish is approximately approximate."

"Where I come from," continued Ahiram, "we have similar traditions. There are things I won't tell anyone unless they are family, and other things I won't tell someone unless I've known them for a long time. And then, there are other things I'm willing to exchange for something else, regardless of who I'm exchanging with. It seems that in your case, you're treating everyone as if they are either family, or your worst enemy."

Orwutt chuckled. "Wrong image. To dwarfs, clans are more importantly important than family, and what's more important than clans are rocks. We believe we came from rocks, and while dwarfs are precious gems that need chiseling, men are mystery stones that must be handled carefully.

"Unfortunately, you don't have time to carefully handle this human," he said as he pointed to his chest. "As soon as the slave is safe, I will return to the castle. Either you ask away, or we can talk about cheese."

Zurwott sighed a deep, sorrowful sigh. "Your hastily hasty ways will lead you in great haste to an anxious anxiety and an anxiety that is anxiously anxious."

"That may be so," said Ahiram with a smile, "but even rocks tumble in haste when pulled by a river."

"Wise wisdom," admitted Zurwott. "Very well then. We have been wonderingly wondering concerning the originating origins and the most original origins of the Silent. What can you tellingly tell us about it?"

"Well, the Silent were founded by Prince Siril of Voltocomb, an Ophirian who came to Tanniin in the year 542 of the Temple."

"So, 1,197... take away 542," said Orwutt, who like most dwarfs preferred to count backward, "is 655, which would be the 7,096th year according to the Tablets of Cosmological Enumerations."

"What are the Tablets of Cosmological Enumerations?" Ahiram asked intrigued, for he had only heard of time being counted since the foundation of the Temple of Baal. That was the origin of the world, and before that, there was only darkness.

"That will be our remunerating remuneration for your telling tale," said Zurwott with a satisfied smile.

"My brother would like to exchange our knowledge of the tablets for your knowledge of the Silent."

"Sounds good," said Ahiram. "Well, Siril was a vain and pretentious prince, and one day, to impress a woman he was fond of—the book does not mention her by name—he revealed to her a closely kept secret of a friend of his in whom she had shown interest. The secret was something shameful, but the young woman carelessly shared it with a friend or two, and soon the entire court knew the secret. A few days later, Siril found his friend hanging from a tree; he had taken his own life to avoid shame and humiliation. As punishment, the king ordered the tongue of the young woman to be cut out and the prince to be sent into exile. Siril left voluntarily and came to Tanniin where he lived as a hermit until he mastered his tongue. He vowed never to speak again unless necessary in order to aid someone or to protect life. So the Silent were born, and over many years they have become an elite troupe defending the kingdom."

"Wow," exclaimed Orwutt, "how did Siril go from living as a hermit to being the founding founder of an elite military corps? We want to know more, more."

"It's a long story," replied Ahiram, "a story for another day."

"How informatively informative," said Zurwott, delighted. "We shall be promptly prompted to prompt promptly the overseer of *Karangalatad* to justly adjust and adjust justly the historically historical knowledgeable knowledge of the dwarfs."

"What is a *book*, by the way?" asked Orwutt.

"I'll tell you in a moment, but first, what is this Kara … thing?"

"The *Karan-gala-tad*," repeated Orwutt. "It is the historical records of the dwarfs. It is our living memory of all things past."

"I see. So you're going to tell me more about it?"

"Yes, but first," replied Orwutt smiling, "what is a book?"

"I don't really know, other than it's what we call the collection of Siril's sayings we are told to memorize. There are 244 of them. They are divided into twelve chapters: Obedience, Courage, Discipline, Endurance, Patience, Justice, Prudence, Temperance, Understanding, Hope, Friendship, and Love. We call the entire collection a book, so I've always thought a book to be nothing more than a collection of sayings."

"Do you knowingly know all 244 of them?"

"Of course. Every Silent does. They govern our conduct. We live by them and train by them. There's a second book called the *Book of Lamentation*, that—"

"One bookish book in its timely time," interrupted Zurwott.

"Was he the greatest amongst the Silent?" asked Orwutt who could not believe his luck; he was getting answers to three questions for the price of one. Like most dwarfs of the southern realm, he was fascinated by the greatest, the fastest, and the strongest.

"According to Commander Tanios, the greatest of the Silent—in our time—is a man named Corintus."

"Corintus?" asked Orwutt and Zurwott in unison.

"You know him?" It was Ahiram's turn to be delighted. "Frankly, I asked the commander to tell me something about Corintus, but he never said much about him."

"Well," replied Orwutt cautiously, "We know of him. A certain acquaintance of ours met him in Alep some years back. We know not where his current whereabouts may be. He may be tied to a prophecy."

To stop his brother, Zurwott stomped his foot, but it was too late.

"A prophecy?" Ahiram, who did not mind a bit of competition, glanced quickly at Zurwott. The dwarf was unhappy. *It looks like I'm getting more questions answered than he is. Not bad.* "What prophecy?"

"A prophecy of a child who would see what cannot be seen," replied Orwutt. "We do not believe a word of it. What we do know is that Corintus has everything to fear from a certain Nebo, a general in the army of Baal, on account of Corintus' wife."

Ahiram looked at them, confused.

"Nebo wanted Corintus' wife for his own," continued Orwutt to Zurwott's discomfiture. "But her parents refused and instead gave her in marriage to Corintus. Nebo is not the forgiving type."

"He holds a grudging grudge for an eternal eternity and is cruelly cruel beyond any unreasonably reasonable cruelty," added Zurwott. "You must be familiarly familiar and familiar most familiarly with Nebo's brother most brotherly and brotherly brother, for he took a parting part in the gaming Games."

"Why did you say 'brother most brotherly and brotherly brother?' Usually, you say it the other way around. Wait, really? His brother was in the Games of the Mines?"

"No, no," explained Zurwott. "This is the properly proper order since Olothe is Nebo's younger brother. I would have said it the way you did, if it were the other way around, and not as it presently is."

Ahiram did not flinch. "Nebo is Olothe's older brother?" *Would this explain why the men of Baal tried to kill me?* He decided to change topics. "So, what are the Tablets of Cosmological Enumeration?"

"A series of sayings that records the history of time or the timely history as we know it," replied Zurwott. This was as good a dwarfish deal as any. He had answered the questions accurately without providing any useful information, which is what every dwarf was supposed to do in these types of exchanges. But his smile quickly turned to discomfiture when Orwutt began to speak.

"That is a long telling tale my friend. From the Tree of Life to this age, the land saw manifold wonders and tragedies. First came the Age of the First Covenant, which led to the rise of Keinuun, the mighty iron city of the Sheituun—rulers of earth and sea—that subdued the land and all races to its will. The Malikuun—Lords of Light—stooped down from their high ranges and fought the rulers of earth and see. The battle was swift and decisive, for unlike us, the Malikuun and Sheituun use silent words of power, which they can use to reshape the world. Had the battle lasted longer, all races would have been wiped from the face of the earth."

"Not so, my brotherly brother and brother most brotherly. Andaxil, the great cave, tenderly cradled and cradled very tenderly her dwarfish offspring and protected him protectively from the wrathful wrath and the mighty might of the Lords of lightning Light."

Orwutt smiled. "As my brother indicates, there are some among the dwarfs who believe we, dwarfs, would have survived the ordeal. Anyway, when the Malikuun spoke the seven words of power, Keinuun, the iron city, was sucked into the belly of the earth," Orwutt removed his right sock, and held it from the toe. "The city was pulled down like so," he inserted his hand inside his sock and pulled it inside out. "The city's inside became its outside, and this transformed, inverted city is what we call today, the Pit of Darkness. Keinuun's foundation became the mouth of the Pit, and the peak of its highest tower, its very depth. In that awful abyss, a mighty fire locks the Lords of Darkness to their thrones of meyroon. The Lords of Light used a rock not of this earth to seal the mouth of the Pit."

"Where is this Pit," asked Ahiram. "Do you know?"

Zurwott shook his head. "The Karangalatad does not revealingly reveal nor reveal revealingly the locating location of this pitiless pit and pit most pitiless. This, the Karangalatad did as a preventing prevention and a prevention of the most preventing kind against foolish and woolly dwarfs who have a constantly constant itch and an itch of the most constantly constant form to deeply dig and dig deeply wherever there is an exploratory hole worthy of any exploration."

"I see, so it was not told for your protection."

Orwutt nodded. "After the Pit was formed, the Malikuun punished all races for dabbling in the deep things of the Pit with the long winter of the Flaming Sword. A bitter cold covered the earth for twenty-two years during which Eden-Elil, the first City of Light, fell. Eden-Elil, the first and oldest of all cities was built by the Malikuun as a gift of friendship for all races. There we were taught the rudiments of the words of power, which we should have used to govern the earth. Alas, our ancestors used these words to subdue one another and that gave rise to the city of

Keinuun. So in that terrible winter, Eden-Elil fell.

"Its fall brought the Age of Tears and Sorrow and the Long Wandering that lasted 205 years. The races separated and mistrust grew. The Age of Blood was upon us. It saw the rise of the Fortress of Enoch, Tessarah, the Unseen Tower of the Lady of Eleeje, and Silbarâd the Fairest. 'O shining city, most beautiful amongst the cities of man, our hearts pine at your loss.'

"But alas, an Empyrean sorceress and her dwarf consort—may their names be blotted from our memory—by a terrible act of magic made a key, a horrific key, with which to open the Pit. We call it *Parixis Morinméa*—"

"Not a dwarfish name," Ahiram noted.

"Very observantly observed," retorted Zurwott, "and observed most observantly. *Parixis Morinméa* is Xargin, an intermediate language between pure dwarfish and the Empyrean tongue. It meaningfully means, and means most meaningfully—"

"A meaningful meaning and meaning most meaningful that must remain unutterably unuttered, my brotherly brother."

Ahiram glanced at Orwutt. The dwarf was visibly shaken.

"I regret regretfully and regretfully regret my impetuous impetuosity and impetuosity most impetuously irresponsible irresponsibility," Zurwott blurted as he bowed low.

"No harming harm has been done," said Ahiram. The twins chuckled, and the tension dropped. "I take it, this is a powerful name."

"A name of tears," explained Orwutt. "May it never be uttered."

"Please continue," prodded Ahiram. He took another chunk of cheese and nibbled at it.

"This magical key which we call 'Parixis Morinméa' is known by many names," explained Orwutt. "I say this so that if you do come across any of these names, you know better than to ask its meaning. It is known as *Mofta Qahor* among the Desert Legion. To the Temple it is called *Baal's*

Bane. Among the Empyrean it is the *Ithyl Shimea*, and to the giants, it is *Onthialamur*, the deadly doorway of sorrow.

"But let us not speak of it any longer. The Karangalatad tells us that when Keinuun was re-opened by the *Ithyl Shimea*, its hordes brought the First War of Knowledge, which lasted for one hundred and thirty-five long years, and after a short lull, the Wars of Riharon, then the Wars of the Wind, which lasted for six hundred years."

"Why is it called the Wars of the Wind?"

"Because," explained Zurwott, who was eager to take part in the conversation in order to have something to barter with later, "these warring wars saw the coming of the dragons."

"There are tales of glory and power. To tell them all would keep us here for a lifetime," continued Orwutt. "Silbarâd the Fair fell, but Tessarah, the Tower of the Lady, was never conquered.

"The Age of the Second Covenant started. Man lived in relatively relative peace for eight hundred years, but he forgot the malice lurking in the Pit. And so, on 1 Teshriin 3333, in the year of the Tablets of Cosmological Enumerations, the Wars of Destruction began—"

"Wait, you didn't tell me who used the *Ithyl Shimea* to open the Pit. How did they do it and why?"

"It would take longer to explain than we have time for," said Orwutt as he glanced at the door where the council was deliberating. "The Pit was closed by the Malikuun, and tragically was opened again."

"So what does the Karangalatad say then?"

"After the Wars of Destruction came the Wars of Fire and the Wars of Meyroon. Somewhere in that span of time that lasted for a thousand years, the Malikuun sealed the Pit once more."

"I wonder," said Ahiram, "are the Lords of the Deep stupid? I mean, you'd think that after being beaten twice, they'd change their ways and make peace. That's why I find it hard to believe in the Pit. Power requires understanding, so if the Lords of the Deep are truly powerful, they can't be stupid. Or if they are stupid enough to be locked up twice, then they can't be as dangerous as we make them out to be. Also, why lock them up again? Why not get rid of them once and for all? I don't know who I should blame more, the Lords of the Pit for being so stupid, or the Lords of Light for being so cruel to leave this Pit to tempt us."

Orwutt and Zurwott faced each other, palms open. To Ahiram's surprise they slapped each other's hand following a complex configuration, which delighted him, for it was beautiful and elegant like a well-executed dance. They faced him and bowed deeply.

"*Xarang kalatad mteinx*," said Orwutt. "Whenever the retelling of the Karangalatad opens wide the doors of the mind to wonderment and questioning, the retelling is deemed successful."

"So what was that slapping all about?"

"A congratulatory congratulation and a congratulation most congratulatory for a performance well performed and a most excellently excellent performing performance," explained Zurwott.

"I am a good storyteller," translated Orwutt.

"Got it, so will you answer my questions then?"

"Not all gems are uncovered with picks and axes," replied Orwutt.

"What picking picks and axing axes cannot bring to a lighting light," corrected Zurwott, "a differently different laboring labor of love will be made known to your beating heart."

"I see," understood Ahiram. "Please continue."

"Then," resumed Orwutt, "in 5694, the great Babylonian tower was erected, and with it, the glory of man and his pride rose to the heavens. Then there is a gap in our account of the cosmological tablets, and in the year 6,554, the Temple of Baal rose to prominence. What happened in the intervening years is muddled and confused."

The three fell silent. Ahiram focused on his open palms.

"Zurwott, can I try that slapping sequence with you?"

"The *xarang kalatad mteinx*?" asked Orwutt. "Do you wish to congratulate us on our ways of eating bread and cheese?"

"No," laughed Ahiram, "I just want to try it."

Zurwott shrugged his shoulders, got up and faced Ahiram. "I shall begin from the beginning with the slow slowness and the slowness of the slowest slow slug."

Ahiram shook his head. "No, no. Do it like you did it with Orwutt."

"But it takes yearly years of painstakingly painstaking preparing preparations," protested the dwarf.

"Hey, no need to bring in the King and Queen. We're friends doing the trust, entrust thing. If I fail, I fail, that's all."

"But—"

"Come on Zurwott, you're not going to lose your beard over this, or your sleep for that matter."

Orwutt slapped his knees laughing, and Zurwott glared at Ahiram as if the Silent had slapped him in the face.

"A challenging challenge and a challenge most challenging you have directly directed to a dwarf of the southern realm, and directed most directly to the dwarfish nation. Be ready in the utmost readiness and in a readiness ready to be discomfited in the greatest of discomfiture."

"Do your best." Ahiram smiled and opened both palms as if he were a mendicant waiting for someone to drop him a coin.

With his left hand, Zurwott slapped Ahiram's right hand who turned it over to let the dwarf slap the back. Ahiram raised his left hand and Zurwott slapped it with his left hand twice. On they went slapping one another's hands in a rapidly increasing complexity and speed until their arms became a blur that moved instinctively to their appointed position. Orwutt's jaw dropped with a bit of cheese hanging from his lower lip. When the sequence ended, he jumped to his feet, threw Ahiram over his shoulder and twirled a half dozen times before setting him down.

"Xarix alik nark, narik alik xark, kora stirix ark, arik stirix kor. Starx avrix silark, salirk avrix starx."

"Orwutt, I don't speak dwarfish," said Ahiram. "But listening to you, I have a better appreciation for the repetition of the language. It sounds melodious."

"Yes indeed," said a puffed-up Zurwott. "Dwarfish is elegantly nimble, whereas the common tongue is a slow, slithering speech."

"Amazing act of amazement, amazement action amazing, intensely beautiful intensity, intensity most beautifully intense," translated Orwutt. "This is as close as I can be to speaking in the common tongue. Now how did you do that?"

Ahiram laughed just as Master Xurgon walked in and immediately started directing his ire toward the twins.

"The council does not consider its deliberation a laughing matter, or for that matter, a matter to be laughed about. You have annoyed the council with your slapping slaps. You are a bear to bear, but the council has asked for your ear. Walk inside and try to reflect most appropriately the brilliance of your paternal uncle."

The brothers bowed courteously and left Ahiram to himself. The Silent waited patiently for the consultation to end. He unwrapped his sword and examined it closely. He could not make sense of the elaborate carvings on the pommel, nor the meaning behind the two stars adorning the dragon wings of the cross-guard. The sword was not his preferred weapon, but like every Silent, he was an accomplished swordsman and recognized a well-crafted blade when he saw one, "This sword is amazing," muttered Ahiram. Hearing footsteps, he wrapped the sword back just as Zurwott dashed into the room and stopped before him.

"The counseling council would like your ear."

Ahiram did not know why he was being ushered into the council, but he followed the dwarf into the adjacent room. About a dozen dwarfs sat around a large, circular stone table. He bowed respectfully and waited.

"Young manly man," said one of the dwarfs, "we are consciously conscious and conscious most consciously of your desired desire to save the breath of the slaving slave who is to be offered as a sacrificial sacrifice to the Xarg-Ulum. We are also pleasingly pleased by your sagacious sagacity and your sagacity so sagacious. You boldly planned a bold plan to constructively construct a trap for the xarg-ulum. You planned to restrain her thus until you could recover, with assured recoverability and recoverability most assured, the slave from the handy hands of the tribe of tribulations. But how do you purposefully purport to do so?"

"A pit is dug for the beast to fall into," replied Ahiram. "She will not be able to make it out in time for the sacrifice. I suspect the slave will be tied up as in any sacrifice. The tribesmen expect the beast to come and take the slave. Instead of the beast, I show up, rescue the slave, and bring him back with me."

Most of the dwarfs winced, for Ahiram's manner of speech was too short and direct to their taste.

"Very good plan," replied Xurgon, who seemed to speak on their behalf, "but if these tribesmen find out that it is you and not their godly god who has come to take the slave, they will surely hack you to pieces; a rather unpleasant possibility. These people are strong, and courageous."

"If I am accompanied by two or three strong dwarfs, they may be able to loosen enough rocks to cause a small avalanche and block the entrance to the cave after the slave and I have made our exit."

"An avalanche is a worthy and good idea. True and trusted by many dwarfs, an avalanche is a friendly friend that will not disappoint," said another dwarf. "He can be strong enough to force a conclusive outcome to our advantage." Ahiram smiled seeing that his idea pleased the council. He hoped this would be the end of the questioning. "But with all due respect for your courageous courage, zeal, and training, you will not be able to face them alone. You will need help. I say we send a company of twelve dwarfs with you."

"Great," exclaimed Ahiram who was relieved to see the dwarfs take part in this action.

"You will make it in the most dire and difficult conditions," said Xurgon. "The unexpectedly unexpected is a dependably fiendish foe. He never fails to rendezvous with you when you least count on him."

"Who?" asked Ahiram, confused.

The dwarf sighed. "The unexpected, of course."

"That was quite unexpected," retorted Ahiram with a smirk.

The dwarf sighed again. "This is the best we can offer you."

"When can we leave?" asked Ahiram.

"In five days hence. We must complete our trap before we can venture into the béghôm's lair."

Five days is all I need. Ahiram felt a tinge of excitement.

"As soon as the company is ready and declares it to be so, Zurwott will guide you with what needs to be accomplished. Are you in possession of a weapon worthy of this endeavor?"

"I am," answered Ahiram nonchalantly.

"Good," replied Xurgon relieved, "we are ill-equipped for the forging of weaponry in this local locality."

"I thank you, Master Xurgon, and I thank the entire council. Dwarfs are known for their courage and boldness, and you certainly live up to this reputation." Ahiram bowed and left the council.

The next three days went by quickly and Ahiram fell into a routine. He inspected the daily progress of the dwarfs as they dug the trap for the beast, and he was amazed at the speed with which dwarfs were able to dig a hole that deep and wide. They used various shovels to move dirt quickly, and then hauled it to a separate cave that Ahiram had visited with Orwutt. It was a brightly lit work area where an odd-looking contraption churned continuously. It would swallow the dirt and mix it with steaming water and strange, black pellets that turned the mixture into a thick, brown clay. The clay was then pushed onto a rotating iron mesh where other dwarfs used a powerful press to cut the set clay into blocks. The blocks were then fed into a brick oven that spat them out from the other end as solid bricks. The whole thing gave Ahiram the impression of a giant dragon plagued by an incurable hiccup that forced him to repeatedly spit out a molar. The bricks were then carted to a giant pile at the back of the work area where they were hoisted into horse-led wagons. The wagons crossed a wide, stone bridge, went up a winding path to an exit point from which the bricks traveled down southward to the port of Tyra-Min, and were finally shipped all over the world.

"Tanniin's bricks are famously famous in many kingly kingdoms," explained a dwarf. "Cheaply cheaper than paying mining miners for goodly gold and profitably profitable for our bottomless bottom line."

"What's a bottomless bottom lining line?" asked Ahiram. "A cave?"

"No, no, no," replied the dwarf. "This is one of the few metaphors we dwarfs use." He spoke in the common tongue for Ahiram's sake. "It means our pockets, see? They're supposed to be bottomless because what goes in, is not supposed to come back out."

"Huh?"

"I mean, we like to make a profit and hate spending money, see?"

"Oh …" said Ahiram prudently. Even though he did not understand what the dwarf meant, he did not wish to embarrass himself again.

After he inspected the digging, Ahiram returned to his training area. He continued to work with his artifacts. As long as the tile was not on him, he could catch the sword and float up and down with the wings with good control—provided he did not attempt any acrobatics. But whenever the tile was on him, his speed multiplied tenfold.

I need to master the basics of flying first, before I can include the tile.

He spent hours honing the use of his sword. He was missing quite a few darts, and wished he could replenish his stash. On the fourth day, Ahiram saw that the trap was completed. The hole was at least thirty-two feet deep and thirty feet wide. It reached from wall to wall, and as he stepped to the edge to take a closer look, he nearly fell in when the béghôm pounded the wall from behind the walls.

"She is painfully close and close in the most painful manner," whispered Zurwott.

Ahiram watched as one group of dwarfs pulled on a metal chain to drag a lid of steel-reinforced wood over the hole, while a second group busily piled up rocks by the entrance of the room where the floor had now been turned into a gaping hole.

"When the beastly beast unfailingly falls into our trapping trap, we will drop this trustingly trusty lid and let this piling pile of rocky rocks roll over her to shut the trap."

Ahiram stood confident, hands on hips, and nodded his head, satisfied. The trap was ready.

7. Sacrifice to a Béghôm

"The béghôm is a mighty foe of the dwarfs. She knows the ways of the rock and the abysmal elements of the earth. She loves the deep shadows of silent caves, and treads in passages never seen by man. Unlike the dwarfs, the creature requires no tools to forge a passage through stone. The caves are her natural habitation."
–Philology of the Dwarfs, Anonymous.

The next day, Ahiram walked into the main hall where ten dwarfs, all members of the rescue company, were breakfasting. He bowed before the oldest dwarf, as per their custom and sat down to eat with them.

His desire to be free was as strong as ever, even though it had temporarily receded to the background. To free another slave from a cruel end made him happy. Any Silent would do the same, regardless of the victim's status, but Ahiram knew how slaves felt. Even though Tanios treated him like a son and the Silent had adopted him, everyone else in the castle treated him as a slave. Besides, he had spent six years in the slaves' quarters of Taniir-the-Strong Castle. He had seen how slaves lived. Their sense of dignity gone, they lived in fearful submission to the one who treated them like cattle: to be bought, sold, and slaughtered at their owner's whim.

"You betook the appearance of a dwarfish warrior," exclaimed Orwutt as he walked in, "dressed as you are in the likeness and mannerly manners of our people."

"When you're with the dwarfs, do as they do," retorted Ahiram.

"A wise saying and a saying most wise," approved Zurwott who came in on his brother's heels. "Is it from the *Book of Siril?*"

"No, from the book of Ahiram," replied the Silent.

Orwutt slapped him on the back amid a profusion of throat clearing and coughing.

"Let us be on to our warring ways," ordered Zurwott after they finished breakfast. "To the armory for arming armors."

They filed inside a nearby storeroom where the dwarf in charge equipped them with weapons, shields, breastplates, helmets, and anything else they needed for their mission.

Ahiram looked at his reflection in a tall bronze mirror and smiled. He had been outfitted with a steel breastplate laced in leather and a round helmet—one that fit him—adorned with two small horns, so characteristic of the northern dwarfs. He had taken a liking to the sandals he had been wearing for the past five days. They were sturdy with a comfortable thick sole and good traction. Dressed for battle, he felt out of his element without his dart belt. The *Book of Siril* 9:2 came to mind. "If your might is only in mighty weapons, great are your victories and greater your defeats."

The day to free the slave has come at last, Ahiram thought.

They left the armory and crossed several caves until they reached a narrow passage where they waited. This was Ahiram's fifth day with the dwarfs, and according to Master Xurgon, the sacrifice was planned for the next morning. The trap for the béghôm was ready; the dwarfs now weakened the wall the beast had been pounding.

As soon as the beast falls into the trap, we're good to go, thought Ahiram.

They waited an hour for the beast to attack, but to no avail. Unable to sit any longer, Ahiram went to check on the trap. He found a group of nervous dwarfs standing quietly by a chain held to a lever.

"No sign of the beast yet?" he whispered.

The dwarfs shook their heads. Ahiram backed out and sat in an adjoining cave where he leaned his sword against the wall. Zurwott and Orwutt joined him. Time passed and the torches on the walls were changed twice, which told Ahiram that two hours had come and gone since he sat there. The béghôm's pounding, faint and far, reached them intermittently. *It looks like the beast will not pay us a visit today.* The Silent wondered if they would have to postpone or cancel their mission. *The mission will not succeed unless we trap the beast.* Another hour went by, during which time he concocted alternative plans to save the slave, but none of them were viable.

There's no use trying to come up with alternative plans. Unless the béghôm is restrained long enough for us to go and come back safely, the plan will not succeed. I can't risk the lives of twelve dwarfs for one slave. I don't know how to fly swiftly, and besides, I wouldn't know where to go.

➣ ⬧⬧⬧ ➢

The four Silent held prisoners by the desert people tensed when the stone moved. A tall woman walked in and ushered them out. Three tall men, including their leader Xendorac, escorted them to a clearing facing the main cave, which Jedarc had spotted during his scouting operation. Their captors had cleaned it out and chained a hooded victim to the pole.

"Is it her?" whispered Jedarc.

"It's her," replied Sondra. "Follow the outline of the arms and legs—that's a young woman."

"Could be a skinny man," objected Jedarc.

"No," asserted Sondra. "You should have paid more attention during anatomy, Tinantel. That is a woman."

Hearing Xendorac grunt, Banimelek told them to sit down. Two men sat on either side of Sheheluth to restrain her in case she felt the urge to run and throw herself into the arms of the beast as a preferred offering. The young girl sighed and closed her eyes.

Even if we reach the cave's mouth, the warriors guarding it will stop us, thought Sheheluth. *They are strong and fast. We cannot defeat them.* She felt her heart constrict in her chest. *It'll take a miracle to save Hiyam.*

Ahiram yawned. By now, all twelve dwarfs from his party had joined them. Two more hours had trickled by in complete silence. *I'm hungry. I wonder what's for lunch.* He yawned again.

"By the mighty Xirik!"

Ahiram bolted to his feet, half-expecting to face the béghôm. Instead, he saw Zurwott, who had been seated next to him, standing up, transfixed. He was holding Layaleen and gazed at the sword in awe.

Ahiram managed to control himself—just barely. "Put it down," he said, a slight quiver in his voice. "That is my sword."

"My deepest deep apologetic apologies," replied Zurwott, crestfallen. "I did not meaningfully mean to rudely intrude."

"But you did," snapped Ahiram as he took the sword and wrapped it quickly back in the shirt, "and I wish that you had not." Ahiram thought Zurwott was about to cry; he had one of the saddest looks on his face. "Your apologies are accepted, but next time, please do not touch this sword or anything else of mine without asking me."

"Keil kzang kazang?" asked another dwarf. Ahiram recognized him as the shoemaker, "Ekal shterm keal?"

"He does not speak the common tongue," explained Orwutt quietly. "He said …" the dwarf struggled to find his words, "… well *kzang* is very difficult to translate. He said 'What a swording sword' and asked if he may look at it."

Reluctantly, Ahiram placed his sword into the old dwarf's hands. The shoemaker held it the way one holds a priceless treasure. The remaining dwarfs congregated around him like children who beheld a treasure. As the older dwarf moved his fingers ever so slowly along the blade, a brilliant blueish streak followed his movements, as if an evanescent light hidden within the sword had been called to the surface.

"This is Korx Terix Tal," whispered Orwutt. "He belongs to the tribe of Karak-Keim, Thunder Cloud. His forefather of ages bygone, the great Thein Terek Al, or Thein, Dragon Eye, lit the great forges of Andaxil and fashioned Layaleen, El-Windiir's sword; Terragold, the sword of Muhaijar, King of the Marada; and Utal, the swift sword of Salfaran the Fair, ruler of the desert legions. The Karangalatad said he forged these swords from dragon scales mixed with meyroon."

Korx Terix Tal whispered softly and Orwutt translated. "What a glad tiding you have brought us, friend." Korx Terix Tal's voice quivered. "This sword was made by the hands by my ancestor. It is very old. The lore has been lost and we no longer know how to forge steel in this fashion. Indeed, great, great tidings this is. Look, this sword has been dipped in liquefied meyroon, from the handle's pommel to the point of the blade. Who would have said that I would live long enough for my eyes to set on such a wonder?"

The old dwarf bid Ahiram to come a little closer. "Do you see how these waves of radiant colors appear as soon as I place the blade under the light?" Orwutt continued to translate. "This is the sign of liquefied meyroon." The old dwarf looked at Ahiram once more. "You could search all sixty-two kingdoms under the sun and you will not find a sword mightier than this. I thank you for letting me look at it. I am so glad."

Ahiram smiled. "Well, perhaps you could find me a sheath for this treasured sword?"

The old dwarf shook his head.

"He does not have the gold and precious stones of the quality this sword requires," replied Orwutt on behalf of the dwarf.

"A sturdy leather sheath will do just fine."

"Very well then. Follow me."

A short while later, Korx Terix Tal, Orwutt, and Ahiram returned with Layaleen in a sheath slung over his shoulder. The Silent looked at Zurwott and gave him a beaming smile. *Something good came out of Zurwott's misplaced curiosity after all.*

Ahiram felt his shoulder vibrate violently. The wall of the adjoining cave exploded and the béghôm thundered as she leaped into the cave. Ahiram and the dwarfs jumped to their feet, but the trap worked as expected. Surprised, the beast fell into the pit but managed to land standing. She roared angrily and jumped, her fingers gripping the edge.

"Drop the lid," yelled a dwarf. "Drop it now!"

The beast roared and pulled herself up as the lever was released. The chain roiled noisily and the lid came crashing down. Despite the lid's weight, the beast did not lose her grip. Three dwarfs shouted a rallying cry and attacked, axes in hand. The béghôm recognized the danger and pulled her hands away just before the axes fell.

"Drop the rocks," ordered the same dwarf. Another dwarf jumped to his feet and snatched a pebble from the large pile, then gave the rock at the summit a quick shove. The entire pile tumbled down, buried the cover, and forced the three dwarfs that had attacked the monster to escape through the crumbled wall.

The lead dwarf turned to Zurwott, "We shall securely secure, and secure most securely the beastly beast within the confining confinement we have constructively constructed for it. You may speedily speed along your peregrine peregrination."

Both dwarfs bowed while the béghôm roared her displeasure and pounded the walls of her subterranean jail.

>◦◦◦◦<

They had walked through a maze of dark, cold hallways deep within the mines for a long time. Ahiram could no longer tell how long it had been since they left the halls of Master Xurgon, and he marveled at the size of the mines. *The caves that I'm familiar with must be no more than a tenth of the actual size of the whole mine system; perhaps even less.* He had so many questions he wanted to ask the twin brothers, but he was barely able to keep up with them. *These dwarfs are amazing, I need all my wits to walk on these slippery steps without breaking my neck, and they walk as if strolling on a comfortable straight path. Even the dwarf with the heavy blanket we brought to carry the slave walks unhindered.*

They had entered the domain of the béghôm and had walked on this slippery ground ever since. Water trickled from the ceiling and the walls were constantly wet, but otherwise, the journey had been uneventful. Dwarfs could be quiet when necessary. They walked as a band of cats on the prowl. Intermittently, Ahiram would hear hushed grunts. He quickly realized they were warnings of holes in the ground, a sudden drop in the ceiling, or rocks that blocked the way. He felt the sword; safe in its sturdy sheath, against his shoulder, for the Silent wore their swords in the Empyrean's fashion. He thought of the wings and the rest of his treasure tucked safely in his small room, hidden in a hole in the wall behind the bed. He wanted to bring them with him to scare the tribesmen while the dwarfs attended to the slave, but he knew he was not yet ready to use them. He could only fly up and down with the wings, and he had not yet dared to use the mask.

A few quick grunts broke his train of thought. The company had stopped. The dwarfs stood in a circle examining a dark mass. Ahiram moved closer and in the dim light saw a massive boulder blocking the way. They were on a ledge that flanked a cliff to their left and a steep ravine to their right. Their torches could barely pierce through the darkness. The rock leaned on the cliff and extended a few feet over the ravine, blocking the way. An animated discussion went on for a while. Finally, Orwutt told Ahiram, "We are not going to move this boulder."

"You mean, you *could* move it if you wanted to?"

Orwutt smiled. "Of course. But if we did, it would make a mighty noise tumbling down the ravine. Can you climb silently?"

It was Ahiram's turn to smile. He ran his fingers on the boulder's surface and crawled up. Supple as a snake, he slithered through the narrow opening between the boulder and the cave's roof and dropped down quietly on the other side. He tapped lightly on the boulder and waited. One by one, the dwarfs crossed over. *They are fast, but not as fast as the Silent*, thought Ahiram, proudly. Orwutt patted him on the back, which he took as a sign of approval. The company continued along its way without any further incident.

After a long, winding passage, the ground was dry, and they were able to move faster. After rounding a long bend, a brightly lit cave came into full view. The rescue team crawled slowly forward until they reached the end of a ledge that sloped gently into a lower and wider cave. A barechested man, skinny and tall, and as pale as the moon stood facing a victim tied to a pole. He was barefoot, with chains of broken bones tied to his ankles and wore shorts and gloves of bearskin and fur. Three claws protruded from each glove, and four fangs were secured to his headcover—a hollowed bear head that reached down to his shoulders. Ahiram glimpsed a pair of eyes glittering from inside the bear's jaw, and as the man began to circle the victim, the Silent saw that his back was branded with an image of a béghôm. The man dipped the claws into a nearby jar, sprinkled the victim with blood, and broke into foreign songs. Next, he sprinkled the ground with a gray powder. Behind him, and hidden from view, drums began to beat in a slow threnody.

"The sacrifice has already begun," confirmed Orwutt.

Ahiram winced. "This complicates our mission."

"What do we do?" asked Orwutt.

Ahiram smiled. "We improvise. Why these drums, I wonder?"

"The béghôm's hearing is acutely acute," Zurwott mentioned.

"She can hear a fly in flight twenty yards away," added Orwutt.

Wrath of the Urkuun – Sacrifice to a Béghôm

Ahiram looked at the man circling the victim one more time. With a short whip, he lightly lashed the victim. The slave did not react and his slumped posture told Ahiram he was most likely drugged. Ahiram gestured to the dwarfs to follow him and withdrew from the cave to a place where he would not be heard. The dwarfs stood around him.

"We must stop those drummers at all cost. They may be calling the béghôm. If we don't, saving the slave will be almost impossible."

"How do you suggestively suggest we stop them?" asked Orwutt. "Their warriors are standing right behind them and not a foot farther. They are mighty and we are only thirteen."

"They are expecting the béghôm to show up. Let's give them what they are waiting for."

Looks of confusion told him the dwarfs did not understand the plan. "Give me the blanket you brought with you." He unfolded it. It was made of a twelve-foot square thin layer of cotton, but when folded, it was strong enough to carry the weight of a man without tearing. Orwutt had thought to bring it with them in case they needed to carry the slave back.

"Which of you can carry the weight of two dwarfs on your shoulders?" asked Ahiram.

"Arax, Xern," Orwutt called out.

"Arax and Xern, stand side by side, one foot apart. Orwutt, we need two dwarfs to stand on their shoulders."

Orwutt called for Birix and Kruxon. The two dwarfs quickly climbed up and stood on the shoulders of their companions.

"Good. Zurwott, stand on their shoulders," directed Ahiram, "then we will throw the blanket over you and that will complete our béghôm."

"But they will see it's a trick right away." replied Orwutt.

"Not if our béghôm stays in the shadows grunting, howling, and pounding. He will trick them long enough for us to rescue the slave and get out. Keep in mind they are expecting the béghôm and are afraid of her. As soon as they see something this big step into the cave, they'll believe it's the creature. They have no reason to doubt it."

"Fine. Suppose they do as you say and we free the slave. What happens when they discover our subterfuge?"

Ahiram was not used to the methodical approach the dwarfs were famous for. The Silent had turned agility and unpredictability into an art of deception. As far as he was concerned, he had the best plan, given the circumstances. "Well, for one thing," he replied as calmly as possible, "they may be too scared to pursue us in these caves, and even if they do, they are not used to this environment, but we are. I believe we have an edge here and we had better use it. Any other questions?"

The dwarfs looked at each other, then at Ahiram. Clearly, they were not at ease with his plan. Yet they did not know what else to do.

"All right then," continued Ahiram, "let's finish our béghôm."

A short moment later, an imposing béghôm, at least twelve feet tall, stood before them with an ominous look.

"Good," whispered Ahiram, "This will do. Walk to the cave, grunting and growling as you go. We will follow you and guide your steps."

Two dwarfs supporting the scaffold moved in lockstep with the makeshift beast. Ahiram and the rest of the crew followed the strange cortège down the slope. The powerful beat of the drums inside the large cave drowned the sound of their movements and grew faster and louder just as they reached the entrance. The officiating magician was reciting strange incantations while bowing to the ground before the victim who was still slumped while held to the post by the iron chains.

Suddenly, the man sprang up as though bitten by a serpent. Though haggard, his eyes were fixed on the back of the cave where the company stood and from where he expected the béghôm to walk in. The man yelled something and gestured violently. The drumming stopped, and all the desert people stood with worried looks on their faces.

Perfect, thought Ahiram, *they are afraid*. Their fake béghôm now grunted and snorted continuously as each of the five dwarfs took turns to produce the cacophony, so much so, that Ahiram feared their trick would be discovered.

"Slower with those sounds," he whispered. "Let Zurwott do it." A grunt answered him. "Good, now move forward some more and let them see you, then roar, all five of you together. The rest of you get ready to storm in and free the slave."

"How are we to break these chains?" asked one of the dwarfs, "they are mighty thick."

"Leave the chains to me," replied Ahiram.

The fake béghôm eased forward, careful to stay in the shadows, and roared. The man yelled excitedly and then bowed to the ground. All the standing members of the desert people did the same.

"Grunt some more to accept their worship," whispered Ahiram, "and then roar impatiently." The five dwarfs applied themselves to the best of their abilities. First, Zurwott grunted in a low voice, and then the five of them roared in imitation of the béghôm. The sound seemed to come from every pore of the creature, and the man lifted his head, then signaled toward his companions, ordering a hasty retreat. They took a few steps back but kept their gaze on the entrance of the cave where the grunting came from. Ahiram peeked into the cave. It was large with a sandy floor and had a narrow back entrance that was blocked by warriors who stood with their backs turned to him. He was about to whisper to Zurwott when Jedarc leaned over to see what was happening. Ahiram saw his friend and stood speechless for a moment.

Since Ahiram was dressed in dwarfish clothing, Jedarc did not recognize him, but his trained eye caught Ahiram's movement.

"There's a rescue party in there," he whispered.

"Who?" retorted Banimelek surprised.

"Dwarfs, by the looks of it. They'll need a diversion."

"Crazy maze?" asked Sondra.

The two Silent nodded.

"Sheheluth," whispered Banimelek, "Get ready to do what I told you."

The three Silent sprang to their feet and started a bewildering dance, like three drunks stumbling in a narrow, confined maze. With arms tied behind their backs, they kicked each other, shouting as they went.

For a few seconds all eyes were on them. *Crazy maze. Jedarc saw me,* noted Ahiram. As all eyes were on him, he allowed himself a longer peek. *They must be here to save this slave as well, so this must not be a slave but a member of the Silent Corps.* He saw the two tall men standing on either side of Sheheluth. *What is she doing here? Beginners are barred from joining a whisper. What's wrong with them? She's under tight surveillance. This is bad, but I'll have a word with Sondra later. Now is the time to move.*

"When you hear my sword hit the chains, roar as loud as possible," he coached the fake béghôm. "As soon as the slave is free, grab him and run back as fast as you can."

"How can you breaking break these chaining chains with your swording sword?" asked one of the dwarfs, incredulous.

Ahiram did not answer. He signaled to the other dwarfs to follow him, and they leaped inside the cave. When Ahiram reached back to grab the sword, the weapon flew out of its sheath and its grip landed into his open palm. He slammed the blade against the chains. The links exploded under the impact and the post was dented. Zurwott roared. Ahiram looked up and saw a few of the desert people patiently trying to subdue the three dancing Silent. He broke the last few links and set the slave free. Sheathing his sword, he aimed four smoke pellets toward his friends, and they landed at Sheheluth's feet. Following the instructions Banimelek' had previously given her, she dropped to the ground, then, as the smoke became thicker, she rolled over and crawled in his direction.

Who threw the smoke pellets? Banimelek wondered.

"Charge!" ordered Jedarc. Quick as a cat, Banimelek snatched Sheheluth and followed Jedarc inside the cave. Two warriors lay unconscious by the entrance.

"Keep running," urged a familiar voice. Jedarc's jaw dropped and he nearly stopped in his tracks. "Not now, Jedarc," snapped Ahiram. "Keep running." Banimelek pushed Jedarc forward and managed to slap Ahiram on the back before disappearing inside the cave.

"Sondra, smoke the entrance," ordered Ahiram as the young woman reached him. Hearing his voice, Sondra's eyes widened then grinning wildly, she whirled around and peppered the entrance with smoke pellets, creating a smoke barrier.

"Banimelek, lend me a hand," called Jedarc who knelt by the unconscious victim, who was still covered with a hood.

"Why is she here?" snarled Ahiram pointing at Sheheluth.

"Jedarc's choice. He is the leader," replied Sondra.

"Ahiram, is that you?" asked the young Silent astonished.

Ahiram gazed at her. He was tense and angry. "Don't slow us down."

"Are they of the Silently Silent stock?" inquired Zurwott.

"The best of the stock," replied Jedarc as he snatched the blanket. "Banimelek, we'll do a carry-ho."

They slid the blanket beneath the victim and wrapped it tightly around her shoulders and legs. Quickly, Jedarc and Banimelek secured the makeshift stretcher around their chests and foreheads, leaving their arms free for action.

"Everyone out," ordered Ahiram. "Move!" They bolted out of the cave. "Sheheluth, what are you doing here?"

She stiffened. "It was Jedarc's idea to bring me along."

Ahiram scoffed. "He's going to be reprimanded when we get back," he muttered. "What was he thinking?" He glanced behind him and winced. The tribesmen had just emerged from the cave and were quickly coming after them. He had assumed they would be able to confuse the desert people and disappear inside the passage before a pursuit was organized. The dwarfs ran as fast as they could, but the company was hampered by the weight of the slave who was still unconscious. Ahiram looked back and noticed they were losing ground. Soon their pursuers would catch up to them and things would get difficult.

Abruptly, the ground became slippery. There, the agility of the dwarfs and the Silent proved to be a real advantage. The pursuers began to lose ground and soon were out of sight. Ahiram began to hope they would rid themselves of the tribesmen, when one of the dwarfs shouted, "The boulder!" Ahiram looked ahead and saw the boulder they had crossed over on their way to the cave. His sword vibrated violently.

"Climb!" yelled Ahiram. "We don't have a moment to lose."

"But what do we do with the slave?" shouted one of the dwarfs.

"That's no slave," protested Jedarc, "that's—"

"We will have to hoist him up," Ahiram cut in, "drag him along the rock toward the other end, we have no choice."

"Look," shouted one of the dwarfs. "The boulder. It's moving."

Everyone froze. The base of the huge boulder shook and was suddenly whisked out of the way as if a child had just kicked a small pebble. It tumbled down and exploded in the valley below. The vibrations on Ahiram's back were now so strong that he was almost shaking. He glanced back to see if their pursuers had caught up with them, when everyone shrieked. Sheheluth stiffened. Ahiram turned around and felt his hair stand on his head. A fourteen-foot monster barred the way: red fierce eyes in a white face.

"The béghôm," he whispered. "Back, go back to the cave."

The Silent reacted swiftly. Jedarc and Banimelek forced their way through the transfixed dwarfs. Ahiram yanked Sheheluth back. "Run," he said, "run as fast as you can. Sondra, go. Now!" Turning around, he shook the dwarfs. They snapped out of their shock and scampered back to the cave. The béghôm stood motionless for a moment, then roared with so much power, it nearly took their strength away and shot waves of fright up and down their spines.

"Faster," yelled Ahiram.

"But what about the tribesmen?" asked Orwutt.

"I don't know. Run!"

They ran as fast as they could, almost breaking their necks on the slippery pass. The intermittent roar of the béghôm grew distant. Evidently, the beast had not decided to give pursuit.

"Why is he not following us?" shouted Ahiram.

"You have my shared wondering wonderment," replied Zurwott. "This is an abnormally abnormal on the part of the xarg-ulum. Normally she attacks with ferocious speed. She delays, and I know not why."

The members of the company kept running as fast as they could until they burst inside the cave. They dashed through the entryway and seeing the cave deserted, Ahiram realized they had not met with the tribesmen on their way. A glance at the exit and he knew why. They stood there, blocking the way.

"Banimelek, any other exit?"

"I can't see one. If we try to force our way, it will be a bloodbath."

"Everyone against the wall. Draw swords. Silent, to your crossbows."

Jedarc was dying to ask Ahiram why he was disguised as a dwarf but thought it best to wait. Feverishly, Ahiram reached inside his pockets and realized he had left the tile in his broken belt in his room.

"I don't have the tile. I forgot the taw," he muttered. Instantly, the tile appeared in his hand. He gasped in surprise.

"Ahiram," Jedarc rasped, "what's wrong with your hand?"

Ahiram grinned and showed his friend the tile. "It just appeared in the palm of my hand," he explained.

"What appeared?" asked Jedarc. "What are you talking about?"

"The tile," protested Ahiram. "Don't you …?" It dawned on him. *He doesn't see it.* He failed to notice the look of dismay and horror on Sheheluth's face, or if he did, he ascribed it to the béghôm. *No one else sees it but me. Why? How did it get here so quickly?* The béghôm roared. *No time to figure this out now. I'm about to fight this creature.*

He placed the tile on the sword's handle and it sunk inside of it like a rock being sucked into quick sand. A streak of bright blue light flashed from the blade as waves of shining colors ran its length.

"Amazing," Sondra whispered. "What kind of sword *is* that?"

"A sword of meyroon," whispered Banimelek. "Meyroon."

The béghôm burst into the cave and Sheheluth felt her heart skip a beat. Ahiram was instantly covered with sweat. "This is as powerful a foe as I have ever seen," he muttered, teeth clenched. His fear flared and for one second, one quick second, he saw himself in the small boat being taken away from the beach, while a bearded man he did not recognize stood in a second boat laughing at him. Instantly, power surged from deep within him; an anger dark and powerful that he had tried repress with the iron-fisted training of the past six years. It had exploded in a violent fury when Prince Olothe had belittled his father, and Ahiram had beaten him senseless because of it.

Ahiram felt it well up again. He swallowed hard. *Not now. This is not the time to lose my temper. I need to stay focused and in control of my actions.* But his anger flared, and this time it was stronger. He could feel his self-control slipping away. *I am losing my mind. Why am I so angry? What is going on?* Unable to control it any longer, he screamed.

The béghôm roared.

The dwarfs covered their faces with their hands, and the victim, who was now awake, shrieked.

Good, she's alive, thought Jedarc, teeth clenched. The crossbow in his hand looked ridiculously small, like a child's toy compared to the size of the beast, but he knew better. He waited for Ahiram's signal.

Ahiram sliced the air before him with his blade. The sword's song was jubilant and strong, which ebbed his fear and steadied his hands. He could see his friends and the dwarfs stand a little taller. The béghôm moaned as if in pain. Ahiram glanced at the sword and eyed the beast who now looked sheepish. He waved his sword and the beast moaned again.

Wrath of the Urkuun – Sacrifice to a Béghôm

This might explain why she did not attack right away. She is afraid of the sword. He noticed then that the béghôm was covered in blood. *Master Xurgon and his dwarfs must have put up a decent fight to keep her in the Pit.* This gave him courage, and he did the unthinkable. He attacked.

He lunged at the monster's heart, but the béghôm sidestepped him and delivered a furious blow, which Ahiram had anticipated. He dropped low when he felt the swift movement of air rush toward him, but the beast had a longer reach. She struck him on the shoulder and sent him rolling on the ground. Fortunately, the shield he wore protected him. He sprang back up to his feet and faced his nemesis. The béghôm roared once more, but this time Ahiram felt galvanized. Somehow, he was confident that the creature was more afraid of him because of his mysterious sword, than he was of her. She edged closer to one of the dwarfs who stabbed her right calf. The beast moaned with pain and delivered a blow to the dwarf, who rolled unconscious against the wall. Ahiram lunged and thrust his sword, but his foe evaded the attack and pounded the ground, hurling fragments of rocks sharp as steel.

She seems a bit slower. The blow from the dwarf was effective.

The beast's tiny red eyes locked on him. He could see deep-seated fear and hatred; a great evil that wanted his destruction.

The Silent shifted his position slightly to the right, and as the beast's head followed his movement, he flicked his left thumb and index finger. Two darts flew from Sondra's and Banimelek's crossbows. One hit its mark and injured the béghôm's left eye, and the other sank right above the right eye, drawing blood. The beast raged, her left fist pummeled the wall just a hair above Jedarc's head, who then dropped to the ground. Seeing blood smeared on the wall where his friend had stood, Ahiram thought him dead.

"Jedarc, no!"

Ahiram had always considered Jedarc and Noraldeen as two beacons of light in a world of darkness. He delighted in their ability to rejoice in a beautiful day, a serene sky, or in a shared meal with friends. True, he sat with them, ate with them, and walked with them, but more so like a shadow visiting the day, or a creature of the night discovering the sun. He did not know how to enjoy what they enjoyed, and was content to warm his heart in the sunshine of their smiles for they enjoyed life to its fullness. They were hope incarnate, hope that one day, someday, he too may step into the light. Noraldeen and Jedarc were his guiding stars, and without them he felt blind and cold. Jedarc and Noraldeen's death would mean the end of a world, an iron door slamming shut on mines too deep to see the snow covered mountains. Jedarc and Noraldeen lived in a world like Hoda's, the world before he was taken away. He was now a wanderer, guided by their voices, back to his sister, back to the days he had danced with her on the beach.

Finally, snickered the voice within, *finally you're ready to let me be free.*

His dark temper rose like a fury. The sword's halo grew brighter, crackling as it shot blinding bolts of light. The beast roared her rage. Ahiram spoke words he did not understand. The halo streaming from the sword flared brightly and engulfed him. Sheheluth covered her ears and screamed but her voice was lost in the beast's bellowing shout. The Silent came down on the béghôm like lightning on a tree, but the creature stepped deftly aside and delivered a blow that should have broken Ahiram's back. Instead, her fists hit and rebounded against the strange halo. Ahiram yelled and turned to face the beast. Fire flared in his eyes, and his voiced filled the cave just as the halo turned into dark clouds hiding him from view. The storm filled the cave with lightning. Everyone covered their ears and dropped to the ground. The béghôm raised her fists to strike once more just as Layaleen tore through the dark cloud and a thin sheath of deadly light slashed through the beast's side. The béghôm screamed in pain, and as the blade retracted, she exploded in a flurry of red flakes. A green oozing hole opened in the ground where the monster stood, sucked the unearthly flakes away, and vanished.

Immediately, the dark storm dispersed and the roaring noise subsided. Ahiram stood breathless for a moment, then staggered forward and dropped his blade. He fell to his knees coughing up blood. Convinced the blade had destroyed their enemy, the dwarfs cheered. Banimelek was the first to reach Ahiram who looked disoriented and confused. He steadied him and helped him up.

"Where am I? What just happened?" He coughed up more blood. "Is the slave alive?"

"Yes, *she's* alive," replied Jedarc.

"A girl? Good, let me see her."

"You're not in a good shape, Ahiram. You'll scare her. She's been through a lot."

"Fine, but she is alive?"

Sondra went over and uncovered the victim's head. Hiyam's hair came cascading down. Her eyes darted from Sondra to Sheheluth, and lingered on Jedarc when she saw his beaming smile. She relaxed and managed to get up. Jedarc signaled to Sondra to quickly get her out of the cave.

"You don't need to carry me," snapped Hiyam. She was still groggy from the effects of the drugs. "I can walk on my own."

This voice, he thought, *I recognize this voice*. He turned around sharply. Hiyam saw his eyes filled with a raging fury and she recoiled.

"You?" he snapped, coughing more blood, "I risked my life to save *you*?" He gathered his strength and got up. Jedarc tried to stop him, but Ahiram elbowed his friend, pushed Sondra out of his way, and raised a hand to slap Hiyam.

"Silently Silent," cried out Zurwott. "Remember the remembrance of your promising promise."

Ahiram remembered: *No one shall touch a hair of the slave as long as I live.* He had made that promise just five days ago. He moved away and leaned on Banimelek, the only one who did not try to stop him. "Never let me see her face again," he muttered, his voice raspy and hard. He fell to his knees and collapsed in Sondra's arms.

"Ahiram, Ahiram," she called, trying to wake him up.

"He must be wounded," observed Jedarc. "He will need help."

"The desert people will help," retorted Banimelek, lifting Ahiram up. "They will know what to do."

"Do you trust them?" asked Sondra.

"They will know what to do," grunted Banimelek carrying Ahiram outside the cave. "Let's go."

Hiyam pushed every one away, stormed out of the cave and faced the desert people. "Once the Temple finds out what you have done to me," she snapped, "you will wish you were all dead at the hand of this beast."

8. Recovery

> *"The Temple of Baal has always straddled two realms: the sunlit world of men, and the Spell World. One is resplendent with life, the other hidden, secret and terrifying. This dual view is dangerous, for the Order of Baal is always tempted to reduce our world to a mere illusion, and to believe that the Spell World is the ultimate reality."*
> —Teaching of Oreg, High Priest of Baal.

When the béghôm vanished, the recluse tribe concluded that a greater force had defeated their god, which meant the beast was no longer able to threaten their crops. The sacrifice had become unnecessary, and they were happy to release Hiyam into the care of the Silent.

"How dare they release me into *your* care?" snapped Hiyam. "I will have them flogged and flayed for what they have done to me."

"You will do nothing of the sort," replied Sondra.

"How dare you order me around? I am the daughter of High Priestess Bahiya—"

"And I am a Silent! And I don't care if you are the daughter of Baal himself. You are under the Silent's jurisdiction and you will follow Jedarc's orders. Is that understood?"

The two young women glared at each other, both unwilling to relent.

"Stay like that," said Jedarc jovially, "and bees will be able to grow entire hives on your heads."

Sondra scowled and Hiyam quietly averted her eyes. She did not want to look at Jedarc.

"High Rider, a word. Please."

Hiyam eyed Banimelek, her hands creeping to where her blade should have been. If his intentions were hostile, he hid them behind an impassible mask.

"This way, please," he added, speaking affably.

She followed him and they walked a short distance away. Sondra and Jedarc observed them. Banimelek spoke a few short sentences and then they saw Hiyam's eyes widen and her expression fall. Banimelek came back, leaving her and visibly shaken.

"What did you tell her?" asked Jedarc. "You didn't ask for her hand in marriage, now did you?"

Banimelek cracked a thin smile and shrugged his shoulders. "I reminded her of the High Riders' code of honor."

Sondra frowned, digesting what Banimelek had just said. Then her features brightened and she slapped the tall Silent on his shoulder. "Brilliant," she said. "Absolutely brilliant. Banimelek you are a genius."

Jedarc slipped his hands in his pockets and began shuffling tiny pebbles with his boots. He had to admit that Sondra was right. Banimelek had found a glaring weakness in Hiyam's defenses, one the proud daughter of the high priestess could not refute, a weakness at the heart of the High Riders' code of honor.

"If a High Rider falls into slavery," he recited somberly, "and is rescued, then that High Rider will become the slave of his rescuer to whom he owes his life. His indenture shall be for one year or until a ransom is paid on his behalf."

Banimelek nodded.

"So Hiyam is now a slave … and her master is …?"

Wrath of the Urkuun – Recovery

Banimelek chuckled. "Isn't it obvious? Hiyam is now Ahiram's slave."

Sheheluth sat at Ahiram's bedside. He lay motionless, his breathing shallow and ragged. An older woman walked in, examined the Silent and signaled to Sheheluth to get Banimelek. A moment later three Silent stood in the cave with the older woman.

"The healer," explained Banimelek, "says Ahiram is too weak and that is why he is not waking up. She will take care of him."

"Can we trust them, Faernor?" urged Sondra. "This *is* Alendiir we're talking about."

"I know, Sondra. Her knowledge of medicinal herbs is greater than that of the dwarfs. I don't think there's anyone better to heal Ahiram than her. I trust her."

One hour later, they carried Ahiram to an adjoining cave where a hot bath had been prepared in a pit dug into the ground. It was filled with aromatic herbs and looked like a thick yellow slush. The old woman asked them to take his belt and shoes off but not his clothing just yet.

"His clothes may be stuck to his wounds," explained Banimelek. They immersed their unconscious friend in the warm water. A moan escaped his lips. The old woman beamed. "She says that's a great sign. She thinks he will recover in a few days."

Later on, as the day waned and night began to settle on the rim of the mountains, they carried Ahiram to a clean bed and sat watch over him. Hiyam confined herself to a nearby cave and refused to speak with anyone. After a hearty meal, the dwarfs and the Silent were all relieved to slide into a warm bed, and they slept well knowing they did not have to worry about the béghôm any longer.

The following day, Zurwott sealed a cooperative agreement with Xendorac; the desert people would ship the bricks the dwarfs produced. In return, the dwarfs would provide Xendorac and his people with clean-burning torches. Furthermore, the dwarfs would provide the necessary equipment to properly patch drafty caves and teach the desert people how to use them. *A mutually mutual agreeable agreement*, thought Zurwott as he stepped into the tunnel that led back to their quarters. This was the primary reason why he had accepted to stay the night. He sealed the agreement without a zakiir, which meant that he himself would pocket five percent of the profit from the sales of the brick—half of the memory man's commission.

"We will be freely free and free to freely roam these caves," repeated Zurwott. He saw them in a new light. Without the constant fear of the beast, these caves would revert to a comfortable, friendly space. While the beast roamed free, these caves had felt like a forlorn uncle who refused visits, but now, with the monster gone, the caves had invited them for a grand tour.

"Xirix Zilal loved his gemstone.
In treasure-caves, he stood alone.
With precious stones and piles of gold,
He danced and dined, or so I'm told."

Zurwott intoned the first verse of Xirix Zilal's famous eulogy and the rest of the band joined in.

"Rich, tall, and proud, Xirix stands alone.
Rich, tall, and proud, he stands so, forlorn.

In ancient caves so deep and dank,
Where no one lived, nor ate, nor drank;
Amid the gold he had accrued,
He stood alone in a cheerful mood.

Rich, tall, and proud, Xirix stands alone.
Rich, tall, and proud, he stands so, forlorn.

No dwarf ever came to visit,
No songs were sung to lift his spirit,

> No beer to share with scrumptious geese,
> No one would dare disturb his peace.
>
> Rich, tall, and proud, Xirix stands alone.
> Rich tall, and proud, he stands so, forlorn.
>
> So went the years beneath the earth,
> He stood content, no joy, no mirth.
> Until one night he turned to stone,
> And still today, he stands alone.
>
> Stiff as a stone, Xirix stands alone,
> No more flesh or bone, he stands so, forlorn."

"It is a goodly good death to die between piling piles of glowing gold," sighed Arax, contentedly. "Blessed Xirix Zilal is a truly true dwarf and a dwarfish dwarf of the purely pure lineage."

Orwutt bit his tongue. Aside from Andaxil and the fratricidal wars of Salsipetri and Alijuun, nothing was more contentious than the eulogy of Xirix Zilal. The northern dwarfs, such as Arax, celebrated Xirix Zilal as a hero, but the southerners considered him a buffoon well deserving of his fate. Two hundred years ago, in an effort to avoid a fratricidal war, the two realms had established a joint commission to determine Xirix Zilal's status of hero or buffoon. This still ongoing commission had just asked its twenty-two current members two questions: How long could Xirix have lived alone without losing his mind? Secondly, a dwarf who did not care for his physical well-being would be called a buffoon. The commission wanted to know the number of monthly grooming a dwarf had to perform to stay in good standing. Once that number was defined, the commission would deliberate on Xirix's ability to meet this requirement, especially as he advanced in age.

Zurwott was a member of this commission. Now that the monster was gone, he hoped to present his answer for the second question. He had concluded, after intense study, that every dwarf required a minimum of a weekly trim; a task an old dwarf could not carry out unaided.

"To groom or not to groom is the heart of the argument," Ashod had advised one day, "the one aspect that would determine if Xirix Zilal was a hero or a fool." Zurwott had never forgotten these words because he was still unable to tell if Ashod had spoken seriously; an answer as ambiguous as Xirix Zilal's predicament.

"By the mighty Xirik!"

His brother's exclamation brought him back to the present. He realized they had reached their quarters. Every room was in shambles. The wounded were many. The béghôm had gone berserk and managed to break through their defenses in under two hours. Despite their fierce resistance, the beast had escaped in a trail of blood.

The following day a frazzled Xurgon convoked a council. Zurwott and Orwutt gave an account of their adventure and concluded by telling the assembly that Ahiram had slain the béghôm. After much questioning, the council disagreed with their conclusion and were of the opinion that the two dwarfs had been hasty.

"That the beastly beast has been dealt a wound is clear to this council," summarized Xurgon. "Whether the Silent definitively defeated the Xarg-Ulum remains to be seemingly seen. I believe a magical trick has spirited the beast away at the last instant to avoid her deathly demise. More I cannot say as an absolute saying in this moment." At this news, silence fell. Master Xurgon stood up, "Let us raise our rising voices to sing the brave, deadly death of our young Silent hero who died a great dwarfish death today and—"

"Ahiram sustained bruising bruises but is breathing breezily." Zurwott stood rather unceremoniously to reassure his master.

"Why have you not brought him with you so we may tenderly tend to his wounding wounds?"

Orwutt explained how Banimelek refused to bring Ahiram back to the dwarfs because of his injuries.

"The desert people have extensive healing knowledge. He will be well taken care of there."

"So the Silent defeated the mighty xarg-ulum," mused Master Xurgon. "He broke the spell-binding spells. This is a mighty deed. Who knew the young man had knowledge of ancient lore to accomplish this feat? Has the venerable Korx Terix Tal seen the sworDing sword?"

They asked the old dwarf who had examined Ahiram's sword earlier to come forward. After an animated conversation with him, Xurgon fell into deep thought. He emptied the content of his pipe into the chimney and filled it with fresh tobacco; then, forgetting to light it up, he tried to smoke it. After a few frustrating inhalations, he realized his mistake, and after lighting his pipe, rose to his feet in a cloud of smoke.

Why would any respectable respecting dwarfish dwarf wish to take on the imaging image of a chimney is beyond my mentally mental capacities to understand, thought Zurwott. He was viscerally opposed to smoking, but he was not about to confront Xurgon on the subject, at least not now.

"Mighty dwarfs, rejoice," said Xurgon with a voice that roused the dwarfs to their feet. "Behold, the bearer of Layaleen is in our midst."

A stunned silence overtook the dwarfs and carried them into the midst of legends, as if El-Windiir were about to walk into the room with their forefathers who had fought by his side. Suddenly, their lives, so humdrum and ordinary, glowed with a brilliance surpassing that of their wildest dreams: El-Windiir's blade had returned. It meant a harbinger of new stories to be told and future glories to be hailed, and generations would sing of them. Still, dwarfs were first and foremost a practical lot, and as Master Xurgon's pipe smoke faded away, it took with it the wonder and elation of the moment.

"Now, onto more mundane tasking tasks," said Xurgon as he left the room. "Rebuild these quarters to decency."

➢ ⁘ ⁘ ≺

Kalibaal, priest of the Temple of Babylon, assistant to the High Priest Sharr, and member of the Inner Circle was perplexed. Never before had he seen such devastation in the Arayat. He floated gently over the evergreen oozing substance that covered the Spell World. His appearance was that of a two-headed bull with hands instead of hooves; hardly anyone controlled how he appeared in the Spell World. The color of his skin was a dark blue, repeatedly crisscrossed by translucent blue streaks of lightning. The right head was fully formed, while the left head flickered in and out of existence. This Arayatian behavior annoyed Kalibaal, which is why he ventured to the Spell World only when necessary, and the unexpected return of the béghôm from the mines required his full attention.

"I had forgotten how loud the Arayat is," he commented.

"It *is* alive, you know," replied Shermas. "It creaks and moans like an old ship, and the wind that blows continuously sounds like a deranged windpipe. Every planted curse burbles and gurgles with a metallic sound, and the slaves whose blood nourishes these fields moan unceasingly."

"You seem fond of the place," remarked Kalibaal.

Shermas would have shrugged his shoulders if he had had shoulders to shrug. His Arayatian form was a headless scarab body with four hyena hind legs and a badger's tail with a face on it. The face being close to the ground was practical for this *shogol*, spell herder, who spent most of his life in the care and feeding of fields of curses. "I am not fond of it. I am familiar with its rhythm, and Baal be blessed, I am not affected by the eerie sounds which drive many a priest crazy."

Kalibaal's right head nodded approvingly; his left head fluttered. He had trained for four long years before he could manage an extended stay in the Spell World. He surveyed the field ahead of him. "What a mess," he sighed. "What a mess."

Outside the Spell World, he would have let loose a series of expletives to shame the most hardened of sailors, but an assertion made here could become a curse in the real world. Every member of the Inner Circle knew the true origin of the gnat infestation that had killed thousands of Babylonians seventy years prior—the high priest of the day had a sister who was an Adorant, and he had called her a "pest," while in the Arayat. The gnats were so numerous, they had moved like a black liquid that drowned every living creature on their path.

"It will take years to heal this field," Shermas pointed out. He was the shogol in charge of these grounds that nourished the now broken béghôm. "The destruction is extensive."

Kalibaal willed to rise up, and he hovered over the devastation. Shermas followed. The area they inspected was shaped like a bowl, half-a-mile wide and half-a-mile deep. In the center stood the béghôm, or what was left of her. Here, she looked like a gray, ragged thorn bush, withered and ashen.

"Do you think she will survive?"

"Hard to say," sighed Shermas. "If the supporting curses were not so extensively damaged, she would regenerate quickly, but look at the extent of the disaster."

All around the béghôm, along thirty-two concentric circles, stood hundreds of odd-looking plants. They resembled lavender bushes and oozed a whitish substance that trickled down well-designed trenches for the béghôm to feed on. Their tips were translucent and they shone with an ominous purple glow. At least that is how the few remaining healthy curse-bushes looked. Most of these Arayatian plants were charred and blackened as if a dragon's breath had snuffed them out.

"Nearly all of these curses are now dead or dying," commented Shermas. "Each took five to seven years to grow and cost the blood of at least five curse providers."

Kalibaal waved dismissively. "You can get all the slaves you need."

"You mean curse providers," corrected Shermas. These were the souls that Baal had exiled to the Arayat to fuel the production of curses.

Shermas glanced at the seven hundred and sixty cocoons lining the rim of the bowl. Each cocoon encased one victim whose blood trickled out at the rate of one drop a week. The shogols then mixed the blood with several other ingredients to feed the curses. Shermas eyed the cocoons with great pride. Before his involvement, it took three drops of blood to raise the same quantity of curses that he could now raise with just one. He did it to reduce the number Arayatian prisoners, but instead, Sharr tripled the production of curses and added to everyone's load.

Sharr deserves what is coming his way, thought the Shogol.

"Incredible," whispered Kalibaal. "I know this curse," he said pointing at the béghôm. "This is not the real beast, but a replica you created from the bones of a dead béghôm. Still, the thirty-two rings of protection surrounding it have been snuffed in one blow. Shermas, if you were to create a countercurse to destroy this field, what would it look like?"

Shermas shook his head, which led the scarab to buzz quickly. "It's not possible. I hardly doubt that even Sureï could have created such a countercurse. When you look at this field you see the bushes, but I see the complex web of roots my Shogols have woven to help these curses protect each other. See that curse over there on the outer circle? That's a paralysis curse. It is defensive in nature. Near the bottom, there's a curse just out of view that triggers and amplifies the anger of an attacker in order to blind his reason. Since their roots are mingled, a threat to one triggers the other. This holds true for the hundreds of curses you see here. To create a countercurse that could rip through this field in a second … the mind staggers …that's impossible. It cannot be done."

"So you don't believe the attacker used a countercurse?"

The scarab buzzed. "It's something else. Something else entirely."

≻⸱⸱⸱≺

Master Kwadil reclined contentedly on his silk cushions. His famed Caravan from Beyond was stationed outside Gordion, the capital of the

Kingdom of Teshub, two thousand miles southeast of Tanniin. He was in a good mood, having received three momentous updates that meant he was now a lot closer to realizing his ultimate goal.

Master Xurgon had just informed Kwadil that the young Finikian boy, who had come to them six years ago, had recently destroyed a béghôm with El-Windiir's sword. At last, this confirmed his hunch about the child's importance. He congratulated himself on his costly investment; for he was the one who had covered the travel fares of Ahiram and his guardians. He had asked Commander Tanios to take the child as a slave for nine years, and had said that if he did not ask for him again, Tanios would be free to do with the boy as he wished. Master Kwadil smiled broadly for he was pleased with his own sagacity.

Now that Ahiram had found El-Windiir's sword, Kwadil knew he could no longer treat him as a slave. Still, there were other ways to get someone to do your bidding. Ashod had just asked him to facilitate the departure of Hayat and Jabbar to the Kingdom of Marada, the Land of Giants. Six years ago, Syreen had freely told Kwadil that Hoda was Ahiram's sister, and since he knew every member of the covert Black Robes, he quickly deduced she was Hayat and Jabbar's daughter. Therefore, he knew the location of the slave's parents; information the slave would be willing to barter against services rendered.

Then, he received the third piece of news—the most important of all. For twenty years now, a secret team of dwarfs had been searching for Andaxil, the dwarfs' mother cave. Their stubbornness, financed by his wealth, had finally paid off, for they had stumbled upon a hole inside a narrow canyon deep within the mountain range of Adiker.

The hole was no bigger than a man's fist; an inexperienced explorer would have missed it, but not Kazak Kerin, the greatest explorer of this dwarfish generation. His scouts had noted the gap but did not think much of it, so he asked them if they had checked the hole's edges.

"An edgy edge, raggedly ragged, would tellingly tell of an erosive erosion, but a smooth slippery edge may tell of an unnaturally unnatural originating origin. When conducting a hunting hunt for the greatest of comely caves, a rounded round should not be ignorantly ignored or ignored in the most ignorant manner."

Kazak's iron discipline had paid off. Upon closer examination, the dwarfs had realized that the hole was in fact a cylindrical passage cut into the mountain to the depth of twenty feet. Its edges were smooth, waterproof, and seared as if it had been formed by a flow of lava. Encouraged, the dwarfs had poured a thin stream of oil down the opening and set it on fire. Kazak's expert eye identified a metallic object at the bottom of the hole. Excited, the dwarfs carved a ten-foot-deep tunnel into the mountainside until they were stopped by an invisible barrier. No pix, axe, or shovel could get through that barrier, however, they could slide an iron cable into the remaining ten feet of the small space without hindrance.

Kazak then instructed them to tie a small flare to the end of the cable and push it into the hole as far as it would go. The flare reached the end and pushed against the metallic barrier, which lifted up without much difficulty. They then shoved the flare through, and the barrier fell back down. Using a second rod, the dwarfs succeeded in lifting the mysterious object, and then lit the flare.

In the bright, burning light, Kazak beheld a river of precious stones. As the flare waned, he recognized the object that blocked the hole: the Merilian medallion, the one his forefathers had *borrowed* from the giants and that had been hanging inside Andaxil for 642 years. The clever dwarf figured that a Merilian blast had created the very hole he was peering into. Their initial joy knew no bounds, but it was quickly dampened when they realized they could not break through the invisible barrier to retrieve the Merilian medallion.

"Kwadil, there is a cursing curse that keeps Andaxil enclosed and closed despite all our continuously continuous effort."

Kwadil had thanked his friend and senior of his clan for the information. The orb had gone dark and his great mind had carefully considered the evidence.

"This cursing curse is the working work of Sureï," he muttered.

A power greater than the sorcerer's magic was required to break the protective curse. No dwarfish cave held such power, but perhaps El-Windiir's blade and its bearer, would be powerful enough to break through the béghôm's protective rings.

Kwadil rubbed his hands and slapped his thighs.

An opportune opportunity will present herself no earlier than is needed and no later than is required, he thought, *and my shrewdly shrewd nephews will be of an impeccably impeccable helping help.*

There was a discrete knock at the door.

"May the highest heavenly heavens protectively protect us from the tormenting torment of importunate opportunists," grumbled the dwarf. Sighing, he clapped twice. "May your inquisitive inquiry be laid to a restful rest." This was the standard dwarfish salutation equivalent to a "come in" in the common tongue.

A bespectacled dwarf leaned forward and squinted. "Your attentive attention is immediately required and required immediately. A zakiir has comely come with a messaging message from a trustfully trustworthy friendly friend."

Kwadil grinned widely. *Ashod has an urgent, requesting request. What a charmingly charming coincidental coincidence.*

"Let him in," he said curtly in the common tongue.

➢ ·:·:· ≺

Ahiram opened his eyes and was assailed by a deep darkness. He closed them, and breathed deeply; opening them once more, he realized he was back in the cave but was not laying on a dwarfish mat. Taking in the vibrant eucalyptus scent, he thought, *This mat is made of fresh leaves. And it's clean.* He raised his head and saw a flicker in the far corner of the cave. He grunted as he pulled himself into a sitting position and was startled when he saw a young girl holding a cup. She prodded him to take it and he recognized Sheheluth. He drank half of it, then gave it back to her.

"I'm not thirsty," he said. His voice sounded coarse.

"Are you hungry?" she asked, on edge.

He gave her a dazed look. "No, thank you, I'm fine, but where are we?"

Sheheluth bolted from the room and he heard her say his name to someone. Dizziness assailed him and he slid back onto the mat. Placing his hands behind his head, he stared at the ceiling. He did not know why, but the darkness was soothing.

"Hey," said Jedarc as he walked in followed by Banimelek, Sondra, and Sheheluth. "How are you feeling?"

"Close that door," grumbled Ahiram squinting. "What is this? Slave's visitation day? What are you doing in my room?"

"You don't remember?" asked Banimelek.

"Remember what?"

"The béghôm, Alendiir," replied Sondra. "You do not remember?"

The name resonated like an ominous threat. A blurry image took shape: a dark mass, a powerful shriek, two red eyes. The image came into focus and he saw a pair of hateful eyes, in want of his destruction. The image faded and he saw himself facing the beast. He remembered jumping ... Ahiram sat up so suddenly, he startled his friends.

"Where is she?" said Ahiram, hands in frantic search of his sword.

"The béghôm is a *she?*" Sondra was astounded.

Banimelek steadied Ahiram. "The beast is gone. You beat him."

"Her," corrected Sondra. "It's a *she* ..."

"I did?" asked Ahiram. His memory was still hazy. "Are you sure?"

Banimelek nodded. "We saw it disappear in a red cloud."

"Her," Sondra corrected again. She was still shocked that the beast was female. "*She* disappeared."

"What happened then?"

Sondra eyed Banimelek. He nodded.

"You coughed up blood," continued Sondra, "then you collapsed."

"I vaguely remember," he said softly, then looked at them in turn. His gaze settled on Jedarc. He looked at his friend, frowned, then jumped up overjoyed and would have fallen back down had Jedarc not steadied him.

"Jedarc," he said squeezing his friend's shoulders. "You're not dead! You're alive! This is wonderful."

"Aren't I supposed to say that?"

"You're not dead, you're not dead," replied Ahiram, relieved. "I'm so happy." Jedarc smiled and helped his friend sit back down. "So, what are you all doing here?" asked Ahiram.

"You don't remember?" asked Banimelek.

"What? What is it that I don't remember?"

"What Faernor is trying to say," said Sondra carefully, "is that you, Alendiir, saved the life of … the high priestess' daughter."

Instantly, Ahiram's face hardened, but before he could say a word, he met Sheheluth's gaze. He was surprised to see how angry she was. "What's wrong with you?" he asked.

"Stop it, Ahiram," she said firmly, her voice quivering. Sheheluth's voice had a sharp edge that was different from her usually soft tone. "I watched over you for six days. I saw you wake up, eat like four men, and drink enough water to drown a desert. While all along you looked at me and yelled, 'I hate you, Hiyam, I hate you.' You said it over and over again. I cannot take this anymore. Stop it."

Ahiram swallowed hard. He gazed at Jedarc. "Did I do that?" Jedarc gave him a sad smile and simply nodded. Ahiram sighed and covered his face with his hands.

"Leave me, please. All of you."

They filed out in silence. He sat looking at the small candle flicker and sputter in the dark, and nearly jumped with fright when he saw a creature that vaguely resembled the béghôm peer into the cave. It was the distorted shadow of a woman, one of the desert people, coming into the room. She spoke in a high guttural tongue. Ahiram noticed then that Banimelek was standing behind her. His eyes widened like saucepans when he heard his friend answer in a halting manner. He spoke this strange language fluently. The woman drew closer and touched Ahiram's forehead. Her hand was soft and warm. She asked him to open his mouth, then pulled on his tongue. She examined under his arms, his chest, and the soles of his feet. She looked at Banimelek and smiled.

"You're doing much better," explained the Silent. "You should be fully recovered in a few days."

They went out together and left him alone. *I hate you Hiyam, Hiyam I hate you*. He did not like the image of himself, raving mad, yelling at Sheheluth. He closed his eyes and saw her face seared with pain and sorrow. He sighed deeply and slumped back on his mat. He slept fitfully until at last, exhaustion caught up with him, and he fell into a deep sleep.

Master Xurgon walked into the common room. The dwarfs had been hard at work cleaning and repairing their living quarters. Progress was steady and he felt confident the dwarfs would remove all traces of the béghôm's rampage within the next two to three weeks. He was however, troubled by a bit of news that he had not paid much attention to until now. On the day that Ahiram had arrived, he chided Orwutt and Zurwott when they warned him that a passage had been elongated. He thought the twins were being facetious, but when other passages began to undergo dramatic changes, he had to admit, the news perturbed him.

"Master Xurgon, she is no more," said Orwutt as he walked in. Speaking to an elder before bowing and receiving permission to do so was rude—unless a sizeable enemy were at the door.

Xurgon saw fear on Orwutt's face. "The lowly or the haughty?"

"Neither the lowly low corridor nor the haughty high passage, but the skinny hallway is no more," explained Zurwott, walking in.

"I see. What of the fat one? Is she still there?"

"She is indeed, but she has lost much fatness," said Orwutt.

"What she has lost in fatness, she gained in length," added Zurwott.

Master Xurgon tapped his pipe with a growing sense of irritation.

"Barely have we begun to enjoy the enjoyment of freedom from the béghôm, when we are careened and marooned on an outlandish isle of sorrow. Of all the godly gods of the dwarfish pantheon, which one is expressing his temper by tampering with the resistance of our walls? The skinny hallway and the fat hallway are no more, you say?"

The twins nodded.

"That would be four more hallways we have lost, and lost everlastingly. This must come to a stopping stop."

"If Master Xurgon would be kindly kind and not discount cheaply the unerring utterance of my brotherly brother, Orwutt," interjected Zurwott, "that would increasingly increase and increase increasingly the numbers of lost hallways to five."

"Indeed, indeed," replied Xurgon rather impatiently. He did not like being reminded that he had previously chided the two young dwarfs when he had not believed their report on the day he had seen them with Ahiram. "I am left bereaved and with dryness of thought. Could it be that these events are not natural in the most natural sense?"

"Your obscurely obscure thoughts and your thoughts, obscurely obscure, pervade the opaque opacity of my mind. I am gripped by a confusedly confused processing process and a processing process so confusedly confused that I am about to fall into obscurantism. An obscurantist obscurantism of such a degree that no obscurantist obscurantism could ever be its equalizing equal in depth, breadth and height," said Zurwott in perfect dwarfish, where a man may have simply said, "I don't get it."

"Rocks are familiarly familiar," explained Xurgon. "They are of good cheer and of good company. We know them knowingly and are acutely acquainted with their comportment since time is time, and there is someone to count. A falling rock, a slide-in, a cave-in, a slip, a crevice, a tremor, a displacement of terrain, a shudder, a tremor, a crack, a crumbling … these are all well-known eventful events whose eventuality is dear to every family. We can predictably predict most of these things and understand their effective effects. This, however, is of an entirely different nature. So different that most dwarfs who have seen the state of these hallways have lost their appetizing appetite."

"And how would you describe them?" asked Orwutt, provoking frowns from Master Xurgon and Zurwott by his nonchalant use of the Common Tongue.

"If this mountainous mountain was a manly man, I would perfunctorily say the man is a cadaveric cadaver in state of decomposing decomposition."

"Ghastly descriptive description," said Zurwott, who did not fail to appreciate the "cadaveric cadaver," which had a lively staccato to it, and a rhythm to which the dwarfs could dance.

Xurgon starred at the twin brothers. Despite their youth, they were masters of rocks and caves, having spent most of their young adult years searching for Andaxil with their uncle. He trusted their judgment. "What is the curative cure?"

"Can we curatively cure a deadly dead man?" replied Orwutt.

"Have you ceased to believe in hope?" asked their grizzled master.

"In naturally natural lore and knowledgeable knowledge of the dwarfs, yes," replied Zurwott.

"Something else is required," added Orwutt.

The twins echoed the old dwarf's own sentiment: An unnatural force was eroding the rocks, causing them to decay like a flesh-eating disease attacking a sick dog. *If this forcing force is ably able to decay the stony stone, what could it do to living flesh of men and dwarfs?* Suddenly, their troubles with the béghôm felt like a pleasant distraction. *A deathly death is spreading its wings, and to oppose it, we have an inexperienced boyish boy.* He knew his greatest challenge was ahead of him and he wondered if he would survive to tell the tale.

9. Northbound

"The realm of magic is an illusion, a mere fabrication of the mind, an attempt on the part of mortal men, to control a matter far more fluid than water, to harness a power greater than fire, and to bring order from a dark chaos. What mortal man forgets is this simple truth: With every act of magic performed, the realm expands, changes, and grows ever stronger."
—Teaching of Oreg, High Priest of Baal.

"Ahiram, Ahiram."

Ahiram opened his eyes and saw Sheheluth. She handed him a mug. "Here, drink this."

"Not thirsty." He yawned and closed his eyes.

She shook him. "Wake up now. You must drink or else you won't heal. You're still feverish. Drink."

"What day is it?"

"The twentieth of Tébêt, why do you ask?"

"Thirteen days since the end of the Games of the Mines. So it's Husèd, right?"

"Yes."

"The last day of the week. Less than thirty days till fall." He sighed. "Where has time gone I wonder?" He closed his eyes.

"Don't fall asleep." Sheheluth shook him harder. "Sit up and drink."

Ahiram pulled himself into a sitting position, took a sip from the mug and grimaced. "This is as bitter as a lonely death," he moaned. "What is it?" he asked. Sheheluth just shrugged her shoulders.

"What is it?" he asked again.

"I don't know," she said irritably.

"I mean what's wrong with you?"

She looked at him for a while. "It's you. That's what's wrong with me." Her voice was soft, almost tender.

"Me?" He took another sip and winced. "Why?"

"You are a *sormoss*."

Ahiram sipped some more of the bitter drink. He wished he could swallow it in one gulp, but the concoction was too hot. "What?"

"A sormoss, you punish anyone who causes you pain. Prince Olothe insulted your father and you crippled him for life. Hiyam tried to kill you, and now that she is in your grasp, you want to hurt her. That's a sormoss."

"If that's true, then a lot of people are a sormoss. She would still kill me if given the chance."

"No, she wouldn't, but you can't see it."

"Sheheluth, what are you saying? I'm not—"

"Most sormossians—at least the ones I have met—are like you, charming and strong. They are leaders, but when they lose their temper and injure someone, they would have you believe they are victim."

"She tried to kill me. I'm the victim here." The hot liquid splashed on his fingers and he bit his lower lip. *Calm down. There's no point in getting angry.* "Is that how you see me?" *How old is she anyway?*

"Did she try to kill you this time around?"

"She hasn't had the chance yet."

"Is that the Silent speaking, or is it the slave?"

"What?"

"Either you rise like the hero you are born to be, or you will die like the slave you think you are."

Ahiram swallowed with great difficulty. He was halfway through the contents of the mug and held back a strong urge to throw it down, or to force Sheheluth to drink it. *What am I thinking?* He could imagine himself holding Sheheluth down, forcing her to drink the contents of the mug. *What's wrong with me?*

"Look who's finally up," said Jedarc as he walked in with Sondra and Banimelek. "How are you feeling?"

Ahiram sighed. "Better." He glanced at Sheheluth.

"So tell us, Alendiir," asked Sondra, "we're dying to know, where did you find this blade?"

"Is that blade ... what happened in the mines?" added Jedarc.

Ahiram thought about the remaining artifacts. "After I left you in the mines, I was chased by ten High Riders to a ledge overlooking the rapids. I don't remember clearly what happened, but I think there must have been an earthquake. Three of us fell in the river and we ended up in the Eye of Death." Ahiram told the rest of the story with an even, quiet voice. He omitted how he found the gold tile, the sarcophagus, and the artifacts, and instead, told his friends he had found the sword laying on an ancient altar. "The temple was huge, and I believe some folks are secretly worshiping Tanniin there, because I found a fresh jar of blood."

"Blood?"

"Yes, blood," asserted Ahiram, happy to stir the conversation away from El-Windiir's tomb. "I can't explain the sword's behavior, but I'm happy it did what it did. We are all alive." This was a half-truth. After all, he did not understand how the tile merged with the sword and why that caused such a transformation.

"Ahiram," pressed Jedarc. "There must be more to your adventure."

"He has to brief the commander first," Banimelek reminded him.

"We know that, Faernor," replied Sondra. "Alendiir, what you did was really incredible."

"What I did nearly killed me," Ahiram corrected.

"Yes, we'll let you rest now," said Sondra. "Sheheluth, make sure he eats something and takes all of the medicine, all of it. He'll need it."

"Hey, I got this."

"Don't listen to him," ordered Banimelek. "Stay and watch him."

Jedarc stood up. "Once you're recovered, I expect a full report."

"Yes, Commander."

They shared a chuckle, then the three friends left. Ahiram slowly finished the drink and handed the empty mug to Sheheluth. She took it and stood up.

"Ahiram, I want to like you." Her voice had changed once more. It was lighter and sonorous. "I don't want to fear you. I wish you could promise someone you care about that you will never ever strike someone when you're angry." Not waiting for an answer, she left.

I'm sick. I just killed a beast, a monster. What's wrong with her? She wakes me to lecture me. I'm her senior, a Solitary. Who does she think she is? He resented her questioning. *Could I promise Nora or Jedarc that I wouldn't strike them if they angered me?* He slid into bed and closed his eyes.

He wasn't sure.

≻·◉·◉·◉·≺

The following morning, Ahiram awoke tired and dizzy. Grunting, he pulled himself up and shivered under the cool draft just as Jedarc walked in with his morning breakfast.

"Hey, hey, Nora's sweetheart is awake."

"I need a bath," grumbled Ahiram. "I'm covered in sweat."

"Cheer up then, My Lord, that's good news." Jedarc placed a bowl of porridge and a glass of milk on a nearby tree trunk. "It means the fever is leaving you and soon you'll be able to stand on your own two feet."

Ahiram grunted. "Where can I wash up?" He clutched Jedarc's arm and sniffed his sleeve. "I knew it, you've managed to clean up. Smells like hibiscus, silver-lemon, and olive oil, or something close to it."

"What?" asked Jedarc.

"The cleaning product they used. Not bad. Come on now, give me a hand and get me to a place where I can wash up. I could use a set of clean clothes too." Ahiram stopped, wide-eyed. "Do they have clothes to loan me? They don't wear much clothing, do they?"

"Don't you worry, My Lord, one of their caves has a spring. You can bathe, wash your clothes, and relax while they dry." Reassured, Ahiram nodded, forced himself up, and began walking. "Where are you going?"

"To that cave with the bath."

Jedarc smiled. "How long do you think your clothes will take to dry?"

"If washed in boiling water, it would take no more than four hours to dry, assuming the sun is out."

"And you're prepared to sit in that imaginary bath for four hours?"

"I'd sit in it for twenty hours if necessary … wait, what? Aaah, another one of your silly jokes. I should have known."

Four men walked in carrying a wooden bathtub and another four filled it with hot water. Ahiram heard a pleasant, refreshing fizz, and he smelled an earthy-lemon scent. "You knew I needed a bath?"

"Needed is debatable. That you wanted, nay, demanded one, yes. The only salve I know who demands to take a bath."

"Commander Tanios is a stickler when it comes to cleanliness."

"And this is why eight desert people are preparing you a bath?"

Ahiram shrugged his shoulders.

"Go ahead, get in, I'll watch the door and make sure no one other than a Silent walks in."

"Fine," said Ahiram as he undressed. "And that's not funny."

Jedarc chuckled. "Don't worry, Sondra and Sheheluth are hunting."

Ahiram slid into the warm, soapy bath, closed his eyes and relaxed.

"So, are you feeling better?" asked Jedarc who came and sat on the tree trunk. "You should eat your breakfast; it's getting cold."

"I'm not hungry."

"Last call. Are you sure?"

"Yes."

"Suit yourself," said Jedarc who dug in with a great appetite, "this porridge is excellent."

Ahiram sighed. He knew he could enjoy a few minutes of silence, for Jedarc preferred to eat without talking, although, he was a fast eater.

"That was good," said Jedarc slapping his belly. "Now, I'll take your dirty clothes and give them to Hiyam to wash. Since she's your slave now, she may as well—"

"What?" Ahiram nearly jumped out of his bath. "If that's a joke it's—"

"Ah, you don't know?" asked Jedarc innocently. "It's not a joke. You saved her life even though she is your enemy. According to the Temple's code of conduct, you now own her until the Temple either redeems her or keeps her in your ownership."

Ahiram set his eyes on his friend. "You're serious?" he whispered. "Dear El, this is worse than a joke. You're serious."

"Dead serious. You're her master, and she's you're slave. So how would you like your clothes washed?"

"Sheheluth said I'm a sormoss."

"A what?"

A sormoss. Someone who hurts others when he's angry."

"She called you a sormoss? Are you certain?" asked Jedarc.

"Yes. Do you know this word?"

"Hmm ... I didn't know Sheheluth was from ... but then why didn't she know what a banana was?"

"What are you mumbling about?"

"That's a word from back home. If she knew what it meant then she should have known what a banana was, but she acted as if she didn't."

"Most Silent protect their past."

"Indeed," confirmed Jedarc, still puzzled.

"Well, *am* I a sormoss?"

"She's observant."

"So, I am?"

"Are you?"

Ahiram heaved a deep sigh. "So I am. Why didn't you tell me before?"

"With your focus on the Games would you have listened? Besides, you hadn't *sormossed* anyone then, not on purpose anyway."

"Why does Noraldeen like me?"

"You mean why does she love you?"

"She's not stupid. Why should she fall for a sormoss?"

Jedarc came over and sat down facing Ahiram. "What are you going to do about it?"

"You haven't answered my question."

"You should ask her when you see her."

"When will that be?"

"Soon. We're moving north. Commander's orders."

"I'll have to change. I couldn't bear Noraldeen looking at me the way Sheheluth did, or Hoda … I couldn't look my sister in the eye. I've got to change. I can't stay like this."

"Do you remember the last mission that Nora, Banimelek, and you and I went on?"

"The diplomatic mission in Togofalk? Don't remind me. Nora and you were supposed to be a dashing young couple from Ophir. And Banimelek and I, your bodyguards. Only, you fell ill, so I had to play your role and Banimelek ended up as a large dwarfish matron." They laughed at the memory of the event. "What a disaster that was."

"Still, the mission was a success. We intercepted the Bar-Tanickian murderers, prevented a war, and saved two Togofalkian elders."

"That we did, thanks to Nora and the dwarfish matron."

Jedarc laughed. "Did you stop to think if these two Togofalkian elders were worth saving?"

"What do you mean?"

"I mean we know nothing of their past, and still, we saved their lives."

"The point being?"

==We don't save someone's life because he is worth saving. We save someone's life because it is the right thing to do.==

"Yes, and …?"

"A sormoss doesn't think that way. He thinks only those worth living should live. Which one are you?"

Ahiram sighed. "Jedarc, Hiyam tried to kill me."

"Yes, and that was wrong of her in more ways than I can think of. Is the person you saved the same person who wanted you dead in the Games of the Mines? Are you the same person who maimed Prince Olothe? Should I freeze you in time and think of you constantly as the sormoss who broke a man just because he was angry?"

In the silence that followed, Ahiram watched a glassy bubble of soap rise and pop. *The soapy surface looks the same, but if I look closer, it becomes a sea of constant change.*

"Fine," he said at last. "I'll talk to her." When Jedarc did not reply, Ahiram knew his friend had already left the cave. He smiled. *He knew what I was thinking. He didn't need to hear me say it.* He heaved a sigh of relief, and even though he noticed the bundle of dirty clothes was still there, he closed his eyes and dozed off again.

"The water is cold, you should get up."

Ahiram opened his eyes and saw Banimelek, sitting cross-legged next to him holding two bowls of porridge. He handed one to him and slowly started to eat from the other.

"Jedarc told me what Sheheluth said to you. Don't you go all mushy on me. You know I can't stand it when you're moping around."

"I won't. Don't worry. But do you think I'm a sormoss?"

"I told you not to go mushy on me. Don't overcomplicate things. You beat that guy senseless. I say he deserves it. He's a scum. There's nothing more to it."

"What about Hiyam?"

Banimelek shrugged his shoulders. "We both hate slavery, so she goes free. But if she hurts Jedarc, nothing will keep her safe from us. You put the fear of the Silent Corps in her heart, or I'll do it. Your call."

Ahiram sighed. Banimelek was the most practical of the three. "I'll do it. What do you think of Sheheluth?"

"Don't know yet. I don't trust her."

Ahiram nodded.

"Come on now, stop playing the pampered prince. Sondra wants a word with you. She's waiting outside."

"Clean clothes?"

"The dwarfs brought you another set. Jedarc hid them by your bed and made me promise not to say anything."

Ahiram chuckled. "You're getting antsy, I see."

"The commander is waiting for us. Then there's the high priestess. She's her mom."

"I thought you hated her."

"Hate the priestess. Respect the mom."

"I'll be out in a few minutes."

Banimelek grunted and left the cave.

<hr />

While Ahiram had been enjoying his bath, Master Xurgon, back in the dwarfs' quarters, was fretting over rocks and stones when Brix barged in and interrupted his train of thought.

"Master Xurgon, Master Xurgon," said the young dwarf, breathless.

"What is it now? Do you not see, young sapling, that Kwadil's nephews and I are in a most respectably respectable meeting?"

"My deepest sorrowful sorrows and apologizing apologies, Master. Yet, I am under obligatory obligation to disruptively disrupt this meeting, for we have a most important visiting visitor." Brix moved closer before he whispered, "A delegation from Amsheet headed by Zirka."

"This is becoming more and more bewildering and bewilderingly intriguing. Usher them in."

Brix left the room in haste. The three dwarfs paced in thoughtful silence as they thought about the events of the last week. Xurgon had to admit that Zurwott's description was apt. The scars were ugly; their edge was jagged and uneven much like what happens when the mighty wind breaks a tree in two. The edge was moist and greenish and exuded a quaint and disgusting smell that was never seen or heard of in the long living memory of the dwarfs.

Brix reappeared and walked slowly this time. He stopped and ushered the visitors in before leaving the room. A dwarf with a long, flowing dark beard walked in proudly, followed by twelve soldiers with the herald of Amsheet.

"Master Xurgon," exclaimed Zirka walking in with open arms.

"My dear Zirka," replied Xurgon. The two dwarfs disliked each other profoundly, but would rather be caught dead than show it. "What glad tidy tidings bring you and your distinguished companions to these solitary walls?"

"The northerly northern walls of Amsheet, the fortified fortress are sickly sick and sick with a sickly disease," said Zirka. "Lord Orgond would like your present presence and presence most present in the fortress no later than what is politely possible and possible under most polite circumstantial circumstances."

Xurgon turned to Orwutt. "Show our honored friend what we have seen. If his gazing gaze witnesses here what his gaze most gazing has witnessed in the north, than we would have to regrettably dispense with the pleasant pleasantries of a dwarfish meal and make hasting haste."

Zirka bowed and followed Orwutt. Xurgon waited anxiously. *If the extent of the northern disease is greater than ours, than the source is closer to Amsheet, otherwise, we may attribute it to the béghôm.* Xurgon's jaw tightened. *The Karangalatad speak of such disease as the signal signature of a formidable foe and a foe most formidable. A foe whose name I do not wish to utter. This would be a nightmarish nightmare proportionally proportional to the worst battle the dwarfs have had to fight against the Pit.*

Less than an hour later, they were back, and confirmed that the walls of the northern fortress were suffering from the same disease but that it was in a far more advanced stage.

Xurgon inhaled sharply and stood, eyes wide-open, as if he were seeing a ghost. He rubbed his deeply furrowed forehead, and sat heavily on a stool. "It is as I have feared," he muttered after a while. He heaved a deep sigh and got up. "Our fate lies up north and a dark hour is upon us, the likes of which none of us have seen before. Northbound we are, and may all the gods have mercy on us."

➤ ⦁⦁⦁ ≺

Three days later, Orwutt and Zurwott dropped by the desert people's camp for a short visit. They were happy to see Ahiram fully recovered. Orwutt handed him a leather bag. "Your dwarfish clothes."

Ahiram undid the knot, peered inside, and was relieved when he did not see El-Windiir's artifacts. "Thank you, Orwutt."

"No thankful thanksgiving or thanksgiving so thankful are necessary," intoned Zurwott. "You slew the beastly beast and beast most beastly, and this baggy bag is but a small expressive expression of our delightfully delighted gratifying gratitude."

Ahiram bowed, and Zurwott handed him a small pouch. The Silent frowned and opened it. It contained a small fortune in silver coins. He whistled. "There is enough silver to keep a man alive for three years."

Bowing, Zurwott said, "We are pleasingly pleased by your accepting acceptance of our tokenized token of thankful thanksgiving."

"Will you be going north?" inquired Orwutt in the Common Tongue, to the chagrin of his brother.

"Yes, to report to the commander."

"When?"

"Tomorrow I believe. Do you mind if we go through your quarters first? It's a shortcut to the castle and I would very much like to replace my belt and change back into Silent's clothing."

"With pleasing pleasure," replied Zurwott.

"Zurwott and I could be your guides through the mines. We're supposed to go with Master Xurgon to Amsheet. I'm sure he wouldn't mind if we went with you."

"Great. My friends and I will be looking forward to your company."

The twin brothers bowed and went in search of Xendorac to get their lucrative agreement with the desert people under way.

>-:●:●:●:-<

Ahiram finally stepped outside of his cave. This was the twelfth day since his fight with the béghôm. Rain had washed the plain anew and the fresh after-storm scent caught him as he stepped into the green grass. He opened his arms, closed his eyes, and welcomed the cold breeze. He watched an intensely blue sky patched with thick white clouds follow their dreamy peregrination. Ahiram wished he could fly with them to another land where he had danced with his sister.

"Beautiful aren't they?"

"Sondra."

She seized him by the shoulders and shook him. "Alendiir, you idiot, we thought you were dead during the last game. Why didn't you come back to the castle?"

True to herself, Sondra did not display her emotions in a large group. Now that she was alone with Ahiram, she let him have it.

"I didn't know where I was, but when I met the dwarfs, they told me there was a slave who was going to be sacrificed for a béghôm, so I—"

"So, you thought it was your duty to save him?"

"Hey, don't yell. Wouldn't you have done the same?"

She let go of him.

==“Slaves live and die every day, Alendiir. You can't save them all.”==

"Sondra ..."

She poked his chest with her finger. "You and you're big heart. Tell me, where did you get that sword? Is it yours?"

Ahiram squirmed. "I'd rather not talk about this now."

"Why? What did Sheheluth tell you?"

"You know?"

"Know what? Something is obviously eating at her."

Ahiram sighed. "She told me I'm a sormoss."

"What's that?"

"She said it is someone who beats people when he's angry."

"The gall of that girl. How dare she?"

"Don't get upset. I let her talk to me because—"

"Because you're too naïve to know what's good for you, that's why."

"But I think she's right. I was going to slap Hiyam when I saw her. I was so angry, but at that moment, she was weak and defenseless."

Sondra scoffed. "I'd have wrung her neck. Nora would have killed her without a moment's hesitation."

"I don't know, Sondra. It's not about her. It's about me. Sheheluth asked me if I think like a Silent or like a slave."

"And?"

"I'm a Silent and I am ... was ... still am ... I don't know. That's the thing, Sondra. I think Sheheluth is right in one respect. I want my actions to be my own. You, you act when you decide to act ... I ..."

She placed her hand on his shoulder. "Alendiir, some will say you ask too many questions. The way I see it, you're searching for something but can't quiet put your finger on it just yet. That's fine, but you'll have to promise me something."

Ahiram froze. He looked at her wide-eyed. "What is it?"

"Don't do it alone. You're not alone. You're one of us and we'll always be there for you. No matter what, we will be by your side."

"Why?"

"What do you mean, why? What kind of a stupid question is that?"

"No. I mean what do you see in me?"

She shook her head. "Sometimes I wonder what's in that head of yours. What do I see in you? You move like the wind, you're like a vengeful wave; you're harder than stone and live with an inner fire that calls to the sun. You're beautiful to watch when you move, that's why."

"You've seen all this?"

"Yeah, and one more thing …"

"Yes?"

"You're a first rate idiot. Now go back inside before you catch a cold."

"I'm fine."

"Clearly, your head is not. Get back in there and rest. We're leaving tomorrow, with or without your head."

Ahiram walked back toward the cave. Along the way, he greeted the desert people and wished he could stay with them a little longer. Somehow, their village had a familiar feeling; a feeling he had not had since he left Baher-Ghafé. *They must be bringing in the boats for the night now. Hoda must be hard at work preparing the meat and …* A lump formed in his throat and his vision blurred. He repressed his feelings and shut these images away. *I'm getting closer. Every step I take brings me closer to freedom, and to Baher-Ghafé.*

He reached his cave and inhaled sharply. Hiyam was waiting for him. She was in her High Riders' uniform but stood with her eyes cast down. Pity washed over his heart, taking him by surprise.

"Are you all right?"

She nodded without looking up. "I would like to know what … what you wish me to do for you …"

He sighed and suddenly felt tired.

"Let's walk," he said. She followed a few feet behind him. His throat constricted. The thought of an assured young woman acting like a slave was too much to bear. He could see himself in her. He pointed to the trees at the edge of the forest. "Let's go and talk over there."

She nodded.

Oddly, Ahiram felt better as soon as he touched the trunk of a tall oak, as if he were reuniting with an old friend.

"I've always loved trees," he said with a smile. "I think I prefer them over caves and stones. I have happy memories of my oak tree in the winter and its cool shade in the summer. That oak was part of the village. It was there with me as I grew up. It was always patient and never complained, and … clearly, I have no idea what I'm talking about. Listen, Hiyam—"

"I would like to offer you my apologies," she said as she sat down. "I grew up as the daughter of a high priestess. From the time I could walk, everyone bowed before me. No one would sit and eat until I sat, and everyone stopped eating when I stopped. I could ask a High Rider to kill himself for me and he would have obeyed. I didn't feel powerful. It all felt normal, like it should be that way. I gave orders and people obeyed. One day, I too, would become a high priestess and people would fear me. Power was not something I desired. It was something I owned."

Ahiram shook his head. "This sounds so far-fetched. I can't conceive of people living this way."

"Think about how I treated you during the Games. I used magic to ensnare you. I toyed with you and ordered my men to kill you."

"So what's changed?"

She sighed. "I've lived on the bright side of power. I did not see its dark side until you won the games. The planning, the killing, the secret assassinations … I did not realize what power truly meant until then. A few days later, I began to despise the Temple. Then, the Game of Gold happened. We were climbing up to the Pit of Thunder, when a powerful attacker assaulted us. He toyed with me, mocked me, jeered at me, and showed me what he was going to do to me …" Hiyam drew her legs against her chest and gripped them with her arms.

"Hoda—"

"Hiyam," the young woman corrected him.

Ahiram bit his lip. *Why am I calling her by my sister's name? What's wrong with me?* He controlled himself. "Do you know who attacked you?"

She looked at him and he saw a deep-seated fear. "He didn't say his name, but his power is beyond anything I've seen. He was so cruel. Despite my shame, I pleaded with him to stop. He laughed and told me that he wasn't doing anything to me that I hadn't done to you …" Furtively, she looked at him. "He made me feel like … a slave."

Ahiram looked away.

"The Games had to go on. The Temple had to win. I pleaded with my mother to let you live, to save your life. I tried to stop the High Riders, but it was all too late. The humiliation I felt, the sense of loneliness, the desperation, the …" She heaved a deep sigh. "This may be hard to believe, and I would not have believed it myself a short month ago, but, I will never be a high priestess. I won't go back to the Temple."

"So what will you do now?"

She glanced at him. "Well, now I truly am a slave … please let me finish. I won't have the courage to say this again. It is one thing to think about being a slave and it is another thing to be one. It's the little things that get you, like can I drink? can I eat? What should I do next? It is debilitating. I don't know how you survived all these years, but the High Riders' code of honor is unbending. The desert people captured me and treated me as their slave. They were going to offer me as a sacrifice to the béghôm. You saved me Ahiram. You saved all of us. So now I am your slave." With a great effort of will, she rose and bowed to Ahiram. "Command me Master, I am here to do your command."

Ahiram nearly exploded, but seeing Sheheluth watching them from afar, he controlled himself. He knew he had to find a way out of this. He breathed long and deep until his irritation subsided, then he reviewed what the young woman had told him, and smiled.

"So, before being captured by the desert people, you had already made up your mind, didn't you? About not becoming a high priestess?"

She nodded. "No matter what, I will not be a priestess of Baal."

Halfway there, thought Ahiram. "What would you have done then?"

Hiyam shrugged her shoulders. "I don't know. I did not have much time to think about it."

Ahiram switched tactics. "So, if you chose not to be a high priestess, would there be consequences? Would the Temple punish you?"

"Not strictly speaking, but I would be ostracized. I would not be able to live in the Temple and the Temple officials would be barred from speaking to me."

"Does this include the military as well?"

She nodded. "Officers of the High Riders would be flogged if they were caught speaking with me."

"And you would have gone to such extremes? You would lose contact with your mother."

Hiyam shuddered. "I know," she added softly, "but my mind is made up. I will not return to Baalbek no matter the consequences."

Almost there, thought Ahiram. "Could you join the High Riders?"

Hiyam laughed a bitter laugh. "I could work in the stables, or assist in the purification ritual, but I would never be a High Rider."

Ahiram smiled. "Therefore, *before* being captured by the desert people, you *knew* you were no longer a High Rider, right?"

"Yes." Hiyam frowned, realizing that Ahiram had been stringing her along. Forgetting that she was supposed to be acting like a slave, she gazed at him, and saw him smile. "I don't ..." The logic of the argument struck her. "So I am no longer bound by the High Riders' code of honor!"

"Glad to know we understand each other, Hoda ... Hiyam. You're no longer bound by their code, therefore, you are not my slave. You're a free woman. Obviously," he added quickly, "you've got to go back with us and report to the commander and your mother."

Hiyam recovered quickly. "Thank you for saving my life."

"Stop it now, all right. Enough thanking me." He sighed. "Did you speak with Jedarc?"

She nodded.

"You know he's in love with you?"

She blushed. "He hasn't told me."

"Well, I'm telling you. And I'm also telling you that if you hurt a hair on his head—"

"You're yelling."

Ahiram tightened his fist and clenched his teeth. "If you hurt a hair of his head, I'll … I'll …"

"You'll kill me."

Her words hit him like a fist. She stated the truth matter-of-factly with a tone that shattered his anger and turned it to grief.

"Yes," he whispered. "I don't think I would be able to control myself if something happened to Jedarc. Most likely, I *would* kill you. It's horrible to say, but it's the truth. What have I become? A monster?"

"I don't know, but if I cared about him as much as you do, I would do the same. I would kill anyone who would try to hurt him. But you do not have to worry about me hurting Jedarc."

"Why do you say that?"

"Because the monster that spoke to me makes the béghôm look like an inoffensive child. Before long, we will be counting our dead and hoping against hope that someone, anyone, will be able to stop him. We're moving into a storm the like of which we have never seen and I am not certain any of us is going to survive long enough for love to blossom." She got up and bowed. "You have my gratitude for saving my life and giving me back my freedom. My blade is yours."

Ahiram waited for her to leave before leaning his head against the tree and closing his eyes. Unexpectedly he saw, or imagined he saw

Noraldeen's face smiling tenderly at him. Involuntarily he smiled. *As long as the sun rises on a world where Noraldeen walks, there will always be a tomorrow to look forward to. There will always be hope.*

Resolutely, he got up, stretched, and the man who dragged a storm wherever he went set his eyes to the north where darkness gathered under the banner of the urkuun.

Ashod's Choice

Part Two

10. Southbound

> *"I am a traveler. Traveling is what I do. I travel. That is what I do. This is what the Temple has commissioned me to do: To sojourn the world in search of strange sights or unnatural events, like springs of golden water or pits that spew back anything you throw in them. One unforgettable site is the breathtakingly beautiful city of Wrok-Atul. Its name is harsh in the common tongue, but it is a hidden gem, a heavenly oasis, a place of abiding wonder and peace."*
> —Memoir of Alkiniöm, the Traveler.

Eighteen hundred miles southeast of Tanniin, deep within the swamps of Kirk in the Kingdom of Mitani, Ashod sat cross-legged behind a low table where an Orb of Seeing shimmered gently. He was a former high priest of Baal who had defected to the Black Robes, a clandestine organization that rescued fugitives from the massacres committed by the High Riders of the Temple. He was deeply perturbed by what he had just heard, and so absorbed was he with the news that he allowed his cup of black tea to grow cold.

He peered into the shimmering orb and tried to decipher the placid expression of his interlocutor. "Are you sure about this, Perit? Are you absolutely sure?"

"If I hadn't seen him with my own eyes, I wouldn't have believed it,"

Perit replied serenely. His features, elongated by the orb's spherical surface were the color of silver. "Like I said, about twenty days ago, the superintendent of the royal kitchen at Taniir-The-Strong Castle told me the butcher in charge of the local specialty, praniti bowls, had fallen ill the week before the Games. She hired me to replace him, so I kept a close watch during the Games and have seen the slave up close."

"And it was him you saw again?" asked Ashod.

Perit nodded. "Also, I managed to speak with the delegation from Ophir. They told me their deal with Lord Orgond has fallen by the wayside. Apparently, the Ophirian who was supposed to marry Orgond's daughter has reneged on the deal at the last moment."

"I am well aware of these details, Perit. Thankfully, you managed to speak with the Ophirian delegation on my behalf and they have agreed to continue the negotiations with Orgond in the Fortress of Amsheet. So, go back to the lad."

"Yeah, well, after the Games, I went back to the dwarfs like you asked me to. I was in the kitchen minding my own business when Orwutt came in and asked for food for a visitor."

"Remind me, who is Orwutt again?"

"Orwutt and Zurwott are twin dwarf brothers, and they are Master Kwadil's nephews."

"Ah yes, Zurwott," Ashod said. "So, they are the crafty twins who always manage to get in trouble. What are they up to?"

"You're not going to like it, boss," whispered Perit.

Ashod gave him a tired look.

"Seriously, boss. It's a xarg-ulum." Ashod's eyes turned into dangerous slits. "I kid you not, boss. The beast is raving mad."

"The béghôm has been in these caves for some time now, and she doesn't get roused unless her quarry is in sight."

"Boss, really strange things are happening all over these caves."

"Strange, how strange?" Ashod was not surprised. He had joined the

Temple when he was eighteen. Thirty-five years of priesthood had taught him to expect erratic ripple effects after each act of high magic.

"Well, the walls around these caves … they are, well, how shall I say it … turning into wet mush. I mean they are *decaying*. In one spot Orwutt showed me, you could stick your finger into flint as if the rock has turned into soggy, moldy bread. Disgusting."

Ashod shivered as if a cold wind were blowing, but the air around him was sultry. "Continue," he said quietly.

"So, yes, I brought the food like Orwutt asked, and that slave boy was there. He looked worn out, but otherwise in good health. Here's why I've decided to use the orb to contact you: He has with him a sword the likes of which I have never seen before."

"You have experience with swords?"

"My father was a blacksmith in the court of Tanniin. I grew up around swords, but this one …" Perit's voice shivered. "I'll tell you this, if a Kerta priest would threaten to curse my children unless I tell him what this sword is made of, then I would say that—"

Ashod gestured impatiently. "Spare me the drama, Perit, and get to the point. You think this sword is made of meyroon?"

Perit inhaled sharply and then slowly nodded.

"I need you to find out if he has a birthmark at the base of his neck."

Perit laughed. "Funny you should ask. I did notice one when serving him. It looks like three circles forming a triangle."

"Excellent work, Perit." Just then, someone knocked at Ashod's door. "Now, I need you to find out if he is in love."

"Seriously boss? Are we getting into the love business?"

"Listen Perit, of all the things I have asked you to do, this is the most, I repeat, the most important task. I need to find out quickly if he is in love with someone or if someone is in love with him. Understood?"

"Yes, boss."

"And, Perit …"

"Yes, boss?"

"Be very careful."

"Got it, boss. I've got to go now. The dwarfs want me to cook three boars and I ..."

Ashod waved his hand and the orb turned black. He wrapped it with a thick black cover and dropped it inside a wooden box. *Not only is Ahiram unharmed, but he has acquired the sword of El-Windiir.* This news troubled Ashod. *The Temple knew the sarcophagus was close to a Letter of Power that Sureï had cursed. How did he retrieve the Letter and survive? He must have evaded the curse ... But, how?*

The door opened. "You have asked to see me?"

Ashod did not look up. *This will have to wait.*

"Yes, yes, indeed. I was waiting for you. Please do come in, Hayat." Ahiram's mother entered. "Sit down, Hayat, if you please. I have a sensitive mission for you."

A few hundred yards away from Ashod's hut, the main barracks of the Black Robe's clandestine camp were abuzz with activity. Refugees from *Wrok-Atul*, Spring-Flower, a city from the neighboring Kingdom of Uratu, were now streaming in under the watchful gaze of their masked guides, all members of the Black Robes. Three hundred and sixty survivors were all that was left of a once proud and prosperous city that had harbored well over seven thousand souls. Men, women, and children filed in silently, wearing dirty gray rags that only a few weeks ago had been bright and colorful linen clothing. The survivors had crossed over two hundred miles on foot through the thick Uratuan forest and the deep canyons at the western border of the Kingdom of Uratu. Exhausted from the harrowing three-week-long journey, they were relieved to walk inside a solid building with a smooth wooden floor. Black Robe guards stood along the perimeter of the hall, while another twenty served the famished refugees a hearty bowl of chicken soup and two slices of bread.

Hayat stepped out of Ashod's hut, which was hidden from the main camp by a dense cluster of oak trees. She fitted a black mask on her face and tied it behind her head. Made of a thin, spherical metallic mesh, it cleverly hid her features without obstructing her visibility or restricting the free flow of air.

As if on cue, thousands of crickets in the pine forest drowned her footsteps with their loud chorus. Not to be outdone, a large colony of frogs from the nearby swamps responded with cheerful, collective croaks. The wind, damp and hot, clung to her like a needy child. Hayat wished she could wipe her sweaty forehead, but it could not be helped. She looked forward to the summer storm the distant rumble of thunder promised to bring in, as if the thunder were a tamer able to subdue the damp wind into submission.

She glanced back at the hut wondering if Ashod would come after her and apologize—just this once. *The day frogs will stop catching flies is the day Ashod will say he is sorry.* She could still hear her voice, shocked and angry, and Ashod's measured, soothing voice detailing her next mission.

"Hayat, I need someone to carry a critical message to a dear friend of mine in the Kingdom of Marada."

Hayat felt the usual frustration mounting. Ashod's utterances were cryptic and very difficult to decipher. She knew the former priest of Baal did this on purpose to protect her and the Black Robes from an eventual capture by Baal. Still, she wished he could explain to her what was going on. She did not bother to ask for his answer: she knew it would be as evasive as the request he had just made.

"You want me to leave my husband behind for a full year, and cross the great desert to deliver a message to a *dear friend?* Ashod, do I look like a zakiir to you?"

Ashod's hut was small and bare, for the former high priest of Baal preferred traveling light and had little need for material possessions. A bed, two chairs, and a small table occupied the hut, and a small lantern hung from the ceiling.

Wrath of the Urkuun – Southbound

"I need you to deliver a message to Lord Lonthi," repeated Ashod, "But Jabbar will not leave camp, so what do you propose?"

"Find someone else," Hayat snapped, "I am not the only trustworthy Black Robe around here, and I am not in the mood to go without my husband and entertain a bunch of vain giants."

Ashod furrowed his brow and scowled. "Lord Lonthi is not vain," he admonished. "The Kingdom of Marada will stand or fall by his word." He relaxed his stance somewhat and cracked a smile. "Besides, I would love to watch you tell a twelve-foot giant princess in the royal court of Marada that she is vain."

"There are female giants?" blurted Hayat absentmindedly. Ashod gave her a tired look. "See what you're making me say? I am telling you, I am not the right person for this mission."

"Yes, you are."

"You could send Hoda and Karadon."

"I have sent them on an equally sensitive mission," replied Ashod in his usual calm, unflustered tone. He was unfazed by her hot temper.

"You could—"

"Hayat, I do not think we have any alternative."

"I will not go without Jabbar," she insisted.

"He won't leave camp. You know that."

"Let me speak to him again."

"You have already done that."

"Then the answer is no. I don't care how important this mission of yours is, I will not leave my husband behind."

"Hayat …"

She had walked out not wanting to hear the rest. *Admit it, Hayat*, she thought to herself, *you're scared of this mission because you wouldn't mind going away alone. You wouldn't mind leaving Jabbar behind.* The flickering light from the large hall surprised her. *I have walked all this distance already?* Resolutely, she chased away her thoughts and stepped into the hall. ==Bracing herself, she tightened her fists, ready to face the shouts of anger, cries of despair, sobs of orphaned children, and wailing of women who had lost their families.==

≻⊙⊙⊙≺

Ashod remained alone, deep in thought. *All along, the Seer had been in Tanniin. How poetic. Only Kwadil could have spirited him away so quickly. Now that is one shrewd dwarf. He did it silently and did not tell me. Good for him.* Ashod pondered his reluctance to share this news with Hayat. *She is his mother*, he chided himself. *I should tell her.* He sipped his hot tea slowly and enjoyed the scalding flavor. Outside, the deafening song of crickets muffled every other sound. *What would happen if I told her? She would rush alongside her husband to Tanniin, right in time to watch their son fall prey to the urkuun. No, our best hope lies with the Marada. By relaying my message to Lord Lonthi, Hayat will be saving her son.*

The old man sighed and closed his eyes. He knew what he had to do; yet wished it could be otherwise. *Things are about to get messy and complicated very fast.*

≻⊙⊙⊙≺

Hayat stepped inside the main hall. It was as silent as the ruins where the Black Robes' camp was hidden. The soles of her leather boots made an irritating squeak as she crossed the large room toward the platform set against the back wall. In the still hall, the squeaking was deafening.

She stepped onto the platform, surveyed the room, and made eye contact with the few who cared to look up. Her motherly heart constricted; Hayat remembered vividly, how six years ago, Jabbar, Hoda, and she had walked into a hall just like this one. Unlike today, the hall had been empty. They thought they were the only survivors until a few hours later, when the Sherabys arrived. Seemingly, they had all gone fishing in the wee hours of the morning and had fled the scene when they saw the burning homes. Hayat had been elated to see them. Then, her elation turned into despair when no one else came. No one else, it seemed, had survived the brutal massacre of Baher-Ghafé.

Hayat would never forget the horror of that night when the High Riders attacked. Her daughter joined them in their hideout near Baher-Ghafé where they had been waiting for her. Her heart exploded with pain when she realized that her son, Ahiram, was missing. Hoda explained that she had left him in her boat, but couldn't say why. Her daughter had tried to run back and get him, but Hayat had held her tightly, refusing to let go for she knew the forces of the Temple would be waiting for them. When a few weeks later, after the High Riders had left the area, a search party had gone to Baher-Ghafé and returned without Ahiram, Hayat refused to believe she had lost him forever. Two years later, Karadon told her that the Temple was compelled to destroy entire villages in order to prevent a greater calamity.

"The priests are sorry for the loss of Baher-Ghafé, but they believe destroying it prevented a cataclysm."

What disaster that could be, she did not know. Hayat had thought the explanation far-fetched. Instead, she believed Baal was a tyrannical, capricious god who toyed with them the way angry waves toss a fishing boat over a dark sea. Slowly, silently, Hayat lost her faith in the gods and believed only in the good and evil men procure one another when living bountifully, or when under duress.

The soft sob of a young girl with frizzy hair and striking blue eyes brought her back to the present. "Friends, I welcome you," Hayat said with a warm and inviting tone. "You are from Wrok-Atul, a village perched atop a lush, green hill, which until last week was a beautiful place to live. You had a bountiful vineyard, and made a rich wine, which the Temple of Baal in Sarg bought from you. The Temple was good to you and you were all faithful citizens of Baal. Your village is now a smoldering heap. This blessed place has become a pile of charred stones. The deadly curses the Temple leaves behind will prevent you from ever going back.

Your village is no more. You cannot return. You cannot rebuild; not if you want to survive."

She stopped to let her words sink in. She had wanted to go back to Baher-Ghafé in search of survivors. She had wanted to bury the dead and save what could be saved. After five years, she had accepted the harsh truth: Baher-Ghafé may one day be rebuilt, but not by the families that had lived there. The same was true for Wrok-Atul.

"My friends, we share the same plight, the same fight. Thanks to the quick action of the Black Robes, you have survived. You are alive. You are here and you are safe, but many, so many of your family are dead." Hayat lowered her voice, "Wives, husbands, children, parents; all dead. Killed by the sword of Baal. You have escaped, but they did not. You could not even give them a proper burial and their souls remain in torment, wandering the land of the dead without rest."

There were no shouts of anger, no protests, no call to arms. The people of the land of Uratu were submissive to a fault. They expected life to be short and bitter and had never even hoped for a bright day they could call their own. They believed that what happened to them was the will of the gods, and who were they to complain? They had learned to keep their pain and sorrow to themselves, trudging along until death overtook them. Hayat knew there was no point in rousing them, but this was not her intent either. Her well-crafted speech was meant to uncover untrained spies, the type the Temple employed to collect simple information—such as the whereabouts of the Black Robes. Trained spies were harder to spot and only Ashod's expert eyes could catch them.

No spies here, she thought, *just a group of folks whose spirits have been broken a longtime ago.* "Here, you eat if you work. You will have a place to call home if you do your part. But first, you will wash-up and rest. Men, move to my left and women to my right. Children under the age of twelve gather in front of me, boys to my left and girls to my right."

Usually, parents, who had escaped the massacre of the Temple with their children would immediately protest being separated from their young ones. Traumatized parents were not be able to listen to reason, as separation from their youngsters was unbearable.

Slowly, the men got up and shuffled to her left and the women went to her right. The children—about thirty of them—dutifully came and sat in front of her. A woman who sat in the back row caught Hayat's attention when she jerked and gazed intensely at the little girl sitting next to Jabbar's wife. There was nothing strange about the woman's reaction. Presumably, she did not want to let go of her daughter; a natural reaction. But the native Uratuan's obedience was flawless, even when anguishing over their children.

If I did not see it with my own eyes, thought Hayat, *I would have not believed it. Only this woman reacted. Maybe she's not from Uratu. She may possibly be a visitor caught up in this tragedy, or a Temple spy. Ashod will find out.* She nodded twice and a man and woman who were fellow members of the Black Robes walked in and took charge of the adults. Another six female Black Robes entered the room. Three of them stood by the young girls and the other three by the boys. These trained women would discreetly question the children. Baal had not yet used children as spies, but it could not be ruled out. Hayat knew that the fate of the Black Robes—hiding in various bases, all inside intractable canyons—was largely dependent on their ability to ferret out spies.

To that end, Ashod had set up a complex system to process the refugees who would come to the Black Robes' camp near Rastoopa in Mitani. This camp was set inside the ruins of an old city in a swampy area that was seldom visited by High Riders. Should the High Riders attack, their sentries would sound the alarm long enough for them to disappear in the swamps, making it difficult for the Temple to hound them.

The camp sheltered the refugees until the reality of their new life sank in: They were no longer citizens of a village or kingdom, but fugitives, with nowhere else to go but one of the remote Black Robes' camp.

After initiation, new members were sent to remote training camps, and when ready, received their first assignment. The Black Robes were members of a clandestine organization created to save as many lives as possible from the massacres of Baal. They had a small trained force to preserve the peace and an even smaller group for special missions. A Temple's frontal assault would destroy the organization, but since their camps were geographically dispersed, such an assault would require the full mobilization of the High Riders; something akin to a global war. As long as they remained in the shadows, the Temple would leave them alone. Still, their number steadily grew, and they were now far better organized than when Jabbar, Hoda, and Hayat had joined six years ago.

During the first four years of their exile, Hayat had feared for her daughter, who had retreated into darkness. Hayat knew she could not reach Hoda. She understood why the young woman was angry with her; she knew the feeling all too well. Her daughter preferred to die than to face a world without her younger brother. Still, what could she have done as a mother? From her years as first servant to a high priestess, she knew the High Riders would have killed or tortured Hoda if she had not held her daughter back that fateful night. But in Hoda's inexperienced mind, her mother had cold-heartedly abandoned Ahiram to his fate.

Refusing to give up hope, Hayat threw herself into the fray and took on a function similar to the role of a first servant responsible for the day-to-day operations of the Temple. With natural ease she led the integration of refugees into the Black Robes.

Jabbar did not fare as well. The destruction of his village, the loss of his son, and their shattered lives had been too much to bear. He retreated behind the fire and smoke of an anvil, and had become a well-respected blacksmith, though he was no longer the man she had married.

"M'Lady, we are ready."

Hayat realized the Black Robes in charge of the men and those in charge of the women were waiting for her signal. She inhaled sharply, and then breathed out slowly to regain her composure. *I am daydreaming again. This cannot continue.* She nodded and the remnant lives of Wrok-Atul left the hall following their guides. Hayat helped with the dishes and the cleanup, and then went out to check on the refugees to make sure everyone was well taken care of. By nightfall, she walked the camp's perimeter to check on the sentries. It was not uncommon for a sentinel to fall asleep. After all, most Black Robe members were not military recruits, but simple civilians.

As she made the rounds, Hayat realized her patience was waning and her endurance weakening. She had reached a breaking point and could no longer carry the weight of Ahiram's disappearance alone. Jabbar's retreat behind the anvil, along with the constant beating of metal—as if he were trying to beat the memory of his son out of his own head—was more than she could bear. They rarely spoke and barely ate together. *A few more years and we will become total strangers*, she thought bitterly. *There must be something I can do to bring Jabbar back, but what?*

She was now close to the two large dormitories set aside for the new refugees. A cluster of pine trees separated the two buildings.

"No, Rajek, staying here I am not."

The woman's voice reached her from the cluster of trees. She spoke with the distinct Uratuan accent, soft and melodic. "My children, I will seek and my path to them must lead."

"But Luliand," pleaded a man, "children of ours are gone to the Wind-End. None shall we see, none left for us to hold."

The couple, evidently from Wrok-Atul, was having an argument, one she had heard a hundred times over, one she could recite by heart. The mother wanted to go back and search for their missing children, and the father tried to dissuade her. Jabbar and Hayat had had that same argument six years ago over Ahiram. She wanted to inquire about their son, find out if he was still alive, but Jabbar had refused. "Our son is dead, Hayat," he insisted. "There's no point looking for the dead."

Back then, his refusal had hurt her deeply, but over the years, seeing the same drama repeated before her eyes, she had forgiven her husband.

"Deter me you shan't," persisted the woman. "Keep me here you can't. A quest my heart calls for, and my heart will I follow."

"Wrok-Atul destroyed it is," Rajek replied softly. "Houses by flames are devoured, bones and shadows, will you find. But Luliand, to Wind-End, our children are gone. From all that could be left, we and their memory are left."

"Wrok-Atul my destination is not," insisted Luliand. "Rajek, the path to the Ancient of Days will I take. A pronouncement will he utter, and on my way must I be."

"The Ancient of Days," exclaimed Rajek. "A legend he is, a dream dreamed by wily minds."

"No, Rajek, a dream he is not, but a legend he is. Where my children are, he will tell, how to get them back, he will show."

"But Luliand, how to him will you go? The road long it is, and the dangers unforgiving they are," Rajek said.

"A caravan I shall take, a seamstress I shall become, through the land of the giants I will cross, and to Salem, I will sail."

This was unexpected. The woman was ostensibly far more learned than Hayat had thought. *She is not going back home, instead, she wants her husband to go with her to ask a prophet about the fate of their children.*

This was not the most extravagant plan Hayat had heard; some refugees wanted to demand an explanation from the Temple of Baal. Unable to believe the Temple had destroyed their village, their first reaction was to seek counsel with the Temple. Others wanted to travel to *Sheit Mot*, the Vanishing Land, where they thought they could find the relatives that they had left behind. Still others were adamant to find the door to the City of the Dead. Some were even ready to bring calves, sheep, goats, or hens as an offering to Mot, the god of the netherworld.

Others attempted to learn the fate of their children through divination by using the entrails of a chicken, a duck, or a serpent. Hayat did not find any of it laughable. She knew all too well that the human spirit could go to extremes and was ready to believe the impossible rather than face the cold, brunt reality of death and muted separation.

"Luliand," called Rajek, "tonight, rest we must. Tomorrow, plan our travel we shall."

"Rajek, Luliand ask not you to come with her. Her mission it is."

"Rajek the heart of Luliand he knows, and where she must, he goes."

Having heard enough, Hayat silently walked away. As she moved toward the center of the camp, a thought that must have been germinating for a long time suddenly turned into a clear and forthright idea. It was so simple that she wondered why it had taken her this long to think of it.

Now, she thought, barely able to contain her excitement, *I think Jabbar will listen to me.*

Purposefully, she walked toward the blacksmith's workshop, but abruptly changed course and strode to Ashod's small hut instead. She stepped inside, and then exited just a few minutes later. Smiling and determined, she returned to the blacksmith's shop and found her husband at the anvil, next to a pile of broken swords.

"Jabbar, we need to talk," she said, beaming.

"Where do you find the strength to do what you do?" he grumbled. "I don't get it."

"From my hope."

"Hope?" he said, confused, "What hope? Don't you see, we are merely surviving here? We are alive today, dead tomorrow. This is not a life, this is a shadow of a life."

Beads of sweat covered his forehead. He set down the hammer and wiped his blackened face with a dirty rag. In the span of those six years, Jabbar had aged fifteen. Still, his arms were strong and his hands steady.

"Perhaps," she answered, "perhaps you are right, Jabbar. But think, they never found his body. What if he's still alive? What if he's out there?"

"Then what?"

"If you knew with certainty that your son was alive, what would you do?" she asked him.

He brought the hammer up close to his face and stared at it for a long time. "There's a dent, right here," he said, "It's a gash actually, and if left unchecked, one of these days, this hammer will break in half."

"What would you do, Jabbar? Answer me."

He looked at her. "What would I do? What *could* I do, Hayat? I am … was … a shark fisherman, content to live in a small little town. My life, my entire life was there, in Baher-Ghafé, in Byblos, in Baalbek, and in Tanooreen. That's it."

"This is a lie," snapped Hayat. "Before you married me, you had been on a ship. You have seen the world."

"So? That was before, when I was young and—"

"Selfish. When you were young and selfish. Go ahead, say it. You could travel when you pleased, but if your son needs you, you are telling me you will continue to hide here, behind this anvil?"

"I am not hiding, woman."

"Yes, you are. You are scared. Scared of the High Riders, scared of what they will do to you if they capture you. Or me. Or Hoda."

"And who wouldn't be? It's sheer madness to stand up against the Temple," he yelled.

"Is it better to submit to fear, to death?" shouted Hayat.

Back in Baher-Ghafé, they had never raised their voices. But these past six years had been filled with acrimony, and their harsh words were lacerations they inflicted on each other. Unable to fight the Temple, they fought each other; afraid that otherwise, they would end up in a sullen silence and slowly decay into indifference, and then despair.

And despair was to be feared at all cost.

He remembered Ashod's warning, *If you despair, if you truly despair of your lives, then rest assured, a Kerta priest will find you. He will slowly worm his way into your mind and your soul. He will convince you to deliver yourselves into his hands. The suffering he would inflict on you would make you long for this life.*

"I don't know, Hayat," said Jabbar. "What is the point of this anyway? What can we do differently today that we did not do yesterday?"

"Come, sit next to me," she said as she removed two boxes filled with nails from a dirty bench. "Let's sit together. I have something to tell you."

He dropped the hammer, wiped his hands with the dirty rag, and joined her on the bench. He smelled of sweat, metal, and burned coal, and had a rancid odor from the cheap wine he had taken a liking to.

"What?" he asked gruffly.

"Today a fresh batch of refugees joined us from the latest village the High Riders destroyed."

"Wrok-Atul," he replied with a smug look.

"You know?" she asked.

Jabbar heaved a deep sigh and explained that even though he seldom left his anvil, he knew what went on in the camp.

"I know that," she had said. "Listen, on my walk tonight, I overheard a couple talking outside their dormitory."

"You mean like we used to do." Jabbar scratched his thick beard, a wry smile on his face.

"Yes." Hayat smiled. "Like we used to."

"And, let me guess," he continued with a sarcastic tone, "he wants to look for their children and she is telling him that he is crazy."

Hayat bit her lip. She refused to reopen that wound. "Something like that," she said calmly, "but not exactly."

"Oh? Don't tell me they were arguing over what to eat or what to wear? Now that would be a novelty."

Hayat had anticipated that talking to her husband would be hard, but she had not anticipated anger and frustration to well up so quickly in her heart. She got up and clenched her fists, ready to leave.

"Hayat," he said in an unusually soft tone. "Sit down. Tell me what you wanted to tell me. I won't talk. I promise."

Something in his voice, a tinge of deep sadness, dissolved her anger. *It's not his fault.* She repeated firmly. *He is the victim here, as much as I am, as much as anyone else in this camp.* Hayat moved closer to her husband and took his hand.

"The woman, her name is Luliand."

"Really?" exclaimed Jabbar, "I met a Luliand once in a jolly tavern of Singatava. She was blond and ..." Seeing his wife's gaze, he coughed and signaled for her to continue.

"Her husband's name is Rajek, and she told him that she wants to go to Salem to ask the Ancient of Days about their children."

"They were discussing a trip to Salem?" asked Jabbar, incredulous. "Now that's a new one."

"So, I asked Ashod about the Ancient of Days, and he confirmed that apparently, there is a sort of a prophet living on one of the mountains of Salem who could answer such questions. He doesn't know of anyone who has met him, but he told me that his sources, which are reliable, were certain the story is not fanciful."

Jabbar sighed. He knew Ashod held greater sway with his wife than he did. The way she spoke now was different from when they had lived in Baher-Ghafé. She used longer words and more complex sentences. But, a prophet who could tell him whether his son was dead or alive? Was that even possible?

"Let's say this man exists," he said, tentatively. "How would we get there, and why would Ashod let us go? We could betray him, you know."

"Exactly. But here is the thing. To get to Salem there are two routes: one, a maritime route through Quibanxe, down to the sea of Babel-Amon, then a dangerous crossing into Salem. It would take us at least three months to get there, maybe more."

"And the other?" asked Jabbar wanting to test his wife's knowledge. *When did she learn about all of this?*

"The other is through the Kingdom of Marada."

"The land of giants?" scoffed Jabbar. "Do you believe such nonsense?"

"Whether the giants exist or not is irrelevant," she protested. "What is relevant is that this kingdom is a destination for caravans, and Ashod would like us to join one of those caravans and go to Marada."

"What for?"

"He wants me, us I mean, to deliver a message to a friend of his there."

"Why can't he ask a zakiir?" He saw her stare at him and realized the absurdity of his proposition. There were no *zakiruun*, memory men, among the Black Robes. In a world where the written word was considered a forbidden act of magic and a capital crime, the League of the Zakiruun consigned to memory—against a handsome fee—the important affairs of others.

"So we go there and deliver this message, then what?"

"Then, from there, we find a guide to take us down into Korridir, we could reach—"

"Adiker and cross to Salem," he completed with a misty voice.

She stared at him with eyes wide open.

"You have been there?"

"Not really," he said. "I have been as far as Merib on the eastern side of Sabea, and I just remembered an old sailor talking about the Island of Salem. He was a leper who wanted to speak with a sage who resided on a mountaintop. Back then, I wanted to find a treasure, so I didn't pay attention to the sage on the mountain."

"And now?"

"If we stay here we won't ever find anything out about our son, and it's not like he is going to come searching for us in the swamps."

"So, we will go?"

"What about Hoda?"

"Hoda is with Karadon on a special mission," Hayat reminded him.

"I know that," he scoffed. "Will she come with us?"

"We will wait for her to return. Then she will let us know."

"Let us know what?"

"If she wants to come with us, of course."

Jabbar looked at his blackened hands, and then slowly shook his head.

"No, Hayat. The answer is no."

"What do you mean?"

"Hoda stays here. We won't take her with us. She stays here with her husband. I don't want to raise her hopes of finding her brother. She has suffered enough. If we go, it will just be the two of us."

"How will we do this?" she asked, even though she had a plan in mind.

"I don't know just yet. Ashod will help. There will be caravans coming this way. We need to figure out how to join them. I'm sure caravans can make use of a blacksmith somehow, don't you think?"

She looked at him and smiled.

"What do you say if we call it a night?" asked Jabbar.

"How about you go wash up?" she replied. "Dinner will be ready before you're done."

For the first time in six years, she felt close to her husband. Though Hayat did not know whether she would see her son again, she was hopeful. *Maybe, just maybe, at the end of this quest Jabbar and I will stand on sunny shores, side-by-side, closer than we have been in the last six years.*

And that, that alone would be a small victory; their own victory over the Temple and the cruelty of men.

11. Tyrulan

"In my travels, I visited Gordion several times. This finely manicured city struck me, but not for the usual reasons. Gordion is elegance and beauty, like a haughty maiden or a solitary diamond. True, its cupolas are unforgettable and its wide avenues are a wonder to behold. But none of this struck me as much as the apparent lack of magical artifacts, as if the city itself abhorred magic, or perhaps, coveted it so much, that it hid it like a mother hiding her child within her bosom."
—**Memoir of Alkiniöm the Traveler.**

Seven hundred miles southwest of the Black Robes' camp, Gordion, the capital city of the confederate state of Teshub, glittered in the bright morning sun. Seen from afar, the cupolas that decked the city skyline looked like beads of diamonds on a finely sculpted crown. Covered with colorful mosaics, they formed an elegant symphony redounding on the venerable Teshubian royal lineage. Here the king was mostly an anointed ambassador for the powerful guild of merchants that funded, governed, and managed the confederation.

The royal palace, cast in the center of the city, was accessible from six esplanades that converged on a wide roundabout where the royal gates stood. Behind the ornamented silver portals and the sixteen-mile-long wrought iron fence lay a trimmed garden with eight hundred and fifty fountains and one thousand alcoves, where white and purple leaves of pruned bougainvillea bushes cascaded gently along the marble base of stolid statues. Their dull eyes stared blankly at exotic trees and lavish gifts from faraway lands, given, no doubt, at the closure of mutually fruitful financial exchanges.

The grass, green and lush, was stretched like an impeccable carpet. It covered most of the ten thousand acres of the garden. It surrounded rosebushes like slaves fanning their queens. It crawled at the feet of butterfly bushes sculpted into green arches over hidden pathways.

Seen from the gate, the garden resembled a manicured maze; a gentle warning that kept at bay anyone without a rich jingle in his purse or a purposeful proposal on his lips.

The palace bristled with a constant coming and going of merchants, noble folks, emissaries, ambassadors, and guild members. An army of servants, two thousand strong, served the two hundred and twenty-two guest rooms, which were almost continually full. Since Gordonian slaves originated from kingdoms that traded with Teshub, they were not allowed on palace-ground to avoid insulting guests from their homeland.

Most guests preferred conducting their negotiations in the secluded alcoves of the vast garden. They could speak freely under the watchful gaze of the *kinbals*, mercenaries, who wore special sound-muffling turbans. The palace handsomely rewarded this league of silent soldiers to preserve the secrecy of transactions and keep the peace.

Four *zakiruun*, memory men, were stationed permanently at the palace, and rumor was, there were at least two *tajéruun*—the powerful league of moneymen who managed the zakiruun's riches—who roamed the palace's four stories.

Everyone walked in the garden with great poise and deliberate slowness. Sporting an air of self-assured complacency—and a quiet indifference bordering on disdain—the traders let everybody know they were in no hurry to conclude any deal. As the placid folks of Gordion were wont to repeat, "The slower the poise, the greater the greed."

Presently, nothing was poised about Corintus who was running as quickly as he could manage toward the palace.

"My apologies … I am so very sorry … But there is a bit of an emergency … I am requested at the palace …" So went his litany of excuses as he avoided small groups of visitors, like a salmon flowing upstream evades rocks. Holding his gardener's pouch high overhead, he snaked his way through the constant streams of visitors flowing from the palace into the garden, until he reached the main plaza and its two hundred-foot-wide, rose marble staircase.

Setting aside all sentiments of propriety, the Solitary bounded the four sets of stairs four-by-four until he reached the western balcony, which overlooked all of Gordion. He veered to the right, followed a servant's path, and barely avoided slamming into twelve hurried waiters carrying condiments, a tureen of seafood soup, and a platter of batter-dipped, fried shark steaks. He slipped through the kitchen door, maneuvered around a host of harried servants busy with their kitchenware and buckets of hot water, and bounded up the main staircase, which was trimmed in diamonds and gold.

Moments before, Vily, his daughter's only friend, had come to him while he sat in his favorite alcove, something the timid young girl would have never done unless she was desperate. Her expression was haggard and she was barely able to control her tears.

"What is it Vily?" he asked while he gently took her hands. They were cold and damp. "What's wrong?"

Vily had burst into tears again. "It's Aquilina. We were supposed to have breakfast together, but she did not come. I went to her room. She wasn't there. I thought that maybe she went to the kitchen to look for me. I sat and played with her dolls when she … she …" Vily struggled to breathe. She was now shaking and Corintus fought the urge to ask her what was wrong with his daughter; but he knew she was doing her best. "She app … appeared over the bed out of no … nowhere in a big bub … bubble of water and she fell on the bed. Everything is wet …" Corintus realized that the little girl's clothes were wet as well. "The car … carpet and the bed and everything is wet and she … she won't wake up …"

Having said that, the little girl's tears doubled. Corintus held her and patted her shoulder.

"Shush, there, there. Don't you worry, I am sure Aquilina is fine." She gazed at him with searching eyes, wanting to believe him. "Listen Vily, I am going to see Aquilina as quickly as I can. Would it be all right if you followed at your own pace?"

"So you…you believe me?"

He had smiled. *More than you care to know, little one.* "Yes, I do," he said gently. "I know you're speaking the truth. Now, listen Vily," he added as he glanced around. "Do not speak to anyone about this, all right? It's best for Aquilina."

She vehemently shook her head. "I told no one. Just you."

"Good girl. I'm going to go straight to the palace. I'll go quickly. You follow me at your own pace, all right?"

Bravely, she held back her tears, nodded twice, and walked away.

I hope I am not too late, he thought as he bounded up the stairs. *She's been going into that other world every day for the past three weeks. She's got to stop.* Having reached the second floor, he veered right and ran unceremoniously along the shimmering rosewood floor of the circular mezzanine that overlooked the main entrance. Portraits of past kings frowned with disdain as he whizzed past velvet drapes framing tall, mahogany, double doors—delicately etched with lilies, the royal symbol of the House of Gordion. Corintus sprinted toward the corridor leading to his daughter's room just as four slow-moving porters emerged from the hallway, blocking the access.

"Make way, make way," he yelled.

They were carrying a gold-plated platform, atop which sat a dignified middle-aged woman on a velvet chair. Instead of stepping aside onto the mezzanine, the startled porters froze. Muffling a string of choice words against placid porters and importunate Ophirians, Corintus sped up, somersaulted and landed gracefully in front of the woman. She let out a cry of delighted surprise. The porters bent their knees, huffed and hoed under the added weight but kept their balance. Deftly, Corintus dropped to one knee and produced a rose from his pouch.

"Madame De La Bambouche," he said with his most charming smile, "I am so happy to catch you before dinner. Please accept this rose as a sign of my affection for you and your house." He dropped the rose on the lap of the woman, grabbed her right hand, kissed it lightly, and gave her a wink. Smiling, he jumped over her head, somersaulted into the corridor, and took off in a run.

"Oh that Corintus," cooed Mrs. De La Bambouche, "what a chaaarmer. What an absolute chaaarmer."

You and your house, what was I thinking? Good thing, Amaréya was not there to hear me. Corintus stopped in front of the sixteen-foot, double-door inside an alcove at the end of the corridor. Two marble columns stood on either side boasting a jade vase which overflowed with arrangements of roses, petunias, daisies, amaryllis, and jasmines. Two light-green, velvet drapes tied to gold rings hung from the two columns; the last barrier between Corintus and his daughter's door. Even though Aquilina was the daughter of the royal heiress, no sentries stood guard by her door, for Gordion was a prosperous and peaceful kingdom and enjoyed the favors of Babylon.

The tall man knocked on the door. "Aquilina," he called, "Aquilina, open the door, right now."

Behind the door, a rectangular space led onto a spherical sunroom where several trees stood motionless in wire-framed planters underneath baskets overflowing with flowers. The room was sparsely furnished on a beautiful silk carpet. It simply hosted a bed, two chairs, a wardrobe, and a trunk where six dolls sat hunched and lonely.

"Aquilina, open the door!"

Eyes closed, the twelve-year-old girl lay on her back, her hands clasped in a gesture of supplication, her face as pale as the shadow of death. She did not react to the loud thuds against the door.

Corintus stood by the window, hands behind his back. *This is the hardest thing I have ever tried to do*, he thought. *Amaréya loves Aquilina, but what choice do I have? I must take her away to Salem and leave her mother behind.* Still lying on her bed, Aquilina slept fitfully. He went back to her side and replaced the wet cloth he had placed on her forehead with a fresh one. *No one must know what is going on here, no one. We leave tonight.*

When his daughter had not answered his repeated calls, he thought of breaking down the door. But just when he was about to put his plan into execution, he had regained his senses. *I am a Silent. What am I doing trying to break a door when I can enter through the window?* He had found Aquilina laying on her bed, shivering, eyes closed, hands clutching her damp nightgown. The bedding was drenched and a pool of water surrounded the bed. He called her name, but she did not respond.

Corintus ran down and asked Drobna and Martha—two of his trusted servants—for help. They changed the bedding, and Martha tended to Aquilina. After the servants had left the room, her fever rose, so he remained by her bedside all day and through the night. Vily kept him company, refusing to leave her friend's side until, unable to keep her eyes open, she had slid down and fallen asleep on the carpet. Corintus had laid her gently on his daughter's bed, knowing that if he had brought Vily to her room, she would be back with him in no time.

The sun rose across the vast plain of Gordion and Aquilina's fever had not yet abated. Corintus paced back and forth. *In the state she is in, I* won't be able to take care of her alone. *Drobna and Martha had already agreed to go with him. They are faithful, they will not speak.* A plan formed rapidly in his mind. *First, Martha and I will take Aquilina to the cottage at the northern foothills of Gordion where she can care for her properly. It is an hour away on horseback and no one will notice my absence. Meanwhile, Drobna will go to Kwadil's camp and will bring Ashod's messengers to the cottage. To the Pit with the protocol, but I can no longer wait five days to meet Ashod's friends. I must have what Ashod has promised to send me immediately. By the time the palace organizes a search party—and Gordion does everything slowly—Aquilina and I will be long gone.*

The thought of leaving Amaréya behind was more than he could bear, but despite Amaréya's stout determination, he could not see how his wife, the heir to the throne of Gordion, could leave the throne without a successor and run away with him to Salem. *I know she said she would do it, but there's a difference between saying it and doing it.* He could not see how she would be able to hide the truth from the King and Queen and leave them without a word about her whereabouts. No, he would have to disappear with his daughter and leave his wife behind.

As if on cue, the door opened and she walked in with Martha in tow.

"Amaréya, how did you…"

His wife gazed at him and smiled. Corintus shivered. Empyreans had a way of smiling just before the kill that was unpleasant, and right now, his wife—who was half-Empyrean—looked like a dangerous warrior on the warpath.

"Martha informed me, dear. You didn't want her to tell me my daughter is unwell?"

Corintus looked at Martha and chided himself. *I forgot to tell her not to inform my wife. How stupid could I be?*

"Well?"

The words "dear" and *"my daughter"* meant trouble.

▷✳✳✳◁

Their marriage had been a matter of state, a politically motivated machination between Gordion and Ophir. It was an alliance that neither she nor Corintus had fully understood when they were first thrown into each other's arms fourteen years ago. They saw each other's face for the first time on the night of their wedding. That fateful night, she tried to kill him when he politely declined the bowl of roasted chestnuts she offered him as a sign of her dedication. "I am not hungry," he had said. His refusal, when translated in Empyrean mores, meant that she was not good enough for him. Naturally, she took her sword and tried to lop off his head. Naturally, he dodged her attacks with a Solitary's ease. He tried to reason with her, citing international laws that govern the rules of dueling, but the more he spoke, the more determined she was to make him to stop. Permanently.

They fought all night, and since their apartments were secluded, no one was alerted of their deadly dance. The following morning, the servants were at a loss to explain what had happened during the night. They found their princess and her groom sitting on the floor eating chestnuts in the midst of total devastation. All that remained of the fine curtains and furnishings that had so elegantly graced the royal suite were shreds of silk and broken pieces of rosewood.

"We used the furniture and the draperies to roast chestnuts," said a jubilant Corintus. "It's a slow roast, so we needed quite a bit of fuel."

◁✳✳✳▷

To an Empyrean, love meant respect, honor, and service. To love meant to speak little and do much. Amaréya prized the palace's garden where she grew up. It held a special place in her heart, and unlike her husband, she did not require words to appreciate its beauty. She would be happy to stand quietly below a tree or sit on one of its branches. Standing by a fountain, she would close her eyes and hear the garden bristle with life like a symphony that blended color and sound into a living song of singular beauty. Silence had been her preferred language; silence, and the deadly whizz of a well-balanced blade, for this was the Empyrean way.

Over the years, she had developed an ear for her husband's words. Neither one was passionately in love with the other, but their appreciation for one another had steadily grown until it became a sturdy bark upon which they knew they could navigate the rapids of the world. As long as they had one another, no harm could come to them. But now, just now, there was a stark determination in Corintus' eyes she had not seen before. Her trained warrior senses told her he was like a fighter on a singular path, preparing to take swift action—alone. *He is a Solitary*, she reminded herself. A Solitary was the highest rank of the Silent. *What are you up to now, Corintus?*

"No, that's not it. Of course I wanted her to alert you," lied Corintus, trying to be nonchalant and failing miserably. He had never lied to his wife before, for he had never had to. Until now.

Amaréya asked Martha to wait outside and to close the door behind her. Corintus tensed, ready for the whizz of two Empyrean blades. Instead, his wife drew close to her daughter and watched her attentively.

"She has a fever, yes?" Corintus nodded. She looked at him. He looked away. "Corintus," she said softly, "to the Empyreans, a wedding is a miracle, for it is like joining a tree trunk to new roots and seeing them become a living tree. We are a living tree, together, and nothing can set us apart. Now, tell me, what have you been planning?"

Corintus looked at his wife, bewildered. This must have been the longest sentence, the most detailed explanation she had ever spoken. *She is really worried.* A wave of relief washed over him. *She is a half-blooded Empyrean*, he thought, *she can take it. Still, how did we end up here?*

Amaréya gasped. Corintus saw her point to the bed. He turned his gaze and inhaled sharply. Their daughter had vanished.

Aquilina opened her eyes and knew she was no longer in her bed. The twelve-year-old girl also knew she was not dreaming. She was in *Tyrulan*, the place that is no place. This vast flat plain with an eternal dusk, empty as emptiness itself, was a place with no visual markers, where left, right, back and front meant nothing, and the same thing. A bewildering, maddening space that seemed as tall as the tallest mountain, and as small as a cup of tea.

She had fallen in this strange world six years ago, when she was six years old. She had been in her room jumping rope, eyes closed and trying to reach sixty jumps without fail, but she tripped after the fifty-ninth jump and fell. She heard a distinct popping sound and when she opened her eyes, she was no longer in her room, but in another world. Scared and confused, she screamed, but instead of hearing her own voice, she saw a beam of light issue forth from her mouth and strike the surface in front of her. Immediately, a bright filament sprouted, grew to be as tall as she was, and began swaying gently. The vision delighted her and she laughed, then applauded. Fireworks of the most dazzling colors erupted from her hands and took root so quickly into the strange ground that she soon stood surrounded by a beautiful forest of throbbing, colorful tree-like plants. Entranced, the little girl walked into the midst of this strange land, observing each shrub, each flower, amazed at what she saw. Strangely, she could not hear her own footsteps or her own breath. The silence was complete, but it felt like a friendly presence.

Aquilina beheld dozens of sounds that stood up like twisted filaments. Some were as small as grass, others as tall as giant pine trees. Some were quaint and subdued with shades of deep blue to light gray, and others were flamboyant and ablaze with brilliant colors that lit the place like a herd of tamed stars. The entire space was wrapped into a total and complete silence where she could not even hear her own breathing or the beating of her own heart. Had she been able to look into a mirror, she would have seen a little girl surrounded by a brilliant halo of dazzling colors with bouquets of bright filaments hovering over her heart.

The plant-like objects had sprouted from the gray plain and remained in one spot, much like plants rooted to the ground. They gently swayed as if moved by a breeze. Some were translucent, while others were as thick as walls—impenetrable.

After some time, Aquilina grew tired. She yawned and rubbed her eyes, and when she opened them, she was back in her own room. Excited, she ran to her mother's bedroom to tell her what she had seen, but her mother did not believe her. She brought the child back to her room and sternly ordered her not to get out of bed again until the rising of the sun. This news confused Aquilina. She did not understand how the sun had disappeared so quickly.

Aquilina had named this strange world Tyrulan, for it reminded her of the game by the same name her mother had taught her. From the first moment, Tyrulan felt like a summer home of a different sort. Just as a bird that falls from the nest instinctively knows how to fly, Aquilina had always known her way around this strange space. Tyrulan, to her, was a rich world where normal, everyday sounds manifested themselves in the guise of incredible shapes—ever-shifting and changing shapes. It was as if she were peering beneath the surface of a sea filled with a brilliance the likes of which she had never known existed. Anyone else in Tyrulan—assuming they could survive—would see nothing but a shocking, maddening emptiness that wrapped around itself, lacking direction and having direction at the same time.

Two years later, when she was eight years old, Aquilina had tried to tell a group of rich girls about Tyrulan, but they had mocked her and jeered at her. Being a half-blooded Empyrean, she challenged them to *paranéva*. In this duel, one participant would throw a knife at a fixed target while his opponent would try to deflect the flying weapon with a throw of a second blade. After a round of three throws, the player that had the greatest number of hits won. When Aquilina produced her mother's set of twelve short, lethal blades, her friends—who were not Empyreans— ran away screaming.

When her mother had confronted Aquilina, the young girl ran back to her room and slammed the door.

"You never listen to me," she shouted, her voice quivering with emotion. "Never."

Amaréya was not easily flustered by her daughter's tantrum. Normally, she would have confined Aquilina to her room for the rest of the day and directed her tutor to increase her daughter's load for a few weeks. She could tell by her tone there was something weighing her down, something that went beyond the usual fickleness that children of men displayed all too easily.

"Very well, Daughter," she said, "I am now ready to listen. You may speak your mind and I will hear you."

Silence.

"Really?" The tone was incredulous.

Despite herself, Amaréya smiled. "Yes, Daughter. This is not a trap. I am not on the warpath. We are at peace. Open the door and let me in. I wish to hear now what you have to say."

Later that day, Amaréya invited Corintus to walk with her in the castle's garden.

"This garden never ceases to amaze me," he told her as they walked side-by-side. "Such perfect harmony between these beds of flowers and the green lush grass, cut in geometric shapes, represent the dance of love between Liluv, the god of love, and Heineh the goddess of order. Smack in the center, these hedges form a maze whose intricate structure symbolizes our journey to the abode of the gods. Walking in this garden is like visiting the cosmic order. It soothes the mind and helps us ponder the deeper things of life."

As the daughter of the royal House of Gordion and heiress to the throne, Amaréya was accustomed to the complicated speeches of the court and the winding discourse of the nobility. Still, her Empyrean side could not fathom the urge men had to explain everything as if their words were collars to subdue a pack of dogs. Her husband was no different.

Whenever he stepped into the garden, he would comment on its natural beauty and launch into a philosophical or religious explanation.

"I wish to speak of Aquilina," she told him.

"Aquilina?" he said abruptly. "Is something the matter? Is she sick?"

She placed a finger on his lips and smiled.

"All right," he said sighing. "I will not speak. I am listening."

She nodded, satisfied. "Our daughter is fit and strong. No physical blemish is upon her."

Corintus has always found the Empyrean language coarse, cold, and unrefined. Nevertheless, the years spent in his wife's company taught him how deeply the Empyreans cared for their children. They showed it in ways different from the ways he was accustomed to. When his wife used two separate sentences to say the same thing, as she had just done, it meant that she was worried, for the Empyreans were people of few words. He resisted the urge to ask his wife what was wrong with their daughter for it was rude to interrupt an Empyrean. He waited.

"She told me today that she has been visiting a different world she calls Tyrulan. A barren world where sounds take on shapes. A world where the beginning and end of a thing are one and the same and different at the same time, where up is down and down is up, and left is right and right is left, and yet they can all be different."

Corintus was devastated. Aquilina meant the world to him and what his wife described could be the early signs of the vanishing—the bizarre manifestation of Sheit Mot in children. Even though the Vanishing Land was thousands of miles to the northeast of Gordion, it claimed children—and only children—from time to time. The poor victims would be afflicted with hallucinations and would have strange visions until, one day, they would fade away like a shadow before the rising sun.

"I shall take our daughter to my ancestral abode," Amaréya said, "where I shall consult the *Onividia*, the Council of Oracles."

"What will they say?"

"Say?" Amaréya asked, confused. "They shall walk with Aquilina under the Vision Tree and we shall know if she is to vanish or …"

"Or?" had asked Corintus. "Or what?"

"The Onividia will tell."

The next six months were the longest and the most difficult Corintus experienced. He stayed behind, for no man was allowed to set foot on Empyrean soil. When finally his wife and daughter returned, Amaréya had disturbing, albeit good news.

"The Onividia walked with Aquilina under the Vision Tree," she told him, "and they passed judgment. She is not vanishing. She is a *Méréléna*."

Corintus almost wished that his daughter was dead. "Are you sure?" he asked, even though he knew this would irritate his wife. There was never a doubt when an Empyrean spoke, and to question their statements was to question her honor. "Are you absolutely sure?"

Amaréya could not fathom the emotional attachment humans had toward their children. She appreciated honor, service, and a heroic death. Children were to be reared in courage, sincerity, strength, and generosity. This was the highest mark of an Empyrean's love. Emotions were to be stayed, and had to remain subdued. Why would such a fearsome and beautiful warrior as Corintus exhibit emotions unfit of his standing was beyond her. Still, she waited for him to finish.

"The Onividia have spoken," she repeated, unable to say anything else. What was there to add?

"Amaréya, if Baal finds out there is a child who is a Méréléna …"

Corintus struggled to find the equivalent word in the common tongue. "A … Seer. Then they will level Gordion. They will destroy every city and every village of Teshub." She nodded, being well aware of the Temple's policy. "Aquilina must never speak of this to anyone. I will talk to her." She waited in silence for her husband to complete his thought. "Let's wait and see," he had said after a while. "If this … tendency of hers is a simple fancy, it will pass and all will be well. If it is real then …"

"Do you doubt the Onividia?"

"'The Silent uses all the facts at hand to distill his own judgment,' *Book of Siril*, chapter seven, verse two. I am not an Empyrean, so I am not bound to the wisdom of the Onividia."

This answer satisfied Amaréya.

Two years had gone by, and Aquilina, now a ten-year-old, had not mentioned Tyrulan once. Apparently, she had lost her ability to fall into the strange world after her return from the Empyrean Kingdom. Her parents breathed a sigh of relief. Well, Corintus did. Amaréya smiled. And Aquilina became a "smacking monkey." At least, that is what her father called her. Upon her return, Aquilina showed him a slingshot her great-grandmother had given her.

"They call it a *raméyél*, wind-master. It throws pebbles like nothing else." Promptly, she had taken a sizeable pebble from a pouch, slid it inside a slit in the slingshot, raised the instrument overhead, twirled it rapidly, and threw her hand forward. The pebble shot out and hit a pumpkin thirty feet away, shattering it.

"I love this raméyél," exclaimed the little girl.

"I guess I'll be eating a lot of pumpkin soup," sighed Corintus.

Simultaneous to her newfound love of the Empyrean slingshot—a lethal weapon by any measure—the young girl developed a dizzying and downright frightening capacity for acrobatics. She could scale walls, dangle from ropes, hang by the tip of her fingers to the edge of tall buildings, and perform mind-bending jumps. With these newfound abilities, the *smacking monkey* learned to evade the guards and slip quietly out of the castle to explore the city of Gordion. It was not long after that she discovered a group of orphans as she wondered over rooftops in the seediest part of the city. Like a shadow, the young princess would jump from rooftop to rooftop and would observe the streets below. So when she met little Vily, an orphan, sitting on the ledge of a door playing with a doll, Aquilina climbed down—for the first time—to the street below. The two girls became instant friends as only children could. Week after week, Aquilina would come and visit Vily, bringing with her sweets, bread, or fruit she would steal from the royal kitchen. Vily and she would play in the dirty streets of the poorest neighborhood in Gordion.

About a year after they had first met, Aquilina came for her daily visit with Vily, but her friend was not there to greet her. Aquilina ventured inside the building down a dark corridor where she heard children talking softly in adjoining rooms. None of the voices were Vily's. The corridor smelled of something rancid, yet sweet, triggering a memory of Tyrulan. When the eleven-year-old took the next step, she was once more in that strange land, walking along a crimson bridge whose edges were on fire. Unafraid, she passed her hand over the flames and the same rancid sweet smell returned. This was a novel experience, something she had not felt before. She followed the flames and they led her to a small cluster of brightly colored trees surrounded by a plain of a dark liquid. Aquilina jumped over the liquid and landed next to the trees. She heard a voice within her mind, a whisper, a gentle whisper, and her heart constricted when she recognized the voice. It was sad and alone, bravely trying to stem the flow of fear that drowned it. She would have recognized this voice amid a crowd. It was Vily, and she was wounded.

12. Contact

> *"Rastoopians are strange folks. They have a great sense of humor, are unassuming, simple, and hospitable. If I did not know better, I would have confused them for simple farmers or servants; inconsequential people of little means. But show them a well-funded purse or make allusions of buying something, anything, and suddenly, the well-meaning, gentle Rastoopians turn into human sharks about to devour your fortune, your name, and your memory. Beware the Rastoopian guile."*
> —**Memoir of Alkiniöm the Traveler.**

Earlier that day, just as Amaréya stepped into Aquilina's room wanting to know about her husband's new plan, Ahiram's sister woke up gasping and sprang to her feet, a dagger in each hand. Tightening her grip on the leather handles, Hoda searched for the assassin that had snatched Ahiram from her, but she was alone  in the large tent. A cold wisp blew in her face and she realized the assassin did not exist. She had been, once more, dreaming about Ahiram. And in that dream, Arfaad, a captain of the High Riders, entered her brother's room holding a bloodied sword. Sighing, she stowed her daggers away and rubbed her eyes. The diffused light of early dawn cast a soft shadow on familiar objects. She fell back on the soft mat and cradled her head in the palms of her hands. "A dream," she whispered to no one in particular, "it was just a dream."

Wiping tears away, Hoda lay on her back, closed her eyes, and brought the thick cover over her. With her right hand, she searched for Karadon, even though she knew he would already be up. Her husband woke before the break of day, while she preferred to linger in bed. Snuggled under the blanket, she felt safe for a fleeting moment. In the quiet darkness, she imagined she was back in Baher-Ghafé waiting for the first fishermen's call. Back then, she too woke with the dawn.

"You're a late riser," Karadon had exclaimed, "Why, that's perfect. You will make a great night watcher. All the Black Robes will be jealous and you'll need me to protect you."

Since I met Karadon, he and I have saved so many lives, especially children's lives, she thought, *so many ... except for Ahiram.*

She turned on her side as tears swelled in her eyes again.

▷ ✳ ✳ ✳ ◁

No one had seen her cry since that fateful day when Karadon and his companions rescued her and her parents from the clutches of the High Riders. She could still remember her mad dash back to the village from the beach where she had left Ahiram. She remembered how Karadon and his companions had appeared at their door.

"Karadon, what are you doing here?"

"There is no time to explain. You must leave now."

"The High Riders. How did you know?"

"Hoda, do you trust me?" he had asked, his voice pleading. "Do you?"

Looking into his eyes, despite the turmoil and confusion, Hoda trusted him completely. "With my life," she had whispered.

He grabbed her hand, and she felt him tremble.

"Then come along. There is no time."

Wrath of the Urkuun – Contact

"But the villagers, we must alert them," she said, barely managing to keep her voice low. "We must!"

"There is no time," he snapped harshly. "If we alert them, we die. Please, trust me." She read pain in his eyes, but she could not accept the destruction of her village.

"He is right," whispered one of his companions. "If you try to save everyone, then you save no one. We all die."

A fifth man joined them. "They're almost here," he said breathlessly. She could see a streak of hatred in his eyes. "You must go *now*."

"My parents!"

"They have already left the village and are waiting for you," Karadon reassured her. "Now come. The four of you," he said addressing his men, "you know what to do."

They ran on the beach toward Byblos and crossed the main road at a deserted spot, and kept running until they had reached the forest. There, Karadon had guided her along a winding path to her parents. The forest was dense and dark, but her burning village's fiery blaze had lit their path. It wasn't until she embraced her mother that she took notice of Ahiram's medallion she had been clasping. She had picked it up where her brother had left it on the beach.

"Mother," she said in a panic, "I left Ahiram on the beach, I must go back and get him."

"You're not going anywhere," her mother had stated in an unflinching voice that took the young woman by surprise.

"Mother ... we must go back! Ahiram is alone, hiding in my boat."

Her father had been sitting on a tree stump, still as a statue.

"In your boat? El be praised. He has yet a chance to survive. We must wait until the soldiers leave."

"I cannot leave him alone. Let me go!" Hoda screamed hysterically.

Her mother, who had previously never laid a hand on her, slapped her, and then slapped her again—and it stung. "You cannot go now," snapped

Hayat. "If you do, they will kill you. You *must* wait until they leave. Do you hear me?"

The roaring fire that consumed Baher-Ghafé muffled her screams of agony. Not waiting, Karadon led them to a flower-filled meadow. In a corner, a brook cascaded along moss-covered rocks into a quiet pond. This setting would have been ideal for the Festival of Light, but to Hoda, the pond had become a pool of blood. They waited there until Karadon's companions joined them.

With a sigh, Hoda pushed her blanket off and got up. She instantly regretted it. The icy-cold wind swirled around her bare ankles like a spider inspecting its prey. It howled as it lifted a fine dusty sheen and swept it against the tent wall behind her. Ignoring the biting cold, she walked toward the entrance and peered through the protective curtain hanging from the main horizontal beam of the canopy door. A turbulent herd of brooding clouds had turned the sky into a thunderous battlefield. Before long, rain would overtake Gordion and the vast plain surrounding the capital of Teshub. Quickly, Hoda slipped into tights and undershirt made of a stringy dwarfish fabric. She strapped a dagger to each of her ankles and forearms, then strapped a leather mesh around her shoulders and waist; it hid another four blades. She then slid into a warm, flowing dress, thick wool socks, and a pair of tall, black leather boots with concealed openings that gave easy access to the daggers tied to her ankles. Mercilessly, she worked the comb through her thick, curly hair until she managed to subdue it into a tight ponytail. She rolled up the sleeping mats and dropped them into a large trunk. Using a soft short-bristled brush that her friend Foosh had given her, she swept the *elmia*, a thin, hand-woven wool rug sporting the design of a balance scale with two gold pans, set between four peacocks.

"*The scale symbolizes Mitani's longevity,*" Foosh had explained. "*The four peacocks represent elegance, beauty, power, and distinction. When they see this rug, the Gordionist inspectors will know you to be a rich merchant from Mitani, worthy to conduct business in the City of Cupolas."*

Carefully, Hoda flipped the elmia over and brushed its underside. Using a firmer brush, she cleaned the thick gray carpet beneath before straightening the elmia back into place. She moved two comfortable chairs to the middle of the living room and placed a small, round, mosaic-covered table beside each chair. Then she rolled up two rugs that hung from the walls, exposing two steel-mesh-covered windows. Grabbing a pitcher, she watered the greeneries hanging in pots from the tent's main pole. Lastly, she dusted the small dining table and four chairs set in the opposite corner. Even though the tent was well insulated, dust still managed to sneak in, and like stubborn flies, it would settle on the table, waiting for her to chase it away.

"There-ah," Hoda said in a near-perfect Mitanian accent, "the room-ah is worthy-ah of couple-ah from-ah the noble-ah city of Torpan-ah."

She crossed over to the small kitchen where she stoked the fire inside a small, movable iron oven—a marvelous little device Master Kwadil had received from the Kingdom of Ophir. The oven's side remained cool, and since its chimney rose four feet above the tent's peak through a sealed opening, it had kept the tent free from smoke and fumes.

"It ah-would been nice-ah if Master Kwadil-ah had servants-ah to cook-ah for us, but no-ah. No servants for Mister Rastoop and his beautiful wife-ah Linlin-ah."

The young woman shook her head, *Linlin, I am Linlin Rastoop, wife of the wheat grower Jermo Rastoop from the southern city of Torpan.* She cracked four eggs into a frying pan. *We have joined the famed caravan of Master Kwadil to trade with the wealthy city of Gordion.* On top of the eggs, Hoda placed four thin slabs of dried meat, slices of cucumber, celery, mushrooms, and zucchini, then added dashes of salt, curcuma, and pepper. *There are thousands upon thousands of people out there who lead normal lives, and I, I have become a trained member of the Black Robes, the covert organization the Temple would love to destroy.*

In a small iron pan, she toasted a handful of pistachios drizzled with butter. She served the omelet on two separate plates and topped them with the toasted pistachios.

She was about to carry the plates to the main room when two hands held her by the waist and she felt her husband's mustache on her neck.

"You're late," Karadon whispered.

"You're early," she replied, closing her eyes. "Morning of Goodness."

"I love you."

"I know. Hungry?"

He grunted.

Involuntarily, Hoda smiled. Syreen had been right, Karadon preferred grunts to words; a very useful trait that had served them well during all the rescue missions of these past four years.

They ate in silence. All around them the vast camp of Master Kwadil was stirring. Hoda could hear the clanging of the smithy and the braying of the donkeys ready to leave their enclosure. Muffled voices reached them; voices of merchants and porters, slaves and dwarfs, all getting ready for another profitable day of trading.

"What day are we today?" asked Karadon.

"It is 4 Tébêt 1191," answered Hoda.

Karadon looked up from his plate and chuckled. "Do you always give the full date when asked for the day of the week?"

"What do you mean?" Hoda was visibly confused. "You asked me for the date and I … Oh," she said smiling. "You're right. It's Nabû today."

"Thanks. Hey, how does that nursery rhyme go again?"

Hoda smiled. Her husband remembered minute details of the massacres perpetrated by the High Riders in so many villages, but not the simple days-of-the-week rhyme that everyone learned as children.

"All right, Karadon," Hoda said playfully, "let's try this one more time.

Remember now that this lullaby was sung by Shalimar the Poet to his favorite daughter, Lulu. Here how it goes:

> Snûnû, Lulu, lost his bright big head.
> Lulu, Nabû, fell from his big bed.
> Their sister, Ishtar, Lulu, showed up instead.
> Next appeared, Lulu, Shamash, bright and red.
> Then came, Lulu, scary Utu the dread.
> Lulu, children ran to be by Mutu fed.
> Lastly comes late and tired, Lulu, Hused."

Hoda's voice was soft and melodious. Whenever she chose to sing, Karadon held his breath, as if he were seeing her through a magical window—the Hoda he had known so briefly before the destruction of Baher-Ghafé. He knew not to prompt her or to ask her to sing, for she would immediately refuse. He wished there were a female-singing zakiir who could sing songs with Hoda's voice.

"Well, that makes no sense," he said gruffly to hide his emotions. "How is that song supposed to help you remember these names?"

"Don't you see it, silly? Seven days of the week for seven verses and each day appears in its matching position: Snûnû is the first day, so it's the first word of the first verse. Nabû is the second day, so it's the second word of the second verse. That's why we teach this song to the children."

Karadon raised his hands to the heavens the way he had seen Jabbar do. "Why are we even discussing this?" he asked.

"Because you asked me the day of the week."

"Ah yes, that's true. I did ask you for the day of the week. So this means we have been camping here for two weeks, yes?"

"Yes."

"Two weeks," he mused. "This is *not* a simple mission."

"If we spend another week, I will turn into a Mitanian turnip," added Hoda. Karadon eyed her, smirking. "Don't you dare say one word, Mister Rastoop, or I will let everyone know how a carpet merchant bamboozled you. You bought sixteen carpets for our living room."

"They were not for our living room. I told you, it was an investment. Besides," protested Karadon, "I returned them."

Hoda shook her head. "No, Master Kwadil returned them. You grunted painfully."

"Well, I mean …" Karadon grunted.

"You couldn't ask Master Kwadil to speak with his friend, the carpet merchant. Instead, you sent me."

An uncomfortable grunt answered her. "Yes, I know. You have a way with words, and me, well …" He broke out in laughter.

He had an easy laugh, and she loved it. He gulped his food down and pushed his plate away. With a satisfied sigh, he leaned back, sipped his tea, and clicked his tongue. How he managed to drink it so hot escaped her, just as his desire to grow a mustache eluded her. She preferred him clean-shaven, but he wanted that silly thing stuck on his face like a haphazard child's scribble. He thought it made him look older, but she knew he would remain forever young, and the sea would always dance in the blue of his eyes.

Seeing her gaze at him tenderly, he blushed. "What?" he blurted while trying to straighten his mustache.

"You didn't comb your hair; you have a balding spot on the right side."

"Really?" he asked, feeling his head. "I didn't notice."

"And the hair on the back of your head is flat against your skull. You look like a wet chicken."

He frowned and grunted. "Anything else?" he asked, sipping his tea. She looked at him with a critical eye. She knew he was wearing the same specialized weapon-concealing undergarments below his black trousers and white buttoned shirt. His shiny boots reached only to his ankles. "What is it with men," she said smiling. "You shine your boots but you can't take care of your hair."

He shrugged his shoulders and grunted.

"I see," she replied. Over the past six years she had learned to interpret his grunts. "So your boots are more important than your head?"

"They're steel-reinforced, ready to deliver a good kick when needed. I can't kick with my head, now, can I?"

Once more, she did not understand how he could think that, but she did not mind it. Karadon declaimed obscure sayings like oracles in the Temple of Baalbek. Whereas the oracles' utterances had filled her with a sense of impending doom, her husband's sayings reassured her. He got up, picked up the dishes and went to the kitchen where he scrubbed them thoroughly before cleaning the pans. She stood at the door and watched him. He sometimes looked and sounded foolish, but she had seen him in action and knew how efficient and deadly he could be. He had taught her how to throw a dagger, then showed her how to throw four daggers in a deadly sequence. He had forced her to repeat the same movement hundreds of times until she could reach behind her back, pull a dagger and hit a target in the blink of an eye.

"Anything new?"

"Oh, yes. This tasty omelet, your talk of turnips and carpets, and this business of my hair made me forget what I wanted to tell you. Our contact was at the meeting point this morning. He came."

"Finally," she said with a sigh of relief. "Two weeks playing a wealthy Mitanian tourist is enough. I can't take this rich food much longer."

Karadon smiled. Patience was not Hoda's greatest virtue. Even though she had learned to handle the daggers well and could fight like the best of men, she was still impulsive and angry. He knew she had been crying, but he had learned to keep his peace. His wife had not forgiven herself for the loss of her brother.

A week after the High Riders had destroyed Baher-Ghafé, they had borrowed a boat from some fishermen in Byblos, and went looking for Ahiram. After a frenzied search, they had found Hoda's empty vessel in a secluded bay, but there was no sign of her brother. She did not speak for days and refused to eat or sleep until Ashod told her about the Black Robe's mission.

"We save lives, Hoda, that's what we do," Ashod explained. "We have spies who warn us of the Temple's movement and we try to save the lives of their next victims before they strike. The Temple's attack on your village came without warning. If Syreen and Karadon had not noticed your brother's medallion, you would be dead. This camp is filled with survivors who have lost loved ones, but who chose to save lives. You can join us, or drift into despair, and despair will lead you to a dark place where the Kerta priests will find you. Choose well."

Hoda agreed to help the Black Robes, but she refused outright to speak with her mother, which pained Karadon. He understood that it was easier for Hoda to accuse her mother than to confront her own sense of failure. Firsthand experience had taught him that the traumatic loss of loved ones and the horrendous destruction of one's own home led many to guilt and a deep sense of shame. His village had been razed when he was fourteen, and he was thrown into a similar inner turmoil. He knew Hoda had to walk the bitter path to its appointed end. He wished he could take her pain away, for he knew he could handle whatever the Temple would throw his way.

A few weeks later, Hoda asked him to train her, and for the next four years, she practiced relentlessly until she could throw a blade like the best of them. Meanwhile, Hayat began welcoming refugees, and Jabbar hid his sorrow behind the anvil of an old blacksmith. Hoda rarely saw them.

Then, one day, Ashod had joined Karadon and Hoda for lunch. He came unannounced and they did not know what to make of it. "Suppose," he had asked them, "you had to choose between saving your family and letting everyone else in your village die. What would you do?"

"I'd save my family," Karadon had replied without hesitation. "That would be my duty."

Hoda nodded.

"Very well," Ashod replied. "Suppose a family member could, with one gaze, one focused gaze, kill everyone in your village. Let's say it was your sister who, through no fault of her own, killed anyone she gazed upon. Worse yet, suppose that by merely looking at a mountain, she could destroy it—"

"A mountain?" asked Hoda.

"A mountain and everything on it. And by gazing at the sea, she would replace it with a deep, dark and empty abyss. If your sister could not help herself from using this terrible power, what would you do? Would you let her live, or would you kill her?"

"That's a terrible choice," said Hoda softly. "I don't know what I'd do."

"Is that what the Temple of Baal is doing?" asked Karadon.

"Precisely. The Temple has every reason to believe that a person with such a power exists, or will exist." His eyes were locked on Hoda. "They call him the Seer of Power, and they believe he will wield this destructive power that will free the Sheituun, the Lords of Darkness, and make him their puppet. He would become the dark overlord to do their bidding in a world as dark as the Pit itself."

Hoda stared at him wide-eyed, refusing to consider the eventuality.

"Is this true?" Karadon asked, bewildered.

Ashod nodded. "You understand now why the Temple feels compelled to do what they do? They have no choice. They do not know who the Seer is. So when they detect the Seer's presence somewhere, they must exterminate everyone in order to protect us."

"Is that why they destroyed Baher-Ghafé?" asked Hoda. "Because of the medallion?"

"Perhaps," replied Ashod. "It's hard to say."

"But what if they're wrong? What if someone faked that sign in order to destroy the village?"

"The Temple is not so easily tricked."

"But they could have spared the women and the aged and only killed the young boys," said Karadon.

"The Seer may be male or female, and no one knows when they will come into power."

"I see," said Hoda.

"The High Riders are so well trained that if the Temple ordered them to kill their own kin, they would do it. This is the Temple's mission. This is what it stands for," said Ashod.

Karadon and Hoda both felt dizzy and weak. "But if this is so," Hoda had whispered, "why are we fighting them?"

Ashod came close, laid a gentle hand on her shoulder, and looked so intently at her that she was frightened by the fiery light in the old man's eyes. "Because, my dear one, although the Temple is sincere, I believe they are sincerely wrong. We keep up our fight until the Temple realizes they were wrong all along."

"Why are you telling us all this?" asked Karadon. "This is so unlike you, Ashod."

Ashod looked at him and grinned. "Indeed, so unlike me. I am telling you this in case, just in case, your brother happens to be this Seer. Your love for him will help keep him safe from the Pit."

"You think Ahiram is alive?" asked Hoda. She held back tears.

Ashod looked at her with his inscrutable eyes. "Time will only tell. In the meanwhile, you must cultivate love and gratitude. Your brother will need you alive and strong. He will need all the help you can give him. You might yet have the occasion to prove the Temple wrong, Hoda. Remember this, child, and do not speak of it to anyone."

The conversation had a profound effect on Hoda. Her appreciation for Karadon had grown into a deep sense of gratitude. "Another day to save another life," he would say, and she would smile. Whether the Temple was right or wrong, together, they would help someone enjoy one more day under the heavens, and perhaps that was enough. They had found a rhythm, a common cause to fight for, a vessel on the high waves of the world to carry them forward.

Two years ago, after an exhausting day of training, they had taken a stroll under cherry trees in full bloom.

"They are so beautiful," Hoda had said.

"I know, and each flower reminds me of you." Karadon stopped and turned to her. "I loved cherries before I met you, but since the first day I saw you, I knew I would love the trees in full bloom even more than the cherries. Marry me, Hoda."

She had looked at him with bright eyes, and her guilt and her deep sense of self-loathing roared like a dragon in its lair. The pain had nearly choked her and she slapped Karadon hard, twice. Dropping to the ground, she had wrapped her arms around her legs and sobbed uncontrollably. He remembered how he stood there, shaken and overcome with grief for her, and for all those who had lost their loved ones by the sword of the Temple. Then, he knelt before her and held her against him. She did not resist but whispered softly, "How could you love me after what I have done? I have sent my brother to his death."

He forced her to look into his eyes and said, "It wasn't you. It was the Temple. You tried to save him, but sometimes we are not strong enough to save those we love. Then we must choose between spending the rest of our lives hating ourselves, or loving those we can love. I love you. What will you do?"

He did not wait for an answer but got up and left. He knew she needed to know he could walk away. She needed to know he would be strong enough to walk away and continue to live even if she chose not to love him, or worse, if the Temple managed to capture or kill her. She needed to know that his love would not overwhelm him, nor overtake him, but carry him forward and give him the strength to face whatever would come. Torn, wounded, afraid and alone he may be, but he would still be standing, still choosing life over death, love over hate, and strength over the murderous weakness of the Temple.

Two weeks later, they were married in a simple but beautiful ceremony. Ashod officiated. Her father and mother stood side-by-side and wept for joy. The cheers and applause of their companions pierced his heart, for there was not one man, woman, or child cheering them that had not lost loved ones.

Secretly, Karadon had hoped Hoda would be with child, but two years into their marriage and still no children were forthcoming. Ashod had advised him to be patient. "She is not yet ready to be a mother, Karadon. She is healing, slowly. Be patient and do not raise the subject. Stand by her side and be there when she needs you and that should be enough for now," he had said.

◈✴✴✴◈

"Karadon? Karadon? You're daydreaming again."

Her husband grunted, then yawned.

"Oh no, you're not going for your morning nap before you tell me what our contact has told you."

Karadon yawned again. "The inspectors are ready to issue our permit today, but the princess, daughter of the heiress to the throne, fell ill. So we should receive the permits in five days hence."

"A little girl falls sick and permits are delayed five days? How do they expect to do business?"

"Ah, my dear Mrs. Rastoop," he said, imitating the surly speech of the palace's intendant, "it is a great honor to do business with you. Please wait a month or two, and we will be with you momentarily."

Hoda sighed in frustration. "I don't understand why Ashod sent us to deliver a package to somebody living in Gordion, of all places. This is not a Black Robe's mission. We're not saving anyone, so why are we involved?"

"Are you asking me, or are you talking to Ashod?" asked Karadon in an innocent tone. "If you're asking me, I would answer that I don't know about this mission any more than I did yesterday when you asked me that same question. If you are mistaking me for Ashod, I would be offended. He is bald and my nose is far better good-looking than his."

Hoda pursed her lips and scowled. Karadon tried to laugh and yawn at the same time and ended up with a loud groan.

"Has he told you who we're supposed to meet in Gordion?"

"Yes," replied Karadon, "by the way, why do you insist on stowing the mats away when you know I'll be taking a nap?"

"If I leave the mats on the floor, you complain that the tent is not up to Mister Rastoop's standards," griped Hoda. "Make up your mind."

"That's true," he chuckled. "All right then, I won't complain about untidiness when I come back from my early morning watch."

"Promise?" asked Hoda who eyed Karadon suspiciously as he retrieved his mat.

"Wake me in two hours," he said as he smoothed his cover over the thick floor bedding. "Two representatives from the Gordion Commerce League and a zakiir will be visiting us this afternoon to begin the necessary negotiations for the permits."

"Wait, what negotiations? I thought the permits have been secured."

"No, the intent has been secured. Before the royal attendant of Gordion can turn intent into permits, he must first verify our claim. There will be two more visits, one this afternoon, and another in four days. If all goes well, we will receive the permits on the fifth day, when we present ourselves at the gate of the city."

"You mean, I have to prepare Mitanian dishes again? They are so greasy, I can't—"

"The good news," Karadon broke in, "is that you won't have to cook. Master Kwadil promised he will take care of the meals. Seemingly, he knows of an amazing cook who is traveling with us, but he refused to tell me who it is.

"Fine, I will, but do you promise?"

"Promise what?"

"That you won't complain about untidiness?"

Karadon stretched and yawned. "Ah yes-ah, my beautiful turnip-ah. I will not complain about untidiness before my nap, only after-ah."

Hoda shoved her husband and he fell laughing onto the floor. She pinned him to the ground and he smiled. "You haven't told me the name of the person we are to meet in Gordion."

"Ah, yes," he said closing his eyes, "The name means nothing to me and I doubt it will mean anything to you."

"Karadon, tell me who we're meeting with or I won't let you nap."

"Fine," he said sleepily, "I got only his first name. It's Corintus."

13. Fire-Storm

> "Empyreans are never to be trifled with. Underestimating them is a deadly mistake. Trying to woo them or bribe them could get you killed. Disrespecting them in any way will result in severe reprisal. Sit on a horse, show yourself a worthy leader and a mighty warrior, and they will respect you. You might still end up dead, but at least you will have won their respect."
>
> —Diplomatic Notes of Uziguzi, First Adviser to Her Majesty Aylul Meir Pen, Empress of the Empyreans.

While Karadon made ready for his favorite nap, Aquilina, still in her wet clothes, had stood in Tyrulan, waiting for her enemy. She remembered the day when Vily had come to live with them at the castle. She had felt the orphan's sadness and vowed never to forget that moment. To this end, she had consigned to memory the very spot where she had experienced her friend's sorrow, and named it Vilytéréyan. It was there that she witnessed the rise of a beautiful silver willow shedding brilliant white tears. She had instinctively known this willow was linked to Vily. She had closed her eyes, lightly touched the willow, and when she opened them, found herself in an inner court next to a grimy iron pole where Vily had been tied. A dark-green bruise covered her right cheek and a streak of dried blood ran from her nose down her chin and neck. Vily had been slumped against the pole and the thick ropes holding her captive dug into her tumefied arms.

"Vily," Aquilina had cried, "Vily!"

The little girl managed to raise her head and had given the young princess a sad smile. Realizing Aquilina was next to her, Vily became afraid. "Run, Lina," she whispered, "Run. He will catch you."

Aquilina worked on the knot. "Who did this to you, Vily? Who?"

"You!" yelled a man from behind. "What are you doing here?"

Aquilina looked behind her. A tall burly man was standing by the door. He was massive and muscular with a neck as thick as a bull's. "Untie her, now!" she ordered.

The man laughed; a loud, sickening chortle. "Look at this, the little twit is ordering me." He stepped into the courtyard, flexing his massive arms. "Tell you what I'll do, I'll slap her twice to teach you a lesson, and then I'll put a nice little collar around your neck and teach you to beg properly. See," he added as he drew closer, "orphans who don't beg properly don't eat; they're punished. Now that's proper, see?"

"Untie her! I am Princess Aquilina of Gordion. Release her."

The man laughed so hard tears welled in his swollen eyes. "A princess? *Here?* You impress me young twit; you'll make a good beggar." He grabbed her by the arm and twisted. "A good beating is what you'll get to know, Highness. I'll—"

"I suggest you let her go. Slowly."

Startled, the man relaxed his grip. Despite the pain, Aquilina looked up and saw her father. *Father? Here? How did he find me?* Aquilina wrenched her arm free and ran toward the back of the court. The muscular man, a former High Rider, recognized the fighter's stance Aquilina's father had adopted.

"I don't know what you're problem is, but it's not worth losing a tooth over it. Take her and go," he barked. "If I see her in my street—"

"I suggest you let the little girl go free as well," Corintus cut in.

Wrath of the Urkuun – Fire-Storm

The man snickered and then pain exploded in his head. A black stone, smooth and swift, punched him between the eyes. Then, two stones pummeled his forehead. He let out a low gurgle as he reeled back and collapsed to the ground, shattering his jaw. Corintus looked up in time to see his daughter charge the unconscious torturer, an Empyrean blade in each hand. She leaped, and screaming her rage, brought her blades down. Corintus' armed moved in a blur and he grabbed her.

"Enough."

"He would have killed her," Aquilina yelled, struggling to get free. "I will finish him."

Corintus' arms turned to steel. "Give me the knives, Aquilina. Now."

"But, Father …"

"Now!" Aquilina was startled. Her Father's voice was hard, unflinching and brooked no complaint. Reluctantly, she complied.

"We're going back to the palace," he said.

"Not without Vily, we're not. I want her to come with us."

"Fine, we will take Vily with us, but you will do as I say, understood?"

Her anger and fury dissolved. "I love you, Father." Wrapping her arms around her father's neck, she gave him a peck. "I can always count on you."

Confused, Corintus wanted to all at once scold his daughter for risking her life, compliment her for her bravery, and thank her for her show of affection. "You are a wonderful monkey, but I should scold you for leaving the palace alone and let your favorite sweets spend the night without dinner."

Aquilina burst into laughter. "You are a flying shadow, Father. I never knew you were following me."

Corintus smiled and released his daughter. She ran to her friend. Vily's sad smile constricted his heart. He cut the thick ropes and steadied her, then held the girls by the hand and headed back to the palace. On their way, Aquilina pleaded with the other orphans to run away with them, but they stubbornly refused and yelled at her to go away.

"Don't be upset, Lina," Vily had told her. "They think you're an orphan too. They don't trust you."

Corintus left Vily in the care of a gentlewoman who nursed the little girl back to health, and being the head seamstress of the palace, put her new protégé in charge of the yarn as a way of earning her keep. Even though Corintus did this out of the goodness of his heart, he had ulterior motives. Now that she had a friend, Aquilina spent most of her days within the castle's boundaries. Her mood improved and her tantrums diminished. The former Silent grew fond of Vily, for he knew she had given them more than they had given her.

Finding her playmate tied to a pole, alone and scared, shook Aquilina's childhood. *I will not give up on the orphans. I will go back and free them all.*

The following day, she had requested an audience with her grandfather, the King, and had asked him to banish slavery from Gordion. "People are people and should not be treated like animals," she had told her grandfather. "Especially the children."

King Domin had just laughed and pinched her cheek—which she detested. "My dear child, your desire for justice will serve you well when you bear this heavy crown. Justice, you see, is often not simple. It requires much patience and fortitude." He had explained how instituting a state-run orphanage would disrupt the social order, for orphans powered a good portion of the Gordian economy. Should he pull them out of the system, he would affect the merchants, artisans, farmers, and other small businesses that affected the local economy. This, in turn, could destabilize the fragile political structure of the entire kingdom. The Temple would be happy to intervene and deepen its control over the royal family. "No, Princess, I do not have that luxury, but the crown does punish those who treat their orphans in an unusually cruel manner."

His explanation did not convince her. She became more determined to take matters into her own hands.

Wrath of the Urkuun – Fire-Storm

▷✵✵✵◁

Not long after, Aquilina fell in Tyrulan again. The landscape had not changed. Though natural and elegant to her, it could be bewildering and confusing to anyone else. The flora was denser and richer, with new words sprouting from the ground. They grew slowly at first, timid like an imperceptible sheen of green moss, then stronger and quicker, until a massive, endless jungle of shapes and colors covered Tyrulan. Still silence prevailed, complete and unbroken like an inverted mountain pushing down from the heavens. The quietude resisted the rise of voices and the light that disturbed its unremitting gray monotony. Aquilina felt lost when she saw the new growth; she did not know what to do. She wished she could do here what she had done in Gordion and walk on the rooftops, or the tops of these strange plants.

"Up," she said.

"*Up*" shot out of the ground; a bright orange leafless oak glittering in the ambient grayness. Carved into the oak, a lighted staircase reached the top and continued far above into the grayness. Without the slightest hesitation, Aquilina began to climb. Her footsteps resonated in her mind like a joyful, comforting song she had never heard before, in a language that seemed familiar, like an old cherished memory she had forgotten. She kept climbing until she reached the canopy of the highest plant-looking object she could see. She looked down and saw the staircase vanish while she remained standing barefoot on the last step. She was no more frightened than a child who says "up" or "down" while standing on the ground. In Tyrulan, "up" and "down" were like words with no real sense of direction. Just as one does not fall by saying "down," nor go up if he utters "up," she did not move within Tyrulan. Even so, her perceived movements in that strange world affected her physical location.

Aquilina stood watching with glee the ever-changing Tyrulian flora. *Like spoken words. We hear them only for a short moment, then they are gone.*

Peering over the colorful forest below, Aquilina realized words came in clusters, a few of them grew in an island disconnected from the rest of the strange world by a gray liquid mass. *The language of the world*, she thought, *how beautiful.*

Over the next year, Aquilina lived happily at the castle. She played with Vily and studied with a warrior's ardor, as if lectures on the history of kingdoms, geopolitical strategies, and etiquette were battles she had to win or summits she needed to conquer. Her favorite subjects were hand-to-hand combat she learned from her father and blade manipulation she learned from her mother. It was her destiny to be a princess, and a princess of Empyrean blood had to be able to defend and protect. She kept her Tyrulian excursions to herself, though she answered her parents whenever they asked her about it. She knew her parents did not understand nor truly believe in Tyrulan, and, for the first time in her life, Aquilina felt truly alone.

As she continued to wander inside this strange land, she caught sight of a giant tree, ablaze with a raging fire that stormed the height of Tyrulan. Mesmerized, she approached it, wondering if the fire would consume her, but it vanished suddenly.

She called it *Arkélad*—a contracted form of *arkétis*, storm, and *ladék*, fire. Her Tyrulian treks became a quest to find it, to find Arkélad. Over time, she had become so attuned to its presence that she could spot it immediately. In the process, she had learned to move swiftly in Tyrulan and could detect the slightest change—like the apparition of new words—almost instinctively. Then, six month ago, Corintus had surprised his now twelve-year-old daughter while they strolled and ate roasted chestnuts in one of the secluded alcoves of the garden.

"Aquilina, you know I find it difficult to believe in … you know …" he lowered his voice to a whisper, "your other world."

"Yes, Father, I know." Her Empyrean side was not offended. If her father's doubt had shamed her, she would have been compelled to challenge him—a duel she knew she could not win. Since her father did not mock her, no harm was done, and no duel would be necessary.

"You told me," continued Corintus, "the things you see there are words that take the shapes of trees, is it not so?"

"Plants, shrubs, and trees, Father."

"Ah, yes. Plants, shrubs and trees ... how about a little test then?"

"A challenge?" She perked up. She loved challenges.

"Yes, a simple, harmless test. Do you think you could go into that other world now?"

She looked at Corintus quizzically. "I can, but I cannot take you there, Father, if that is what you have in mind."

He shook his head. "Something far simpler. Ah, careful, these chestnuts are hot."

"I know, Father," she said giggling. Reaching up, she kissed him on the cheek. "I love you, Father."

Startled, he smiled. "This is not your Empyrean side, child."

"I know," she said smiling. "I learn much from Vily."

"You like her, don't you?"

"She's like a sister to me."

"Well, daughter, are you ready for the test?" She had nodded. "Here is what I would like you to do. I will go sit by that fountain over there. I will quietly repeat the same short sentence over and over again. You will go into Tyrulan, hear what I am saying and come back and tell me."

"But, Father, Tyrulan is big. I don't mean like this garden, but more like the idea of bigness." A quick glance at her father and she realized she was losing him. "The words of the world fill Tyrulan. How could I possibly—"

"Ah, yes. Good observation. Remember when you rescued Vily? You were in Tyrulan and you somehow figured it was Vily yes? Then, you came back to our world and you ended up near her, yes?"

She nodded thoughtfully. "I see, Father. You think that when I enter

Tyrulan, I will be close to words spoken in this garden, yes?"

"Yes."

"This means," she added mischievously, "I could spy on all the trades taking place here and make a few gold coins in profit, heh, heh, heh." She rubbed her hands with great satisfaction, the way she had seen many a zakiir do after a good deal. A quick glance at her father told her to stop; he did not appreciate the joke.

"Still, Father, there are too many conversations in this garden—"

"Conversations, yes, but not repeated words," he corrected gently. "If what you say is true, you should be able to see a cluster of things that look identical. I bet they will look like a small forest of indistinguishable trees. You need only reach this forest to know what I will be saying."

"This test is worthy of an Empyrean, Father. But, I do not know what the plants in Tyrulan are saying."

"What do you mean?"

"I get ideas in my head when I stand next to these plants. I don't actually hear the words."

Corintus thought about it for a while. "Well, Aquilina, why do you think words take the shape of plants, grass, shrubs, and trees? Why don't they show up like dogs, cats, or chickens?" She laughed at the thought, but had to admit she did not know why they appeared that way. "Think, daughter, what do Empyreans like?"

"They like the forest, the trees, the plants …" It dawned on her. "I see, so you think Tyrulan is Empyrean?"

"I don't know, but what would an Empyrean do when standing before a beautiful tree?"

"Touch it?" replied Aquilina. And then she understood what her father was inferring. "So, you think, if I touch the plants in Tyrulan, they will speak to me?"

"Not speak to you, but you may hear what they are saying."

Excited, Aquilina clapped her hands and did a few pirouettes. "I am ready," she said. She looked at her father and smiled. *He is smarter than I thought.* Ordinarily, Corintus gave an impression of a daydreamer who loved to talk about simple facts, seemingly missing important clues. Had she had the occasion to meet another Silent, she would have understood his demeanor to be part of their standard training: "Appear harmless, avoid drawing attention to yourself so you may be free to act."

"Good," said her father getting up. "I will go now and sit by the fountain. It is far enough from where you are standing so you will not hear me whisper. As soon as I am seated, you can go to Tyrulan and find out what I am repeating."

Getting in and out of Tyrulan had become much easier. She only needed to close her eyes, empty her mind, take a few deep breaths, and she would cross over. Aquilina opened her eyes in Tyrulan and quickly climbed to survey the landscape.

After only a brief search, she found a cluster of identical bright shrubs that were pulsating quickly. As soon as one vanished, another would take its place. *That's Father's sentence.*

Just then, in the distance, she glimpsed Arkélad. The massive burning tree was in the midst of a firestorm. She said, "Run," and found herself riding rapids that moved her at a dizzying speed—assuming she was moving at all—to her destination. She said, "Stop," and the rapids vanished. *Let's see if Father is right.* Timidly, she laid a finger on the fiery trunk and felt such overwhelming grief and deep longing that she burst into tears. *Father was right,* she thought, *but how sad are these words.*

The voice's inflection told Aquilina that the one who spoke was a lonely young man, aloof and angry. *He is seeking someone or something.* She wanted to console him the way she had consoled Vily. Despite the flames, she gripped the trunk and willed to cross over but ended up with a searing pain, as if the power in the young man's words stopped her from going to him. No other words in Tyrulan had thus far behaved this way. After several attempts, she stepped back in frustration.

Father! Oh no, I forgot about him.

Swiftly, she went to the cluster of bright shrubs, touched one of them, and broke into a giggle that lit the Tyrulian skies. She closed her eyes, and when she reopened them, she found herself standing next to her father by the fountain.

Seeing her appear out of nowhere, Corintus jumped and almost knocked his head against the marble fountain.

"Where did you come from?" he asked, confused.

"From Tyrulan."

Nervously, Corintus scanned the garden half expecting to see High Riders running with swords drawn.

"All right then," he whispered. "What was I saying?"

"Oméléya tu ovo marinaya," she said. Unable to hold back, she burst into laughter.

"So it is true, you can hear and travel in the land of words."

"Do you believe me now, Father?" She laughed again, until tears streamed down her cheeks.

He nodded. "Yes, I do. Why are you laughing?"

She hugged and kissed him. At last, her father believed her. As they walked back toward the palace, Aquilina described Tyrulan in detail. She had been relieved to confide in her father and told him everything she had known about this strange space, but for some obscure reason she omitted Arkélad. He had listened intently and in complete silence. As they were about to step inside the palace, he asked her again why she laughed when she told him what he had been saying.

"Because," she had said in a giggle, "you said, *I love you, my precious cow.* That's what *Oméléya tu ovo marinaya* means. Mother says *Oméléya tu ova marinéya*, which means *I love you, my little darling*, but I understood what you were trying to say, Father."

That exchange with her father was etched in her memory. Thinking about it brought a smile to her face despite her dripping wet dress. As each drop of water splashed on the Tyrulian ground below, it produced an evanescent pink-freckled blue plant that looked oddly like a candle. She felt bad for vanishing from her room the way she had, but she needed to be sure, absolutely certain that her enemy was no longer in Tyrulan.

High over the flora she stood still, watching and waiting. *Will he scream again? Is he still here?* She shivered from fatigue, for she had been exerting herself for two weeks now, helping the young man behind Arkélad. It started when a young woman had wanted him dead. Aquilina had heard her distinctly say, "Kill him." He had thrown an object in self-defense that, in Tyrulan, took the shape of a small cone with a fat tip. *A small blade or an arrow*, had realized the young girl. As the object crossed the air, the sound it made appeared as an icy blue streak. Aquilina saw a tight net around the dark green shrub representing the young woman. *The net is too tight for the weapon to cut through.* Aquilina touched the net and whispered, "Open." The mesh loosened. With one hand, she guided the bright blue trail through the net. Deep in the mines, during the Game of Silver, Ahiram had just thrown his dart at Hiyam and Aquilina had broken through the protective spell that should have prevented the dart from reaching Hiyam's neck.

Then, she heard Ahiram when he had just completed the Game of Silver. Feeling desperately lonely and disheartened over what he had done to Prince Olothe, he had said, "I will always be alone." Instinctively, Aquilina had gripped the tree and whispered back, "You are not alone. I am with you." Once more, a searing pain flooded her senses. It shot through her eyes, momentarily blinding her. She did not know that Ahiram had heard her.

Her desire to speak with him turned into mounting frustration when we he would not return the favor. Instead of his voice, she would hear a whooshing sound, as if he preferred to sleep and snore rather than converse with her. Impulsively—and to punish him—she started calling him Snoring Man.

Later, at the start of the Game of Gold, Ahiram had stood precariously on the shoulders of two athletes while surrounded by a ring of fire and had shot his dart toward a cluster of stalactites. She had guided his dart to its target.

These experiences had left her giddy. It did not matter that no one could witness what she did, for Empyreans disliked public displays of valor. Snoring man was safe, and that was all that mattered. Then, the enemy surfaced. When she heard his voice the first time, she nearly fainted from fright; it sounded like a giant wave about to swallow Tyrulan. This was when the urkuun mounted his attack against the athletes while they were climbing the Pit of Thunder. Her fear turned to anger and she became determined to stop the enemy, but it vanished.

Then, during the Game of Meyroon, she witnessed her friend's fall into dark waters, which appeared as a hollow pipe full of raging "noise" in Tyrulan. She had seen him fall in the water, and the water rushed into an enclosure that appeared as a subterranean hole streaked by bright filaments. But Aquilina could see a way out: a passage that looked like a tangled vine swirling upward. "Up," she had said, directing her words at the drowning young man, but he banged his head against the roof of the siphon in the maelstrom. She jumped into the Tyrulian hole, touched Arkélad, and repeated the command. This time, he managed to find the exit, but she was suddenly sucked into the dark waters and nearly drowned in his place. In extremis, she managed to cross back into Tyrulan where searing pain welcomed her. Drenched, frozen, and aching, she refused to leave until she saw the fiery tree flare in the distance. Elated, she forced herself to move and reached the tree in time to hear the young man utter a word unlike any other. Ahiram had just called the tile by its name, "Taw." The word he spoke lit Tyrulan from one end to another, nearly blinding her. She felt a rush of power flow through her like nothing

<mark>she had experienced before</mark>. That all happened when the one she called "her enemy" spoke words of power and command in Tyrulan and for the past three weeks, she had been waging a secret, protracted battle against him. Whenever he tried to speak, she would order his words to stop growing and they would reluctantly obey her. She could not stop him from speaking but she continued to stunt the power and extent of his control. This enraged her opponent who began seeking her with words of despair and destruction that affected her deeply. Still, she was a fighter, not one about to give up. She began spending long hours in Tyrulan, fighting him with the determination of an Empyrean warrior and the battle dragged, sapping her energy away. *He has not weakened*, she had thought. *Where does he get this energy?*

▷✷✷✷◁

Earlier that day, her foe filled Tyrulan with dark words of power and overwhelming fury. So vicious were they, they silenced every other word around them. Exhausted, her mind wandered, seeking a place of refuge, a place where she could be safe. The memory of her Father repeating that funny sentence below the fountain in the garden popped in her mind. She closed her eyes and when she opened them, she fell in the basin of that fountain in a grand splash that raised a correspondingly grand outcry from the dignitaries and merchants of Gordion.

They must not see me, she had thought, and she vanished from view, back into Tyrulan where she came face-to-face with the words of commands. Exhausted and at the end of her strength, Aquilina knew she could not continue the fight alone. Impulsively, she gave an order, "Tyrulan, speak against him."

Immediately, hundreds, then thousands upon thousands of words had risen from the Tyrulian soil. They converged on the dark words of the being of power, surrounded them, forming a deafening and chaotic barrier. The dark being of power reeled in fury, trying to disentangle itself from the tight web of voices, and after a long fight—at least it seemed long to Aquilina—it retreated. Her little trick had succeeded. Relieved that she had stopped the attack, she returned to her room exhausted and fell on onto her bed. Unwittingly, she had brought with her a bubble of water from the fountain. The water fell, scaring Vily, but the young princess was too tired to hear her friend's cry. Aquilina was too young to know the toll the fight had taken on her, and did not yet realize that her extended exposure in Tyrulan had nearly killed her.

◈✻✻✻◈

Now standing over the Tyrulian landscape, she searched for the words of fury. *I must be sure*, she thought. *I cannot leave Tyrulan to this monster*. For the first time, she was afraid in Tyrulan and wanted to confront her fears. *I must know*. She walked toward the spot where the scream of the urkuun had erupted. *There it is*. She looked at an ashen forest of thorny trees. Their size was beyond anything she had seen before. As she craned her head back to see their tops, she shivered at the thought of the creature that had uttered these words: *These are words—words that stand like gigantic thorny trees*. She drew closer, and one of the trees, lithe as a whip, lashed at her. Instinctively, Aquilina averted her face, raised her hand before her and said, "No." She did not hear her own voice but instead saw a lightning bolt issue forth from her mouth that hit the tree. The ugly thorny tree recoiled like a serpent and lashed at her once more with greater ferocity. The other trees followed suit, and the little girl thought she was fighting a many-headed, giant serpent. She could not say how long the fight had gone on, but she began to feel very tired.

Just then, a beautiful rose sprouted at her feet. It glowed joyfully, and its light gave her strength. Instinctively, she touched it.

"It's a trap," said a voice stemming from the rose. "These serpent-trees are words of power. If you hear them, you will not be able to leave Tyrulan on your own." The rose dissipated quickly as other sounds did in Tyrulan. The voice was kind and strong, and she trusted it.

I am not leaving these ugly words in Tyrulan.

"Faraway and up." Instantly, she lifted and floated high, looking at the monstrous creature down below. "Fire," she commanded with great determination, "Burn." Tyrulan erupted in flames. *Oh no, I meant to say burn these trees. Now everything is burning!*

People in and around the Fortress of Hardeen—farmers, merchants, and shepherds—experienced a sudden and unexplained lapse in memory. Conversations were abruptly interrupted, and people were momentarily confused. Some thought Arika, the goddess of good health, had sneezed; others assumed Tanniin had bellowed from the void to which Baal had confined him. Still others believed Tiamat, the earth goddess, was stirring. A wave of thin filament flooded the Tyrulian spot where the burned-up trees once stood. In Tyrulan, a thick dense forest sprouted, consisting of one sentence repeated thousands upon thousands of times: "What was I saying?"

Aquilina felt dizzy and weak. She knew she had to leave. She closed her eyes, dropped down, and landed back in her bed.

"Aquilina!"

She opened her eyes and smiled weakly. "Hello Mother, hello Father. It's always nice to see you."

She closed her eyes and fell into a deep sleep.

14. Permission To Kill

> "When an Empyrean weds outside of her kin, she changes allegiance. She is no longer a servant of the empress, she becomes a servant of her marriage-not her husband. The empress is a symbol for the endurance of the Empyrean Kingdom, and it is the kingdom that an Empyrean serves selflessly. When she marries outside of her kin, her marriage becomes her kingdom, her purpose, and her end. Nothing else matters."
> —Diplomatic Notes of Uziguzi, First Adviser to Her Majesty Aylul Meir Pen, Empress of the Empyreans.

"Do not fall asleep, Aquilina," urged Corintus, as he lifted his daughter to an upright position.

"But Father, it is *sooo* late," complained Aquilina, "and I'm *sooo* tired."

"Amaréya, hold her. Do not let her fall asleep, or else we may lose her again." He ran to the door and yelled, "Martha!" The old maid, who was sitting by the door, jumped in fright. "Oh, sorry Martha, could you please bring food? Aquilina is hungry."

"Yes, Master." She hurried down the corridor and as she reached the main staircase, she met Drobna, on his way up with two hooded figures. "My, oh my, it is finally happening," whispered Martha, going down the stairs as fast as her stiff legs allowed.

Earlier, Drobna had left the palace grounds disguised as a rich merchant from Gordion. He had crossed Royal Avenue and went into the exclusive district of Rithar, and walked past the mansions of the wealthy noblemen and merchants. He wore a diamond insignia on his chest—the highest distinction of the Merchant Guild. As he passed the impeccably manicured lawns and pavilions, the slaves who toiled in the gardens, prostrated themselves when they saw him. He then crossed Thontar Avenue and reached the eastern edge of Rithar, and instead of crossing the bridge over the Hent River, he went down to the docks where a covered barge waited for him.

"You're late," grumbled a woman so tanned and wrinkled one would think she had seen the first day of creation. A gray apron covered her from the shoulders down, and she smelled of fish and herbs.

"Don't mind me, Gilna," said Drobna as he stepped quickly inside the barge. "It's going to happen soon. Master Corintus is ready."

"About time." She let loose a strident whistle, and six young men got busy moving the barge away from the docks and upstream. "About time. Now, where to?"

"The caravans. You'll wait for me at the pier, and we'll have two more passengers to bring back."

Gilna grunted. Neither spoke the rest of the way. Progressively, the simpler structures of the poor replaced the four-story-high buildings of the middle class. After a mile-long strip, they reached Orol, the City of Lepers. Orol had been, in times past, the capital of a much smaller Teshub, and Gordion had supplanted it six hundred years ago. The old capital had decayed into a ruin where now only lepers lived. Drobna and his crew glimpsed them fishing by the shore. At the sight of the barge, the sickly figures hid their faces.

A few miles southeast from Orol, two tributaries of the Hent swelled the river, turning it into a lake where the caravans' port lay. Hundreds of barges were docked while thousands of slaves loaded and unloaded wide assortments of livestock and goods. This commercial zone was reserved for merchants judged unfit to do business within the capital.

"This camp is getting bigger by the month," grumbled Gilna. "A bit more and it'll turn into Tirkalanzibar."

Drobna had a dry chuckle. "Obviously, you've never been to the largest caravan city in the known world. This camp is child's play compared to Tirkalanzibar."

To trade inside Gordion was a dream come true to most caravaners, but not to Kwadil. His exotic merchandise already allowed him to trade with the established businesses of Gordion without incurring the exorbitant tax the city levied.

"Between taxes and the plague," he would say in the common tongue, "A wise dwarf chooses the plague. It is short lived and therefore far less demanding than taxes."

Drobna left his expensive merchant's coat on the barge and crossed the twenty-two docks unnoticed., He followed a dirt road that smelled of horse manure and swine until he reached the gates of Kwadil's camp. *More like a small city than a camp*, he thought. *There are a thousand tents in there*. The gates and the barricades around the large encampment were portable, made to travel with the caravan wherever it went. *The dwarfs charge the cost of transportation and maintenance of this enclosure to the caravaners. Now that's being savvy and shrewd in business.*

"I have business with a rich merchant from Rastoopa who is seeking access to Gordion." He said this impatiently, the way inspectors from Gordion would.

An old dwarf manning the gate smiled obsequiously and spoke softly to a young dwarf child who nodded.

"This way please, sir," the dwarf said in the common tongue. "The lad will take you to them."

Wrath of the Urkuun – Permission to Kill

As he crossed the camp, amazement seized Corintus' servant. Unlike Gordion's market, which sold familiar products, Kwadil's camp featured items he had never seen before: tempting spices, alluring jewels, and bizarre clothing. There were even brightly colored birds that uttered oracles, curious steel containers with twisted winding tubes, and smoking pipes—some as tall as a man. On and on the shops went with a bewildering assortment of colors, smells, and sounds. *No wonder they call it the caravan from beyond*, Drobna thought. He gasped when he saw a mummified giant, fourteen feet tall, and the stuffed head of a monstrous shark with three rows of razor-sharp teeth. *I could spend days here and never be bored.*

Eventually, the dwarf child took him away from the busy market to a quieter area and brought him before a clean, well-kept tent. He asked the child to wait for him across the street then struck a small bell with a wooden hammer. A young woman came to meet him. She was, in his own terms, dangerously beautiful, reminding him of the Empyrean race. Her long and curly black hair, dark eyes, and somewhat shorter stature, told him she hailed from the shores of the Great Sea.

"How can I ah help-ah?" she asked in the Rastoopian accent.

"Master Corintus needs to see you right away," he said. "It's urgent."

A man walked out of the tent and eyed him suspiciously. "Pardon-ah me my friend-ah, but-ah, we do not know-ah any Corintus-ah. We are-ah waiting for our-ah permit-ah, which ah—"

"Which will be ready in five days, I am well aware of that," Drobna interrupted. "Please, I am sent by Corintus himself. He bids you to come with me and bring what you have with you to him."

"Corintus-ah? Who is Corintus-ah?" asked the woman. "I have-ah never-ah heard of him-ah before-ah."

"Please, the master's daughter is very ill, and you have what she needs," replied Drobna. He then remembered what Corintus had told him. "Oh yes. My master said if you do not believe me then I should tell you about his breakfast. He enjoys alligator meat on a bed of salad and a cold mug of goat's milk, but …" Drobna struggled to remember the rest. It was such a weird message that he had difficulty recalling it precisely. "Let me see: 'That this is the wrong season for alligators and that my master is sighing three times.' Does this mean anything to you?"

Karadon and Hoda's eyes met. "Fine," replied Karadon, dropping the Rastoopian accent. "We will follow you, but at a distance. You will walk ahead of us and will remain in plain sight at all times."

Drobna had thanked them profusely and asked the dwarf child to bring him back to the gate. He glanced back a few times. He could not locate the young couple until he was outside the camp, then he noticed them walking behind him. They joined him on his barge, and two hours later, they stepped inside the palace's garden.

❖✻✻✻❖

Presently, Drobna brought them to the second floor where they stood before Aquilina's door. Drobna knocked and stepped aside. The door opened and they came face-to-face with Amaréya.

"Evening of goodness," said Hoda bowing.

"Evening of roses," replied Corintus who joined his wife by the door. Amaréya watched the curious exchange, pondering its deeper meaning.

"Evening of peace," answered Hoda.

"Evening of friendship," said Corintus.

"May El bless you."

"May El keep you."

"May he grant you long life."

"May he gift you with children."

"May he grant you to see your grandchildren," said Hoda.

"May he grant you to kiss your children's children," replied Corintus.

Hoda gazed at Karadon and nodded. Her husband breathed a sigh of relief. This was indeed their contact. The tall blond man had given Hoda the proper greeting and in the right order. This was a peculiar practice of Ashod's, who loved to use the Finikian greetings as an introductory signal between parties. Finikians had over fifty such greetings, which they used in a sort of friendly competition, heaping salutations and praises on one another until one party drew a blank or gave up. These greetings could be said in any order. But by selecting ten such greetings in a specific order, two parties could confirm they were addressing the right person, whereas a casual passerby would only hear a friendly greeting.

"How did you know where to find us?" asked Karadon.

"When you inquired at the gate, I followed you," replied Corintus, "but first, let me introduce you to my wife, Her Highness Princess Layaléa Amaréya, heiress to the crown of Gordion."

"Please call me Princess Amaréya. Layaléa is my official name."

So shocked were the two Black Robes, they forgot to bow.

"The princess?" whispered Hoda.

"Your Highness," said Karadon, bowing deeply. "We are so very sorry for speaking in your presence the way we did. We did not know."

They removed their cowls.

Amaréya smiled. "You have not done anything to be sorry for. Have you brought the package?"

"A package?" interjected Aquilina, who had been following the exchange with great interest. She perked up. "Is it a present?"

"Aquilina," snapped her father, "stay in bed."

Too late.

The young girl had already jumped out of bed. Resolutely, she walked toward the two strangers, and ignoring Karadon, she went straight to Hoda and looked at her with great intent. Hoda smiled.

"Hello," she said, "I am Hoda."

"What a funny name," said the young girl in a giggle.

"Aquilina, apologize," said her mother. Her voice suffered no protest.

"I am sorry," said Aquilina with a curtsy. "I found your name funny because it is so close to another name I heard Snoring Man say."

"Who is Snoring Man?" asked Corintus suspiciously. *Is she calling me Snoring Man, now?*

"A friend. Sometimes when he sleeps, he speaks a name like yours. That's what's so funny."

Corintus rolled his eyes. *They must be thinking we're terrible parents to allow our child to associate with some random snoring man.*

"What name is that?" asked Hoda. Instinctively, she liked this young girl with a commanding spirit and bright mind. With her long, straight blond hair and brown eyes blazing with the light of spring, she had a natural beauty, simple yet enduring. Even though she wanted Karadon to give Corintus the little package so they would be on their way, she had to admit that she enjoyed this little exchange.

"Doda," replied Aquilina giggling, "isn't it funny?"

Hoda staggered back as if someone had struck her with a dagger. Karadon steadied her. She glanced at him and his stern gaze told her to control herself. *Breathe, Hoda, breathe.*

"Aquilina, mind your language," Amaréya reminded her.

"I'm sorry," said Aquilina with an altered voice. She glanced at her parents. "Did I say something wrong?" She could tell Hoda was reacting as if she had seen a ghost.

"No, you did not, but it is best if you go back to bed now," said Corintus smiling. Amaréya knew the name had distressed and saddened the young woman, but she did not perceive any threat to her daughter.

"Dinner for the little princess," said Martha as she walked in with a silver covered plate. "A dish of praniti, just the way you like it."

Forgetting what had just happened, Aquilina clapped effusively, somersaulted back to bed, and then jumped until she was out of breath. Her father caught her mid-air. Surprised, she stared at him, mouth open, and he pinched her nose.

"Not fair," she exclaimed, "put me down and see if you can catch me again. This time I'll pinch *your* nose."

"Aquilina," called her mother, "your language, please."

Immediately, the young girl quieted down.

"I am sooo hungry." she said. She glanced at Hoda, smiled, and was relieved to see her smile back.

Just then, they heard a gentle knock on the door.

"It's Vily," exclaimed Aquilina, "Come in," she shouted loudly.

"Please forgive our daughter's lack of manners," said Amaréya.

"Not at all," replied Karadon. "She's lively."

The freckle-faced young girl came in running, then, seeing the group of adults in the room, stopped in her tracks and gave a deep bow.

"I am so sorry," she said, glancing at Amaréya. "You have guests …"

"Come over here, Vily," said Aquilina. "Come on, I'm hungry … I mean, I *am* hungry. You can eat with me."

"Great idea," said Corintus, "Why don't we let the two girls eat together, and we can continue this conversation in our apartment? I am certain you have much to tell us about Grandfather."

Is he calling Ashod Grandfather? wondered Karadon. He was about to walk out when Hoda went over to Aquilina and knelt by her bed.

"Are you certain you heard 'Doda'?"

Aquilina looked at her and nodded. "Yes, he said it often in his sleep."

"Do you know his name?"

Aquilina shook her head.

"Why do you call him Snoring Man?"

Aquilina shrugged her shoulders. "He doesn't want to talk to me when I speak to him, so I called him Snoring Man to teach him a lesson."

"Does he snore?"

"I don't know."

Hoda wanted to ask her more questions but knew this was not the time. She smiled a sad, gentle smile and moved a lock of hair from

Aquilina's forehead tucking it behind the young girl's ear. She whispered a quick, "Thank you," then stood up and followed her husband.

"Vily, Aquilina," Corintus said as he was about to close the door, "I want you to eat and to wait for us here."

"Yes, Father," replied Aquilina. "We won't go anywhere. I promise." He gazed at her and she smiled. She loved his deep blue eyes when he smiled at her so. "I promise," she repeated.

He nodded, left the room, and closed the door softly behind him.

>·:·❖·:·<

When Corintus reached his quarters, he found Amaréya, Karadon, and Hoda standing around a table with a small wooden box in the center. A comfortable fire burned gently in a large chimney behind them, warming the cold, humid wind that blew from the north. The box must have been five inches wide and long, and two inches high. Its cover had a slight curvature that gave the box the appearance of a miniature hope chest. Corintus could tell it was made of cheap pine, and overall, the workmanship was simple.

"Is this it?" he asked.

Hoda nodded.

"The box has a keyhole, but it looks flimsy. A thief could smash this box with a hammer or rock."

"Or with a swift blade," said his wife.

Hoda smiled. "Please try," she offered.

The half-Empyrean did not need a second invitation. She went into their bedroom and came back with a long, curved sword in a leather sheath hemmed with silver etchings.

"Beautiful," exclaimed Karadon. "That is one beautiful blade."

Amaréya smiled broadly and handed him the sword. Karadon knew enough about Empyrean culture to understand the meaning of this gesture. Deeply moved, he bowed and received the sword with both hands. He let his fingers run on the handle.

"Amazing," he said. "This blade can be held with one or both hands." He pulled it from its sheath and held it at arm's length. "Beautifully balanced." He twitched his wrist and the blade fluttered. "As if made of liquid steel. I am a great admirer of Empyrean blades. Thank you, Your Highness, for allowing me to examine your sword." He carefully returned it to its sheath, bowed, and presented the sword with both hands.

"Here is a man who knows how to properly hand a sword to an Empyrean," said Amaréya, glancing quickly at her husband. Corintus rolled his eyes. He preferred darts. Amaréya unsheathed the sword, held it with both hands, and in the blink of an eye, brought it down on the box. The blade bounced back as if it had hit diamond.

The box did not move. "I see," said the King's daughter as she inspected her blade. It was not chipped, but she knew she hit a barrier she could not cut through. "This box is deceiving."

"It cannot be broken by normal means," said Hoda picking it up, "Nor can it be burned," she added as she threw the box into the fire. "Water will not affect it either, and no hammer can shatter it." She smiled mischievously and added, "Karadon and I call it Ashod-in-a-box."

"Why?" asked Corintus.

"Because it is as stubborn as he is, that's why," replied Karadon who retrieved the box from the fire with gold tongs. He dropped it gently back on the table.

"So the Black Robes use magic?"

"When necessary," replied Hoda, "After all, we have nothing to lose. The Temple is our sworn enemy, so why not make use of the Temple's weapons to protect ourselves?"

"I see. All right then, where is the key to open this box?"

Karadon and Hoda gave Corintus a confused look. "Ashod did not give us the key. That would have been foolish. All along we assumed you had the key."

It was Corintus' turn to be confused. "Me? How would I have the key? I did not even know you were bringing me this box."

Hoda sighed. "Figures," she said, "this has Ashod all over it. All right then, why don't you start from the beginning and tell us what happened. We may be able to figure out where the key is and what's in this box."

"So you are ignorant of the box's content?" asked the heiress.

Karadon nodded. "We cannot reveal what we do not know." Amaréya and Corintus exchanged a quick glance. "Or we could leave now," offered Karadon. "After all, our mission is to bring this box to you, and we have acquitted ourselves of our duty."

"Please sit," offered Amaréya. "You must spend the night here. I think we have much to learn from each other." The heiress to the throne of Gordion waited for her guests to be seated. "Let us start from the beginning then," said Amaréya. "Our daughter has a special gift the Temple finds dangerous, which is why we turned to Ashod for help. In the eyes of the Temple, we are outlaws, so you share a common fate with us. As such, we must pool our resources and help each other."

"When did you find out about her special abilities?" asked Hoda.

"Six years ago," said Amaréya, "when Aquilina challenged her friends to a knife-wielding game."

Six years ago? The coincidence perturbed Hoda. *This is when Ahiram's medallion betrayed us on the beach.*

"How old was she?" asked Karadon.

"Six years old. She was *six years old*," replied Corintus with great emphasis. "I can't imagine what we would have done if we had had twins."

Seeing Karadon smile his dreamy smile, Hoda felt like kicking him. *Now is not the time to think about babies.* Seeing her scowl, he regained his composure. "And that is when you sought Ashod's assistance?" he asked.

"No. We did not fully understand her special ability back then," explained Corintus. "That happened fairly recently."

"So that's when you decided to seek advice from Ashod?"

"Yes, we need some way to help our daughter control her abilities so she can hide them from the Temple."

"Very wise. A mere suspicion is sufficient for the Temple to act," confirmed Karadon.

Corintus told Karadon and Hoda about his meeting with Ashod, omitting the exchange he had had with his wife before his departure.

◊ ✶ ✶ ✶ ◊

"I will leave tonight and visit Ashod," he had told her. "He is far more learned about these things than we are."

"You mean far more learned about Seers?"

Corintus had nodded. "That, and there may be a connection between Aquilina and the Pit of Fire prophecy."

Amaréya perked up. Corintus had already told her he would be seeking Ashod's help. Repeating an already agreed upon line-of-action was tantamount to telling her he could no longer trust her, but a connection with the prophecy was a new fact. Sharing new facts with an Empyrean was the most common way to honor them.

"You are like a vorlogh, Avinilé, quiet and dispersed in the heat of summer, but deadly and fast like lightning in the depth of winter."

He smiled. A *vorlogh* was a fearsome creature of the Empyrean forests, and *Avinilé*, White Falcon, was her Empyrean nickname for him. Corintus gave her a charming, youthful smile. Involuntarily, she blushed.

"The Empyreans cannot help us," she told him. "They do not have knowledge of this magic."

"Be careful, Amaréya. We should not use this word lightly."

That night, Corintus had left Gordion, traveling southeast until he reached Rastoopa where he took lodging at the Three Pleasant Pheasants and asked for a guided tour of the local swamps. The following day, his guide arrived and they departed for a boat tour of the swamps which were reputed for their alligators. Midway through the trip, Corintus told his guide how he liked alligator meat for breakfast on a bed of salad and a cold mug of goat's milk. His guide responded that this was the wrong season for alligators. Corintus sighed deeply three times. His guide then blindfolded him and they followed a meandering path that led him to the Black Robes' camp. King Domin, the present ruler of Gordion and Amaréya's father, had been a longtime supporter of the Black Robes and Corintus was his representative. Corintus met with Ashod and told him about Aquilina.

"I have never heard of such a place," said Ashod. "This is amazing."

"So, you believe her?"

"I have no reason not to. You said the little one does not lie. She is of an upright character. She has Empyrean blood coursing through her veins and is courageous. She could tell you precisely what she heard, and she suddenly disappeared and reappeared next to you. Given your background as a Silent, I doubt a twelve-year-old could take you by surprise. All of these facts lead me to believe she is sincere, and that this place is real. What did she call it again?"

"Tyrulan."

"The name of a child's game, how fitting."

"What shall we do then? I fear for her and the entire city of Gordion."

"You had better fear for Teshub," corrected Ashod. "The Temple would rather level the entire kingdom than let her survive."

"What shall we do?"

Ashod grabbed Corintus by the shoulder and leaned forward. "You must prepare for exile," he said with his usual measured tone of voice.

"Exile? What? Where? Where would we go?"

"Salem. You must reach Salem before the Temple finds her."

"Salem? Why Salem? What is in Salem?"

"Get there and you will find out. So, she has never met anyone there?"

"In Salem?"

"No, in Tyrulan."

"You're confusing, Ashod, you know that? That is what she told me."

"This would explain why the Temple has never heard of such a place. I wonder if … well, never mind."

"What?"

"Nothing. I need to think about this a bit more."

"Ashod, how shall we explain the disappearance of my wife? She is the heiress to the throne. She—"

"You do not explain," said Ashod abruptly. "You disappear. The kingdom will have to take care of itself. Your wife would never be able to rule, not with your child. Therefore, the good king will have to find another suitable heir. The Temple, no doubt, will offer its services, but it cannot not be helped."

"But the Temple of Baal will—"

"Conclude that Empyreans can never be trusted. The Temple must be convinced that Amaréya crossed over to the Empyreans and that you went with her to stay close to your daughter."

"Is this really happening?" asked Corintus, crestfallen. "I mean, my own father will be so angry to learn that—"

"You shall not say a word to your father. As an Ophirian, your father will simply not understand and will think you a coward. You shall not tell King Domin either. You will wait for me to send two trusted messengers to Gordion. They will bring you a small box and when you open it, you will know how to use its contents to shield your daughter from the searching eyes of Baal. Once my messengers reach you, relay what I have told you and they will realize the extent of their mission. They will help your family evade the Temple until you reach Rastoopa where you will join a large caravan to the Kingdom of Marada. I will alert my contacts among the giants. They will help you reach Salem."

"This is insane, Ashod. I cannot do this to my family. My wife will ascend the throne in a few months. Can you imagine the consequences if she were to suddenly disappear?" Corintus had said, almost pleading.

"No, but I can imagine all too well the consequences if she does not. The Temple will capture your daughter. They will torture her and kill her. They will raze Gordion and destroy Teshub. Baal will take no survivors. This unprovoked act of violence will lead neighboring kingdoms to rebel, sparking a regional war, or worse, a global one. Baal will commit atrocities in an ever-widening circle until it has restored order. The Black Robes will not survive. All of this because a Solitary refuses to listen to reason. Do I have to spell out your choices, Corintus?" Ashod had been resolute.

◆✷✷✷◆

Corintus threw another log into the chimney. The fire protested by fizzing, crackling, and then licking the sides of the log, like a dog lapping the bottom of a bowl. "As crazy as this may sound, my wife and I have been preparing for our departure."

"Amazing," said Hoda. "I can just imagine how hard this must be for you, but as survivors of the Temple's massacre," she added in a low voice, "I can assure you this is the better option."

"Absolutely," concurred Karadon. "You must avoid bloodshed at all cost. The Temple is ruthless… Hoda and I have seen it countless times."

"And they don't stop," added Hoda. "Just four or five weeks ago, the High Riders raised Wrok-Atul…"

"So the rumors are true," said Corintus. "It was hard to believe because Wrok-Atul was one of the High Riders' favorite place."

"They will kill their own kin if ordered," added Karadon. "Keeping the Pit closed is the only thing that truly matters to the Temple. And your daughter would be considered a worse danger than Wrok-Atul."

Corintus sighed. "I knew all this … I guess it is different when you hear it from … those who witnessed the Temple's atrocities first-hand."

Hoda smiled. "We will do whatever in our power to help you, but you must leave as quickly as possible. You are in danger here. The Kingdom is in danger because of you."

Karadon looked at his wife. "Now we have a real mission on our hands. I didn't understand why Ashod asked us to deliver a simple package," he added for the benefit of Corintus and Amaréya. "After hearing your story, it all make sense."

"Your Highness," asked Hoda, perturbed by the Empyrean's lack of reaction, "are you willing to leave everything behind? Are you ready to leave without a word to your parents? Forgive my disbelief," added Hoda, "but this I find hard to believe."

Corintus eyed his wife with a triumphant gaze. *See, I am not the only one who finds it difficult to believe.*

"Empyreans are not so easily troubled by strange turns of events," explained Amaréya. "They think of life as an endless sequence of battles leading them to *véréya*, serenity. I understand the need to disappear. Either I suffer to save many, or sit on the throne and watch the multitude perish. My path is straight. I have no reason to doubt what must be done. The Temple is after our daughter. By running away, we are declaring war on Baal. This war is worth every sacrifice."

"So, I take it you have a plan and are ready to execute it?"

"Yes," confirmed Amaréya eyeing her husband. "Unless Corintus …"

He shook his head. "If you say you are ready, then so am I," he said quietly. The matter was settled. *I won't pretend to understand you, Amaréya, but I will never doubt your resolve.*

"Great," said Karadon. "Now, back to the box and the key …"

Corintus shook his head. "I am baffled. Where could this key be?"

"Did I hear you correctly when you said Ashod touched you when you were speaking with him?" asked Hoda.

"Let me think …" said Corintus. "I walked into his hut, he was sitting there and I was sitting here, then there was tea, we talked …" he fell silent for a short while. "Yes, when he told me I had to go into exile, he placed his right hand on my left shoulder. I don't recall anything else."

"Can I look at the cowl you wore that night?"

"Sure." Corintus walked into his bedroom and came back with a dark blue, full-length cowl with two large pockets. The seam was cut into a red velvet cloth with thick gold stitches, and a large moon crescent with two stars—the emblem of Gordion—was stitched on the right side.

Hoda took a small ring with a lone ruby stone and slid it onto her left index finger and waved her hand over the cloak. A key appeared on the right shoulder, then fell silently onto the carpet.

"Has it been there for the past two months?" asked Corintus.

"Hum ... yes and no. I don't fully understand how this magic works but somehow, Ashod attached this key to your cowl and kept it there until I released it with this ring. I don't understand how the ring works, but Ashod told me to use it in cases such as these."

"Remarkable," said Corintus, but his eyes betrayed his discomfort.

Hoda picked up the key and handed it over to him. Reluctantly, he slid it into the small keyhole. He gasped when the small box vanished, taking the key with it. It was Hoda's turn to gasp when she saw Ahiram's medallion. Ashod had given it to Corintus without telling her. She remembered vividly the day Ahiram had yanked it off when it suddenly became burning hot on his skin. He left in on the shore before hiding in her boat. Hoda picked it up before rushing back to the village to warn her parents of danger, moments before her village was burned to the ground and its inhabitants all murdered. She had kept Ahiram's medallion. A year later, Ashod had asked her of its whereabouts, and when she told him she still had it, he offered to keep it safe for her. "This medallion has powers we do not understand. I have a box that will keep it safe from Baal. Hoda had consented, thinking that Ashod believed her brother to be alive, and he would be keeping it for Ahiram.

"I must ask," she said with an altered voice, "did Ashod mention to you that we would be bringing a special medallion for your daughter?"

"No," replied Corintus. "He told me that when I see the content of the box, I would know what to do with it to keep Aquilina hidden from Baal. I suppose he wants her to wear it?"

Hoda struggled to keep her emotions in check. There was no room left for doubt. *I am certain this little girl has seen Ahiram. How, I don't know, but somehow, they are connected. Ashod is giving her Ahiram's medallion. She has to run away from Baal and she is twelve years old. That's the same age Ahiram was when he had to flee. I must talk to her.*

As if on cue, the door opened and Aquilina barged in with Vily in tow. "Father, we have been waiting a long time. I'm getting sleepy," she said teary-eyed. "You said I should stay awake, but I'm sooo tired, and afraid I will break my promise."

"She told me to slap her if she closed her eyes," said Vily softly. "I don't want to slap her."

"Some friend you are," said Aquilina, pouting. "If I fall asleep, I'll break *my* promise, and I can't do that."

Corintus embraced his daughter and held her close to him. She wrapped her arms around his neck and leaned her head on his shoulder.

"I'm so tired, Father. I want to sleep."

"Look, Aquilina," said Hoda, "We have a gift for you. Do you like it?"

Aquilina lifted her head and saw the medallion Hoda was holding.

"It's nice," she said with a yawn. "But I want you to give it to Vily."

"I don't want it," replied Vily. "I have everything I need."

Aquilina yawned again. "Nobody gives her gifts," she said, glancing quickly at her father and mother. "That's not right. She deserves a gift."

"Aquilina?" interjected her mother.

The young girl sighed. "Fine, Mother. *But that is* not right."

Karadon smiled. He produced a small object from his pocket. "Here," he said, "Please receive this small gift from me. Blow in it."

Vily looked at him with fearful eyes.

Aquilina perked up. Nimbly, she pulled away from her father's embrace and stood by her friend. "Come on, silly, Take it and blow."

Vily shook her head vehemently. Karadon took her hand, placed the object in it and said, "You don't have to worry, Vily. This one comes from Master Kwadil's caravan."

The eyes of the two young girls became as wide as a full moon.

Vily looked at the object in utter disbelief, wanting to blow but still afraid to do so. "Is this true?" she whispered.

"As true as the day is day and the night is night," replied Karadon. "Go ahead, try blowing in it. You'll be happy you did."

Vily looked at her friend who nodded energetically. "Go ahead, Vily, I want to see what it does."

Vily blew. The small object brayed, as if a donkey were in the room. The two girls shrieked in delight.

"Shake it and do it again," said Karadon.

Vily shook the strange object and blew once more. They heard a plaintive meow, as if a kitten were walking by their feet, hungry and lonely. Vily's face brightened and she clasped her hand on her chest while Aquilina jumped and danced around her. Vily looked at Karadon as though he were a heavenly messenger. Unable to contain herself, she gave him a quick peck on the cheek.

"She accepts your gift," said Aquilina in a loud voice. She bowed before him. "Sir Karadon, you are my official hero. I am in your debt."

"Well thank you, Princess Aquilina," replied Karadon, "I shall most certainly call on your services in time of need."

Hoda sat next to Aquilina. "Now, Princess, I would like you to hold my right arm with your left hand."

Aquilina, instead, snuggled close to Hoda. Hoda laughed. "You can sit here, but I need you to hold my right arm with your left hand."

Aquilina did as told. "You are running a fever," exclaimed Hoda.

"True," confirmed Amaréya. "Some Empyrean children run a fever for a few years. Even though our daughter is only one-quarter Empyrean, running a fever is not abnormal for young children of our kin."

"I'm tired," moaned Aquilina. "I want to go to bed."

"Yes, Princess," answered Hoda, turning her attention back to the young girl. "Let us do this little exercise quickly then." Hoda held the medallion in her left hand and presented it to the young girl. "Listen carefully, Aquilina. I want to make sure this medallion will be nice to you. It does have a tendency to behave like a wild dog. It is a bit unpredictable. So I want you to bring your index finger as close as you can to it, but do not touch it. Can you do that?"

Instantly, Aquilina's index finger hovered just a hair's-width above the medallion. The movement was perfect.

"Very good," said Hoda. "Do you feel anything? Any tingling in your toes? Do you hear a high-pitched noise, or feel like sneezing?" Aquilina shook her head. "Very good. Go ahead and now place your index finger on the medallion, but be ready to take it off if you feel any odd sensation." Aquilina felt nothing. She yawned, leaned her head on Hoda's shoulder and gently fell asleep.

"Aquilina is sleeping," whispered Vily.

Hoda touched the girl's forehead. "Her fever is gone," she said with a strangled voice. Unable to contain her tears, she released Aquilina to Amaréya's care and abruptly left the room.

"What is wrong with the lady?" asked Vily. "Did I upset her?"

Amaréya and Corintus looked to Karadon for an explanation. He looked at Vily, winked, and tousled her hair. "It's a long story," he said, smiling. "No, Vily, you did not say anything wrong. This whole thing is bringing back some painful memories for Hoda, but not to worry. She will be her usual self tomorrow."

"Very well," said Corintus. "Drobna will lead you to the guest room."

"Certainly." Karadon bowed. "Good night, Your Highness. Good night, Master Corintus."

After his departure, Corintus brought his daughter to her room and sent Vily back to hers. He sat by his daughter's bed and watched her sleep. He could tell something had changed. Her breathing was steady, and she did not toss and turn as she usually did. For the first time in a long while, Corintus felt like any father would when watching the peaceful sleep of his child, and it moved him to tears.

The door opened and Amaréya walked in. She sat on the side of the bed, facing her husband.

"Our daughter is strong," she said. "No harm shall befall her."

He nodded. "Amaréya, as a Silent, I know what it means to disappear. I know how to live as if I am someone else, but you are an Empyrean and you are royalty. You are used to commanding people. What would you do if I were to give you a direct order? What would you do if, say, a stranger were to insult you?"

"You think my behavior will betray us?"

Corintus nodded. Gone was the playful, carefree man. Her husband had always liked to hide great strength behind a veneer of weakness; a Silent technique apparently. She knew he was now his true self, the one who could defeat her in combat if he set his mind to it.

"What do you think I would do?"

"You would lop his head off without a moment of hesitation, and you know it as well as I do. Do you understand now what it means to disappear?" he added with a pained voice. "It means I will have to take your blades away from you and you will not get to use them again. Ever."

Amaréya blinked. He had just told her he would have to take her honor away and force her to live like a slave. Even less than a slave.

"This is why I thought it would be best if I left with Aquilina," he added softly. "Frankly, I am not certain you can live like that."

She looked at him squarely, placed her hands on his shoulders and said with a firm voice. "I will yield my blades to you, but to no one else, and you shall return them to me when it is the right time. Further, if I place you or our daughter in danger, in any danger whatsoever, I give you permission to kill me with my blades."

Standing up, she left the room.

Corintus sighed. *That's what I was afraid of,* he thought. *Soon, she will realize the greatest battle for an Empyrean is to live without a blade in each hand. To best your enemy with a blade is hard, but to best your will by your own hand is harder still. Now, we shall see of what mettle you are truly made, Amaréya. And may the gods have pity on us.*

15. Tirkalanzibar

> "Do not go to Tirkalanzibar. Under no circumstance, should you set foot in this maddeningly confusing city. Tirkalanzibar is a nightmare hiding behind empty promises, a spider's web pretending to be a haven and a refuge. If you must transit through this accursed city, blindfold your eyes, cover your ears and do not breathe until you are out in the open, away, far away from Tirkalanzibar."
> —**Memoir of Alkiniöm the Traveler.**

While Corintus spoke to Amaréya, Tamri—the soloist who had helped Bahiya save Hiyam during the Games of the Mines—ran as fast as her silver, open-toed heels allowed. Her mistress, Sarand the Soloist, had summoned her into the Arayat.

"I have need of your counsel, daughter, in a matter that cannot wait," she had told her. Tamri ran for she feared her mistress more than the Pit itself. Reaching the main entrance to the Adorants' wing, she sang the "Elikan", and the marble double-door silently opened. Adorants used magic in social settings to control, manipulate, and subdue the minds of men. One of their techniques, known as *arayin*, or transposition, consisted of a quick mental shift from this world to the Arayat world where they called on a specific spell or curse, then switched back. Elikan was one such spell that protected the main door of the Adorants' wing in Babylon. Since arayin spells were weak and limited in range, they were ideally suited for use in social settings and for localized effects such as opening or closing a door. For more potent magic, the Adorant used other ways, which required them to enter the Spell World, and this is where Tamri was headed.

Outside, the Temple of Marduc—as Baal was known in Babylon—blotted the setting sun. *Sarand would not have interrupted our communal meal if this matter was not urgent*, Tamri thought. *Urgent and evil.*

Tamri reached the end of the third balcony, which graced their wing, and stepped onto the stony pathway that ran the length of the inner garden. Across the way, she glimpsed the Meridian Gate as it glittered in the dying light of the day. According to ancient lore, Sureï had set this gate in place as a final defense against the Pit, and there it still stood. Tamri wrapped her scarf around her bare shoulders as Babylon was uncharacteristically cold for a summer night. Shivering, she wished she had time to change from the flowing silk dress into warmer attire. *I will be cold in the Arayat anyway. Nothing can keep me warm there.* An imperious wind whipped her ankles as she passed between two rows of tall statues. High priests stood to the left facing the Adorants to her right, as if each consecutive pair of statues were about to embrace and dance. The base of each priestly statue was cut into black onyx while the statues of the Adorants rested on pink marble stones. A chiseled face lined each dark stone, and in the rays of the setting sun, the faces seemed to be alive, contorted in pain, as if they were caught inside the stone itself. Tamri shivered, *No wonder we call them the Kerta pillars.*

She left the inner garden through the Meridian Gate, and climbed two flights of stairs to a side door and walked into the Temple of Marduc. Two of her sister Adorants stood barefoot with arms outstretched before the altar of Baal, while three *Shogols*, spell herders, performed the ritual of purification. Even though they were in their thirties, they looked much older. *They are deathly pale. They must have spent several weeks in the*

Arayat. I can barely last one day there. Tamri looked across Baal's massive altar and gave a start. A Kerta priest looked at her, his eyes glittering beneath his thick gray cowl. *What is he doing here? Kertas do not worship Marduc.* The sound of her silver shoes on the marble floor suddenly became deafening. *I cannot believe it. That lousy Kerta touched my mind.* She closed her eyes and let out an inner sigh—which could only be heard in the Arayat. The touch disappeared instantly. *He will have a lingering headache. Who does he think he is?*

Directly behind the main altar, an eight-foot-wide, silver plate, cut in the shape of an arched doorway, hung inside a recessed alcove. Smooth as a mirror and cold as death, it absorbed the faint reflection of the candles. Tamri stood in front of it and did not see her reflection either. Taking a deep breath, she sang an inner song, a song that resonated inside the Arayat. The silver plate flashed a bright light and Tamri walked forward, hands outstretched. Her fingers touched the plate and the metal liquefied, turning into a frigid, gray pool. When Tamri walked through the pool, she emerged in the Arayat looking like a sunflower.

"Come hither, daughter."

Obeying her mistress' command, Tamri flew over rolling hills that oozed a thick green substance, then down into a steep yellow canyon covered by a bubbling silver mist. *The spellflow is as thick as syrup tonight. The Shogols must be seeding a new field of curses.* Emerging from the canyon, she felt a stronger tug and crossed a vast plain in minutes. A brilliant speck appeared on the horizon and grew steadily into a fearsome creature. Tamri shuddered. This was Sarand's appearance in the Spell World: a shattered millennial oak as dry as dead bones, fused with the upper iron body of a three-headed dragon. Sarand was the Soloist, the leader of the Adorant and a favored daughter of Baal. A high-ranking servant of Baal taking the form of a three-headed dragon may have led some to suspect Sarand of secretly serving Tanniin, the dragon-god. Still, since no one could control their appearance, no one took umbrage.

The middle head turned in her direction. "So you have come, daughter," it said. The other two heads stayed motionless and gazed at a spot hidden by a ridge.

Tamri wanted to bow, but her sunflower persona performed a pirouette. "Yes, as soon as I heard your summons, Your Ladyship."

The dragon cocked his middle head. "I seek your advice in a troublesome matter, daughter. Follow me."

Inwardly, Tamri shivered. Sarand was not to be trifled with. The Soloist's powers rivaled those of the High Priest Sharr. Endowed with a superior intellect, she was learned, cunning, and remorseless. Sarand was known to relentlessly pursue her goals with the patience of a spider and the strength of a tigress. She was a formidable magician, one who could easily challenge and perhaps overtake Sharr as the head of the entire order of Baal. From her Adorants, she demanded complete submission and blind obedience. She would often muse and call them her butterflies who feed a giant spider, which is how she saw herself; as a spider who brings all into subjugation to Baal, lord of rain and sunshine.

Dutifully, Tamri followed her mistress. *Have we stopped moving?* she wondered after a while. *We are not getting closer to the ridge.*

As if reading her mind, Sarand explained, "I have placed an Elongation Spell to protect this spot. It will take longer to cross. What I will show you is for your eyes only."

An Elongation Spell in the Arayat? Normally, this spell is used against advancing armies to demoralize or fatigue them before they reach the line of battle. Suddenly, Tamri realized the danger she was in. *I will not be able to cross back. Sarand can leave me here to die, or worse, to be slowly absorbed by the Spell World.* She wanted to flee, but Sarand's grip was iron-fisted. Like a butterfly caught inside a net, Tamri was forced to follow. After a long agony, they broke free and crossed over the ridge into a gray plain.

"Gray?" asked Tamri, forgetting her worries. "I have never seen a gray plain in the Arayat."

"The closer to the Pit you are, the lighter the Arayat becomes. Normally, no creature raised outside of the Pit ventures here; it is too dangerous."

Tamri wondered how Sarand knew these things and whether her mistress had gone near the Pit. A wave of terror choked her.

"Look up ahead, daughter, what do you see?"

Tamri inhaled sharply, which led her sunflower representation to perform a few turns.

"Stunning, are they not?" said the dragon's middle head.

Beyond them, thousands upon thousands of Whisper Spells formed a huge, continuously circling tower over a spot Tamri could not yet see. Whenever a Shogol noticed a failed spell, they would starve it to death and let the Arayatian ground reabsorb it. Occasionally, a defective spell would evade detection until harvest time. Destroying a broken, full-grown spell was a dangerous and time-consuming process. Instead, the Shogols moved these useless spells to a deserted corner of the Arayat. Most of these spells would eventually die, but some have taken on a life of their own. A Whisper Spell was a failed spell that looked like a headless bird; these spells came in all sizes and shapes, and were recognizable by the swirl of color along their underbelly and their dark gray wings. Like parrots gone mad, they whispered garbled words without ceasing, as if they were trying to undo the incantation that had brought them into existence. No one knew why these broken things perdured or why they flocked together. Owing to the vastness of the Arayat, the Temple had never bothered with them, considering them inoffensive magic trash.

"I have never seen anything like it," whispered Tamri. "I have seen a flock of Whisper Spells, but never this … gathering. Why are they all here? What is attracting them?"

"Excellent questions," hissed the dragon. "Come and see."

They descended onto the plain, flying below the broken spells. "Do not look up, daughter," snapped Sarand. "In proximity to one another, these broken spells can combine in unexpected and deadly ways."

"They can do that?"

"It is rare, but it can happen. I brought you here out of dire necessity."

Tamri relaxed. *Perhaps, she does not want me dead after all.*

The three-headed dragon looked up and screamed. Tamri winced, for the scream was a modulated, high-pitched screeching sound. Like concentric waves pushing away thousands of small fishing boats, Sarand's scream forced the Whisper Spells to scatter. "That ought to do it," said the dragon in a slur. "Tell me now, what do you make of this?"

Tamri looked down and saw a wide black patch in the gray vastness where a monstrous plant lay. It looked like four palm leaves, each the size of a mountain with edges sharper than the sharpest blade.

"Do not go any lower, but examine this spell. Tell me what you see."

Tamri shuddered. "This spell is not made by human hands. Its roots are throbbing red, which means it is sourced from the depths of the Spell World, beyond mortal reach. A Pit Spell," she whispered. "This spell is the work of the Pit. It has four parts, equally distributed, which means it is universal. Its size shows its strength and the sharp edges are meant to break through a counter-spell. The color tells me it is curse-filled. Its hatred is overwhelming. I do not understand, Your Ladyship. I thought the Pit was closed. Did a creature of the Pit manage to escape?"

The dragon's three heads produced a sharp click. "The Temple has, shall we say, *visitors* from the Pit. It has kept them in the Arayat from before the closing of the Pit. They are held behind a series of curses that Sureï created. Our current leader, in his arrogance and stupidity, has released an urkuun." Tamri stiffened, then nearly panicked. Calling Sharr arrogant and stupid was a declaration of war. *She is going to challenge him soon.* "Do you know what an urkuun is, daughter?"

Tamri needed all her self-control to stay focused. Standing in front of this monster in the Spell World and listening to her mistress speak of the urkuun as nonchalantly as one might speak of a lazy summer day was too much to bear. She struggled to contain her emotions and stay recollected, for Sarand was unforgiving.

The dragon grunted, "An urkuun is a like a scream that all listeners are bound to memorize and imitate. It turns you into a willing copy of itself, as much as your nature allows. The urkuun needs no army. Its staunchest enemies become its willing soldiers."

"Why did Sha—"

"Careful, daughter," snapped the dragon, "do not utter anyone's name in the Arayat. The Spell World can seize on your intent and tag a curse to the name, and it will drain life from you to feed that curse."

Tamri chided herself. She knew this. "My apologies, Your Ladyship; it will not happen again. Why did our leader do this?"

The dragon-oak tree shook under a boisterous laugh. "Because he is a coward. He fears the Seer."

"The Seer? Is he among us?"

Please, enough, thought Tamry. As the dutiful daughter of a high-ranking soldier of Baal, she had joined the Adorants. Her brother was a commander of the High Riders, and her family had been in the military service of Baal for as long as anyone could remember. But this, nothing had prepared her for this.

The dragon grunted. "Yes, he is, but he is not a worthy foe of the urkuun. Most likely, the Seer has no clue how to use the Letters of Power and we could scoop him up the way a tiger snatches a baby lamb. The High Priest of Babylon has gone mad."

"We know how to stop an urkuun, don't we?"

"Our *leader* thinks the four orders of Baal combined can control the beast. He is a fool. Only a spell-storm could overpower an urkuun."

Tamri blanched. "A spell-storm? Thousands upon thousands of spells bound by a curse of anger so strong that once released, it must run its course. It would wipe out—"

"Three or four kingdoms. I know," replied the dragon dismissively. "Now, daughter, focus on this spell. What else do you see?"

Confusion, anger, and bewilderment threatened to cloud Tamri's judgment, but her fear of Sarand overcame all other sentiments and she regained her composure. She inspected the four sides of the spell but nothing came to mind. Tamri knew the cardinal rule of magic: Nothing should be observed unless it comes to mind. She let her gaze glide up and down, waiting for a signal, but quickly abandoned her search. Instead, she focused on the root of the spell. At first she saw only blackness and the feeble, red throbbing light. She was about to move away when something caught her attention. *The light ...* Tamri gasped.

"Excellent, daughter. You saw it then."

"I don't understand. How could this be?"

"What do you think it is?"

"A ... hole in the ... fabric of the Spell World. It is like saying there is a hole in the heavens. This hole, it is like a void sucking away the fabric of the Spell World."

"Very observant, Daughter. There is a hole close to the roots, which the red light hides. Someone inflicted a deadly wound to this spell and pierced the Arayat. In your estimation, could you and the priestess of Baalbek have done this?"

Sarand's question confused Tamri. "Done this? You mean when I helped the High Priestess fend off an attack against her daughter?" At last, Tamri understood why Sarand summoned her to this place. After the Game of Gold, she related to Sarand how she had lent Bahiya a hand. She had relayed the incident to Sarand, who saw it as routine cooperation between a Methodical priestess and an Adorant.

"I do not believe so, Your Ladyship. We were hard-pressed and barely survived the onslaught. No, most certainly not." Tamri carefully avoided pronouncing Bahiya's name. Instead, she called her by the order of priesthood Bahiya belonged to. "The Methodical priestess could not have caused this." Realizing what she had just said, she looked at her mistress. "*She* fought the urkuun?"

The dragon snickered. "Do not commit a man's mistake, my daughter. Their inflated sense of self led them to dismiss a woman simply because she is a woman; as if a bramble would dismiss a pine tree for being a pine tree. The Methodical's priestess strength is buried deep within her soul where she has kept it hidden from sight. She knows the deep things of the Arayat." The three heads nodded, and the middle one grinned a bone-chilling, metallic grin. "You did very well, my daughter. I have underestimated you."

Seeing the glint in the beast's eyes, Tamri shivered. "Thank you, Your Ladyship."

"Indeed, none of us has the wherewithal to destroy a spell of this magnitude, let alone create a hole in the Arayat. But clearly, the urkuun has directed this all-encompassing spell against someone."

"But you just said, Your Ladyship, that no one can withstand the might of the urkuun."

"Unless …"

Tamri saw Sarand look at her with expectant eyes. The Soloist had an answer in mind and she expected her Adorant to know it. "Unless," Tamri continued slowly, "unless the Seer is alive."

"Indeed," said the dragon as she smiled a murderous smile. "Unless she is in our midst."

"*She?*" asked Tamri, confused, "the Methodical priestess?"

"No, daughter, I mean the Seer, the *female* Seer, the one who holds the key to the Pit. You are exhausted, daughter. Let us leave the Arayat for now. I have much thinking to do.

➤ ⁘ ⁘ ⁘ ⁘ ≺

The following morning, a caravan carrying Hayat and Jabbar waited for the High Riders to complete their inspection before admitting them into

Wrath of the Urkuun – Tirkalanzibar

Tirka—short form of *Tirkalanzibar*, City of Caravans. Tirka was set in the eastern foothills of the low Mitanian Chain on a narrow plateau. It overlooked the dusty lowlands of *Uratu*—Kingdom of Caravans. Tirka, the millennial city, stood behind a forty-foot wall, which the High Riders had manned for the past three hundred years.

The city benefited from clement weather and good pasturage. The Aliferaaz River, which took its source sixty miles northwest, became a forty-foot-wide channel by the time it reached the city. The Tirkanians had created specialized barges to ferry the caravaners east to Kapor, the last outpost before the desert. From Kapor, they could follow a safe transit to the Kingdom of Marada. The barges continued south to Sargussal, which offered a shorter but far more dangerous crossing to the land of the giants.

Arfaad, the newly appointed commander of the High Rider division, opened the door to his apartments and stepped outside. Even though the sun was still on the horizon, the air was warm and dry. The raging cacophony rose from the city below and hit him like a fist. Human shouts tried desperately to rise over the braying of camels, like survivors trying to stay afloat on tumultuous waves. He stepped onto the parapet and gazed at the sea of tents, which occupied the interior of Tirka. Apart from the High Riders barracks and the three hundred and fifty large water basins, there was no other building in the city. A chaotic mishmash of colorful tents prevailed. Some were barely large enough for a man and his horse, while others were wide enough for an entire caravan. Tirka was a city without streets and a city without rest; a place where caravans came and left all hours of the day and night.

"Amazing, isn't it?" asked Omead.

"Amazing indeed," replied Arfaad, impressed.

"Remind me, how long have you been here?"

"A week."

"Ah yes. I'll be leaving tonight, so all of this will be yours to command.

I have not briefed you on your duties, have I now?"

Arfaad glanced at Omead, the commander he was replacing. Omead was tall, with a full head of white hair and a trimmed mustache. The Temple had picked him to lead the diplomatic mission to Tanniin, and he was well suited for his next assignment. *A man who can govern Tirka can govern anything*, thought Arfaad. "How many tents are there in Tirka?" he asked for no specific reason.

Omead chuckled. "That was the first question I asked when I arrived here. I never could get a straight answer. You may as well ask how many waves, or how many dunes. As the locals say, 'Tirkalanzibar barzibar toh barzibar Tirkalanzibar.' Loosely translated, it means, Tirka is change, and change is Tirka. This is a city of caravaners; it has no equal. On any day, you'll have over ten thousand tents, fifty thousand souls, another fifty thousand slaves, and five to ten thousand camels."

"How many caravans a day?"

"Factual, I see. No worries, Tirka will wear that out of you the way a rope smooths an oak tree. Close to fifty caravans come into the city each day and about the same leave as well."

"How do they move in and out?"

With his chin, Omead pointed toward eleven gates. "The central gate is reserved for the High Riders. The five gates to the right are for caravans moving in, and the other five are for caravans moving out."

"Security?"

"Lax, I'm afraid. As long as a caravan pays its dues when it arrives, and as long as they keep the peace, we leave them alone. After all, no sense in disturbing the golden geese, now is there?"

Arfaad caught the bitterness in Omead's voice but chose to ignore it. *A soldier's wounds and shadows are his own, unless they interfere with his job.* Arfaad thought about his own wounds and shuddered.

"Anything else I should know?"

Omead slid a bony finger down his collar, trying to ease the pressure of his trimmed uniform. "Oh, look there, that's one of them."

A camel had escaped from one of the enclosures specially designed for the care of the animals. It ran gracefully, braying as it went, causing pandemonium. The camels nearby became agitated and brayed as well. Their voices were now deafening.

"They should have called this city *Arikinkaja'ar*, for it is a braying city of camels," shouted Omead over the din. Arfaad smiled briefly. Dust blocked his view and he could barely follow the action between the tents. "It's a real maze down there."

"Which is why you do not enter the city without a significant show of force. Caravaners are not regular folks. They're used to defending their own. Some are cutthroat assassins who have no regard for the law. This city teems with killer-for-hires, bodyguards, spies, wailing women for a wage, poison suppliers, and all the rest. There are even renegade priests from the Temple who sell their magic to the highest bidders. Caravaners seldom call on the Temple for justice. They have their own courts, and you would do well to leave them alone."

"It seems they have subdued the animal," said Arfaad evenly. He was not certain if the last thing Omead had told him was friendly advice or a direct threat.

Omead scoffed. "A camel is no slave to be subdued. These people have more respect for a camel than you and I have for a horse. See that large, colorful tent in the center with the bright oriflammes?" Arfaad nodded. "That's your other trouble right there. That tent is Cahloon's, and no one, I mean *no one*, will ever tell her what to do. Don't even try."

"Who is Cahloon?"

"You'll find out soon enough. Listen," he added with a tired voice, "this place can be a gold mine for your career. Set your pride aside, act as a good caretaker, and levy a bit more taxes than the Temple expects. Then, in about four to five years, you'll be promoted. You'll become emissary for the Temple. You will live the life of kings. But if you step inside that hellhole, if you let your curiosity get the better of you and you start to meddle with the Pit-spewed rubble and filth below, you will wish a Kerta priest had come to take you into the depths of the earth—"

"Do not say that," snapped Arfaad, livid.

Omead gazed at him and smiled sadly. "I should have known." His voice was soft now, almost friendly. "Ah, a High Rider's nightmares are his constant companions." He sighed. "I'll be leaving by the end of the day. I guess you and I won't be seeing much of each other, and that's a good thing." He grabbed Arfaad's arm and looked him in the eye, "Whatever you do," he hissed, "do not go down there."

"Why?" snapped Arfaad? "What's worse than the nightmares?"

Omead laughed a soft bitter laugh. "The sweet sound of a lullaby that promises to take your nightmares away. Do you understand? Down there, Cahloon, she'll take your nightmares—"

"She will?"

Omead shrugged. "I guess sooner or later you would have found out. The Nephral take it all! I hate this place, I can't stand it anymore. I wish I could burn it all up. But we can't touch the golden geese, now can we? Yes, we can. For a price." He eyed Arfaad with the severity of a teacher. "You will lose your sanity, your sense of direction. You will reveal to her every secret of your heart, and she will take the nightmares away, sure enough, so you will keep coming back for more and more." His voice was a quiver now. "And then, one day, you'll wake up and realize the nightmares are gone but so is your soul. You're a walking shadow, an empty smile, a shell." He bowed his head and chuckled silently. "I miss them, you know?"

"What?"

"The nightmares. I miss the nightmares."

Arfaad closed his eyes. He could still see Baher-Ghafé burning in the early dawn. Six years ago, he did not think twice when he received the order to raze the town. He was a High Rider, a captain, and a good soldier. An order was given, an order was executed. The high priestess had praised his swift action and he had been promoted by the Temple, who sent him to Bragafâr, a beautiful city by the sea, indolent and as quiet as the breeze that quelled the heat. The two divisions he commanded had spent most of their days in training, for nothing ever happened in Bragafâr. Two years ago, the nightmares began. Rare at first, they became more and more frequent until they filled his nights. Baher-Ghafé was on fire, and he could hear the dirt crunch beneath his boots. The sound was loud and strident. He walked with his bloodied sword in his hand, unaffected by the smoke and flames. All around, villagers were killed by fleeting shadows of soldiers. One by one their voices were silenced, until at last, only the fire, the purifying fire, could be heard. Invariably, he would stop in the center of the burning town. There, in the middle of a high fiery wall, in the bright incandescent light of the flames, Hoda's head would sprout from the tip of his sword. Only her head. She would look at him sweetly and whisper "Arfaad, will you marry me?"

For two years now, this nightmare had filled his nights, turning his mat into a bed of torment, his rest into an exhausting wrestle with shadows. At first, he thought the nightmares were his punishment for lying to Bahiya. She had asked him if he had killed everyone in Baher-Ghafé and he had lied to her. Hoda's home was empty, and so he knew they had escaped.

While still in beautiful Bragafâr, the relentless onslaught of the nightmares took its toll on his mind. He started hearing voices and seeing the faces of his dead victims. Having seen these symptoms in other soldiers, he knew all too well where this path would lead: to despair, then, a muted loneliness enclosed in cold stone, then darkness filled with the howling screams of regret. Then the unfettered madness before the loss of all hope, the deepest form of despair, where the Kerta priests would find him. Hundreds of camels braying savagely brought him back to the present. He gripped the parapet, scrapping his fingers hard, trying to drown his regret with pain. He wished with the intensity of a thousand stars that Hoda were still alive. How he wished she had survived, for then, he could find her, kill her, and perhaps his nightmare would end. He laughed bitterly for he knew this could not be. There were no survivors in Baher-Ghafé. They were all dead.

Ahiram's father, was bewildered and amazed as he overlooked the sea of travelers with their burden-laden camels. "Look at all this," Jabbar whispered, "Incredible."

His wife, Hayat, who was seated on one of the camels, arched her neck to get a glimpse of the front of the caravan. She could see two High Riders in animated discussion with Kwadil's master caravaner, a shrewd dwarf who knew his business. "I hope they won't keep us waiting too long. I'm exhausted. Riding a camel is not as easy as I thought."

Jabbar smiled. Ever since they left the refugee camp at Kirk and crossed the sixty miles down to Tirka, Jabbar's mood had been steadily improving. They both felt like prisoners who had suddenly recovered their freedom. She was surprised by his desire to leave as soon as possible.

"Don't you want to say goodbye to Hoda?" she had asked him.

"No. If we wait and see her again, I may not have the courage to leave," he explained. "Besides, we don't know when she will be back, and we're just leaving on a mission."

Still, she wished she could have spoken with her daughter before leaving, but Ashod had prevailed.

"Good, good. This is very good. He wants to go, and there is a caravan leaving in two days. Don't worry, Hayat," Ashod had assured her, "After you have spoken to Lord Lonthi, ask him to show you the surpassing beauty of the moon, and he will show you your daughter."

Hayat had not asked Ashod what he meant, for she knew he would not tell her. Still, his words gave her comfort. Ashod was often obscure and confusing, but he always meant what he said.

I wouldn't mind that, she thought with a slight quiver of anticipation, *I wouldn't mind seeing my daughter again.*

A long trumpet blast jolted her. "We're going in," said Jabbar with excitement. "What a city. What a city."

The master caravaner gave the signal and beasts and men began to move. Within a short moment Tirka swallowed the caravan like a hungry beast swallows a herd in one gulp.

>·:·:·:·<

Standing by the door of his hut, Ashod enjoyed a moment of peace. The refugee camp was quieter than usual, a peaceful lull that crickets and toads had decided to respect. *The quiet before the storm*, thought the former priest of Baal. Eyes closed, he smiled as a westerly crisp, clean wind blew gently through the woods. His heart was in turmoil and his mind reeled from the difficult choice he had made earlier, but he would not let it steal away the peace and quiet of this scene. *These moments are all I have these days. Everything else is sweat, toil, and pain.*

▷✵✵✵◁

Earlier that day, he had received a summons from Sarand.

"How is my favorite priest of Baal doing?" she had cooed. Even in the hazy reflection of the dark orb, Sarand's charm was overwhelming. Early in his career, Ashod had discovered, quiet accidentally, that fasting was a powerful defense against the wiles of the Adorants, and he had stuck to a severe regimen. He looked at her and smiled. She blew him a pouty kiss and began to play negligently with her long necklace. He kept his eyes firmly locked on hers.

"What can I do for Her Ladyship?" he asked. As a member of the Inner Circle, he was Sarand's equal, but mollifying the Soloist was more important than his rank and honor.

"Now, here is my Ashod," she cooed like a tigress. "I have been protecting you from Sharr's searching eyes. He has not managed to locate your camp, has he now?"

He shook his head. "No, Your Ladyship. Thank you for your protection, it means much to me."

Her smile widened. "Anything for my favorite priest. You know how jealous I am of the Black Robes. They keep you away from me. When will you be visiting me in Babylon?" she implored. "I miss you," she added seductively. "Come to me, Ashod. I want you by my side." So powerful was the allure of her voice, it could lead men into lunacy and even kill one another for her sake. Ashod felt a powerful urge to get up and leave; to run to Babylon and throw himself into Sarand's embrace.

"I wish I could be by your side." His voice cracked and his mouth became dry. "Unfortunately, it will have to wait a little longer."

"I do wonder what keeps you away from me," she added. "One of these days, I will come to you disguised as a refugee. I shall want you to take care of me personally."

"But of course, Your Ladyship. This camp could—"

"Now, *Shoshod*," she cut in, "I need a small favor of you."

His face remained impassible even though he hated that nickname. "Yes, Your Ladyship, anything."

"You know the Seer is among us."

He decided to tell the truth. Properly lying to an Adorant required preparation, and he was tired.

"As I understand it, he is in Tanniin."

"Yes, yes, I am not talking about him. I am asking you if you know that *she* is among us."

"Since the Seers come in pairs, I would say that I am not surprised. But no, I did not—"

"She broke a curse. The curse of the urkuun."

"So it is true then," he sighed. "Sharr did unleash the urkuun."

"You do not have to worry about Sharr, my love. My coalition is growing. Soon he will be howling in the Arayat next to a field of curses I have prepared just for him."

Ashod shuddered. "How may I help Your Ladyship?"

"Her name. Her name, Ashod. You are the greatest seeker the Temple has ever known, perhaps even greater than Sureï." Sarand's voice was implacable. "I need you to find me her name."

"Yes, Your Ladyship, I am at your—"

"Now, Ashod. Right now. She defeated a spell from the urkuun. We cannot wait. Now. Do it now!"

Ashod smiled a slow, gentle, reassuring smile.

"Your Ladyship need not worry, I was about to say I am at your service. I believe I know who she is."

Sarand furrowed her brow and gazed at him with murderous eyes. "Do you mean to tell me you knew all along?"

Ashod chuckled and gave Sarand his most dazzling smile.

"Why would I do such a thing, Your Ladyship? I am your humble servant. Based on the information you have provided me, I arrived at a conclusion. May I share my thoughts with Her Ladyship?"

"Proceed." Her tone was calmer but still on edge.

"The Seers come in pairs, always. In the *Teaching of Oreg*, it is said that the male and female seers are destined to find each other and fall in love. We know where the male is, and you just told me the female has fought the urkuun, so—"

"She is in Tanniin then."

"Precisely. And," he added with a confident smile, "my sources tell me that Lord Orgond's daughter is in love with the Seer."

"Lord Orgond? Who is he?"

"He governs the northern realm of Tanniin, and his wife was an Empyrean who died while giving birth to their only child."

He watched as Sarand's expression went from gloom to elation. "And Sureï asserted that the female Seer will always be of Empyrean lineage. Are you certain she is in love with him?"

"This is a well-known fact. She has been in love with him for the past five years."

"Five years. It fits. It all fits together. Her name?"

"Noraldeen."

"What a pretty name," cooed Sarand. "Very well, Shoshod, you have earned the peace of your Black Robes for another year."

"Is there anything else I can do for Your Ladyship?"

"You have helped me well enough, Shoshod. Once I dispose of the girl, the male Seer will fall into despair. You will bring him to me and get rid of that Black Robe trash you have been using as your cover." She purred mischievously, "I can hardly wait to have you by my side." Sarand blew him a sulfurous kiss before dropping from sight.

◁✳✶✶▷

The wind raged stronger than before. Eyes closed, Ashod stood in the wind, savoring the moment. *How did Corintus' daughter cross paths with the urkuun, I wonder. To protect her, I have condemned an innocent young woman to death.*

He pondered the situation a little longer. *Did I do the right thing? My master believes that if Ahiram and Noraldeen are in love, her death will certainly leave him hopeless, and we cannot have that.* Immediately, a plan formed in his mind. *He must find out that his sister is alive. This will give him hope and will bring him to me. I will see to it.*

Ashod sighed. *Must we always toy with people's lives like children with their dolls?* He tightened his jaw. *I have promised I will keep the two Seers safe and I will keep my promise, no matter the cost.*

He pulled a hood over his head, and with his hands behind his back, disappeared into the woods. He walked like a man hunched under a heavy burden; the burden of a choice he had just made.

Night fell. Hoda, with her heart in turmoil, could not sleep. She kept pacing back and forth while Karadon slept peacefully. *At least the carpet is thick enough to muffle my footsteps. One of us is getting some sleep tonight.* She found it difficult to concentrate on any one idea, instead she bounced back and forth between bits of sentences she had heard today: "Doda", "She has a fever", and "Her fever is gone".

Hoda felt queasy yet hopeful. And that sense of hope angered her. She felt betrayed by Ashod who had given away her brother's medallion without asking. She felt she had betrayed Ahiram again by allowing this to happen. Still, the way Aquilina said "Doda" led Hoda to believe that Ahiram was still alive. *Aquilina may know where he is and may be able to reach him.* She stopped in her tracks. *Careful, Hoda, careful. You will lose your sanity if you think this way.* She looked out the window as if the night were about to part and reveal her brother to her. *Perhaps,* she countered, *but I cannot believe these are mere coincidences.*

"Hey," said Karadon, "I think you've scrubbed the carpet clean on this side of the bed. You may want to scrub it on the other side."

She sighed and sat down beside her husband.

"I know," he said with a sleepy voice. "You can't stop thinking about it and you can't draw a conclusion, but we will be traveling with Aquilina and who knows what the conversations may uncover along the way."

Hoda smiled and heaved a deep sigh.

"You're right, my love. I've become so focused on what I heard today I nearly forgot that there will be a tomorrow. Nothing is lost then."

"Come to bed. We have a long day ahead of us. The dangerous part of this mission is about to begin.

Middle Road

༺༻

Part Three

16. Magdala

> "The Silent shall not tempt the gods. No one has entered the Forest of Magdala and survived. The Silent shall avoid Magdala at all cost."
> —The Book of Siril 7:5.

> "I stood at the rim of Magdala and wondered what secrets it harbored. The locals have so many superstitions related to Magdala that if I were to tell them all, they would fill many volumes. As I peered through the tall trees, in the stillness of the shadows, I, unlike so many others-including the great Oreg-felt that Magdala was not accursed. As extraordinary as this may sound, I felt that the forest was hallowed."
> —Introduction to the Book of Knowledge, Ussamia the Togofalkian.

A shadow chased Ahiram along a narrow bridge that ended abruptly over a burning abyss. He was lost, frightened, and searched frantically for an escape route. Below, the flames of the deep roared. The shadow drew closer, covering the Silent's field of vision. Eyes wide open, Ahiram faced the advancing terror. A soundless scream escaped his lips as he fell to his doom. *I am dreaming*, thought Noraldeen. *This is just a dream.* The dark terror stood over the abyss, and its searching gaze rested on her. She recoiled in fear, and the scene abruptly switched to a peaceful meadow where Noraldeen found herself standing in front of a monolithic gate hinged into a circular hulking wall of black stones. Made of steel, the gate was set in a tri-foiled, cusped stone arch that stood sixteen feet high and six feet wide. A garland of lilies and amaranth, carved into a coralline backdrop, ran along the triple-arch molding. A single etched rose set between four rubies covered the seamless face of the gate.

"Welcome, daughter. I have been expecting you."

The gate faded like a wisp of fog, revealing a woman dressed in dazzling colors. Her face was ageless; young and regal. Filled with compassion, her green eyes bristled with power.

"Walk with me, daughter," invited the woman. Inside the circular wall stood a tower made of the purest white alabaster. *How did they build such a high tower?* Noraldeen knew enough about rocks to appreciate the incredible feat accomplished with such a weak stone.

As they drew closer, the Silent saw alcoves carved inside of the thick wall. They housed the statues of winged men and women standing with arms extended forward in warning. The effigies were cut into dark dull steel that the sunrays streaked with a bright blue light. Under the constant brisk motion, the statues looked alive, ready to spring into action to defend the tower.

Meyroon! Noraldeen was astounded. *Every one of these statues is made of meyroon.*

Between the alcoves, arched windows framed by green limestone shimmered in the light. Behind the alcoves, from somewhere within the tower, Noraldeen heard a choir sing a melody that filled her with a deep longing for a day of unending peace. She breathed deeply and arched her head back to glimpse the tower's pinnacle where four giant horns soared like the extended wings of eagles.

"You stand in the garden of Tessarah, the Unseen Tower, the last unvarnished remnant of Silbarâd the Fair," said the woman.

Thinking she may have heard wrong, Noraldeen confirmed, "Silbarâd the Fair? The city of legends built before the Age of the Temple by the Lords of Light?"

"You have learned your history well, daughter."

"Tessarah, the Unseen Tower did not fall," continued Noraldeen, feeling suddenly dizzy. "This tower was built in the center of Silbarâd, and from within its walls Eleeje, the fountain of life, flowed." Disbelieving what was coming out of her mouth, she continued, "When Silbarâd fell, the steward of the Tower remained faithful until the last." She looked at her companion and her heart skipped a few beats. "The steward is …" she stammered, "the Lady of El …" Realizing with whom she was speaking, Noraldeen fell to her knees. "Forgive me, My Lady, but how can this be? How can I be in the presence of the Lady of Eleeje?"

"Rise, Noraldeen, daughter of Orgond. I called you to me the day you had pity on a lonely slave," replied the lady. "The shadow that invaded your dream before I brought you here is an Urkuun of the Ninth Order, a being of the Pit whom I fought over two thousand years ago." She produced a thin staff of pure sapphire and held it over Noraldeen's heart. "Be strengthened Noraldeen and do not fear him. The one you love is coming, and the balance of power will rest in your hands. The day of restoration is drawing near. The broken covenant shall be mended. I have made my presence known to you because you love selflessly, and selfless love is the essence of Eleeje. Take courage, daughter, your longing for a day of peace shall be answered soon." A tinge of sadness troubled the woman's gaze. "But," she continued, "a peace not according to your heart's desire. Take heart and be strong. I shall call for you, and I will show you what must be accomplished."

Noraldeen bowed and as she straightened her posture, her vision blurred. As darkness was about to hide the tower and the lady from view, the Silent saw the mysterious woman smile, and that smile led her to a peaceful lake bristling with hope, and she woke up. *This is the fourth time I have seen this monster in my dreams, but today, I do not fear him.* Her heart was serene, her mind peaceful and content. *The Lady of Eleeje,* she thought. *Can this be true?* The quiet strength animating her spirit told her that it was. *The Lady of Eleeje.* She recalled the lady touching her heart with a shimmering staff and the light flashed in her mind once more. *I do not fear you any longer. I am ready for you.*

A soft breeze gently tugged at the drapes covering the large windows. She threw the covers off the bed, rose to her feet and stepped onto the large balcony overlooking Iliand, the vast northern valley of Tanniin. The fertile plain of Iliand ran east to west, from the foot of the Karian Chain to the Mayorian Chain and functioned as the cellar of the kingdom. The northern territories of Tanniin were prosperous despite many wars. To the west, Togofalk bounded Iliand, Thermodon to the north, and the Empyreans to the east. Togofalk and Thermodon had tried to invade Iliand several times, but each time, the forces of Tanniin repelled them. The Empyreans were a different matter. Twice they invaded Tanniin, and twice they ruled the land. However, the Tanniinites were tenacious folks who could endure hardships when freedom was at stake. They waged a one-hundred-year war of attrition against the Empyreans and won their freedom back.

Shortly after the second Empyrean invasion, King Saliniir II commissioned the building of Amsheet and Hardeen, the two great fortresses of the North. They were completed under the reign of his great-great-grandson, King Namiir XII, one hundred and four years later. Amsheet guarded the western gate of the kingdom against Togofalk, and Hardeen guarded the eastern gate against the Empyreans. Both fortresses ran deep into the mountain and benefited from high, fortified walls. Amsheet protected the Karian Chain, and Hardeen protected the Mayorian Chain. The two fortresses served as powerful outposts for the kingdom. Namiir XIII, successor to Namiir XII, planned a third fortress to protect the northern road to Thermodon, right where the Somarian Chain met the Mayorian. However, he died before he could start the project, and his son, Namiir XIV, was too frivolous to carry the plan forward.

Noraldeen lingered on the balcony. She loved to feel the air blow against her face in the dead of night. Closing her eyes, she remembered the evening when Ahiram and she had parted. The startling light they had seen, the furtive kiss, the goodbye. *Ahiram, Ahiram, are you in the land of the living, or have you left us to be among the dead? My heart longs to see you and to behold your gentle smile. Where are you, my love? Have the days treated you well? Did you survive the Games, or have you been left to die in some dark corridor of the mines?*

Directly across the great northern plain, deep in the bowels of Hardeen, the twin fortress of Amsheet, the urkuun stood behind a wide pool filled with a strange red liquid. The creature was nine feet tall with shoulders to match a giant and fists made to break stone and skulls. His wings had a span of thirty feet and were made of a thin, retractable membrane that no steel could cut. The urkuun's eyes were completely white with no eyelids and they were filled with a blazing fire where an intelligent, evil malice brooded. He walked bare foot and his claws raked the ground in a steely strident screech. A green breastplate of dragon scales protected his torso, and he carried a tall sword exuding a dull gray fume. Standing by the pit, he watched the unending stream of men, women, dwarfs, and empyreans who had answered his call of seduction. From the fortress of Hardeen, he had cast his net into the Empyrean realm and as far south as Taniir-the-Strong. He did not have to coerce or threaten, nor force or enslave through violence. He whispered, and his words, like an invisible poison, oozed through the walls and carried forth into the air where they licked the minds of his victims. Anyone who had made ambition their consolation, greed their driving force, gold their purpose, answered his call. ==He was the ninth urkuun, known as the Seducer, the one who amplified and nurtured every selfish and heartless desire of man==. He fanned them, cultivated them until they broke their owner's will. Then he made them surrender to the comforting song of the urkuun, the song that promised them everything their hearts desired but turned them into his willing and faithful slaves.

Being a creature of the Pit, the urkuun had access to every curse and spell the Arayat offered. Using his powers he created this liquid portal into the Spell Word. As his willing servants entered the pool, they stepped into the spellflow he had diverted from the Shogols in a spot where a monstrous Whisper Spell storm raged. As soon as a willing victim—be it a human, an Empyrean or a dwarf—stepped inside that pool, their skin sucked in the spells of seduction from every pore. The victims yielded their will to the urkuun, wanting to be made into his image. If the urkuun had relied on the spellflow alone, his victims would have required repeated immersions into the pool for weeks, if not months, before the transformation was complete. But the storm of Whisper Spell transformed the other spells into a raging magical fire. By the time those who had entered the pool left it, they were turned into uncanny monsters, images of the urkuun, bony, gray creatures, wheezing sounds resembling the sound "sylveed."

The urkuun knew that this acceleration had unintended effects: It sapped his victims from their strength, reducing their lifespan to mere months. In addition, it allowed the Arayat to seep into the neighboring rock, rotting it to its core. He knew that this second effect would not be localized, but wherever the Arayat had found a way to seep into the real world, even for a brief moment, the rocks in these spots would rot and decay as well.

He moved his right foot forward and winced under the pain. Things had not gone entirely as he intended. *This Seer is surprisingly stronger than*

I expected, he thought. Recently, he had seen, in an Arayatian vision, the face of the female Seer. She was a young woman living across from the great plain, in the fortress of Amsheet. Earlier today, he had invaded her dreams for the fourth time, showing her, once more, the death of her beloved. He used these nightmares to expose hidden vices, faults within her character he might be able to exploit. But today, she threw him out, confirming in his mind that she was the female Seer. Despite all his cunning, the urkuun did not sense the presence of the Lady of Eleeje and attributed the counter-attack that threw him out of Noraldeen's mind to the Silent herself.

Unaware that Tyrulan existed, he also attributed to Noraldeen the wounds Aquilina had inflicted on him. Unwittingly, Corintus' daughter had curtailed his influence, preventing him from raising an army twice the size of the one he had mustered. She had weakened him sufficiently so that he was no longer able to simultaneously attack Ahiram's mind and devote his energies to the building of his army. *No matter*, he thought, *I will crush her soon enough and I will turn the male seer into a willing slave. He shall open the Pit for me.* He bared his lips into a blood-curdling smile. A few months was all he needed to kill the Seer, and once his foe was dead, he would take the time to mount an army; an army whose shadow would blot out the light of day, an army so vast, nothing would stand in its way. He would then destroy Babylon and reign over its rubble. Setting his piercing gaze on the Fortress of Amsheet, he saw Noraldeen standing on her balcony. He let out a domineering roar. The Sylveeds around him groveled in fear. The beast from the pit sneered.

He was the Urkuun of the Ninth Order, the Seducer.

≻ ⁘ ≺

"Awake I see, my daughter."

Noraldeen smiled. Her father stepped onto the balcony and stood by her side. He surveyed the valley the way a general of an army would survey a field of battle. *A man of rectitude and courage, that's how the folks of Tanniin describe my father.* He governed the city of Amsheet, and his people loved him. He was renowned for his sense of justice and the care with which he managed the affairs of the bustling city at the edge of the turbulent western Kingdom of Togofalk. Many Togofalkians crossed the border daily to work in Amsheet. Similarly, Togofalkians employed Tanniinites in the adjoining port of Prat and the inner fortress city of Lionides. Incidents erupted on either side of the border where locals would threaten the migrants, and Orgond was often involved in thorny negotiations to prevent bloodshed.

To mend the bruised relationship between the two kingdoms, Amsheet had agreed to host The Carnival of Jaguar-Night; the annual celebration of the main Togofalkian deity. In return, Prat and Lionides would celebrate the Carnival of Tanniin. The city of Tanniin prepared a grandiose celebration in honor of Jaguar-Night, which was to open with the procession of his statue. The date was set for the tenth of Shubat, in twelve days time. Yet tonight, Orgond's mind was far removed from festivities.

"What is the matter, Father?" asked Noraldeen.

"The inner wall has crumbled."

"For the third time? I thought the dwarfs took care of this problem."

"So they said. Yet tonight they confessed their inability to remedy the situation."

"What is the solution then?"

"A delegation left a week ago to escort Master Xurgon here from Taniir-On-High. His knowledge of stone is without compare among dwarfs. Yet the road from the east has grown increasingly dangerous. I fear he may not make it here safely."

Noraldeen's heart beat faster.

"You have only to ask," the young woman offered with a note of hope, "and I will lead a small force to assure his safe passage."

Her father looked at her quizzically and then laughed slowly, as if she had told him a good story. "You have not changed your mind, have you, daughter? Even though Braird Mistlefoot is witty, charming, and of noble birth, you sent him away as though he were a sultry miscreant—"

"Father, I did no such thing. He left of his own accord when I refused to dance with him."

"You may just as well have slapped his face."

"But he hates dancing. He told me so himself."

"Which has nothing to do with propriety or protocol. He asked you to dance at the bidding of his father; you should have accepted this as an act befitting the daughter of the House of Orgond."

Noraldeen gripped the parapet and tightened her jaw. Her father looked away. He did not wish to trouble her with the additional bad news he had received. His spies from the northern Kingdom of Thermodon had told him that Lord Derek Mistlefoot, Braird's father, overstayed his presence in Orlan, the capital. *Bar-Tanic is seeking an alliance with Thermodon to attack Tanniin. I need to know why, and when.*

He leaned against the stone rail and watched his daughter closely. "I underestimated this slave of yours. What is so exceptional about him?"

Noraldeen's face lit up instantly. "Oh Father, I wish you could meet him, you would understand right away," replied Noraldeen, her eyes brimming with joy. "He is handsome, brave, gentle, and strong. He is much like you, Father. He is quiet and kind. And he is patient, although he sometimes has a bad temper that he cannot control well. He is not pretentious, and he is so natural in his ways."

"And he is a slave," interrupted her father gently. He raised his hand to prevent any further discussion. "My daughter will not marry a slave. He must be free to contend for your hand."

"The Temple cheated during the Games," replied Noraldeen, hardly controlling her anger. "How do you expect him to win?"

"Not the Games," whispered her father in a somber tone.

"Then what?" asked Noraldeen impatiently, not noticing the slight change in her father's voice.

Omitting the second bad news, he moved to the third. "I have received disturbing news from Hardeen. Peasants have left their villages, and they speak of terror and darkness. Though peasants are inclined to believe a rumor as truth, the concordant reports I have received lead me to conclude that something is amiss in Hardeen."

Noraldeen shivered. "How does this concern Ahiram?"

"Daughter, you amaze me. The fate of this young man leads you to ignore the plight of our people. Many of them have lost loved ones and abandoned their homes."

"I am sorry, Father."

"In any event, I sense a great battle is forthcoming, one that will require forces beyond our limited strength." *We will not survive a double assault from the mysterious power in Hardeen and the combined armies of Thermodon and Bar-Tanic.* He forced himself to smile. "If your friend takes part in this battle and distinguishes himself by his courage and deeds, I will set him free."

"Is that true?" asked Noraldeen, barely able to contain herself. "You would set him free?"

"Yes. Go back to sleep now. We have a long day ahead of us."

Noraldeen kissed her father and returned to her room, followed by the tender gaze of her father. She slipped under the covers and smiled as she fell asleep, a sleep that was long in coming.

➤ ✦✦✦ ≺

Three hundred miles south of Amsheet, at the southernmost edge of Magdala—also known as the Forbidden Forest—a group of riders stood still. They waited for Master Habael's signal. When it finally came, they dismounted with a sigh of relief, and spoke with hushed voices.

"Care for the horses," ordered Commander Tanios. "Form camp. I want six Silent on the first watch. Protect the Priestess."

The rain finally stopped. The Silent set up camp quickly at the edge of the valley facing Magdala. They huddled in small groups around pit fires to keep warm. Commander Tanios did a mental review of the remaining portion of their journey. They were near Middle Road, which ran the length of Tanniin from its northern plain to its southern ports. It was scrupulously maintained against the constant encroaching of Laymiir and Magdala, the two forests that hemmed it from the east and the west. Once on the road, they would head toward Iliand, the great northern plain, until they reach a three-way fork: west to Amsheet, east to Hardeen, and north to Thermodon. They would continue east to the seat of Lord Orgond where Tanios hoped to find a boat for Bahiya that would be sailing to Byblos. He sighed. It was a long and dangerous detour for the high priestess. *Without this avalanche, we might have reached Mitreel, and she could have been sailing to Byblos by now.* But the avalanche blocked the access to the south, forcing them to seek the port of Amsheet. *This detour from Tanniin-The-Strong to Amsheet was supposed to last two weeks, but it took us twenty-one days just to reach the edge of Magdala. I did not expect the castle to fall so quickly or for the new ruler to mount a search operation to locate Bahiya.* He glanced at her as she sat by a small fire at the foot of a tree. Ever since they lost contact with Hiyam, the priestess had hardly said a word. Her face was as hard as flint and while a different mother would have been filled with angst and guilt, Bahiya's face was expressionless—the result of years of priestly training. *What do they do to them in their training? Do they wrench their hearts and replace it with a piece of coal?* He clenched his jaw. *The quicker we reach Amsheet, the better. I hope Jedarc and his team have managed to find the priestess' daughter.*

Tanios heard a rustle. He looked back and saw nothing. He gazed forward at Magdala, wondering why the forest was forbidden. Hardly anyone else, including the King, had ever set foot inside this forest. Legends surrounded it like a dense fog, and it was difficult to weed out fact from fiction. One thing was certain: no one entered Magdala and came back to tell. *No one, except Master Habael*, the commander thought. *I wonder, why did he ask if we could rest here? Why here?*

He got up and joined Master Habael by a small fire that crackled despite the ambient humidity—an incidental tribute to the Silent's mastery over chemistry. He threw a log on the fire and watched thick steam rise as the damp wood hissed and popped. Unwittingly, he glanced up to seek the approval of the nearby trees. He shrugged his shoulders, unable to shake the feeling that they were being closely followed. His trained eyes searched through the semi-obscurity for watchers, but found none. Perhaps those surveilling them tolerated their presence and did not necessarily mean harm. Habael started whistling and chanting in a foreign language. Tanios looked at the old man and beheld an expression of pure joy. Habael's face was like that of child. He seemed to embrace the trees with his gaze and want to dance for joy. Tanios knew these trees were not the cause of his joy, for the gardener had often seen *zalinty* trees, the noblest of Tanniinite trees that did not grow in Magdala. Even though the sight of these trees was breathtaking, Habael's reaction had remained even. No, something else in Magdala was provoking the joy of the old man; something or someone Tanios could not see but secretly wished he could.

The trees around them stood watchful, and in the silence that followed the long storm, one could hear the last droplets of water cascade down the dense cover. Tanios looked up and could barely see the clouds above the canopy. It was dark, unnaturally dark, but dawn was near, and he hoped the sun would dispel the gloom. After three consecutive days of unusually heavy rain, the rays of the sun would be a welcome respite for the weary travelers.

Once more, Tanios glanced at Bahiya. Her eyes glittered in the dark as she sat alone by the small fire. In the dancing flames, he saw once more the young, impetuous girl he had loved long ago.

Images of the two of them in the distant past came to mind: Bahiya and him riding white steeds from Arvalaad. Never had they ridden such noble horses, swift as the wind of Aribona—the great lake between the Kingdom of Milengu and that of Marada, the land of giants.

She had ridden ahead of him, her long, red hair flowing. As she looked back at him she would laugh, and her laughter thrilled him. He shunned these memories away and refused to think about that small cottage on the outskirts of Merieb, which overlooked the lake and where, nearly twenty years ago, he had shared with her the happiest days of his life. *Reaching Amsheet safely is what matters now*, he thought. If the high priestess were hurt, Baal would be merciless. He could still remember how the Temple reacted to the murder of a Baalite ambassador. Farmers had found the man dead on the road to Taniir-the-Strong. The High Riders hanged thousands of men, women, and children in response. Tanios shook his head. Time was against them.

A strident shriek interrupted his train of thought. He jumped up, sword drawn, and looked around. He glanced at Bahiya and was relieved to see her surrounded by Silent with their crossbows also drawn.

"Commander Tanios, no need for weapons here," whispered Habael.

"Whatever produced that shriek may not be so easily convinced," replied Tanios.

"The shriek is far from here. We are safe."

Tanios looked at his friend with bemusement. Here they stood in hostile ground before the Forbidden Forest that had swallowed untold numbers of adventurers. Surrounded by darkness and lurking danger, Habael smiled. Had he gone mad?

"I assure you, Commander Tanios, I have good reason to say that swords are not needed here. We are well protected, better than you think." Habael placed his hand on his friend's shoulder. "I suggest you try to sleep. We are all tired and in need of rest."

"Very well then," said Tanios as he sheathed his weapon. "The Silent will keep watch over the camp. They will alert us in case of danger."

"Your stubbornness is legendary, my friend," replied Habael.

"As long as I do not become part of a legend tonight, I do not mind."

Habael stood in the circle of light, a vast opening deep within the forest of Magdala that very few men had ever seen. His face was resplendent with joy, shining and youthful. His clothes, usually drab and old, shimmered under the light with dazzling color. Across from him, a young man wore a bright white tunic with twelve stars surrounding a moon emblazoned on it. He wore a crown of meyroon studded with pearls of the purest white and held a scepter in his right hand. Habael knew him as Sabael, one of the twelve guardians of the covenant. To his right stood a second young man, in a shimmering purple tunic. Whenever his hem touched the grass, vibrant flowers would spring up; and when the wind swayed, the flowers would leave a fleeting, golden imprint on the fabric. There was a braided rope around his waist, and two strands of meyroon held a translucent crystal over his forehead. He was Lorian, guardian of Magdala and master of sky and wind.

To the left of Sabael stood a third young man with a deep, vibrant green sash. It reflected the starry night, or rather, the sky seemed like a dim reflection of the living stars on its surface. On his forehead, he carried a large topaz held also by thin threads of meyroon. He was Ariond, keeper of the heavens.

Master Habael bowed low.

"Where have you been and wither have you come, O lover of El?" asked Lorian. His purple tunic flashed like lightning, his voice a whisper seeping from the forest—as if the forest itself had spoken, and not he.

"Since the days of Silbarâd, you have wandered the land, O lover of El," said Ariond. His eyes flashed as if a star had come to existence in their depths. "Why have you come here? What seek you now?"

"You have called to us, and we have answered," said Sabael, with a voice of command and power seldom heard among mortals.

"The time is upon us," said Master Habael. "The time long expected has come at last. The prophecy will be fulfilled."

"Twice, the prophecy was fulfilled, and twice it failed," said Lorian. A deep sigh rustled the leaves, as if the forest were mourning a loved one.

"Men's hearts grow dark. They have sundered the covenant, broken the living bridge that bound us in friendship. We stand and watch, unable to aid," added the youngAriond.

"Still," said Sabael, "mercy is granted to the merciful."

"But will mercy be shown?" asked Lorian. "Will there be an act of love of such depths to move the heavens? Is man capable of greatness?"

"What do you think, O Habael?" asked Sabael.

"Hope is still with us. Much remains to be done, and much is still hidden, but hope is before us. As we speak, unrequited mercy is being shown across this hallowed place."

"Your prayer shall be granted, O lover of El," said the one in command. "As for hope, the Seer will be given a measure through strength, a second measure will be added through grief, and a half measure he will be asked to supply. This, you shall witness later. When you return to camp, the man of courage will tell you that someone had been sobbing nearby. Find him and bring him here. Go in peace now."

≻·:·:·:·≺

"Commander Tanios."

"What is it?"

Tanios looked at Alviad. Slowly, he stood up. The young man's bearing told him the matter was important, though not urgent.

"Something in the valley is moving."

"Show me."

Alviad led them silently. Tanios looked up and saw the night passing away before the rising of the sun. Dark clouds hovered overhead, although at a higher altitude than the previous day. *It will not rain today.* The young man knelt next to two other Silent. The commander recognized Allelia and Corialynn.

"The bush, over there," whispered Corialynn who was almost as tall as the commander. She was a consummate archer who excelled at hand-to-hand combat.

"What do you think it is?" asked Tanios.

"Not sure, Commander," replied Allelia, the youngest of the three. She was short, but wiry and fast. "Alviad thought it may be a large animal rummaging for food.

"Could be," muttered Alviad. He was nearly as large and strong as Banimelek.

"The forest in the valley is not forbidden ground, is it Master?" inquired Corialynn.

"No. Still, the silence in the valley is deafening. No crickets, no birds, no movement. A stillness covers this land."

"So you don't think we are dealing with an animal?" confirmed Allelia. "I didn't think so."

The Silent waited for the commander to decide on the next course of action. "Where is Master Habael?" he asked.

"We do not know," replied Alviad.

"Explain yourself. I was not aware that he had left the company."

"He told us he had to visit a place dear to him. He said he would not be gone long."

"How long ago did he leave?"

"Difficult to say, but I would guess no more than one hour."

Suddenly, a whimpering noise came from the bushes, as if someone was softly crying, and between the sobs, one could faintly hear a cry for help. Instinctively, the three Silent leaped forward.

"Stop."

They froze. Tanios' voice acted as a powerful restraint. "Where do you think you are going?"

"Someone is calling for help, Commander," protested Corialynn. "Should we not lend a hand?"

"We have heard a voice, and we do not know what lurks in this valley," replied Tanios in a whisper. "Appearances can be deceiving. There are powers we do not command. We will wait for Master Habael before we move."

"But what if someone needs our help?" persisted Corialynn. "Behind us is a forest from which no one has returned. Ahead, a valley covered by an unnatural stillness. I will not allow my Silent to venture in without some assurance that they will come back alive." He raised a hand to stay Allelia's rebuttal. "We have a mission to complete, and I intend to fulfill it and return to the castle. Help or no help, I forbid any one of you to move outside this camp under any condition. Have I made myself clear?" They nodded. "Very well. Now fan out and keep an eye on these bushes. Alert me as soon as Habael returns."

17. Northern Plains

"Once, a Thermodonian noblewoman—if there is such a thing—fell in love with me while visiting the Royal Court of Tanniin. I, on the other hand, fell off my seat. She asked the King for my hand, and I asked him if he wanted my head on a platter instead. She wanted to take me back to Thermodon, and I wanted to take my own life. She was afflicted with love for me, and I was simply afflicted. When the King explained my function, he told her, "He is a jester," but she heard, "He is a tester," and since all testers take a vow of chastity, she relented, and we both cried; she of sadness, and me of onions."
   –Soliloquy of Zuzu the Hip, Jester of the Royal Court of Tanniin.

While Commander Tanios waited for Master Habael to return, five hundred miles north of the Silent's camp, thick smoke rose from the center of Orlan, the capital of Thermodon, a city built entirely from wood and surrounded by a thick forty-foot stonewall. Built as a lowly hamlet centuries ago, Orlan had grown into a sprawling city, home to seventeen thousand souls who built their homes on the banks of the mighty Valan. Rivers were as important to the Thermodonians as the Great Sea was to the Finikians. The homes were one or two stories high, built with oak beams from the nearby forest.

Their windows were small round holes set high next to the ceiling. At night a heavy beam locked each main door. Short, flat wood slats of different colors and grains covered the facade of every dwelling in Orlan. So bewildering was the arrangement that each home looked like the next, yet each home was unique. To further confuse a would-be invader, the streets of Orlan formed a chaotic maze that seemed to lead at once everywhere and nowhere.

The city hall—the only three-story building in Orland—proudly stood in the square. Oddly, the first two floors were storage units for an assortment of weaponry such as swords, axes, saddles, helmets, and shoes as well as household goods like bearskins, pots, pans, and a large collection of ladles; there were also nonessentials like wooden toy soldiers and knickknacks of all kinds. Only the third floor had usable space consisting of a large circular room with an open hearth at its center. Fur-covered square blocks were set around the fire in a wide circle. Rows of axes decorated the back walls and between each pair hung stuffed heads of bear, elk, and moose.

Despite the late hour, twenty-two chieftains sat on the fur-covered blocks. Some smoked pipes, others stared blankly at the fire, still others used the tip of their blades to clean their nails. They were the Thermodonian chieftains, whom Archchieftain Yanneen Gothney Ravind had summoned to a late meeting.

Time went by as silent as the eternal northern ice. No one complained or even spoke. Thermodonians were patient folks, used to the long hours of a hunt before closing in on prey. Their archchieftain had asked them to wait, and so they did. If it turned out that her ask was unwarranted, a quarrel could follow. The quarrel would turn into a brawl, and the brawl into a tribal battle that could spawn a fresh batch of vendettas, enough to last a century. Thermodonians were, therefore, a stern lot that took everything seriously. They would never joke lest it led to an unwarranted quarrel that could turn into a brawl and the brawl into …

"The archchieftain says someone from Bar-Tanic is visiting," announced one of the chiefs.

Grunts and chuckles answered him. Thermodonians were very familiar with Bar-Tanic. Amused smirks lit their faces for a moment before the cold dullness of the wait wiped them away.

Located in the far northwestern ranges, Bar-Tanic was a land of incessant rain, where a sunny day was always a bad omen; a sign that it would rain tomorrow. Thermodon and Bar-Tanic had a long and tumultuous relation, much like an ill-conceived marriage between an Empyrean and a sailor—the Empyrean refusing to leave her beloved forest and the sailor unable to relinquish the Great Sea. Bartanickians were as phlegmatic as the Thermodonians were choleric. Nothing ever surprised Bartanickians or bothered them, but a Thermodonian's temper could be roused instantly. Some within the Temple ascribed this difference to the lifestyle these two kingdoms led. Bartanickians were anglers, while Thermodonians were hunters. Bartanickians' emotions were buttoned up like a closed infected wound that grew fatter every day until it burst. Thermodonians were given to singing and cheering, and they could shed tears of joy or sorrow easily. Every Bartanickian learned proper etiquette and civil participation in the life of the community. "Clean as a Bartanickian tavern" was an insult hurled at someone who was perceived to be hiding a dirty secret while pretending to be innocent. "Jolly as a Thermodonian" was a sarcastic snide thrown at drunkards who had a propensity to switch from joyful exhilaration to depressing gloom.

Bartanickian society was well ordered, and their cities were tidy and clean. Their roads were well maintained, their children well dressed and were never seen running in the streets barefoot. The boots of every Bartanickian soldier had a special shine not found elsewhere.

Thermodonians were, on the whole, brawlers. They loved a good fistfight and would willingly engage in one without caring about the cause or the reason. Thermodonians did as they saw fit as long as they were not the leading cause of the brawl. Even their battles took on the form of a large fracas, which made them difficult to contain since their warring strategy had no rhyme or reason. Their societal rules governed mostly property ownership, honor, and the division of spoils. Thermodonians shared in the worship of *Skein*—the goddess of war—a fear of the Empyreans, and a love of fur. Besides that, the tribes were free to do as they saw fit and governed themselves according to their own laws.

Before Baal pacified these two kingdoms, raids and counterraids occurred with a depressing regularity every fifty years or so. Out of boredom or a perceived slight to their honor, the Thermodonians crossed the Northern Sea to raid and plunder the Bartanickian coast. Occasionally, they pushed inward as far as Lanudonis, the capital, until they tired or were routed by the Bartanickians. The people of Bar-Tanic would then mount a swift, punitive expedition to subdue the Thermodonians for a generation or so. Between these destructive battles, the two kingdoms were happy to engage in trade even though a dispute sometimes occurred over the price of an item or the size of a shipment. No zakiir would agree to a meeting with these two parties without the High Riders' protection. Indeed, Thermodonians, when slighted, would draw swords and lop off heads. Bartanickians who felt cheated would politely poison the other party, then smile as they watched them die.

Over time, the Temple of Baal built a major temple in the northernmost Thermodonian city of Sherborg. Soon after, a second temple rose in Ordon, the Bartanickian city facing Sherborg. The High Riders in these Temples had managed to keep the peace between the two kingdoms by stopping the frequent raids that ravaged both coasts. The Temple had pushed mercilessly inland until its presence was felt everywhere. To Babylon, Thermodon had a strategic importance since it shared a long border with the Empyreans, and the Empyreans had escaped Baal's control up until now.

Rich in tin, Bar-Tanic was of strategic importance to the Temple. Tin was an essential ingredient in the fabrication of glass orbs and concentrators. Furthermore, Bar-Tanic would be an ideal launching pad for any swift maritime action required to rescue the people of Halon-Sted who weathered the worst snowstorms known to mankind.

At last, the door opened and Archchieftain Yanneen Gothney Ravind walked in followed by a thin, tall man. At six-foot-six, the archchieftain stood a head taller than the rest. Her braided blond hair fell to mid waist and was ornamented with five silver skull-shaped clips, the symbol of her authority. The archchieftains' sword was as broad as her arms, and her girth gave her the appearance of a mother bear, fearsome and powerful. Her green eyes were cast into a wide face that age and beer had begun to transform from svelte to pudgy, yet she was still appealing. She slowly surveyed her kin. Thermodonians' faces were as solemn as a statue of Baal, and they excelled at detecting shifts in facial expressions; a slight smirk may signal that someone was about to unsheathe a sword.

The man who accompanied her was none other than Lord Derek Mistlefoot, the Bar-Tanickian who had formally asked for the hand of Noraldeen on behalf of his son, but was refused. His tall, shiny boots, leather belt with its intricate tin buckle, and thin furless surcoat made it clear to the assembly that he was from the upper class of Lanudonis, the capital of Bar-Tanic.

Being that Lord Derek Mistlefoot had arrived unaccompanied by a priest of Baal, and that Archchieftain Ravind had not invited their local priest, meant trouble was brewing. Either the two kingdoms were headed to war, or they were seeking an alliance against a third kingdom.

Lord Derek bowed, right arm on the hilt of his sword, left arm behind his back. The chieftains grunted in unison. This was the extent of the formal introduction.

"Dis is Kein Derek Mistlefoot. He is from Bar-Tanic. His vife is my sister. Dey have a thaine dat is twenty suns old. His name is Braird."

Lord Mistlefoot's perfectly manicured eyebrows came together in a fleeting frown. *Thain? Thain? … Ah yes, that's their word for son, and thaina means daughter.* He sighed inwardly, *Good thing I remembered.* The Thermodonians would be greatly offended if he showed the slightest lack of understanding when their Chieftain spoke and would then lop off his head with great alacrity and enthusiasm.

"Good Thermodonian name, da," cheered one of the chiefs in a thick cloud of blue smoke.

"Yes, I know," Yanneen said, "I chose de name."

Lord Mistlefoot sucked a breath inward. Had the chief spoken mockingly, a brawl would have followed.

"Kein Derek here asked Kein Orgond from Tanniin for de hand of his thaina for Braird. De thaina insulted my nephew."

"How did she insult him?" asked another chief. Thermodonians valued a man by the strength of his sword and the length and variety of the insults he could hurl. Any new insult, especially foreign, was a welcome addition to their repertoire.

"She said, 'I will not marry you.' Dat is what she said. Dat is an insult."

The chiefs nodded in silence. Refusing to marry a Thermodonian—even a half-blooded Thermodonian—was insulting. Why? No one knew exactly, but whenever a Thermodonian felt slighted by an alien, righteous Thermodonian anger flared.

"So why did you bring us here today, Yanneen?" asked another chieftain. "I could have hunted two more bears."

"To do what with them?" added another chieftain. "You already have fur to cover your fat belly fifteen times over."

The chieftain who spoke first unsheathed her sword and pressed its tip against the second chieftain's throat. He ignored her and continued smoking his pipe.

"Will she forthwith do him in?" asked Lord Mistlefoot. "It would be rather unpleasant and would bode ill for our southern peregrination."

Inwardly, Yanneen muffled a sigh and the urge to unsheathe her sword to chop off the lord's head. "Oh why, oh why did my sister marry him?" she mumbled. "Dat is no brawl," she explained patiently. "Dis khaina is Von Coenig Bru and dat man is Varin Var, her twice-removed cousin. She is showing him dat she value da compliment."

"By thrusting a sword against his throat?"

"Do you expect her to kiss him in public?"

"Oh gods no. That would be ghastly."

Lord Mistlefoot shook his head. *This mission is proving far more intricate and complex than I had thought. Oh well, if I must drink this mug's dreg to the bitter end, so be it.*

Von Coenig Bru, visibly satisfied with Varin Var's seeming indifference, sheathed her sword and regained her place.

"Continue," she said.

"Do we go with the Bartanickians to lop off some Tanniinite heads, do we let them pass through our lands, or do we lop off their heads?"

Lord Mistlefoot wanted to roll his eyes in utter scorn. *What negotiating skills are these? Are these brutes incapable of civility? Why have the fates decreed that we must find solace in their numbers by our side?*

The chieftains considered the question silently. Yanneen had craftily sandwiched the least pleasing options between the only two her kin would consider, for to let foreigners cross their territory without helping or hindering them was tantamount to treason. She also knew that a brawl in Tanniin was a novelty the chiefs could scarcely resist.

"Tell me someding Bartanickian," said Varin Var, "Once we've destroyed Tanniin, what will you do?"

"Well, I firmly intend on killing the father in front of his daughter, and taking her back to Bar-Tanic to be given as a slave to my son."

"I say we go, if we get to lop off Orgond's head."

"Is there a prior vendetta between you and him?"

"No. He is a great one. It would be an honor to lop off his head."

The other chiefs grunted their agreement.

"No disagreement there," replied Lord Mistlefoot, trying hard to speak as plainly as possible. "So long as I give the order to do so."

"You can talk all you want, as long we get to do the lopping off," guffawed Von Coenig Bru.

The other chieftains joined her. Lord Mistlefoot smiled and bowed. *There will be poison aplenty to go around once our little revenge is complete,* he thought.

Yanneen extended a hand as large as a paw, and reluctantly, Lord Mistlefoot inserted his hand into hers. They shook on it, and he winced. He felt as if he had inserted his hand into a bear's jaw.

"Good den," she said beaming. "You take care of your High Riders, we take care of ours, den we go enjoy ourselves in Tanniin. Anyding else?"

"I suppose not," replied the lord.

She slapped him on the shoulder nearly dislocating it. "Very good. Now we eat and drink." She clapped and yelled, "Bring food and ale."

==Servants made their way into the spacious room with large trays of roasted wild boar, stuffed turkey, and enough ale to drown a boat. The festivities had begun. And so did the drums of impending war.==

> ⁘ <

Midnight rang in Lanudonis, six hundred miles northwest of Orlan. Milaniöm stepped outside his apartment and onto Kharen Street. He muttered a profusion of vile imprecations against the Bartanickian's punctiliousness and their cold, wet weather. *Do they have to ring the blasted bell at the hour, every hour?* It was drizzling, as it always did in Bar-Tanic's capital, as if the elements were the progeny of an ambivalent god and an insecure goddess. "Should we open the heavenly spigots or shall we let the sun shine? Oh well, better not be hasty, better be temperate and settle for a cold, wet drizzle to last a lifetime."

Despite his thick cowl and wool mittens, Milaniöm was chilled. His bones were cold, his muscles were cold, and his nose, as red as a scarlet macaw, sniffled miserably. He wished he could be back in Ano Kartag, the beautiful aestival city by the seashore of Oronoque. Stationed there for well over twenty years, he had enjoyed a carefree life surrounded by beautiful women and the best wine that gold could afford. Then, two years ago, almost to the day, an extraordinary thief managed to break into the tajéruun's safe while it was under Milaniöm's care, and stole 174 pieces of gold. Even though the heist was puny, it mattered. Someone had broken through the tajéruun's defenses, all twelve rings of bloodcurdling curses and spellbinding traps. Galliöm, the head of the tajéruun, had rightly concluded that an insider was complicit in the theft. Naturally, suspicions fell on him, and naturally, the investigation yielded no proof. Still, someone had to be held accountable for the break-in, so Galliöm sent Milaniöm to Lanudonis. The thief knew the order would never report the theft to the Temple. Still, to dare defy the tajéruun, the thief had to have been a master planner with experience and a skilled team. The heist bore the telltale signs of the most wanted robber throughout the sixty-two kingdoms: Slippery Slued.

"Why me?" muttered Milaniöm incessantly. "Why me?"

He hated Lanudonis with its interminable rows of look-alike buildings, each with six apartments arranged on three floors. *You could go anywhere in this city and would know before you walked into these blasted apartments how they were arranged.* According to Milaniöm, the nobility in this idiotic kingdom preferred to live in apartments instead of palaces like any sane, well-to-do-person would. But no, the nobility were indistinguishable from the gentry, who were also nearly indistinguishable from the commoners. *And don't let me mention their food*, thought the tajèr bitterly. *Meat, taters, and parsley. May the Nephral take this blasted kingdom to the Arayat.*

"Greetings to you, Lord Abélard Neoman."

Milaniöm stopped in his tracks, smiled and bowed.

"All the same to you, M'Lady Niral Bristletoe, splendid day isn't it?"

Lady Niral Bristletoe made a quick gesture and the two slaves carrying her large canopy moved forward to shield Milaniöm—known as Lord Abélard Neoman, for few knew the real names of a tajèr.

"You meant splendid day, did you not, My Lord?" she asked. Seeing his confusion, she continued, "It is. Now it most certainly is."

"Will you grace us by your presence at tonight's game of Salamander?" asked Milaniöm, playing the role of a Bar-Tanickian lord to perfection. "I am told most of who's who at Lanudonis shall be there."

Lady Niral removed her right glove and played nervously with the trim of the delicate material. Absentmindedly, Milaniöm priced the exquisite garment. *Finely laced cotton, probably of Zemorian origin, three white pearls from Emet no doubt, worth three pieces of gold.*

"That may be so," pleaded Lady Niral softly, "but I would venture that a short stroll along the Tarulin River may prove more satisfying. I dare say, these Salamander games leave me rather languid. I heard," she added with a hint of excitement in her voice, "that we may even spy silver runners making their way to the sea."

Milaniöm was pleasantly surprised. He eyed the widow as if seeing her for the first time and noticed how young and pretty she looked. "Splendid enterprise," exclaimed the man she knew as Lord Abélard Neoman, "I shall forthwith meet your grace this evening at Liy Street. We could go for a refreshing stroll along the northern side of the river and catch a glimpse of these most excellent fish."

Lady Niral placed her bare hand on his wrist. "I so thank you, my dearest Lord, for your kindness towards a lonely widow."

The tajèr felt a streak of excitement up his spine. He was positively flattered. "Your grace is much too kind to me. On the contrary, it is I who must thank Your Grace for bestowing such goodness upon me."

Lord Abélard bowed and Milaniöm regretted ever having cursed the day when he had first met Lady Niral. Confusedly he had thought of her as a pesky spider trying to suck life out of him, niggling him over every penny. He had endured these frequent trials, for Lady Niral was a wealthy widow who traded extensively, which enriched the tajéruun's coffers. ==That the coffers were already full mattered little. Milaniöm had fallen in love with gold and his insatiable appetite for the scintillating metal had darkened his heart beyond recognition.==

They parted ways after she made him promise that he would meet her that night. *My, she is far more agreeable than I thought*. Invigorated, he resumed his walk.

The rest of the way to the tajéruun's vault was uneventful. The moneyman had ample time to ruminate on the latest muted rumor that began to snake its way around town. Fanning its dark wings, it moved from rapacious hearts to avid eyes, from one indolent gossip spoken in a moment of hollow hilarity, to a sulfurous whisper inhaled with the perfumed wisp from a mother-of-pearl pipe. As it moved from the burning fire of a cozy chimney to another, it gained strength and substance until it became an undeniable fact, an investable future that would surely bear fruit: Bar-Tanic was about to invade Bar Tan, its southern, smaller neighbor. Baal had decreed it and preparation for war was already under way.

For Milaniöm, the protagonists were inconsequential. ==War was as much a part of life as fresh bread. As long as men warred, the tajéruun would finance. The tajèr knew Bar-Tanic was not invading Bar Tan. This== was a cover-up to distract the Temple. Bar-Tanic played a far more daring and more dangerous game. Being Bar-Tanickian, this game was subtle and contrived.

Let's see if I can keep this straight in my head, for Galliöm will be sure to ask me the next time we speak. The Temple's high demand for tin is depleting Bar-Tanic's reserves and in two years, their mines will dry out. Tin powers this economy and the Bartanickians are desperate for new mines.

The Bar-Tanickian ambassador to Togofalk has relayed to the Bar-Tanickian king that his men have found mines of tin in the north of

Togofalk. *The Bartanickians are ready to invade that kingdom, but as usual, they need a cover-up. They sent Lord Mistlefoot to Tanniin asking for the hand of Orgond's daughter for his son. If Orgond ascents, a gang will massacre her escort in Togofalk, prompting reprisal. If he refuses the union, the Bartanickians will convince the Thermodonians that Orgond has slighted their honor. The Thermodonians will attack Amsheet. A Togofalkian gang will suddenly appear and slight their honor, and the predictable rowdy tribes will promptly invade Togofalk. Once the Togofalkian forces are busy defending their border, the Bartanickians will invade quietly and gain de-facto control over the mines of tin in that kingdom.*

Milaniöm calculated mentally the draw this war would impose on the tajéruun's coffers in Lanudonis. *I am able to finance the Bartanickians and the Togofalkians, but Tanniin would have to draw on other coffers.*

Naturally, I have not told my Bar-Tanickian clients that Lord Orgond's late wife was the sister of the Empyrean empress. If this war provokes the Empyreans, the Temple would want a more active role. Our profit would quintuple; all good for business.

The tajèr reached his destination; a nondescript building at the end of a cul-de-sac. He walked through a narrow door, removed his coat, went down a flight of stairs, and stood in front of a wooden door encrusted with twelve medallions. A low table to the right of the door held a glowing lantern. Milaniöm opened a drawer, took out a tiny candle, dropped it inside a copper bowl set on the table, and lit it from the flame of the lantern. Then he stood motionless and waited for the candle to be consumed, after which he opened the door and walked in. Two clerks were busy emptying bags of gold into a silver box. Three zakiir watched them, repeating the amount, originator, beneficiary, and the reason for the exchange associated with each sum. They worked quietly, efficiently. After filling a silver box to the brim, the clerks locked it and carefully loaded it into a wagon that could hold four such boxes. Once the wagon was full, they gave it a quick shove and it slid silently into a dark corridor that went down to the vault below. Satisfied, Milaniöm turned to leave, when a clerk gave a start.

"What is it?" asked the tajèr.

"That's 636 transactions," said the clerk, "is that not so, My Lords?"

"It is," replied a zakiir. "These are the transactions for this week."

The clerk pointed to a bag sitting on the table. "We have 637 bags."

"Are you certain?" asked Milaniöm, who knew the answer already. The clerks counted the bags every day for seven days before emptying them. They were never wrong.

"Count the empty bags," ordered one of the zakiruun.

The clerks divvied up the empty bags into three piles and went about counting them. They rotated the piles until each clerk had counted all the bags. They looked at one another and nodded.

"Sir, we counted 636 bags," said another clerk.

All present focused on the one bag sitting untouched on the table.

"Could it be a trap?" asked one the clerks.

"Impossible," snapped the tajèr, "there are 144 spells protecting this door." He pulled an oblong medallion with a dull surface from under his shirt. "Without one of these, you would die trying to cross this door."

"What should we do?" asked a zakiir.

"Open the bag," commanded Milaniöm. "See what's in it."

One of the clerks took the sack, loosened the leather tie and stretched open the mouth of bag. Cautiously he peered inside and pulled out a woman's glove sagging with its heavy contents. He peeked inside the glove and breathed a sigh of relief. "Gold coins, sir," he said, smiling.

"Count them," barked the moneyman. "Count them now."

While the clerks were counting, Milaniöm grabbed the glove and examined it closely. It was a refined garment, with an intricate design lacing each finger and three small white pearls on the right side of the cuff. It looked vaguely familiar. An image formed in his mind that slowly came into focus: Lady Niral playing with a glove, while speaking to him.

"We finished, sir," said the clerk.

What is this glove doing here?

"Sir?"

"What?" he yelled. "What?"

The clerks and the zakiruun were taken aback by the sudden change.

"We have counted the gold, sir."

"How much?" yelled Milaniöm, nearly losing control.

An agonizing moment went by, during which he held his breath and then felt his heart explode when the clerk told him the number of gold coins in the glove, "There are 174." He began sweating and vertigo seized him. He staggered toward the door and slammed into the wall.

"Slippery Slued," he moaned. "Slippery Slued is back!"

18. Undying Love

"Magdala, love of my youth,
Your wind is soft like the gaze of a mother.
As from the palm of her hands, you fed us;
You gave us the grapes of joy, and the honey of tenderness.
You covered us with the stars.
A mantle of love to teach us of love.
With open hearts, with joyful deeds, with generosity.
I carry you in my heart, O beauty of my youth.
I remain forever your son.
Would to El that I may see your blessed fields,
Kiss the ground of my dreams that lulled me in the meadows,
In the tall grass of spring, like the arms of my mother,
Who rocked me to sleep."
–Memoirs of Shalimar, the Poet.

"Commander Tanios, Master Habael is back."

A short moment later, Tanios stepped out of his tent. He stretched and was relieved to see dawn break through the thick canopy. The sun had not yet risen, but a light pinkish hue breathed hope into the vanishing darkness of the night. Seeing the old man approach, he went to meet him.

"Well, dear friend, I am glad to see you. May I remind you that you ought to inform me before taking leave? We were concerned."

"My apologies, Commander Tanios," replied Habael humbly. "I needed to visit a friend and time did not permit for much preparation."

"I hope your visit was pleasant," replied Tanios. He scanned the surroundings half expecting the Malikuun, Lords of Light, to dispel the night and animate the trees with a thinking mind and a mouth to speak.

"It was, Commander Tanios, it was."

Master Habael's words brought him back to reality. "We have heard someone crying outside camp."

"Where was the cry coming from?" asked Habael.

"From the bushes over there. We heard someone whimpering and calling for help."

Habael smiled his usual, mysterious smile. "Unless the high priestess disagrees, I would suggest we look into this event further. It may delay us, but if someone needs help, we should not tarry."

Bahiya welcomed the suggestion warmly. At first, her reaction surprised Tanios, but after further thought, he concluded that she must have looked forward to being distracted from her worries.

The Silent quickly found muddled footsteps around the bush.

"It is indeed human," reported Corialynn, "a man with a heavy gait, pulling a small wagon."

The trail was easy to follow. It led them deep within the valley among large trees that gave shadow to a grassy meadow, where the tracks suddenly disappeared.

"How could a man and a wagon vanish?" asked Alviad.

They combed the ground in ever-widening circles searching for footsteps but failed to find any.

"I don't think we're going about it the right way," commented Allelia.

"Agreed," added Alviad. "We're missing something."

Tanios smiled and waited. He cherished these moments when his Silent acted in accordance with their training.

"Suggestions?"

The Silent looked at Commander Tanios who chuckled and pointed at Corialynn. "She can mimic my voice so well, she could even fool me," he said. The Silent laughed.

"Up," pointed Allelia, smiling. "He went up."

Giant trees reaching to the sky surrounded them, but Allelia pointed to one specific tree. Midway through its trunk, they could see a man-made scaffold. Their mysterious visitor must have climbed up instead of continuing ahead. Tanios questioningly turned toward Habael and drew closer to touch the thick trunk. He closed his eyes, listened intently, and looked at Bahiya. "What does the high priestess say?"

Bahiya fixed her gaze on the scaffold as though trying to pierce through its intricate lines. Tanios remembered, when, years ago, she had stood by his side on the shores of Bragafâr. She now had that same look on her face that once had pierced his heart; serious and beautiful. He waived the memory away with a slight irritation. All of that happened long ago, and he was now dealing with a high priestess of Baal. *She no doubt had her share in the death of Ahiram.* The commander closed his eyes to hide his anger.

"I do not sense any danger," she said after a while. "Only deep sorrow and unspeakable sadness."

"Exactly my thought," said Habael in a murmur. "I believe it would be best if you, my dear Bahiya, Commander Tanios, and I were to climb this tree. You, my young friends, should wait for us here."

Immediately, Allelia loaded a vanishing dart into her crossbow and released it toward the camp. The dart flew swiftly and slammed into a tree, producing a white flash. In response, three Silent joined them.

"Perimeter," commanded Allelia. "This tree."

Bahiya glanced around, and smiled. The Silent had vanished.

"There's a ladder built into this tree," whispered Tanios.

"Do not touch," said Bahiya. "Curses may be protecting this place. Let me check first."

The commander glanced at Habael who nodded. They took a few steps away to give Bahiya the space she needed.

≻·❂·❂·❂·≺

Just then, some fifty miles south, seven hooded individuals walked north on the main road.

"I much preferred you as a dwarf. Those buttons were cute on you."

Ahiram rolled his eyes. "No offensive offense Master Zurwott, but I am far more comfortably comfortable and comfortable in the most comforting way in my silently silent and silent most silently garbs."

Orwutt grinned. "You're dwarfish grammar is improving, my friend."

"Perhaps," grumbled Ahiram, "But, as we were taught in the Silent Corps, 'My tailor is rich,' see?"

"Huh?"

"Silly expression we learned in our language class," explained Sondra. "Another one, 'my master's garden is smaller than his wife's boat,' and—"

"I have one," added Sheheluth. "This one is funny, 'The pants of my brother are wider than the table of my mother,' which is—"

"This is nonsensically nonsensical and nonsensical beyond any sensibly assembled sentence," protested Zurwott.

"'And my tailor is rich,'" chorused the five Silent, sharing a chuckle.

"That's the first sentence we learned in dwarfish," explained Jedarc.

"But there are no rich tailors among dwarfs," protested Orwutt. "Each clan tailors their clothing according to long-standing traditions."

"Hey, I'm not the one who made this up," said Jedarc with a yawn. "I wish I had a few bananas with me. I'm hungry."

"What is a banana?" asked Hiyam.

"Oh no, not that again," muttered Sondra. "It's an imaginary fruit Tinantel made up to console himself whenever he's hungry."

"For the umpteenth time, Sondra, it's *not* an imaginary fruit."

"We just ate," commented Banimelek.

"Catch," said Ahiram throwing Jedarc an apple.

"Yum," beamed Jedarc. "You wouldn't have a piece—"

"Catch," interrupted Ahiram as he tossed him a chunk of cheese.

"Double yum," exclaimed Jedarc.

"Is he a mind reader?" whispered Orwutt to Sondra. "How did he know his friendly friend asked for cheese?"

==“Tinantel's eating pattern follows a long-standing tradition.”==

==“A sign of wise wisdom,” added Orwutt, who failed to see the irony in her statement. “A man who fills his belly with tradition will protect his tradition with his belly.”==

"Faernor, what does that mean?" asked Sheheluth, who was walking beside Banimelek.

᛭ ✷ ✷ ✷ ᛬

It had taken them four days to return to Taniir-The-Strong, three days longer than expected. A major avalanche had blocked the main passage linking the dwarfs' quarters to Royal Road. At first, they tried to dig a tunnel through the rubble. After a full day, they gave up and went back to the dwarfs' quarters, then continued farther south to the desert people's settlement. A violent storm grounded them. Despite Ahiram's desire to leave, they decided against venturing into the forest while the storm still raged. By midmorning of the third day, they reached the main plaza where the Games of the Mines had begun twenty-five days ago. They spent the rest of the day carefully planning their infiltration of the castle when Frey Leifa, the head servant, was returning from a visit to her folks and spotted them.

"Ahiram?" she said overjoyed. "Is that you?"

"Frey Leifa," replied the Silent, beaming with joy. "I'm so happy to see you." Without thinking, he hugged the older woman. She smiled.

"The commander left so quickly, we didn't know what to do, then this giant of a man invaded the castle and his brother came. His name is

Soloron. He is handsome and unmarried, I'll have you know. He appointed himself as king, but I don't think he wants to be a king. He hasn't said it just yet, but I won't be surprised if he abdicates shortly to Lord Orgond."

"So everyone at the castle is safe?" asked Ahiram. "Even the slaves?"

"Yes, life is almost back to normal.

The Silent were relieved. "So, he is treating you well?"

"Oh, very well. I am certain he would love to chat with the Silent."

"Are you sure, Leifa?" asked Sondra. "I thought he was our enemy."

"Oh, gods no." She lowered her voice. "He doesn't like them gray owls, you know," she said pointing with her chin to indicate the High Riders' barracks in the south. "But harm us? Oh no, he loves Tanniin. Come, come, I bet you're hungry and could benefit from a good breakfast."

"A breakfasting breakfast and a breakfast for the breakfasters would be most appropriately appropriate and appropriate in the most appropriate of fashionable fashions." Zurwott bowed.

"My brother is hungry," translated Orwutt, bowing.

Leifa laughed with delight. "Master dwarfs, it is a pleasure to meet you here. Please come, there is breakfast aplenty for all."

"One of us is from Baal," pointed out Banimelek.

"This is Lady Hiyam," replied Leifa, reproachful. "She is an athlete. Besides, if anyone asks, you could always say that you are bringing her to Commander Tanios and that would be that."

"Which is the truth," Sondra commented dubitatively.

"It'll work," added Jedarc. "We're the Silent after all."

"What happened to King Jamiir?" asked Ahiram.

"Soloron locked him in the star room, up in the Lone Tower. He's not sure what to do with him, but hey, what do I know, I'm just a kitchen girl."

Ahiram did not answer. *Strange how one's fortune can turn. One day you are a king and the next, you are less than a slave.* He reflected on his heart's desire. *I never wanted freedom for freedom's sake. I wanted to be free so I could return home. Home is what I want. Home is where I am free.*

They were relieved to see that the castle was in good condition, and the servants were performing their duties as usual. The soldiers staffing the castle were Tanniinites and greeted them with a military salute.

"Those guys are properly trained," commented Jedarc, impressed.

A captain escorted them to Royal Hall where Soloron sat. Banimelek thought he looked deeply bored, as if he had been flopped onto the throne. Every so often, the new king would take off his crown, inspect it carefully, and place it back on his head.

The Silent stood before him and bowed respectfully.

"Five Silent I see. Is this Hiyam, daughter of High Priestess Bahiya?"

"I am," replied Hiyam.

"Is the high priestess well?"

"She is under the commander's protection," replied Sondra.

Soloron sighed in relief. "All praise to Tanniin. I was concerned that the chaos of these last days had indisposed the high priestess. No wonder my search party could not find her. Tanios knows how to hide when he wants to hide." Again, he took the crown off, and inspect it carefully before placing it back on his head. "This does not fit me."

"So you did not mean the high priestess harm?" asked Jedarc with surprising frankness.

"Harm? Why? I don't want Baal's soldiers at my doorsteps. I have no qualm with their priesthood. They can do whatever they want, but not in Tanniin."

"We are under orders from the commander. We must bring Hiyam to Amsheet. Is this order agreeable to Your Highness?" asked Jedarc.

"Highness, Highness," grumbled Soloron. He sighed. "Yes, that's fine. I do want you to carry a message to Lord Orgond. Please let him know I would like to meet with him to discuss the future of the crown. The meeting can take place at his earliest convenience."

"We will do so," replied Sondra with a bow. "I am certain Lord

Orgond will be relieved by your message. Thank you, Your Highness."

"Would it be possible to visit our quarters?" asked Ahiram abruptly. "I would rather change back into Silent's clothing."

Soloron looked at him uncomprehending, then, realizing he was in dwarfish attire, nodded with approval. "Though you may wish to keep your dwarfish look," he said. "In case you're looking to wed a she-dwarf."

A stunned silence answered Soloron, and he sighed deeply. "We need a jester here. I'm losing my mind, sitting on this throne. You may go now." he grumbled under his breath.

Back in the Silent's quarters, Ahiram stood with a satisfied smile. He had found not one, but two fresh uniforms and a new belt with all the darts he needed. He even found a sturdy leather bag, which he now carried on his back. *After six years, I have managed to lay my hands on a second set of Silent clothing. Now I can wash one set while wearing the other and stay clean.* He smiled gleefully and rejoined his friends in the kitchen for a scrumptious lunch, courtesy of Frey Leifa. They ate quickly, for Jedarc wanted them to be on their way as soon as possible.

"Please tell Master Habael we are taking care of his garden. He shouldn't worry one bit."

Ahiram nodded. "Frey Leifa, thank you for everything."

She handed him a bag of goodies. "For the road," she added. "I know my Silent, you will be hungry soon."

As they were about to leave the castle, Ahiram grabbed Sondra by the arm and pulled her aside. The others noticed him say something to her, then saw her throw her arms in the air, lash at him, and storm out in anger. The dwarfs went out after her, followed by Jedarc, Sheheluth, and Hiyam. Banimelek waited for Ahiram and they walked out together.

Soon they were gone. Frey Leifa stepped out the door and peeked into the sun. *Will we see the Silent back at the castle, I wonder?*

Presently, Banimelek and Ahiram were walking behind the rest of the group on the main road.

"What happened?" asked Banimelek.

"When?"

"When you spoke to Sondra as we were about to leave the castle. She stormed out, upset."

"Oh, that. She called me stupid."

"Why?"

"I don't know. She can be odd at times."

"What did you tell her?"

"Well, I thought since Soloron is king and all, I mean he *is* the current king, isn't he?" Ahiram looked at Banimelek for approval. His friend smiled. "Well, he is sitting on the throne and wearing a crown, so …"

"Let me guess," said Banimelek gently. "You asked Sondra if you should ask Soloron to set you free. Didn't you?"

Ahiram was shocked. "How did you know?"

"Seriously? That's all you've talked about for the past six years."

"It's not the *only* thing I talked about," protested his friend.

"Anyway," continued Banimelek, "you asked Sondra if you should run back and ask Soloron to give you your freedom back, didn't you?"

"Yes. What's wrong with that?"

"Nothing," retorted Banimelek, "unless you want every member of the Silent Corps to call you an idiot for the rest of your life; there's nothing wrong with that. Do me a favor, don't mention it to anyone else."

"Come on you two," called Jedarc. "Enough secrets. Let's move."

Ahiram and Banimelek rejoined the group.

"Jedarc, what's wrong?" asked Banimelek.

"I'm still hungry," moaned Jedarc. "I want a banana."

"Do you always complain when you're hungry?" asked Hiyam.

"Of course, don't you?"

"I have never complained," she answered after a moment of silence.

"Never? Never as in not once, not even a smidgen, not one complaint, ever? Wow. That makes you a prime target for marriage." She shoved him and he laughed. "Come on, I was teasing, so what do you mean by never?"

She shrugged her shoulders. "Growing up, I grouped people and objects into two camps. Those I owned, and those I did not. I used what I owned and asked for nothing else. This is the Temple's way." She jerked back when Jedarc's hand appeared in front of her face.

"This one is for you," he said, smiling.

"A daisy?"

"Yep, It's a flower, and it's for you. Here." Before she could protest, he slid the stem through her thick, curly hair. "It suits you. Would you like an apple?" He turned back and called to Ahiram, who was, once again walking behind them with the rest of the group. "Hey, Ahiram, do you have another one?"

"Please," she interjected, "do not ask him for anything on my account."

"You're joking, right? This is Ahiram we're talking about. I can ask him for anything. I can even ask him to bring me the moon and he will. He's my friend." Turning around he yelled, "Ahiram, do you have an—" Jedarc's hand moved so fast it startled Hiyam. "There," he added with a beaming smile while handing her the apple he had just caught. "A green apple. It looks good with the daisy. It suits you."

Sondra rolled her eyes. "Why can't the gods spare us? Tinantel in love? He was impossible before. Imagine him now."

"Ah, love," replied Zurwott, "the gleaming gem of a beating heart. The hearty beat beaming like a majestic gem. It is the crowning crown and the achieved achievement of a life well-lived."

"Are you in love too?" asked Sondra.

"Not yet," explained Orwutt. "Dwarfs are not allowed to fall in love before they have secured their inheritance in the clan."

"You mean, gained their heritage?"

"No, secured. The clan inherits part of our wealth when they reach adulthood. Once we have secured our clan's inheritance, we are then allowed to seek a she-dwarf for marriage."

"I see. Who can you marry?"

"Any she-dwarf of our choosing."

"Do you only choose a mate of your clan?"

"We prefer not to."

"Why?"

"Since the she-dwarf's clan provides the dowry, we prefer to dip into another clan's wealth."

"That's sooo complicated! How can a dwarf *ever* get married?"

Orwutt had a dry chuckle. "It happens routinely, and once a year, representatives from all the clans come together for rebalancing."

"Rebalancing?"

"Yes, we tally all weddings and dowries then exchange the difference in wealth between clans. While each clan's wealth may vary from year to year, over longer periods, it evens out."

"From year to year," added Zurwott.

"Then why go through this ritual?"

"Because it is tradition," replied Orwutt, slightly offended, "and because the wealthiest clan chooses the next king."

"I sure am glad I am not a she-dwarf," scoffed Sondra.

"How is it among your kin?" asked Orwutt.

"The man brings half the dowry, the woman brings the other half."

"How sensible."

"Isn't it? And after the wedding the newlyweds go through a ritual fight with dull daggers. The winner becomes the lawful owner of the dowry and rules over the household. See? Sensible."

≻◦◦◦◦≺

About two hundred and fifty miles north, in the Fortress of Amsheet, Noraldeen walked into her room. She had just returned from her daily visit to the orphanage in Amsheet. The previous month, at her father's suggestion, she had visited the orphanage for the first time and the young children had taken an instant liking to her. For the past thirty days, she had visited the orphanage daily where she played with the children, helped to feed them, and even sang lullabies before putting them to bed. Noraldeen's voice was beautiful—though the other Silent had never heard her sing.

"Lady Noraldeen?"

Noraldeen looked up and saw her first maid waiting by the door.

"Yes, Mamameer, what is it?"

Marialeen walked in followed by two maids carrying a silky white dress. Noraldeen cringed. She looked at her *mamameer*, her second mother, the woman who had taken care of her after her own mother had died in childbirth.

"An Empyrean messenger came yesterday. A delegation of the empress is on its way to meet with your father. They will reach Amsheet by nightfall, and they are under the leadership of Princess Gaëla Meïr Pen."

"Gaëla Meïr Pen," replied Noraldeen, astounded. A chill ran up her spine. "The heiress to the Empyrean Kingdom is coming to us?"

"In person."

"Why?"

"I don't know M'Lady." Even though Marialeen had raised the young woman, she always kept protocol. "Your father has sent me for you. He requires your presence by his side when Princess Gaëla arrives."

"But—"

"Your father, Lord Orgond," said Marialeen, who could be firm when necessary, "is convinced the empress would find it regrettable to know that her daughter, the heiress, was in a hall full of men."

"That is not what I meant. As a Silent, I am bound to protect and—"

"And as the daughter of Lord Orgond, you are duty-bound to stand by your father."

"Well, I refuse to wear a dress. I am a Silent."

"And I will not have you dishonor your mother's memory."

The two women glared at each other.

"I will not dishonor my mother's memory, but every time I wear a dress, men stare at me."

"You lift their thoughts by your bearing and conduct. Either you stand before men by the truth within you, or you kneel before the lie within them. The choice is yours."

"You are worthy of the Empyreans, Mamameer."

Marialeen smiled. "I was honored to serve as your mother's first maid for four years. I learned much from her; the best of women."

Noraldeen beamed. Since she had never met her mother, hearing Marialeen extol her virtues warmed her heart. "Fine," she sighed. "Bring the flaming dress and let's be done with it."

"Not so fast, M'Lady," said Marialeen. "The Empyreans respect Lord Orgond for his fairness and strength, but they prefer dealing with a woman. You will welcome the princess."

Noraldeen moaned and plopped down on her bed. "Me? But I am a Silent. I trained for combat and negotiation, not to heap praise on Empyreans who believe the ground should turn gold beneath their feet."

Marialeen laughed and swiftly grabbed Noraldeen by her arms, yanking her off the bed. Noraldeen gracefully rolled into a somersault, and landed gently in front of her father, who had just walked in. He took her by the waist and spun her around.

"Ah, daughter, how much I cherish the days when you were three apples high. I could lift you up in one hand, then toss and catch you. All behind your mamameer's back, of course; she could not bear to see those acrobatics. Now, look at you. How much you have grown. You remind me of your mother in temperament and beauty." Lord Orgond became serious. "I had a say in the training program of the Silent. I believe Commander Tanios has prepared you for diplomacy better than you think. I should like to see my daughter in a dress for a change. Come to think of it, a visit from the princess may have a salutary effect on your demeanor."

Noraldeen looked at him dejectedly, but her mamameer's stern gaze kept her quiet. She sat on her bed as though she had been condemned to death. The maidservants closed the door behind the lord and lifting their sleeves, surrounded Noraldeen with the determination of generals about to wage a fierce battle.

➤ ✦✦✦ ≺

"Lord Orgond, the great statue of Jaguar-Night is here."

"Ah, yes." replied Orgond.

The effigy of the Togofalkian god had reached the fortress ahead of the midnight procession where it would parade through Amsheet. This was the long-awaited, grand opening of the carnival named for the god.

"Bring it in," commanded Lord Orgond. He stood in the great hall where the statue would be kept. A group of men pulled a cart in. It rumbled slowly and stopped before the pedestal reserved for the statue. A thick velvet cloth covered its content. Lord Orgond inspected the cart, carefully and methodically, as agreed with the Togofalkians. The men waited patiently, hoping to catch a glimpse of the Togofalkian god.

"Uncover it," said Orgond.

Immediately, the men removed the cloth. A mahogany crate with a thick gold frame occupied most of the cart. Carefully, one of the men climbed onto the wain, gripped a gold handle, and pulled the front of the large box. Working quickly, he released a series of locks and removed the top and the four walls, revealing its content. Even Orgond was taken aback. The statue was a lifelike representation of a black jaguar leaping forward. Its jaws were of gold and its teeth made of precious stones. The front paws—cut from zephyr—were air-born with protracted jade claws. But what struck the men most were the eyes. They covered almost one third of the face and were made of red corundum rubies; one of the rarest and hardest minerals on earth. The upper eyelids looked like two large gold triangles. The face would have been comical had it not been for the bloody reputation of this god.

"Very well, gentlemen," whispered Orgond. "Let it remain here."

The men bowed, stowed the disassembled crate beneath the wagon and left in haste. *They must be scared.* Standing before the uncovered statue in the large deserted hall, he gazed into its eyes. *I do not blame them.* Leaving the hall, he ordered the guards to stop anyone from walking in the hall without permission.

※ ※ ※ ※

Two hundred miles south, near the edge of Magdala, Bahiya had just completed her thorough inspection for magic.

"No curses here," she whispered. "Still, there is a powerful magical presence. Something I do not recognize."

"Friendly?" asked Tanios.

She shook her head. "Not friendly, but without evil intent." Seeing Tanios' confusion, she explained: "This evil is not set against us."

He nodded. "Shall we climb?"

She nodded back.

A moment later, Tanios reached the last rung of the ladder and stepped onto a rugged platform, high in the tree. He turned around and lent a hand to Bahiya. She grabbed his hand and for a split second, their eyes met. He looked away and sat down on a bench. She reached the platform and sat beside him. They waited in silence for Habael to join them. She looked at Tanios, wanting to say something, but he looked down. He was relieved to see Habael resuming his ascent. This closeness with Bahiya was starting to weigh on him. He stood up and went to the edge of the platform. All around him, giant trees stood silently, as if watching. He craned his neck but could not glimpse the treetop. He heard someone weeping and glanced at Bahiya, half-expecting to see her in tears, but she pointed to a dark structure behind them.

At last, Habael reached the platform. Tanios lent him a hand.

"Have you found anything?"

"Yes, someone is crying behind these branches," replied Tanios.

Habael pushed the branches away and opened a door. A disheveled man walked out.

They gasped.

"Garu!" exclaimed Tanios.

"What happened to you?" added Bahiya. His appearance was ragged. He had not washed or shaved in weeks, his eyes were red and swollen, and his tussled hair was covered with dirt and debris.

Still weeping, Garu ushered them into the small room and did not bother to ask how they found him or what they were doing in this part of the kingdom. They entered sedately and immediately saw a poor creature, barely human, deformed and eaten by leprosy, lying on a thin mattress made of fresh leaves. Only their perfect self-control prevented them from running away. Instead, Habael moved closer to Garu, placed his hand on his shoulder, and spoke softly.

"Garu, who is this?"

"My poor Ramel," said Garu in a choked whimper. "Oh, my love, my love," he exclaimed and he fell to his knees sobbing.

"The Queen?" replied Tanios in hushed amazement.

Bahiya knelt by Garu. "This is then the source of the evil I sensed," she whispered. "She is under a powerful curse. Garu, what happened?"

The Queen started to shiver violently. Garu quickly grabbed a blanket and gently placed it on her. He signaled for Tanios to bring the candle closer. Garu placed his hand on the forehead of the Queen, and Tanios had to resist a gag. The face was no longer human.

"She has a high fever. I do not know what to do," said Garu rapidly. "I tried every medicinal herb I know of in the forest to no avail. I cannot cure her. Curse you, Ibromaliöm. Cursed be the day that I trusted you, the day that you enchanted this innocent creature with your lies and deceits. All you wanted was the book. The book! What to do? What to do? Master Habael, help me, I beg you, bring back my Ramel to me, please."

Habael looked at Garu with eyes full of pity. "Master Garu, I am so sorry, but I do not think there is much anyone of us can do. She is dying."

Garu slumped to the floor sobbing uncontrollably now. Even though he knew the Queen was dying, hearing it was a shock. He looked at Habael and Bahiya with pleading eyes, imploring them to do something. Bahiya knelt by him and held him in her arms. Garu sobbed quietly. Habael placed the deformed hand of Ramel, which only three weeks ago, had been so beautiful, into the hand of Garu. The Queen's respiration had become short and erratic.

"Ramel, my poor Ramel, do not leave me," moaned the former judge. The Queen's body tensed, she sighed one last moan, then became still. Queen Ramel was dead.

Garu was inconsolable. Gently, Bahiya helped him to get up and go outside. His resistance was broken by the strain of these past days, and he followed her like a child.

How did he manage to bring her up here? wondered Bahiya. *What he did is nothing short of heroic.*

Tanios shuddered. The thought of Garu carrying the deformed, rotting body of Ramel sent cold shivers up his spine. Lepers were unclean, and Ramel was far worse. By touching her, Garu accepted to be unclean. *Unclean out of love,* Tanios mused. *Poetic.*

"How will we bring him down?" asked Habael. "He is too weak to climb down on his own."

"We will lower him with ropes. Two Silent will do it."

"We must also bury the Queen," Habael pointed out.

"What?" Tanios snarled. "Bury a cursed leper? *We* would become unclean. Why not burn the body?" But he already knew the answer to that question. "I see. The forest. We cannot start a fire on this platform. Leave the body to the crows. They will do a fine job picking the bones."

"It is proper to bury a body, Commander," replied Habael.

"Only if we remain clean."

Bahiya walked back in. "For once, just this once, can't you think about someone else's need?" she snapped.

Tanios was dumbfounded. Bahiya had spoken the way she used to when they were together. "I warn you, Priestess," he replied angrily, "do not cross this line again. I am not your lapdog to carry out your whim."

"Commander," interjected Master Habael, "What if Master Garu were to wrap the body in a cloth? We would lower the body to the forest ground using ropes. The Silent will carry Ramel on a stretcher."

"That would work," replied Tanios. "We could give her a proper burial while remaining clean. Great plan, Master Habael," he added while eyeing the priestess angrily. "I will supervise."

"The commander is a man of principles," commented Habael after Tanios had left. "He does not bend easily."

The priestess nodded. If Habael noticed her tears, he said nothing. It took the Silent an hour to bring both Garu and the body of Queen Ramel down from the safe haven. Habael knew the Silent carried forth this heartbreaking task out of respect and admiration for their commander.

After they laid the body on a stretcher, the commander instructed them. "We will give the Queen an honorable burial. You have not touched the body, therefore, you are all clean. You will not speak of this event to anyone. That is an order. Understood?"

The burial was simple, yet dignified. Four Silent carried Queen Ramel's ravaged body on a stretcher between two rows of honor guards. Garu stood by Bahiya and followed her with great docility. He was in shock. The Silent buried Ramel at the foot of the tree. Habael told Garu that without his love and devotion, she would not have received a burial at all. As a leper, she may well have died alone in some dark alley, or even have been killed by a mob. Instead, she died with dignity and had the Silent to pay her homage. Garu could console himself in knowing that he had made her last days full of comfort and love.

The company of Silent departed. As they walked back to their camp, Tanios questioned Garu further. But he gained nothing more than jumbled answers about a book that Ibromaliöm had stolen. Apparently, Ramel had looked inside this book and a curse had fallen upon her. She lost her sight, then leprosy began eating at her with unbelievable speed. Garu had brought her here in the hopes of finding a treatment, though all his efforts were in vain. She quickly withered away.

Tanios slowed his pace and let everyone else pass him. He needed to think. Even though the kingdom was in shambles, he still considered it his responsibility to find the murderer of the four men of Baal who had been killed during the Games of the Mines. When he had held the candle close to Ramel's face, he could clearly see her reddish hair, something he had not noticed before. *She must have dyed her hair while in the castle. Was she not the mysterious woman who met the Junior High Rider in the garden? Was she the murderer? If so, why? Was Ibromaliöm involved in these crimes? The judge had great physical strength despite his age. But why? What could be the motive? Wait, if she had dyed her hair, how could she have left a clump of red hair in the soldier's hand?*

Tanios knew he was standing in the center of a cobweb deeper and more complex than he could fathom. All the facts he had gathered seemed related, but nothing thus far made sense. Habael called to him.

"I need to bring Master Garu to visit with my friend," said Habael with a charming smile on his face. "We shall not be gone long. Could you please wait for us here?"

"Do not tarry, my friend. We have a mission to complete."

"I will see you soon." Habael held Garu's arm and bid him forward with a warm smile. "Come, Master Garu, I want to show you something that will gladden your heart."

"What is there to gladden my heart after what has befallen my Ramel?" asked Garu.

"Come now, come." Master Habael's face glowed with warmth.

The two men retraced the small company's footsteps, and when Habael was convinced no one was following, he quickly entered Magdala with Garu in tow. They walked along a wide path that led to a small and odd-looking wooden bridge. They crossed it and stepped into a circular clearing. Habael stood there with Garu and bid him to wait silently. Garu looked at the trees around him. They seemed normal, no different from any other trees he had seen before. Suddenly, a sheet of pure light appeared, and moving slowly, it surrounded them in a wide circle. The light was pure, but did not blind them. Garu could see waves of color dance along the sheet's surface, which grew taller than the trees and soon hid the forest. ==Two figures then appeared. They moved forward and stood before the two men. Garu opened a gaping mouth. He could not believe his eyes. Even though he had read about the *Malikuun*, he never imagined he would one day be standing in their presence.==

"Master Garu. We have witnessed your devotion to Queen Ramel, and it has pleased us to see you have served her in her time of need with faithful love and great charity. Charity moves the heart of El. Would you like to be the tiller of this forest? You will find peace and true contentment until the day when you will serve once more. Do you accept?"

Garu could feel waves of supernatural joy fill his heart. The beauty of the Malikuun soothed his pain. He did not know what tilling the forest meant, but he accepted without hesitation. *I could be home here.* The peace he felt brought to his memory the days when he walked alone, content to reflect and think. He could do the same here. *This may soothe my pain and help me cope with Ramel's death.*

Nodding like a child, he let go of Habael's grip and crossed the sheet of light. He turned, waved good-bye, and disappeared.

==Kindness begets kindness, Habael,== said the Lord of Light. "A word of power awaits you at the foot of the bridge; the first fruit of Garu's self-sacrifice. Use it as you see fit. Go in peace now."

Habael bowed low. When he looked up again, he was alone. As he was about to cross the bridge, he noticed a small brass horn. He picked it up and left Magdala.

≻ ◦•◦•◦ ≺

"Commander Tanios," whispered Corialynn, "horsemen on the road."

"Silent, vanish." In an instant, Tanios stood alone on the path. He surveyed the road in front of him and saw no one, yet he trusted Corialynn's senses more than his own. *She is remarkable. She could hear a mouse treading slowly on tufts of cotton.* Tanios stood motionless in the depth of the forest. Time was suspended. Nothing moved. Tanios glanced at the young woman perched on a nearby branch, as she pointed to the road ahead. *She is always right. Let's wait some more.* Suddenly, something moved between the trees to his right.

"A platoon of riders, about thirty of them," she called out.

He waited until he could see their standard and then relaxed. It was white with an empty, broken sheath and two jewels on its upper rim. Tanios stepped out.

The riders stopped, and their leader dismounted. He came forward and saluted the commander.

"Commander Tanios, it is an honor."

"Enryl of Amsheet, the honor is mine. What brings you here?"

"I am on an official mission for Lord Orgond and we are now making great haste to rejoin the fortress."

Tanios glanced at the platoon and recognized at least two dwarfs: Xurgon and Zirka. "Why have you followed this detour instead of riding swiftly on Middle Road?"

"We took it as far north as we could. A heap of boulders and dirt blocks it, the size of which we have never seen before. It reeks and is an eyesore. Whoever blocked the road is mighty and has no good intentions; that much we can say. Rather than attempt to open the road, we decided to go around it, guided by our good friend, Zirka, the dwarf."

Tanios looked in the direction Enryl pointed to, and saluted the dwarf. "A dwarf who knows his way around forests, now that *is* unusual, would you not say, Master Dwarf?"

"We refrain from any inadvertent advertence and keep from any advertence whenever inadvertent." The dwarf bowed.

"Yet, I am surprised, Master Zirka. Do you not know that you are treading near forbidden ground?"

"We take precautionary precautions and precautions of the most precautionary nature."

Tanios bowed back and hid a smile. The dwarf's manner of speech brought back warm memories of his good friend Kwadil.

"Do tell Lord Orgond that High Priestess Bahiya of Baalbek and the Silent will be in Amsheet in a few days. We seek safe passage for the priestess on her return to Byblos."

"Would you like to ride with us?" offered Enryl. "I would be honored."

"My warmest thanks, Enryl. I have a platoon of my own to care for."

"Captain Enryl, a word."

Surprised, Tanios eyed Allelia. *What is she doing?* He was, of course, well aware of the authority his Silent carried throughout the Kingdom. The nature of their missions and the dangers they faced required them to give direct orders to ranking officers, which if not followed could lead to disaster. Still, the fact that Allelia chose to speak to Enryl *now*, when she had no assigned mission puzzled Tanios.

Enryl dismounted from his horse, followed the young woman below the shadow of the tree, and returned a short moment later.

"The Silent asked me to give her uncle, who lives in Amsheet, this token of her affection." He said this while showing Tanios a vanishing dart. "It is my pleasure to help your corps in any way I can."

Tanios gave him a warm smile. "You have my gratitude, Enryl. Until we meet again."

Enryl bowed his head and the platoon past by him. As Xurgon drew close, he leaned sideways toward the commander who wondered if the dwarf was not about to fall off his horse.

"The priestess' daughter yet lives and so does your slave. There is a mighty tale to be told later."

Tanios' face remained impassible even though relief washed over him. *Ahiram is alive! He survived. How will Bahiya react when she hears the slave she tried to kill is alive?* He chose to keep this news to himself.

"Allelia, what did you tell Enryl?" Tanios wanted to know.

"I asked her to relay a message for me," Bahiya said as she walked briskly toward him. "He must beware of Zirka. Dark magic hides his intent. Given Magdala's closeness, I dared not pierce through his cover."

"Ally or enemies of Magdala?"

"I can assure you, my dear friend," said Habael, who stepped forward, "that Magdala is by no means evil."

"I agree with Habael," said Bahiya. "Magdala harbors a power unlike any I have seen before. But I am puzzled why they refrain from using their power." she said in a dreamy voice.

Tanios looked at Habael, and then at Bahiya. She looked back at him. *Those eyes. Those bewitching eyes*, thought the master of the Silent. *They remind me of someone …* In a flash it came to him. Tanios knew who that someone was, and it distressed him greatly. Troubled, he mounted his horse and sighed. Looking up, he stared at the trees and shook his head as though their mute weight had begun to oppress him. *These trees. This forest, it is making you impatient*, he chided himself. *We must reach the open air, but we must do so safely*. Gruffly, he gave orders to the company to move. *I have a mission to complete, forces or no forces.*

They reached Middle Road at dusk. It stretched northward as far as the eye could see. The men were relieved to be back in the open, and

Wrath of the Urkuun – Undying Love

Tanios was eager to arrive at the fortress as soon as possible.

"Commander Tanios, do you smell the stench?" asked Habael.

The westerly wind blew, carrying with it the smell of rotten food, decaying trees, and decomposing carcasses. "Yes, my friend, I do. This stench does not bode well, does it?"

"Is all well in Hardeen, I wonder?"

"The eastern fortress is miles away," replied the commander, "but let us not delay. The sooner we reach Amsheet, the better."

They trotted at a comfortable pace for a few hours and came upon a group of villagers traveling on foot.

"Where are you from, and where are you going?" inquired Tanios.

Recognizing him, the villagers cheered.

"From Santiir," replied an old man. "We're on our way to Amsheet."

"I know your village, old man," replied Tanios. "It is near Hardeen."

"Commander. Santiir is no more. The terror from Hardeen swept it."

"What terror?" asked Tanios.

"Don't know. All's I'll say is that a bit o' time past, somethin' terrible went inside the fortress. Doors slammed shut for two nights. They opened and let lose the stench and the terror. Santiir fell. We ran for our lives. Ain't seen my brother, my cousin, and all 'em Limen, good family of twenty. Gone. All of 'em."

"To Amsheet we go," said another. "Lord Orgond, he is our last hope."

Tanios looked at Habael and Bahiya.

"I feel the same power flowing from across the forest," said Bahiya shivering. "I dread what is coming."

Dark clouds loomed above their heads as they advanced down the road. They passed shadowy figures: men, women, and children as they walked by the side, heavily burdened with their belongings and their hunger. Tanios felt like a man riding the crest of a giant wave of destruction about to crash. He wondered if any of them would survive what was coming next.

19. Gaëla Meïr Pen

"*Jaguar-Night is one of the principal deities of the Togofalkians. He is a god of the night, a god of stealth and power, and he is revered for his magical powers. Of particular interest to the Temple of Baal are the protuberant eyelids encrusted in one of its most famous statues. The Temple believes these eyelids were not there originally, that Jaguar-Night had acquired them after some somber dealings with Tanniin. Baal had tried to be rid of the eyelids for some time now, however, fearing the unrest and upheaval that would result from their vanishing, has thus far not tried to remove them.*"
—Teaching of Oreg, High Priest of Baal.

"*The Great Council was providential. It made the right decision for the wrong reasons. Most of all, it revealed what was hidden and allowed the bearer of Layaleen to acquire an indispensable weapon.*"
—Chronicles of Yardam, Third Stewart of the House of Hiram.

Ahiram ran along a narrow ledge while being chased by a dark shadow. He seemed frightened and lost and searched frantically for an escape route. Below, the gushing fires of the deep roared with a deafening sound. The shadow behind him grew larger and
more ominous until it swallowed everything. Ahiram stood with his back

to the void, paralyzed and unable to resist the approaching terror. He opened his mouth to yell, but fell back. The dark terror advanced. Noraldeen struck at it with her sword. Pain wrung through her arm, and she woke up. She sat with her back against the bed, her arm still throbbing with pain. Pondering the meaning of these dreams, she gazed at the brightening sky, for the sun was about to rise. *I am convinced you are alive, my love, somewhere out there you stand with your will to be free. I sometimes wonder what the price of your freedom is, my love. Oh, how I wish you were here now. Is distance keeping us apart, or your desire to be free? In your slavery, you are worth a thousand princes, O source of my joy and sorrow.*

She slid back into bed and closed her eyes. Her dream was a nightmare, but it no longer held sway over her. *If I cannot see you by day, my love, then I long to see you in my dreams.* In a way, this recurring nightmare had strengthened her love for Ahiram. Noraldeen loved him deeply. She knew she wanted to be with him, grow old with him, and love him for the rest of her life. Since their separation, she had the time to reflect and ponder the events that had taken place in her life during the past six years. She noticed Ahiram the first day Commander Tanios had brought him in. Ahiram had a worried, serious look on his face; a sense that he did not belong in their group. Tanios ordered him to sit and observe. Then he told the students that among the Silent, valor, aptitude, and strength were the measuring rods. "True nobility," he said, "expressed inner strength and magnanimity." Back then, she did not know what magnanimous meant, but she knew it was an important quality they ought to strive for.

Ahiram sat by the training course that day, and soon no one else but her paid attention to him. For weeks on end, he sat and watched their movements. He never spoke, never said a word until the day when Tanios ordered him to enter the game of tagging. He stood and faced Noraldeen and smiled his disarming smile, as though apologizing for being her opponent. Even before the game began, Noraldeen knew she had lost.

A few days earlier, Noraldeen had broken her staff during an outdoor exercise. She ran back to grab a spare rod and was surprised to see the door leading to the Silent's quarters left ajar—a rule violation. She heard Master Habael encouraging someone. She tiptoed to the open door, peeked inside, and was seized with amazement. In the middle of the training hall, Ahiram was a whirlwind of color and movement.

The Silent Corps main mission was to guard the king and protect innocent life. In a world that favored the double-edged sword, the Silent opted for the lowly dart. When a Silent throws one dart, one enemy falls. When several darts are combined in a lethal sequence, the Silent becomes a formidable foe. Combining martial art moves with the throw of darts was essential. The faster the better.

Before they could use a dart efficiently, the Junior Silent needed to gain strength, endurance, and stamina. They needed to develop greater self-control and precision. Wood staff training served this purpose well. The study of bones and muscles, history, culture, geology, and botany occupied the rest of the day. The intermediate two years intensified their physical training. Dart and dagger throwing, hand-to-hand combat, swordsmanship, and fighting on horseback were all introduced. The last two years of training were intense as the students were focused on the dart crossbow, vanishing techniques, advanced martial arts, poisons and antidotes, as well as the manufacture of darts. They memorized essential facts about every royal family across the sixty-two kingdoms, and learned the fine art of diplomacy and proper court etiquette. And finally, they studied the structure and design of the Temple of Baal.

Most students in Noraldeen's first-year class could combine twenty consecutive martial art forms in a sequence that Commander Tanios considered acceptable. "Flowing like a river," the commander repeated, "faster than a horse, more powerful than a bear, these are the moves of the Silent." They trained for four hours each day with the staff; persevering through injuries and painful bruises. She prided herself in perfectly executing her fighting form; a sequence of sixty moves. Jedarc and Sondra could string together seventy moves each. Alviad and Banimelek, eighty, and Allelia and Corialynn could perform sequences of ninety moves, which was exceptional. An accomplished Silent would do one hundred to one hundred and fifty coordinated moves and the Solitaries, those outstanding Silent, topped it all with a sequence of three hundred moves of the highest difficulty. Tanios did not tire of repeating, "Performing a form of one hundred moves means nothing if they are poorly executed. Your moves must flow, one into the next. Your attack must be purposeful, efficient, and when needed, crippling. Dance on water and I will see a Silent. Give me a dance, dangerous and beautiful."

Before her eyes, in the empty room, Ahiram danced like a Lord of Light. There were moves she had never seen before, and the staff in his hand became liquid water flowing in space. As the staff flew in the air, his movements remained graceful, focused, and purposeful. Instinctively, she knew that what she was seeing was extraordinary, and she felt privileged to be the first to witness it.

Noraldeen rejoined her class without a staff and incurred the commander's ire. She kept Ahiram's secret and felt that eventually he would have to join their ranks. The next day, she saw him sit quietly by the wall watching them and wondered why he did not feel bored seeing how clumsy they were compared to him. She remembered looking into his eyes and could see nothing more than studious attention to their moves. She then understood the meaning of magnanimity.

When Tanios gave the signal of the game of tags, Ahiram's dart hit her before she could reach for her weapon. She had not even seen Ahiram's hand move, but she could still remember how everyone else froze and looked at her with amazement. As the game advanced, she stood by the side and watched Ahiram expel each of his opponents with the same speed and deadly precision, until he faced Banimelek and won the game.

The students teamed around him and started asking questions. She saw how embarrassed he was. She stood by him and smiled. He smiled back and relaxed.

Over the years, Noraldeen had ample occasions to witness his talent and ability. While in their third year, a visiting Solitary, had dropped by to observe the students and had given them the privilege of facing him in one-on-one combat.

Solitaries were the highest-ranking Silent who could take on any mission unaided. Their numbers and location was a secret the Commander protected jealously. They lived away from Taniir-The-Strong Castle and relied solely on their own resources.

Most students fared well partly due to their training and partly due to the magnanimity of their champion. Banimelek fared better than most. Then came Ahiram's turn.

Most beginners were nervous when they faced an accomplished Silent. Ahiram looked nonchalant and eyed his opponent with the same wry smile he bestowed on his teammates; a smile that said, "I'm going to win." Noraldeen knew what Ahiram was thinking and was simply awed. The two fighters stood in diagonally opposite corners. Tanios gave the signal and they leapt forcefully into the arena; the visiting Silent moved like a prowling tiger, but Ahiram charged like an angered viper. Powered by an unnatural fury, he displayed a complex sequence of moves that surprised and confused his adversary, who lunged forward, aiming for the young man's ankle and missed it by a fraction of a second. Ahiram had been already air born. He landed behind his fellow Silent and said "tag; you're it." The attack had lasted less than five seconds. The bemused Solitary felt the dart on his forehead and burst out laughing. He turned around and slapped Ahiram on the shoulder.

They faced each other again. This time the secretive champion was ready. He knew he was facing a challenger of extraordinary talent. Yet the best talent is no match for experience. Ahiram lost the following two rounds. Later, the visitor admitted that he relied on all his wits to defeat his young opponent. "I will think twice before facing you again next time around, young man."

Yet, Noraldeen was not attracted to Ahiram's prowess. She vividly remembered how he had patiently mentored, and freely taught all those who approached him. She could still see him sitting quietly, lost in thought as he admired a sunset or flight of birds migrating south at the beginning of fall. They had taken long walks in the mountains talking about his life in Baher-Ghafé, shark fishing, and sailing the sea without boundaries, without restraint, without limits. Noraldeen had fallen in love with Ahiram despite her rank and her upbringing. She felt she was dealing with a prince, not a slave.

"Lady Noraldeen?"

Noraldeen woke in a start and realized she had fallen asleep sitting on her bed. She massaged her neck, stretched and got up.

"Yes?"

"Lady Noraldeen," said Marialeen walking in with two maidservants in tow. "Your father would like you to join him now in the reception hall. The Empyrean delegation is at the door of the city."

"Already? But it's so early."

"M'Lady, it is past noon," replied Marialeen with a note of concern. "You have slept all morning."

"I did? I must have been exhausted then." The young woman sighed. "Let's get that dress on."

After a frenzied wardrobe makeover, the maidservants managed to turn Noraldeen into a royal princess. "Your father will be pleased, M'Lady," said Marialeen. "Now, please follow me and try to walk with poise, not like a tigress on a hunt."

The Empyreans had sent word saying they would arrive early afternoon. Lord Orgond had commanded everyone to be ready to receive them at a moment's notice; he wanted a full royal reception for the delegation. Noraldeen felt awkward in her white dress and was grateful the Silent were not there to see her—though she would have been surprised to see their reaction, for she was simply stunning. She reached the hall and forced herself to walk slowly as instructed by her mamameer. She noticed all eyes were on her. *I must look stupid*, she thought.

"You are ravishing, my daughter," said Orgond with a tender smile.

She could not help but frown. Her father meant what he said, yet she had never thought of herself as ravishing before.

"Sir, the Empyrean delegation requests an audience."

"Have they come amiably?" asked Lord Orgond, in accordance with Amsheet protocol.

"Yes sir, they have."

"Open the gates, allow the delegation in, and may these walls protect them as they protect us."

They waited in tense silence. Noraldeen knew any slight misdemeanor would offend the Empyreans and could mean war. In the past, the master of Amsheet had intervened personally in two different cases where the Empyreans had felt insulted by representatives of Tanniin. Only the respect they owed him, and his great sense of diplomacy, had saved the day and averted war. The peaceful result was especially good for Tanniin. The odds against the formidable Empyrean army were slim. Even the mighty Baal had left them alone.

The Empyreans had never crossed into Tanniin amicably. This was the first delegation to come in peace, and it was headed by the daughter of the Empress, Princess Gaëla Meïr Pen.

The doors of the reception hall opened quietly and a servant announced the visitors. All present bowed, save Lord Orgond, who held his daughter back, preventing her from bowing. He nudged her forward and she stood in front of him. He surveyed the members of the delegation and was surprised to see a turbaned man dressed in colorful clothing and of phenomenal proportions. *The Empress has sent Uziguzi Aor Jar. This is going to be a remarkable visit.* Uziguzi Aor Jar—known among the lowlanders as Heehee-The-Fat—was one of the closest advisers to the Empress. Lord Orgond had employed him during the War of Ar-Gaeer that had ended the uprising of the lowlanders. Despite his silly name and embarrassing appearance, he was a brilliant strategist and a great diplomat. Uziguzi had one of the sharpest minds, and he remembered everything including the minutest details.

Three standard-bearers processed in first, then twenty-four Empyrean warriors clad in full military attire. Next, Princess Gaëla entered in her full military regalia. As a sign of peace, she carried her sword on her shoulder and not at her waist as in battle.

The military dress heightened her stark beauty. Her black eyes shone softly in her oval-shaped face, the hallmark of Empyrean beauty. The contrast between her long, black hair and opaline skin was striking, and the effect was enhanced by her tall, lean frame. The whole image created an ethereal aura around her, as though she were more spirit than flesh.

Noraldeen was impressed by the princess, despite the early misgivings the Silent had had of her. Gaëla moved with grace and simplicity. To all those who knelt and bowed on her approach, she responded with a thoughtful, quiet smile. Noraldeen wondered how the princess could tolerate the fat man dressed like a buffoon. He saluted everyone by waving a silky handkerchief that hung from a protuberant ring. Four Empyreans of exceptional height flanked him. Finally, another twenty-four Empyrean warriors walked in, closing the delegation.

"That is Lord Jar," whispered her father. "You must salute him after the princess. Now, you may take your seat."

Noraldeen showed no reaction. Keeping her eyes on her guests, she waited until they drew closer before she took her father's place on the seat of authority. The delegation stopped before her.

"Princess Noraldeen of Tanniin," said the princess, "I salute you in the name of my empress, Aylul Meïr Pen."

"Your Serene Highness graces this fortress by her presence."

"Princess Noraldeen, in the name of Her Royal Highness, the Empress Aylul Pen, I wish to extend to Your Ladyship and your household our warmest wishes of well-being and peace."

"And how is Her Highness, the empress? In good health, I hope?" Noraldeen's own ease surprised her. She knew her father was pleased.

"She thanks you for your solicitude toward her and has expressed a wish to meet with you."

The Tanniinites breathed a sigh of relief. This delegation was not here to avert war or settle accounts. Something else was in the offing.

"Lord Jar," continued Noraldeen with a voice strong and firm. "I welcome you to the Fortress of Amsheet."

"Tatata Doopeleedo, do not lord and butter me," replied Uziguzi Aor Jar with a distracted tone. "I am Her Highness' fool and have come here to entertain, and to be entertained. Now, Doopeleedo, you are scrumptious in your dress, and fresh as a lilac in the first days of spring. This mission is parsimoniously political and politically atypical, thus, the red in my turban. Do you like red roses, Doopeleedo dear? I love roses. Red is my favorite color when I travel and you know me, or you should know me, I hate to travel. It is dizzyingly monotonous. The weather, ah, the weather, I get hot when it is humid and humid when it is warm and my horse caught a cold and was killed by accident. I miss him, Doopeleedo, I miss my horse. Animals have feelings you know, and he loved ripened apples. Since he is gone, there is no one to share apples with. I have a splitting headache doctors would die for. Life is a river, is it not so, Doopeleedo dearest? We are but floating lilies that gasp for the light and then are gone in the mist of the past. Past the falls of yesteryear lie the dreams of tomorrow. They rise to the sun and fall back, dew of the children to come. This trip has affected me. Where is the chicken? I am hungry. No, do not tell me, I know all is ready and waiting. I shall leave you to rest, dine as your guest, and have a bite or two at best."

Unceremoniously, Uziguzi left the hall behind two attendants who ushered him into the dining room. Orgond breathed a sigh of relief. He needn't look at his daughter to know how she felt about Doopeleedo.

"Lord Aor Jar is highly esteemed by my mother," said Gaëla. "Please excuse his eccentricities."

"The house of Tanniin is Lord Jar's house," replied Noraldeen. She was mechanically repeating what she had learned over the past six years. *The commander trained us well.*

Lord Orgond could not help but admire the fat man. *He still remembers our secret code after all these years.* What had appeared to be a gibberish rant was well-disguised information. And the message was loud and clear: Red meant danger, the dead horse meant war, the eaten ripe apple meant the enemy was on the move, the floating lilies meant an absence of strategy, and the children of tomorrow was a reference to urgent readiness. Uziguzi's wish to eat right away suggested that immediate action was required. To the uninitiated, the message was absurd, but to Lord Orgond, Uziguzi made perfect sense: The enemy is coming. The Empyreans were ill prepared to fight him, and so was the Kingdom of Tanniin. *The situation is much worse than I thought.*

Noraldeen could not decipher the message, but Doopeleedo was one of several terms of endearment the allies used to warn a Silent. Her cheeks flushed red when she heard Uziguzi speak, but her training kicked in and she quickly realized that what Commander Tanios had prepared them for was unfolding before her. An ally sought help, and if he spoke in riddles, then the enemy was among them.

She stood up. "I believe Lord Aor Jar is right," she said cheerfully. "You must all be famished. With permission, Your Highness," she said addressing Princess Gaëla, "Your retinue is welcome in the great hall, and I should like for you to dine with me at my table."

Orgond and Gaëla were taken aback. Noraldeen was dumbfounded. *What did I just say?* The words flew out as if she had said them hundreds of times. *It was my favorite greeting during diplomacy classes.*

"Do as Princess Noraldeen has commanded," said Gaëla. Immediately her retinue followed the butlers into the dining room.

Noraldeen breathed a sigh of relief. *Wait a moment,* she thought, nearly panicking, *I don't have a table that I can call my own.*

"My apartments," whispered her father as he squeezed her shoulder. He had read her confusion. They walked in silence through the halls to his chambers. A table was placed near a warm fire for them. Noraldeen ordered the doors closed and asked that no one disturb them, save for Lord Uziguzi.

"Please forgive Uziguzi," said Gaëla, "not everyone can be trusted."

Noraldeen nodded thoughtfully. "I gathered as much. I know the Silent understand the meaning of the term Doopeleedo when used by an ally. How did he become advisor to the empress?"

In another diplomatic context, her questions would be considered forward, almost aggressive. Orgond knew the Empyreans preferred this direct style and refrained from speaking.

"He is not Empyrean, but his extensive travel and knowledge of the world makes him a highly qualified and trusted adviser. I believe his ridiculous name means *wise one* in his native land. That he called you Doopeleedo," she added while glancing at Lord Orgond, "is high praise. He reserves this term of endearment for the royal Empyrean family."

The idea of the fat man calling Empyreans Doopeleedo brought a smile to Noraldeen's face.

Uziguzi walked in followed by three servants. "You may thank me now, Princess." He carried as many dishes as the servants, and helped set the table. "I was once a cook," he said looking at Noraldeen. "Cookery is the best diplomatic school, right before crookery," he added with a grin. "The table is now ready. You may leave my friends, I shall take care of the service. Thank you very much and do please keep that chicken soup warm for me. I shall have it for desert." He walked the servants out and came back a short moment later. "Your men and the princess' elite guards are standing outside your quarters. We are safe to speak freely. Doopeleedo, sit next to me. I am so happy to see your ruddy face. It is a pleasure."

"The pleasure is all mine, Pottiporo," replied Noraldeen. "I am enthralled to see that you have grown a prickly mustache."

Uziguzi, about to shove a massive piece of chicken into his mouth, froze and eyed Noraldeen. She grinned. A silent chuckle shook his frame and he exploded in boisterous laughter. "That impossible Tanios. I cannot believe he used *my words* to teach you diplomacy. So you knew what Doopeleedo meant then?"

"Yes, Pottiporo, I did."

"Impressive, Lord Orgond. Go ahead, what are you all waiting for? That's why I became a buffoon. We eat warm food, while royalty eat cold food, like slaves. Dig in, dig in."

"If you ever get bored, Lord Jar," said Noraldeen, "you are welcome here in Amsheet. The house of Orgond needs a buffoon of your caliber."

"Ha. Spoken like a true Empyrean." exclaimed Uziguzi. He noticed Orgond and Gaëla glare at him, but he continued. "What? Orgond? My friend," he said pointing a fork at Lord Orgond. "This one will cost you."

"Father, what is Lord Uziguzi alluding to?"

"That's Uncle Zuzu to you, Doopeleedo," added Uziguzi smiling. "Oh boy, this is entertainment."

"Princess Gaëla, this must be serious," said Lord Orgond, trying to change the topic.

"It is. I fear for our kingdoms."

"For the Empyrean kingdom?" Orgond was visibly shaken. "Is the empress in danger?"

"Not imminently."

"Pray tell."

Gaëla smiled at Noraldeen who followed the conversation with controlled surprise. Her father had called the Empyrean princess by her first name which was unusual. "How much does your daughter know?"

"Not much. I suppose I should have told her earlier."

"This chicken is scrumptious, is it not, Doopeleedo? Could you pass the salad to uncle Zuzu? Thanks a bunch, you're a treasure. Orgond dearest, are you going to tell her, or do you wish me to do it? Time is running out."

"Tell me what? What am I supposed to know?" Noraldeen straightened.

"You don't usually wear dresses, do you?" asked Uziguzi. "No, this is not about your dress. And by the way, you are ravishing, Pumpkin. But don't worry, no one will confuse you with a ravishing pumpkin."

"Lord Uziguzi," said the Empyrean princess, "I do not believe this strategy to alley Princess Noraldeen's fear is working well."

"Ah," said Uziguzi looking up from his plate. "Odd. Usually it works well with full-blooded Empyreans. I can't count the number of times my silliness has averted the spilling of Empyrean blood."

"Let me handle it," said Lord Orgond.

"Great," muttered Uziguzi, "I thought you'd never ask."

"Ask what? Handle what?" interjected Noraldeen. The meeting was not going as she had imagined. "What am I supposed to know?"

Lord Orgond sighed heavily. "Daughter, how much do you know about your mother?"

"What you have told me, Father. That she died giving birth to me, and that she was a beautiful and fair woman. You told me you loved her very much, and she loved you even more."

Orgond bowed his head and whispered, "Yes, my daughter, much more." He looked at her before continuing. "You know that I was involved in the battle of Ar-Gaeer, do you not?"

"Yes, Father."

"And you know that we fought side-by-side with the Empyreans?"

"Yes, Father."

"Well, during this war, I met a beautiful Empyrean and we fell in love.

Her name was Layal Meïr Pen, the youngest sister of Aylul—"

"My mother was Empyrean?" interrupted Noraldeen.

"Yes, she was. By marrying me, she renounced her birthright and had to leave her home, her beloved kingdom and all her riches. She came to start a life with me here. She fell ill while pregnant with you, but she told me that giving you life was to be her greatest battle, her highest victory. It became her final triumph. Your mother was a warrior of unmatched skills amongst the Empyreans. She fought for your life until the very end when she held you in her arms and kissed you. She handed you to me, and was gone. She gave you life, then gave her life to you because she so loved you. There is so much Empyrean in you, daughter."

Conflicting feelings overcame Noraldeen. She felt privileged to have been given so much love, but sad that she had not known her mother, and angry that her father had kept the truth from her for so long.

"Why did you not tell me, Father?"

He looked down and whispered, "To prevent a war."

"I don't understand."

"Your father feared that a child may not realize the full meaning of these events, and as a result, many would know that an Empyrean princess had married a man of Tanniin," replied Gaëla softly.

"And so?"

"So, my dearest daughter, this valley would have been sacked and I would have burned at the stake," continued her father.

"By who? Who would do such things?"

"The Empyreans," replied Gaëla with a sad tone. "We have a strict code of conduct. Any Empyrean is free to marry a worthy warrior of another race; any Empyrean, except for a member of the royal family. It would have been preferable for my aunt to marry an Empyrean slave than for her to marry your father."

These last words struck Noraldeen's heart like a sword. Her eyes welled with tears and she silently looked at her father. He understood immediately the meaning of this look. Unable to keep her composure any further, Noraldeen left the room. Lord Orgond sighed.

"See," said Uziguzi who was busy cleaning his plate, "my silly ways may have been a bit easier to handle, don't you think?"

"I wish it were that easy," sighed Orgond.

"Can I be of help, Uncle?"

Lord Orgond smiled. He knew what it meant for the princess to call him Uncle. "Perhaps. As you know, my daughter is a Silent. Commander Tanios trained her himself."

"A worthy teacher whose fame is known to us."

"Worthy indeed. Tanios enrolled a slave as a member of the Silent Corps. Noraldeen spoke highly of him. At first, I did not pay much attention to her praises. By the end of her training she could not stop talking about him and saying his name, 'Ahiram this, Ahiram that.' I argued with her when she refused a wonderful suitor from Ophir. She told me she loves Ahiram and she will not wed anyone else. I called her to my side and invited many worthy men of great valor and nobility. They found Noraldeen charming and fit for marriage, but she rejected them all, maintaining that she loves him and him alone. I had not realized how serious she was until now."

Uziguzi chuckled silently. "Charming as usual, Orgond. You do know how to make a romantic mess of things. First your wife, then your daughter. Now that the princess has told Noraldeen the truth, it would have been more preferable for her mother to be with a slave than to have been with you. Ha. The irony of it all."

"She is so much like her mother; independent, determined, and stubborn. I wanted Tanios to teach her how to control her Empyrean temper. Who would have thought she would fall for a slave? Yes, it is ironic. Still, I am glad it is in the open now. I shall speak with Noraldeen later. Tell me all and do not hide anything from me, I beg of you."

Uziguzi became suddenly serious. "We need your help."

"Incredible. Who could do this to the Empyreans? The lowlanders?"

Princess Gaëla's shoulders sank a little. "No. Empyreans."

"What?" Lord Orgond could hardly believe his ears.

"Much of what we know is incomplete at best. About a month ago, Empyreans began disappearing in great numbers from the Avaleyyan valley. We organized search teams and they disappeared as well. Gone without a trace and no search party could find them. We closed off all roads leading to the southeastern realm and warned everyone. Despite our best efforts, entire villages were abandoned."

"The only adviser who followed these events was Uziguzi," continued Gaëla. "No one in the court paid attention to him and despite my concerns, my mother did not follow his advice. He suggested we raze and burn the forest. But she found this measure excessive, and the worries of the court kept her from giving this matter her full attention."

"Naturally," surmised Orgond. "After all, you are talking about events that started four weeks ago; hardly a reason to burn a forest."

"Aha, Orgond, ahaha. You were never a cook my friend. Once a fruit is diseased, the disease spreads quickly to the other fruits and vegetables, and anything else nearby. If you do not take drastic measures, you won't have anything left in your kitchen for your guests." He cut the air with the flat of his hand. "All would be rotten."

"So you think this is what is happening."

He nodded forcefully. "Some magic works slowly, and some magic works faster than the wind."

"I see. Then what happened?"

"They attacked."

"They?"

"The sylveeds," continued Uziguzi. "Five days ago. Thin, small creatures with ash-white colored skin. They walk in darkness and fear the light. Fire scares them. They have no fear and spread terror anywhere they go and we don't know how to stop them."

"How can this be?" exclaimed Orgond. "The might of the Empyrean army is without compare. I cannot believe these sylveeds could defeat it."

"They cannot," replied Gaëla with pride. "If this were a matter of military might, we would have crushed them long ago. But it is not."

"Then what is it?"

Gaëla looked Orgond in the eye before continuing. "Many of the sylveeds are our sisters."

"I do not understand."

"Many of these creatures are Empyreans," explained Uziguzi. "They are our own people. Like I said, there's a mighty evil magic behind this. Something or someone is taking Empyreans, dwarfs, and humans and turning them into these monsters."

"It is happening with frightening speed," continued Gaëla. "There is now an army of sylveeds."

Orgond shuddered. "Someone or something is attracting Empyreans, humans, and dwarfs, turning them into sylveeds, then throwing them back at you? This seems unbelievable. Are you sure?"

"Yes," replied Gaëla with a quiet voice. "If a sylveed dies shortly after the ghastly transformation takes place, it reverts back to its former self." She looked at Orgond again with imploring eyes. "It is disheartening to see a being as ugly as a sylveed turn back into your best friend. Our army is paralyzed. Each one is afraid they would be killing her sister, her mother, or her daughter."

"How can we be of help?" asked Orgond.

"Uziguzi urged me to come down to the Avaleyyan valley to see for myself. Three days ago, we tracked a group of sylveeds, and they lead us to Hardeen. The fortress has become their lair."

"Hardeen?" Orgond gazed at the advisor. "Lord Awaniir commands the fortress. I know him personally. He is incapable of such evil."

"Princess Gaëla did not say the commander of the fortress is the cause of this evil, rather that—"

"The evil that had decimated the Empyrean Kingdom," continued Lord Orgond, "and has taken residence in Hardeen."

Princess Gaëla nodded.

"Evil with immense power," continued Uziguzi. "And left unchecked, none of the kingdoms are safe." His voice was now a whisper.

"We must overtake Hardeen," added Gaëla. "We must."

"Overtake Hardeen?" repeated Orgond. "This will be supremely difficult. King Jamiir has been deposed. I have sent a delegation to meet with Soloron, the man who sits on the throne now, regarding his intent and I have yet to hear from him. Besides, most of my men would balk at the idea of attacking their beloved fortress, and even if I were to muster such force, the death toll would be very high."

"My Empyreans are ready. We do not wish to invade Tanniin, yet it is imperative to be rid of this evil," insisted the princess.

"I see," replied Lord Orgond. "So, you are doing this without the formal approval of the Empress, are you not?"

Gaëla gave him a hard stare. "My mother is busy with the affairs of the court. I will not trouble her with this matter."

"So, Uziguzi, you thought it best for me to initiate the attack then ask the Empyreans for help? This would give further justification for Gaëla to act without seeking the consent of her mother?"

"Exactly."

"Brilliant, as usual. How much time before the Empyrean attack?"

"Gaëla's will meet us at Hardeen in ten days," disclosed the advisor.

"Let us wait to hear back from Taniir-The-Strong. Meanwhile, I will ready us for the move against Hardeen. We are in the midst of the preparations for the Carnival of Jaguar-Night; we will leave the day after. It will be a three to four day journey to Hardeen if we keep the troops moving for ten to twelve hours a day," said Orgond.

He sighed. This was much worse than he had expected. He knew the Empyreans would attack, and if Tanniin refused to cooperate, they would take it as a sign of loyalty to the enemy. And if evil forces had overtaken the fortress, the responsibility would fall on his shoulders to see that Hardeen was freed.

"This requires planning. For now, let us eat and get some rest. I do not know when you will be able to get much of either in the days to come."

The princess smiled and helped herself to the food being served. As a soldier, she valued her uncle's advice. Lord Orgond excused himself and left to go to his daughter. He had a difficult conversation ahead of him and wanted to address it before the coming of the storm.

20. Sylveeds Prowling

"What are forests for? I haven't the faintest idea. They're made of prickly things that stand all day long like the prickly hair of a prickly beard on a prickly face. Shave it I say. Shave it all, and turn it into an open space for the nobility to parade around all day long like chicken outside the coop. That way, we may enjoy a few hours of peace at the castle while everyone is away."

—Soliloquy of Zuzu the Hip, Jester of the Royal Court of Tanniin.

The following morning, Soloron walked into the Royal Hall at sunrise, hoping to get some peace and quiet before the start of another day. He sat on the throne, and savored the silence.

"Frajil bored," exclaimed Frajil.

Soloron nearly fell off his throne. "Bored?" he roared. "I am trying to run the kingdom, and you are bored? What do you want me to do? Dance on my head?"

"You can do that?" asked his giant half-brother. He was impressed.

"No, Frajil, I cannot. It's a manner of speech."

"Oh," said Frajil, disappointed. "What can you do then? Frajil bored."

Soloron dreamed of an edict that would appoint an adviser to the king who would strangle his exasperating brother. *Only a mindless boar would attempt to strangle Frajil, though.* He shuddered at the thought. He heaved a deep sigh and tried once more to sit comfortably on his throne, as it was made of two cold, marble slabs. *I expected the kingdom to run itself.* His appreciation for Jamiir's rule was rising. Secretly, he regretted overthrowing the King. *These royal clerks fill my days with dreary meetings and endless ceremonies. They'll be the death of me.* Soloron ached for a mug of cold ale, but the royal clerks warned him he would be breaking protocol. Four hundred years back, King Arindiil XIV amended the royal protocol that forbade a Tanniinite king from consuming ale. His father, King Arindiil XIII, died of an excess of ale on the very throne Soloron now sat upon. *Amending a protocol takes six months of hard work.* Soloron itched to fire the court. *However, a king without a court is nothing but a shepherd on a throne.*

The visit with Captain Enryl, Orgond's messenger, had been informative. He had received with honor the young lad who relayed to him a Togofalkian message: "Togofalk disapproves of the takeover. Their treaty with the Temple compels them to military action should Baal demand it. Furthermore, the Empyrean empress favors Lord Orgond." Soloron got up and paced. Frajil mimicked him. Like a living shadow, he stopped, turned, and scratched his head in perfect cadence with his brother. Soloron ignored him. *Soon, Baal will send an envoy before unleashing their armada. They will want to discuss alternatives. Togofalk to the north, and the High Riders' barracks to the south. A war on two fronts. Is this what I want?*

Soloron knew the armada would reach his shores within the next three months. *I have to control the ports.* Even though he had the muscle to do it forcefully, he hoped he could take them peacefully. He sighed. He was a man used to roaming freely. *I am no politician. I am a man of action. Truthfully, I wanted to rid the kingdom of King Jamiir, not take his place. Let someone else sit on this marble slab.*

He stopped pacing and noticed his brother standing in a corner.

"What are you doing?"

"Frajil wants to be un-bored."

"I know that, but what can you do that does not bore you? Do you want to eat chicken?"

"No," replied Frajil with distaste. "Yesterday, Frajil eat five chickens. No more chicken for Frajil."

"Five, huh?" mumbled Soloron. *No wonder I had to eat parsley and mushrooms.* "Fine," he continued out loud, "no chicken for Frajil."

"Never?" asked Frajil with a worried voice.

"I did not say never. I said *for now*, until you are not bored anymore."

"Not bored?" Frajil was confused. "Frajil bored or Frajil not bored?"

"Frajil bored, no chicken. When Frajil not bored, Frajil eat chicken. Frajil understands?"

"Yes, yes. No chicken."

"Good, no chicken. What does Frajil want to do?"

"Frajil wants to be un-bored again."

"You mean you do not want to be bored, right?"

Frajil's thought process seemed to reach a climax. His eyes lit up and he said excitedly, "Yes."

"Good, so what do you feel like doing?"

"Frajil wants carnival."

"But I told you, we cannot go to the Carnival of Jaguar-Night. I am the king now, and my rear is tied to this throne."

Frajil came closer and inspected the situation. "I see no rope from Soloron's rear to throne," he said waving his hand. "Soloron free to go."

Soloron sighed. "No, Frajil, I am not free to go. It's complicated."

"Complicated is boring. Frajil wants carnival."

Soloron opted for a different tactic. "Listen. Middle Road, which leads to the carnival, is blocked. You can't go." Frajil shrugged his shoulders. "What can you do? Force your way through the barricades?"

Frajil's eyes lit up. "Yes." he replied. "Frajil wants to do that. This is un-bored for Frajil."

"Right. This would be exciting, but it will also get you killed."

"No, Frajil careful. Frajil will not go there alone."

"No?" asked Soloron, amazed that his half-brother made sense. "You mean you would take men with you?"

"Men?" asked Frajil confused. "Frajil takes chicken, when Frajil excited, Frajil un-bored and hungry. Frajil eats chicken and he is well and not badly dead." Proud as a peacock, Frajil stood tall; he had said three related sentences in one breath.

Soloron sighed. A crisis brewed along the northern road. Someone had erected a large barricade that disrupted communications between Amsheet and Hardeen. Soloron needed to reopen the road, but the southern High Riders' barracks was a more pressing matter. Thus far, he had reestablished order at Taniir-the-Strong, restructured the army, and sent delegates to the southern ports seeking their submission and they had yet to return.

"What does Frajil do? Frajil not un-bored."

"You want to go to the carnival? Go to the carnival," exclaimed Soloron exasperated. "I do not care. Go!"

"Frajil goes. Frajil back with candies, dates, pomegranates for Soloron. No more upset Soloron."

➤ ◦◦◦ ≺

"This an improbable probability and a probability most improbable," whispered Zurwott.

Ahiram nodded. They sat on tree branches east of Middle Road and peered at a monstrous barricade. After leaving the castle they had followed Middle Road without incident until it led them to this barricade and the foul smell that surrounded it. The stillness, the lack of noise, and the destructive power behind the barricade all spoke of hidden danger.

"It's as if a giant scooped up a village, a herd of cows, and a mountainside, and mixed them into a giant barricade," whispered Jedarc.

"Apt description," replied Sheheluth. "I've never seen anything like it."

"The avalanche south of us looks like a mound by comparison," Sondra added.

"Hiyam."

The young woman nearly jumped when she heard Ahiram call her name. "Don't be nervous," whispered Jedarc. "He doesn't bite."

"And if he does," added Sheheluth, who had taken a liking to Bahiya's daughter, "I'll kick him."

Hiyam smiled as she dropped down several branches. "Yes, Ahiram?"

"Can the Temple do this?"

Hiyam had already thought through the possibility. "Yes, it can."

"What about your mother?"

The tone was quiet, restrained, and neutral. Still, the question stung. "My mother? Yes. If she wills it, she could do this, but why?"

"Is it magical?"

"I would have to take a closer look."

"Sondra, Banimelek, go with Hiyam. I'll stay behind for backup. Jedarc and Sheheluth, keep watch from up here. Orwutt and Zurwott, keep an eye on the forest ground. Let's go."

An hour later, they were back in the safety of the trees. Hiyam was shaken. "This hill reeks of magic. It's evil. It's the same source as …" she struggled to complete her sentence, "as the magic behind the giant geyser."

The urkuun, thought Ahiram. He saw fear in the young woman's eyes.

"What can you tell us about intent?" asked Sondra.

"What would it take to remove this barricade?" added Banimelek.

"My kingdom for a banana," sighed Jedarc. "What? I'm hungry."

"Don't touch the barrier," said Hiyam. "It's ringed by powerful curses."

The dwarfs, who could be silent when needed, listened intently.

"So we need magic to remove it?" confirmed Banimelek.

Hiyam nodded. "You need to defeat its maker."

"What's its purpose?" asked Ahiram.

"It is a landmark of sorts. He is marking his dominion a bit the way dogs mark their territory."

"That's a mighty dog if he could drop one this size," mused Jedarc. "What? Why are you staring at me like that? I mean look at it … it's an apt description."

"So where's his territory? Can you tell?" asked Sondra.

"The forest east of the road," replied Hiyam.

"Including or excluding the road?" asked Jedarc.

"Excluding the road," clarified Hiyam.

"West of the road is Magdala, the Forbidden Forest. The curse would have no effect on it," explained Banimelek. "But why not the road?"

"Ancient and powerful spells protect this road," clarified Hiyam. "Something only Sureï the Sorcerer could have done."

"That makes sense, I suppose."

"What should we do now?" asked Sondra.

"How do we cross?" added Banimelek. "We cannot step inside Magdala, so we would have to cross through Laymiir."

Hiyam shook her head. "The curses extend far into the forest of Laymiir. We cannot pass."

"We would have to travel back to Taniir-The-Strong, down into Renlow Valley, and follow the river upstream to the edge of Magdala," explained Sondra. "I see no alternative."

"That's a ten-day detour, at least," objected Banimelek.

"What choice do we have?"

"This is a reasonable reasoning and a reasoning of the most reasonable reason," commented Zurwott. "When facing a stubborn stubbornness, the wisdom of the wise demandingly demand a properly proper retreating retreat." He was out of breath for having spoken so quickly.

"My brother agrees. We should retreat."

"Zurwott and Sondra are right," sighed Ahiram. "Let's rest now until the sun is high before we go back. Jedarc, take the first shift."

Wrath of the Urkuun – Sylveeds Prowling

Ahiram sat cross-legged, and waited for the sun to crawl up the sky. The ten-day detour angered him, but he knew this was the right thing to do. He heard a quiet rustle and saw Sheheluth walk swiftly on the branch to come sit next to him. She gave him a thoughtful gaze. *Why is she not upset with me?* thought Ahiram.

"I am not upset with you, you know?" she said, with a quiet sweet voice. "I was afraid for you. Hatred is not the way of the Silent."

Ahiram heaved a sigh. "I've been so busy with my own loss, I never stopped to think about anyone else. How strange. I'm becoming like the people who took me away. I don't know what I can promise to whom, but now that I know I'm a sormoss, I will do everything I can to fix it. This I can promise."

She smiled. "For a sormoss, you learn fast."

"I always do. Don't forget that."

Their eyes met, and she could see the deep, burning fire, the iron-fisted will and something else; something she had seen before.

"It's *théléos*, your ability to channel energy from a remote source to a proximate target."

"It's what?"

"What you call your temper is a powerful energy you're tapping into; and you've used it to defeat the monster."

"It's not just temper?" asked Ahiram, bewildered.

"Of course not," laughed Sheheluth. "A temper, at least a bad one, leads you to raise your hand to strike a defenseless woman. Your temper couldn't defeat this monster, not with the thirty-two rings of spells protecting it. Come on, Ahiram! You should know that by now."

"Thirty-two rings of what?"

"Of ..." She looked at him wide-eyed. "You didn't see them?"

"See what? Listen Sheheluth, I've got the part of being a sormoss. You showed me that and I can see it clearly now. Got that. I'll work on it. But energy? And thirty-two rings of what? I recall seeing a beast in front of me. Was there something else I was supposed to see?"

He cut through the protective curse rings without seeing them? She was astonished. *How is this possible? Who is he?* "This explains why you nearly killed yourself," she added. "But how could we know if you're telling the truth?" she said in a hushed distant voice, as if speaking to someone else. "You could be lying."

"What are you talking about, and how do you know these things?"

She looked at him as if seeing him for the first time. "You attacked the béghôm without seeing the curse rings around her? What were you thinking?" Her voice was harsh once more, demanding, imperious.

"What else was I supposed to do?" His anger was mounting. "The monster chased us. I had to face her. What else could I do?"

She breathed deeply and closed her eyes. When she opened them, she was in control once more and smiled gently.

"Sheheluth, one minute you're cold and the next you're about to blow up. Make up your mind. These mood swings are hard to put up with."

She laughed. "I know, I'm so sorry about … my behavior," she added sheepishly. "But never mind that. Listen, when you throw a dart, it moves in the air because of the energy in your arm, right?"

"Yes." Ahiram sighed.

"Magic works in similar ways. In the end, magic is a different way to throw a dart. Instead of using your own strength, you use someone else's strength, or *something* else."

"So, you mean to say I was using magic?"

She looked at him aghast. *He knows nothing. How could this be?* "I believe so." She could sense how lost he was and avoided chiding him. "How else did you manage to kill this monster?"

"Frankly, I don't know. I mean I didn't stop to think about it. When I found the sword—"

"El-Windiir's sword?"

He glanced at her. "You knew?"

She smiled and refrained from rolling her eyes. "*We* know, Ahiram. What other sword could it be?"

He sighed and closed his eyes. "That's the thing, Sheheluth. That's the thing. I don't want this sword. I didn't want to be the one to kill the beast. I don't want to be in charge here. I —"

"You just want to go home."

"Yes, and I want to take Noraldeen with me."

"Do you love her?"

He laughed a bitter laugh. "Can you imagine Noraldeen as the wife of a shark fisherman?"

"No, but I can imagine you as a prince." Sheheluth's voice was tender.

"I don't want to be a prince. I want to go home. I want to see my sister and my parents. That's what I want."

"So, you chose not to speak to us about the sword, because if you told us you had found the sword of El-Windiir, we would do everything we could to keep you in Tanniin, right?"

He nodded. "I should have been gone by now, Sheheluth. I should have been free by now and on my way home. What am I doing here?"

Gently, she placed a hand on his arm. "Théléos is the energy you must use to defeat the monster behind this mound. Think of it as a … a spigot. You know, you turn it, water flows, you turn it in the opposite direction, and water stops flowing."

"But I don't recall doing any such thing."

"Listen, if you want to stop the flow of water, you build a dam, right?"

"You mean across the river?"

"That's right. The béghôm was like a castle protected by thirty-two walls. When you attacked her with your sword, you managed to cut through all thirty-two walls at once."

"That's impossible," scoffed Ahiram. "I did no such thing."

"You beat the monster. It's gone."

"I didn't see any dams or walls or anything."

"I saw them," said the young girl.

He glanced at her and smiled awkwardly. "Sorry, Sheheluth, I believe in what I see. You'll have to show me if you want me to believe you. That's just how it works with me."

"Does it now?" she replied. Her voice had slightly changed once more, it was sarcastic. "Haven't you ever seen something no one else could see?"

He was about to scoff at her when he remembered Jedarc's reaction when he showed him the gold tile. *Jedarc did not see it*. Ahiram pulled it from his pocket, laid it in his open palm, and presented it to Sheheluth. "Do you see something?"

She glanced at his hand and shook her head. "Do *you* see something?"

"I do," he replied, embarrassed.

"Very well, now hold whatever you see with both hands, close your eyes, and tell me what you see."

"That sounds ridiculous."

"Just do it, Ahiram."

Ahiram shrugged his shoulders, held the tile in both hands, and closed his eyes. At first, he saw nothing, that is, nothing more than the usual. He felt the cool hand of Sheheluth on top of his.

"Keep looking," she whispered.

"I see blackness, like the sky at night and …" he hesitated, "yes, there are stars, so many stars."

"Stars?" she asked shaken. "Are you certain?"

"Yes. They're getting closer. It's like I'm in the abode of the gods."

"Are you scared?"

"No, it's exhilarating. The stars are moving in my direction and there are so many of them. They are clumped into clusters, like sand in the air."

"Ahiram," interjected Sheheluth, "grapes are in clusters. Throw sand in the air, and it disperses. Don't be poetic; just tell me what you see."

"I'm not being poetic. I'm telling you they look like … like a bunch of bright grains of sand frozen in the air."

"That's poetic, but I get the idea. Now what?"

"They are so white … bright white. Wait, one of them is getting closer. It is now the size of the sun and is growing larger. It's huge. It stopped in front of me. It's so big … I don't see anything else, its …"

Sheheluth pulled her hand and the vision was gone.

Ahiram opened his eyes and blinked. "That was amazing, Sheheluth, amazing. I didn't know stars could be that big." He looked at her. In the dim light, she was white as a sheet. "What?" he said. "What did I do?"

"You're théléolyss," she said shaken, "the god-crusher."

"I'm the what now?"

"Your source of energy is from the gods. The stars are the sign of their presence, and you are harnessing the stars to do your magic. Only a god could do such a thing, or a Malikuun, a Lord of Light."

"Hey, I'm a sormoss okay? I am not a god, nor am I a Lord of Light."

"No, you are much more," she said, "and I have yet to decide if you are friend or foe."

Before Ahiram could say anything, she vanished.

≻⁙≺

When the sun rose over the eastern Karian Chain, the town of Amsheet was abuzz with activity. Preparations were well under way for the Carnival of Jaguar-Night. News that the famed statue of the god was already in town heightened everyone's expectations. The sick and the lame poured into town. Healings and cures were ascribed to these processions. Tourists and souvenir vendors with hoards of trinkets filled the streets. One could always buy a plate of *tamril or rumanil*, the local desserts that made Amsheet famous. Tamril consisted of fresh dates stuffed with roasted walnuts, pine nuts, and sweet blackberries. Rumanil was the famous golden pomegranate treat. Orange blossom water mixed with honey was injected into four small incisions made close to the stem of the fruit to add fragrance and sweetness. The incisions were then sealed with wax and the pomegranate was dipped in ice.

"Give me one of each," said a tall man with a slight tone of impatience in his voice. The young lad manning the booth placed the tamril and rumanil into a small wicker basket and handed it to the man. He was relieved to see the tall customer leave.

Despite its name, the Tavern of the Hot Potato and Three Turnips was not a tourist spot. Located deep within the city's bowels in a shady neighborhood that had seen better days, the tavern served exclusively Togofalkian gangs. Admittance was by invitation only. Wanderers were summarily ejected and warned never to come back. The tavern was comfortable and quiet; small rooms dimly lit by fireplaces had all the intimacy needed for plotting and scheming. The tavern served as a neutral zone for representatives of warring gangs to meet and resolve their differences or form alliances against other gangs. As local tentacles of the Togofalkian hydra that operated in most kingdoms, these gangs plagued the trade road that linked Hardeen to Amsheet.

Ibromaliöm threw the wicker basket away before knocking on the iron door of the tavern. A bald waiter with a hydra tattoo on his scalp—and enough arm muscles to wring water out of a log—ushered him into a cozy room where a fire, already lit, was waiting for him. He took a sip of cherry wine and clapped his tongue with satisfaction. The tavern made a point to serve the best wine in town. The price of reserving a small discussion room was exorbitant, but if his plan went as expected, it would be well worth it. He finally saw the two men he had been waiting for. Ibromaliöm closed his eyes. A slave carefully added two logs to the fire, then closed the door and left the three men alone. The newcomers sat on two chairs opposite Ibromaliöm. The pair was striking; they were from Togofalk and belonged to a major gang. Orag was frail, weak, and sickly. The other, Tophun Makack, was tall and muscular, with a nonexistent neck, and a head shaped like an anvil. In the Togofalkian language, Orag meant *the planner* and Tophun Makack meant *fists of stone and ice*.

"So?" asked Ibromaliöm without opening his eyes.

"It can be done," replied Orag in a hushed, elegant tone.

"When?" snapped the former judge.

"During the procession."

"The procession? Daring. I like it. How?"

"We bribed the organizers to slightly adjust the itinerary for the procession. They will take the statue under the widest bridge in Amsheet. Our men will be waiting to take the relay and carry the statue away. While under the bridge, they will replace the true eyelids with fake ones. They will then pass the statue to another group of carriers before leaving. Simple, really."

"Are you certain the fake eyelids will fool the examiners?"

"Per your request, dwarfs from Poytal, in Thermodon, have forged them. They charge an arm and a leg for a rushed job, but no one will ask questions this far north. They may not fool the examiners, but they will fool everyone else. By the time the examiners inspect those eyelids, we will be long gone."

The plan was simple, but it did not satisfy Ibromaliöm. "The tourists will hear of the change and will flood that bridge to be close to the statue. Anything can go wrong then. How should we handle it?"

"Good question as usual, Master Ibromaliöm. To protect the statue, the organizers will restrict access to the bridge. Only members of the procession will be allowed on it."

"And those members will be our own men," concluded Ibromaliöm. "Be sure to add me to the list. I want to oversee the entire operation."

"Sure boss, consider it done."

"Very well. I shall see you in three days, on the bridge."

"Four days, Master Ibromaliöm, the carnival is in four days."

"Is it, now? Four days then. Succeed and you will be handsomely rewarded." He closed his eyes. When he opened them again, the men were gone. He sipped some more of the cherry wine and stretched out by the fire. Ever since he had the book in his possession, his hunger for its secrets had known no bounds. It consumed him and gnawed at him until he surrendered to its demands. He knew the book was under an unimaginable curse, but he would not be deterred. Whenever other readers looked at the open book, they would trigger the curse upon themselves, affording him a safe window to hear a voice read to him just a few words. Who was behind that voice, he did not know; but for the sake of the secrets held inside the *Ithyl Shimea*—the book which was a maleficent key created by a dwarfish sorcerer and his Empyrean consort to open the Pit—he was willing to listen to it. *The reading window is short*, thought the former judge while sipping his wine, *but long enough for a dying man to breathe his last. Oh well, there is no dearth of fools around here.* For the past few days, he had slept by day and haunted the shady parts of town by night, waiting for drunkards to stumble out of taverns. He would stop them and ask if they wanted a drink then shove the open book before their faces. Initially, the effect of the curse had overwhelmed him, reminding him of Ramel. But after his tenth victim, the feeling of guilt dissipated and each victim became a safe, five-second reading window into the book.

He had already deciphered the first page. It told him of three ways to alter the curse. The eyelids of Jaguar-Night would afford him a longer period of reading time, perhaps a full minute. The Cup of Eleeje, hidden somewhere in the Kingdom of Marada, might break the curse, giving him unimpeded access to the book's content. The third way was a spell that could turn cripples into mediums who could suffer the full brunt of the curse without dying. Eventually, the curse would consume them, turning them into something he did not understand, a *raayiil*. He had a vague memory of the fat judge—what was his name again, Rabu? Blubu? He could no longer remember, but that judge had once mentioned a raayiil.

Raayiil, jmaayiil, what do I care? I'll grab the eyelids and then the cup. If I can't lay my hands on that cup, I'll open a hospice for cripples and use them for my book. Wait, why wait? I'll open one anyway, for cripples, orphans, unwanted babies, the elderly, I'll be the city cleaner. I'll be a good citizen. The gentry will love me. A murderous smile slit Ibromaliöm's face that caused the hair of the tattooed waiter, who had just entered, to stand on end. He retreated and refused to go back inside the room.

Four days, that's time enough for Galliöm to act. Ibromaliöm needed wealth. Being a former tajèr, he knew the location of the tajéruun's vault in Amsheet, and had stolen enough gold to last him three lifetimes. In his wake was a pile of cursed, dead bodies. *It won't take the tajéruun long. They'll find out I did this and will come after me.*

"My dear Ibromaliöm," a soothing voice whispered, "soon the book will yield its secrets. You will become the high priest and combine the secrets of the Temple with the secrets of this book. No one will stand in your way." He felt inebriated by a glory that just a few weeks ago he did not know existed. And now he was about to walk with the gods.

"What about the slave?" whispered a second voice.

Ibromaliöm threw his glass violently into the fire. The fire flared for a brief moment. "He is dead," he shouted. "Dead, I tell you."

"Maybe," replied the second voice. "And maybe not."

Ibromaliöm sprung from his chair and paced. While listening to the first page of the *Ithyl Shimea*, he had seen, in a vision, the slave from the mines rise with great power against him.

"The vision is no dream, Ibromaliöm," whispered the voice. "He will wrest the power from your very hands at a moment you do not expect, unless you be rid of him first."

"Speculation. No one knows how to interpret these visions?"

"You saw the face of that slave."

"Bruised and battered and near death, yes." snapped Ibromaliöm. "And I also saw the priestess of Baal, and that idiot, Baru, or what's-his-name, and a slew of others as well. Who is to say that this slave will wrest anything from me?"

These self-inflicted arguments tired Ibromaliöm. To test his own internal logic, he had grown accustomed to argue opposite sides of the same point. He wished he could stop but could not help it. The stakes were high, and the face of Ahiram kept popping up like a distracting fly. Deep down, Ibromaliöm sensed Ahiram could mean trouble—even though he did not know why. Moreover, no amount of logic could shake his conviction. He tried once more to convince himself. "So far there is no trace of him. When he appears, we will take good care of this lad." Ibromaliöm smiled at this prospect and breathed deeply trying to whisk away his doubts. Soon, the eyelids of Jaguar-Night would be his.

When it was his turn to keep watch, Ahiram leaned against a tree trunk, his hand cautiously resting on his sword, and his senses alert. He had learned to relax his muscles and rest even in the most awkward positions. He glanced up and sighed. *How long is the night when you're hoping for dawn.* He was impatient to meet with Tanios and Habael again. He needed answers. Tanios had told him that he had been demoted from the privileged rank of Solitary. Was this still true? Now that he had found the real wings of meyroon, was he free or still a slave? He looked to his right and saw Banimelek assuming the same posture. Jedarc slept a few feet away from Hiyam. *Jedarc in love with her? Who would have thought?*

He remembered how sad Jedarc had been when, while on the road, he had pretended to keep Hiyam as a slave, after he had told her he would set her free. It had been a misplaced jest of poor taste. Jedarc's composure had fallen, and Ahiram immediately stopped. Jedarc was one of two people he could not bear to see sad. The other was Noraldeen. He called them the Innocents, an endearment he had shared with Banimelek who grunted in approval. Banimelek and him were like brothers. They carried deep wounds and losses of loved ones. Jedarc and Noraldeen were polar opposites who radiated joy and levity of heart. Gazing at them always gave him hope that good things were possible. The beauty and goodness he saw in them meant his belief in good things to come would be realized one day. His hope, wistful today, may become tangible reality tomorrow. Therefore, he could not bear to see either of them sad or forlorn. Incapable of feeling their joy, he lived by their side like a mendicant who, unable to afford a good meal, sits by the door and is content with the delicious smell. Ahiram needed Jedarc and Noraldeen far more than they ever knew. He needed them to feel whole and be happy, and to that end he would do anything for them.

Ahiram stretched and leaned once more against the tree. Thus far, Hiyam had not given him any cause for concern. Banimelek had tried to talk some sense into Jedarc, but without success. Hiyam surprised them by holding a straightforward conversation with Jedarc. She told him her mother was on her mind, and once they have reached Baalbek, she would invite him over for a formal visit. More than that, she could not offer. This had a sobering effect on the Silent, who calmed down and returned to his good-natured self. Ahiram and Banimelek breathed a sigh of relief.

≻⋅⊙⋅⊙⋅⊙⋅≺

"Ahiram, someone is standing in front of the barricade."

Instantly, Ahiram was up and standing next to Sondra. Light had finally begun to streak the dark sky and they knew dawn would break soon. A giant of a man, and his horse, stood before the barricade. The monstrous size of the barrier did not seem to faze him. The stench was stronger now. Frajil had but one question on his mind: how to get to the Carnival. He worked out a brilliant plan: *Frajil not climb. Horse too heavy on shoulders. Frajil not dig. Frajil go around.*

He was about to enter Magdala when he saw a young man running in his direction. He did not bear a sword and did not look hostile.

"Excuse me, sir," said Jedarc, "I am a Silent of His Majesty."

"Yes?" said the giant, putting on his best manners. "Little one hungry?" which was his way of asking, "Can I help you?"

"Well, you shouldn't enter this forest, it's forbidden."

Frajil sneezed. He was allergic to the word 'forbidden.' "Frajil not understand. Frajil want go to carnival, and Frajil not want to tire by carrying horse over mountain, so Frajil go around."

"But you may not be able to come back."

"Frajil not want to come back. Not till after carnival."

"No, I mean you may not be able to come back at all."

Frajil looked at the young one who spoke to him and saw concern in his eyes. "Young rooster should not worry. Frajil show you he can go and come back. Hold Frajil's horse."

"What are they doing?" grumbled Banimelek.

"I don't know Faernor. We had better go find out," replied Sondra.

The rest of the group joined them. Sheheluth avoided Ahiram; she was still pondering the meaning of her latest discovery about Ahiram, for he was now, in her eyes, théléos, god-crusher.

Ahead, Jedarc tried one more time to stop Frajil. "You mustn't …"

Frajil ignored him. He chose to go around the barricade by way of the Forbidden Forest. He went into the forest and walked through undergrowth until he reached the opposite side of Middle Road.

"Frajil back on road," he yelled. "Frajil not smitten. Frajil come back now." A short moment later, Frajil emerged from the forest. He gripped Jedarc, lifted him, and gave him a bear hug. "Young rooster not worry. Frajil is not, not unharmed."

"Extraordinary," whispered Zurwott. "In the most extraordinarily extraordinary manner."

"Indeed," added Sheheluth. "He managed to get in and out of Magdala unharmed."

"Young roosters want come with me?" asked Frajil. "We go to carnival together." With that, Frajil, who considered it proper to share the load with his horse, lifted the steed and stepped into Magdala.

"Wow ..." said Ahiram.

Everyone else was just as flabbergasted as he was.

"Let's go," said Sheheluth. "What are you waiting for?"

"The Silent shall not tempt the gods," quoted Sondra. "No one has entered the Forest of Magdala and survived. The Silent shall avoid Magdala at all cost."

"The *Book of Siril*, chapter seven, verse five," completed Banimelek.

Sheheluth peered through the opening, then fixed her gaze on Ahiram. In the ambient darkness, her eyes glittered and without warning, the Silent found himself standing once more in front of the massive star.

"Ahiram, what do you see?" Sheheluth's voice was commanding.

"I see ... a star ..."

"Do you see anything *else?*"

Ahiram looked around him. Aside from the light of the star—that somehow did not blind or burn him—there was only the cold hollow space filled with an unbearable silence.

"No. There is nothing else."

Ahiram blinked and was back with his friends standing before the giant mound. The strange experience had only lasted the span of two breaths, and none of his companions noticed anything. He gazed at Sheheluth questioningly. *Not a word to anyone*, she seemed to say.

"I think we can cross," she said.

"How do you know this?" asked Banimelek.

She shrugged her shoulders. "Like I said, I am no stranger to magic, and I can tell you we can cross now." Not waiting, she went ahead.

"Sheheluth, wait," shouted Sondra.

"It's all right," replied the young girl from the other side. "I'm on the main road now. I'm safe."

The Silent and the dwarfs exchanged confused glances.

"What's going on?" whispered Hiyam. "Are we allowed to cross through a forbidden forest now? I am from the Temple …"

"This is forebodingly foreboding, and foreboding in the most forebodingly foreboding manner," stuttered Zurwott.

Jedarc shrugged his shoulders. "Well, Magdala, or whomever lives within, does not like this mound and they're helping us. That's all. I say we cross. Hiyam? What do you think?"

The young High Rider peered into the forest. "I am like Sheheluth; I don't sense any danger."

"Sondra, what do we do?" asked Jedarc.

Sondra exchanged glances with Ahiram and Banimelek. They nodded. "We go then," she said. "Me first."

A moment later, the entire team had joined Frajil and Sheheluth on the opposite side. Was it because Frajil was a simpleton, or because he had the heart of a child that they managed to cross safely? No one knew, but the small company stepped inside Magdala and reached the other side of Middle Road unharmed. They were awed by Frajil who had no understanding of what he had just done. *I'm like him*, thought Ahiram, *a simpleton of sorts. I am dabbling with powers I don't understand.* He glanced at Sheheluth, but she ignored him. *What was the point of showing me that star anyway?*

Frajil hooted. "Good things at carnival. Frajil cannot not, not wait."

His horse snorted. Had his steed been able to talk, he would have yelled at his rider, wondering why Frajil had carried him when he could have easily walked beside him.

➤•◆•◆•◆•≺

By nightfall, their situation had become dire. The stench was now unbearable and still the road dug deeper between the two forests. West of the road, Magdala bristled with unseen life and pleasant scents that reached them from time to time, temporarily subduing the stench that flowed from Laymiir. Alone, Frajil was not excessively bothered by the smell, and his good humor was not dampened. As long as the sun stayed its throne in the heavens, it seemed everything would remain peaceful. When the heavenly orb fell like a soldier onto the battlefield, shadows crept forward and glittering eyes gazing out from beneath the trees followed them. Like an unholy fire, they flowed from bush to bush and from tree to tree. Orwutt and Zurwott each held a torch to keep the creatures at bay.

"Sylveeds, Sylveeds, Sylveeds ..."

The refrain grew and became louder and stronger.

"Silent, draw your crossbows," ordered Sondra. "Hiyam, Sheheluth, inside the circle."

"We can't stay on the road," said Banimelek, "We're too exposed."

"Back into Magdala," ordered Jedarc. "Stay on the edge of the forest but step out from the road."

Everyone followed his command, including Frajil's horse that had taken a liking to the Silent's leader. *At least, this one won't try to carry me, the steed seemed to be thinking.* Alone, Frajil commanded the road when they heard the twang of a bowstring being released.

"Frajil!" shouted Jedarc. "Watch out."

The giant looked back as his hands sprang to his blades. The blades became a blur breaking the strength of the arrows into inoffensive shrapnel. "Woo-hoo," hooted Frajil, "More, more. Frajil love games. Send more. Frajil ready."

Attackers swarmed from the wood and surrounded the giant.

"Ahiram, keep Hiyam and Sheheluth safe," ordered Sondra. "Banimelek and Jedarc, with me. Dwarfs, if you care to fight —"

"We are fitting fighters fit for a fitful fight and not fitful fighters fit for a frightfully fleeting flight," replied Zurwott.

"Zurwott, stop trying to speak in the common tongue. It's dreadful."

"Attack!" shouted Sondra.

==Before the small group reached Frajil, he had mowed down half of the assailants. His long blades in his powerful arms were like windmills caught in a tornado. They were deadly and invisible. A passing shadow, a slight flick of the wrist, and more sylveeds fell.==

"Roosters want help me?" he boomed, seeing the Silent coming to his aid. "And chicks too?" he added when he noticed the dwarfs. "Frajil make one big space."

Ahiram stood and watched the battle. Oddly, his sword did not vibrate. Seeing more of the ashen creatures join the fray, he looked at Hiyam. "I'm going to help them," he said. He was about to unsheathe his blade when Sheheluth placed a hand on his arm. "What are you doing?" he asked.

"You do realize," she snapped, "that as soon as you unsheathe this blade, *he* will know you're here?"

"What do you mean?" Ahiram was confused.

Sheheluth sighed. "I don't understand how you could be wielding this *blade* and not possess even the basic rudiments of magic."

"Let go of my arm, Sheheluth," said Ahiram not listening. "This is my last warning."

"Ahiram," interjected Hiyam, "Sheheluth is right. Use your blade and the magician behind all this will know you're here."

"He is after you, you do realize that, don't you?" pounded Sheheluth.

On the road, the ranks of the sylveeds were swelling.

"Then why hasn't he attacked me before?" snarled Ahiram. "If you're so smart, Miss-I-know-everything, then why didn't he attack me when I used my blade to save Hiyam from the béghôm?"

"I don't know," Sheheluth admitted, "but here you can see his power everywhere. If he knows you're here this skirmish will turn into a desperate battle for us."

"Fine," spat Ahiram yanking his arm away, his temper exploding. "I don't need a sword after all."

"Ahiram!" yelled Sheheluth, but he was already gone.

Like a whirlwind he fell on his attackers. Bones snapped, ribs cracked, and bodies flew. A dark rage animated him, moving him forward, carrying him from one foe to another, his fists and legs working like a tireless beast of old. Nothing stood in his way and still the enemy surged from under the forest threatening to overwhelm the Frajil and the Silent. Despite their resistance, four Silent, two dwarfs and one giant could not sustain the onslaught of hundreds of determined sylveeds—many of whom were trained Empyrean fighters.

Hiyam stepped onto the road, raised her hands to the heavens, then slapped them together. Opening her palms, she willed to repel the attackers. A strong wind surged and forced the sylveeds back. The friends shouted for joy, but then Hiyam screamed and fell holding her head.

Jedarc ran back and held her. "Hiyam, Hiyam what's wrong?"

Sheheluth joined him. "She cannot hear you. She's under attack. Quick, we must take her back to Magdala." Jedarc lifted Hiyam and carried her to the forest.

"They're coming back," warned Ahiram. Without looking away, he tapped with his left foot according to an established pattern. Banimelek lit a torch and threw it high overhead. It streaked the night sky and fell into Laymiir. In the brief moment that the torch lit the night, they saw the forest crawling with sylveeds that lashed out without fear or restraint. Like the head of a viper, they struck with blinding speed, snatched Orwutt and Zurwott, then ran back into the forest.

"After them!" yelled Ahiram.

He felt a heavy hand grip his head, which immobilized him. "Little one stay here. If little one go under trees, little one die. Too many of ugly creatures," said Frajil quietly.

"They have our friends, we must rescue them."

Ahiram grabbed his bag wanting to use his artifacts but recanted. *I am not ready to fly*, he thought with mounting frustration.

"Serpent caught chicks," said Frajil, struggling to string a series of ideas into a comprehensible argument. "Serpent below ground. No hand can catch it. Only fire and smoke. Serpent gone, chicks gone."

"He is right, Alendiir," added Sondra. "We cannot hunt them in the darkness of the forest. We are ill-equipped and we do not know what we are facing."

"Jedarc, how's Hiyam?" asked Ahiram, his eyes locked on Laymiir.

"Recovering," replied Hiyam, still shaken. "His counter-attack is incredible," she said. "I've never faced anything like it."

"By the way," interjected Sondra, "why do you keep saying 'he' this and 'he' that. How do you know it is a 'he'? This bothers me."

"Really, Sondra?" protested Banimelek. "Now?"

She shrugged her shoulders. "Just saying."

"I'm going to start calling you Zurwott," said Jedarc.

"You can all go now," said Ahiram. "I will go rescue Orwutt and Zurwott. They are my friends. I told them they could come with us. I am responsible for them."

Banimelek came and placed a reassuring hand on his friend's shoulder. "You're not betraying them if that's what you're thinking. They wouldn't have gone after you if you had been in there. There's foul magic at play here and we're not equipped to face this horde in the dark."

"Are you sure?"

"Plain as the day is day," said Banimelek. "Besides, don't count them out just yet. Dwarfs are far more resourceful than we give them credit for."

"Ahiram, a word."

He glanced at Sheheluth. "Quickly, then."

"Not on the road," she protested. "In Magdala."

Sensing that Sheheluth wanted to speak alone with Ahiram, the rest of the company stepped a few feet away while remaining under the protection of the forest.

"Your heart is in the right place, but your behaving foolishly."

"Foolishly? These are my friends and if I can help them I—"

"Your action is foolish, even though you are not," cut in Sheheluth impatiently. "Do you remember what I told you about théléos? You are tapping into a powerful source of energy. Well, so are these creatures that attacked us and so is the one behind them."

"And your point?"

"Listen, Ahiram, I know this is hard for you to understand, but with a little experience this will become obvious. ==Your capacity to tap into energy is terrifying. What you can do, what you will be able to do is unimaginable. Anyone with knowledge of these things will want you gone as quickly as possible.== This attack may be a trick to ferret you out. These creatures may have grabbed the dwarfs by mistake. If you go after them with whatever means you have, your enemy, who is stronger than you, will capture and most likely kill you. You are not ready for this."

Ahiram looked at her, trying to assess her intent. "What do you know about the urkuun?"

Sheheluth blanched. "An urkuun? What degree?"

Ahiram shook his head. "He didn't say."

"He spoke with you?"

"On several occasions."

She started pacing nervously. "I don't understand. This makes no sense, unless of course—"

"Sheheluth, I am sorry to say, but I am reaching my limit. My temper is flaring and I don't know—"

"If an urkuun found you, he would have snatched you by now. Once this creature sets its gaze on its victim, there is no escape. So, why are you are still here?"

"Sheheluth, I am going to ask you this one more time." Ahiram's tone was dark, threatening. "Who are you and how do you know these things? How can I know you are not an agent of the urkuun trying to convince me to let my friends die?"

"First sensible question you've asked me. Where I come from, théléos is common. Since childhood we are exposed to it. I know of the urkuun from stories my folks have told us. More I cannot say without endangering the life of a dear friend of mine."

"Which is why I am not sure I can fully trust you. You can't tell me why the urkuun has not attacked yet. But then again, the commander accepted you as a Silent, and if he vouches for you, that's enough for me. All I know is that my friends are in danger and I will defend them."

An inhuman scream, searing like the fire of the Pit and commanding like a dark storm, stilled Laymiir. A sense of dread fell on the company, as if their fate had already been decided. As if defeat awaited them at the end of the road.

"That's one *biiig* chicken," chuckled Frajil. "Who is hungry?"

21. Confluence

"The tajéruun are to the Temple what money is to magic; money requires magic to grow and magic requires money to flow."
—**Philology of the Dwarfs, Anonymous.**

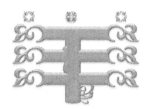

That same night Master Galliöm entered the Hall of Medallions. As head of the tajéruun, or moneymen, he oversaw the main vault of the zakiruun's fortune. The Hall of Medallions was built over the vault and was the tajéruun's nerve center; the central command from which Galliöm directed his empire.

He sat on the chair of command; an iron seat welded out of actual medallions of power. Set on a raised deck, it overlooked an oval pit three hundred feet long and one hundred feet wide with a raised ceiling standing sixty feet overhead. Two identical sets of rails covered both the floor and the ceiling of the pit so that one hundred and fifty iron ladders locked to the rails moved soundlessly in a dizzying dance. Each ladder carried five silver seats that pointed in different directions, and each seat carried a clerk who wore a silver helmet with a retractable glass visor. These were the *observers*, who mediated all distant exchanges between thousands of zakiruun across the sixty-two kingdoms. As the ladders moved silently, they scanned the thousands of red medallions that hung from the giant circular wall. Whenever a medallion flashed, an observer would lower the visor, slide a black medallion into a slit, and wait until the requester's face appeared on the visor's surface. The requester, typically a zakiir, would tell the observer whom he wished to speak with. The observer would slide a white medallion into the same slit and wait for the recipient's face to appear. Each of the requesters and recipients would use a red medallion identical to those on the wall, along with a glass orb. The observer would listen and consign the conversation to memory.

"Any news from Tanniin yet?" asked the leader of the tajéruun.

Iron bars welded to the platform in front of him held seven orbs. A disembodied voice flowed from one of them.

"Not yet, Master."

"What of Milaniöm? Any progress in the Slippery-Slued case?"

"Nothing new, Master. They cannot explain how the thief managed to slew the scene and slip the extra bag past our defenses. His action is baffling. Why would a thief give us gold instead of stealing it from us?"

"What of Ibromaliöm? Do we know why he stole from us?"

"No Master, we are still investigating the crime. Shall we report him to the local authorities?"

"No. This is strictly the tajéruun's business. Alert me when our men in Amsheet have found him."

Galliöm dismissed his interlocutor. He spent the night in the hall, waiting and observing. The night had been uneventful with most conversations being mundane or technical and not warranting his attention. Morning brought no more details about Ibromaliöm nor the mystery behind Slippery-Slued's actions. Leaving the hall, he followed a ten-foot-wide circular walkway. Thick cork panels, encrusted with four dull-looking iron medallions covered the floor, ceiling, and walls; they were equipped with interlocking curses that shielded the hall from magical attacks. Galliöm stepped out through one of the four available doors. Two creatures stood guard and opened an iron gate for him. As tall as giants, with green translucent skin and eyes slit like snakes, they wore iron chain mail, high leathery helmets, and carried fuming gray blades. They were the *Massrifuun*, guardians of the Hall of Medallions.

Galliöm stepped onto one of the four bridges that linked the hall to the walls of a huge cave. Seen from below the hall's exterior, it resembled an iron egg suspended by massive iron beams from the cave's ceiling. Below the bridge, the main vault lay in a colossal oval pit, six hundred feet wide, twelve hundred feet long, and four hundred feet deep. Slaves had excavated the hole, smoothed out its surface, and sealed it.

Ages ago, the tajéruun had commissioned dwarfs to build a device to showcase the size of their fortune. The dwarfs proposed the alignment of the planets as a measure of wealth and influence. Every gold coin falling into the Pit would help nudge the planets forward. When all seven planets will stand aligned in the center, the pit will be full to the brim. The moneymen immediately commissioned the project.

The dwarfs went to work. They designed a weight-sensing device for the pit's floor. It consisted of a thick iron platform with seven holes through which mechanical arms were bolted and set over the pit. Like the legs of an inverted spider, they ran along the edge of the pit, rising thirty feet over its surface where the monstrous arms each stood clasping a crystal sphere. To hold the tajéruun's massive wealth, the dwarfs had used a strong gold alloy to build a container the size of the pit, which rested on the iron platform. When the coins started flowing inside this container, their weight tripped the pressure-controlled mechanism, which then began to move the smallest sphere toward the center.

The pit is already half-full, thought Galliöm as he approached the exit. From the bridge, he watched the shimmering lake of gold with elation. Three planets were already aligned, with the fourth not too far behind. *There is enough here to buy forty kingdoms.*

The cave that housed the hall and vault was huge but ordinary. There were no curses protecting it, no glittering statues lining its sides, and no elaborate carvings along its walls. Despite this lack of magical protection, the cave terrified the slaves and clerks alike, for no one, not even Galliöm, knew of its precise location. It was completely sealed with no natural way in or out. The Arayat was the only known way to access the cave. Over the years, slaves had dug secret tunnels to escape, but they all led back to the starting point. Some tajéruun speculated that it was right above—or below—the City of the Dead. Others swore it was in the Vanishing Land, but none of them knew with any degree of certainty where the vault was located.

The dwarfs had dug a spiral passage into one of its walls. Outfitted with a complex of rails, it transported white carts filled with gold coins and returned them empty. A parallel system carved into the opposite wall used black carts; they were wheeled in empty and then returned filled with gold. With this simple system, the tajéruun kept a meticulous count of all their credit and debit operations.

Stepping off the bridge, Galliöm entered one of the five elevators, each powered by twenty slaves. Like the thousand other slaves Galliöm had acquired for the service of the vault, they lived and died there, never to see the light of day.

With bent backs, the slaves turned a large wheel that powered the elevator, which wormed its way up into a vertical tunnel. Galliöm waited for the fifty-sixth level, and then pulled the rope. A muffled horn sounded down below, and the elevator came to a stop at the fifty-eighth floor. He stepped out of the elevator and walked along a circular iron platform ringed with ten elliptical doors. Each of the remaining 199 levels was identical: a circular platform with ten elliptical doors. He covered his face with an oddly shaped mask, slid into leather boots, and put on a thick leather coat with gloves sewn into the cuffs. A group of clerks opened a door a few floors below him, and another group opened a door a few floors above. They brought in the gold, then pulled on a rope and two elevators moved up. Opening one of the doors, Galliöm stepped onto a small metal platform with a circular hole in the middle where a thick green soup oozed and bubbled. Carefully, he grabbed a medallion that hung on a nearby hook and placed it around his neck. Immediately, the coat, mask, and boots fused, and became one seamless, impermeable garment. The mask expanded and covered Galliöm's head, then inflated until it became the size of a large pumpkin. He jumped into the green soup, which quickly sucked him downward. He dropped inside a tunnel somewhere in the Arayatian underground, a place where the priests of Baal never ventured. He waded through the green soup toward an elliptical door held in place by four medallions. He opened it, grabbed a ladder, and pulled himself up until he stood dripping on a smaller metal platform. He removed the medallion, hung it on a hook, and waited for the mask, coat, and boots to regain their original form before removing his outer garments.

The two hundred levels, with their ten doors and underground Arayatian tunnels, were the only way in or out of the main vault. Two thousand doors took the tajéruun to nearly every kingdom and provided them with unimpeded access to every major city in the world.

Galliöm opened an elliptical door and stepped inside a meager empty room, then into a small cave where gold trickled from the roof through a hole. This cave, the vault of a tajéruun's outpost, was a worthy treasure by any measure. Still, it was puny compared to the central vault. But thousands of locations such as this one fed the central vault through the Arayatian underground passage.

Shortly after, he emerged inside the Lanudonis tajéruun's operation where clerks and a few zakiruun worked quietly. He pulled his hood onto his head and passed by them silently. Outside, the Lanudonis' sky drizzled its usual sulking gray cover. Indifferent to the cold, he walked briskly to the Prickly Peacock, a select tavern for the well-to-do. He walked in, and a fawning lackey ushered him to a velvety table in a quiet corner where two men waited. Seeing him, they rose to their feet.

"Milaniöm, Silvaniöm, may gold preserve you from harm."

The two men bowed and they all sat down to a scrumptious dinner. As an appetizer, they had pheasant marinated in an eggplant and basil sauce and a side dish of Thermodonian lemon truffles. A refreshing rosé wine formed the perfect accompaniment. The next course was honey-glazed duck in a light sesame sauce with a rich, smooth red wine. Next, they enjoyed the best ale-basted venison in all of Lanudonis. Finally, they washed it all down with a parsimonious green salad sprinkled with roasted almonds and dowsed with a raspberry sauce.

"Ah, this wine, I tell you," said Galliöm, clapping his tongue with satisfaction. "The best in the northern realm."

"Indeed, Master," concurred Milaniöm. "The Prickly Peacock is by far the best inn in town."

"I understand a second breach of our vault occurred under your watch, is that not so, Milaniöm?" The short, balding man clasped his hands and waited. Anguish kneaded his forehead and constricted his breathing. "Nevertheless," continued Galliöm with a reassuring paternal smile, "this time around, someone added to our treasury instead of stealing from us. How odd. What do you think, Silvaniöm?"

"I don't like it. We have a breach and maybe a mole." Galliöm nodded in approval. "We must find out who is behind this and why."

"Agreed. Nevertheless, this matter is of regional importance. Most likely, it is related to the covert war between Bar-Tanic, Togofalk, and Thermodon. We have dealt with similar situations in the past and this one may not be different. Milaniöm, I'm going to assign Silvaniöm as your assistant. He will help you manage this annoyance. More importantly, he will coordinate our regional response to the theft in Amsheet. Milaniöm, you will direct your Bar-Tanickian clients to delay their invasion of Tanniin until further notice. Understood?"

"Yes, Master."

"You will cooperate fully with Silvaniöm and facilitate his work here."

"Yes, Master."

"Dismissed."

Milaniöm got up, bowed deeply, and left the inn. He was relieved that Galliöm had not killed him on the spot. The League of the Tajéruun owned the inn and no one would have objected. The Lanudonisian sky looked friendlier and gentler than he had ever seen it before.

Inside the Prickly Peacock, Silvaniöm waited for his master to speak.

"Hire a group of murderers, the best you can find, and send them to Amsheet. I want Ibromaliöm dead, is that understood?"

"Yes, Master."

"Be careful, he is growing stronger day-by-day, we may have underestimated him. Dispose of him quickly."

"Understood."

"Silvaniöm, one more thing: Once you complete your mission, get rid of Milaniöm, and blame his death on Ibromaliöm."

"Yes, sir."

≻ ◦∶◦∶◦ ≺

"Fool, shameful idiot, unrepentant failure. The Rahal take you! Lothan drag you to the deepest waters, and the Nininth carry your sorry self to the hellhound of the pit. You have shamed our family name, dishonored our parents, and brought a stinging rebuke to my title. If our father's curse did not bind us, I would kill you and leave your despicable body to the carrions. I should have sold you in Metranos long ago. You are a sham, Olothe, a wicked miserable slime. May the Nephral devour your soul!"

Olothe, unable to speak, shook violently. He knew his older brother was right, he had brought shame to the family and disgraced his ancestral home. He was a cripple now, condemned to a life of misery. He wished he could die, oh how he wished his brother would pass his sword through his heart and release him from his misery; but he knew no one would dare touch him. Powerful curses hung over his head like a murder of crows in a darkened sky—curses his father had spoken when he was born to guard against anyone who tried to take his life. To cast self-proclaimed curses against assassins was the House of Lurca's long-standing tradition. But these curses forbade suicide, and no assassin worth their salt would go near the Lurcas. Since the fate of Olothe's servants was tied to his, they protected him with their lives. They would die when he died.

Nebo, Olothe's oldest brother, paced angrily. Despite his anger, he had managed not to yell, for he did not want everyone in the inn to know that he, a high-ranking officer of the Baalite army, had a cripple for a brother. He would not recover from the shame.

"You did well to wait for me here, in Taleb," he said addressing Olothe's servants. "Taleb is the busiest port in the kingdom of Baraknun, a great ally of the Temple. A cripple will go unnoticed. Who among you is in charge here?"

"I am, Your Lordship," said a short woman with a pudgy face and a fat mole on her chin.

"Do not continue on to Lurca. Instead, I command you to go to Babylon and spend the rest of your lives there until this trash is dead."

"Babylon, sir? Under Baal's nose?"

"Precisely," replied Nebo. "No one will look for him there. Go to Babylon, purchase a mansion, and buy a husband or two. Enjoy life and lock Olothe away. When he dies, kill everyone, and kill yourself, or the curse will spread to your villages. Understood?"

"Yes, Lord, we will do as you command. Our lives belong to the Pit."

Leaving them to their own devises, Nebo fetched his horse and galloped away under the cover of night. *May Antral, the god of the dead, be praised, for I managed to travel secretly to Baraknun. I am an hour or two away from Sowas. The slave that maimed my brother will pay dearly. He will taste the bitter blade of the Sowasian assassins.*

"What does Lord Sharr command?"

Sharr, High Priest of Babylon, looked at Kalibaal kneeling before him. Kalibaal's balding head was creased and wrinkled, and his neck was beginning to look like the trunk of a millennial tree. *Age does not befit you my friend*, he thought.

"Would you do me the favor of asking Lady Sarand, the Soloist, to join us here for a meeting?"

Does he know of the attempt to overthrow him? We are a few weeks away from carrying out our plan. "Certainly, My Lord. I will do so at once."

Kalibaal rose from his kneeling posture, walked back while keeping his head low, and left the Hall of Judgment. Outside, he slipped into his leather boots and walked briskly down a wide marble hall. Tall statues of former high priests and priestesses eyed him somberly as he descended a short flight of stairs and stepped outside the Temple. He clambered down an additional seven flights of stairs that had been constructed in honor of Baal—the first among the seven major deities of the world. After a short walk in the streets of Babylon, he rang the Adorant's doorbell. It had rained the night before, and a Babylonian storm in the month of Shubat was a bad omen. Still, the air was brisk and fresh.

The door opened silently and an Adorant welcomed him. He averted his eyes and asked to speak with Sarand. The Adorant told him she would be delighted to take him to her, and he replied that it would best if they could speak outside. The woman gave him a bewitching smile and disappeared behind the door. Kalibaal breathed a little better. Women had always been his weakness and he knew he had little resistance to the Adorants' charms. *Control yourself you idiot. You are a member of the Inner Council, not some minor priest.* His words had little effect. *Women will be my damnation*, he thought with a trepidation that scared him. *I should not think this way.* Had he known how deeply attached he had become to Sarand, he would have called himself even worse. Any sailor devoted to his bottle would have told Kalibaal, had he asked, that Sarand's noose was wound too tightly around his heart for him to escape. Sailors knew of only one way to kick the habit: Enroll for a year on a liquor-free boat and hope for the best. Even if boats were to sprout from the ground, Kalibaal would have refused to leave Babylon. He had ventured too deeply into Sarand's web and did not even know it.

Sarand came to the door, bringing with her the ravishing Adorant he had seen before.

She roped her arm through his and whispered gently, "My dear Kalibaal, what brings you to me today?" The Adorant behind her chortled, and Kalibaal felt alive, strong, and invulnerable.

"Sharr is asking to see you," he answered.

"Alone?"

"I am not sure, My Lady."

Sarand looked into his eyes. "You are not lying, Kalibaal. I can see that. Did he say why?"

Kalibaal shook his head. "I do not believe he knows of our plans. It may be unrelated."

Sarand fell silent for a short while. The young Adorant drew close and whispered a few words in Kalibaal's ear causing his heart to race. He clenched his fists and tried his best to ignore her sultry words.

"Do not mind Quinn, she is anxious to see if her new charms are working," muttered Sarand, "and she is trying to impress me. Fine, let us be on our way. I suppose we cannot ignore Sharr's summons."

Their walk back to the Temple was uneventful, but they grew concerned when a Shogol priest met them at the door.

"Lord Sharr would like you to join him beneath the main altar. All other members of the Inner Council are waiting for you."

Sarand glanced at Kalibaal who avowed ignorance.

"He told me it would just be the three of us."

Sarand and Kalibaal joined the remaining fourteen members of the Inner Council. Four were Shogol priests and another four where Kerta priests. There were three other Adorants besides Sarand, and three other Methodical priests besides Kalibaal. Sharr joined them and invited everyone to step with him onto a large shield held by four gold bolts. It had no markings and resembled the portal Tamri had used to cross into the Arayat. This was the transference platform and the council used it to ferry people or objects in and out of the Spell World. All who were present understood that Sharr was leading them into the Arayat, and by stepping onto the shield they were placing themselves in his hands.

A moment later, they were hovering over a cultivated field within the Spell World. Sharr assumed the appearance of a two-headed bull with a human torso. "This, my dear friends, was the field where we grew our own version of the béghôm."

That's right, thought Kalibaal, *this does look familiar, but something is different now.*

"Is this the remnant of the béghôm?" asked one of the Kerta priests.

"Indeed. I checked on this field two weeks ago and back then the béghôm was still alive, barely, but still alive. I have brought you all here to show you this."

Sarand followed Sharr's bony finger. The high priest's torso was discolored, his limbs appeared as dried up twigs, and his fingers looked like spider's legs. She peered inside the ruined, empty fields. Gone were the slaves feeding the field with their blood. Gone also, were the curses protecting the creature which stood frigid as stone; a sign of imminent death. Sarand focused on the base of the dead creature. *What is this?*

Kalibaal was no less puzzled. A light flickered at the base of the creature and a bright, yellow flame burned right beneath the Arayatian surface. *What madness is this? A candle in the outside world produces a flame such as this. In the Arayat, this flame is alien.*

"You have guessed right, my friends," explained Sharr. "This flame, this most ordinary flame, is not of Arayatian origin."

"How could this be?" asked another priest.

Sarand felt a streak of fear grip her. She gazed at her colleagues and saw that many shared her anguish.

"Yes," added Sharr with a slithering, angry voice. "This is the Seer's doing. He successfully used a Letter of Power when he fought the béghôm and he used our creature—the creature we created—to kindle his fire in the heart of the Arayat." Sharr waited a moment for his acolytes to grasp the full meaning behind his words.

"How do we stop this?" asked Kalibaal.

Sharr laughed. "We depend on the Arayat for our magic. How do we stop something that burns the fabric, the very soil of our spells? We never prepared for this, nor do we have the knowledge to face such an attack."

"We could extract this knowledge from the Seer," whispered a Kerta priest whose Arayatian appearance looked like a dislocated dog.

"Indeed, my friend, indeed. Initially, I had released the urkuun as a precautionary measure. If our béghôm has not killed him, the urkuun will take care of it. Somehow, the Seer managed to wound the urkuun, destroy the béghôm, and cause havoc in the Arayat." He gazed at them. "This seer is young and inexperienced and has no knowledge of magic. He is not supposed to know how to damage the Arayat. Somehow, someone helped him," he added. Raising a hand to quell protests, he added: "I am well aware that not a few of you are plotting to take my place. Our god expects this strife. Through it, he preserves a strong priesthood. But if anyone of you has been helping the Seer, I ask you in the name of reason and all that you hold sacred to stop. He is burning the Arayat, the very source of power you depend on."

"You released the urkuun already," protested another priest. "This beast is uncontrollable and will kill the Seer. How do we know it is not *you*, who is working for the destruction of the Arayat?"

A murmur ran through the group.

Sharr sneered with great disdain. He drew an imaginary circle in the air that created a portal into which they could all see the urkuun standing by a dark pool. Sharr flicked his fingers and the urkuun fell to his knees. The monster snarled and shrieked, but he could not break the invisible fetters holding him back. Sharr flicked his fingers and the portal disappeared.

"You may disapprove of my methods," he said sternly, "and you may wish to overthrow me, but do not underestimate my power."

"If this is so," persisted the same priest, "why haven't you taken the Seer yourself? Why all this complication?"

"I control what I know," replied Sharr. "But this?" he said pointing at the flame, "Do any of you know how to snuff it? We are dealing with a Seer of Power," he added. "The urkuun should suffice."

"What if it doesn't? What if the Seer manages to destroy the urkuun?"

"Then," said Sharr in a threatening dark tone, "other, harsher means will be necessary. If he overtakes the urkuun, I will—"

"I will take care of it," Sarand cut in. She was scared. They were all scared, for none of them had ever dealt with events such as these. "If the urkuun fails, I will unleash the khoblyss. They will bring the Seer to me."

"Excellent initiative, my dear Soloist," replied Sharr. "We must capture the Seer at all costs. We need to extract from him the knowledge to help us fight this evil."

The members of the Inner Council accented. *This makes sense*, thought the Soloist, *but why do I have the feeling that Sharr is still pulling all the strings?*

She wondered if she should mention the existence of the female Seer, but decided against it. *If the urkuun does not kill her first, and if she escapes my clutch, then we shall see …*

Kalibaal, who knew what Sharr would do next, stood motionless. He prayed and hoped the urkuun would succeed.

The following morning, twenty tents were huddled in a secluded meadow. A short distance north, over a hillock, the road leaving Gordion ran in a straight path and traffic was already heavy. Caravaneers, couriers, merchants, farmers, slave traders, and countless others shuttled between the capital and Tulin—a town that bordered Teshub and Mitani. Aquilina stepped barefoot out of her tent and darted over to Hoda's.

"Miss Hoda," she said while standing before the tent, "I am ready for a new adventure." Four days ago, they had left the palace in Gordion for their cottage two hours northeast of the capital. There, her father had told her they would not be staying in the cottage after all.

"Where are we going?" she had asked as she rubbed sleep off her eyes.

"On a grand adventure."

"Great. Is Vily coming too?"

"Yes."

"And Mother, and you?"

"Yes."

"Then I am ready," she told her father with a beaming smile.

She giggled when she saw her father dressed like a Finikian itinerant merchant. She gawked when she saw her mother dressed in similar fashion. "Mother, you are so beautiful," she exclaimed. "I would have mistaken you for a queen."

"Aquilina," whispered Vily, "Your mother *is* a queen."

"I know *that*, but before, she was just called a queen. Now she looks like a *queen* queen. A real one."

Amaréya managed a smile. To wear anything but Empyrean attire was harder than she had expected. Still, Corintus had not asked for her blades, which she had conveniently hidden beneath her dress. Now that she walked like a merchant, she began to understand her husband's concern. *This is far more demanding than I expected.* Still, there was no going back. She would have to adapt, just like she did when she had married. *As long as Corintus is by my side, I know I can do this.*

Wrath of the Urkuun – Confluence

The first day of travel had been truly enjoyable. The countryside had enchanted Aquilina, who found everything new. But by the next day, she had begun to miss her room in the palace for she loved her routine, her habits and the familiar environment. That stable life counter-balanced the chaotic Tyrulian landscape, and she craved it.

"Father, when are we going back to the palace?"

"Not just yet, Aquilina. Your mother has a mission from the Empyreans. She must fulfill it before we can return."

"But Mother is the heiress to the throne. She can ask someone else to carry out this mission for her."

"She could, but this is very sensitive and she wants to handle it herself."

Aquilina found this explanation strange. Questions swirled in her head, but she knew she could not ask her mother directly; she would have to wait for Amaréya to speak first. The day before, Hoda had sensed how restless the young girl had become and kept her busy with memorization games. Vily and Aquilina memorized the names of trees, plants, and bushes, and called out the names of critters they periodically met. Each time they stopped for a break, Hoda would race the young girls to keep them physically busy. When they had their camp set up, Aquilina and Vily had quickly fallen asleep, which explained why, on this bright morning, Aquilina stood by Hoda's tent at sunrise.

"Sir Karadon is my prince," Vily had told her, blushing. "He is the best prince I know. He is wonderful."

Aquilina smiled. She liked Karadon, but Hoda fascinated her. Something about her, her expressions, her voice, reminded her of the mysterious figure she had been calling Snoring Man. Whenever Aquilina heard the young woman speak, she could not fail to notice that Snoring Man spoke with similar intonations. Hoda stressed certain sounds, and so did he, and in the same way. She stressed other sounds whenever she spoke quickly, and so did he. It was uncanny. *Perhaps they are from the same land? That would make sense*, she had thought.

"Aquilina, you're early this morning," said Vily, joining her. She was shivering. The sun had not yet appeared, and the air was still brisk. "It's not polite to stand by someone's tent," she whispered. "They may hear us."

"And hear you, we did," said Karadon as he emerged from the tent dressed in Finikian clothing. He wore a pair of pleated purple trousers with a light brown leather belt ornamented with a clasp of Baal on his chariots and a beige V-neck linen shirt with long puffed sleeves. His braided hair flowed from under a tall conical hat. The thick light brown laces of his sandals climbed to his knees.

The two girls giggled. "Sir Karadon," said Vily mimicking Ophirian nobility in Gordion, "You are most gallant in your merchant attire."

Hoda peeked outside. "Good morning, girls. You're up early."

"I'm an early riser," said Karadon, "Missy over there is not," he said in a fake whisper. Vily giggled and Aquilina smiled.

"I can come back later, Miss Hoda," she offered.

"I'll be out in a moment."

When Hoda emerged, she too was wearing Finikian clothing: a bright red tunic with a belt from which two tassels hung over a long purple skirt. A large decorative pendant in the stylized shape of Uropa—the Finikian goddess of safe travels—hung over her matching purple blouse. Her hair was braided down to the back with two shorter braids on each side. Her sandals were similar to Karadon's but with two small clasps each bearing a cobra, the head deity Etersis of Edfu, with whom Finikians had a rich and long-established commercial relation.

"Wow, Miss Hoda," whispered Aquilina. "You are beautiful."

"*Beautiful*," repeated Vily.

"Well, well," said Karadon, "I can see that my protégé has good taste. I kind'a agree," he added with a glint in his eyes. "She *is* beautiful."

Hoda laughed. "Thank you, girls. But something tells me you didn't wake me up this early to stare at my clothing, now did you?"

"Well then," said Karadon as he bowed before Vily. "I shall see if I may be of service to this most gallant young maiden over here."

Vily blushed. Aquilina giggled. Karadon's Finikian accent was funny. Corintus looked out from his own tent and waved.

"Good morning, Father," shouted Aquilina.

"She must not shout so," protested Amaréya. "Someone may recognize her."

"Soon, we will have to leave our names behind," replied Corintus. "We will have to use Finikian names."

"What we are doing is crazy," said his wife. "Tell me, do we have to do this? We can still return to Gordion, to the palace."

"It is necessary, Amaréya. You know it as well as I. Aquilina vanishes. You have seen it with your own eyes. The Temple *will* find out, then they will come after us and we will lose everything: our daughter, the palace, and our lives. I know how strange this feels. I know parents who would not think twice of bringing their child to the Temple for a generous reward. Here we are, going into exile, leaving everything for her sake."

"I am ashamed, Corintus. I should not have spoken the way I did."

"It's a good thing that you are ashamed. Most humans would feel ashamed. There is nothing wrong with your feelings. It's how you act on them that counts." He drew closer and added in a softer tone, "Do you want return to Gordion, Amaréya? You still can."

"How long before we reach the border?" she asked, determined.

"Good," he said, relieved. "Now, you must not doubt our resolve. We need to see this through."

She nodded and grabbed his hand, which surprised him in a pleasant sort of way. He squeezed her hand and hummed a sultry song about a sailor in love with an Empyrean.

Outside, Aquilina was helping Hoda prepare breakfast. "Miss Hoda," whispered Aquilina, "You and Snoring Man are related."

Hoda froze. "Have you … seen him lately?"

Aquilina placed her hand on her chest and felt the Merilian beneath her clothing. She shook her head. "The medallion you gave me keeps everything quiet. I sleep better now. But your accent is so much like his."

"Next time you hear him, see if you can ask him his name. I lost my brother when he was a little boy about your age. I had given him a doll that he called Doda. He carried this doll everywhere and was inconsolable when he lost it."

Aquilina opened her eyes wide. "That's why you were so surprised when I told you." She looked down. "I'm sorry. I have been careless."

"Don't be. I'm glad you told me. But yes, we cannot afford to be careless. Do not speak of this to anyone without your parents' consent."

"Not even you?"

"I have already spoken to your parents. They understand."

"Vily?"

Hoda was silent for a moment. "Ask your parents. As far I'm concerned, the less you speak of it, the better."

"Why, Miss Hoda? Why should I keep it a secret?"

"Has anyone bothered you about this?"

"Well no …" Aquilina's voice trailed when she remembered the one she called her enemy. The terrible voice she had heard in Tyrulan. "Yes, someone did."

"This is why. There are people, terrible people who will do you harm if they know what you can do."

"Is that what happened to your brother?"

"You are one perceptive little girl, you know? Yes, I believe that is how I lost him. I do not want to lose you too, so be very, very careful."

Aquilina smiled. "I will."

Deep within her, a resolve as hard as steel and brighter than the stars was growing. She would be by her friend's side. She would help him and would use all the power of Tyrulan to stop her enemy, and his.

22. Northern Council

> *"O Silent, beware the wiles of your heart and the secret desires of your dreams. They are like a silent, giant wave behind you, and you do not see it crashing down, and you do not hear it."*
> —The Book of Lamentation 7:1.

"Amsheet," shouted Tanios.

The company cheered. They were worn out from the five-day forced march on the road between the two forests. Initially they had traveled on horseback, but soon after their ranks swelled with refugees from the city of Hardeen and the horses were made to pull  chariots for the elderly and the sick, and for mothers and their children. As they walked, many more joined them, turning their small group into a large multitude of at least five thousand. The commander had spread the Silent among the people to keep order. All were hungry, tired, and afraid, but no one wanted to stop until they reached Amsheet. The Silent raised an alert when aged folks began to collapse from exhaustion. Tanios requisitioned all chariots to carry those too weak or too tired to walk. Everyone else continued on foot.

Along the way, they stopped several times to bury the dead. Unless they reached Amsheet quickly, provisioning this large crowd would become a serious problem.

Habael and Bahiya walked among the people and listened to their stories. Invariably the tales included creatures with ashen skin who attacked houses, farms, and markets.

"Can we dismiss all these tales?" asked Master Habael.

Bahiya shook her head. "There is a power in the forest," she whispered, "and its presence is spreading."

"I can vouch for Awaniir, Lord of Hardeen. He is an upright man. We need to speak with someone who was in the fortress. We need to know what happened there. See if anyone here has been to Hardeen recently."

As they pressed on, Habael, Bahiya, and the Silent continued to listen. The closest they came to finding someone who had been inside the Fortress of Hardeen recently was Sohol, an old woman whose brother was a cook in the fortress.

"When did you last see your brother?" asked Tanios as they walked.

"Six days past," replied the old woman.

"Did he notice anything unusual? Anything out of the ordinary?"

"Methinks he said nothin' surprisin'," replied the woman with her thick lowlander accent. "He ain't no talker ya know, a brick of a brother he is, yes sir, nothin' against bricks, but no talkin' sure is."

"So he did not mention anything that was out of the ordinary?"

"Nope, he kept talkin' about his kitchen. Hmm, ya may like this."

"What?" asked Tanios. Habael and Bahiya listened intently.

"Two weeks before today and another three weeks before'em—"

"Five weeks prior," translated Tanios.

"So you says," Sohol confirmed politely, "right, then, about this hour, he said he had a mess in his kitchen. Da same mess three times."

"Is this extraordinary?"

"Sure is. Ya know not my brother. A brick of a man sure he is, but ordered. Yesseree ordered like an ant colony."

"Did he tell you why he had a mess in his kitchen?" asked Habael.

"Yep. There was three earthquakes."

"Earthquakes?" asked Tanios bewildered. "But there has never been an earthquake in the north, ever."

"Dat's what I told him. He said he knew dat, but it was an earthquake all right, a rumblin', and tumblin', and cracks and the whole bit. Somethin' to behold, dat's for sure. <u>The worst of it was the Temple of Tanniin. He said there were strange cracks and round things in the Temple.</u>"

"Were the cracks round or square?" asked Bahiya with an altered voice. "This is important, so please, try to remember."

The old woman thought for a moment. "Ya know, he did say somethin' about dat," said the woman pensively as she scratched her tanned and leathery face. "He said somethin' about three squares and a bunch of small circles around them," added Sohol.

The colors drained from the high priestess' face. "How many circles?" she asked in a trembling voice.

"How many?" replied Sohol alarmed by Bahiya's reaction. "I ain't no knower of numbers, but my brother did this." She showed Bahiya her hands with nine fingers up and one down. The High Priestess placed her hand on her mouth and closed her eyes. "Did I say somethin' to upset the pretty lady?" she asked the commander.

We are in deep trouble, thought Tanios. *Whatever the circles and the squares mean, it cannot be good. And whoever is behind them must be very powerful to scare a high priestess of Baal.*

"You did well," said the commander gently, "and thank you. Your help has been invaluable." He tried to give Sohol a gold coin, but she refused adamantly saying she was doing her duty. He caught up with Master Habael, and placed him in charge.

"I need to speak to Bahiya privately. This is serious." Habael nodded and settled comfortably at the helm of the long column moving precariously toward Amsheet.

"People."

Frajil pointed to the distant town of Yaneer. He had been yelling, "People," since the morning. More peasants stepped onto the road to join the legion of Tanniinite refugees, all eager to reach the safety of Amsheet.

None of these folks—except for Frajil, that is—traveled to Amsheet for the carnival. They were refugees from the farmland surrounding Hardeen, having escaped the great terror there. It was a mass exodus. All had abandoned their land, farms, crops, and livestock, and many left with only the clothes they had on. Others, more fortunate, pushed carts full of belongings. Ahiram was anxious. *What are we to do with this multitude? They will have to sleep on the streets, yet with the approaching carnival, the streets will not be safe.*

Sondra tapped Hiyam's arm, who looked at her. "You sensed a curse in front of the barrier we crossed with Frajil, didn't you?"

"Yes, I did," said Hiyam.

"Do you think this curse extends to the entire forest? Are all these people cursed? Will we be cursed?"

Hiyam shook her head.

"The curse was for the barrier. To blanket a forest this size with a curse requires the power of the Pit ..." Hiyam's words trailed. "If the Pit were open, then the world over would be cursed beyond saving."

Sheheluth and Banimelek, who were near the front of the exodus, signaled to Ahiram. They neared Amsheet's gates. Ahiram motioned to his friend to go on ahead. An old woman had grabbed his arm and would not let go. Her young grandson walked beside her, and Ahiram did not have the heart to leave them.

"I will join you as soon as I can," he shouted to Banimelek. His friend nodded and pressed on. The old lady gave him a wary smile.

"I have family in Amsheet. They will take care of us," she said.

The child, not more than ten, smiled valiantly. *Strong boy*, thought Ahiram as he smiled back. "What's your name?" he asked.

"Tinn," replied the young boy.

"Strong Tanniinite name. What will you be when you grow up, Tinn?"

"A Silent, like you," replied the young boy.

Ahiram tousled his blond head. "Great choice," he said.

Behind him, Jedarc was patiently describing bananas to a few folks. *Even now, he finds ways to lighten the mood,* thought the Silent. *Incredible.*

Farad was a young man who had grown up on the shores of Baalbek. He left when he was still a lad and worked as a sailor on many ships. Eventually, he settled in Togofalk and became an assigned carrier of the statue of Jaguar-Night. This envied position was both lucrative and honorific. Farad liked his position. He liked it a lot.

Until now.

Farad was out of breath and his side was killing him. He forced himself to move until he reached the great hall where the likeness of the god was being kept. The guards recognized him and let him in. He closed the door behind him and frantically ran to the statue, reached for the eyelids and tried in earnest to remove them.

"It's no use," he whispered. "No use. I had better tell Lord Orgond everything."

He dashed back out, climbed a flight of stairs, and ran through a long corridor that lead to the main hall where Lord Orgond held audience. Farad froze when he saw a shadow that stepped away from the wall.

"No!" It was too late. The dagger reached his heart. Farad gripped the handle and fell to the ground, dead. His killer moved silently and began dragging the body when he heard footsteps. He dropped the body, jumped through a nearby window, and disappeared into the darkness. The moon glided lazily between quiet clouds and shone on the statue that silently eyed the dead man sprawled on the cold marble floor.

"Beautiful view."

Noraldeen whirled around and saw Princess Gaëla by her side on the balcony. "Yes, the valley is always beautiful at sunset."

"You look so much like your mother," said Gaëla softly.

"How do you know?" asked Noraldeen.

"There is a family portrait of her when she was just sixteen. One would easily mistake you for her."

"I would love to see that portrait," replied Noraldeen, excited.

"Then you should come and visit us sometime."

"I suppose I should … Are we preparing for war?"

"Yes, we are."

"Are you afraid of dying?"

"I do not think in those terms. We live. We die. That is normal. Failure is not. The kingdom gave us our lives, and we give it back. The kingdom must remain in order for others to live."

Noraldeen shuddered. "I am afraid of death," she said slowly.

Gaëla looked at her curiously. "An Empyrean afraid of death betrays the kingdom."

"'O Silent, only a fool ignores death. Prepare to die every day, and your name will be remembered beyond your mortal years.' The *Book of Lamentation*, chapter 12, verse 7," quoted Noraldeen. "A Silent may fear death before the action, and perhaps after, but never during."

"If what we heard about the Silent is true, then it must be an impressive group."

"It is," said Noraldeen proudly. "Would you like a demonstration?"

"I would love one."

"Great, come with me." Princess Gaëla smiled and followed the Silent into her apartments. Noraldeen had naturally assumed command of the situation and forgot that she was speaking to the liege of the Empyreans.

A true Empyrean, thought Princess Gaëla as she watched Noraldeen closely. The Silent fetched her training darts and showed them to the princess. "These darts are for training. They have a sticky head. We will stay inside this square. To step out of it means defeat. You can use your favorite weapon and I will use my darts. The first to score a hit wins."

"Very good," replied Princess Gaëla. "I will use my stick and flail, both are for training purposes. I carry them with me." She opened the door and asked one of her guards to fetch them for her.

The two fighters assumed their positions diagonally across the square. After a brief salutation, they circled each other slowly. Noraldeen sized up her opponent. *Princess Gaëla is tall and strong, but how fast is she?* As if reading her mind, the Empyrean attacked with a suddenness and force that surprised Noraldeen. She barely escaped the flail and the stick through a series of complex moves. Gaëla was unrelenting. She was in command and would not give Noraldeen a moment of rest.

O Silent, if you forget your opponent is your greatest ally, you will be fighting a losing battle. This was a quote from the *Book of Lamentation* 2:3. The Silent waited for Gaëla to attack her with her stick, and then caught it with both hands. The Empyrean princess pulled it back hard and pulled a willing Noraldeen toward her. She whipped the air with her flail, but the Silent used her momentum to leap over the princess' head. Gaëla whirled around and Noraldeen threw her dart. It hit the princess just as the flail grabbed Noraldeen by the waist. The two women dropped to the floor laughing.

"You are very good," said Gaëla.

"Your speed is amazing. You remind me of …" Noraldeen became serious again.

"Of Ahiram," continued Gaëla softly.

Noraldeen looked at her, surprised. "Yes. Of Ahiram," she said and smiled. "Of Ahiram." She stood up, picked up her darts and walked toward the balcony. Gaëla followed her.

"Your mother had much to suffer when she married your father. He does not wish to put you through the same suffering. He loves you." Noraldeen did not answer. "Your father is a great man, perhaps one of the greatest the Empyreans have seen. Yet, we consider him less than a dog in my kingdom."

"Why?" asked Noraldeen. "I do not understand."

"There is not much to understand," said Princess Gaëla. "This is how it was, how it is, and how it will always be. We stand and we fall by our word, by our sword, and our empress. We are Empyreans, one of the four elder races. Our kingdom's surpassing beauty is our joy and our peace."

"Perhaps, but I would rather love and suffer than behold the most beautiful kingdom on earth," said Noraldeen.

"I do not understand that," the princess replied.

"Neither do I," said Noraldeen with a smile. "There is one man out there whom I long to see and be with. For me, it is enough that I love."

Gaëla looked at her and smiled. "You would have been a great Empyrean."

"And you, a great Silent."

They both laughed, and their laughter echoed in the garden and out in the valley surrounding the fortress. Habael lifted his head and smiled. At last, the company had reached the fortress. Tanios pounded on the outer door. Before reaching the fortress, he had organized the refugees into small groups under the Silent's care.

"Commander Tanios," said Captain Enryl, "I welcome you in the name of Lord Orgond. Please follow me."

>-:◦:◦:◦:-<

Alviad met Jedarc and the Silent Whisper of four men he was leading at the gate of the city. He was overjoyed to see his friends alive, and pulled Banimelek aside. He wanted to give the tall Silent a hug, but knew

Banimelek, who was one of his closest friends, would not appreciate even a simple accolade while on duty and in public.

"What are you doing at the gate?" asked Banimelek.

They were walking toward the temporary refugee camp that was now under the control of the military.

"Waiting for you, what else? Commander's order. What kept you?"

"Some folks captured Hiyam to offer her as a sacrifice to a béghôm," explained Banimelek.

"A bé ... what?" replied a shocked Alviad. "The creature of legends? It exists? Wait ... You're serious?"

Banimelek nodded. "You should have seen this beast, Alviad. It was as tall as a giant and ... but I'm getting ahead of myself. We sneaked in to free her, but they caught us."

"Who?"

"The desert people. They were going to offer her as a sacrifice."

Alviad let out a low whistle. "Imagine what would have happened had they succeeded. The Temple would have burned the whole area."

Banimelek nodded.

"How did you manage to save her?"

"Ahiram showed up at the last moment—"

Alviad hooted and slapped Banimelek on the shoulder. "I knew it! He is alive then!"

Banimelek smirked. "Come on, Alviad, it'll take a lot more than a few gray owls to kill shark-boy."

Alviad nodded. "So what happened then?"

"He killed the beast and then fell ill."

Alviad eyed his friend. He was visibly confused. "Has anyone ever told you that you should be a story teller?"

Banimelek frowned. "Not that I remember."

"Good. You tell stories so quickly, one would think your listeners all have an extreme urge to go to the—"

"No latrine jokes," Banimelek cut in.

Alviad chuckled. "So then, Ahiram is alive. Amazing. Everyone in the Silent Corps has been worried sick about him. This is great news."

"Indeed. He survived the High Riders."

"Is he all right now?"

"Yes. He recovered and will be joining us soon. He's walking an old lady and her grand-son home."

"Huh … most likely he was hoping to find a clean la—" Banimelek elbowed his friend who smirked. "Anyway, I know a young lady who's going to be very happy to see him."

"I guess so," replied Banimelek. His tone was noncommittal. "He'll be relieved to see her too."

"Relieved?" Alviad shrugged his shoulders. "He'd be an idiot not to be thrilled to see her."

"He will be happy to see her, that's certain."

"But not thrilled?" insisted Alviad, a glint in his eye.

"You can't order love around. It doesn't work that way."

"Since when do you know so much about love?"

"Since I've seen Sondra look at you."

"What do you mean?" Alviad asked nervously. "You're not serious, are you now? I don't like the sound of this."

"You'd be an idiot if you didn't."

"You're not serious."

Banimelek sighed. "I'm surrounded by clueless oafs who can't tell the difference between friendship and love."

"Hey, there's Mr. Prince Jedarc, you know?" protested Alviad. "He's the good-looking one, so why would Sondra … I mean, you're sure Sondra—"

"You're an idiot."

Alviad stuck his hands deep into his pockets. "So, what am I supposed to do now?"

"Stop being one."

After leading the refugees to the camp, they went to the fortress and presented themselves before the commander. Tanios was happy to see them and relieved to see Hiyam. He grinned when they told him Ahiram was alive and would join them soon. Hiyam went in haste to meet her mother. Bahiya held her daughter tightly in her arms.

"It is so good to see you again, daughter," she whispered. "So very good to see you."

"Thank you, Mother." Hiyam avoided any show of emotion—a weakness the Temple despised in future priestesses. Still, relief washed over her. She was with her mother. No matter the gravity of the situation, her mother would know what to do. She always did.

"Mother, where is my team?"

"On their way to Baalbek. After the events of the Games, I decided to grant them leave."

"What about us, Mother?"

"I have my orders from Babylon. More I cannot say. You are free to leave, if you so wish. I am not certain I will survive what is to come," she added softly.

Hiyam blanched. "Mother—"

"Not now, Hiyam. If you leave, you will be safe in Baalbek. If you stay, you might not survive. Choose well, daughter."

➢ ⋅◉⋅◉⋅ ≺

Jedarc had struck up a friendship with Frajil. He had brought him into the kitchen where a succulent smell of roasted chicken filled the air.

"Young rooster good to Frajil," said the giant. "Frajil take care of you."

"Do you have a place to stay?" asked Jedarc.

Frajil was confused. "Kitchen is place. Frajil is in place. Frajil stays."

"Yes, but what about after you're done eating? Where will you go?"

Frajil lived in the moment. Any future dealings were Soloron's realm.

"Listen," said Jedarc. "I'll find you a place to stay. You can go into town if you like, and you can come back here for the night."

Frajil beamed. He grabbed Jedarc, and hugged him the way he hugged his brother.

"Put me down, Frajil," whispered Jedarc. "I can't breathe."

"Ha! Young rooster like Soloron." Unexpectedly, he burst into tears. "I miss Soloron," he hiccuped. "My brother!"

"Frajil, look," said Jedarc. "A pomegranate."

Instantly, his tears stopped. He saw Jedarc smile and he relaxed. *People happy. Frajil like people happy. Frajil like pomegranates. When people happy, Frajil get pomegranates.*

≻ ⚬⚬⚬ ≺

Refugees and Togofalkian tourists filled the city of Amsheet. Tophun Makack had to wade slowly through crowd-filled streets, which soured his mood. He was late to an important meeting. His massive frame was not cut out for crowded streets, which slowed him down. His temper got hotter and hotter by the minute.

Ahiram looked up and saw the fortress. *I'll be there soon.* He was impatient to rejoin the group of Silent and speak to the commander and Habael, but he restrained himself and walked slowly, guiding the old woman. She was tired, yet she pressed ahead. She leaned on Ahiram's arm saying, "Soon, soon." Tinn, the ten-year old young lad walked quietly beside his grandmother, helping her as much as he could. The city was lit in preparation for the carnival and buzzed with excitement. Happy visitors filled the streets alongside carnival jesters and musicians.

A joyful laughter rose above the noise. Ahiram turned around and saw a beautiful woman and a young man walking side-by-side, filled with hope and joyful expectation.

How strange, thought the Silent. *I wish I could do what he is doing; walk carefree with someone I wouldn't be afraid to love. I faced a béghôm and now an urkuun, and if I survive the next battle, who's to say there won't be a worse opponent? I don't want those I care about to die ...*

A booth of delicious rumanil distracted the old woman's grandson, and he accidentally stepped on someone's boot. Tophun Makack looked down and saw dirt on his shoe. He slapped the boy and sent him rolling on the ground. His grandmother shrieked.

"You dirtied my boot," he snarled.

"*You* should apologize," said a voice behind him.

Tophun Makack whirled around and faced a tall young man. His curly hair fell untidily around his face. *Like mutton's locks*, he thought. The fierce hazel eyes did not impress him. Even if Makack had paid attention to Ahiram's muscular build, he would not have been impressed. His mind had no use for the word *impressed*. He believed in his strength alone.

But less than a minute later, he lay on the ground writhing in pain. He was indeed strong, but strength without training is no match for the speed, accuracy, and power of a Silent. Ahiram drew closer and looked him in the eye.

"Next time, think twice before hitting a child. You may avoid unnecessary pain."

"Thanks, Ahiram," said the lad.

Tophun Makack was glad to see them leave. Wearily, he stood up and rubbed his head and chest. "If we ever meet again, Ahiram, you will be lucky if I let you die," muttered the man as he continued his walk. By now, his boots were filthy.

> ⋅⋅⋅⋅ <

Master Habael looked at the group of men and women sitting around the table. *So it begins again*, he thought wistfully. *These are extraordinary times.*

The day after they reached the fortress, Lord Orgond had called a council, but there were complications: Princess Gaëla refused to sit at the same table with a high priestess of Baal. Lord Orgond explained the

413

priestess would disclose the identity of the enemy was and assured her of Bahiya's good will. Master Xurgon threatened to leave when he saw the Empyrean princess—for there was much old blood between the two races. Master Habael spoke in favor of the princess and the dwarfs agreed to sit at the council table. Xurgon reserved the right to leave if his suspicions were confirmed that the Empyreans had weakened the fortress' walls before they attacked.

The Lord of Amsheet presided. Princess Gaëla was at his right, followed by Lord Uziguzi, Master Xurgon, High Priestess Bahiya, Master Habael, Commander Tanios, and Enryl. The company of the Silent waited in an adjacent room. Hiyam was with them. Noraldeen's features hardened when she saw her, but she said nothing. *She knows who I am. I do not belong in Baalbek anymore, but I do not belong here either. What am I to do?* She caught Jedarc smiling at her. He winked, and she blushed. *Don't be an idiot, Hiyam.* She chided herself. *Why am I blushing?* She watched him talking with Noraldeen who kept looking in her direction. *What is he telling her, I wonder?*

"I will refrain from killing her and will want to hear what Ahiram has to say," Noraldeen was saying in a low, unbending voice to Jedarc. "You can be too trusting for your own good."

"He saved her life," insisted Jedarc. "Be patient, Nora."

In the council hall, Lord Orgond stood-up. "I have convened this council," started Lord Orgond, "to prepare for our next step. You know we face an enemy of considerable might and ability. Many here have had some exposure to his dark trade, whether in confronting the sylveeds or witnessing the decay of rocks. From the concordant accounts we received, we must assume Hardeen is now the enemy's lair. Our plan is to attack Hardeen and oust the invader."

Orgond stopped talking when the main door opened. A guard ushered Ahiram in and closed the door quietly behind him. Ahiram was overjoyed to see Commander Tanios and Master Habael. The old man looked at him with a warm smile, but Tanios' countenance was severe. "You are late, Silent." Tanios had wanted his voice to be even, but even he could no longer hide his joy.

Ahiram walked toward the table and saluted. "My apologies, Commander. I am late."

"And what is your excuse?"

"An old woman asked me to walk with her and her grandson until she reached her house. 'The Silent is faithful to his call, especially to the elders to whom he owes respect and consideration,' chapter one, verse five of the *Book of Siril*." Ahiram bowed.

"Offer your apologies to Lord Orgond for having disrupted the council and join your peers in the next room," replied Tanios.

Ahiram turned around and bowed respectfully before Lord Orgond, who nodded. Orgond glanced at Gaëla. She met his gaze with a smile. *Is this the wonder of wonders?* Orgond seemed to say. *Appearances can be deceiving*, the princess seemed to reply. This young man with a comely appearance did not impress them. Ahiram left the hall, and Orgond resumed talking.

"Before I explain the details to you, I would like to ask each one of you to share with us what he or she knows about the enemy."

A shout of joy could be heard from the other room as the Silent welcomed Ahiram. After the cheerful noise had subsided, Master Xurgon stood up.

"As you knowingly know …" Master Xurgon cleared his throat and reverted to the common tongue. "These creatures have taken two of my dwarfs. I have heard rumors that these so-called sylveeds are related to the Empyreans. Yet I see present among us a worthy representative of the empress. I must confess my confusion." He sat.

"You are both right and wrong," Gaëla corrected. "This evil revealed itself first in our empire, leading you to conclude that we had created it. The empire itself is in a precarious position. We do not know how to respond adequately to such evil. This is why we are here seeking advice."

"I might add," continued Uziguzi, "that whatever is attacking you is attacking us. We have a common enemy, and I wonder," said the rotund man while glancing at Bahiya, "if this 'common enemy' of ours is not behind this."

Bahiya met Uziguzi's gaze. "The Temple of Baal subdues magic wherever it finds it," she said. "It has done so precisely to protect the world from calamities such as this one. This protection extended over every kingdom, including the empire you serve, Lord Uziguzi. The Temple is the strong wall that has held these powers at bay." She shuddered. "But after what I heard, I am compelled to admit the Temple has either allowed a being of great power to enter this world, or the Temple has been overcome."

"Lady Bahiya," objected Uziguzi, "the Temple may be callous and tyrannical, but not reckless. I must ask, is this an attempt to overtake the Empyreans?"

"It may be," replied the high priestess thoughtfully.

Her straightforward words, which was so unlike her, surprised Tanios. He could feel the tension mounting in the room and knew Lord Orgond refrained from intervening on purpose. Uziguzi's pointed question demanded a valid answer from the priestess.

"I do not know what the Temple's intent is," she said after a pause. "We may never find out," she added, staving the protests. "However, I do know what we are dealing with."

"What?" demanded Uziguzi.

The high priestess clenched her fists and looked down before answering in a whisper. "An Urkuun of the Third Order."

A deep dread came over those who knew what an urkuun was. At the same moment, a second whoop of joy answered, and it startled them. They could hear the Silent chanting Ahiram's name. Lord Orgond's plan to invade the fortress sounded hollow, for how could they hope to overtake a being who nearly defeated the mighty legions of the Marada? In the adjacent room, the name of Ahiram rose to a crescendo as sunrays splashed the council room.

"No matter the evil we face," said Lord Orgond, "our call is to meet it and work unceasingly until we defeat it. If we fail, then let us be a beacon of hope to those who will come after us. For evil is but a passing shadow, a fleeting agony, a sorrow we must endure. In the days to come, those who will walk in our footsteps must know we have not wavered, that we have not surrendered, that we have not been overcome. Darkness is falling. Let us stand and raise a shining sword to subdue the depths of the Pit."

23. Broken Sheath

*"A sword that was once hidden shall now be revealed.
By the power of a broken sheath the steward had concealed.
A sheath, a mighty sheath of silk, gold and precious stone,
For the mighty hand of El-Windiir's heir, and him alone."*
 —The *Chronicles of Yardam,* Third Steward of the House of Hiram.

The Silent had been speaking quietly to avoid disrupting the meeting when Ahiram joined them. Noraldeen, who had been standing with her back to the door, did not see him enter. She chatted with Banimelek and Sondra when a hush fell on the room.

"Look," whispered Banimelek pointing with his chin to the door.

A thunderous shout filled the room as the Silent, carrying Ahiram on their shoulders, stood and chanted his name until the chanting became a protracted applause. Finally, Ahiram jumped down, and Corialynn punched him.

"That's for scaring us," she said.

Allelia smacked him on the head. "And that's for refusing our help."

Alviad elbowed him. "And that's for taking this long to come back."

"Hey, don't hurt Alendiir," protested Sondra. "He's barely recovered."

"I'm fine," grinned Ahiram.

Each one of his companions wanted to congratulate him personally and time passed amid relieved laughter. The Silent were not only glad to be reunited, but Ahiram's victory was also their victory. Jedarc did his best to include Hiyam in the general euphoria, but she could not bring herself to rejoice. Seeing the Silent's joy in welcoming Ahiram increased her sense of shame. That the Temple of Baal had wanted him dead just to allow her to win a Game seemed unreal now.

Noraldeen was the last to greet him. She approached Ahiram and looked at him with such tender eyes that he blushed.

"You are alive," she said in a hushed voice. She was not one to display her feelings publicly, yet now she could barely hide them. Her relief and elation surrounded her like a graceful aura, a beam of pure light. And she stood ravishing before him.

"Yes," replied Ahiram, flushed. "And gladly so."

"I am so happy to see you."

"And I am so happy to see *you*," replied Ahiram with a soft, gentle smile. "I heard you wore a dress yesterday. I would like to have seen that," he added with a snicker.

Everyone laughed. Noraldeen joined in, unconcerned with yesterday's outfit. He was here, with her. Nothing else mattered now.

"Tell us, how did you do it? How did you survive?" She wanted to move the attention away from her.

"Well, there is not much to tell, really," replied Ahiram.

The Silent booed him.

"Come on, Ahiram, cut the modesty routine," yelled Allelia.

"The commander is not here, now is he?" added Corialynn.

"Tell us what happened," called Alviad. "We really want to know."

"Well, it came down to this, as I ran by the water, I fell in but managed to get out and make my way to the top. By the revolutionaries overtook the castle and you were all gone, and here we are now back together."

"That won't do," protested Allelia. "Tell us more."

it insisted, so Ahiram began relaying the events of the past few weeks—though omitting El-Windeer's artifacts and minimizing his fight with the béghôm. He handed his sword to his teammates and they passed it around in silence. Noraldeen let her fingers glide lightly along the sword and it produced a joyful, thrilling sound; calling, *commanding* all to battle. The Silent rose like one man, ready for action.

She handed the sword back to him. "I have always known you were a true prince," she whispered cryptically. "This blade is yours to keep. It will be with you until the end."

Hiyam breathed a sigh of relief. Ahiram did not mention her participation in the High Riders' plan to murder him during the Game of Meyroon. She noticed that Jedarc looked at her, smiling. He bent down and whispered in her ear, "I told you, didn't I? He quickly forgets his anger." She nodded affirmatively.

"Is that all?" asked one of the Silent. "Did you find the wings?"

Ahiram misunderstood the question. The Silent, naturally, had meant the fake wings, the ones hidden in the mines by the judges. But Ahiram thought the Silent had asked if he found the real wings of El-Windiir. He didn't know how to answer for he did not want to reveal his findings before first discussing it with Tanios. Fortunately, the door of the meeting room opened and Habael spoke. "Follow me please, all of you." Ahiram breathed a sigh of relief. As the company moved toward the meeting room, Ahiram grabbed Noraldeen's arm and gently pulled her aside. "It's so good to see you, Nora," he whispered. "Let's talk some more later." Noraldeen was overjoyed and in her joy misunderstood his intent. He was like a mariner who had just found his anchor, like a lost child found by his older sister. So focused was he on his relief to be with Noraldeen again, that he did not stop to think how she might receive these words, how she could misinterpret them. Indeed, Noraldeen thought Ahiram was finally ready to reciprocate the love burning in her heart for him. *At last, we will be together*, she thought, while Ahiram was thinking, *I am reunited with my friends. Everything will be just fine.*

The Silent filed into the council room. Lord Orgond directed them to stand around the table. Ahiram leaned against the wall with Noraldeen by his side. Her father waited for silence to settle, then rose to his feet and pointed to the broken sheath before him. "Do you know what this is?"

"The emblem of the north, Your Lordship," answered Banimelek.

"Correct, young man, but can you tell me why?"

As was the habit for a Silent, Ahiram surveyed the room. His eyes settled on the high priestess, who was looking at him; and when he met her gaze, she smiled. Ahiram looked down and thought, *A serpent's smile, no doubt. What is she up to?*

"A long time ago," continued Lord Orgond, "towards the end of the Wars of Meyroon, a major battle was fought in the north of our kingdom. This was the year 2,925 in the Age of the Second Covenant. El-Windiir commanded a great army of men, dwarfs, giants, and even Malikuun, those beings of light and great power. They fought a great evil that plundered the earth, one of the great beings the Lords of the Deep had brought fourth: the urkuun. The Lords of the Deep fashioned nine urkuuns, three of the First Order, three of the Second Order, and three of the Third Order. Each order was more powerful than the previous one. The ninth urkuun, the greatest of them all, was stronger than all the previous eight combined."

Orgond paused and looked at the Silent to prepare them for what was to come. "Urkuuns of the First Order were called Destruction. They were unleashed to stem the advance of the Malikuun in the wars bearing their name. These Wars of Destruction stretched from 876 to 1,436 of the Age of the Second Covenant. The urkuuns each led their own army and turned the land into a heap of desolation. They destroyed entire kingdoms, burned large forests, and left nothing standing. Yet their tactics were predictable. At the Battle of Sufian, Escalion, the general of the federated army, stopped their terror.

"Peace reigned for nearly five hundred years, during which time the Lords of the Deep patiently readied their second assault. In the depth of Jaheem, the deepest cavern of the dead, they brought forth the Urkuuns of the Second Order. These three were known as Fire, and with their coming, the Wars of Fire began. They were stronger and smarter than their predecessors, and having a primitive knowledge of magic, rained fire on the land. The urkuuns led an immense army and laid siege to the fair city of Ea. This ushered in the Age of the Seven Battles of Light. The urkuuns and their armies won the first four battles and were about to overtake the armies of the Malikuun when the Marada, who were nonaligned, joined the army of men. On 29 Kislev 2223, in the Age of the Second Covenant, the great king of Marada, Muhaijar I, slew these urkuun by the power of Terragold, his royal sword.

"As you know, the Marada are giants of incredible strength, aloof and unconcerned by the affairs of men. Why they joined the battle at such a desperate moment, we may never know. They came like thunder, and fell on their enemies. The urkuun blazed fire on them but could not pierce through their stony shields."

This part of ancient history was not new to the Silent, but hearing it told by Lord Orgond in the Fortress of Amsheet turned the shadows of the past into sinister figures lurking in the darkness. This was no longer a mere remembrance of great deeds done by characters frozen in the stream of long forgotten tales; this had suddenly become their struggle, their fate, their future.

"Again, peace reigned for three hundred years. We forgot our enemies. But while the Wars of Fire raged, the Lords of the Deep had begun fashioning the Urkuuns of the Third Order. These last three creatures were called Power, and they were masters of magic. The last of them, the ninth urkuun, was called the Seducer because he enticed the hearts of men to follow and serve him. With them began the last and most terrible wars of the Age of the Second Covenant, The Wars of Meyroon that lasted two hundred years. These three urkuun nearly succeeded in conquering all the kingdoms.

"To fuel their conquests, these monsters required a great supply of meyroon to sustain themselves, and meyroon was plentiful in the Kingdom of Tanniin. The urkuun enslaved the dwarfs and forced them to dig the mines. Then they enslaved men and forced them to work the mines. El-Windiir was one such slave. Even though despair turned men into beasts, El-Windiir remained true to his first love, Layaleen, and in so doing, became acceptable to the Lords of Light. They tasked him with an impossible feat: to block the supply of meyroon from the Lords of the Pit for four days. How this lonely man managed to inspire his fellow slaves, we may never know. Despair turned to hope and fear into resplendent acts of courage. These nameless heroes blocked the mines of Meyroon and paid with their blood the ultimate price. They weakened the three urkuuns and gave the third army of light an edge in the battle. Then the Temple of Baal joined forces with El-Windiir and confronted magic with magic. The weakened two urkuuns fell under the golden arrows of Ximban, the legendary archer of Quibanxe. The last, the Seducer, stood defiant. He repelled every attempt and derided the army. Even the Temple of Baal could not overtake him. El-Windiir drew closer, unnoticed to the Seducer. He was terrified, yet he forced himself to continue. The Seducer boasted, confident in his might. This proved to be his downfall. The Malikuun had revealed to him that only a sword forged of pure meyroon could pierce an urkuun's magic. The dwarfs who were enslaved with El-Windiir forged such a sword for him. He called it *Layaleen*, the name of his beloved wife. With one masterful blow, El-Windiir drove his sword into the Seducer's heart, and the urkuun fell. El-Windiir and his allies took charge of the mines and defended them. In the ensuing battle, the Lord of Light defeated the Lord of the Deep. Peace was restored. We believed the Seducer had been destroyed, until now."

Orgond looked at Bahiya. This was her cue. She stood up.

"We know that every creature of the dark has a landmark signature," she explained. "When an urkuun sets his lair, he surrounds it with strong curses and marks the area with squares and circles dug into the ground or carved into trees or rocks. The simplicity of the signature is purposeful; it is meant to alert his allies that they are in his territory. The number of squares indicates the urkuun's order and the number of circles, the urkuun's level—"

"So then," interjected Lord Orgond, who could see many confused faces, "the First Urkuun of the Second Order would carve two squares and four circles, is that not so, Lady Bahiya?"

"Precisely. On the way to Amsheet, a woman told us her brother had worked as a cook in Hardeen. Her cousin saw three rectangles magically appear in the fortress's ground surrounded by nine circles."

A hush fell in the room as they pondered the priestesses' words.

"The Third Urkuun of the Third Level," whispered Jedarc.

Banimelek nodded.

Noraldeen stomped on Jedarc's foot. "Be quiet or my father will have us leave the room."

"This woman," continued Bahiya, "a farmer by all accounts, could not have known what this meant. I am convinced the Seducer, the ninth urkuun, and the third of the third order has taken over Hardeen. The presence of these so-called sylveeds is another sure sign that the Seducer has emerged: He is turning people into monsters by seducing them."

Orgond lifted the sheath with great care before continuing. "When El-Windiir defeated the urkuun, he ordered a special sheath be made for his sword. The sheath would not accept any other sword but Layaleen." He unsheathed his own sword and tried to slide it into the broken sheath. An unseen power blocked the sword, preventing it from moving forward. "No other sword will do," he added, sheathing back his sword. "Only Layaleen. Before leaving for his last battle, El-Windiir broke the sheath and commanded the keeper of his house to watch over it until the return of the sword." He raised his hands to let everyone see the sheath. "I am the current keeper of El-Windiir's house. We have faithfully kept the sheath from generation to generation. The sheath will only be restored when both pieces come in contact with Layaleen."

"With Layaleen, we may have a chance to defeat our enemy," continued Tanios. "But without it, our chances are slim."

"What does the urkuun want?" asked Ahiram.

His question surprised the council. They had assumed everyone knew what the Seducer wanted.

"The urkuun is at the service of the Lords of the Deep," answered Bahiya. "His sole purpose is to raise an army and open the Pit of the Abyss. Once freed, his masters will unleash their destructive power on the land and usher in a reign of darkness and chaos."

Silence fell. "How can we, so few, hope to defeat such a powerful foe?" asked Banimelek, voicing nearly everyone's concern.

Ahiram saw the sullen faces of his friends. As he looked around, his gaze met Master Habael's, who looked at him as though saying, *what are you waiting for?* Ahiram sighed. All he wanted was to be free, to return to Baher-Ghafé. Yet without him, what would become of his friends? Slowly, he drew closer to the high priestess. Both Commander Tanios and Lord Orgond scowled in disapproval, but he ignored them. He stood before Bahiya.

"Supposing I had the sword in my possession and *I* faced the urkuun. Would I be able to return home a free man?"

Bahiya looked at Ahiram with sorrowful eyes, as if he had reopened a deep, hidden wound. All council members noticed how pale she was.

Is she seeing a ghost? Uziguzi wondered.

At last, Habael broke the silence. "Do what you must, lad." Ahiram looked at him, and Bahiya slumped in her chair as if freed from a powerful spell. Ahiram could not resist the old man's warm smile. He relaxed and smiled back.

"I shall do what my sister would bid me to do." he replied. He went and stood in front of Lord Orgond.

Tanios was about to order him back to his place when Habael whispered in his ear, "Let the lad speak."

Ahiram looked at the broken halves of the sheath. "May I hold them for a moment?" he asked Lord Orgond.

"Ahiram," interjected Tanios, for whom this was too much. "Go back to your place immediately."

"Give the lad a chance," cut in Master Habael in a soothing tone.

This surprised Tanios, who was not used to an assertive Habael. The Lord of Amsheet looked at the young man sternly, thinking this was indeed an impertinent slave. *Let him make a fool of himself, and let Noraldeen see how preposterous he is.* He glanced at his daughter. She had an indefinable smile, something between relief and elation. Orgond felt foolish but did not know why.

He stepped aside and signaled for Ahiram to draw closer. Ahiram unsheathed his blade and raised it in the presence of all.

"Lord Orgond, I ask your permission to sheath my sword with these two pieces," he said.

Commander Tanios was about to jump from his seat and slap the slave when Habael stood up and spoke.

"Commander Tanios, Your Lordship, and all who are present. I would like to vouchsafe my humble word in favor of this lad. I will take the blame if you consider his action impertinent."

Reluctantly, the commander nodded. Lord Orgond looked at Habael, then surveyed all those who were present. Clearly, most of them did not approve of the actions of this young man.

"Father, I add my word to that of Master Habael," said Noraldeen. "Please, let Ahiram sheath his sword."

Lord Orgond looked sternly at Ahiram.

"Young man, do you know the penalty for forgery? This is a most sacred object, and we do not treat impostors lightly. Only Layaleen will fit inside this sheath. Do you claim that you," continued Orgond with a note of chastisement he could not hide, "*a slave*, hold in your hands the legendary sword of El-Windiir?"

"Ahiram," interjected Hiyam. "Tell them about the monster."

Sheheluth nodded. "Tell them, Ahiram."

The Silent felt the familiar irritation well up inside him. He wished this useless discussion would end so he could sheath the sword. Habael's reassuring gaze once more invited him to patience.

"The monster, ah yes," said Master Xurgon. He stood up. "Your Lordship and all you benevolent and mighty present, I am not one to be entwined in hum-drums and topsy-turvy fables of dubious origins, whose source cannot be tracked to solid facts embedded in the rock of reality, and realistically verifiable by obvious means and means within reach. I am one to attest that this young man has accomplished the unthinkable and has done so impeccably, so much so, that peace reigns in our corridors where once strife and impediments to lateral movements were the norm. He has indeed made way with the beast."

"Which beast is that?" asked Uziguzi, intrigued.

"A béghôm," replied Ahiram lightly. "Killed by *this* sword I hold in my hands." He whisked the sword through the air and it rang joyfully.

"You killed a béghôm?" asked Lord Orgond, incredulous.

"Yes." Ahiram sustained his glare.

"My Lord," interjected Tanios, "I have known this lad for six years now. He may be impulsive and ill tempered, but a liar he is not. If he says that he killed a béghôm, I believe him."

Lord Orgond looked at Gaëla, who nodded. "Sheath your sword."

Silence fell on the room. Ahiram bowed before Lord Orgond. He took the first half of the sheath and slid it easily over the sword until it touched the handle. It locked in place. A gasp filled the room. He then took the second piece, took a breath, and effortlessly slid it after the first.

The fit between them was flawless. Everyone rose to their feet. Ahiram felt a slight tremor along the blade and light flashed through the hairline seam between the two parts of the sheath. Ahiram unsheathed the sword, gripped the sheath, and held it high for all to see. The two pieces had become one. He placed the sheath on the table, raised his sword and proclaimed:

"I am the bearer of the sword! Layaleen is mine!" He looked at the astonished crowd as he vowed, "I will slay the urkuun and free the land from its evil. By this, all will know that El-Windiir is claiming the land once more. I am Ahiram, Son of Jabbar, and by the honor of my father, I will confront the urkuun and slay him. His blood will spill on the land!"

Lord Orgond knelt before Ahiram. Then Commander Tanios, Master Habael, Master Xurgon, and the entire body of the Silent Corps followed suit. Bahiya bowed, as did Uziguzi, and Princess Gaëla.

Though he felt unworthy of it, Ahiram accepted their homage. "Never ask more than what the meat is worth," his father had once told him. "In all things, deal honorably. And above all else, be truthful." Ahiram did not know why these words came back to him, but he knew he had to live by his word and fulfill what he had promised.

>·:·:·:·<

Down in the dungeons of the fortress, an Empyrean, a member of Princess Gaëla's retinue, had made his way into Zirka's room. Behind her, a strangled guard lay on the floor.

"Quick," she said, "go alert the master. The sword of defamation is found, and has been raised against him by El-Windiir's heir."

Zirka rose quickly and slipped out of the dungeon. Soon he was out of the fortress and on his way to Hardeen.

>·:·:·:·<

Ahiram stood on the balcony that overlooked the gentle valley below the fortress. The city basked in quiet obscurity beneath a star-studded sky. Oddly, he could not see the moon. The air was brisk and reminded him somehow of the air back home. *Hoda, where are you? Why didn't you come back? Why did you let them take me away?* He heard a noise from the road below: a heave, a screech, and wood creaking under the heavy weight of an object sliding noisily on a rough surface.

"Be careful," said someone. "You almost dropped it."

"Careful, careful." repeated the echo.

He saw a group of men hunched over a cart, straining with effort as they wheeled it. Ostensibly, it carried a large, heavy object that a thick cloak concealed from view. Ahiram stood mesmerized. Something beneath the cloak was calling his name.

"Hello," said Noraldeen gently.

Unable to tear his gaze, he spoke abruptly. "What's in the cart?"

His tone was hurtful, but she ignored it. "The statue of Jaguar-Night. The procession will start in a couple of hours. Why do you ask?" She looked at him and moved closer, but he kept his gaze on the cart as though troubled by it. She had hoped he would ignore their surroundings and pay attention to her alone.

"You miss your family, Ahiram?"

"Yes," he replied. The pull weakened as the cart moved away.

"You are a free man now," she observed, trying to cheer him up.

Ahiram laughed bitterly. "After all these years, what is the use of my freedom if I cannot return home? Now I must fight the urkuun, and who knows if I will survive this battle."

Noraldeen did not flinch. The anticipation of seeing him again had turned into a bittersweet disappointment. "What if you cannot see them?" she asked softly. "What if they are not … in your village?"

"What do you mean?" asked Ahiram, incredulous.

She smiled a sad smile keeping a close watch over her feelings. "You might want to ask the commander," she said at last. "I had hoped we could talk about … other things but I guess it cannot be helped. You should go and ask the commander."

"But, where would they be? What are you hiding from me?" Noraldeen slowly stepped back and Ahiram closed in until her back was against the wall. "Noraldeen, tell me! Don't hide anything from me. If you know something about my family and you do not tell me, you cannot call yourself my friend."

This last word stung, more than she expected. She pushed him violently. "I am not your friend. I love you. Ahiram, your parents are dead. Do you hear me? They are dead!" she screamed. "Ask Commander Tanios, he will tell you." Noraldeen slowly slid down the wall sobbing. She did not need to look up to know that Ahiram had left.

The council finalized their strategy. It was daring; some might call it insane, but this was their best plan of attack.

"Defeating the urkuun inside Hardeen is impossible," Lord Orgond summarized. "But it hates the light of day and passes on this hatred to the sylveeds. The high priestess will cross into Empyrean territory, with Commander Tanios, and they will sneak into the Fortress through a secret door. Bahiya will mount an attack to weaken and force the Urkuun out of his lair. The Silent will accompany them since Princess Gaëla cannot guarantee their safe passage. The Empress is not aware of her daughter's initiative and therefore to most Empyreans outside the Princess' immediate followers, the Commander and the High Priestess would be considered spies."

Orgond sighed before continuing. "In the meantime, the urkuun will unleash its forces against us. The Empyreans will join in battle on the plain of Hardeen. We will need to hold the Sylveeds back until the urkuun is flushed out and Ahiram confronts him. The thought that victory rests on the shoulders of a single young man is enough to send cold shivers down my spine. Yet, as Lord Uziguzi mentioned, there is a worse fate than defeat: Ahiram could join the urkuun. If this were to happen, who knows what calamity may come to us all?"

"This is why," interjected Princess Gaëla, "I am against allowing the young man to face the urkuun alone."

"It is too dangerous, Your Highness," replied Commander Tanios. "Anyone who comes close to the urkuun may easily fall under its spell. You know this as well as anyone. We must keep our distance."

"But you will face him in Hardeen," replied the princess.

"An unavoidable risk," replied the commander. "Not so when he is in the open. There you have the option of staying behind the lines of defense and acting with greater liberty. I think the wisdom of this plan will become manifest once we confront the urkuun."

"If none of us can withstand the power of the urkuun," said Uziguzi pensively, "how can we let this boy face the monster alone?"

"What is necessary is fateful, and what is fateful is to pass," answered Master Xurgon. "That the boy must face an ancient horror requires our consent and helpful participation, beyond an uncompromising boundary that none of the most august present can cross."

Ahiram stormed through the door, startling them.

"Ahiram, what is the meaning of this?" asked the commander.

Ahiram ignored him. "Are my parents and my sister dead?"

"What?" Tanios felt as if someone had punched him in the gut.

Bahiya covered her face. *How did he find out? I only shared this information with Tanios recently so that he could break it to Ahiram and help him better prepare for battle. I knew the urkuun would want to torture him with the events of Baher-Ghafé. Did the monster attack him here despite my protective spells?*

"Is it true that my family is dead, Commander? I must know."

Tanios looked hard at Ahiram, but the young man did not avert his eyes. For the first time ever, Ahiram sustained his master's glare. The commander knew Ahiram would not accept anything but the truth.

"Who told you this?" he asked cautiously.

"Noraldeen. She said I should ask you. She said you knew all along." Ahiram added this last bit of misinformation to test his commander.

"I do not know for sure that your parents are dead," replied Tanios as calmly as possible. "All I know is that your village, Baher-Ghafé, was raided shortly after you were taken, and there are no known survivors."

His eyes locked on Tanios. A silence followed that lasted an eternity. "Why did you not tell me?" asked Ahiram quietly. He raised his hand to prevent Commander Tanios from speaking. "I know, you don't have to say it. It is not permitted for a slave to ask questions, right? A slave does not have the right to know anything. You repeated this to me so often, so I just kept to myself. I did not ask anything, or question anything. But then, why did you say you cared about me, why did you let me take part in the Games and risk being killed? What was the point of it?" Ahiram hit the table with his fist and ran out of the room.

"Ahiram," shouted Tanios. There was no response.

Ahiram was gone.

Battle of Hardeen

෩෬

Part Four

24. Jaguar Night

"The dwarfs are dangerous. Their lore is foreign to Baal. There are great magicians amongst them, yet not once was Baal able to pinpoint one single act of magic that could be attributed to the dwarfs. It is said that they perform their acts deep within their mountains through secret ways known to them alone.
"Priests of Baal should fear their presence greatly."
—Teaching of Oreg, High Priest of Baal.

"Whether El-Windiir faced an Urkuun of the Third Order or not remains a matter of contention. To think that a mere mortal could face such a powerful servant of the Pit requires a great deal of faith. To believe that he was capable of defeating him is downright absurd."
—Diplomatic Notes of Uziguzi, First Adviser to Her Majesty, Aylul Meir Pen, Empress of the Empyreans.

While Tanios sent the Silent to search for Ahiram, Ibromaliöm stood inside a private room of the tavern The Hot Potato and the Three Turnips. A smell of rancid oil and fried fish hung in the air like a giant albatross hovering over a fishing boat. The smell pervaded the walls and floor, and clung to people as fog to trees.

"You bungling fool!" He yelled and pounded the table. "I told you to dispose of that idiot quietly, but instead, you stab him in the hall of the fortress and leave his body there? Are you trying to frame me?"

Ibromaliöm's interlocutor bowed his head like a scolded child. "Farad was suspicious," he finally said while raising his shoulders in a gesture of resignation. "You wanted him dead. He is dead. Besides, I did not nab him *in* the hall. I got him in a hallway."

"I wanted him dead in a dark alley where no one would find him, you dull-headed, full of third-grade duck feathers! Not dead and lying in the fortress. That rat Tanios is there. It will not take him long to figure out the dagger you left belongs to the gang of Teheromac Ud-Palda."

Orag looked at Ibromaliöm with exasperation. This was the third time this southerner had mispronounced the gang's name.

"Tahoramac Ur-Pagday, Ibromaliöm, sir," he said in a soft voice as he walked toward the ex-judge and faced him up close. "*Pagday*, hum? You will remember, yes?" Tahoramac Ur-Pagday meant the deadly snake, whereas Teheromac Ud-Palda meant the respectful donkey.

Ibromaliöm sneered. "If it suits me to say Teheromac Ud-Palda, I will say Teheromac Ud-Palda. And you should know better than to argue with me on linguistics. I take linguistic very, very seriously. Besides, Teheromac Ud-Palda or Tahoramac Ur-Pagday, Tanios will find out."

"So what?" interjected Tophun Makack. "So what if he finds out we quacked Farad, what's he gonna do? Old Orgond has been trying to lay his fat hands on us, and so far he's gotten nothin' but cold air and lots 'a sweat." Tophun walked toward Ibromaliöm and patted him on the shoulder. "You're a tall guy and dat's good, but you worry too much. You keep worrying like dat and you'll shrink."

The members of the gang erupted in laughter. Ibromaliöm surveyed them and wondered how long he would be able to suffer this rough, dirty and vulgar lot. He noticed that Tophun had a black eye.

"You are one to give advice," he snarled. "You seem to have had a rather unpleasant encounter."

Though Tophun did not understand what Ibromaliöm had just said, he noticed his boss gesture toward his eye and deduced that Ibromaliöm wanted to know how he hurt himself. "I was on my way to a gentlemanly meeting when a brat walked on my leather shoe and dirtied it. Da lady I was going ta see hate dirty shoes so you may say my gentlemanly meeting was turnin' sour. I whacked da cockroach and a nervous lizard got on my tail. He moved so quick I could barely see da crook. Da kid said his name was Ahiram. If I ever meet dat lizard again I will pin him on a rock and leave him to rot. Dat's what I'll do."

Ibromaliöm, upon hearing the name of Ahiram, broke into a cold sweat. He tottered back and dropped into an armchair with his eyes wide open. His gaze was transfixed on Tophun Makack who wondered what had suddenly gotten into his boss.

"What's da matter with ya? Are ya seein' a ghost or somethin'?"

Ibromaliöm managed to get a grip on himself. "What was the name of that boy again?" he asked with a faint voice.

"Ahiram," replied Tophun. "Why?"

Ibromaliöm inspected his fingernails carefully. "The first one who brings this young man to me alive will receive twenty gold diegans." A respectful silence followed Ibromaliöm's words. Twenty gold diegans was enough to keep anyone fat and merry for a full year. "Let us move now, each to his own post. I want this operation to be a total success."

The men stood up, and as they left the tavern, they wondered who this Ahiram was and why Ibromaliöm had placed such a high price on the young man's head.

➢•❖•❖•❖•❖•➣

"A Togofalkian gang member," said Tanios as he stood, having finished examining the body of the dead man.

"What do you make of it?" asked Orgond.

"As you know, Lord Orgond, Togofalkian gangs busy themselves by emptying travelers' pockets between Hardeen, Amsheet, and beyond into Togofalk. Typically, these gangs will commit a cold-blooded murder for treason, or when they feel threatened. Lord Orgond, who had access to the fortress lately?"

"The porters of the statue."

"They are our prime suspects," replied Tanios. "Where are they?"

"They are parading the statue in the city."

"I'll send a few Silent to trail them. Once the parade is finished, we will bring them here for interrogation."

"Do you think this may be related to the urkuun?" asked Orgond as the two men left the scene of the crime.

"I do not think so, but it gives me cause to worry. This gang may be trying to steal the statue. We do not want to deal with a diplomatic incident with Togofalk right now. It is enough that they choose to remain neutral in the current conflict."

"Togofalkians do not deal well with Empyreans."

"Apparently, this goes both ways," said Tanios.

"It does," replied Orgond with a sigh.

"Lord Orgond." A guard ran toward them.

"Yes?"

"We found a guard strangled in the dungeon near Zirka's room."

➤ ⁙ ≺

"The carnival, the carnival of Jaguar-Night has begun!"

Fireworks signaled the start of the festivities. Tourists, locals, and refugees all walked elbow-to-elbow; the former invoking the god's protection for a fruitful and rewarding year, the later asking the gods to release them from the impending terror.

Three days had come and gone since Ahiram had stormed out of the fortress; three days during which he had wandered the streets aimlessly, unable to think clearly or to make a plan. He felt rudderless, so he let the excitement and festivities carry him everywhere and anywhere. The purse

Zurwott had given him before he had left the desert people came in handy. He rented a small room in one of the inns for one copper diegan—an exorbitant amount for a servant's room, but he did not care. For the first time in his life, he acted as a free man and not as a slave. He breakfasted, dined, and supped wherever he liked. When night fell, Ahiram would fly for hours on end high above the countryside. He quickly gained full mastery of the wings and moved through the air faster than any bird of prey. He resisted the urge to land until he could no longer suffer the cold air.

On the third night, while flying, he considered calling the golden tile to him. The first three days he had left it behind in his room. He vividly remembered when he had first found El-Windiir's artifacts. He had unwittingly tried to use them with the golden tile and had nearly killed himself. But now, he felt more confident and decided to try it out again.

To his knowledge, no one else could see the tile, which is why he did not try to hide it. *Besides, hide it where? Anyone who can see it will probably find it no matter where I hide it.* As he flew over a plain, he whispered the name of the Letter "taw" and the tile materialized at once in his hand. Instantly, Ahiram careened uncontrollably, so fast that the world became a blur. Down below, a pack of wolves was moving stealthily through the country when they suddenly heard a massive BOOM overhead. *I can't see anything*! He frantically dropped the tile from his hand, knowing he could call it back at will. He decelerated rapidly and found himself flying over the northern border of Tanniin.

Amazing. This tile packs more power than all the artifacts of El-Windiir combined. If only I knew how to use it properly. Well, actually, I have not tried to use the mask yet.

He waited until he was back over the plain, where down below, three shepherds were spending the night with their flock. He slid the mask onto his face and peered through the slits, but he could not see anything. He lost control for a moment. The mask glowed, dissipating the darkness within, then it became translucent. Its edges burst into flames that quickly subsided, forming a bright outline. Warmth spread through his entire body and shielded him from the cold air.

"Wow," whispered Ahiram who managed to steady his flight. "This is amazing. Even though it's night, I can see as if it's bright day."

Down below, sheep stood still and three shepherds huddled around a small fire that he had not noticed before. Then, out of his peripheral vision, he saw a pack of twelve wolves creep up on the unsuspecting shepherds. The wind blew in their direction and hid their scent from their sheep. Tanniin, much like Finikia, considered dogs to be unclean, but the Tanniinites took their disdain for dogs a step further. They believed dogs to be so vile they avoided sheep that had been guarded by them and to eat their meat, milk, or cheese would bring a bad omen. That is why sheep herds in Tanniin roamed the land without the protection of dogs. Not giving it a second thought, Ahiram dove straight down, and at the last moment straightened his posture so he now hovered just a few feet above the ground. He cut through the herd and moved in a straight line toward the wolves. *I'll scare them so they'll scamper. This will alert the shepherds and it will become an even fight. After all, a wolf has got to eat.*

As he drew closer, he realized he did not have the faintest idea what he was supposed to do with the mask. *This is El-Windiir's mask, so it must somehow be connected to the dragon Tanniin.* The mask had a small opening that was level to his mouth. He had assumed it was meant for breathing, but the mask in its current state allowed warm air to blow freely on his face. Ahiram thought of Tanniin blowing fire and without further thought, he blew through the opening. The two eye slits flashed hot red and pandemonium ensued.

The shepherds saw a giant flame erupt from the edge of the field. Their sheep scampered for shelter. Wolves howled as they darted away, and a tree burst into flames.

"Lightning," said one of the shepherds. "Lightning hit the tree."

"Where's the storm, pea brain?" interjected another. "The sky is as clear as your balding head."

"It's the god Tanniin protecting us," explained the third.

The two others nodded. This was the best explanation. Tanniin had saved them from the wolves.

High overhead, Ahiram fled the scene at breakneck speed. *I didn't know the mask was that powerful. The blast killed three wolves and burned a tree and I barely blew through it.* Suddenly, he felt tired and dazed. He found himself over Amsheet and quickly alighted on the highest rooftop near the main road where the statue of Jaguar-Night would process. All eyes were on the brightly lit street, so no one saw him land. Quickly, he removed the artifacts and stowed them inside his bag, which he carried over his shoulder alongside his sword. He sat down and watched the road below where throngs of visitors stood on either side in anticipation of the idol. The city had lit giant torches spaced at regular intervals along the road to honor the Togofalkian god, and many bystanders held candles in homage. From his vantage point, Ahiram could clearly see a long stretch of the main street as well as the small bridge that crossed over it.

Ahiram noticed three riders step onto the deserted bridge. They dismounted and watched the street below. *Lax security*, he thought absentmindedly. *There's at least three ways I could get on and off this bridge without being noticed.* Ahiram yawned. Below, the crowd started to chant slowly. It would be another hour or two before the statue arrived. Pangs of hunger reminded him that he was famished. *Wearing the mask took a lot more energy than I thought.* He jumped onto a set of stairs and went down to the streets below in search of food.

Jedarc looked at Banimelek and knew from his friend's expression that he had no luck finding Ahiram. "That's why Ahiram is a Solitary," he mumbled. "If he wishes to disappear for three days, he can do so despite being chased by the Silent Corps."

"He's not in the fortress' caves," reported Alviad, joining them.

"No sign of him either in the Togofalkian Highlands," added Allelia, filing in after her.

"And no one in the city has seen him," said Corialynn as she arrived next to the group. "Where could he be?"

They had regrouped on the fortress' first wall, overlooking Amsheet.

"We have been searching for him for three days with no luck. What should we do?" asked Hiyam.

"We think," replied Banimelek. "There is an old saying that states, 'No Silent is lost who has friends that cherish his ways. They think like him, they act like him, and they find him.'"

"Chapter eleven, verse seven of the *Book of Siril*." Noraldeen completed the quote out of habit. Banimelek looked at her, and with his hand under her chin, lifted her head, then smiled and winked at her. She smiled back. "I should never have told him," she repeated bitterly.

"You mean you would have left Alendiir in the dark about the most important event of his life?" asked Sondra as she landed gracefully next to Noraldeen. She yanked on her rope and reeled it in. "I don't think so."

"It was not my place to tell him," replied Noraldeen. "The commander must have had a good reason to keep the truth from Ahiram."

"His temper," whispered Sheheluth, stepping onto the wall.

"What do you mean 'his temper'?" Noraldeen snapped.

Everyone stared at the Junior Silent. "You should realize by now that he was never meant to be a Silent, don't you? He's not an order-taker."

"Ahiram is the greatest Silent there is," said Noraldeen as she stood up. "You should not judge what you do not understand."

Sheheluth looked at her with unflinching eyes. "Did he hit you when you told him?" she asked softly.

"Hit me? No. Ahiram would never do that. How dare you ask?"

Sheheluth sighed and smiled sheepishly. "We should talk later." Suddenly she changed her tone. "For now, we need to find him. He may be in grave danger."

"How do you know?" asked Noraldeen.

The Junior Silent shrugged her shoulders. "With that temper of his, who knows what he might be up to?"

"Most of us know Ahiram," interjected Banimelek. "Some of us more than others." He glanced at Hiyam as he spoke, and she smiled. "So ask yourself, if you were Ahiram and someone told you that your family was dead, what would you do?"

"Well," began Jedarc, "Ahiram would be itching for action. That's his way of dealing with pain. I mean, imagine, you've been a slave for six years, and for six years you keep thinking about your parents, your sister especially, and you long to go back and see them. You are a slave who will not run away lest you dishonor your family. So you train beyond the limit of your abilities. Some of the things I saw Ahiram do are unbelievable. Next, you pester the commander until he allows you to take part in the Games of the Mines. Getting the commander to yield to anything is no small feat. Then, you're in the mines, alone, only to face certain death—"

"And you gain the respect and admiration of your foes," added Hiyam.

"Yes," continued Jedarc. "Finally, you emerge from the mines with El-Windiir's true sword. You are a hero; you are free. Then you learn that your parents and sister are dead."

Noraldeen stood up and tightened her fists. "I bear responsibility for what happened," she said forcefully. "I will find him."

Banimelek glared at her with an expression that said, "You did not have to say that."

Sondra grabbed and squeezed her friend's shoulder. "Noraldeen, listen to me. You and I have known each other forever, right?" She nodded. "Let's deal with it." She eyed the young men. "Boys, you're in this too. Sheheluth, watch your tongue, or so help me, I will whack you so hard you won't be able to sit for three days. Hiyam, you're in this as well, so wipe that annoyed look off your face. I won't tolerate any soppiness from either of you," she added addressing Hiyam and Noraldeen.

"Don't you love her when she's like that?" whispered Alviad in Banimelek's ear.

"That question is troubling on so many levels," grumbled Banimelek.

"Sondra, I will listen to what you have to say now," replied Noraldeen, a glint in her eye. "Speak your mind."

"Start by telling us exactly what happened," said Sondra.

"I should not have reacted like I did, but I wished that once, just once, he would pay attention to—"

"You," added Allelia with a smile. "Instead, he asks you about the statue of Jaguar-Night without even looking at you."

Corialynn rolled her eyes, "Predictable."

Noraldeen is upset because he asked about a statue? thought Jedarc. *Really?* "Can you believe he did that?" he said in a reproachful tone.

"How shocking," added Banimelek. *What did he do wrong?*

"Dreadful, I say," echoed Alviad. *Good thing it was him and not me. I have no clue why Nora is upset.*

"I don't understand why that upsets you," interjected Hiyam. "Show of emotions are not allowed within Temple precinct for the high priestess and any close relative: it defiles the Temple."

The two young women locked eyes and neither backed off. Noraldeen could see that Hiyam was sincere yet did not understand, and it reminded her of Gaëla. *How strange are the ways of the world,* she thought.

"Ahiram asked Nora to meet him," explained Corialynn, "but instead of paying attention to her, or even looking at her, he asked her about some statue. Nora had been waiting to meet him because she loves him. How insensitive can he be? Don't you agree?"

The three young men gave her a cacophony of "Sure. Yeah. Absolutely. Imagine that. How insensitive."

"Clearly," continued Corialynn, "these three don't get it either."

Alviad glanced at Sondra and gave her an embarrassed grin when he saw her glare at him.

Hiyam sighed. "I would have not noticed it," she said, "but that's me."

"You're one lucky guy," whispered Alviad in Jedarc's ear. "She's *way* less complicated than the others."

Banimelek elbowed him, "Idiot. They can hear you."

"Did you stop to think that there may have been a good reason why he asked you about the statue?" Sheheluth asked. Her voice was gentler this time around, almost maternal, but the tendency of this Junior Silent to command the conversation was starting to annoy the rest of the group.

"What do you mean?" asked Noraldeen.

"If he does not defeat the urkuun, we will all die, or worse …" Her voice trailed and everyone quieted. "Where I come from, we are far more sensitive to the flow of magic than the rest. We … we see strong sources of magic the way you see strong sources of light." She pointed to a specific spot in the city. "For example, the statue of Jaguar-Night gives off a very powerful beam of magic. It is nearly blinding."

"What does that have to do with Ahiram?" demanded Noraldeen.

Everyone could feel the tension mounting but no one intervened.

Sheheluth sighed. "I'm telling you this because it may help explain his actions a bit more. Sure, he was rude and insensitive, but he has to conquer a being from the Pit."

"He has the sword of El-Windiir," observed Corialynn. "Shouldn't that be enough to protect him?"

Sheheluth was about to let out a derisive laugh, but caught herself. *They don't know. They have no idea what we're up against.* She shook her head. "Against an Urkuun of the Third Order? You'll need all the magic you can get your hands on. In addition to the sword, he has five magical weapons with him."

"Six in total? Wait, you mean five, right?" asked Sondra.

"He has four artifacts in his bag," Sheheluth replied patiently, "and another one in his belt."

"Wait, wait," stuttered Jedarc. "He has four in his bag? Could it be …?"

"It must be," added Banimelek rising to his feet.

"El-Windiir's artifacts," said an incredulous Alviad. "The belt of silver, the shoes of bronze, the mask of gold, and the wings of meyroon," he said almost dreamily. "Amazing."

"It makes sense. They must have been with the sword."

"That sneaky Ahiram. He kept it to himself," commented Corialynn.

"Well, we all know Ahiram, don't we?" said Jedarc. "He hates attention because all he wants is to—"

"Go home," finished the other Silent with the exception of Sheheluth.

"So, what is the fifth one?" asked Hiyam. *Look at me. A few months earlier I would have alerted the High Riders.*

"I don't know," replied Sheheluth, "he didn't tell me." She did not want to share her misgivings with Ahiram's friends. *I cannot tell them he is a god-crusher, they would not understand. In fact, I don't either.* "Anyway, one of the four artifacts in his bag gives off the same magical light as the statue."

Astounded, the rest of the Silent looked at her as if she were an apparition. Sheheluth sighed. "You know how we beginners gawk when we watch you do your incredible moves with the darts? Where I come from, a three-year-old child could tell you what I just told you. It's nothing special really, not for us at least."

"So, Ahiram saw magical artifacts on that statue?" asked Hiyam, who understood more than Sheheluth assumed.

"What's odd is that he has no clue," continued the young girl. "He is unaware of the powers in his possession. And whenever ancient artifacts with magical powers like these are in his presence, he cannot help but be drawn to them. So no, he wasn't trying to ignore you," she added for Noraldeen's sake. "The statue must have called to him. Since he doesn't know how to control this … penchant, he asked you about the idol."

"Thank you, Sheheluth, that's extremely helpful," replied Sondra. "Listen, Noraldeen. When he asked you to tell him what you knew about his parents' death, you did not hold back. You answered him truthfully. You did it for him, even though you knew he would be upset. You did not think of yourself, but of him."

"Knowing Ahiram, your selfless concern must be gnawing at him," added Corialynn with a gentle smile.

"All right," said Jedarc, who felt it was time to say something. "Noraldeen, let's face it, Ahiram is not the easiest Silent to deal with when he is pining for his family. He can be annoying at times; my father this, and Hoda that. It makes you wonder if we even exist."

Noraldeen smiled and chuckled. "So I'm not the only one who feels this way. I should have known."

"The only one?" asked Alviad. "He is so obsessed by his 'I will return to my village,' it makes you wonder if he ever *left* his village."

Jedarc slapped his friend on the back. "Bull's-eye," he said. "It's as if his body is here, but his soul is still there."

"Wow," said Banimelek. "That's deep."

"Are you making fun of me?" A quick look at Banimelek convinced Jedarc that his friend was serious, which he should have known, for he had never seen Banimelek make fun of anyone.

"That must be it," said Noraldeen in a sad, distant tone that nearly broke their hearts. "His soul is not here, but back home."

"Now wait a minute," said Banimelek, deeply troubled by what he was hearing. "There's something you two should know …"

They looked at him and saw how conflicted he was. "What are we supposed to know?" asked Jedarc.

"Banimelek," interjected Noraldeen, "don't say it unless—"

"I know he told me never to tell anyone, but I think for once, he's wrong. Listen carefully because I will not repeat this, ever. One day, Ahiram told me that of all the people he has ever known, none have given him more joy and consolation than the two of you." Banimelek pointed to Jedarc and Noraldeen.

A stunned silence followed.

"Seriously?" asked Jedarc. "He never laughs at my jokes."

"This has nothing to do with your jokes, silly," said Sondra. "I find them lame and so does everyone else. He's talking about who you are."

"For reasons I won't get into," added Banimelek glancing at Noraldeen, "he is grateful that you both exist, that you are here, and that you are close to him."

"He said that?" asked Noraldeen.

Banimelek nodded. "He told me when you meet people who are more beautiful than a sunset, purer than the fresh air of the highest peaks, and joyful like the soft wind of spring, and you do not lay down your life for them, then you have never lived."

They looked at Banimelek, dumbfounded.

"Ahiram said that?" asked Jedarc, disbelieving his ears.

"That's so poetic," said Hiyam deeply touched.

"He loves me, but cannot give himself to me for his soul is trapped back home," said Noraldeen. "Now I understand. If I were to die, the world around him would become dark, and the hope to right what was wrong would fade away. I am his light and he is afraid, more afraid than I have ever known. Poor Ahiram. Lost between two worlds, two moments; a past that will never be again, and a future he cannot begin to consider. Ever since he was ripped away from his village and brought here, he has been desperate to return, and he will not stop until he does."

"Noraldeen," muttered Banimelek, confused by the turn of the conversation. "I—"

"No Banimelek, thank you. That helps."

Time went by as each of them tried to absorb what had just happened. Hiyam was deeply touched by Noraldeen's words. Unlike Ahiram, her childhood had been undisturbed. As she pondered the latest events, she

n the present moment. She missed the Temple, the city
 he golden shores of Finikia, but there were no regrets, no wounds tying her back to her past. If truth be told, she was becoming fond of Jedarc. She understood Banimelek's allusion; Jedarc was a ray of sun and his joy was contagious. He marveled at everything, small or big, and enjoyed whatever came his way. She felt safe and content with him.

"Poor Ahiram," she said at last. "Ripped from his home and his past and nowhere to go."

"He may not have somewhere to go," said Noraldeen smiling, "but, he who has friends is never alone."

"Right," said Jedarc springing to his feet.

Banimelek stood up, "We'll find him. He'll defeat the monster."

"Then he will return home to make sure his family is not there waiting for him, and then come back to marry you," added Jedarc.

Hiyam winced. "How do you know that?" she asked as she glanced at Noraldeen.

"Easy," replied Jedarc laughing. "What do you think his father would say if instead of fighting the urkuun, he went back to see him?"

"I don't know what his father would say, but I know what Ahiram would say," and Noraldeen assumed Ahiram's serious composure and mimicked his tone of voice. "I will not bring dishonor to my family."

Everyone laughed, even Sheheluth. The imitation was near perfect. Then they all fell silent. In more than one way, Ahiram meant a lot to each one of them. Banimelek had, at first, looked haughtily on the little fellow that Tanios brought into the training room years ago. He thought that Ahiram was not worthy of becoming a Silent. Then came the day when Tanios had asked Ahiram to take part in the game of tagging, and Banimelek quickly learned to respect Ahiram.

Hiyam broke the silence. "I remember I was so sad to hear that Baher-Ghafé had been destroyed." They looked at her not understanding what she meant. "My mother told me Ahiram comes from Baher-Ghafé."

Wrath of the Urkuun – Jaguar Night

"Did you know his parents?" asked Noraldeen, hopeful.

"No. I went there once or twice to watch them fish for shark. It was a beautiful village on the seashore, and the fishermen were strong and efficient. When I heard the village had been destroyed, I cried. I felt so sad and this feeling of sadness has never really left me. I don't know why."

The wind blew. Like an old man sweeping away unpleasant memories, it shuffled dead leaves into the night. The city glittered with thousands of candles that were lit for the carnival.

"So you think he is down there, somewhere?" whispered Noraldeen.

"Knowing him, he must be on some rooftop watching the carnival," replied Jedarc, stretching.

"Rooftop!" exclaimed Banimelek. "Ahiram will perch himself on the highest roof he can find to get the best view."

"So do you want us hopping on rooftops like monkeys?" asked Jedarc. "There are too many rooftops in Amsheet. How will we find the right one?" inquired Corialynn.

"The statue," Sheheluth said. "Follow the statue, it will draw him."

They exchanged glances, knowing what they had to do. Noraldeen spoke first. "The procession of Jaguar-Night is a major attraction. I wouldn't be surprised if Ahiram is following it right now. The procession will begin shortly. We can start with the rooftops along the way."

"Any objection?" asked Sondra. None came. "Allelia and Corialynn, you will work the southeast rooftops. Alviad and I, the northeast. Banimelek and Sheheluth, cover the northwest side. Jedarc, Hiyam and Noraldeen, the northeast buildings. The first to find him signals the rest."

➤ ·❖·❖· ⋖

"This is unfittingly unfit and unfit most unfittingly for dwarfish consumption. I am dishearteningly disheartened, and disheartened most dishearteningly," whispered Zurwott, chewing on a stale piece of bread.

"It is the least of the worst I could find," replied Orwutt. "That we have been able to escape those slimy creatures and are well and alive should suffice."

The sylveeds had dragged the two dwarfs along a muddy path in the forest for nine long days and had forced them to run, prodding them on with spears and swords. They ran most of the night and rested during the day, but on the second night, Empyrean scouts located them and the hunt began. The Empyreans forced the sylveeds to change course several times as they desperately tried to evade their pursuers. On the seventh day of this exhausting chase, the sylveeds ended up in a clearing where the Empyrean forces attacked. A group of sylveeds yanked Orwutt and Zurwott away and managed to escape while their companions stayed and fought to their last breath.

Once the battle was over, the Empyreans piled the bodies. Despite being in a forest, they burned them before the corpses had a chance to revert to their former selves. The Empyrean warriors did not want to know whom they had killed. They secured a fire containment, lit the large pyre, and left the bodies to burn in the dead of night.

The group of sylveeds who had escaped with the dwarfs rationed what little food they had, but the morsels they gave Orwutt and Zurwott, the twins would not have given their dogs. Yet they ate them in an effort to keep their strength. The cuts and bruises they had suffered during the escape from the battle were still healing. They were kept in a tight circle with barely enough space to move. Despite the mistreatments, they were in fair condition.

Two days later they stopped in front of a steep mountainside. The moon was high and splashed the mountain with a silver light. The dwarfs realized they stood before the western side of the Tangorian Chain, the eastern border of the kingdom. The mountainside extended from north to south like a giant white wall as far as the eye could see. The small group of surviving sylveeds became agitated and forced the dwarfs to move to a specific location where loud shrieks erupted among the creatures. One of them, who could barely talk, pointed toward the mountain and said, "Door, open." He repeated the command several times.

"They want us to open a door," said Orwutt, mystified. Reluctantly, he forced himself to chew the last bit of what one may call bread.

"While this may seem absurdly absurd, and absurd in the most absurdly possible manner," said Zurwott eyeing the cliff before them, "these sycophantic sycophants may have reasonable reasons to reason reasonably that a hidden door may be presently present, and present most presently in this mountain's facade."

"So what do you purportedly purport to daringly do and do most daringly?" asked Orwutt, curious.

"Whether a daring door and a door so daring existentially exists in this local location is a questionable question, and a question most questionable. Nevertheless, it may be less questionable than to question questionably the honorably honorable calamities that surround us with a completely completed circular circle. Therefore I would wholeheartedly recommend, and recommend most wholeheartedly that we look for a daring door rather than consider the ill-considered proposition that we may be factually facing, and facing in the most factual manner; a wall."

"A wall of misunderstanding perhaps," replied Orwutt, who had not lost his wry sense of humor.

The sylveeds grew impatient, and one of them stuck the butt of his spear in Orwutt's back, forcing him to move closer to the mountainside.

"Their acts bespeak of serious intent," said Zurwott.

"Very serious," replied Orwutt who tapped on the wall.

The spear moved away from his back, and the sylveeds took cover under the nearby trees. Orwutt and his brother knew there was no sense in attempting to escape. They would be nailed to the wall at the first suspicious move.

Orwutt placed his ear against the cold rock and started tapping gently. Zurwott moved ten feet away from his brother and started doing the same. They tapped and listened, tapped and listened, and repeated the process over and over again. As time passed, the sylveeds became uneasy and moved nervously back and forth under the trees. Orwutt looked up and noticed the clouds had become lighter; he could almost see the pale disk of the sun gliding behind them. He repeated his taps. So far, he could not detect any difference in the constitution of the rock. Dwarf's ears were particularly attuned to detect variations in substance, or structural differences. What the two dwarfs looked for was called a *maxo-rock*.

A maxo-rock is a portal; a door made of two stone slabs. These doors guarded caves and passageways. They were so well made that one could distinguish them from the surrounding surfaces. Only a dwarf could find the portal and open it. This required time and attention to detail.

Orwutt walked toward his brother. "This is rather strangely strange. The inflective resonating resonance of the rock is not what a faithful maxo-rock ought to produce, and is distinctly distinct from, and contrary to, the inflections of a mountain."

"My own concluding conclusions lead me to a similar confusing confusion," replied Zurwott. "This is extremely puzzling, and puzzling in the extreme. It would have been an excellent rhapsody in starkly distinct circumstances."

"If my thought process is leaning toward your thought process, and both are meeting in a convenient abstraction, I would prognosticate an internal adipose suppuration of the rock," concluded Orwutt.

"A viscose viscosity shall we sayingly say?" asked Zurwott. But he was dissatisfied. "A viscose viscosity would productively produce a lighter after effect of the tapping tap." He tapped again on the wall. "Pay attentive attention, my brotherly brother, to the returning return of the tap." He tapped slowly three times. "It suffers a slightly slight delay, yet its reverberating reverberations are strongly stronger than what a polite reverberation sounds like."

"Indeed, and a viscous surfacing surface would not retain the after-tap. Then what is it that we are dealing with?" wondered Orwutt.

"Lend your ear with attentive attention."

By now, the two dwarfs had but forgotten all about the sylveeds and the precarious situation they were in. Dwarfs loved rocks and mountains, and to be able to listen to the stony breath of a mountain was sheer delight. The twin brothers placed their ears on the mountainside and listened attentively, eyes closed. Suddenly, they felt the tip of a spear between their shoulder blades. Behind them, a small group of sylveeds waited impatiently, and they jumped in place as though trying to hide from the light.

"Open door, open door," said one of them, presumably the same one who had spoken to them earlier—although it was hard to tell them apart. In the light of day they looked pathetic and weak.

"We are attempting to locate the contour of the portal," replied Orwutt patiently. "Now, if your legitimacy could be relatively patient and patiently resolute, we shall succeed in acceding to your demands shortly." This said, Orwutt closed his eyes and tried to listen once more. The sylveeds went back toward the shade and mumbled in a strange language, having no other option but to wait.

"I hope, my brotherly brother," said Zurwott, a glint in his eye, "that you have spoken the truthful truth and the truth most truthful. If not, these troubled souls will force us to rest in pieces."

"Are you trying humor in the common tongue?" asked Orwutt frowning. "If you are, you should stop." He raised a hand to stave the incoming objection, "You should refrain from complaining in front of a stranger; that is unbecoming."

Zurwott harrumphed, but his brother ignored him. The two dwarfs listened attentively for several minutes without any exchange of words. Finally, Orwutt announced, "Water."

"Watering water, and water most watering. There can be no confusing confusion nor confused confusion about it," confirmed his twin brother.

"The main cave must not have been well insulated," continued Orwutt, "and water has made its way in. This explains why the portal rendered our taps so poorly."

"Concerning what is poorly poor and richly rich, my brotherly brother, your spoken speech tends toward sullenly sullen expressions and overworked adverbial adverbs when events overcome you by their surprising contours."

"It is a matter of lively life and deadly death, my dear brother,"

"All the more then to maintain elegant elegance in spoken speech and a refined refinement in courage."

In joyful response, the two dwarfs shook hands and bowed, then turned away from each other. They clapped their hands, then raised their arms and faced the clouds. Next, they turned and faced each other, bowed once more, and again shook hands. Finally, they clapped, turned around while raising their hands and faces up, then repeated the sequence once more. This was the closest a dwarf could get to expressing jubilation. They knew now that they had found the portal, and presumably, there was water behind it. All that remained to be done was to open the portal, a thing easier said than done. The two dwarfs stood facing the mountain with their powerful hands pressed flat on the surface of the rock. They looked at each other, Orwutt nodded, and the two dwarfs began to slap the surface at full speed. They passed each other as they moved from right to left without ceasing to strike the surface. This was the famous *Raks Sochor*, the Dance of the Wall. The dwarf brothers, in fact, slapped the surface at different angles with their hands. They were on the lookout for a ringing sound, one that is not usually produced by the rock when it is slapped. Typically, two to three rings controlled a maxo-rock. To open the portal, they needed to slap the rings in the proper order. This would release a lever and set the portal in motion. Zurwott was the first to hear a ring. He hit its position fast and lost it. He repeated his last movements until he found it again. Using a small rock, he marked its placement.

They searched for the second ring without success. They multiplied their slaps, repeated their moves, and tired themselves out. Dark clouds started to assemble above their heads, which caused the sylveeds to come out from hiding once more. Their menacing figures grew closer until they had surrounded the two dwarfs who continued to strike the rock.

"Open door," said one of the sylveeds. The two dwarfs stopped and stood panting with their backs against the wall.

"We are considerately considering the requisite options with attentive attention to the details," replied Orwutt.

The sylveed placed the tip of the spear against his neck. "Open door," it shrieked, "or dead."

"But we have not found the second ring," said Orwutt, exasperated. "We need at least two rings and we have found only one."

By now most of the sylveeds had come out of the forest and swarmed around the two dwarfs. Zurwott shook his head and hit the ring hard out of frustration. The portal instantly flung open, and its twelve by ten feet panels slammed each of the dwarfs against the mountain face. The sylveeds shouted in victory, then screamed in terror. A high wall of water gushed with the might of the gods, and turned into a wrathful tidal wave that carried the sylveeds into the forest, smashing their bodies into trees and rocks. The portal that nearly crushed the two dwarfs against the mountain had in fact saved their lives. After the water subsided, they stepped out cautiously. Three sylveeds leaped from the forest and attacked. Fortunately, axes and swords littered the ground.

"This is what I call a fortuitous fortifying turn of tide," exclaimed Zurwott as he picked an axe and a sword.

"A dance to tap a portal and a dance to make axes sing," added Orwutt, grinning dangerously.

The battle raged and remained uncertain, for both sides were accomplished fighters, but when the sun rose over the forest, the sylveeds ran back and disappeared in the trees. At last, the two brothers were alone. They stepped into the damp, deserted cave and closed the portal after them. Light seeped in from the sides through hidden openings, as expected from a cave dug by dwarfish hands.

"A one-ring portal. This must be primordially primordial and primordial primordially, perhaps one of the first, and first and foremost amongst the portals our ancestors built," said Zurwott.

"Probably," replied Orwutt, inspecting the doors. "This may explain its bad manners when it opened. This portal does not know how to contain its zeal. We should remedy this situation."

"We will, my brotherly brother, in a timely manner and a manner most timely when the situation is more auspiciously auspicious. In the intervening interval and interval most intervening, let us freely roam and roam freely while trying to cogently discern and discern in the most cogent fashion, the meaning of all this."

Unwittingly, the sylveeds had brought them closer to the heart of the mystery. Orwutt and Zurwott forged ahead, wondering what waited at the other end of the great caves.

25. Trapped

> *"The dwarfs, having carved the mines, knew them better than anyone else. Yet, the mines remained shrouded in mystery, as though the mountain itself housed ancient beings of great power deep within its bosom."*
> –Philology of the Dwarfs, Anonymous.

Just as the dwarf brothers, Orwutt and Zurwott, stepped into the cave, Tophun Makack stood on the bridge overlooking the street through which the statue of Jaguar-Night was to process. Legs spread, hands behind his back, he stood like a general surveying a battleground. Ibromaliöm  stopped his pacing, and froze. The statue was finally in view. Singers walked in front of it droning sacred chants with cymbals, tambourines, and the *fyrad*, the sacred lute of Babylon. The crowd cheered and applauded when the idol finally came into view. The statue was secured on a golden ceremonial carriage, and in the trembling light of the burning candles, it looked alive with its glittering eyes beneath the disproportionate eyelids.

"Are your men ready?" whispered Ibromaliöm.

"Stop worryin,'" replied Tophun, grinning, "They know what ta do. Da plan is easy ta follow."

"Is my horse ready?"

"Over this way," said Tophun pointing toward the street behind Ibromaliöm. "A fine steed I found ya. Dat's if ya got da gold."

"The coins are in this purse," said Ibromaliöm. "All one hundred and fifty of them, as we agreed."

Tophun peeked into the purse. He quickly counted fifteen rolls of ten gold diegans each, which satisfied him. Besides, If Ibromaliöm double-crossed the gang, he would not reach the port alive.

"Perfect," he said. "Dat's a good dealin for all us."

Ahiram stood up, mesmerized by what he saw. He was unable to take his eyes away from something pulsing rapidly above the green pupils. The object called to him with flashes of white and blue. It throbbed randomly, increasing and decreasing in intensity. A single word bubbled on the surface of his consciousness and he felt a strong need to utter this word from a spot that was close to the statue. He did not know why, but the urge was compelling. He quickly unrolled a rope and tied it to a beam, then checked that his sword and bag were fastened securely in place. Holding the other end of the rope, he ran and jumped.

Jedarc spotted Ahiram minutes before on a neighboring rooftop. Frenetically, he signaled to Hiyam whom had stayed on street level, and to Noraldeen, a few rooftops away. Sondra, who faced Jedarc across the street, signaled back. Noraldeen relayed the signal to Banimelek before joining Jedarc, just as Hiyam reached them.

"There," said Jedarc. "He just leaped off that rooftop."

"What is he up to?" wondered Banimelek.

Ahiram threw his weight forward, which yanked the rope behind him. He waited for it to tense, then arched his body along a wide semi-circle that brought him over the corridor bridge where the statue was about to enter. Ibromaliöm and Tophun leaned over the handrail and closely watched the slow progress of the procession. At the point of his trajectory closest to the statue, Ahiram said the word that had formed in his mind.

"Tiir!"

The two eyelids immediately flung off the statue faster than soaring arrows and flew toward Ahiram. He caught them in his hands and was about to turn around to flee when the rope snapped. Ahiram instinctively adjusted his position to soften the approaching blow, but his head hit the pavement. He lost consciousness just a few feet from Ibromaliöm.

The crowd cheered thinking this was part of the procession. Ibromaliöm bowed and forced Tophun to do the same.

"This is da lizard dat I was talkin' ta ya about," snarled Tophun as he barely restrained himself from crushing Ahiram.

"I know. Turn around slowly. Slowly, I said. Carry him carefully to my horse, tie him on, and I will give you twenty gold diegans as promised."

These words immediately mollified Tophun. "This lad must be somethin' if ya're willin' ta spend dat much on em."

"More than you think," said Ibromaliöm in a jubilant tone, unable to believe his luck. "Far more than you think." He grabbed Ahiram's bag and deftly slid the eyelids into it, then followed Tophun Makack as nonchalantly as possible. "More for me and less for you," he muttered as he waved to the cheering crowd.

He settled on his horse, waited for Tophun to secure Ahiram, then briskly took off after paying the gang member. Meanwhile, the statue emerged from the tunnel with its false eyelids intact. The crowd cheered and chanted, "Jaguar-Night." They were more convinced than ever of the god's power and protection.

➤❖❖❖❖❮

When Noraldeen and her friends reached the bridge, they found it deserted. Alviad knelt and inspected the pavement.

"Blood. He must be injured."

"Are you sure he fell?" asked Allelia.

"I saw him," replied Alviad.

"I saw him as well," confirmed Corialynn. "It was a nasty fall."

"Look over there," said Jedarc pointing toward the building from which Ahiram had leaped, "The rope. It snapped."

"Who was that man who picked him up?" asked Hiyam.

Banimelek looked at each of them in turn before responding. "I know you will not believe me, but it was Ibromaliöm."

"The judge?" responded the others.

"In person," replied Banimelek. "Let's go. We don't have one moment to lose." They ran toward the end of the bridge just in time to see Ibromaliöm disappear with a slumped Ahiram. "A horse. He is well prepared. We must run."

"No, not this way, he must be headed to the Togofalkian gate. I know where we can find fast chargers nearby," replied Noraldeen. "Follow me."

>-◉◉◉-<

"But dat's all I know, I told ya. Ya keep yakin' and yakin' and I know nothin' a dat Bramolum of yours."

"*Ibromaliöm*," replied Tanios severely. "You have not told me where he is taking the young man."

"Bramolum says 'Get me da lids and I will shell da gold.' I says fair deal cause we all know da lids are cursed and ya must be crazy to want to touch thems. Da gold is bettar. What he does after is none da my business."

Tanios had interrogated Tophun Makack for over three hours, but was getting nowhere. The Togofalkian was as stubborn as a mule and no amount of cajoling or threats could make him reveal where Ibromaliöm was going. The commander was forced to conclude that he truly didn't know. He left the prison and returned to the meeting room. The two Silent that Tanios had assigned to follow the gang led the soldiers of Orgond to their bandit's hideout. When the gang members saw the soldiers, they ran away and fell into the Silent's traps. The soldiers rounded them up, including Tophun, along with the gold.

"Any results?" asked Orgond when Tanios entered the council room.

"I am convinced that Ibromaliöm did not share his destination with the gang."

"What should we do then?" asked Lord Orgond. "The festivities concluded yesterday. As we speak, the Empyreans are marching toward Hardeen. If we delay further we may not be able to meet them in time."

"Did Noraldeen say anything else to the keeper of the horses yesterday?" asked Bahiya.

"No more than what Tophun told us," replied Tanios. "Ibromaliöm has taken Ahiram hostage and has left the city. Banimelek, Hiyam, Noraldeen, and Jedarc are on a quick chase behind them. They hope to catch up with him soon."

"Why did the high priestess' daughter go with your Silent, Commander?" asked Lord Orgond. "Her safety is paramount."

"I don't know," replied Tanios. "I will find out when they return."

"Hiyam is an accomplished Junior High Rider," interjected Bahiya. "If need be, she can call on the High Rider camp in Togofalk for aid. I am not concerned for her safety."

"Thank you, Your Ladyship," replied Lord Orgond who knew he would have to negotiate with the Temple eventually. "Now, this Ibromaliöm, is he not a former tajèr?" he asked.

"Yes, why?" replied Tanios.

"Two weeks ago, thieves broke through a private residence in Hardeen. Apparently, the tajéruun own the home."

"How much did they steal?" asked Master Xurgon.

"Roughly five thousand gold diegans."

Tanios whistled. "It takes three carts to transport that much gold," he said. "I can see why he was in league with a Togofalkian gang."

"How did he manage to break in?" wondered Bahiya. "Several curse rings protect the tajéruun's house of gold. If he is this powerful," she added, "perhaps the Silent should avoid a direct confrontation."

Orgond sighed. "I wish my daughter were not …" Clenching his fist, he changed the topic. "The tajéruun actively seek the perpetrators. From what I have learned, three men were found inside the house in the same state as the Queen."

"Are they still alive?" asked Bahiya. "I would like to speak with them."

"I am afraid they are all dead."

"A pity," she whispered.

"A thief who robs the tajéruun forfeits his life. They will hunt and kill him," added Tanios. "Ibromaliöm must know he is a wanted man now. He knew the risk when he stole the gold. This is one dangerous man."

Habael placed his hand on his friend's shoulder. "I trust in the Silent," he said with a warm smile. "I trust they will use stealth and the techniques you taught them to avoid confrontation."

"There is no point in worrying," interjected Uziguzi. "Four young Silent with excellent training and the experienced daughter of a powerful high priestess will handle this mission. We do well to trust their judgment, as our good friend Habael just said. We should worry about the forthcoming battle and move quickly."

"But without the lad, what hope do we have?" asked Master Xurgon.

"There is always hope," replied Habael.

"When can we move?" asked Tanios.

"We should be ready to leave Amsheet in four hours," replied Lord Orgond. "The army is ready. I need to give specific directives to my men. I suggest you take advantage of this short lull to rest. This may be the last time you will be able to do so comfortably."

The room emptied, save for Tanios and Bahiya.

"Are you certain you wish to do this?" he asked. "A ship will sail to Byblos tomorrow morning."

Bahiya shook her head. "I will see this through. I am staying."

Tanios kneaded his forehead. "Why?" he asked. "We both know this beast rampaged through Tanniin with the Temple's consent." He stepped closer to her. "Did you release it?"

Bahiya sustained his intense gaze. "I did not. Babylon did so without consulting me."

"Then your fight against the urkuun is treason. Frankly, I do not understand your motives, Bahiya."

"That may be so," she replied softly but firmly. "Still, I have made up my mind. I will see this through."

"Fine," he said after a short moment.

"Will we be traveling with the army, or on our own?" she inquired.

"With the army until we reach the main camp north of Hardeen. An Empyrean scout will help us cross into their kingdom. We will enter Hardeen through a hidden door high up the mountain. It is a steep climb. Will you be up to it? You have not climbed mountains in a long time."

She smiled briefly. "I will be fine."

≻·•·•·•·≺

Ahiram opened his eyes, then closed them quickly. The ground beneath him was dancing frantically and his head throbbed in pain. He tried to move his hand but could not. *Where am I?* he wondered. He forced himself to open his eyes again and lifted his head. He was surprised to find he was on the back of a horse. A rope ran under the animal's belly and was tied to his hands to his feet. He could barely see the rider's back but tried hard to recognize him. *He was standing on the bridge when I fell. What does he want with me?* Ahiram closed his eyes, exhausted and in pain. He returned to his jostled slump and let the horse carry him.

Briskly, Ibromaliöm crossed the border bridge between Tanniin and

Togofalk. Due to the festivities, the bridge was unmanned and the border wide open. Ibromaliöm had counted on this. *Tomorrow evening, I will reach Prat. There will be multiple ships headed south to Gilgal and not a few captains willing to take a fugitive for gold. In Gilgal or any other Zemorian city, I will find at least one corrupt zakiir willing to remember a fake identity on my behalf. That will grant me safe passage into the Kingdom of Marada. Once the Cup of Eleeje is mine, Babylon will mine as well.* Ibromaliöm grinned madly and laughed into the wind like a wolf on the hunt. He goaded his horse up the deserted main road of Togofalk, across the tail end of the Somarian Chain, the northern mountain range between Togofalk and Tanniin. The road snaked upward and into barren hills. Ibromaliöm was so pleased with his plan that he felt the urge to stop and rid himself of Ahiram. *He will look into the book and die.*

Dawn was about to break. He had been riding for a good part of the night and decided to stop and rest soon. *There is a shepherd's shelter close by. It will be a great place for a reading lesson.* Ibromaliöm burst out in a malevolent laughter that echoed like ice shards slicing through the hills.

≻⁘⁘≺

"He went into Togofalk," said Banimelek as he sprang back on his horse. "He is an hour ahead of us, no more."

"We must hurry, the extra weight is slowing him down," replied Jedarc.

The four riders now crossed the bridge and followed Ibromaliöm into the hills. After leaving the bridge where Ahiram had fallen, they followed Noraldeen to a stable where they found only four horses. Sondra, Alviad, Allelia, Corialynn, and Sheheluth had agreed to return to the fortress and leave the pursuit to Noraldeen, Jedarc, Hiyam, and Banimelek. They rode through the night. Every time they reached a fork, Banimelek inspected it carefully. He was thorough, whereas Jedarc was impulsive.

"Come on, Banimelek," he said after the third fork, "Ibromaliöm is still on the run, and there's nothing to run to in those barren hills."

"Do I have to remind you what the *Book of Siril* has to say about impatience?" asked his friend.

"'Better a mindless parrot than an impatient Silent.' At least the parrot is pretty," quipped Jedarc.

"The *Book of Siril*, chapter five, verse six," added Noraldeen. "Banimelek is right to be prudent. One mistake and Ahiram is lost."

Hiyam smiled when she heard Jedarc mutter about pretty parrots and stubborn friends. Surprisingly, it was Banimelek who had asked her to accompany them. "Togofalk is on friendly terms with the Temple," he had explained. "We might meet High Riders and you can help."

"Keep your eyes open," said Banimelek. "We're catching up."

"I can't believe the commander did not want us to help save Ahiram," grumbled Alviad while picking hay from his pants. "Ahiram needs us."

"Cut your complaining," replied Allelia. "I can't sleep."

"You are traveling comfortably inside a covered chariot with three charming young women," Corialynn quipped. "What more do you need?"

"What? Now, wait a minute, I—"

"You are a handsome Mitanian Lord with three female servants from the elegant city of Rastoopa. You should-ah, speak-ah like-ah them-ah."

"Firstly," protested Alviad, "the commander came up with this crazy plan because you didn't offer him a better way to infiltrate Orlan."

"We came up with several ideas," protested Corialynn, "the commander did not like any of them."

"That's because they all required that I shave my head," replied Alviad.

"That's not the reason, Alvy," added Allelia. "Togofalkian ladies travel with a well-supplied wardrobe and nothing was available in Amsheet."

Alviad looked at Sondra, "Did she just call me Alvy?"

"Why are you asking me? She's right in front of you."

He looked at Corialynn, "Did she just call me—"

"She did Alvoovoo," replied Corialynn with a wide grin.

"Would you—"

"Alviad," Sondra cut in, "You're a Rastoopian Lord with three female servants. What's your problem?"

"I didn't want to travel with three female servants."

"You mean-ah, you do not-ah enjoy-ah our company?" said Corialynn with an offended tone.

"What, well, no that's not what I—"

"Ah," added Allelia, joining the fun. "The young-ah master-ah is not-ah happy-ah with—?"

"Stop it," Allelia cut off a blushing Alviad. "We do not have to pretend to be who we are not,"

"Oh, but I think we should," replied Corialynn. "Very much so. What is ah Your-ah Lordship-ah's command-ah?"

Alviad glanced at Sondra with pleading eyes. *Get me out of this one.*

Sondra, who sat next to him in the cart, smiled. "You will do just fine, Alviad. You can play the part." She closed her eyes and thought about the commander's order.

"Bar-Tanic is creating an alliance with Thermodon. They plan to attack Tanniin. Go to Orlan, learn about their command structure, the size of their army, their supply lines, and their plan of attack. Report as quickly as you can. If you can disrupt them, or slow them down, do so."

"Hey Sondra," called Corialynn. "Do you like Alviad's nose? Doesn't he have a lord-looking nose?"

"Hey," interjected Alviad feeling his nose. "Leave my nose alone."

Allelia moved closer to the young man who pushed against the side of the chariot as if he were trying to squeeze his large frame between its panels. Corialynn joined her and together they inspected his nose.

"He's got hair coming out of his ears in bushels," observed Allelia.

Instinctively, Alviad felt his ears. "No, I don't. Stop it you two."

"And a receding hairline," added Corialynn.

He looked at Sondra. "I have a receding hairline?"

"It's a sign," signed Allelia. "No doubt about it."

"Indeed, a sign," confirmed Corialynn. Sondra tried not to laugh.

"A sign of what?" huffed Alviad. "What?"

"That your servants are about to die of ..." replied Allelia, solemn.

"You're going to what? Are you out of your mind?"

"Of laughter," said finished Corialynn. "Die of laughter."

The three girls looked at each other and burst into giggles. Alviad rolled his eyes and smiled. He knew the young women were hiding their own anxieties and concerns for their friends behind sarcasm directed at him. He closed his eyes. *Why do I feel guilty?* Then he knew. *We're leaving the worst of it behind. Whatever awaits us in Thermodon is not as bad as facing the monster here.*

Orwutt and Zurwott were not used to paralyzing fear; fear so powerful it wrenched their guts and turned them to mush. Fear so strong it paralyzed their legs and sapped their strength. But they were dwarfs, sons of the deepest caves, and every rock was their friend, and every cave their home. They refused to bow down and relent to this fear or let it pin them like a spider pinning two miserable bugs, so they crawled slowly, so slowly that life came to a stony halt. They felt they had been in this tunnel for as long as time itself. The inclined space was just wide enough for them to maneuver side-by-side but not high enough for them to walk upright. They crawled silently, inching their way up. After many twists and turns, the corridor straightened, widened, and opened into a small cave. Exhausted, the two brothers sat with their backs against the wall and fell into a restless slumber.

They jumped and nearly died of fright when the most alarming shrieks snapped them out of their slumber. Compared to this terrifying sound, the béghôm's shriek now seemed like baby babble. The wail created a sense of helplessness and irremediable defeat. It paralyzed the mind and deprived all who heard it of strength and courage.

"What is that?" asked Orwutt, as he tried to stop his jaw from rattling.

"I do not knowingly know," replied Zurwott.

Orwutt breathed deeply and crawled forward. The shriek came from somewhere below. At first, his body refused to obey, as if he were paralyzed. He lay inert and unable to make the slightest movement. It was not until much later that he managed to move slowly. Zurwott, not wanting to stay behind, followed him. Luckily, whatever produced that shriek did not repeat it. The path veered left and led them through a narrow entrance to a huge cave twenty feet below. They realized they were on a wide ledge circling the igneous cavity. They crept forward to the edge and peeked. The cave beneath them was expansive.

"A temple," muttered Orwutt.

In the center of the cave, nine burning candles surrounded nine circular holes. Three rectangular holes stood in the middle. A dim light hid most of the cave. Evidently, the cause of their terror had left. Massive beams carved into the rock sustained the imposing ceiling that was just a few feet above their heads. The beams stood along the walls, and glowed under the bright light of candles at their feet. Orwutt looked up and noticed the ceiling. Large marble slabs with delicate carvings formed a sealed, smooth cover. The beams lent support to the slabs, but they did not seem strong enough to keep these massive marble segments from falling. Orwutt did not need to crawl between the marble ceiling and the roof of the cave to know how this structure stayed in placed. Dwarfs had drilled large iron rings into the slabs and the cavern's ceiling, and secured them with a single chain. This had been standard dwarf architecture in times past, but was subsequently abandoned in favor of better designs.

Someone spoke in the cave below. The two dwarfs moved back quickly. The voices were harsh and piercing, and difficult to understand.

"Temple must be ready. Master expects visitors." rasped the sylveed.

"Temple ready." replied another.

"Not ready, must be with accursed, bright candles. Hate light."

"Why bright?"

"Master expects visitors," screamed the sylveed.

"But door not open,"

"Not dwarfs. He expects others. Also, he is unhappy, door not open."

"Water killed all. Door closed. Dwarfs dead."

"Door must be open. Army ready to invade."

"Master powerful. Master can use magic. Master break door."

"Walls weak. Walls sick. Magic breaks door and walls. No magic. Door must open with no magic. Dwarfs open door."

"Why walls sick? Master powerful, master cure walls."

Orwutt and Zurwott heard a thud, then a moan. Carefully, they crawled forward and peeked. Dwarfs had excellent vision even in dim light. Below them, one sylveed stood rubbing his hand. Next to him, the other lay on the ground rubbing his head.

"Walls sick, because of pool that Master built. Pool gives life to Sylveeds but makes wall weak," whispered the one who was standing.

"Walls sick elsewhere too," whispered the one who was on the ground.

"Pit makes walls sick elsewhere."

"What to do?"

"Wait. Master knows ugly ones attack soon. Ugly ones have priestess from Baal. Master makes her servant, then attack with her and conquers all. Master strong. No one resists Master."

"How can master capture her?"

"Master does not capture. She will come to master. Master knows all."

The dwarf twins covered their ears as strident shrieks filled the cavern. The screams slowly faded as the sylveeds left the temple. *This master of theirs,* thought Orwutt, *is of the unpalatable kind, and I hope we will not have the displeasure of becoming one of his acquaintances.* Orwutt guessed the so-called master was the author of that terrible shriek they had heard earlier. He was aware that the high priestess would come, and that the master planned to make her one of his servants. The sylveeds started preparing a reception in her honor. The dwarf knew this monster had to be stopped. He formed a plan and signaled for his brother to follow him back into the small cavern.

Ibromaliöm tied his horse to a tree. He had stopped by the shepherd's refuge in the mountains to give his stead a rest. He drew his sword and forced Ahiram to come down, and pointed to the door.

"Walk slowly and keep your hands in front of you. Disobey and your head will be a lot closer to the ground than you would like it to be."

Ahiram was in no condition to argue. He was dizzy and weak and staggered like a drunkard toward the door. Despite his feeble condition, he managed to reach the door without falling and leaned on it heavily. It gave way under his weight with a sinister creak. Ibromaliöm pushed him unceremoniously and he stumbled in, falling against the wall. He heard a loud ruffle followed by piercing shrieks. Bats came flying out and whizzed by his ears. Ibromaliöm kicked him in the stomach, which took his breath away and shot waves of pain through his body. He made Ahiram sit against the wooden wall and tied his wrists before going to the fireplace. Ahiram felt warm, thick liquid trickle down his face. The fall had reopened his wound. Ibromaliöm looked back and sneered.

"It must hurt," he said over the crackle of the wood. The former judge tied a piece of cloth tightly around Ahiram's head.

"Thank you," said Ahiram. He watched Ibromaliöm return to the fire and asked calmly, "Where are we going?"

Ibromaliöm erupted in laughter. "You don't know what I am about to do to you?" Ahiram did not answer, but he stared at Ibromaliöm and tried to read his next move. He needed to find a way to free himself. "A fine Silent you are," continued Ibromaliöm grinning while he warmed himself by the fire. "Let me show you something interesting." Ibromaliöm opened a bag and took out the book he had snatched from the hidden Temple of Tanniin deep below Taniir-The-Strong Castle. "Do you know what this is?" he asked as he waved the thick book in one hand before Ahiram.

I'll have one chance to get out of these ropes, Ahiram thought. His hands quietly started to work on the knots.

"You do not wish to answer?" continued Ibromaliöm. "I am so chagrined by your silence. I am showing you one of the greatest treasures that exists, a treasure to unlock powers beyond your imagination, and you look at it as if it were a piece of dirt."

"What is it?" asked Ahiram who wanted Ibromaliöm to keep talking.

"It is a *libre*, a book," replied Ibromaliöm triumphantly. "The ancient called it Byblos, like the ancient city in Finikia. Those eyelids you tried to steal are magical. I can use them to read this libre more efficiently."

"What do you mean by 'read' and what is the libre for?" asked Ahiram.

"You'll have to thank the Temple of Baal for your ignorance," spat Ibromaliöm. "A book is a device that records information for later use."

"You mean like a zakiir?"

Ibromaliöm scoffed. "A zakiir is a poor man's book. I'd much rather deal with objects than with men. But since the Temple has banned the written word, we invented the zakiruun. A book is compact, simple to carry, and sturdy. A book is a storehouse of power."

"I thought a book was a collection of sayings one memorizes like the *Book of Siril* or *Lamentation*," said Ahiram. "Why go through the trouble of recording information when memorization is so easy? I can get twenty Silent to memorize the *Book of Siril* in half the time it will take you to record a single book. That's silly."

"Because," replied Ibromaliöm all wound up, "people die, kingdoms can be destroyed, and memories fade away like the leaves of summer under the ice of winter. Knowledge is too precious to entrust to the fading memory of men."

"Knowledge changes with situations," replied Ahiram. *These knots are real tight.* "You will have to record your information over and over. A zakiir can replace one thought with another."

"A book is far more potent," countered Ibromaliöm. "It sits in darkness, waiting for someone to find it, to open and read it. Now … I have heard," continued Ibromaliöm in a friendlier tone, "there is a book which is key to the Letters of Power." He said these words with rapture.

This last statement pricked Ahiram's interest, but he gave Ibromaliöm an innocent and confused look. "I may have heard about these Letters of Power before but—"

"Pah! You are a Silent, are you not? You're supposed to know everything about power and there is no greater power than the Letters. Listen well, because I will not repeat what I am about to tell you. After the Wars of Meyroon, which pitted the Lords of the Deep against the Malikuun, there was peace, 'troubled peace', the Temple calls it. When ships began to ferry goods across the sea, they used a cumbersome recordkeeping system. The merchants wanted a better method, more compact and efficient, to keep track of their goods, their letters of credit, and other financial notes."

"Why not hire a zakiir? He could remember all that."

"A zakiir on every ship? Are you mad?"

"No, not on every ship, but in every port."

"Hum, I see your point. Well anyway, back then the League of Zakiruun did not exist. Wealthy merchants from Byblos commissioned Hemilco, the greatest mariner ever to cross the seas. 'Travel to the end of the earth and find us the best bookkeeping system there is,' they said. When Hemilco returned, he told them of the *aleph-bet*, twenty-two Letters with which they could reshape the world." Ibromaliöm stopped and looked at Ahiram pitiably. "Of course, you do not know what a letter is." He sighed, then continued. "To ordinary folks, a letter would be a symbol to represent a sound."

"Huh?" Ahiram wanted to prolong the conversation in order to extract as much information from the former judge as the tall man was willing to give. "What do you mean a symbol to represent a sound? That makes no sense."

"That's because the Temple forbade writing," snarled his foe. "It's a brilliant idea that will make sense shortly when I'll get you to read this book," he added with a murderous grin. "In any case, Hemilco explained to the League of Merchants that by stringing these letters together, they could form words and the words would carry thoughts in a compact object such as this libre. Although the merchants saw merit in his approach, they simply could not wait for someone to conceive of such a system and make it sufficiently precise to serve their mercantile needs. But they were wrong, for long before their time, books had been written using these letters, exactly as Hemilco planned to use them."

Ibromaliöm threw a few logs in the fireplace and faced Ahiram. The reflection of the amber fiery light in the tall man's eyes turned the dancing flames of the hearth into a swirling mad intelligence, a boundless ambition to consume the world and then consume itself into a dark abyss, a pit of lifeless flames to last an eternity. Ahiram shuddered.

"What these merchants missed," continued the former judge in a low, tense tone, "and what Hemilco may not have known is that the alephbet—these seemingly, simple, innocuous twenty-two Letters—could become a doorway to twenty-two storehouses of unbelievable power, if they are in the right hands. The Letters of Power," he said raising his fist and his voice, "Letters so powerful they could reshape the world and give their master complete dominion over the land."

Stubborn knots, thought Ahiram, *the judge knows his business.* "If so, why didn't Hemilco use them to further his ambition?"

His kidnapper slapped him. "Pay attention now," he snarled. "I hate repeating myself." He sighed and shook his head like a tired teacher. "Youth these days, what do they teach you? I said *if* in the right hands, haven't I? I believe that at one point in time, anyone could draw into this storehouse of power, but for some reasons, this knowledge was forgotten. Only a Seer of Power can still see the Letters in this way and use them."

So the tile is a Letter of Power then, and that star I saw is the storehouse of power? thought the Silent. *God-crusher, that's what Sheheluth called me. Is this what she meant?* He reeled at the thought of so much power.

The former judge drew closer to Ahiram and smiled like a friend about to share a good news. "But there is another way, a sneaky way to tap into the same storehouse of powers, without relying on the Letters." Languidly, he caressed the cover of the book, "And I have it. I, Ibromaliöm, am the recipient of this amazing gift. This book, here, the *Ithyl Shimea*, written long ago by the dwarf Kertal with Evanéya, his Empyrean companion, will tell me how to tap into this power."

Ahiram blanched. "The *Ithyl Shimea*? But that's a key to open the Pit!"

"Precisely," said Ibromaliöm, his eyes flaring. "It *is* a key, and a key can have many uses. To open the Pit, you need power, power that the storehouse of the Letters will provide. And once I have access to that power, what would compel me to share it with the Lords of Chaos?" He smiled and his smile sent chills down Ahiram's spine.

He is mad, thought the Silent, forcing himself to stay calm. "So you can read this book?" asked Ahiram.

Ibromaliöm shrugged his shoulders. "Not really. It is written with the Letters of power but …" Ibromaliöm glared at Ahiram, then smiled. "Oh well, I might as well tell you because in a little while, it won't matter. I can't see the Letters, which is frustrating, but this book *is* powerful. There's a voice with it, or *in it*. The voice whispers the words to me when I look into it. Convenient, don't you think?"

"And you're not bothered that there's a *voice* reading the words to you? How do you know you're not deceived?"

Ibromaliöm shrugged his shoulders. "I know this voice wants to use me. I am *well aware* of that. But who is to say that I am not using it?

Besides, my lot is better than the Seer's. The Temple of Baal, aware of the enormous power of these Letters and unable to control them, sent Sureï the Sorcerer to curse them."

"I don't understand," replied Ahiram, "The Temple sent Sureï where?"

Ibromaliöm slapped him again, harder. "Do I look like your teacher? Who knows where? Apparently, these Letters, in their true form, are hidden all over the world. Sureï couldn't destroy them so he cursed them to keep people away from them and the curses are triggered if the Seer merely draws near to the Letters."

That make sense: After all, I found the Letter hidden in the mines, pondered Ahiram. *I have it and I don't feel anything. Could I still be curse?* "So, to use these Letters," said Ibromaliöm standing up, "the Seer would have to go past Sureï's curses, survive the wrath of the Temple, and then find the hidden zakiir, the one zakiir, who according to the legend, has memorized a book that describes how to use these Letters. As you can see, it is a much harder route than mine."

"So, why can't this voice read this book to you? What is it waiting for?"

"Another excellent question," replied Ibromaliöm who forced the young man to look up by grabbing his hair and jerking his head up. "Excellent question indeed. Unfortunately, I cannot read the book, not directly, no. Like all libres, this one is cursed. If I open it and look at its pages, *I* will be cursed. When I found this book with Ramel and that idiot Garu, an earthquake shook the ground so fiercely, we all fell. The book landed under the Queen's nose and she saw its pages." Ibromaliöm slapped his thighs as he burst into a cynical laughter. "Imagine that, under her nose. She looks at it thinking to find a treasure, instead she is cursed. Cursed! The irony of it all. Oh …" he snickered, wiping his tears, "she must have turned into an ugly thing, a real mess." He continued with a glint of pure malice. "After the curse fell on her, I glanced in the book by accident and instead of being cursed as well, I heard a voice whisper in my ear the first few words. Later, I understood what happened. After someone is cursed, there is a small window of time when one can read the book safely, or, in my case, hear the words. I will need to curse ten thousand worthless lives to get through the whole thing. It is an expensive way of reading, but then, life is cheap."

"And you want me to look at the book?" asked Ahiram. He thought of the gold tile, and suddenly felt it in the palm of his hand.

"Precisely," replied Ibromaliöm.

"The curse is deadly?" asked Ahiram.

"Yes indeed," gloated Ibromaliöm. "Did you really think I was sharing all of this for your instruction? It was merely for my enjoyment. Now, young man, do not annoy me with these trifles, and look inside the book."

"What if I don't?"

"Oh, in that case I will kill you with my sword."

Ahiram bolted to his feet and head-butted his tormentor in the stomach. Ibromaliöm fell back hard. With his hands now free, Ahiram jumped up and pounded his opponent with his fists. Ibromaliöm's eyes flared and he uttered an incantation. The fire lashed out with a sudden intensity and spewed burning coals that singed the Silent. Ibromaliöm grabbed the young man's right foot and yanked. Ahiram suddenly dropped and hit his forehead. His head swelled with pain. The judge got up and quickly opened the book before Ahiram, who unwittingly gazed upon it. When Ahiram realized what Ibromaliöm was doing, he felt his hair stand on end. *I am cursed*, he thought. A wave of intense heat irradiated from the tile in his hand, nearly scalding him. The pages he was looking at were mostly white with the symbol † on it, the same symbol that was on his strange tile. It was written multiple times in a seemingly random pattern on the page.

Ibromaliöm's eyes widened. "What are you doing?" he yelled.

The flames in the hearth became black with a blue hue as a voice, steely and without pity, whispered, "He is the Seer. Whatever Letter of power he has in his possession, he can read on these pages." As the flames returned to their normal form, Ibromaliöm howled, slammed the book shut and went for his weapon. He was about to bring his sword down on Ahiram when the wall behind him exploded under Banimelek's weight. The door shot open and Jedarc ran in. The window over the fireplace shattered and Noraldeen jumped in followed by Hiyam. Ibromaliöm ran toward the hearth, grabbed a hot coal, muttered words in a foreign tongue, and threw the coal on the ground. Thick smoke filled the hut. When the smoke scattered, Ibromaliöm had vanished.

"What took you so long?" asked Ahiram with a tired smile.

"Are you all right?" asked Noraldeen.

"I'm fine," he said. He grabbed her hand and tried to stand, but was suddenly too weak.

"Not so fine, I see," said Jedarc with a smile. "You're just tired."

"I could have been *dead* tired," replied Ahiram. "Let's get going."

He tried again to get up, but could not. Hiyam took out a small pouch and sprinkled a pinch of a red powder over Ahiram. It turned instantly to gray before dissipating. She gasped.

"Impossible, how are you still alive?"

"What do you mean?" said Noraldeen.

Hiyam skirted the question. "He can't walk. We need to take him to a healer as soon as possible."

"Your mother?" inquired Jedarc.

"Most likely she left with Lord Orgond," Banimelek reminded them.

"What's wrong with me?" wondered Ahiram.

"I … I cannot explain," replied Hiyam. She was shaken. "We should leave," she added and glanced at Noraldeen.

"We will bring you in a cart as you need to rest," said Banimelek.

"But what if the urkuun attacks?" asked Ahiram.

"So be it," replied Jedarc. "From what we have heard, you are the only one who can stop him. You had better be in shape."

"Do you have your sword?" asked Banimelek.

Ahiram glanced around the room. "Over there, bring me my sword and my bag," he asked. He looked in the bag and was relieved to see the rest of his treasure, including the eyelids he had caught earlier. "It looks like Ibromaliöm had every intention of taking my bag with him but didn't have the chance."

"Should we go after him?" asked Hiyam.

"No," replied Ahiram. "He is far more dangerous than we thought and besides, we need to deal with the urkuun. Let the judge go hang himself somewhere."

Banimelek picked up his friend's bag and walked out. Jedarc and Hiyam followed. Noraldeen helped Ahiram stand up. "It is so good to see you," she said with a tender smile.

"Sorry about earlier, Nora. I was rude. I should have—"

She placed a finger on his lips. "I know. No need to say anything more."

He held her hand. "Thanks," he said softly. "Thanks for not giving up on me." She smiled and squeezed his hand. He felt unusually dizzy and weak. Suddenly, he slumped, unconscious. She gasped and tried to wake him, but without success. She touched his forehead. It burned with fever.

"What happened?" asked Banimelek as he walked back in.

"He has a high fever and lost consciousness," she said frantically. "What should we do?"

"We move," Banimelek picked up Ahiram in his arms. "We need to find someone who can take care of him and quickly."

"What is going to happen to him?" said Noraldeen.

"What will happen to all of us if we don't find someone to help us," replied Banimelek.

They placed Ahiram on a hastily made stretcher and left for Tanniin. They couldn't help but wonder what lay ahead and how things were holding at the Fortress of Hardeen. Jedarc gazed up at the distant stars and whistled the song of El-Windiir, and his whistling surrounded them like wisps of hope in the cold of the night.

26. Hardeen

"Hardeen, like its sister fortress, Amsheet, was built to withstand the greatest Empyrean assault. It is not a fortress in the usual sense, but a mountain transformed into a formidable wall to stem the staunchest attack and defeat the greatest siege."
     –Diplomatic Notes, Uziguzi, First Adviser to Her Majesty Aylul Meir Pen, Empress of the Empyreans.

"Amsheet—Hardeen—Amsheet—Hardeen, my head is bobbing. Which to choose? Where to die? Where to die? What choices we have in time of war. Die here, die over there, die everywhere!"
     -Soliloquy, Zuzu the Hip, Jester at the Royal Court of Tanniin.

Two days later, in the late afternoon, Lord Orgond and his company reached the army's main camp. Six hundred riders and four thousand footmen were already camped in the foothills of the Mayorian Chain. Immediately, Lord Orgond checked in on his soldiers. His calm presence and  assured tone lifted their morale. He spoke to them about family and friends, and enjoined them to eat and rest. After the meal, he instructed them on the battle to come.

For his part, Master Xurgon regrouped with his dwarfs and started the forge fire. He told the dwarfs that Master Kwadil had sent his nephews, Orwutt and Zurwott, on an important mission. *It would be a nonsensical sense to alarmingly alarm this commune of dwarfs about the twins' absence. Time, well timed, will tellingly tell what fate they have met.*

Tanios, Bahiya, and the Silent left camp the following morning at sunrise. They followed a deep ravine into the Empyrean territories through a seldom used path that climbed up steadily along a zigzagging incline until they reached the highlands. There the path became a treacherous, stony ridge along the mountain's spine. They faced howling winds and endured slick and smooth stones covered with invisible ice. Wearily, the small company forged ahead until they reached the Pass of Oranil. Known as The Howling Wind Pass, this narrow canyon, two hundred feet long, cut through the mountain from side to side.

"We will cross quickly," the commander ordered. "Cover your face, neck, and hands if you don't want frostbite."

The icy-cold wind howled like an angry monster as they inched their way through the pass. They were frozen to the bones by the time they reached the Empyrean side of the mountain. Even though they would have welcomed a break, the commander ordered everyone to keep moving. Several hours later, the snow-covered terrain made way to dry land, but the air remained bitterly cold. Evening caught them midway through their descent from the peak. Tanios led them to a ridge that overlooked a vast forest.

"We will spend the night here. No fires. I want four watchers at all times. Empyreans and sylveeds will be patrolling this area. Stay vigilant."

≻·❖·❖·≺

Tired, Bahiya closed her eyes. She tried to rest despite the biting cold, knowing tomorrow would be even harder. Wearily, she dozed off, and then fell into a fitful sleep. In her dream, she stood on a beach before a small, unadorned hut. The sand was bright yellow like the surface of the sun, and the water was a thick green slush. *Someone summoned me to the Arayat*, she realized. She went through the door of the hut and found herself standing inside a multi-storied maze wider than the Temple of Babylon. *A Maze Spell*, she thought, *and a mighty one*. Anyone could walk inside the maze but the only way out was through a locked door that could only be opened with a Spell Key—a special spell created at the same time as the maze. Bahiya closed her eyes and moved her hands slowly in front of her until she felt a draft of damp air. She extended her right index finger and moved it slowly until the draft began to flow around it. She then bent her finger and pulled her hand up and the draft followed. *Good. I hooked the spell*.

Minutes later, each of her right fingers had hooked a different spell. Forming a fist, she pulled all five spells to her ear and listened to the spell song—the distinct sound spells produced when combined. It was familiar. She smiled and whispered, "*Urakuun alamayn allalm*," which loosely means "Above us, the powers of the world." This was an obscure reference to a map kept in Babylon and one of Ashod's favorite sayings.

The maze vanished and the building shrunk down, turning back into the hut she had first seen. In the center of the empty space stood a tall, bony-looking plant. Its head was green, vaguely resembling an apple. *Ashod's avatar*, she thought. *He called me to the Arayat*.

"Hello pretty daisy," said Ashod's avatar, taking the precaution of not pronouncing actual names in the Spell World.

"Hello bobbing apple," she replied, smiling. "I wish I could see what I look like," she added. No one looked at one's reflection in the Arayat, for a reflection was an unpredictable spell, and mirrors, a destructive portal.

"I, don't," grumbled Ashod. "Wish to see my reflection, that is. I don't want to know what I look like."

"Why are we here?"

"Take this," he said, and handed her a curious object resembling a dark blue worm oozing a slimy orange substance. "You're going to need it."

Ashod's avatar dropped it in her open palm. It felt warm and fuzzy.

"A Furtive Spell," she said. "Who do you want to trail?"

"Put it on the creature," he added. "Without it, the wielder of the sword may not find his mark."

"Can the boy defeat the monster?" asked Bahiya. "He is so young."

The apple-like head bobbed several times. "What will happen is hard to predict, but we are not without hope," replied Ashod.

"I will cast this spell on the creature. Anything else?"

"Things may get worse after the battle," added Ashod cryptically.

"I know. I am prepared," asserted Bahiya.

"I did not mean you."

"For the sword's wielder? Why?"

"It is imperative that he does not lose hope. If he does, the Temple will capture him and make him a high priest."

"I will not let that happen."

"You may consider telling him about his sister. He will need to know she is alive. He will need something to hope for."

Bahiya's heart constricted. "I will see what I can do. I must leave. I have already overextended my presence here."

Ashod opened his mouth and blew. Bahiya felt a rush of air push her out and into darkness. *Ashod's breath is the key to the maze,* she thought. *How ingenious … and how predictable.*

After her departure, a cloaked figure moved out from the shadows. "Well done, my son." The voice was a faint whisper.

"Do you think he stands a chance to defeat the beast?"

"As good a chance as we can possibly hope for."

The next morning, at the break of dawn, the company resumed their trail. Despite a brisk pace, it took them seven hours to reach the valley floor. Heat and stifling humidity replaced ice, snow, and wind. A shorter, direct path existed through the highlands, but it passed within a stone's throw from Vumax, an important Empyrean military outpost.

The Silent are true to their namesake, thought Bahiya. *We have been walking for hours and they have yet to speak.*

The sun was high when they reached a wide, still lake.

"The mountain wall you see opposite this lake is the northeastern edge of the fortress," the commander said for Bahiya's sake. "We will trek along the lake's eastern edge," he told his Silent. "The entrance is on that side. Keep your wits about you. Vipers are common in this area."

"Better snakes than Empyreans," muttered Bahiya.

Two hours later, they reached the opposite side.

"Keep moving," the commander told them. "We need to reach the door before nightfall." *Assuming the Empyrean forces in this area are under the Empyrean princess' authority,* he thought. Tanios was worried. He knew the Empyrean army followed a decentralized command structure, and the regional commander could choose to launch a frontal attack on the fortress without prior notification from Gaëla.

Bahiya surveyed the landscape but could not spot the entrance.

"Where is it?" she asked at last.

Tanios pointed up to a cliff that hung two thousand feet over the lake. "Atop that cliff there is a plateau. At the southernmost end of the plateau there is a small, unprotected cave which leads into the fortress."

"An open cave leading straight into the fortress?" *How clever,* thought the high priestess.

"The dwarfs reworked the cave's mouth. It's very difficult to spot, even when you're looking for it."

"How do we get up there?"

"We climb," said the commander, giving Bahiya a wink. He firmly secured a belt around her waist and in doing so, drew the priestess near to him. She gazed up at him. He smiled a faint, crooked smile and said, "Like old times, right?"

She gave a reserved smile back. *Oh Tanios, if you only knew.* This was not the first time Bahiya had climbed up a straight mountain face. She found herself repeating old, familiar moves that she had sworn never to repeat. *It is different this time*, she thought as she dangled off a rope seven hundred feet over the lake. *I am doing this for a vital purpose. Besides, we have the company of the Silent with us now. Before, it was Tanios and I alone.*

They reached the summit by dusk. They were exhausted yet relieved, for their climb had gone without a hitch.

"We'll camp here tonight, and we should reach the fortress by early tomorrow morning."

The night was uneventful despite the howling wind. It was again frigid, and the company huddled for warmth as the commander would not allow the smallest fire.

"Empyreans have keen eyesight. They will spot the faintest flame."

The following morning, after a quick and cold breakfast, they resumed their walk. On several occasions, they were forced to lie low to avoid detection by the sylveeds. Despite their hatred for the light, the urkuun's servants heavily patrolled the area, so even though the entrance was relatively close, it took them all morning to reach it.

"There it is." Tanios finally pointed to a wall ahead of them.

"Amazing," said Bahiya, "I do not see it."

As they drew closer to the wall, she searched for the cave but could not see it. *Where is it?* she thought. *Did we miss it?*

"Halt," ordered Tanios. "We have reached our destination."

"Where is the entrance?" asked Bahiya. She knew the Silent did not see the cave either.

Tanios smirked and pointed to the mountain face two feet away from Bahiya. "Right here."

She gasped. The entrance was right there in front of her; a narrow slit in the mountain. *Ah, rounded edges and a steep, narrow path that looks just like the rest of the mountain.* "I thought the cave was part of this wall."

Wrath of the Urkuun – Hardeen

"Are you ready?" asked the commander.

She nodded. "This has been too easy."

"Does he know we are coming?" asked Commander Tanios.

The high priestess nodded. "We share the same magical realm. He knows I am here."

"Well, we shall attempt to live up to his expectations," replied Tanios. He looked at the Silent before continuing. "Return from where you came and report to Lord Orgond."

The Silent did not move. This was the first time they had refused a direct order from their commander.

"You have heard my order," repeated Tanios. "A large group will be easily detected inside the fortress. You have protected us until now, but in Hardeen a large group becomes a hindrance. I want you to return."

"Who will defend you?" asked one of the Silent.

"We will take care of ourselves. I do not wish to argue any further. Return from where we came. Obey Lord Orgond as you would obey me. Now go. You are wasting my time."

The Silent put one knee to the ground and bowed their heads in a promise of fidelity, fully aware they might not see their commander again. Tanios smiled slightly, almost tenderly, then abruptly turned his back and walked into the cave. The priestess followed.

➤ ⋅⊙⋅⊙⋅ ≺

After a wide right turn, Tanios and Bahiya reached a dead end lit by a shaft overhead. The commander examined the wall carefully for a long while. After a frustrating search, he heaved a sigh of relief and tapped the wall lightly at a precise location. After the second tap a section of the wall silently sprung open to reveal a narrow passage. Tanios scanned it quickly before signaling to Bahiya to follow him. Once inside he tapped on the wall three times and the door jolted back into place. Dwarfish workmanship never ceased to astound her. The door vanished as if the wall had swallowed it. She traced the ragged surface lightly with her fingers without detecting an edge. The door was completely gone.

"Let's move," whispered Tanios.

They went down a flight of stairs and reached a narrow platform where two additional staircases connected.

Not here, thought Tanios. *We're too exposed.*

High up inside the Fortress of Hardeen, they were now headed to the lowest level. The commander chose the left stairwell and Bahiya followed. As they moved, he listened for the faintest sound and searched for the right spot to speak with the priestess. As they made their way down, they glimpsed vast empty storage areas and some long narrow corridors. Tanios was familiar enough with the fortress to know that these secondary quarters were empty and now served as a sanctuary in case of invasion. Eventually, they would reach the main arteries of the fortress where they would make contact with the enemy.

Here, he thought, *this room is perfect*. He signaled to the priestess to follow him as he stepped into a small, secluded room. A frown creased her otherwise perfect forehead when she saw him glare at her, anger contorting his stealth features. She looked at him questioningly.

"Why?" he asked.

"Why what?" she said.

"Why did you murder those four young men during the Games? Why did you kill your own men?"

Bahiya looked at Tanios with stunned eyes, teetered back, and slid down against the cold wall.

➤ ⋅⋅⋅ ⋞

Just as Tanios was confronting Bahiya, Noraldeen bowed. "We thank you for your generosity and we gratefully accept."

"You do not have to thank me. It is I who thank you," replied the old woman. "Lord Orgond, helped us when my husband was away, and gave us shelter and food. Come in and bring this poor young boy with you."

It had been five days since they set out in search of Ahiram, and since then, had not a moment of rest. After finding him, they moved back along the mountainous road of Togofalk, toward Tanniin. Ahiram's fever had not subsided, and carrying the stretcher on which he lay slowed them. The journey back became dangerous. After the festivities ended, Togofalkian gangs plagued the roads once more. Then, a prolonged hailstorm forced them to take shelter inside a ruin, and a few hours later, the storm turned into a snow blizzard—which, even this high in the mountains, was rare during the last weeks of summer. As the snow fell, violent lightning and thunder filled the sky. Worried that Ahiram might not last much longer, they had taken to the road and inched their way through the storm. Soaked to the bones, cold and weary, they reached the first Tanniinite village past the border where the hospitable old woman now received them. She recognized Noraldeen and opened her house to them. They dried off, and she served them hot lentil soup and large chunks of steaming bread. She watched over Ahiram while the four of them slept. Noraldeen had wanted to care for him, but could not keep her eyes open. The old woman gently led her to a mat.

The following morning, Jedarc woke up to an empty house. He stepped outside and saw Hiyam sitting on a chair on the porch. The sky was still covered with clouds, but the wind had abated. The snow began to melt in the morning sun, revealing dark puddles here and there.

"Where is everyone?"

"Noraldeen, Banimelek, and the old woman took Ahiram to a medicine man."

"How is he doing?"

"Worse. His fever rose despite the woman's treatments." *As I feared,* thought Hiyam, her heart constricting.

"How long did they say they would be gone?"

"A couple of hours."

"Did you eat?" Jedarc could see how worried Hiyam was.

"No. I'm not hungry."

He drew close and whispered, "How do two fresh eggs prepared according to my secret recipe and served on a fresh piece of bread sound?"

Hiyam looked into his cheerful eyes. Their faces were close and she had to admit that she felt very comfortable around the tall, lanky blond Silent. Since their last conversation, he had not broached the subject of love, so she did not feel pressured by him. He had won her respect, and there were elements of his character that she had not seen in other men.

His sense of humor is a derivative of being at ease, observed Hiyam, *and he acts naturally around me despite my rank. He must hail from a high court with its own share of intrigue.* She recalled a conversation she had had with Bahiya on the way to the Games of the Mines.

"*The Silent train in accordance with the virtues*," her mother had explained while they were still at sea, on their way from Baalbek to Tanniin. "*Temperance forms passion, prudence develops reason, justice guides reparation, and fortitude teaches the heart to undertake worthy tasks, even at great personal cost.*"

"What about the High Riders?" Hiyam had asked.

"The High Riders are bred for one singular goal; to make sure the Temple prevails. They are known for strength, stamina, courage, and unwavering fidelity to the Temple."

"Which one is better?"

Her mother had not replied.

This short exchange stayed with her. Whenever her mother had been required to take Hiyam to a feast of the Temple where wine flowed freely and morals were set aside, Bahiya's fearsome reputation protected her from any lewd attention. In an attempt to spare her the spectacle, her mother would confine Hiyam to a discrete corner, but she would still witness the slow descent of revelry into utter madness. She saw High Riders whom she admired, men—normally disciplined, stout, and loyal—lose all control and give into their passions during these unbridled parties. *They acted like blind, uncontrollable animals*, she remembered. Standing alone, she would wonder if she would ever meet a good man, a man truly worthy of her, who would respect her and act lovingly.

Here I am, sitting in this kitchen, at ease with a man I barely know. It troubled her to admit that she felt far more at ease with Jedarc than she ever had with any of the men on her team.

"Can I ask you a question?" she said sheepishly.

"Ask away," replied Jedarc who turned to face her.

"What can you tell me about temperance?" she said blushing.

Jedarc cocked his head and raised his eyebrows in surprise. He had not expected that, but was not one to seek out the reason for a question. A question was asked and he was obliged to answer.

"Hum," he said, "do you want the long answer or the short answer?"

"The short answer," she replied.

"Very well." He tapped her knee with the side of his hand. Her leg jerked. "See that?" he asked.

"What?" she replied, confused.

"Your leg responded the right way, wouldn't you say?" he asked.

"Yes."

"And yet, you did not say to your leg, 'Hey, Oh leg of mine, you will obey my command as I instruct you to jerk thusly and in no other way.'"

"You are beginning to sound like a dwarf," she said, straight-faced.

"Really?" His eyes shined brightly. "I have always dreamed of being a dwarf with the overgrown beard and long hair."

She giggled at the thought of a dwarf Jedarc. He impressed her with his princely allure. She noticed how tall and slender he was, with deep green eyes, high cheekbones set in an oval face, and straw-blond hair that fell untidily over his face no matter how often he pushed it away. She imagined him with a long, bushy beard and laughed even harder.

"Well," he said pretending to be hurt, "I would have made a great dwarfish dwarf," he said. "Hey, did I ever tell you what one chicken said to another when they …."

She raised a finger and said gently, "Temperance?"

"Temperance, right," replied Jedarc. "Well, when I tapped your knee, your leg reacted the right way. When I did it again, your leg repeated the same motion. You didn't have to think about it did you? So, in a manner of speaking, your leg is trained to do the right thing. In the same way, temperance guides us to act according to right reason. That's Master Habael's fancy way of saying we do the right thing."

"But how do you know what the right thing is?"

"It's easy. You eat when you're hungry, you sleep when you're tired, and both in moderation." Jedarc flushed slightly and softened his tone. "And you never take advantage of a woman for your own selfish desires, but you love her as she deserves to be loved."

Their gaze lingered on each other for a moment, though these last words had taken her by surprise. They were bold, straightforward, and carried a depth of meaning that she had not anticipated.

"It all seems so simple."

"Love or the chicken eggs?"

She sighed, exasperated. High Riders never joked around, so she had difficulty keeping up with Jedarc's meandering mind.

"If everything is ordered like you say, what of spontaneity?"

"Does your leg bore you when it acts according to right reason?" he asked. "Or would you like it to spontaneously dislocate itself from its socket and go gallivanting after a chicken? No, but if your leg acts the right way, it gives you the freedom to walk, run, and dance. Spontaneity leads to peace of mind when it is virtuous."

"But this is my leg. It's not me."

"Indeed, and my passions, but they do not define me." He went to her and lowered his face so their eyes met, and added, "one thousand passionate acts do not amount to a single act of love if they are done selfishly." He moved away and bowed. "All right, how about we satisfy our appetite with some tasty food?"

"Isn't this against the virtue of temperance?"

He sighed. "Not when it is in the service of justice, and justice demands we eat. Please, follow me."

He led her outside and turned around. He walked her back, arm over arm, head raised with the solemnity of an imperial ruler. Reaching the doorstep, he let go of her arm and signaled for her to wait. Switching roles, he pretended to be a dutiful waiter and prepared her table. She laughed at the precision of Jedarc's gestures. She could almost see the tablecloth and candles. He then unrolled an imaginary carpet and ushered her in. He sat her down at the table, bowed ceremoniously, and began cooking. Before her fascinated eyes, he flipped the flat bread on the saj, and prepared eggs with the mastery of the chief cook of Baalbek. Hiyam tasted them and was pleasantly surprised. The bread was delicious, the eggs scrumptious.

"What is this recipe?"

"That's a secret," said Jedarc, laughing. "It's quite simple. You chop garlic and cook it lightly in a little bit of grease, then you cook the eggs sunny-side-up. I like to add a pinch of rosemary, thyme, and sumac whenever I can find them. And then," he whispered, "you serve the eggs on a plate and you top them off with two spoonfuls of yogurt."

"Yogurt?" said Hiyam, shocked.

"Absolutely," replied Jedarc. "If you add yogurt, it gives them a rich and smooth texture. It's the best."

"I never knew eggs could taste this good," said Hiyam, pensively.

"You mean you have never eaten eggs before?" asked Jedarc with a pained expression on his face. "Admit it now, it's a good thing you met me," he continued, with a sparkle in his eyes.

"I've had eggs, of course," she protested, "but somehow they taste so much better when you prepare them." Realizing what she had just said, she blushed and looked down at her plate. *He makes me say things …*

Jedarc laughed. She smiled and relaxed. She felt peaceful and content. They finished their meal in silence while exchanging glances and smiles.

"What do we do now?" she asked after they had finished eating.

"Groom and saddle the horses," replied Jedarc. "I have a feeling Banimelek will want to move on as soon as they return."

They readied the animals in silence.

"Tell me, Jedarc," said Hiyam while brushing one of the horses.

"What do you wish me to tell you?" he replied.

Hiyam smiled and stopped brushing. She looked at him. "How can you be so cheerful in a moment like this?"

"My mother's gift, I suppose. She was the most joyful person I have ever known. I like to think that I honor her by keeping a high spirit."

"You do her great honor," replied Hiyam with a charming smile.

Banimelek, Noraldeen, and the old woman returned with Ahiram just as they finished preparing the horses. The news was not good.

"We must leave at once," said Banimelek.

"How is Ahiram?" asked Jedarc.

Banimelek did not answer.

"What happened?"

"The medicine man examined him and said the fever is not natural—"

"Meaning?" cut in Jedarc, exasperated by his friend's laconic style.

"The medicine man said Ahiram is cursed," clarified Noraldeen. "And unless the curse is broken, he will surely die. He added that the curse is old and powerful, and he did not know of anyone who could break it."

"As I feared," said Hiyam. They looked at her. "The red powder I used, it detects the presence of spells. When it turned gray, I thought he was cursed, but when it dissipated so quickly I was confused."

"Why?" asked Jedarc.

"The change in color tells us what type of spell it is and the speed of dissipation shows its strength. So when it instantly vanished, I knew the curse was beyond anything I have ever seen, but then …" She glanced at Noraldeen before continuing, "someone cursed this way … he should have been dead already. Since Ahiram is still alive, I thought that perhaps what Ibromaliöm did had disturbed the powder."

Noraldeen nodded. "You acted prudently. This was the right thing to do. What you told us explains why the medicine man was so frightened and why he refused to help us."

"So what do we do now?" asked Jedarc.

"We move," replied Banimelek. "We must take him as fast as possible to Master Habael. He may know what to do."

After thanking the old woman profusely, they took to the deserted road. Banimelek firmly held a slumped Ahiram on his horse. Soon rain began to fall, gently at first, and then, a downpour. They were soaked. Banimelek looked up and was startled by the low clouds. The sky was dark with a green tinge and a large wall of clouds was visible just northeast of them. The rain became hail, and they heard a loud roar above them. *I have never seen anything like this. I don't like it one bit*. He surveyed the plain. The few trees seemed frantic under the lashes of the wind, waving their branches like weeping mourners waving handkerchiefs at a Tanniinite funeral.

"Gang!" Noraldeen yelled over the din of the storm. Behind them, in the distance, a group of riders was fast approaching.

"Quick, to that farm," she added pointing at a low-ceiling building a short distance away.

She prodded her horse, which leaped forward. They followed her in a gallop to keep the gang at bay. Inexorably, the distance began to shrink.

"Faster!" screamed Jedarc. "They're getting closer."

Banimelek looked back and winced. Confrontation was unavoidable. He counted eight riders, maybe more. In the open, the gang had the advantage. They needed to balance the odds somehow.

In one graceful movement, Hiyam swung her body around so she was riding her horse backward. She raised her hands to the heavens and brought them together in a powerful clap. *If only I had an orb and a concentrator,* she thought, *but this will have to do.* A wall of dust surged from the ground in front of the forward gang members, hiding them from view. Hiyam pivoted back and screamed in sheer terror. Banimelek looked at her, and she pointed to the right. He turned to look. Just ahead, outrunning the horses, a monstrous, dark funnel of spinning wind, full of dust and debris careened across the open land. It twisted at incredible speed, uprooted the scarce trees, and destroyed everything in its path. And they were on its path.

Banimelek held Ahiram tightly, spurred his horse, and locked his eyes on the farm. *We will make it, Ahiram, don't you worry. Even if I have to carry you on my shoulders myself, I will get you there.* The horses, under the impulse of fear, bolted. Suddenly, the tornado seemed right on top of them. They were too terrified to scream. The twister lifted and touched down again behind the farm. They rushed through the gate, still on horseback. Like most farms on the great plain, this one was built out of large slabs of stone. It consisted of one main room with a narrow door.

"Hiyam, get the horses to the back of the room—"

"You want the horses inside the house?"

"Yes, otherwise we will loose them. Take them to the back and calm them down," yelled Banimelek as he carried Ahiram to a mat in the corner. "Noraldeen, take care of Ahiram. Jedarc, follow me."

The two Silent, armed with two dart-crossbows each, stood by the door and waited. Despite the gale, the gang converged on the farm. Banimelek was about to release his darts when the tornado suddenly landed in front of the farm. It hurled the two Silent against the vine that snaked through a pergola. They frantically grabbed the branches and remained pinned against the pergola by the power of the vortex that wanted to suck up everything else. This lasted only seconds as the tornado moved away, but it felt like an eternity to the two Silent. Finally, the strength of the pull weakened, and the two young men fell to their feet, facing the door. They turned around and watched with horror as the vortex swallowed the gang. It snatched up horses and men, carrying them in the air, and tossed them away like broken toys. The few gang members that escaped the dreadful fate turned tail and ran. Suddenly, the tornado scattered and died out as abruptly as it had started. The two friends looked at each other and sighed.

"Well, I'm cured," exclaimed Jedarc.

"Of what?" asked Banimelek.

"The desire to fly."

"Stay here and keep an eye out," said Banimelek. "You never know, they may decide to come back." He stepped into the farmhouse and saw that Noraldeen had found enough kindling and wood stacked inside the house to start a fire.

Wow, he thought, *how did she manage to keep her cool in the midst of this madness? Must be her Empyrean side, I guess.*

"How is he?" he asked.

"No change," she replied with an even voice. "High fever and still unconscious."

He knelt beside her, placed his hand on her shoulder and smiled. She leaned back against him and closed her eyes. Hiyam, having succeeded in quieting the horses, came over and looked at Ahiram. She sighed. They all felt powerless, unable to cure him, unable to bring him back. She went to the door and saw Jedarc leaning on one of the posts that supported the pergola. He looked back at her and smiled weakly. She walked onto the porch and hugged him. Surprised, he folded his arms around her, and held her against him.

In the distance, a thin line of blue sky broke through the once sinister clouds, like a ray of light in their darkness.

27. Revelation

> "*Of all living gods, there is only one who is uncreated, and who has created all things: El.*"
> —Chronicles of Yardam, Third Stewart of the House of Hiram.

> "*Ultimately, it all boils down to courage, integrity, and generous love. These are the three most important qualities a soldier must possess in order to win a war.*"
> —Lost discourse of Ramael, son of Shatumael, son of Hanayel, son of Zarubael, son of Lamatael, great-grandson of Habael the Wise.

"Why? Why did you kill those four men, Bahiya?"

"I wondered how long it would take you to figure it out," said Bahiya. Before he had a chance to reply she added, "How did you?"

"By elimination and luck. Initially, I ruled out Habael, the King, and Olothe: Habael for obvious reasons, the King and Olothe because I had Silent watching them and knew of their whereabouts when the first murder happened. It could not have been Hylâz, because he is a coward and a heartless zakiir who cares only about money, and Ramany is a spy of Baal."

"So you knew."

Tanios repressed an amused smile. "Yes. My suspicions centered on Ramel. She hungered for power. She was heartless and driven. The Queen would have had no qualms with sacrificing a husband she despised to nurse her ambition. She had the means and the clout to do as she saw fit. She could have tried to pin these murders on the King and convince the Temple to be rid of him."

"The Temple doubted the King's allegiance," said Bahiya.

"Which is why they sent you to Tanniin, but that's a different matter which I will get to in a moment. One factor prevented Ramel from assassinating Jamiir. She was childless, and the people of Tanniin would not take too kindly to a foreign, childless queen, yet, she was too proud to have sought a pregnancy out of wedlock. Furthermore, I considered Garu to be an inoffensive fool and Ibromaliöm, a pompous nincompoop. They were two of the Queen's puppets and would not murder men of Baal on their own.

"I was stumped. We were forced to leave the castle and I thought the case lost, but then your eyes betrayed you. On our way to Amsheet, after we met with Enryl by the forest of Magdala, you told us the Forbidden Forest harbored no ill will."

"I remember saying that, but how—"

"It wasn't what you said, it was in your eyes. You looked at me, and in that shadowy light, your eyes reminded me of someone; someone I had seen recently."

"Who?" she said, already knowing the answer.

"During the fourth day of the Games, the Game of Meyroon, the King asked the High Riders to protect the castle. He did it to please you. Someone had killed three of your men. How then could the King refuse such a request? You are a brilliant strategist, I'll grant you that much. Your request had less to do with Baal's politics, and more with your next murder. In the Star Room, Garu and Ibromaliöm had been dabbling in magic. I asked you to look into it. Naturally, you wanted the soldiers of

Baal to protect the Lone Tower while you conducted your inspection. As I was on my round, I heard a commotion in the tower. That is when the event of the black sun occurred. You were in the Star Room, behind the locked door, supposedly examining the magic of Garu and Ibromaliöm. The men and I were in the cramped hallway gazing at the eclipse. I looked back and came face-to-face with a soldier who then jumped through the window. Why did he look me in the eye? Because he wanted me to remember his features, features which were different from yours. The soldier then jumped from the window. Some among the men of Baal think of Tholma, the sun losing its power, as a deadly curse. Thinking it was suicide, rare, but not unheard of, I looked down expecting to see a shattered body. But I saw no one.

"That's when the soldiers behind me screamed. I turned and saw one of them leaning against the wall. He was dead. Murdered like the other three victims. I realized the soldier who jumped through the window must be the killer. That is when I noticed the rope hanging by the window that I had not seen before. I gave chase on the rooftop of the tower, but inexplicably, he escaped.

"I came back down, and found you standing by the door of the Star Room. I did not think the murderer would have had the gall to jump into the Star Room from the roof. After all, you are a high priestess of Baal and the murderer was killing your men. It would be sheer madness for the killer to enter the Star Room knowing the powerful priestess of Baal was there. Unless of course, the assassin was you."

Bahiya's expression remained placid, which did not surprise Tanios.

"All four murders were committed close-up with identical darts which convinced me there was one principal murderer behind them all. The events that led to the last murder made me realize how clever your strategy had been. Before the eclipse of the sun, you asked the men of Baal to come down the stairs, except for one. They were too afraid to question you. You asked the soldier to wait for you outside the room. You went in, changed into a soldier's uniform, hid your long hair beneath a helmet, and darkened your features. When you came back out, you killed your unsuspecting victim and let him slump against the wall in the darkest corner of the tower."

Bahiya smiled a dismal smile. "I tried to hide all this from you, but everything happened so quickly, I did not have enough time to prepare."

The commander cocked his head sideways and glanced at the high priestess. *What is she hiding, I wonder? No matter, I will soon find out.* "Tholma then occurred," he continued, "creating a deeper shadow. You called for the men to come upstairs. They rushed in and saw a soldier standing by the door whom they mistook for the dead one. You immediately directed their attention to the darkening sun. As a priestess of Baal, you knew the black sun was coming and had planned accordingly. Presumably, you did not expect me to show up, but you knew I would not suspect you to be the murderer. I would see what I wanted to see. You knew that and took advantage of it. All along, you convinced the soldiers and me that you had been in the Star Room studying the remains of Garu's magical acts. When I turned away from the window the first time, we came face-to-face. I looked at you and you grabbed a rope, jumped out the window, and made your way to the roof. You are a high priestess of Baal and it's easy to forget how athletic you are. During our climb yesterday, I saw your strength and ease, like that of a Silent."

"You trained me before training the Silent," she replied softly.

Tanios ignored her. "To get back inside the Star Room, you leaped through the open window. I remember noticing that someone had removed the slats that shuttered the windows. While I searched for the murderer on the roof, you were changing back into your priestly garments and then emerged as the indignant High Priestess Bahiya. It was perfect. You almost succeeded in creating an imaginary killer and moving all suspicion away from you."

"Your presence at that moment complicated my plan," said Bahiya quietly. "I was desperate, time was running short. I had to do it—"

Tanios had been pacing. He interrupted her as though lost in his own thoughts.

"This, of course, does not explain how the assassin could carry the body of the third unfortunate victim from the officer's garden to Ibromaliöm's room. I followed the footsteps and they ended in front of the wall. There was no secret passage at this point, so where did the assassin go? How was he able to transport the dead man?" He looked at her with realization before continuing. "When I spoke with the Queen, she reminded me that you are a Methodical, your shields of power can easily lift a body, and you are able to cloak yourself, therefore, it was easy for you to move unnoticed in the castle.

"As I investigated these crimes during the Games of the Mines, I did not suspect you. How could I? You are a high priestess of Baal. I could not find a motive for you to go about killing your own men, and I still cannot understand why you killed them. This strikes me as madness. It is plain suicide. The Temple will find out and put you to death. Why? Why Bahiya?" asked Tanios with a pained exclamation. "Why did you murder those four men? Tell me."

Bahiya sighed heavily and looked at Tanios with a somber expression. "I wish you had not found out," she said. "Besides, I did not murder them as you put it. They willingly sacrificed themselves."

"Do not lie to me, Bahiya," said Tanios gritting his teeth. "I wanted to wait until after this crisis, but we are about to face the monster and you are tasked with forcing him to leave the fortress." He drew closer to Bahiya and looked her in the eye. "I need to trust you. I need to know why you will not side with the enemy. If you killed four men in cold blood, why would you not side with another murderer?" His eyes turned cold and determined. "I will never allow this, do you understand me?"

"You do not need to worry," she replied softly, "I am more determined than you or anyone else to fight this beast. I am not lying when I say the men sacrificed themselves. I officiated, but they willed it."

"You mean to say they knowingly sacrificed themselves to Baal?"

"They thought it was for Baal, but it was for Tanniin."

"You offered human sacrifice for Tanniin?" replied Tanios, bewildered and disgusted. "Since when does Tanniin accept human sacrifice?"

"All gods do," replied Bahiya with aplomb.

"But why? This seems senseless to me. I do not understand."

"I was trying to protect Ahiram."

"Ahiram?" said Tanios dumbfounded. "But you ordered your High Riders to kill him. You wanted him dead."

"Babylon issued this order," snapped Bahiya. "Not I."

"Babylon?" said Tanios shaking his head. "Why would the high and mighty Babylon involve itself in all of this? Stop talking in riddles," said Tanios raising his voice, forgetting his surroundings.

"Do you remember the last moments of our stay on the Beach of Emerald, nineteen years ago?"

"How are those memories relevant?" replied Tanios exasperated.

"That is why we are here. Bear with me, please. Do you remember?"

"Yes," he said quietly. "It was the day after our wedding. Back then I thought I was the happiest man on earth." He shook his head as though staving off the pain and the loneliness of the past years.

"Then what happened?" she asked softly.

"I don't remember."

"You don't remember the cavern with golden walls?"

"No," he replied unconvincingly.

"You remember the prophecy, don't you?" He did not reply. "The prophecy of the Letters of Power?"

"Yes, I remember," he said bristling with anger. "Empty promises, hollow words. We were young and impressionable. We found the Cave of Gold and we convinced ourselves that a being of light had spoken to us. We were stupid. It was a cheap, fanciful dream, nothing more."

"Cheap, fanciful dreams?" replied Bahiya, shocked. "The Order of Baal exists because of this cheap, fanciful dream. Since the fall of the Great Tower, the Order has destroyed entire villages in order to repress any knowledge of the Letters of Power. Baal destroyed every libre it could, and those it could not destroy, it foredoomed with every conceivable curse. Those it could not curse were hidden in dark places, and inhuman watchers were assigned to protect them; watchers I do not want to meet in my worst nightmare. The Letters of Power scare the Temple. According to the lore of Baal, a Seer will find these Letters and use them to bring chaos and destruction to the world. He will open the Pit and set himself as the archlord of darkness—"

"Archlord of darkness," interrupted Tanios on a sarcastic tone. "It sounds trite and stupid."

"You are right. Pure evil always sounds trite and stupid because one of its greatest weapons is to convince us it is a harmless charade. We use poor labels to speak of what we cannot fully understand. I assure you, the Pit is real. Every high priest and priestess experiences the Pit."

"You're losing me, Priestess."

"I destroyed Baher-Ghafé because of these Letters, do you understand? I loved this village. I loved its people. They were dear to me. I killed them because of the Letters."

"You're confusing me. Stop speaking in riddles."

"Why did this being of light reveal the prophecy to us?" asked Bahiya.

"I don't know and I don't care to know."

She glared at him, barely repressing her anger. "Let me remind you of this prophecy first, then perhaps you will care."

Tanios shrugged his shoulders and waited. He was a man used to action, not historical tirades or reflections on obscure prophecies. Nevertheless, Bahiya had killed four men for Tanniin in order to break a cryptic curse. *I am not certain I believe any of this, but I need to find out if I can trust her before we meet the urkuun.*

Bahiya looked at Tanios as she recited:

> "'A Seer each of you is given in this vale of tears,
> To find what was lost and bind what was broken.
> A joyful light shall shine in the fullness of years,
> To reveal what you heard and what I have spoken.'

Now before I go on, Tanios, I want you to think about the 'joyful light', and then think about what happened right before the start of the Games."

"What are you getting at Bahiya?" he replied in a guarded voice. She could see he had connected the show of lights the night before the Games and the "joyful light" of the first stanza of the prophecy.

> "'Twenty-two uncreated Letters of Power,
> To heal and redeem by a shout of command,
> Or free the Lords of the Pit beneath the fallen tower,
> Lay scattered to the four corners of the land.'

"This part is clear. There are twenty-two Letters of Power hidden all over the world. The Temple believes there are only twenty Letters," she said with an intensity that surprised him.

"All right, Bahiya," he said heaving a deep sigh. "I'll humor you and assume that any of this makes sense. I am doing it because I need to know if I can trust you. So, what are these Letters of Power?"

"We don't know. Sureï alone, who had cursed these Letters, could have shed some light. The Temple believes the Letters can break the *Rohmarim*, the Seal of the Pit, and free the Lords of Darkness."

Tanios threw his arms to the heavens. "I am starting to lose my patience, Priestess, I—"

"I never wanted to involve you in any of this but now that you are involved, I need you to understand. Please, listen to the rest.

> 'They must be gathered by one of the two Seers,
> Who will bind them in a final word of light.
> The second Seer must lead in this vale of tears
> To eternal darkness into the depth of night.'"

"So there were supposed to be two Seers then," said Tanios. "Funny, I don't remember any of this."

"Who was in the Cave of Gold that night Tanios?" she asked softly.

"You and me, Corintus and his wife Amaréya, and two others."

"Two others?" she asked surprised. "I did not see anyone else."

"You were not looking," he replied with a wistful smile. "I am certain Balid and Kwadil were hiding in one of the lateral passages, listening in."

"Kwadil?" she asked dumbfounded. "I should have known," she added in a whisper. "I should have known."

"How does Kwadil have anything to do with this?" asked Tanios, losing his patience.

"Listen to the last stanza:

> 'A boy will be carried by a double-finned shark.
> And when unexpectedly the night will be lit,
> By supernal light across the sky so dark,
> The Seer will rise against the wiles of the Pit.'"

Her eyes never left his while she recited the verse, and she could see in his eyes, that at last, the truth had begun to dawn.

"You mean to say that Ahiram is—"

"The first of two Seers," she completed softly.

Tanios frowned. "What does this prophecy have to do with Ahi …" He was starting to relate Bahiya's statements. "But that would mean that he is—" He looked at her with eyes filled with a fearful disbelief.

"Your son." Tears fogged her vision and she struggled to control her voice. "*Our* son, Tanios. Ahiram is our son."

Tanios was stunned. The words hit him in slow motion.

"Our son?"

"Yes, when the Lord of Light told us about the prophecy, I did not yet know I was pregnant with Ahiram."

"You were what?" asked Tanios who had not yet registered the full impact of her words.

"Pregnant with Ahiram. With your son and mine, Tanios." Tears were now streaming down her cheeks. "I am his mother and you, his father."

Tanios suppressed his raging emotions—something he was all too good at—and focused on the facts. *If Ahiram is her son, that would explain why she tried to save him.*

"Are you certain? When did you find out?" he asked.

"After I joined the order of Baal."

"You mean after you ran from me?"

"Yes. I was young. We had run away, and I married you against my father's wishes. Tanios, I loved you, but I was frightened. You were so wild and adventurous, you cared nothing for order and stability, and I needed these. I desperately needed structure in my life, to go back and tell my family about you, about us, but you wouldn't listen. The prophecy had scared me and I didn't …" she heaved a deep sigh. "I didn't want to be with child, not from you. The Temple offered me security and honor. I ran away, Tanios. I ran away from you. I embraced the Temple."

Focus on the facts, thought Tanios. "What happened then?"

Bahiya breathed deeply before continuing with a low, anguished voice. "Shortly after joining the Temple, I discovered I was already pregnant. I was so stricken with fear that my child, your child, would be the Seer of the Prophecy. If the Temple would ever find out, they would kill him. Kill *our* child, Tanios."

Tanios drew close to her, his eyes now full of concern. Bahiya felt compelled to continue.

"Back then, Hayat, one of my maids, was serving in the Temple. She had married a man from Baher-Ghafé and was to leave my service. She was pregnant as well. I was desperate, Tanios, I had to save our child. I used herbal potions to quicken her delivery and we gave birth within hours of each other. If a woman gives birth on Temple grounds, she must undergo the Right of Purification, during which time, a wet nurse cares for the baby. The midwife had briefly shown Hayat her baby wrapped in swaddling clothes. Following my orders, she told Hayat that it was a boy. Two months later, she left the Temple with Ahiram, and I kept Hiyam."

"And the midwife and wet nurse knew your secret."

Bahiya shook her head in agreement. "A Mist Spell works wonders on recent events. They both forgot what had taken place."

"Why did you keep all of this hidden from me? Why did you not tell me? I would have helped you."

"I tried," said Bahiya with deep sorrow. "I sent you many messages, asking you to come and see me, but either you did not receive them, or you refused to come." She looked at him, and he looked away. She had deserted him and he had been too proud to respond. "I tried, Tanios."

Still looking away, he said, "Then what happened?"

Bahiya took a deep breath and continued, "Six years ago, a few months before Kwadil had brought Ahiram to you, an order came from Babylon. It was like a sword piercing my heart. 'Destroy Baher-Ghafé.' I sent someone to warn Ahiram's family, but more I could not do. I gave the order to kill my own son. I was the high priestess of Baalbek, Tanios. The order came from Sharr. One act of insubordination and he would have exiled me to the Arayat. Later I found out that Ahiram's family had survived, but there was no news of our son. Six long years went by without a word, without a glimpse of hope. For six years I thought our son was dead. I silently grieved for him without hope, until that fateful evening when I told the King the slave should sit by my side. Ahiram. The slave who was trying to win the Games of the Mine, the one person I had orders to eliminate, the one I had set Prince Olothe after."

"I remember," said Tanios. "You cried out loudly and dropped to the ground. How did you recognize him?"

"By his birthmark. Ahiram has three small dark circles at the base of his neck. When he sat by me at the table of the King, I looked at him and noticed the circles on his neck. I knew he was my child. The shock was so great, I fainted."

"So you thought about the lights before the Games and you figured out he was the Seer? A bit outlandish don't you think?"

"Not when you consider the prophecy. Don't you see? Many high priestesses will gladly sacrifice their sons for power and the chance to join the Inner Circle. Something held me back. The raid in Baher-Ghafé should have killed him, but he survived. Six years later, he is a trained Silent, an accomplished athlete. Then, the incredible lights that no magic could have produced—"

"Still, this does not explain why the four men are dead," replied Tanios, matter-of-factly. "I believe in facts. In facts and in objects I can touch and see."

"Sureï came to Tanniin," she began to explain.

"Yes, the Queen told me," said Tanios who leaned against the wall. He was dizzy and nauseous, and for the first time in his life, he felt lost. "She told us that whenever Sureï traveled far from Babylon, it was to curse a Letter. To break the curse, one must shed blood on the corners of the Letters of Power."

"Sureï's curse would have killed him as soon as he got close to the Letter," continued Bahiya.

"You knew then the location of this Letter?"

She looked at him, taken aback. "Yes, why? Does this surprise you? The Temple has spared neither effort nor expense to locate these Letters. The location of the Letter in Tanniin is ancient news to the Temple."

"Why can't the Temple take them if it knows where the Letters of Power are? Why all this complication?"

She shook her head. "The Temple cannot touch the Letters because none of its members can see them. What the Temple wants is to make the Seer a high priest, a servant of Baal who would help the Temple control the Letters. The Seer alone knows the shape of the Letters. Have you not heard of the enchanted cedar tree in Laban-Arz?"

"Who has not heard of this wonder of wonders? A tree the wind

507

cannot move, the rain cannot touch, and time cannot change."

"It's not a real tree. It is one of the Letters. Everyone knows where it is. We see its appearance, but no one can get close enough to touch it."

"Why?"

"Because you need to see it in its true form. Sureï cursed the area around it and Baal keeps watchful eyes on it day and night. Ahiram would see its true form; a Letter. He would call it by its name, the tree would vanish, and the Letter would appear to him. But the curse would kill him before he could call the Letter."

"If he were to have all the Letters, what would happen then?"

"No one knows, but the balance of power would shift irrevocably and I am not sure the Temple would survive." Bahiya looked hard at Tanios before continuing. "This is what you have set in motion by allowing Ahiram to enter the Games." Tanios looked at her and she sustained his gaze. "When the Inner Circle of Babylon realized the Seer was here, they unleashed the urkuun to destroy him. 'Better that one child dies, than see the entire order perish,' they said. Well, not my child." Bahiya fell silent and Tanios peered down the corridors once more. All was quiet in this deserted part of the fortress.

"Did you act on your own or were there others involved in these … sacrifices of yours?"

"Alone." Bahiya hesitated. "Although, I admit I do not understand how he managed to hit Hiyam with his dart."

"What do you mean?"

"During one of the Games—I do not recall which one now—he threw a poisonous dart at Hiyam."

"The Game of Silver, and it was not poisonous. He was bluffing."

Bahiya waved the explanation away. "Hiyam had used a spell of protection. Not the strongest spell, but strong enough to stop his darts from reaching her. Yet it did. Someone must have helped him then."

"Could he not have done this? I mean, as the Seer—"

Bahiya shook her head. "No. Without the Letters he is powerless. Someone helped him. But aside from this event, yes, I worked alone."

"But you did not protect Ahiram from Hiyam. She could still have killed him during the Game of Silver."

"She is my daughter," snapped Bahiya with exasperation. "What was I to do? Shackle her and …" She took hold of herself before continuing. "I had to rely on your training. He is a Solitary after all. The Temple watches my every move. I did what I could."

"Then what?"

"Ibromaliöm asked me if the Temple would be interested in recovering an ancient libre, written before the fall of the Tower of Babel. I reminded him of the curse. He shrugged his shoulders and left. This was the only conversation I had with Ibromaliöm concerning his search. I must admit, I did not take him seriously. I thought this was the whim of a bored judge and would soon pass when confronted with the difficulties of finding this libre—supposing it does exist. I should have acted a lot quicker."

"But you said that the blood—"

"The sacrifices allowed Ahiram to come out of the mines alive and well. I know nothing about him looking at the pages of a cursed book. It is beyond my understanding. Had I not done what I did, the curse would have killed Ahiram if he had gotten too close to it. He would have died a horrible death, alone, and unloved. I could not bear the thought of losing him again. I did what I did so that he may live. When I saw him walk into the council, my heart leaped for joy. I was elated and relieved. My son is alive and he wasn't cursed. I broke the curse."

"But you killed four innocent lives."

"Don't you care about your son? Are you not happy he is alive?"

"I was not aware I had a son! I have been living with these murders on my conscience, and I just found out the woman I loved, the mother of my child murdered them."

"They were *hardly* innocent. Besides, these sacrifices were worth it."

"How could you be so heartless? Those boys have parents who will miss them. How could you justify their deaths with the life of your son?"

"He is your son too, Tanios."

"I have loved him like my son. I have always loved him like my own son. But I could not have shed innocent blood to save him."

"I do not believe you."

"You do not have to. It is enough that I do."

"Then I stand condemned in your eyes," she said in a tone of complete resignation. "What are you going to do? Are you going to help me fight the monster, or will you help it destroy me? I do not fight for kingdoms, nor do I fight for Baal. I fight for my son." Bahiya looked at Tanios and he held her gaze. Despite their arguing, their love, though wounded and distraught, had withstood time and space. Mistrust and wounds, had perdured in spite of their will to break away from the warmth of shared memories. And now, standing between them, unseen, unheard, unstoppable was Ahiram. To Bahiya, Ahiram meant an unbroken world, a reunion with the only man she had ever loved. Tanios, had embraced a life of unremitting discipline as Commander of the Silent Corps to atone for the chaotic life he had imposed on Bahiya. If he were complicit of the priestess' crime, a violation of justice, he would then betray his discipline and the woman he had loved with all his heart. In the vast loneliness of Hardeen, in passages given to cobwebs and unbroken silence, their love stood between them like a chasm, an abyss where the extended and open arms of Ahiram was now the only bridge back to each other. Tanios was the first to break the silence.

"Promise me that if we survive this mission, you will stand before a tribunal and abide by its judgment."

"I promise," replied Bahiya without hesitation.

He breathed a sigh of relief. "Fine. One last thought. I do not believe the prophecy. Corintus disclosed to me that his wife gave birth to a stillborn boy. If you were hoping their son was the second Seer, then I hate to disappoint you. You need to look elsewhere to find him."

"But that is impossible," she said with a quiver in her voice. "There must be another Seer hidden somewhere, someone powerful enough to guide Ahiram through it all."

The commander shrugged his shoulders. "Let's move on."

"Watch out!"

Bahiya yanked Tanios back; Empyrean soldiers, lances in hand, stormed the room.

"In the name of Her Highness Gaëla Meïr Pen," called Tanios with a voice of command, "State your purpose!"

The name caught the Empyrean's attention. Uncertain of what to do, they waited for their captain who walked in with her sword drawn.

"If Empyreans try to stop you," Lord Orgond had told him before they left camp, "show them this royal amulet. They will listen to you."

Slowly, Tanios lifted the amulet. *I hope it will subdue them. If not, Bahiya will have to take them down.*

The Empyrean captain inspected the amulet closely but without touching it. "How is it that you, a man, hold in your hand an Empyrean tévana? Who gave it to you?"

"Lord Orgond. I am Commander Tanios of the Silent Corps. This tévana belongs to the empress' daughter."

Reverently, the captain examined the amulet once more. "Indeed it is royal. Why were we not informed of your mission?"

Tanios refrained from smiling. "The enemy has spies everywhere, wouldn't you say, Captain."

She saw Bahiya and her eyes hardened. "What is she doing here?"

"I am not at liberty to disclose the purpose of our mission. Princess Gaëla herself has approved our plan. Her word should be enough."

"I will seek confirmation."

Tanios winced. *It is as I feared,* he thought. *The regional commander must have ordered an assault on the fortress and this is the scouting party.*

"Do not draw close to the Seducer," said Bahiya. The Empyrean captain's eyes flashed with anger. "You know who I am. As high priestess, I am warning you, you cannot defeat the Seducer by force. Your sisters did not fall into his hands out of weakness. They did not surrender or betray the empress. He showed them a world where Empyreans are victorious. The Seducer convinced them that the better way to serve the empress is to serve him."

By now, a full Empyrean contingent stood at the door, waiting.

"I do not understand," replied the captain.

"Physically, the Seducer is as powerful as any one of his brethren. Mentally, he is far superior to them. He cannot bend your will to his own, but what he can do is show you the future you crave. The stronger your desire for power, the greater is his hold. He will take you to this future, make it real for you, and when you freely choose it, you will submit to him willingly and serve only him. He will lie to you and deceive you, and in the end, your own desires will break you. The Pit created the urkuun to fight the Marada and anyone else who trusts in the might of their shield, swords or spears. I beg of you not to confront him, else you fail like your sisters did and end up serving him."

"Why are *you* different?" asked their captain.

"My defenses will hold long enough for me to do what I must. I … you may not believe me, but ambition and power no longer compel me. Someone dear to me needs my help. The Seducer does not understand motives of this kind."

The captain looked at the amulet once more, then she gave it back to Tanios. "I shall seek confirmation. Wait here." She then left behind a dozen of her soldiers by the door. Time wore on and the Empyrean captain did not return before dusk. Darkness fell, oppressive, depressing.

"The power of the urkuun is stronger at night," whispered Bahiya. "We better not speak until tomorrow morning." They spent most of the night awake, listening to grunts, shouts, shrieks, and moans of pain that turned into howling.

"They are the sylveeds who have not been completely transformed," said Bahiya softly. "They know they are transforming. They know they have been deceived, but their word binds them. If we can rescue them, they will revert to their human form, but in two days, it will be too late."

<hr />

"Tanios, wake up." The commander opened his eyes. "The Empyrean commander is back." Slowly, Tanios rose to his feet. "You will need all your strength when confronting the monster. Here, drink this, it's a restorative elixir. No magic. I promise."

Tanios gulped down the content of the small gourd that Bahiya handed him. He quickly felt alert and energized. Moments later, the Empyrean captain walked in.

"You are free to go," said the Empyrean captain. "If in two days you have not returned, we will launch a full-scale attack inside the fortress. That is all I can do."

The Empyrean forces retreated. As the tornado moved away from the farm where Noraldeen and her companions had taken refuge, Tanios and Bahiya continued their descent into the depth of Hardeen. In full stride to meet the urkuun, Bahiya had no hope of surviving the ordeal that awaited them. She quickly glanced back at the man who was, in her eyes, still her husband. Tanios lived and died by a great sense of justice, but he was still willing to trust her, and nothing else mattered.

28. Guiding Light

> *"The realm of magic is manifold, strange, and twisted like a man's conscience. Hiding within its folds are spells and curses that defy the imagination. It is my stated belief that the world of magic is like a dormant volcano that could be triggered by a seemingly benign act of magic; but once awake, will burn our world through and though, leaving behind the charred remains of the natural beauty we have come to take for granted."*
> –Teaching of Oreg, High Priest of Baal.

"We're losing him," shouted Noraldeen, panic-stricken. "What can we do?"

It had started to rain once more; a gentle, soft rain. Ahiram lay at her feet by the door of the farmhouse. They had hoped the cool air would lower his temperature, but his fever still raged. Banimelek looked away, seeming to survey the large, open fields around them. Dark clouds hovered above like a sign of impending doom. Never before had he felt so powerless. What can sword and might do against fever and sickness? He looked at his friend lying on the floor and bitterness engulfed his heart. He wanted to yell at Ahiram, to tell him that had he stayed with them in the castle rather than acting hastily, they would not be where they were now. They needed Ahiram to fight the terror. *He* needed Ahiram to fight the terror. Banimelek looked at his friend quivering with fever in the rain. *How can you fight the urkuun now? He asked silently. Why did you do this to us?*

Noraldeen sat eyes closed, still as a statue. Banimelek looked at her and felt ashamed. *She is worried about him, and I am worried about us.* He had to admit that for the first time, he was afraid. Afraid of dying at the hand of the beast.

"Look," whispered Jedarc pointing in the distance, "Over there, a rider. Someone is coming."

>·❀·❀·<

When Noraldeen opened her eyes, she was kneeling on a vast ledge that overlooked snow-covered mountains she did not recognize. Ahiram was still lying on the ground. She looked around and was bewildered. Straight across the canyon a waterfall flowed from the heavens above into the abyss below, seemingly with no beginning and no end. A trumpet blast filled the air. Turning around, she saw Tessarah, the Unseen Tower of the Lady of Eleeje. She heard another six trumpet blasts, as loud as the first one and then the gate opened.

"How did we get here?" she whispered. Ahiram stirred. She felt his forehead and her heart leaped for joy. *No fever, what is going on?*

A procession streamed through the open door. Maidens filed in with candles set in gold handles. They wore long, flowing white dresses that shimmered in the light, and they carried wreaths of flowers on their foreheads. As they walked, their hair and the candle flames remained steady, unmoving, even as the wind flowed around them. Behind the maidens, a woman in a gold silken dress carried a coat-of-arms. It was white and blue with the design of a gold cup framed by two roses.

The Lady of Eleeje, the woman she had seen before, closed the procession. She wore a crown of dark metal that glowed white and blue, with a brilliance to rival the stars.

The maiden stood in a circle and the Lady of Eleeje stood before her.

"I have summoned you here in spirit. You are still in that farmhouse, daughter," she said softly. "The Seer is under a formidable curse, one you and I cannot cure. Do not despair, for there is a power that will heal him. It is not far from you."

"Thank you, My Lady." Noraldeen pleaded, "But please, I beg of you not to delay. I fear for his life."

"The curse has no power in my dominion," replied the Lady of Eleeje. "He has been summoned."

"Summoned?" said Noraldeen. "I do not understand."

The Lady raised her right hand and said with a voice of command, "Ahiram, Seer of Power, stand up! You have been summoned." Ahiram opened his eyes, got up, and walked to the edge of the mountain. Noraldeen wanted to go after him, but the Lady stopped her. "No, daughter. He cannot see you. Watch."

A gray velvet cape richly ornamented with elegant symbols floated to the left of Ahiram. Beneath this cape, Ahiram saw tornadoes form above the clouds while volcanoes erupted below. Loud thunder boomed and lightning streaked the sea of clouds with ragged blasts of blinding light. At the extreme range of vision, he could detect a vast sea where waves of water rose with incredible speed and might to engulf the clouds and wash over the volcanoes. The volcanoes raged, spewing lava and brimstone. The wind, fierce and unrestrained, blew constantly. All about was chaos and unceasing destruction.

To his right, a light blue standard floated gently. It bore the Cup of Eleeje with twelve stars in its upper right corner. Ahiram, alert and well, saw a gentle meadow beneath the flag, where a millennial cedar tree rose. Under its shade sat a group of children. He saw a man and woman enter the meadow. They must have been in their fifties, but they walked like two mighty warriors who had seen many a battle.

They joined the children and sat among them. The man raised his right hand and began to speak. Judging by the way the children listened,

Ahiram understood the man was teaching them something, but what it was, he could not hear. The serene setting filled his heart with hope.

A voice, steely and jarring, spoke. It came from the gray velvet cape. "Who gives you the right to stand here, Sabael, guardian of the covenant? They broke the covenant. I claim the Seer as mine."

"Has he made a choice yet?" replied a second voice, quiet as the breeze, as commanding as cloud-covered mountaintops. It originated from the floating blue standard.

"An implacable curse owns him," snickered the first voice. "He is ours."

"The young maiden intercedes on his behalf."

"They broke the covenant," replied the first voice with a brooding anger. "She is forbidden from interceding."

"Her intercession is selfless love, and love is the fabric of the covenant."

The velvet gray cloak was violently thrown back. Ahiram followed until he could no longer see it. *Who are these voices and what were they talking about? Where am I?*

"Son of man, listen to my voice and what I am about to say to you," said the voice of Sabael. "You are here because Noraldeen's selfless love pleads for you. A test is set before you, a choice for you to make, to reveal your heart's desire. Consider what is being offered and choose wisely."

"What am I to choose?" asked Ahiram still confused.

"Much you will not understand, but this you will discover: the inner movements of your soul, and the dictates of your heart. This you shall see, and you must then choose for you, and you alone."

The gray cape returned with terrifying speed. It expanded to become a giant dragon. Its wings blotted the sky just left of Ahiram. The blue standard flashed brightly and sent out waves of light, which crashed against the dark wings. Lightning and thunder broke out in a violent tempest. Ahiram closed his eyes, and when he reopened them, the gray cape and the blue standard were back, floating to his left and right. *What's going on? Where am I?* He glanced back and now saw an empty meadow.

He could not see the Lady of Eleeje or the Unseen Tower. He could not see Noraldeen either. He was alone.

The two heralding standards moved closer to the waterfall.

"I am here to ask for what is rightfully mine," said the gray cape. "This miserable creature is mine and I intend to take him with me."

"Selfless love is the fabric of the covenant. Her voice must be heard," replied the blue standard.

Ahiram perceived that the two voices spoke to the waterfall, or to the being it represented.

A voice whose power penetrated to the depths of his soul spoke a plenary command, so absolute, no one could protest. "A choice is given him." No objection was possible, as if the wind and the sea suspended their activity and the entire cosmos was listening. *This must be El*, thought Ahiram and he collapsed face down.

"Come now, my dear," said the gray standard, "let me show you what I can give you if you follow me." The gray cape whisked Ahiram from the ground and took him away at great speed.

"Ahiram!" screamed Noraldeen. "Where are they taking him?"

"This is the choice he alone must make," said the Lady of Eleeje.

"That is not true," protested Noraldeen. "No one is ever alone if he has someone to love him. As long as I live, Ahiram will never be alone."

"Careful, daughter, words such as these in the presence of the steward of Eleeje have the weight of an oath."

"Then let it be an oath: as long as I live, Ahiram will never be alone."

"So be it," said the Lady of Eleeje. "It is done."

"You will conquer the earth and be its master." The voice of the gray standard confided to Ahiram. "I will make you a great and powerful king." Both Ahiram and Noraldeen heard the voice as if the unseen speaker stood next to each of them simultaneously. But Noraldeen knew the words were not addressed to her. They were meant for Ahiram.

He saw himself leading a powerful army. The sound of battle thrilled him; the conquest of cities and powerful fortresses enchanted him. His mightiest enemies fell under his sword. "You will be a god, and they will worship you." The gray mantle took him to the top of a great tower. He saw men bring down the statue of Baal and raise one of him instead. They bowed down and worshiped their new god. He now sat on a tall throne of meyroon set on five consecutive thrones of emerald, lapis lazuli, gold, silver, and cedar. Embedded above his head were four diamonds that surrounded one large pearl. His right hand wielded the scepter of justice and his left, the balance of life and death. People came from the four corners of the earth to venerate him and give him homage. His word was uncontested, and his will was obeyed.

"I will preserve your youth for one hundred years. You shall not suffer pain, sorrow, or disease. You shall have everything your heart desires," continued the voice in charming tones. Ahiram saw himself walk in a heavenly setting surrounded by women of breathtaking beauty, each one competing for his attention. He saw one hundred years of uninterrupted bliss. He wanted it, and he now knew he could have it.

"Your reign shall be one of justice and peace, and your name shall be exalted among the nations." Ahiram saw himself freeing slaves, defending the land, and ending wars. He saw a long line of mighty kings, all first-born sons that began with him. "Your dynasty shall be remembered as the greatest among the most powerful of the earth. All of this is yours and more, if you choose to come with me."

They were back on the platform. Ahiram felt impatient. He desired what the gray cape offered and he wanted it now. The gray cape appeared to be full of power and determination. In contrast, the blue standard looked feeble and ordinary.

"My Lord," said the voice behind the blue standard. "Would you not let the young woman speak?"

"No!" boomed the opposite voice, "they broke the covenant."

"<u>Man has broken covenant with the Lords of Light</u>," replied the quieter voice. "We cannot come to his aid as in the days of the First Covenant. Yet love is the fabric of the covenant. She should be allowed to speak to him."

"Ahiram," called Noraldeen as she strode to meet him. "Why do you want all of this?" she asked.

"Nora!" he exclaimed. "You are here."

She smiled. "Answer me, Ahiram. Why do you want this?"

"Don't you see, Nora? No more sickness, no disease, life forever."

"A life unloved, is the life of stones; it is the life of the living dead."

"But don't you see?" he protested, "There would be nothing to fear anymore. We could live in peace."

"What do you fear, my love?" she asked with a lamentable smile that broke his heart. She gazed at the waterfall. "You fear death," she said after a while, "the awful separation, and the dark silence when the beloved is no more, don't you? You fear death the way you fear being yanked violently away from your family. Instead, you are willing to turn life itself into a stony silence. Look," she said pointing to the waterfall. "No end, and no beginning. Don't you see, my Ahiram? This life is a shadow of things to come. To fear death is to fear love. Do you see this throne you long for so much? It has no memories, no children around it, no joy blooming in shouts of glory. It is not a throne, but the mausoleum of tyrants. I cannot live like that."

Ahiram did not understand everything Noraldeen had said, but he believed her. He dealt with facts; undeniable, verifiable facts. And his reasoning was simple: Noraldeen *was* beauty. Not just beautiful. She was beauty, and beauty was Noraldeen, and beauty was truth. He did not expect to understand the essence of beauty or truth, but once he made up his mind, all doubt vanished.

Does it make sense to trust someone this much? I trust Banimelek with my life, but I trust Noraldeen with the truth. Am I crazy? An image came back from his childhood; his sister Hoda holding him tight. *Yes, I do. If I don't, then Hoda is a lie, my whole life is a lie. Yet, I know as surely as the sea is the sea and the stars light up the heavens, that Hoda was not a lie. If she was truth, then so is Noraldeen. Even more so.*

Whatever truth Noraldeen saw—what he himself could not see—he now believed to be true. She was his moral compass, the trustworthy sure guide leading him home.

"Nora," he said softly. "Say it, and it will be enough for me. You do not want me on this throne?"

She looked at him tenderly and pointed to the cedar tree where the children had fallen asleep. "Do you see the grass beneath the cedar tree?" she asked softly. "It is a throne far more glorious than this. That is where I would rather see you. That is where you belong."

He smiled and relaxed. "What a fool I am. My sister would agree with you. This throne is not for me. I don't belong here."

"The choice is made," said the majestic voice behind the fall.

Ahiram crumpled and Noraldeen caught him before he hit the ground. The light around her began to dim.

"Daughter," said the Lady of Eleeje as a fog rose from the earth that surrounded them. "A guide is coming who will show you what you must do to break this curse."

"Who?" Noraldeen asked. "Who is coming?"

≻·❊·❊·≺

"Noraldeen, are you all right?"

The Silent opened her eyes with a start and saw Sheheluth standing over her. "Are you all right?" Sheheluth repeated.

"She found us," said Jedarc.

Sheheluth knelt down and touched Ahiram's forehead. "We must act quickly," she said. "Everyone, help us bring Ahiram inside. Quickly now."

Encouraged by her sense of purpose, they carried Ahiram back into the farmhouse. "Do you wish for Ahiram to live?" she asked.

"Of course," said Jedarc.

"Will you do everything in your power to help him?" she asked again.

"Why?" replied Hiyam. "What do you have in mind?"

"Time is running short. I come from a place where spells, curses, and magic run freely. I won't get into the details, so please do not ask me. I can see the curse around him. It's like a series of complicated knots, one on top of the other. The entire structure is complicated. It is constricting him and soon he will—"

"Die?" finished Noraldeen.

Sheheluth shook her head. "Curses like this one don't kill you … you become a shell, a wraith."

"So what should we do?" asked Banimelek, who preferred not to dwell on the news. "How can we help?"

"Normally we would undo the knots, one by one, but since time is running out we will have to burn them, so to speak."

Hiyam gasped. "Burn the curse? It cannot be done." Hiyam said.

Sheheluth gave her a reassuring smile. "Ordinarily, you are right because when you try to burn a curse, especially one as complicated as this one, you may kill the victim. In this case, we have a fighting chance because he possesses something very, very powerful. My plan is to nudge this power and cause it to burn the curse."

"What will happen if you fail?"

Sheheluth shrugged her shoulders. "We all may die, or be sent to the Vanishing Land, or we may stand here and watch him fade away."

They all glanced at each other.

"You don't have to do it," said Noraldeen. "I will. I am strong enough."

Sheheluth shook her head vehemently. "No, you can't do by yourself. There aren't even enough of us to do it right, and everyone must agree."

"We're all in, Sheheluth. Tell us what we must do," said Jedarc.

"Let's start," urged Banimelek.

Sheheluth looked at Hiyam who came and stood by Jedarc. *You're the only who understands magic*, she seemed to say, *are you ready for this?* Hiyam smiled and nodded. The young Silent nodded in return. "Everyone turn your back to me, close your eyes and keep them shut until I tell you." They turned their backs to her. She inhaled sharply, vanished for an instant and reappeared calm and refreshed. "All right, you can turn back now. Banimelek," she ordered in a softer voice, "please sit on the floor next to Ahiram." With her dagger she cut the outline of a wide circle into the stone floor. She waved her finger over the circle and the stone collapsed as it turned into dust. The others gasped. Sheheluth smiled. "Any child in my hometown can do this. Commander Tanios forbade me from using my skills, but I don't think he would object now. Noraldeen, remove your shoes and stand in the circle." Next, Sheheluth asked Jedarc to stand by the window and finally, for Hiyam to stand next to the fireplace. "Add another log to the fire," she added.

"But he's burning up," protested Noraldeen.

"I know," Sheheluth replied. "Either we succeed, or he is gone."

She opened one of her Silent-equipped belt pockets and removed five smooth white stones. She gave one to each of them. "Hold this stone in your fist and do not let go. You will feel a burning sensation in your hand, as if your flesh is on fire, but this is just a sensation. Your hand will be fine. Now, clasp the stone tightly, and do not let go."

"We got that," Banimelek snapped. "What next?"

"Stay where you are. You may be a bit surprised, but do not move."

Sheheluth removed her shoes and sat behind Ahiram's head. She placed both hands over his heart, closed her eyes and said, *Enteraka!* which meant, let it flow.

At first, nothing happened. Then Hiyam screamed. Flames from the burning logs behind her had slithered out of the hearth and now climbed along her leg.

"You are not on fire," said Sheheluth. "Remain calm. All is well."

Banimelek nearly panicked when he felt his limbs turn to stone. They were so heavy he could not move them. Jedarc found himself floating in the air and hooted. Noraldeen remained calm and collected even when roots shot up from the ground and ran along her arm until they reached her fist, the one gripping the stone.

Sheheluth breathed deeply. "Good. Everything is in place. Now, we must hope that what we are about to do will wake the magic in Ahiram. I want each of you to keep your eyes shut and think of a reason—the one reason— why you want him to live. Banish every other thought from your mind. Close your eyes now." She made sure they obeyed before vanishing for another quick moment. She reappeared and continued with an imperious tone. "Are you ready? Focus on the most important reason you want Ahiram to live."

"Yes," said Jedarc. "Because he is my friend."

"Because I owe him a debt of gratitude," said Hiyam softly.

"Because he has to defeat the urkuun," added Banimelek.

"Because I love him," said Noraldeen.

"Very good. Different reasons. Different motives. Very, very good. Now, no matter what, no matter how horrible you feel, keep your eyes closed and focus on your reason. Above all, do not let go of your stone."

A drowning sensation came over each of them. Hiyam felt as though fire was coursing down her throat and she grasped her neck with her free hand. Coughing sputtered from Banimelek, who thought he was swallowing dirt. Jedarc gasped with the sensation that he was suffocating under a windblast so strong it would not let him breathe. Noraldeen hallucinated that she was turning into grass.

"Stay focused. Ignore the sensations. Focus on your reason to see Ahiram through." Sheheluth's voice rang strong and clear, but it was unsettling. It sounded like the voice of a very old woman.

Abruptly, the strange sensation was gone and replaced by a very real burning feeling in their hands. Hiyam nearly dropped the stone but managed to keep her hand closed at the last moment.

"The feeling is real, but the burning is not." Sheheluth's voice was a whisper; a dreamy, faraway whisper.

How long did the burning sensation last? No one could tell. The suffering was intense, and the desire to drop the stone was overwhelming. "A bit longer," said Sheheluth. "Just a little bit more. Now, release the stone! Drop it now!"

They followed her order and opened their eyes. Hiyam, Jedarc, and Noraldeen collapsed onto the floor. They were weary, drained beyond anything they could have imagined before. "The weakness will fade soon," said Sheheluth, exhausted herself. Slowly, she got up. "Now, everyone out. We need to leave now."

She went around and helped each of them to stand. "Quickly now, we do not have much time."

"Why?" asked Noraldeen, breathless. "What is happening?"

"His power is awakened. I can see it but you cannot. It is about to burn the curse. We cannot stay here."

She forced everyone out of the farm and urged them to mount their steeds. "Gallop away, quickly now."

Sheheluth nudged her own horse, and as it fled, the other horses followed. Though dazed, Hiyam wondered what she smelled. *Something is burning*, she thought.

"Look!" snapped Jedarc. "Look at the ground."

Hiyam gasped. She gripped the reins and screamed. Everything around them, as far as they could see, was crumbling. The meadows, the trees, and every living thing was turning into ash before their very eyes.

Sheheluth slowed her horse, came to a full stop, and turned around. "We can watch from here." She said.

"What happened?" asked Hiyam. "What is this destruction?"

Sheheluth shrugged her shoulders. "You want him alive?" she asked. "This curse he's under is mighty. It takes a lot of energy to get the power he is holding to react." With her chin, she pointed to the farm. "Now—

"What's that?" wondered Banimelek, bewildered. "What's that light?"

A blinding arc shone from inside the farm and grew into a sphere that swallowed the entire building.

"Is Ahiram safe? What have we done?" asked Noraldeen.

"We have awakened his power," said Sheheluth.

The sphere continued to grow until it became ten times bigger than the farm. Then suddenly, it vanished.

"Is that it?" asked Banimelek. "Is it over?"

"Let's go back," said Jedarc, prodding his horse.

"Don't move," snapped Sheheluth without taking her eyes from the farm. "It begins now."

The walls of the farm exploded in a tempest of flying stone. Instinctively, Hiyam placed a protective arm in front of her face, but from the chest of Ahiram, who was still lying unconscious, a gray flame burst free in a strident shriek and drew the rocks back, shattering them in the process. Fueled by the matter it had just consumed, it grew in strength and girth until it dwarfed the tallest of trees. A second flame, bright as the sun, came forth from the Silent's side and the tongues of unnatural fire fought viciously, like two serpents vying for the same territory.

"Ahiram, please," whispered Noraldeen. "Please live!"

As if on cue, the bright flame surged past the gray one and swallowed it. The friends cheered, not knowing why they were cheering. The bright flame went out and dust progressively settled.

"Is it done?" asked Jedarc hopeful. "Is he alive?"

"Let's go and find out," said Sheheluth.

"Sylveeds. They are coming this way," whispered Tanios as he quickly drew back into the tunnel.

They had finally reached one of the main passages that led to the heart of the fortress. This was their first contact with the enemy.

"There is no point in hiding," whispered Bahiya. "The urkuun must have detected our presence by now."

"What do you suggest we do?"

"I suggest you go back and let me continue alone," said Bahiya. "You cannot help me in what I am about to do now."

"This we shall see," replied Tanios. "There is no turning back. We're in this together."

"Death is certain, Tanios." She was pleading with him even though she knew he would not change his mind.

"We do what we must. Let's go and face him."

"When we get there, stay behind me. I want you to promise that under no circumstance will you look at the urkuun. It will mesmerize you, and you will be lured into becoming one of them." Bahiya pointed toward the direction of the sylveeds.

"Very well," said Tanios.

"Good. Keep your focus on my left hand. Ignore everything else. When you see me wave my left hand back and forth, run, and do not look back. I will take care of the rest."

"Fine," replied Tanios as he stepped out of the room. *I may not know anything about magic, but rest assured, my dear Bahiya, I have a little surprise for this urkuun, one he may not be expecting.*

They resumed their descent until they reached one of the lower levels. Stepping off the staircase, they barely walked a few feet when a sylveed spotted them. Immediately, a threatening horde carrying spears and swords swarmed around them. They stood motionless until the movement subsided. Tanios could tell the sylveeds were ready for war. They filled the caves with continuous motion. Throngs of the creatures passed them on their way to the surface.

"Take us to your master. We wish to speak with him," said Bahiya in a commanding tone.

There was a hush in the ranks. One sylveed came closer.

"Master is strong. No one stronger than Master. You want join us?"

"Yes," replied Bahiya. "We recognize the strength of the master and we wish to join you."

"Fine. We take you to Master. If Master wants, you join. If Master does not want, you die."

The sylveed yelled some orders. Soldiers escorted them down a large corridor. The walls of the passageway oozed a foamy green substance, which turned the stone into gelatinous puddles that reeked of decay. *If these poor creatures are willing to endure this ordeal, then the urkuun must indeed be powerful*, thought Tanios.

Bahiya knew the urkuun would try to entice her to join him, to side with him, and to swear an oath of servitude to him. *The fortress is in worse condition than I expected. This is going to make things a little bit easier.* She counted on the monster's self-confidence to act. *Today, we shall see what happens when concentrators and orbs meet.*

➢ ⚬⚬⚬ ➣

Orwutt and Zurwott crept cautiously out of their hiding place. The urkuun's servants had hung tapestries on the wall and unrolled a thick lush carpet in the center. They had set a table and lit a dozen torches. Smells of roasted meat reached them and increased their suffering. A full legion of sylveeds stood along the walls and wore hoods that shielded them from the bright light. The twin brothers felt a cold, terrifying presence straight below them but could not see who it was coming from.

"Does your state of prepared preparedness match my readied readiness?" whispered Zurwott. "Will you be willing to actively act in the utmost certain certitude, and certitude so certain it is without a doubting doubt indubitably indubitable?"

Orwutt responded quietly, "Indubitable most indubitably. We need to conclusively conclude and terminally terminate this pugnaciously pugnacious terrorizing terror. I must admittedly admit that the ceiling must fall on the grounded ground below and not the other way around."

"The successful failing of the roof will meaningfully mean, and mean most meaningfully, that those beneath the falling roof will unfailingly fail to rise and will, without fail, fail to responsibly respond to a summons."

"Indeed, my brother, indeed. They will be dead."

"How uncouth, my brother," protested Zurwott. "It would be most appropriately appropriate to say that some who were short shall be tall, and those who were incongruously fat in incongruous areas, shall be slimmed down to the point of exaggerated thinness."

"Apt descriptive description, my brother."

"This is one link in the chain of causality that neither us who are above nor those who are beneath can escape. It must come to pass." Zurwott spoke as closely as possible to the common tongue as was allowed by dwarfish propriety.

"And if the falling fall does not stop the terrorizing terror below?" whispered Orwutt.

"Then it may bruise it sufficiently, and sufficiently bruise it to weaken its strength and strengthen its weaknesses, so that someone else can put an effectively effective ending end to it."

"When faced with the possibly possible, do the impossible …" started Orwutt, with a forced grin.

Zurwott completed the worn-out but well-known dwarfish proverb, "…And when faced with the impossibly impossible, do the possible."

"This suggests that our successful success is plausibly plausible."

"Not only is it plausibly plausible and plausible most plausibly, but I would also say that it is possibly possible."

A cohort of sylveeds silently crept into the room. The two dwarfs nearly gasped when they saw Tanios and Bahiya walking among them. The sylveeds bowed and joined the legion on the side of the temple. Bahiya and Tanios bowed.

"We have come to do you homage," said Bahiya as she struggled to control the tone of her voice. It was too joyful to her taste. She looked at Tanios furtively and saw that he was looking down. *He must be feeling it more than I*, she thought.

"Did my hearing hear what I think I hurriedly heard?" asked Orwutt.

"My eyeing eyes saw what your hearing heard," replied Zurwott. "Two of our great ones are giving in to treason. This should not be."

"Now is the time to act," said Orwutt.

The urkuun took Tanios by surprise. The commander expected the beast to terrify him, but instead, he was pleasantly surprised and relieved to feel the warm friendly atmosphere that now surrounded them. He wondered why they had decided to fight the urkuun, who struck him as a caring, harmless being. He was about to look up when he remembered the promise he had made to Bahiya and his iron-fisted discipline prevented him from breaking his promise. Bahiya was barely able to keep her focus in check. *I won't be able to wait much longer*, she thought. Keeping her eyes on the beast, in her peripheral vision she saw the concentrators and orbs fly mere inches below the ceiling. *Good, he has not noticed yet.* She had released them on the way and kept them hidden from view high overhead. When they stepped inside the temple, she saw them dash along the walls of the circular room. By nature, concentrators held the magical fuel needed to ignite orbs. *A little longer and the concentrators should be ready*, thought Bahiya. Priests used their bodies to transform the energy stored in the concentrators into an energy suitable for the orbs. If an activated concentrator and an orb touched, they would cause a massive explosion, provoke a rift in reality, and therefore, lead to an Arayat spillover into the real world. The power of the explosion was magnified tenfold when two concentrators and two orbs were used, which is what Bahiya was about to do. She knew the blast would level the fortress and annihilate most of the sylveeds. She also knew that neither she nor Tanios would be able to survive. *If the urkuun tries to smother the explosion, I have another surprise waiting for him.* Her breathing quickened, and beads of sweat covered her forehead. The urkuun focused on her while keeping Tanios under his control.

He is wounded. Bahiya was shocked. A white substance oozed from the monster's side. *Someone wounded the urkuun.* She was exhilarated. *That explains why he did not attack earlier. Who could have done this?*

Powerful images rushed at her, images of glory, might, and dominion. She pushed them away by an act of will and focused on the concentrators and the orbs. The images came back relentlessly, tempting, tantalizing, and surrounded her from all sides. They were in her own mind at first, but soon, they crept into her senses. They became visual hallucinations; first blurry, and then all at once in clear, full color. Bahiya could no longer resist, and the urkuun whisked her into a world of light and glory to a makeshift illusion inside of the Arayat. At the last moment, she managed to pull her magical artifacts with her into this Arayatian illusion. Since these objects were created inside the Arayat, they were easier to control here than in the real world. *The concentrators are not yet ready.* Bahiya knew she had to somehow stall the assault.

She was now the greatest priestess Baal had ever known: Bahiya the Mighty. In every city, loyal subjects placed her effigy in their temples. Everywhere she looked, she saw her glory made manifest in the lives of the multitudes. She had become a goddess to them. Thousands of slaves had built a seven-storied temple of jasper, topaz, and onyx with three gold cupolas and fourteen silver ornate doors, all in her honor. The priestess stood on an esplanade flanked by giant torches that proclaimed her eternal reign, and a great multitude filled a capacious marble plaza in front of her temple. *The concentrators, they are almost ready,* she thought breathless. *I must keep them in orbit.* She waved at the throng of people and knew that she was the cause of their joy. An evildoer had been desecrating the kingdoms of the earth and many heroes had risen and died trying to stop him. They had all failed. Only her might and wisdom could stop his tyranny. With one imperial move, she struck him down and forced him to kneel before her, bound in heavy iron chains.

Bahiya had only to drop her handkerchief, and the executioner's sword would end the life of the miserable creature that dared to challenge her reign of peace and justice. He awaited her signal. She looked contemptuously at the malfeasant and was about to let go of her handkerchief when he raised his head and looked at her. His eyes were full of sorrow as if asking, "Why?" She gasped. The creature was no other than Ahiram. "No," screamed Bahiya. She was thrown out of the hallucination and was now back in the room of the fortress. At that very moment, however, the urkuun became aware of her secret relationship with Ahiram. *At last! The concentrators are ready*, she thought. Immediately, she released them from her control, grabbed Tanios and they both dropped to the ground.

The concentrators hurtled toward the orbs and the four devices collided in a decimating explosion. A blinding light filled the expansive cave, leveling the pillars and pulverizing the dining table. A wave of fire erased the carpet the way a wave on the beach washes away footprints. Oddly, a platter of meat flew up and landed intact before the two dumbfounded dwarfs. The Arayatian energy Bahiya had just released shattered reality. The ground reeled and sundered as a massive fungus sprouted, and turned to stone. The fortress' ground crumbled to dust, and from this dust, a pool of dark water emerged threatening to swallow Tanios and Bahiya. Climbing vines quickly crept from the waters and covered anything that was left standing, killing any sylveeds who had not managed to escape. Half the walls boiled and became lava, while the other half froze under thick ice. Lightning and thunder filled the air. Tanios and Bahiya were thrown out of the pool, and its water instantly evaporated. A subterranean force sucked in the temple's floor and walls crumbled.

The urkuun, clapped his hands and sneered, "Did you not know priestess that your cheap tricks have no effect on creatures of the Pit?"

The orbs and concentrators appeared before him. With a flick of his hand, he neutralized Bahiya's attack. The climbing vines, lava, and ice all vanished, and the storm was over as suddenly as it had started.

He took the bait, she thought.

My turn, thought Tanios. He quickly produced two crossbows, drew the darts, aimed and released. To pull attention away from the darts, he shouted as he released them, "May El rebuke you, we humbly pray." To the commander's surprise, the urkuun reeled under an invisible blow.

"Say this little prayer when you see the monster, Commander," Master Habael had instructed. "Do it for me."

There you go old friend, thought Tanios. *I did what you asked and delivered a small gift, courtesy of the Silent Corps.*

The wall behind the urkuun exploded.

Perfect timing, Tanios, thought Bahiya. *You prevented the urkuun from destroying the concentrators. Well done.*

Tanios grabbed her hand and they bolted toward the exit. They were about to exit the cave when the urkuun bellowed and both of them fell in sheer terror. They managed to look back and saw a gray light flowing from the concentrators into the creature's chest. The monster wailed with pain and struggled to free itself.

"What is going on?" yelled Tanios.

Bahiya smiled. "The best way to fight an urkuun is with an urkuun."

The last time she had used these concentrators, the monster had attacked Hiyam in the Game of Gold, and she had asked Tamri, the Adorant, for help. Neither of them had realized they were contending with an urkuun. Back then, Tamri had used eight absorbers to deflect the attack, but the energy had been too much to bear. Desperately, Bahiya had directed the overflow of energy back into the concentrators and unwittingly charged them with the creature's own power.

"To stop my magic," she explained, "he absorbed the explosion. The concentrators are blind objects. Once energy flows out of them, it is impossible to stop it, so the concentrators are tearing through his insides."

"Can you breezily breathe my brotherly brother?" whispered Zurwott.

Orwutt nodded his head. He could not speak. The last few moments had been horrific beyond any measure, but something had changed and the hold of the beast on their consciousness weakened. "As they say in the common tongue," added Zurwott, "It is now or not now."

"You mean, now or never, my brotherly brother," corrected Orwutt. "Let us be done with this maddening madness."

The urkuun staggered forward but managed to remain standing. *We must force him out of the fortress*, thought Tanios, *but how?* In the eerie silence they heard a heavy iron chain slide off of metallic rings.

Am I terrified? Or am I going mad? Tanios wondered. Then he heard the awful moan of stone under unbearable pressure, and he glanced up just as the marble ceiling began to cave in. The stone columns that suspended the enormous marble slabs could not keep them in place without the chains. Mustering all his will and strength, Tanios leaped to his feet and grabbed Bahiya. Together, they staggered out of the hall and took shelter behind a large column when the ceiling collapsed and crashed to the floor. Stone shards showered the room in a deadly blast. The walls of the cave, weakened from Bahiya's magic and Tanios' explosive darts, could no longer resist. They fractured. The urkuun shrieked in rage. The walls exploded, creating a chain reaction. Multiple caves were leveled, entombing legions of sylveeds. The outer walls of the fortress severed and crumbled. A huge gaping hole exposed the inside of the fortress like a wound in the side of a giant beast.

Orwutt hung in midair by a rope and Zurwott held onto his brother's feet. Without waiting for the rope to stop swinging, Zurwott climbed over his brother, reached the rope, and continued to climb as quickly as possible. Orwutt followed him inside the small cave and they inched their way forward, back into the tunnel. Debris partially blocked it, but the dwarfs managed to snake their way through. They heard and felt a powerful explosion come from the larger cave. They heard but did not see the urkuun, wings deployed, crawl out from underneath the rubble with a deafening roar and dive outside.

Now, the battle begins, thought Orwutt. *A battle someone else must win.*

29. Sylveedian Pool

"Words are like dead leaves that wither and are forgotten; they are inadequate to describe the supernal depth of human love. Deeds speak plainly. They lodge themselves firmly in our hearts and bear fruit aplenty: undying hope and treasures of beauty."
—Memoirs of Shalimar the Poet.

After Tanios and Bahiya left camp in the company of the Silent, Lord Orgond staggered his men on the northeastern hillsides directly opposite from the Fortress of Hardeen. They spent the next two days fortifying their camp across this plain. Large ditches  were dug and lined with rows of protective spikes long enough to break the stride of a galloping horse. The soldiers toiled without rest despite the fetid smell rising from the charred remnants of homes and barns that littered the landscape.

On the morning of the third day, Lord Orgond took counsel with Master Habael, Master Xurgon, and Uziguzi to review the situation.

"Something troubles me," confessed Uziguzi. "If I were the urkuun, what would compel me to attack now?"

Xurgon nodded approvingly. "I would not movingly move my forces unless my foe was within view."

"Ahiram, you mean?"

Uziguzi disagreed. "The ninth urkuun is called the Seducer because he trusts his own power above all else. He favors submission and adulation over the clanging of weapons and shouts of war."

Addressing Uziguzi by his formal title, Master Habael added, "Wise assessment indeed, Lord Jar. I expect an envoy from our foe to come with a formal offer of capitulation. Having you, Lord Orgond, submit willingly to the monster would redound on his conflated sense of honor."

Lord Orgond agreed. "It is one thing if Orgond, Lord of Hardeen and Steward of the Broken Sheath of El-Windeer, bows down before the urkuun, and quite another if Gaëla, Heiress to the throne of the Empyreans, submits to the monster of Baal, don't you think?"

They nodded in agreement. "I can see the hand of Sharr in this matter," commented Uziguzi. "I knew him even before he joined the Temple, and he has not wavered from the path he chose to follow after the death of his sister. Back then he was a captain of the High Riders stationed in Mycene, and he had quite foolishly provoked the ire of the Empyreans by setting foot on their beach with three thousand soldiers. Because of his pride he thought the Empyreans would negotiate first. Tragically, he miscalculated and saw his forces mowed down. He managed to escape with less than one hundred soldiers. His twin sister died at the hands of the Empyreans, and he has never forgiven them. This would be a fitting way to avenge her and may help explain why he would unleash such a monster."

"Insightful Empyrean advising advisor," replied Master Xurgon. "We dwarfs have had our daring dealings with the Empyreans, but only a foolish fool would cross over to their land and expect to survive."

"Foolish, indeed," added Master Habael, "and if the hand of Sharr is behind this, we must remain vigilant. He has a keen mind and tend to think several steps ahead of the rest."

"When should we expect the Empyrean forces?" asked Lord Orgond. "Princess Gaëla left us a few days back. I expected her to be here by now."

"Indeed," sighed Uziguzi.

"Her delay is concerning me. I will fear the worst if she is not back here by tomorrow."

Orgond rose to his feet and grabbed his helmet. "Well then, I had better join my soldiers. The children of Tanniin will do all in their power so that in days ahead, the name of Amsheet remains a beacon of hope and not a source of shame."

The urkuun stood by the sylveedian pool, a wide hole where the waters of the Arayat bubbled and flowed. He used the caliginous water to accelerate the transformation of his victims into sylveeds. The monster's features were accentuated in the fluorescent green light seeping from the pool, and the sylveeds around him cowered in fear. They hid in the darkest corners of the wide cave, deep below the fortress' complex. A lone figure emerged from the pool. Unafraid, Sharr stepped out of the murky green liquid and faced the creature of the Pit.

"What does the master of Baal command?" asked the urkuun in a soft sultry voice that betrayed no emotions.

Sharr waved his hand with an annoyed expression. "Do not mock me, creature," he snarled. "I am not one to be toyed with."

"Far be it for the Seducer to toy with the master of Baal," replied the beast. "To what do I owe the honor of your visit?"

"How many sylveeds have you produced?"

The urkuun was bound to speak the truth since the curses Sureï the Sorcerer had used to shackle the urkuun forced the beast to obey the current high priest of Babylon. "Twenty thousand strong."

"That many?" replied Sharr, surprised. "How did you do it?"

"Humans, dwarfs, and Empyreans expose their vices the way dung is exposed by its smell. They come to me faster than I can transform them. You think it is too many? I think it is too little. Once I leave these walls,

I will show you the true meaning of power."

"You will bind and deliver the Seer to me, unharmed. Then, you will defeat the Empyreans and you will bring me the head of their empress on a platter." The urkuun chuckled, producing a sound similar to the screech that iron sheered by iron produces: strident, loud, and mind numbing. Witnessing this sound coming from the mouth of the urkuun, Sharr smiled while anyone else would have screamed. He raised his left hand and gestured rapidly. With a moan of pain, the urkuun bent one knee. "I am happy to know that my command amuses you, but do not forget to whom you owe obedience. Stray from my orders and I will show you the real strength of the curses Sureï used to bind you. You may be of the Pit, but the Temple *rules* the Pit."

By the time the urkuun straightened his posture, the sylveedian pool was as still as a dead man's face. Sharr was nowhere to be seen.

➤·◦·◦·◦·◦·◾

Ahiram pushed his horse faster. He was eager to get to Hardeen. The life of many hung at the edge of his sword and every minute he delayed was counted in blood. He knew what he had to do and he was ready. Noraldeen was saddled behind him, her hands around the waist of the man she loved. Like the others, she was taken aback when they had found him sleeping peacefully after the two giant flames that sprang from his chest had vanished.

"What are you doing in my room?" he had asked, visibly confused. "Is breakfast ready?"

Noraldeen had helped him up and hugged him fiercely. He held her against him. The others left them alone.

"Ahiram, I am so sorry," she said. "I should not have told you about your family, not like that. Please forgive me."

He pulled her gently away and gazed in her eyes, a wry smile on his face. "I want to thank you for telling me." Noraldeen took a breath to speak. "No, let me finish. It was devastating, the worst thing I have ever heard, but when Sheheluth told me I was a sormoss—"

"Yes, you told me already."

"She is right you know. When I'm angry, I think it is my right to attack, like when I attacked Olothe."

Noraldeen bristled at the name. "He deserved his punishment."

Ahiram shook his head. "No, Nora. That was no punishment. What I did to him was evil. I was angry and believed I had the right to break him. When Sheheluth told me what I was, it tormented me. Well, I was already worried even before she told me."

"Worried? Worried about what?"

He averted her eyes.

"About hurting you. I was afraid that in one of my fits of anger, I would strike you. Then you told me about my parents. The news hit me like a giant fist. My anger flared, but then … just then, I knew that no matter how angry I become, I would never hurt you."

"So, you conquered your anger?"

Ahiram shook his head. "No, Nora. You did. I had this dream, this strange, powerful dream, something about a choice. I don't remember all the details, but I do remember the end. I chose what you wanted because I trust you more than I trust myself."

She looked at him tenderly. "So what are you saying then?"

"I don't know what the future holds, I don't know if I will survive this beast. All I know is that I am happy, so very happy because I met you, Noraldeen, daughter of Lord Orgond. I don't want to lose you … ever."

"And you won't. I will always be by your side."

Ahiram was fully healed. And he now felt rejuvenated and strengthened. As they watched him eat ravenously, his friends felt overjoyed and awed, hopeful and fearful, the way mariners feel aboard a ship cresting a storm—fleeting atop a giant wave between the howling maw of a vengeful sea and the dark furies of an implacable sky.

Wrath of the Urkuun – Sylveedian Pool

He ate and laughed at them, as if he himself belonged to that great storm that toyed with the ship of their hopes. Or rather, as if *he were* that storm, surging forward to conquer their fear to show them a world they had never dared to imagine.

As they moved swiftly forward to Hardeen, toward the battle, Ahiram coaxed his horse with the vulpine impatience of a lion on a blood trail.

They looked like they were watching a ghost, and he made fun of them. It was unbelievable to see him sitting and talking among them, and then to declare he was anxious to get to Hardeen. Yet there they were, moving swiftly toward the fortress, toward the battlefront. Unlike the others, Noraldeen stopped questioning, stopped trying to find answers. She had been witness to Ahiram's choice, and now she too had a choice to make. She had thought him dead, yet he was alive. She knew he was the holder of a hidden power, but she also knew that her love for him was an even greater force, one that would embolden him to fight until the end. She closed her eyes and savored the moment. An old song came to her mind and she wondered why this particular song, one that spoke of separation and forgetfulness, came to her.

> I sing your name, O my love, in everlasting song.
> You write my name, O my love, on the seashore sand,
> And when waves will carry you to where you belong,
> I alone shall fade away in the misty land.
> I alone shall fade away in the misty land.

> And tomorrow, when the rain
> Will carry softly my name along,
> Only your name shall remain
> In everlasting song.
> Only your name shall remain
> In everlasting song.

They rode while there was light, then climbed the easternmost slopes of the Mayorian Chain and set up camp in a small nook hidden from prying eyes. Ahiram spoke with Sheheluth, then told his friends he needed to train with his weapons and left them for the rest of the night.

"Won't you need our help?" asked Noraldeen.

Ahiram shook his head. "I need to train alone. There are a few things I still need to learn to control."

They were exhausted and quickly fell asleep. Banimelek took the first watch, and Ahiram had still not returned when Noraldeen took the last watch of the night. She regarded the stars lacing the night sky like joyful children dancing in the heavens. She was delighted to be with her friends and the man she wanted to be with. Another song came to her from her childhood.

> Up where the lilies shine in the starry night,
> Where the moon embraces the snow peaks tenderly,
> A bench, a lonely bench, where you used to hold me
> With eyes shining brighter than the lilies of the stars.
>
> I walked by the lilies, the lilies of the stars,
> Walked by our bench where you comforted me.
> Two children holding lilies stole so tenderly,
> the bench of starry lilies where we so loved to sit.
>
> O fleeting lilies, happy days so long past,
> Come back to me, O please do come back.
> And bring, won't you? The love of my heart
> On the starry bench beneath our peaceful skies.
>
> Behind the bench, a quiet cabin with an open door.
> Inside, a candle on an empty table wiped clean.
> All those long gone who will not be.
>
> I sat on that bench and waited for you,
> Waited like a river that longs for the sea.
> Nothing came to me except the dead leaves;
> Tears of the forlorn tree.
> Shadows of the faithful departed.

Wrath of the Urkuun – Sylveedian Pool

O fleeting lilies, happy days so long past,
Come back to me, O please do come back.
And bring, won't you? The love of my heart
To the starry bench beneath our peaceful skies.

Now I walk alone, the bench is no more.
Pray tell where are the children who sat after me?
They are gone like a forest in winter,
In snow, and shadow, and mist,
Beyond the river and the years.
Fleeting like the wings of migrants,
They slowly drift, the years do not return
Alone, the bench, the lonely cabin, and mist.

O fleeting lilies, happy days so long past,
Come back to me, O please do come back.
And bring, won't you? The love of my heart
To the starry bench beneath our peaceful skies.

Noraldeen thought of Ahiram, and she smiled contentedly. *At least no one can take these days from me.*

When dawn came, Ahiram returned. Quietly working side by side, he helped Noraldeen start a small fire and then woke up the others. After a frugal breakfast, while their friends readied the horses, Ahiram took Noraldeen aside and walked with her until they reached a clearing by a weatherworn boulder, in clear view of the snow-covered peaks.

"We are going into battle," he said quietly, purposefully. "I don't know if we will survive what we are about to face, so just in case I don't, I want to thank you for all you have done for me. Not just now, but all through the six years we've lived together, trained together, and learned everything together. You've always been there for me. That gives me courage." He fixed his gaze on her. "There is one thing I want you to do for me."

"What is it Ahiram?" she asked with tenderness. In the morning dawn, she looked like an ethereal maiden, filled with light, pure, beyond mortal reach.

"Stand down," he said in a guarded tone, for he knew he was asking her to betray the code of the Silent. "Do not …" his voice faltered under the strain of emotion, "do not expose yourself to danger. Please."

"Ahiram," she said, deeply touched, "you are going to face the greatest danger and you are asking *me* to stand down?"

"It's not the same thing," protested Ahiram strongly. Though his temper flared, he was controlled and resolute. "*I* have no choice. No one else can fight this monster."

"And if you did have a choice. If it were I who had to fight instead of you," she replied with her usual disarming smile, "What would you do?"

"This is not about me," he said. "This is about—"

"What?" she cut in. "What is it about, Ahiram?"

He lowered his gaze and bit his lower lip. He was shaken and upset. "See this boulder?" he said after a while. "See how worn out and gray it is? Now, do you see the snow on the summit of those mountains? How brisk and beautiful it glitters under the rays of the sun? This old boulder would rejoice if it could turn to dust and lie on the mountaintops to protect the falling snow. And the snow, high on these mountains, looks up to the sun, the blue of the sky, wanting to soar in the glory of the day. This is how things are meant to be," he added, looking at Noraldeen. "It is the fate of a slave to die for a princess, not—"

"Not the other way around," she completed. "Yet, my sweet Ahiram, has it occurred to you that the pure white snow, when spring comes, melts with joy at the thought of the life it will nourish? The snow might look to the sun and the sky with longing, but it knows that its fate is not to fly with the eagles, but to nourish the land so that we may celebrate new life." She pointed to an old nest Ahiram had not noticed on the boulder. "Life on old boulders, like this one."

"Noraldeen, please." said Ahiram choking under the emotions. "I don't know what I would do if something should happen to you."

"You would go on, Ahiram," she asserted. "You will carry this fight to its end. You would carry me in your heart, and should anything happen to me, know that I will never leave you. I will always be with you. No matter what happens, I want you to know that what I choose to do, I choose to do it freely. So you see, my Ahiram, you would give your life for me, and I would do the same for you. In this, at least, we are together."

Ahiram grabbed Noraldeen and held her tightly against him. She held him closely and felt him tremble. She knew he was sobbing.

Soon after they returned to camp, they were all on their way to the Fortress of Hardeen. If any of their friends noticed how solemn Ahiram was, they did not ask any questions; none were needed. This was the last leg of their journey, the last moments before the dreaded confrontation. Now, their thoughts turned toward the battle, toward those who would be waiting for them. Would they find anyone alive when they reached Hardeen, or would the urkuun and his legions have devoured the land? Would they find their beloveds alive, or worse, turned into sylveeds, into unrecognizable foes whom they would have to battle? And beyond all this, beyond their personal worries, would Ahiram be able to defeat the powerful urkuun? Even though they did not have answers to these questions, they rode forward, hoping against hope that they would live to see another day, another glorious sunrise.

Dusk fell on the plain of Iliand, bringing with it heavy clouds that tossed and turned in a dark sky like insomniac sailors before the onset of a storm. The western tip of the plain was deserted, save for a fitful wind that darted here and there as if a pack of mad skunks were ferreting the charred ground for who-knows-what. Wafts of decay and decomposition traversed the military camp of Lord Orgond, leading soldiers to believe that ghosts wrapped in the smell of death had come to torment them.

The trenches were complete and the camp was in order. Uziguzi stood with sentinels peering over the plain toward the edge of the western forest, beyond which lay the lands of the Empyrean. He was anxiously awaiting the arrival of Gaëla and her forces. *This respite has allowed the men of Orgond to rest and prepare. But they are not battle-ready, not like the Empyreans. What is keeping the princess, I wonder?*

A sentry signaled an archer standing behind them and a fiery arrow flew overhead toward the plain below. Uziguzi followed the yellow streak and gave a start. A short distance outside the range of the arrow, four hooded figures waited while a fifth was on approach. Immediately, archers advanced, ready to let their arrows fly. The enigmatic figure drew near the camp and dropped its hood.

"It is a sylveed," whispered one of the sentinels.

"Find out what it wants," directed Uziguzi.

A short moment later, Uziguzi informed Lord Orgond that the urkuun had sent an emissary for a parley. After consulting Masters Xurgon and Habael, he sent a small delegation to find out more.

"Most likely a trap," surmised Uziguzi while they waited for the exchange to end. Down below on the plain, Captain Enryl, his herald bearer, and three other captains stood facing the sylveed.

"It looks like they are done," Master Habael pointed out.

Enryl and his men walked back up to camp, and Enryl joined Lord Orgond and the others in his tent.

"The urkuun offers us peace if we submit to him."

Lord Orgond gave a start. "He wants to turn us into sylveeds?"

Enryl shook his head. "No, he promises not to do us harm if we submit to him."

"To whom is his offer directed?" asked Orgond.

"To you, Lord," said Enryl.

"How long do we have to reply?"

"The emissaries are waiting for your answer, Sir."

"I see," replied the master of Amsheet, "he wants to concentrate his forces on the Empyreans. Sharr must be behind this."

Wrath of the Urkuun – Sylveedian Pool

"I think there must be more to it than that," added Uziguzi. "Your forces are limited, Lord Orgond, and with time the urkuun would have no trouble subduing Tanniin. There must be something else."

Orgond saw that Enryl was troubled. "What is the matter, Captain?"

The young man drew a breath. "Lord Orgond, the envoy of the urkuun. The sylveed that spoke to me … he was … that was Awaniir, Sir."

Orgond was startled. "The Lord of Hardeen?"

Enryl nodded.

"Did you recognize him?"

Enryl shook his head. "Right before he left, he whispered to me. He said, 'I am Awaniir. Please kill me.' I wanted to, but my hand would not move to my blade. I felt paralyzed. I betrayed him."

Orgond went to Enryl and placed a reassuring hand on the young captain's shoulder. "You were not ready for this, Enryl. No one is. However, once the urkuun's scouts tire of waiting and then report to their master, I want you, I need you, to be ready to fight. You have heard what Lord Awaniir has asked of you. This he would ask of every soldier. Do not think, do not hesitate, and do not hold back. When the battle begins I will need you to lead and not look back. Understood?"

"How can we win against such evil?" Enryl was visibly shaken.

"One sylveed at a time," replied Orgond, fixing his gaze on the soldier. He smiled. "Do not underestimate our forces, do not underestimate the Seer. But for you and me, our calling is to fight, and fight we will. We shall not surrender, and we shall not weaken. Understood?"

Enryl breathed more freely, as if he were rousing from a deep spell. "Yes, Sir," he said with a loud voice, "To the glory of Tanniin and the honor of Amsheet!"

Lord Orgond grabbed his helmet. "Master Xurgon do you require anything of me?"

"No, Your Lordship. My dwarfish dwarfs have worked tirelessly and all soldiers are fittingly equipped with fitting military equipment."

Orgond nodded. "To battle then. We will leave the victory to the holder of Layaleen."

> ⋅◉⋅◉⋅◉⋅ <

Ahiram waited until his friends had left before opening his bag of treasures as he called it. Sheheluth sat by his side and watched him intently. He took out his sword and felt it. Oddly enough, it was still. Ahiram thought that with the enemy being so close, his sword would be quivering strongly, but he felt nothing. It was as though the sword was just some inert, cold piece of metal. It also felt heavier than usual. He glanced at Sheheluth, was about to say something, but changed his mind and carefully emptied his bag on the ground in front of him.

"Wow," she said, inhaling sharply. "So this is why I was getting these conflicting signals."

"What signals?" he asked. "Sheheluth, there is no time for you to speak in riddles, or to yourself. Speak plainly."

"These artifacts: the mask, belt, shoes, and wings give off a different signal than your sword and that other thing you have in your possession. Very different."

"Do you see the signal now?" He showed her the sword.

She looked again at each of the objects. "No … I don't."

"As I thought," he said.

"Thought what?"

"Don't you see?" he snapped. "They're cursed. They are all cursed."

"You're right, Ahiram," she said after a short moment. "They have lost their power. You cannot use them to fight this monster."

"They were fine yesterday. I spent the entire night training with them."

"That's not surprising," explained Sheheluth. "Some curses are proximity curses. They trigger when you are close to their source. Ibromaliöm's libre and the monster must somehow be connected."

Of course! How did I not think of it before? Orwutt and Zurwott told me the Karangalatad, their account of the history of the world, speaks of the Ithyl Shimea *as a hidden doorway to the Pit. The urkuun is a creature of the Pit, so they must share the same power.* Ahiram sighed. "What am I supposed to do now? How can I hope to defeat the urkuun?"

"Wait for me, here," said Sheheluth. "I need to … go somewhere."

"What? I need you to help me figure how to lift this curse."

"That is what I am about to do, but I need to speak to … never mind. Wait for me here. I'll be back."

Sheheluth ran down the hill, and as she rounded a corner, she vanished from view.

30. God-Crusher

"A Silent must never heed whispers of self-doubt or bouts of despair, lest they lead him to a lonely demise without honor."
—Book of Lamentation 11:6.

"Dying we die and rising we rise. It is to the second that our eyes must yearn and our strength must lead, for death is a muted, meaningless void without the hope that carries us to the everlasting flow of love."
—Memoirs of Shalimar, the Poet.

Standing in the midst of his men, waiting for the battle to begin, Orgond looked like an unmovable rock, a fitting symbol for the resistance of Tanniin. A scout joined him and bowed.

"What of our northern border?" asked Orgond.

"No forces in view," whispered the scout.

"Excellent. Continue to watch and report if you see any movement of Thermodonian forces."

The sentry bowed and left and Lord Orgond breathed a sigh of relief. He had shared with Tanios alone the latest alliance between Bar-Tanic and Thermodon. The commander had immediately sent a shadow of four Silent to Orlan, and he thought, *Whether the Silent manage to disrupt the attack, or whether the Thermodonians decide to turn on the*

Bartanickians, either would be welcome news. Assuming we survive the urkuun, we will then deal with the northern berserkers.

Without warning, the sylveeds attacked. They rose from the plain like a gray massless form. As they drew closer, the mass became a sea of soulless soldiers, two thousand strong. There were no banners, no drummers, no trumpets, and no shouts. Just a deadly march of placid puppets that then turned into a trot, and the trot became a surge rising to kill and destroy.

Their forward charge leapt in the trenches with a blind, carefree style, as if they were happy to die, hoping to attain a promised bliss in the afterlife. Arrows from the entrenched camp flew in successive lethal waves, mowing down the attackers who fell the way broken dolls fall when dropped by a child; as still as a cemetery, listless like ancient ruins. "Hold your positions," bellowed Lord Orgond, "Do not let them break the lines. Hold your positions."

As the night wore on, the fighting became a bloody, messy chore with the sylveeds surging relentlessly and the soldiers hacking and hewing. The blood of the dead soaked the tired grass, turning the hill into a slide.

Then, abruptly, like puppets in the hands of a puppeteer, the sylveeds stopped. Turning their backs on the soldiers they retreated slowly, soundlessly, and became a gray mass once more before vanishing from view. Even though they made easy targets, none of the archers had the heart to shoot them in the back.

"He is taunting us," said Lord Orgond. "He wants us to know that life is cheap and he is willing to throw it away recklessly. We will show him that every drop of blood is precious. Stand your ground, warriors of Tanniin. Do not lose heart."

More than one hundred soldiers died, and more were wounded. The bodies of countless dead sylveeds littered the plain. Orgond knew this was an initial skirmish to assess their power and detect any weakness. *They now know we are fighting without Empyrean forces.*

"Tend to the wounded and move the dead to the back of the camp. Keep your formation and repair the trenches," commanded Orgond.

As the night began to recede and a sickly light turned the plain into a field of ashen grass, the sylveeds came back, ten thousand strong this time. Orgond's army was ready. Riders set the plain ablaze, crippling the sylveeds' advance while archers rained more arrows. But the urkuun held sway over his forces so they could not be demoralized or scared. They kept coming, and Orgond's army was barely able to hold them off when a freezing blast of wind lashed out from the fortress and sundered the army's trenches.

"Urkuun's sorcery," muttered Orgond. "Where is Ahiram?"

The situation was precarious. The sylveeds attacked with renewed vigor, and spread their troops on three different fronts.

"What are they trying to do?" asked Enryl.

"Surround us," replied Orgond.

"Your orders, Lord Orgond?" asked the captain.

Lord Orgond mounted his horse and gave the captain a reassuring smile. "We do what Tanniinites have always done. We attack."

Orgond had been puzzled by the lack of riders among the sylveeds, but he now understood why. He mounted a swift attack, outflanked the enemy, broke its leftmost rank and withdrew before the sylveeds managed to react. Standing at a distance, he saw the rest of the sylveedian army move in unison while the enemy troops he had disrupted fell into confusion. They began hacking at each other mindlessly, then abruptly stopped. Forming their ranks anew, they joined the bulk of their army.

Lord Orgond thought, *The urkuun's hold on the sylveeds is strong but uniform. He is unable to direct them individually, and he did not delegate subordinates to lead them. Presumably, he thinks numerical superiority will be enough to overtake us.* He rejoined the infantry and relayed orders to Enryl who set the archers behind the soldiers while the riders flanked his battalion to the right and to the left.

"If we break their ranks, they will attack each other," explained Orgond. "Rain the rest of our fiery arrows in their midst. We will divide the riders into two groups and they will lunge laterally, breaking their flanks. Let the infantry stand its ground and be ready to defend as the sylveeds draw closer."

At that moment, a sentry bawled an alarm. All eyes turned to where he was pointing. "Who is that running on the plain?"

It was Frajil. When the carnival had ended, having had his fill of pomegranates, Frajil saw soldiers leave and naturally assumed these soldiers would lead him back to Soloron. The fact that they were moving toward the east instead of going south meant nothing to the dim-witted half-giant, for he had no clear sense of direction. So, he happily followed them. Along the way, they came across an abandoned farm with a destroyed chicken coop. Frajil lagged behind until he had finished repairing it. He then went about gathering every stray chicken and stray chick he could find. Having secured them in the reconstructed coop, which looked now like a mini-fortress, he went his way, happy as a rooster, and kept walking until he reached the field of battle. His eyes darted from the men of Orgond to the sylveeds and he recognized the soldiers as friends of Soloron, and the sylveeds as the "smelly ones who attacked young rooster on the road." Having made up his mind whom to fight for and whom to fight against, he unsheathed his twin double blades, and with a mighty roar, fell on the enemy as an army of one, tearing through their ranks like a tornado.

Galvanized by this show of courage, the infantry charged down the middle, following the trail Frajil was leaving behind him. The riders followed suit and the sylveeds, controlled by a single mastermind, reacted slower than a normal army would have. Confusion ensued in their ranks, which was what Orgond had been counting on. He attacked the sylveeds and broke through their ranks, outflanking them on each side. His infantry went on the offensive and the sylveeds found themselves sandwiched between the horsemen and the infantry. They fled the battlefield and retreated to the fortress. Lord Orgond pursued them as far as the edge of the fortress when the mighty gates of Hardeen were flung open, spewing sylveeds by the thousands. This was an all-out attack, and the sylveeds were determined to break through their ranks.

Enryl was about to sound the retreat when a different trumpet blast filled the air. Everyone stopped to look, except for Frajil, who continued his private assault on the enemy forces. Lord Orgond lifted his sword triumphantly and shouted, "The Empyreans!"

Riders on approach raised the crimson Empyrean standard, and the trumpets sounded again. A shout of victory echoed and the balance of the battle quickly shifted. The Tanniinites resumed their offensives and as the deadly combat continued, a strong rumble filled the plain. In the distance, two thousand Empyrean riders went into a trot; the trot became a quick canter, and the canter turned into a stormy gallop. They charged with deadly force and precision, decimating the enemy's troops and bringing much needed relief to Orgond's troops.

After hours of fierce combat, the sylveeds retreated to the fortress. The forces of Orgond were now stationed in the fields directly across from the main gate of the enemy's fortress. A welcome respite followed, and Lord Orgond called a meeting. He sat by a low fire with Master Habael, Princess Gaëla, Uziguzi, Master Xurgon, and Enryl.

"Enryl, how long do you think we will be able to last?"

The young captain shrugged his shoulders. "It depends on what the enemy will do next. If they attack again with the same strength, we may manage to last another day now that the Empyreans are here."

"Princess Gaëla, do you agree with this assessment?"

"Yes. We have battled our way here from Vumax. The sylveeds have besieged the city. We cannot hope for more reinforcements. I do not think we can last more than a day or two."

"Master Habael, what do you say?"

"I say we keep hoping against all hope. Let us fight as though victory were ours. Despite the dire conditions we find ourselves in, let us keep up our spirit. Ahiram is sure to come, Layaleen in hand, and when he does, he will conquer the beast."

"Master Habael, I respect your opinion," replied Lord Orgond, "and I believe that you are a man of deep wisdom. Yet my men demand more than mere words. They demand signs to live by. What sign can you give them that victory is indeed ours?"

Habael thought for a little while, and then smiled broadly. "Very well, Lord Orgond, Princess Gaëla, assemble your warriors at dusk tomorrow morning and a sign shall be given them."

The soldiers assembled in battle array. Across the battlefield stood legions of sylveeds, more numerous than before. *This is our final battle,* thought Lord Orgond as he surveyed the land. *We cannot hold against these odds much longer, not with our reduced forces and our waning strength.* He looked to Master Habael and wondered what sign the old man would give these tired soldiers whose fate would be sealed at the hands of these creatures. That day, the sun did not rise. Thick, dark clouds covered the heavens, forming a perfect shelter for their foes.

The urkuun is protecting his own, thought Habael as he watched the brooding clouds. He stood at the front of the army. Turning his back on the enemy, he looked at the soldiers that stood before him. "Warriors of Tanniin and loyal Empyreans, take heart," he said with a booming voice. "You have demanded a sign to know that El is with you. I spent the night interceding on your behalf so you may not lose hope or be overcome by despair." He then placed his hand in his pocket and revealed a petite brass horn. "Do you see this bugle? It is so small that some of you may not believe it will be the cause of the wonder you are about to witness. I will blow this horn three times. When you hear the third blast, I ask of you to attack, and do so as one sword. I promise that before you reach their lines, you will receive aid."

This is the most absurd thing I have ever heard, thought Enryl. He was stunned and bewildered. He had hoped for a secret weapon, some potent magic, and instead Habael exhorted them with a trinket. *Unbelievable!* He was about to say something when Lord Orgond moved forward.

"Do as Master Habael has commanded you," he said.

The men stirred but stood in place. Enryl looked at Princess Gaëla and saw her take command of her troops. *Looks like the Empyreans are ready to charge*, he thought. "I've always enjoyed the company of beautiful women," he muttered while taking his place at the head of his army.

Habael sounded the meager bugle. The tone was feeble. He blew a second time, and then a third. Enryl waited. No friendly forces came to fight by their side, but Gaëla lunged forward and advanced at full speed in front of her Empyrean army. *I hate it when I'm second*. Raising his sword Enryl charged, and his men followed. The enemy covered the plain like a plague of ants, and this time their small army would not be able to break through the sea of sylveeds.

Right before the armies made contact, a sunray pierced through the thick clouds. They parted and the sun shone through. The soldiers, realizing how much the sylveeds were repelled by the light, felt the odds suddenly turn in their favor. They plunged into battle with renewed force. The clouds gathered strength and covered the sun once more, wherein the sylveeds attacked anew. But the sun pierced through again, and the enemy fled, blinded and weakened by the aster. The battle raged, ebbing and flowing in cadence with the weather, moving closer and closer to the fortress. Each time the sun dispersed the clouds, the unified forces of Tanniinites and Empyreans gained the upper hand, but when the clouds blotted the sun, the sylveeds attacked with vigor.

Enryl coordinated his moves with those of the Empyreans, so even in retreat they could inflict heavy losses on the enemy. His constant problem was to get Frajil to retreat, which was a foreign idea for the giant who systematically continued his merciless attack even when surrounded by sylveeds. More than once, he had to rescue the giant and drag him back.

Lord Orgond led the riders on the left side while the Empyreans covered the right. Uziguzi and Habael stayed behind. One of Orgond's men tapped him on the shoulder and pointed to the road from Amsheet. Four riders were fast approaching. One of them waved and Orgond recognized his daughter. He left the battlefield and rushed to meet them.

"Where is Ahiram?" he asked as he joined them.

"He is on that hill," replied Noraldeen, breathless, pointing toward the highest peak of the Mayorian Chain. "He will join us shortly."

"Is he all right?"

"Yes, Father."

"Where is the high priestess?" asked Jedarc. His concern for Hiyam made him forget whom he was addressing.

"She went into the fortress with Commander Tanios and the rest of the Silent to force the urkuun out of his lair." Lord Orgond straightened his posture and prodded his steed forward to the incoming assault. "We have a full battle ahead of us. Stay with me and follow my orders."

≻⋅⋅⋅≺

The outcome of the battle was still uncertain, but the forces of Lord Orgond and Princess Gaëla steadily gained ground. There was not much respite, for the sun came out more often now. Enryl pressed the sylveeds and commanded his soldiers to pursue them closer and closer to the fortress. The creatures wanted to retreat inside, but a greater fear than the sun forced them to stay and fight. Enryl kept his forces organized to avoid the slightest mistake, for the sylveeds still outnumbered them. In his peripheral vision, he saw Lord Orgond move the fight closer to the walls of Hardeen. The move was daring, but deadly for the enemy if successful. The riders tried to overrun the sylveeds and attack them from behind. Lord Orgond charged just as a powerful explosion blasted the outer wall of the fortress, crushing many sylveeds as it fell. Noraldeen was locked in a vicious hand-to-hand combat with three of the creatures. A rock, the size of a fist, slammed into the sylveed to her right; her head snapped back and she fell dead. A hail of stone shards hit Noraldeen and the sylveeds around her, and she saw them all collapse. Noraldeen raised her sword high in a shout of victory when the battle around her began to spin rapidly. She felt weak and dizzy as a warm liquid ran down her neck. The Silent touched her head and looked at her bloodied hand uncomprehendingly. Darkness overtook her, and she collapsed.

The battle stopped abruptly. The clouds closed so suddenly that everyone thought that night had fallen. A powerful creature leaped from the fortress with a shriek that chilled their souls. He landed among the sylveeds and shrieked again to claim dominion over the land. He splayed its clawed wings and struck the ground with its tail. The Third Urkuun of the Third Order was demanding obedience. Raising a dark, clawed sword, he commanded the entire battlefield.

Master Habael whispered to himself, "If Ahiram does not show up now, we are truly lost. Come on, lad! Delay no longer."

≻ ⁘ ≺

"Hot, hot, hot!" yelled Aquilina as she quickly yanked the Merilian and threw it on the carpet before her.

Blood drained from Hoda's face. She had been enjoying a moment of rest with the young princess and her friend, Vily. *Not again!* she thought in a panic. *Not again! I am about to lose her the way I lost Ahiram.*

"Aquilina," called Vily. "Are you all right?"

Aquilina saw fear in her friend's eyes. She smiled at her reassuringly. "I'm fine, but what is the matter with this medallion? It nearly burned me." Aquilina jumped to her feet, with wide opened eyes. "Oh no, he's attacking. He will hurt him. I must go!"

Hoda grabbed her hand. "Stay here, Aquilina. Put the medallion back. I won't let your parents lose you the way I lost my brother."

Aquilina tried to free her arm, but Hoda's grip was steely.

"Let me go," she pleaded with Hoda. "He needs me."

Hoda shook her head. "I lost him six years ago. The medallion, his medallion, did the same thing. It became suddenly hot. He took it off, and we lost the village and everything was destroyed. I should have never let him take the medallion off." She grabbed the pendant. "Put it back on, Aquilina, put it on right now."

"You do not understand," pleaded the young girl, trying with all her might to free herself. "I have to help him. Let me go!"

➢ ⦂⦂⦂ ⪡

"Ahiram, I am back."

The Silent jumped to his feet. "What took you so long?" His voice quivered with restraint.

"I know," replied Sheheluth. "It wasn't as easy as I thought, but I think I found out how to remove this curse."

"Where did you go anyway?" he asked.

She glared at him. "Didn't I tell you not to ask?"

"But you've been gone forever. I have no idea what we're going to find out when we—"

"Ahiram, listen," she snapped. "Listen carefully to what I am about to tell you. It will sound harsh, it will sound cruel, but I have no other way of telling you this: you might get to Hardeen only to find out that everyone died. Jedarc, Banimelek, Noraldeen, everyone—"

"No, I don't want to hear it. I can't."

"You must! If you weaken your resolve and allow fear or anxiety to show, he will seduce you, do you understand? He will gain the upper hand over you and then all will be lost. He could order you to kill Noraldeen and you would do it willingly. Do you understand? You cannot win if you are going to fight him to ease your fear and your anxiety. You can only win if you are willing to fight him no matter the loss and no matter the cost. Your weapons are strong and powerful, but your ultimate weapon, your strength, is in your heart. Without it, we're all lost." She stood breathless before him, and as she expected, he calmed down.

"I see," he said. "I see. If I don't stop him then …" He clutched his fists. "All right, Sheheluth, tell me what I must do."

"Grab the piece of magic you have I cannot see and hold it tight."

"Like so?" he asked, showing her his left hand.

She covered her eyes. "It's light blinds me. Cover it." Ahiram closed his fist. "Now, hold it tight and close your eyes. Seek that star you saw, seek it with all your will."

Instantly, Ahiram stood facing the star. *That was fast*, he thought. Everything became silent and cold beyond imagining, as if death itself had died and left behind a muted, icy wraith to strangle silence into a frozen eternity. Ahead of him, covering his field of vision, was the star, or rather, an unbelievably large fireball. *Is this what stars are made of? I thought they were candles burning in the abode of the gods.*

"*Do you see it?*" He nearly jumped. Sheheluth's voice was in his head. "*If you do, just nod.*" Ahiram nodded. "*Good, now touch the star with the object in your hand.*"

"*I can't.*" He had not spoken aloud, but Sheheluth heard him.

"*Why?*"

"*The star. It's not what you think. It's huge. It is impossibly huge. I can't reach it, and I can't get any closer.*"

"*I see*," came the reply. "*Throw it.*"

"*What?*"

"*Throw the object you are holding toward the star. Trust me.*"

Ahiram froze. *What if Sheheluth is in league with the urkuun? What if she wants me to lose the tile, then what? How can I possibly win?*

"*What are you waiting for? Don't worry about losing the tile. It is powerful, Ahiram. It will always find you,"* she insisted.

That's true. How could I forget? Whenever I think about the tile or invoke it, it appears in the palm of my hand. With one brisk motion, he hurled the tile toward the star.

"Did you do it?" The tone in his head was impatient.

"Yes."

"Good. I've stowed the artifacts in your bag and strapped it to your shoulder just in case."

"In case of what?" He watched the tile sail silently, spinning as it went. Abruptly it sped up and flew higher at an unbelievable speed. A dark spot appeared on the surface of the star, and a tongue of fire lashed out tearing the darkness apart and engulfing Ahiram. He yelled, opened his eyes, and flew faster than the wind.

Darkness now shrouded the land. Noraldeen lay in a heap, unconscious, then the sylveeds cheered and their voices woke her. She moaned in pain as she reached for her sword, her hand dripping red with her own blood. She looked up and saw the urkuun standing just several feet away from her. Her heart missed a beat or two. Noraldeen closed her eyes, pretending to be dead.

The urkuun shrilled. A charged bolt of fire struck him in the face, and he lost his footing and staggered back. The clouds quickly scattered, and in the widening space, the Tanniinites and Empyreans saw a figure step out of their legend and into the sky. They saw a man with shoes of bronze, a belt of silver, a mask of gold, and glorious wings of meyroon holding a sword that radiated dazzling colors from the sun.

"It's El-Windiir come back from the dead!" a soldier shouted.

"It's Ahiram!" replied Jedarc.

Ahiram descended slowly and stood before the urkuun while the crowd of soldiers and sylveeds stood transfixed. He pointed his sword toward the beast. "I have come to reclaim the land. I shall slay you and make your name a mockery among the living. I am Ahiram, bearer of Layaleen, the sword that cut through your flesh once before, and the sword that will slay you today."

In a terrible shriek, the urkuun dove at Ahiram, who became a whirlwind. He pounded the beast with bolts of fire and he responded with thunderous red flares. Ahiram increased his speed and focused his attacks on the head of the beast. He fired blazing bolts from his mask. Bolt after bolt pummeled the reeling monster. As he drew closer, he lashed at him with the sword of El-Windiir. The urkuun's own dark sword met Layaleen. Metal screamed against metal in a volley of blinding sparks. The two blades racked each other, vying for dominion. The monster wailed, then roared angrily. *Great*, thought Ahiram. *The beast still remembers Layaleen*. He shot into the air and circled the beast. His first attack had been a test. Ahiram wanted to measure the strength of the urkuun and his sword. It was incredibly powerful, so he knew he had to weaken it still. *It is only a matter of time.*

The clouds parted and the sun splashed the plain with its warm rays; a sign that the strength of the urkuun was finally waning. Ahiram dove down once more, this time at full speed. The beast pounded the ground and powerful geysers erupted, spewing boiling water and nauseating mud. The steaming jets of water threatened to knock the Silent down. The battlefield had come to a complete standstill. Entranced, friends and foe watched the battle knowing their fate depended on its outcome. *This explains the geyser in the Game of Silver*, thought Hiyam. She stood by Jedarc, her eyes riveted on Ahiram. He now had to avoid the geysers and dodge the red bolts. He plunged to the ground, adjusted his flight, and fired a string of fiery bolts. The urkuun managed to stave off some, but others slammed into his head. With Layaleen in hand, Ahiram advanced on the monster, and though his flaming sword blocked Ahiram's, it was markedly weaker. Ahiram pretended to take off, but this time he lunged back and took the urkuun by surprise. Layaleen sunk deep into the monster's flesh and the beast wailed, yet with a blow from his left arm, he sent Ahiram rolling on the ground. Ahiram bounded back, but winced with pain from two bruised ribs and a dislocated right shoulder. Blood trickled down his leg.

He took to the air, sheathed Layaleen, and with one quick pop reset his shoulder back in its socket. The flash of pain was more intense than he had expected. *At this rate, I'll be exhausted before I can defeat him. I may not be able to sustain another blow like that one.* Without Layaleen, the urkuun would certainly have destroyed him. His mind drifted for a moment, and he saw himself back at the lair of the béghôm. He remembered the vision of the book, the specific page, and the four pieces he had seen fly together: The eyelids of Jaguar-Night were part of El-Windiir's wings! Ahiram suddenly realized he could join the eyelids with the wings to become a powerful weapon. 'Weakness is strength when it fools your enemy', he remembered from the *Book of Siril*. He quickly formed a plan, dove back down, and landed fifty yards from the urkuun.

≻ ·:·:·:· ≺

What is he doing? thought Noraldeen. She had been following Ahiram's strategy and could not understand why he had landed so close to the urkuun, or why he was divesting himself of the wings. He dropped them on the ground and walked with confidence toward the monster. *Why is he walking toward the beast?*

The urkuun waited for Ahiram to get even closer, then shot two powerful bolts of dark light, but Ahiram blocked them with bolts of fire and walked confidently to the beast who was waiting for him, sword raised. They were now at arm's length, too close to work effectively with bolts. Ahiram attacked with Layaleen, and the urkuun met his blow.

Banimelek had been following the duel closely when he saw a disheveled creature leap from the ground and attack Ahiram with a knife.

Michael Joseph Murano

The Silent shouted, "Ahiram, look out behind you!" Ahiram jerked to the side, but the knife caught him in the shoulder and he staggered in pain and fell back. The mask slipped from his face. Zirka, the dwarf, stood triumphant until a quick arrow from Xurgon sent him tumbling down. Zirka the betrayer was dead.

Ahiram forced himself to sit upright. He yanked the blade from his shoulder and threw it to the ground. The monster was slowly approaching. Terror seized Ahiram. He looked confused and dazed. Thus far, the mask had shielded him from the mental power of the beast, but now that he had lost it, he was feeling the full force of his influence. The urkuun pounded the ground with his tail, splitting the earth into a crevasse like a knife slicing open a piece of meat. Several boiling geysers shot up nearly scalding the young man. The beast bellowed like the waters of the deep. Noraldeen looked at Ahiram. He seemed frightened and lost while he searched frantically for the mask. Below, the gushing waters of the rift roared with a deafening sound. The urkuun's shadow grew larger and loomed more menacing until it covered Ahiram and all of his surroundings. Ahiram stood on the rim of the ledge, his back turned to the deep crevice, starring at the approaching terror.

"Miss Hoda, please, if I don't help him, something very bad will happen."

Hoda held the young girl tightly against her. "I won't lose you," she said. In her state of desperation, she could not let go of Aquilina. Anguish and guilt pounded her, overwhelming her reason. She wanted to keep Aquilina safe no matter what and could think of nothing else. Just then, a donkey brayed in her ear. She screamed and relaxed her hold. Aquilina vanished. Hoda turned and saw Vily shaking with fear, clutching the little whistle that Karadon had given her.

"I trust Aquilina," Vily said fiercely. "I will always trust her."

"What have you done?" shouted Hoda. "She is gone!"

"She'll come back," Vily said with a firmness that surprised even her. "She always, always does."

> ◦◦◦ <

Like a stormy wind, Aquilina moved through Tyrulan and located her nemesis. He was facing the one she had affectionately called the Snoring Man. In Tyrulan, the attack taking place in Tannin looked like five massive gray plants—like the ones that had attacked her—surrounding a thin, bright filament. Just then, a large inverted flower filled the Tyrulian sky. *That flower is glowing like the filament. I know what to do.*

As she was about to move, Aquilina saw a beautiful lily shine brightly. It was dangerously close to the gray plants, which were the deadly words of power her opponent was speaking. Aquilina's heart skipped a beat. *She will be injured. I must save her.*

"Fly faster than the wind," she commanded, and a hurricane rose in Tyrulan and carried her toward the battle.

> ◦◦◦ <

Moments earlier, Noraldeen had recognized the scene before her. *This is my dream*, she realized. *The dark terror ... Ahiram ... the gulf.* While Aquilina came riding in on the wind in Tyrulan, the Silent gathered her strength, and forgetting her fear, drew her blade. She sprinted as fast as she could toward the unsuspecting urkuun, and with her sword raised, drove it deep into his back.

"No, no, no!" screamed Aquilina. In Tyrulan, she saw the white lily throw itself onto the horrible words. She saw her wilt, falter, and fall.

Noraldeen's arm instantly grew numb, and she felt cold all over. The urkuun howled with pain and turning around, he faced her.

"Daughter of Orgond," he said softly. "I was expecting you."

Suddenly, Noraldeen found herself standing in a beautiful temple of Tanniin, being wed to Ahiram, who stood by her side smiling. The images were real, the emotions powerful and overwhelming. But with one act of the will, with one simple gaze sourced from the depth of her heart, a loving gaze that mortals scoff and deride because they seldom understand its true power, Noraldeen destroyed the illusion and set her unbending eyes on the face of the monster. "You do not scare me, urkuun, and you will never command my heart. Go back to the Pit where you belong. You do not hold sway over my heart and you never will."

The urkuun felt a streak of fear, something he had not felt for two thousand years, not since he faced another young maiden, a woman of similar beauty, the stewardess of Tessarah the Unseen, who broke his will and forced him to retreat. He struck Noraldeen full force. She rolled on the ground like a broken doll. The monster, howled with triumph. *The female Seer has fallen; now I must bring the male Seer into subjection.*

By forcing the urkuun to focus on her, Noraldeen had freed Ahiram from the monster's mental clutch. He rose to his feet and saw Noraldeen, not ten feet away, lying crumpled and motionless on the ground. He could tell she was still breathing, but could also see that her leg and arm were shattered and that she had lost consciousness. In that moment, he understood his worst fears were coming true. The one thing he had feared all along was becoming reality, and he had been powerless to stop it.

"Nooo!"

His scream was primal, savage, haunted, and absolute. It then turned into something else entirely, as if the storm within him was now howling.

"May the heavens have mercy on us," whispered Sheheluth as she watched helplessly. Lord Orgond had given an order to stay behind in the safety of the camp, but she had crept out slowly, and was now less than a hundred yards away from the battle scene. She saw Ahiram stand up and she shivered in fear. "The god-crusher has awakened. May the stars have mercy on us," she said, gritting her teeth.

Fury—unadulterated and beyond the reach of mortals—rose in the Silent's eyes and overflowed until his sword began to pulse with an unnatural light. Ahiram attacked without the protection of the mask, forgetting his pain, his wounds, and his fear. There was only rage. The Letter of Power, inscribed on the tile, flashed like a great light around him, and he assailed the urkuun with a surge of renewed strength, his own strength. He fought like a storm for his mother, for his father, and for the sister he had lost. He fought for all the years of loneliness and separation, for the sake of the fallen, for Baher-Ghafé. But above all, he fought for Noraldeen, who had risked her own life to save him. Layaleen met the monster's dark sword in a thunderclap, and blow after blow, Ahiram forced the urkuun into retreat.

He is holding his power within, thought Sheheluth suddenly hopeful. *But he does not see the urkuun's trap. The monster is drawing him in. Use the star power, god-crusher! Use the star!*

Flying high above the battleground, in Tyrulan, Aquilina drew close to the gray plants. They looked like the thorny tail of a massive lizard and they lashed at her, wanting to ensnare her.

"Be still!" she commanded.

Like wild dogs before a lioness, the plants kowtowed instantly.

The beast peered across the field to Noraldeen. *The female Seer still lives? My blow was not powerful enough.* Switching tactics, he went on the offensive. Ahiram was taken aback by the ferocity of his assault. He was now losing ground as the powerful urkuun pushed him back toward Noraldeen, who still lay silent. As they drew closer and closer to her, Ahiram grew desperate to protect her from further harm. He redoubled his efforts, but all was in vain. He exerted himself to the limit of his strength, but could not keep the beast away from Noraldeen.

I will kill her and crush him in one blow, thought the urkuun.

"Connect!" commanded Aquilina.

The filament of light—a icon of the Letter of Power in Tyrulan—linked up with the massive, inverted flower—an image of the star.

"Burn!" she ordered fiercely. "Burn him to death!"

The hilt of Ahiram's sword flashed. High up in the abode of the gods, a star, a heavenly torch, exploded and lit the heavens with the power of a thousand suns. In Tyrulan, the inverted flower became a volcano, and the white filament, a massive flow of white-hot lava. On the field of battle, Ahiram's sword turned into a fiery, blinding rod of light. The hot flare swallowed the Silent, and he became a blazing sun that struck the urkuun with a beam of light, two feet wide. The creature reeled under the unearthly attack but held his ground. Summoning the power of the Pit, he counterattacked. Ahiram yelled, and the beam became twice as powerful. The sylveeds groveled on the ground and the warriors shielded their eyes. The urkuun raised his fist and pounded the ground, tearing it asunder. A gray dull flame slammed into the beam, held it in place, and slowly began pushing it back.

And then Ahiram screamed.

"Noraldeen!"

The beam exploded, tore through the gray light, and broke through the urkuun's defenses. It ripped the Arayat like a fiery river. No one knew how long the blast lasted, but when it subsided, Ahiram stood inside a bright halo. Everyone looked with awe at the one who moved like a shark honing in on its prey, a lion claiming victory; a storm rider.

"Tiir!" he commanded.

The wings and the eyelids flew not to Ahiram, but to the left and right of the urkuun. They joined and became a lethal arrowhead. Ahiram struck with his sword. The monster countered and groaned. Both blades were raised high when the arrowhead hurled, slicing off the beast's arm. Ahiram leaped upward, and in one perfect motion, slashed off the head of the beast. The head dropped as flames tore through the ground and consumed the body of the urkuun. A powerful roar filled the camp and drowned out Ahiram's cries of pain. Invigorated, the army resumed the attack, but the remaining sylveeds retreated hurriedly inside the fortress, locking the doors behind them. The battle was over.

Aquilina saw the four terrible curses vanish from Tyrulan. She saw the inverted flower fade away, and as she landed back on Tyrulian ground, she saw a field where lilies faded as quickly as they bloomed. She saw crystalline drops of water fall and dissipate soon after. She touched the delicate lilies, and burst into tears. Each one was a laboring, pain-filled breath. The drops of water were tears of deep sorrow.

Noraldeen looked up at Ahiram's face bathed in tears.

"Oh Nora, Nora, why you? Why did it have to be you? Why did you do such a foolish thing? Why should you pay such a high price to save me? I should be lying here, not you."

With great difficulty, she raised her hand and placed a bloodstained finger on his lips. Gathering her last strength, she spoke. Her was face peaceful despite the pain. "Ahiram, my sweet love, you are finally free. Remember me by my love for you. Love me as I have loved you, and keep me close to your heart all the days of your life." Ahiram held her closely. "I promise." His tears mingled with hers, their eyes locked on each other. Noraldeen, content in Ahiram's arms, smiled weakly. "Fare thee well, my Prince," she said, and then was gone. It was the sixteenth of Shubat of the year 1197 in the Age of the Temple. Forty-three days after the start of the Games of the Mines, Noraldeen, beloved daughter of Lord Orgond and Princess of Tanniin, who had fallen in love with a slave, had just breathed her last.

≻ ⁘ ≺

"No, no, no!" screamed Aquilina, bursting back into the tent.

"See, Miss Hoda," said Vily, heaving a sigh. "She always comes back."

Aquilina threw herself into Vily's arms. "She died Vily, she died, she died. I should have been there, not her. She died, Vily."

Hoda, feeling guilty but not knowing why, took the young girl in her own arms. "Go get Amaréya," she mouthed to Vily, who left quickly.

Aquilina pulled away from Hoda.

"I am sorry, Aquilina," said Hoda, "I was trying to protect you."

The young girl looked at her. "It is not your fault, Miss Hoda," she said between two sobs. "You did not kill her. He did. He killed her."

"Killed who? Who died?" asked Hoda.

Aquilina did not reply, and remained lost in her thoughts, sobbing quietly until her mother walked in.

"Aquilina, why do you cry?" she asked.

The young girl gazed at her with imploring eyes and Amaréya's heart seized. What she saw in her daughter's eyes was the look Empyrean warriors would have after witnessing, for the first time, the death of one of their sisters on the battlefield. *You are two young for such sorrows, my daughter.* She sat by Aquilina's side and softly hummed the Onyévérah, a psalmody to Vronde, the god of the dead, to grant her fallen sisters a blade of eternity.

Vily took Hoda's hand. "Come, Miss Hoda," she whispered. "Do not worry about Aquilina. She is very strong. She knows you were trying to keep her safe. She's not upset at you."

Hoda walked out with Vily and returned the young girl's warm smile. *What just happened?* She wondered. *Who died? Is Ahiram safe?*

Inside the tent, the Onyévérah had an unexpected effect on Aquilina. Instead of soothing her pain, it sparked a storm in her heart, a fiery storm, seeking to consume the perpetrators behind the death of Noraldeen.

The Second Seer of Power had awakened.

A long time passed until the forces of Lord Orgond and the Empyreans cleared the battlefield from any surviving sylveeds. Shouts of victory echoed all around them. Ahiram finally rose, still cradling Noraldeen in his arms, and carried her across the battlefield to Lord Orgond. He had just returned from pursuing the sylveeds and was straining to make sense of what happened. Ahiram knelt down and laid her gently on the ground in front of her father. Ahiram tried to speak. He wanted to explain, but could only weep. Lord Orgond, heartbroken, took his daughter in his arms. Clutching her to his chest, he softly called, "Nora, Nora."

A procession formed and they escorted Noraldeen back to camp. Ahiram walked behind Orgond. Tanniinites and Empyreans knelt as Lord Orgond passed with his daughter in his arms. They knelt to honor the one who gave her life for the sake of their freedom. And they looked upon Ahiram with awe. In their eyes, he had entered the legend.

Ahiram paid attention to no one. The one who had become a legend was weeping for the princess who had loved him to the last.

31. Come What May

> *"Shortly after the Battle of Hardeen, the refugees returned and rebuilt their homes. Life went on, yet the villagers honored the memory of those who freed the land from the dark evil. Year after year, they commemorate these events and reenact the final victory.*
>
> *"I have been told that the day of celebration is filled with weddings. The open space in front of the Fortress of Hardeen, where the final battle took place, welcomes newlyweds with their joyful processions, and soon the plain is covered with flowers as though to celebrate the renewal of life."*
>
> –Chronicles of Yardam, Third Stewart of the House of Hiram.

Intense activity marked the following days. The people of Tanniin piled the bodies of dead sylveeds and cremated them. Princess Gaëla officiated at the Empyrean funeral rite. Her warriors stripped their dead of their weapons before laying them on the  pyre. Later, they would gift the weapons of their fallen companions to young, new recruits to the Empyrean army. In their eyes, a sword held a mighty tale, a song, and an expression of love to carry forward. Gaëla intoned the Onyévérah. This was the solemn ceremony imploring Vronde, the keeper of the dead, to grant each of her fallen sisters a blade of eternity. She burned incense and pleaded with Vronde to grant them safe passage to Skéné Varéla, the glorious, boundless forest where their bliss will never end as they go from glory to glory.

Since the Tanniinites had lost their priesthood to Baal a few centuries ago, they relied on a *morespherini,* shepherd of the dead, to lead their loved ones home to Tan-Adeen, the land of peace. There, in the company of their forefathers, they feasted bountifully in the presence of Tanniin. The morespherini—traditionally a woman—sprinkled the dead with a mixture of wine and garlic to fortify them during their last journey. Then, she and a large crowd lit candles and kept vigil all night long, praying for Tanniin to guide their loved ones through the fog of nothingness where one could be lost forever. The following day was spent burying them.

A large heap of stones was placed to cover the spot where the urkuun had fallen, and the exhausting cleanup and rite of purification followed. Frajil roamed the camp in search of something to do. The end of the battle had disappointed him. He was bored again. *I miss Soloron*, he thought. *Soloron knows how to unbore Frajil. Frajil goes back to Soloron.*

Three days later glad tidings reached the camp: Tanios and the high priestess had survived the fall of the fortress. After Orwutt and Zurwott dropped the ceiling, the Silent, who had disobeyed Tanios, rescued their commander and the priestess from underneath the rubble. They made their way back to the hidden door where they had entered, and battled through sylveeds' territory, back to camp.

More glad news followed when Orwutt and Zurwott reached the camp. Xurgon rejoiced and let them know how happy he was to see them by expounding the virtues of their ancestors twenty generations back. His panegyric lasted two hours.

A clean breeze flowed in from the sea and swept away the remnant of the stench. Despite all the happy tidings, there was none of the buoyant clamor or shouts of joy characteristic of victory. The loss of Princess Noraldeen weighed heavily on everyone's hearts.

"Poor Lord Orgond," a woman sighed. "He lost his wife and now his only child. He is all alone."

"He won't be for long," replied a friend of hers. "He will be king soon, and as king he will have to marry."

"Yes indeed, but who can replace fair Noraldeen in her father's heart?"

"True," sighed her friend. "Of all those who were on the battleground, it had to be her. Why?"

Ahiram sat on a barren rock, high above the main camp. The wind, cold and cruel, blew continually as though a deranged beast were trying to unseat an intruder. It seemed the wind wanted Ahiram to go; to leave and disappear. But the Silent paid no attention to the natural elements. Oblivious to his surroundings, he sat as still as the rock itself and gazed into the distance. He saw nothing, and heard nothing. He reviewed the last moments of the battle hundreds of times. He wondered what had gone wrong and chided himself for his weakness. The wound Zirka had inflicted was healing well, but he didn't notice or care. How could he have abandoned Noraldeen at that crucial moment, and why had he not seen her when he descended? Why had he not moved the battle scene away from her? Was he so focused on victory that he had forgotten Noraldeen?

The questions became a host of carrion birds flying overhead, and their insistent cacophony pulled him away from the shore of sanity into a troubled sea. The fragile raft of his mind struggled to keep afloat. *Why did you betray her? Why did you let her die? He killed her because of you* ... Despair rose like a dark storm over razor-sharp waves. Loneliness closed in like a shark and pulled him down into cold and still waters. In this iron-frozen depth of despair, where no human hand seemingly could reach, he imagined his sister Hoda standing before the dead body of Noraldeen.

"I died because of you, Ahiram, and now you killed her. You destroyed Olothe, destroyed our village, and allowed your mother and father to die."

She gazed at him with eyes filled with sadness. "You killed me, Ahiram."

Exhausted from the battle and still fighting the aftereffects of the powerful Ithyl Shimean curse, Ahiram lost the will to live. In that dark moment, at that terrible point of utter dejection and weakness, he slowly pulled out one of his daggers and pointed the blade to his heart. He tightened his grasp and ... was slapped hard. Twice.

"How dare you? How dare you?"

Ahiram regained his senses. He managed to focus on the form standing in front of him and finally recognized Sheheluth. Her cheeks were flushed, her breathing labored, like someone who had been running for a while. His anger flared. "What do you care, Sheheluth? You think I'm nearly as evil as the urkuun, so what do you care if I live or die?"

"Selfish idiot," she yelled, tears streaming down her cheeks. She pounded her fist on his chest. "Selfish, arrogant idiot. Can you for once think about the feelings of others before you wallow in your own sorrow?"

"Others?" he yelled back, "I saved everyone else. I saved them all except for the one that mattered the most to me."

"And what do you think she would say if she saw you trying to kill yourself now?" Sheheluth shouted back.

"It doesn't matter anyway. Nothing matters."

"Wait until you hear what Hiyam has to say."

"What?"

"You may want to compose yourself. The others should not see you like this. Control yourself for Noraldeen's sake."

A short moment later, Jedarc, Banimelek, and Hiyam reached the promontory. They too were out of breath.

"Where have you been?" asked Banimelek. "Everyone is looking for you. What are you doing here?"

Ahiram lowered his gaze.

"He is not well," interjected Sheheluth. "You can imagine the—"

"I was going to kill myself. Sheheluth stopped me." Almost in a whisper he added, "I'm not sure she should have. Why did Nora die?"

At first, no one said anything. Then Jedarc knelt in front of Ahiram and looked at him closely. "You know, I'm not shocked. Losing her is too hard, isn't it? I mean, it hurts me beyond belief, and I wasn't nearly as close to her as you were. You already know that's not what she would have wanted, but hey, sometimes the pain becomes unbearable and you don't know what to do with yourself, right?"

Ahiram glanced at Hiyam then looked at Jedarc with concern. "Since when do you know so much about pain, Jedarc?" His tone was bitter.

"What? No, it's not what you think. Hiyam has done nothing to hurt me." The young man laughed nervously. "I mean, we all come from somewhere, and where I come from, they do teach us a thing or two about pain. But not to worry," he added quickly. "I am my usual self, see?"

"Ahiram," said Hiyam as gently as she could. "Hoda is alive."

The words registered slowly, like a heat wave moving over water, or a sandstorm approaching on the horizon. Hazy and vague at first, the meaning became clearer and more certain until Ahiram took in the full significance of what she had just said.

He sat up and asked softy, "How do you know this?"

"I overheard my mother speaking to the commander."

"What of my parents?"

"She only said your sister was alive. Chances are they're alive too."

"Where is she?"

"The commander wanted to tell you first, but seeing you like this … I couldn't wait. My mother didn't know, but she said that one of the servants to the first priestess knows."

"Which one?"

"She didn't tell him her name, but she mentioned you would be able to recognize her quickly."

"So then, Hoda is alive," he repeated mechanically. He scoffed. "Are the gods so cruel that they must take Noraldeen away to give me Hoda back? My sister is alive and Noraldeen is gone? What meaningless evil is this? Why? Please tell me, why?"

"I don't know, Ahiram," answered Banimelek. "But if you find your sister you may be that much closer to finding the answer."

Ahiram smirked. "Ever practical, Banimelek." He sighed. "Thanks though, this helps." He smiled slightly. "You don't have to worry," he said glancing at Sheheluth. "The dark storm has passed. I'll be fine."

≻⋅⋄⋅⋄⋅≺

"Why? Why Master Habael? Tell me, why did she have to die?"

Two days passed since Hiyam had told him about Hoda. At first, Ahiram had focus, direction, and hope. But the dark clouds began to gather once more. Despair, sticky as mud, and damp as everlasting rain flooded his mind with dark thoughts. *What if it's a trap? What if the high priestess is telling me Hoda is alive to taunt me? How can I trust her?*

He refused to come down to the camp, preferring to stay high in the hills. His friends had set up a tent for him and a few more for themselves, and they did not leave his side day and night. He sat, unmoving, on the same rock where Sheheluth had found him. His eyes were lost in a daze. He barely ate and spoke to no one. Then Habael came for a visit, and Ahiram pounded him with questions.

Habael placed his arm around Ahiram's shoulders and did not reply.

"You loved her?" he asked after some time.

Ahiram did not answer right away. "I loved her, but I never felt worthy of her. She, on the other hand …" tears streamed down his cheeks, shaking him. "She loved me more than I deserve to be loved."

"No one deserves to be loved, Ahiram," replied the old man softly. "Love is a gift. A mystery. Sometimes it can be difficult to love. Sometimes it can be harder to *be* loved, especially if that love is powerful, good, and better than we are. Her love is hard to bear, is it not?"

"Yes. It hurts. She was fair and beautiful, passionate about all things, just and joyful, intelligent and kind. She was the first to welcome me, to encourage me when I needed it. She was never jealous, never envious. She was far better than me. Nora died for me. I don't deserve that. Master Habael, this is too much to bear."

"So you think you're guilty? You think you betrayed her?"

"Yes, I do. I feel guilty that she cared so much about me, and that I did not care enough. Why should she care so much? I should have never spoken to her. I should have not spoken to anyone. Noraldeen, Jedarc, Banimelek, none of them. I'm just a slave. How could she love a slave?"

"Because she saw in you more than a slave."

Startled, Ahiram looked up and saw Lord Orgond. "Because," he continued as he drew closer to the two men, "she saw a prince and more than a prince. My daughter knew what she was doing when she ran toward the beast. She was in full control of herself. She knew no one could defeat the urkuun but you. What she did, she did for you, for me, and for this land and its people whom she loved so much. Do you see?"

Despite his turmoil, Ahiram perceived, obscurely, that Noraldeen's father was also addressing these words to himself.

"No father should ever have to watch his daughter die. My daughter knew how difficult her death would for me, for all of us. But this did not stop her, because she was free, truly free to choose what was right. Even though it tears my heart to see her gone, I honor her decision. I respect it. I will do what I must to honor her memory, to make her sacrifice count. She trusted you, Ahiram. She is worthy of your trust and mine. She gave you her life. You may not understand why, you may wish it were not so. But you are a Silent. A Silent that honors a fellow Silent. This you can do, as you should, for Noraldeen's sake."

Realizing he was still sitting, Ahiram sprang to his feet and bowed before Lord Orgond.

"Thank you, Lord Orgond. I will always honor her. I will."

Noraldeen's father nodded before taking his leave.

"What did Noraldeen tell you before she died?" Master Habael asked.

Ahiram lowered his head. "To love her as she loved me." He looked away. "I promised I would, but …"

"You don't know what she meant, do you?"

Ahiram shook his head. "I would have gladly died instead of her."

"I know, lad, I know. We all know that, but she did not want you to die for her. She wants you to love her as she loved you."

"Well she's dead isn't she? How am I supposed to do that now? How am I supposed to show her my love when she's no longer with me?"

"That is for you to discover. Nonetheless, would it be fair to say that you know what she loves and what she hates?"

Ahiram nodded. He could still see her pointing to the tree, the children, the peaceful setting, away from the throne of glory. *It was a dream. Still, Nora would have chosen the children sitting under that cedar tree. That's what she would have chosen.*

"Then, if you do what pleases her, especially when you do not understand or wish it, you would be honoring her, would you not?"

Ahiram reluctantly nodded once more.

"It would be pleasing to Noraldeen to see that you uphold her name, carry her memory, and honor her desires. This falls short from perfect love, but it is an act of love. Do you see that?"

Ahiram did not answer. Master Habael's words made sense, but he needed more. He wished he could ask her himself. *I wish I could talk to you, Nora. I wish …* A thought crystallized in his mind. *Hoda would know what I should do to honor Noraldeen. But what if she is dead? What if the priestess was lying?* Oppressed and heartbroken, he did not know how to escape the obsessive back-and-forth his mind was playing between the unbearable pain of Noraldeen's death and the joyful hope of seeing Hoda.

"Master Habael, if the high priestess said that my sister is alive, would you believe her?"

Habael was relieved to see Ahiram focus his mind on a matter he could do something about. "She is not one to speak casually of such things," replied the old man.

"But what if it's a trap?"

"One does not exclude the other," explained Habael. "She may be speaking the truth, and it may still be a trap."

"I will ask the commander."

"He would vouch for the priestess as I would."

"She tried to kill me."

"And she saved your life by weakening the urkuun, did she not?"

"I don't know what to believe anymore."

"One thing you can believe is that the Temple of Baal wants to capture you. You are now a threat to them."

"I don't care about their threats," he sighed in anger. "That's the other thing, Master Habael, Sheheluth told me I'm a sormoss, that I can gravely injure people when my anger turns to rage."

"Thyme and mint soothe an angry mind," whispered the gardener.

Ahiram managed a smile. "That's why you had me work in that garden of yours. You knew about my temper then."

"You carried it in your eyes wherever you went."

Ahiram remembered then that he had wanted to ask Master Habael about the golden tile. He opened his palm and said the name of the Letter softly. The title materialized in his hand. He looked at the old man questioningly. "Do you see it, Master Habael?"

Habael glanced at Ahiram's hand. "What is it?"

"I'm not sure. I found it over a small door that led to the tomb of El-Windiir. No one else but me can see this tile. Well, Sheheluth can sense it, but she can't see it like I do. She helped me. She showed me how to see this star. Stars are scary when seen up close, Master Habael, did you know that? She told me how to use that star to defeat the urkuun."

Habael listened intently as was his custom. Whatever thoughts or feelings Ahiram's words elicited, he kept to himself.

Ahiram's posture slumped. He rubbed his forehead. "I feel hemmed down, tangled up in a web that holds me back, and all I have ever wanted was to be a shark fisherman."

"I know someone who can help you with this tile," said Habael quietly.

"You do? Who is it?"

"If you go to the Island of Salem, he will find you."

"Salem? How do I get there?"

"Through the Kingdom of Marada."

"The giants?" said Ahiram. "And go with the caravan from beyond?"

"You mean Master Kwadil's famed caravan?"

"Yes. That's what we used to call it because he traveled beyond our mountains to the land of the giants. I never thought I would be traveling that same route. By the way, Master Habael, why are you keeping from me the name of the person who can help me? How do you know him?"

Habael smiled. "This is the first time you have questioned my intent."

Ahiram was mortified. "I'm sorry, I didn't mean to—"

"Do not be sorry. I am proud of you. I have been waiting for this day for a long time. It means you are ready to act as a free man. This is good. See, when a child is taken from his home and sold as a slave, he sets limits in his mind to the things he is allowed to know and he lives in a mental cage. You have been living in that cage for six years, and it seems that you have just opened the door."

"I never thought of it that way."

"Much like you cannot think of Noraldeen's death in any other way than through your grief, see? Now, to answer your question, in the magic of Baal, there is this place they call the Spell World. It is a dark and disturbing realm where the Temple uses conjurations to know when someone utters important names. The one I want you to meet in Salem has a special name, one of those names Baal watches in the Spell World."

"So if you pronounce his name here, they will hear it and will know about my plan to go and see him?"

"It is a bit more complicated than that, but yes, they will know a lot more about your plans and whereabouts than you might like them to."

"Do you think I can reach the Island of Salem without being caught by the Temple?"

Habael looked at Ahiram with a sly smile. "You killed a béghôm and slayed an urkuun. It won't be easy, but yes, you can. Remember who you are: a Silent and a Solitary. In time, you will learn all you need to know about the tile. As long you do not forget the fragrance of mint and the flavor of thyme, all will be well."

Ahiram breathed deeply. "Fine. I will search for Hoda. If she is dead, I will avenge her death and the destruction of Baher-Ghafé. Then I will go to Salem, and I will find out what this tile is all about."

"What will you do once you discover what this title is for?"

"I don't know. I'll figure something out once I'm there."

The old man chuckled. Ahiram placed a tentative arm on Habael's shoulder. "Thank you, Master Habael, for everything. I won't forget the mint and thyme. I can promise you this much."

Habael smiled. *If you only know the true depth of your promise, Ahiram,* he thought. *It is not you who should thank me, but I who should thank you for what is to come.*

⊱ ✦✦✦ ⊰

Evening came and the campsite glowed within a circle of torches. Enryl's men had set the torches around a gaping hole in the damaged Fortress of Hardeen. An emissary of Baal had arrived by boat and negotiations were underway between him and Lord Orgond inside a tent set up for the occasion. Meanwhile, the people of Tanniin strolled quietly, enjoying their recovered freedom. The terror of the night had passed. Tanios walked thoughtfully with Master Habael.

"What have you decided?" asked Habael.

"That is not so easy. It would not be just to have Bahiya stand trial before Baal when I do not believe in its justice. Yet I cannot, in good conscience, let these crimes, sacrifices as she calls them, go unpunished. However, if this becomes a public concern, I fear it may risk the diplomatic discussion Uziguzi has agreed to undertake with Baal on behalf of Lord Orgond. I am weighing the issues."

"And Bahiya, what is her position?"

"She is resigned to whatever decision I make. She gave me her word. I must say that I find it difficult to bring her before a court when at last I find her to be so peaceful and content. The emissary has asked her to remain in Tanniin a while longer. The politics of the Temple is complicated, but the urkuun's death relieved the emissary."

"Would you accept a tribunal of my own?"

"You, Master Habael, providing a tribunal?"

"Yes," he replied with his usual smile. "An unusual tribunal. You and she would have to travel with me to the Forbidden Forest."

"Hmm … I have wondered what is in that forest." He looked at his friend. "Why not? I am willing to return there with you, and I will decide then if your tribunal is to my satisfaction."

"Very well, when the time is right, we will head to Magdala. It might take longer than your forbearance allows, but it will come to pass." Habael looked at Tanios and placed his hand on his friend's shoulder. "What about the lad?"

"What about him?" asked Tanios knowing what was coming.

"Are you going to tell him?"

"That he is my son?" asked Tanios. The commander had confided Bahiya's words with his old friend. "There is nothing I want more. I am very proud of him."

"So, you will tell him then?"

"No," replied Tanios in a low voice. "I cannot. Ahiram put his life on the line before the urkuun. He competed in the Games to be free. His parents may be dead and he has just lost Noraldeen. Shall I now take his childhood dream away by telling him his true mother, the woman he believes has tried to kill him, switched him at birth instead of running away with him?"

"Did you know they were dead when the Games started?"

Tanios shook his head. "No, I did not. Bahiya told me shortly before Ahiram interrupted the council in Amsheet," He sighed.

"What will you do next?"

"Well, the situation in Tanniin is dangerous still. Lord Orgond will have to negotiate with Baal, normalize Tanniin's relations with the Empyreans, assure himself of Togofalk's intentions, and figure out what to do with Thermodon."

"Thermodon?"

"The Thermodonians are in league with the Bartanickians. Lord Orgond is concerned it may involve Tanniin. We have dispatched four Silent to learn more. Then, there is Soloron, the self-styled king in Taniir-The-Strong. Did you know that he is Frajil's brother?"

"No, I did not," replied Master Habael in a chuckle.

"In any event, we need to find out what his intentions are and then determine what to do with the garrisons that Baal keeps in the south. As you can see, there is plenty for my Silent and me to do in order to defend the kingdom."

Habael nodded. "How are you feeling, my friend?"

"I live now as if I had wasted twenty years of my life. Had I been willing to reconsider and listen to Bahiya's pleas back then, I could have been with her when she was pregnant with Ahiram. Had I been less haughty and proud, this all may never have happened. Discovering that I am Ahiram's father and now having to let him go without telling him is the greatest sacrifice of my life. Yet this is how it must be."

"So." said Jedarc.

"So?" replied Hiyam.

"Are you leaving?"

"I don't know yet."

"I thought you would be leaving soon for Baalbek."

"Well, my mother has decided to stay. She is stepping down from her position as the high priestess of Baalbek."

"Will you be replacing her?"

Hiyam smiled. "No. I will never be a priestess of Baal."

"That's true, you've told me that already. So, what will you do?"

"For now I am staying here."

"You are?"

"Yes. Lord Orgond has asked me to be part of the delegation that will meet with the ambassador of Baal, and I have accepted. We will be signing the peace treaty at Taniir-the-Strong Castle."

"You will need an escort as you move back to Taniir-the-Strong. The roads are dangerous, you know."

"My mother has prepared everything."

"Oh, and who is escorting you?"

"Well, Master Habael suggested the trip could be profitable to Banimelek. He has not been himself lately."

"Of course it would be profitable for Banimelek, but can he protect you? I mean, the roads are really dangerous."

Hiyam glanced at Jedarc and laughed, unable to keep a straight face. He lifted her up and twirled her. Slowly, he brought her down, and they held the embrace.

"You know," whispered Jedarc, "if you keep me company long enough, something wonderful may happen."

"What?" whispered Hiyam.

"I may marry you."

"That is a risk I am prepared to take."

They both laughed.

"I wonder if this is all right," said Hiyam.

"What?"

"To feel so joyful when …"

"When Noraldeen's death is still so close? Every time I think of her death, tears well in my eyes. I can't help it. I feel the separation bitterly. Then I think about what she has done. She gave her life so that we may live fully." He held Hiyam's hand. "I say to myself that by defending those I love, I am honoring her memory. So, I rejoice in this victory. I force myself to do what is right because I want to honor her. We can't yet share our joy with others, but we can prepare the future."

"I agree," said Banimelek who joined them.

The three friends sat silently, Hiyam between the two. Banimelek moved over, leaving an empty spot between them. "We'll never forget her." he said, "She'll always be will us."

"Noraldeen," said Jedarc. "I miss you." There was nothing more to say.

⊱ ⋅ ⋅ ⋅ ⋅ ⊰

The following day, the camp came together for Noraldeen's funeral. The Silent carried her coffin, while a mournful crowd showered it with white roses. The Silent laid her on a raised pyre and four Empyreans placed a wreath at the foot of her coffin. Princess Gaëla Meïr Pen gave a pledge of peace to the Kingdom of Tanniin in honor of Noraldeen and told Lord Orgond that a statue of his daughter would grace their pantheon. This was the highest honor Empyreans could give anyone.

Lord Orgond asked Frajil to come forward. The giant of a man wanted to know where the chicken was but for once controlled himself.

"By now, you all know Frajil. His bravery on the battlefield is unequaled and I am grateful he fought at our side. Frajil fought selflessly and with all his heart. I would like to commend you for what you have done and I want you to know you are always welcome in northern Tanniin. By the power given me, you have my word that you will no longer hunger. No matter where you go, or where you stay in Tanniin, you will always have a warm dish and a roof over your head."

Warm dish and roof over head was all that Frajil understood, but it was all he needed to hear. He wanted to hug Lord Orgond, but Princess Gaëla's expression told him it wasn't a good idea. He wanted to shake someone's hand, but there was no hand to shake. He would have liked to get into a scuffle of some sort, but no one wanted to fight, so Frajil cried for joy. Everyone thought he was mourning Noraldeen.

After Enryl managed to guide Frajil down from the elevated platform, Lord Orgond spoke of his daughter and the meaning of her actions. He told the crowd what he had told Ahiram: Noraldeen knew well the risk she was taking. As a half-Empyrean, she knew the meaning of sacrifice and embraced it. She acted out of love, and that love allowed all of them to be alive this day. "If you wish to honor Noraldeen's memory, if you believe in what she did, then you must *do* as she did. Like El-Windiir and Layaleen before her, my daughter loved this kingdom with all her strength. As I speak, I am convinced she stands radiant among my ancestors, in whose company she is proud to be."

The morespherini came forward, bowed before the dead princess, then sang a dirge in her honor:

> "Night fell over the Plain of Iliand when you fell, my princess,
> Pure lily of early dawn whose fragrance will never cease.
> Starry light, shine upon us with an everlasting brightness,
> Be our beacon of hope, our steadfast guide to peace."

Ahiram and the Silent sat transfixed. The woman had a haunting voice; deep, velvety, pure, and able to soar like eagles over eternal snow. The melody mourned Noraldeen but remained hopeful, like a cheerful smile can sometimes soften the face of a widow.

> "O fearless one, you defeated a heartless tyranny.
> Your selfless, loving sacrifice broke my heart.
> Your courage shaped our lives, our fate, our destiny.

Must you then, my beautiful princess, leave us and depart?"

Ahiram heard his friends of the Silent Corps sob softly. His tears flowed freely, as if the woman had read his innermost thoughts and put them to song. "Must you then, my beautiful princess, leave us and depart?" This verse, he knew was etched indelibly in his own heart.

"Night has fallen over the mighty plain of Iliand.
I weep now for our children, the fallen, the brave,
Those who left us and went to the everlasting highland
Shining like glorious stars beyond the power of the grave.

They are gone, never shall we see their faces again,
Never to hear their voices echoing in the merry night,
Never to watch them dance when spring colors our plain,
Or see them fall in love in the fullness of light.

They walk on the final path that takes them away.
Away from us they go to everlasting shores
Where darkness never overtakes the light of day,
Where they rest at last beyond the pain of wars."

The verses were sobering for Ahiram. *I've been so taken by Noraldeen that I forgot the many other losses.* He surveyed the crowd. *That young woman over there, she may have lost her husband or her brother.* For the first time, Ahiram considered what would have happened if Noraldeen had not intervened. *Many would be dead, and many more would be dying still.*

"Say, my love, who it is that walks ahead of them.
Who is this beautiful woman, this young maiden of eighteen?
More precious than the dwarf's treasures and their lonely gem,
Orgond's beloved daughter, she is Princess Noraldeen."

Ahiram instantly memorized this stanza. He knew he would never forget it. He wished the woman had used it as a refrain for her elegy. Slowly, he realized the singer had stopped and a deafening applause filled the camp. Spontaneously, the crowd began chanting the name of

Wrath of the Urkuun – Come What May

Noraldeen. "Noraldeen, we love you, Noraldeen, we miss you," and "Princess Noraldeen, we thank you," were some of the expressions Ahiram heard, and he struggled to stay afloat on the waves of maddening sadness toying with his heart.

Gradually, silence fell once more, and all eyes were on him. Slowly, he got up and faced the crowd. He was shocked to see many of the same faces he had seen at the start of the Games of the Mines. *How much has changed in such a short time.*

"I am not one to speak before large crowds," he started hesitantly. "I don't know if I could say anything more than what you heard in that beautiful song. Noraldeen is dead," he said pointing at the pyre, "and so are many of your sons and daughters, husbands and parents. I wish I were the one on the pyre and she were standing here." He let out a nervous chuckle. "At least she would know what to say. She would have said great and wonderful things about me. You would have believed her because you would not have been able to resist her smile, her warmth, and her joy. That is who Noraldeen is. I say *is* because I cannot bring myself to say *was* before you. I don't know if I will ever will."

He wiped tears from his face with the back of his hand and struggled to control his emotions. "You know, Nora meant everything to me. I owe her my life twice over." Ahiram unsheathed his sword and held it high for all to see. "This is El-Windeer's blade. I slew the urkuun with it, and before that, I slew a béghôm. This blade is magnificent, isn't it? Wouldn't you say that Noraldeen is worthy of it? Why is it that she was not the one to bear this sword? She may not be dead if this sword had been in her hands, but this blade answers only to my voice. Why? I don't know." He then noticed Sheheluth standing with the crowd and not with the Silent. She was shaking her head. *Cut it out Ahiram, stop the whining.* This is how Ahiram interpreted her gesture. *They want to hear something great from you, not hear you whine.*

Ahiram sliced the air with the blade. His movement was swift and powerful. The sword sang, and the crowd gasped when they saw a deep purple halo crown the steel as it cut through the night. "El-Windiir called this sword Layaleen, the name of his beloved. Today I, Ahiram, Urkuun Slayer, I declare before you, I shall no longer call this blade Layaleen. I call you Noraldeen." Immediately, the halo blazed a clear, bright blue. Ahiram gasped. *Nora.*

The crowd clapped and cheered.

"Noraldeen has accepted."

"It is the princess. She said *yes*, the princess said yes."

"Noraldeen, Noraldeen!"

Somewhat shaken, Ahiram waited for the crowd to quiet, and moments of silence passed before he spoke again. When he finally lifted his face to the multitude, his posture was different. He no longer looked haggard and sad. He stood tall and resolute, and his tone became harsher, even dangerous. The crowd stiffened. "The urkuun has masters who did not value your lives, the lives of your children, or the life of Noraldeen. These heartless leaders unleashed this horror on us. I swear by Noraldeen that I will not rest until I have avenged her death. Nothing less than their utter destruction will be enough to pay back the precious blood they drew in Tanniin."

The crowd erupted in a sustained applause. *Why did I say that?* he wondered. *I didn't know I was going to say that. Do I wish someone's utter destruction? I'm so confused.*

Keeping his inner turmoil hidden from the crowd, he waited for the applause to quiet down, then sheathed his sword and went to the throne where Lord Orgond was sitting. He knelt before him. Lord Orgond stood, stooped down, and reached for Ahiram, thereby conferring on him the dignity of a prince with all of its privileges.

"Ahiram, you were a slave of Commander Tanios. I, Lord Orgond, declare you now a free man, and raise you to the dignity of a prince of my kingdom." He stood by the Silent and faced the crowd. "People of the mighty Kingdom of Tanniin, I present to you Prince Ahiram."

The crowd stood for Ahiram. He bowed deeply. Then, an Empyrean officer walked over.

"Urkuun Slayer," she said, loud enough for all to hear, "receive this amulet from Her Highness Princess Gaëla Meïr Pen, heiress to the Empress." The pendant was a clear, brilliant diamond tear, two inches long. "This amulet grants you free passage throughout the entire Empyrean Kingdom. You may come and go as you please, a privilege never accorded to any man since the days of El-Windiir the Great."

"Do your eyeing eyes behold what my eyeing eyes are beholding?" whispered Zurwott in the crowd.

"Aye, my brotherly brother and brother most brotherly," replied Orwutt, a quiver in his voice. "A *Séréléna Gléna*, the goddess' tear, one of three such incredibly incredible and incredible in the most incredible exquisitely exquisite jewel."

"Please, convey my gratitude to the princess and assure her I will not set foot on Empyrean soil without her consent."

The officer smiled and nodded. Ahiram had answered in the correct way. All applauded. It was a strange spectacle of joy mixed with sorrow.

Subdued music hung over the camp as the evening went on in solemn celebration. Ahiram spent the evening with Banimelek, Jedarc, and Hiyam. He looked for Sheheluth but could not find her.

"We are sorrowfully sorry for your loss," said Orwutt as he stepped out of the darkness and into full view.

"The sweet bitterness and the bitter sweetness of this bittersweet momentous moment is sweeter than honey and saltier than salted salt," added Zurwott, so shaken that he lost his usual unblemished control over dwarfish grammar. "I am disheartened and ..." unable to continue, he began to sob.

"Thank you," replied Ahiram, visibly touched by the twins' solicitude. "Noraldeen has touched the hearts of many."

"Her victorious victory and victory most victorious," said Orwutt, who when troubled or sad resorted to full dwarfish speech, "shall be memorably remembered and remembered most memorably in the Karangalatad, and a melodious melody shall be sung to her name." He bowed before Ahiram, and he too, began to sob.

This was the highest homage dwarfs could show a stranger. Ahiram looked up and saw Amalseer, the northern star shining brightly. "A new hope is rising," he said softly. "There will be wonders to be remembered in the Karangalatad, but none as momentous as Noraldeen's death."

He was yet to understand these words he had spoken as a Seer.

32. Departure

> "O Silent, do not waver in your friendship, nor take what is given you in vain. Friends who are true are more precious than gold and the strength of a thousand warriors."
> —Book of Lamentation 3:9.

> "Life is never ashamed to dance
> Atop the tombs of the fallen.
> And they, the gentle fallen,
> Do not take umbrage
> When we dance and clap without them."
> —Memoirs of Alkiniöm, the Traveler.

One week later, a small procession reached the port of Tan-Aneer located thirty miles south of Hardeen. Everywhere along the way, the devastation the urkuun had left behind was visible: destroyed villages, ashen trees, decaying rocks, and rotting wildlife. Nothing was spared. Surprisingly though, the port was in relatively good shape. Several vessels resumed the ferrying of passengers to and from Hopp, the port across the thirty-mile-wide channel separating Tanniin from the Kingdom of Mycene.

"Ahiram, are you sure you want to journey alone?" asked Tanios.

"Ahiram let us go with you," pleaded Hiyam. "I know the Temple better than most, I can help reach Baher-Ghafé safely. I know the way."

"No," replied Ahiram firmly. "I cannot bear to lose any more of you." He shook his head and took a deep breath. "I cannot. Maybe you can join me later."

"Take this with you," said the commander handing him a new weapons belt. "Orwutt and Zurwott have looked personally after this one, and they have added a few surprises."

"Thank you, Commander," said Ahiram, grateful. "I have never thanked you properly for all that."

The commander placed both hands on his shoulders and did something that took Ahiram by surprise. He hugged him.

Resuming his forceful stance, he looked at Ahiram and said, "When you find your father, Ahiram, I want you to return to Tanniin with him."

"I will, Commander," replied Ahiram.

As he approached the high priestess, he saw her look at him with such tenderness that he was confused and concerned. He gave her a shy quick look. "Thank you for your help and for the information about my sister," he said hurriedly. He bowed before Master Habael who grabbed him in a hug, and then gave him a blessing.

"Remember, lad, never lose hope. Believe in what Noraldeen has given you. Believe in her choice."

"I will, Master Habael. Thank you for everything."

"When will you return?" asked Banimelek.

"I don't know yet. It may be a while, but I *am* coming back." Banimelek nodded. "Tell Sondra and the rest of the Silent that I will miss them and they should not slack off. When I'm back they'll have to show me some great forms. I'm counting on it."

Sheheluth surprised him, as usual. She gave him a quick hug and whispered. "Don't act surprised when you see me next time. I haven't finished training you yet."

Ahiram smiled. She was cryptic as usual. "Thank you, Sheheluth for everything. I would not have been able to do any of this without you."

"I am not so certain," she said, a frown creasing her forehead. "But never mind that. Watch that temper of yours; do not yield to anger."

"I won't, Sheheluth."

"Hey, do you know what the chicken said to the—"

Ahiram did not let Jedarc finish. He grabbed him by the shoulders and hugged him. Pulling back, he wiped his tears. "Don't you do anything stupid, do you hear me, Jedarc?" he said threateningly. "Don't get yourself killed. If you do, I will travel to the abode of the dead and pull you out so I can yell at you. It won't be pleasant for you, for the dead, or for me. So don't you ever, eve, die on me."

"Don't you worry, Ahiram," answered Jedarc with his usual disarming charm. "I'm as sturdy as an oak."

Ahiram looked away. "I swear Jedarc, I'll prove you right."

"Right? About what?"

"I'll bring back a banana, even if I have to go to the ends of the earth, just to show them you're right. I don't know why they don't believe you, but I do. I always have."

Resolutely, Ahiram walked toward the *Terion*, a two-masted merchant vessel setting sail for Byblos. While slaves in the underbelly began to pull the vessel away from shore, Ahiram stood on the stern, starboard side, and waved to his friends until he could no longer see them. He turned around to the south, saw the immense open sea flowing without boundaries, and knew he was truly gone.

≻ ⁘ ≺

"Master, the Seer has left Tanniin."

Sharr lifted his head and looked at his assistant, Kalibaal. "Very well. Have you alerted Sarand?"

"She knows. Her khoblyss are on their way."

"How did he leave?"

"By ship. He is aboard the Terion, a Quibanxian merchant ship sailing straight to Byblos."

"Surprising. I thought he would have taken greater precaution. Has his grief from the passing of the princess made him so careless?"

"Possibly. We have seen such careless behavior before, have we not?"

"Indeed, we have."

"What do you bid me do?"

"Have a military vessel intercept the Terion. The captain will make this offer to the Seer: The Temple of Baal and all of its power is at his disposal. We will help him find his parents and are prepared to rebuild Baher-Ghafé. Whatever he needs, he can have, including the head of the high priestess who is responsible for the destruction of his village."

"Is what I heard true?"

"It would seem so. She is the bearer of the Seer. From what I have been able to gather, the Seer is unaware of this fact; a weakness we can exploit. If he kills his mother with his own hands, his mind will snap and he will no longer be a threat to the Temple."

"Is that why you agreed to Sarand's plan?"

Sharr nodded. "If Sarand's demons can catch him, all is well. We bring him in, fuel his hatred against the priestess and let him exact revenge."

"If he manages to evade them?"

Sharr sighed and rubbed his forehead. "We will have to consider far more drastic measures. The béghôm and the urkuun were the least dangerous agents of the Spell World we could release. We are now confronted with the possibility of releasing the—"

"No," whispered Kalibaal as he staggered back. "Not him."

"What other choice do we have?"

"I shall speak with Sarand. The khoblyss shall not fail."

"Fine," replied Sharr. "Do what you must."

"How devious are the ways of the gods," said Kalibaal. "To think that all along she hid in the Temple. Shall we exact judgment?"

marada TODAY -483

			-442
-400	-409	-418	-443
-402	-410	-419	-447
-403	-410	-420	-448
-404	-411	-421	-448
-404	-411	-421	-449
-405	-411	-421	-450
-405	-412	-422	-450
			-453

~~* error pg 406 "princes"~~

		-422	-462
		-423	-462
			337
-406	-413	-423	-467
-406	-413	-428	-4MM
-406	-414	-431	-471
-406	-416	-432	-471
-408	-416	-435	-471
-408	-416	-438	-473
-408	-416	-440	-474
-408			

488 [533 Tamri? with an i]
488
489
491
491
501
502
503

[Hiyamt Ahiram were switched ?!?!]

508
510
514
518
520
520
525
529
533

Sharr shook his head. "How did she elude us so well, I wonder? Whoever helped her has used the highest form of magic to keep her from me. I need to know who this is. We will bring Bahiya for questioning. Leave this matter to me. Focus on the Seer. You have three months to subdue him."

"Yes, Master."

The high priest dismissed the priest of the Inner Circle. "Fools, they do not understand what is at stake," he muttered. *If the Seer manages to gather all the Letters of Power, he will open the Pit and release the eternal hatred locked within. An age of darkness such as man has never seen will blanket the earth. This can never be. No matter the cost, this must not be.*

>◦◦◦<

"You called for me, Master Galliöm?"

The head of the tajéruun turned and faced an older tajèr bearing a striking likeness to Ibromaliöm.

"Ah yes, Dariöm, thank for joining me in the vault in person. I know how much you dislike the Arayatian crossing, but this conversation needed to be face-to-face. Please follow me."

The two men left the Hall of Medallions and went into an adjoining small office where they sat facing each other across a small jade desk with twelve small drawers on each side.

"Here," said Galliöm glancing at the door which closed silently on its hinges. "Now, I believe you are Ibromaliöm's cousin, are you not?"

"Indeed, on our mothers' side."

"Have you been informed of the latest news?"

Dariöm nodded. "Ibromaliöm has the *Ithyl Shimea*. The Assassins you sent after him are dead, and Silvaniöm's whereabouts are unknown. The mission was a failure."

"What do you know of the *Ithyl Shimea*, and what do you suppose Ibromaliöm will do next?"

Galliöm respected Dariöm, and more importantly, considered him inoffensive, for he thought the older man was more enamored with knowledge and lore than he was with money.

"What little we know is that a weapon was meant to open up a rift between this world and the Spell World. Whosoever falls in its snares will lose all sense of reality and become obsessed with serving that darkness."

"Didn't Sureï curse it?" asked Galliöm.

"Yes, indeed he has."

"So how can anyone use the *Ithyl Shimea* without feeling the effects of the curse?"

"By transferring the curse to unsuspecting victims, thereby allowing one to peek into its content for short periods of time."

"I suspected as much," said Galliöm wincing. "This explains the bloodied trail Ibromaliöm has left behind. If he continues, he will put the entire order in jeopardy. This cannot be. Tell me, Dariöm, if you were in Ibromaliöm's shoes, what would you do next?"

"I would do everything in my power to acquire the Cup of Eleeje. The Annals of Amrafel states that whoever drinks the water of Eleeje will never fall under the curse of the *Ithyl Shimea*."

"Indeed," said Galliöm smiling. "So we must acquire the Cup before he does."

"This is not possible, Master," said Dariöm calmly. "We have often tried, and so has Baal. None of us can see the Cup, much less obtain it. Only the Seer has this ability."

"Then we are safe," said Galliöm, "for neither will Ibromaliöm be able to see it."

"Not so. If he continues to read the *Ithyl Shimea*—"

"How can he do this, I wonder?" interrupted Galliöm. "Isn't the *Ithyl Shimea* written with the Letters of Power? How can he read it?"

"We do not know, but such high magic must have its own dark ways.

Now, if he has figured out that Tanios' slave is the Seer, he might want to acquire the Cup and—"

"Get the Seer to read the book for him."

"Yes indeed," confirmed Dariöm. "I would have never thought we would be living in such times."

"That may be so, but face it we must. The Temple will hunt the Seer down. Ibromaliöm will try to grab him as well. Others, no doubt, will want his capture as well. Anyone sufficiently versed in magic knows that when the Seer masters the Letters, there will be no one strong enough to oppose him. We catch him now or we are done for."

"What do you propose, then?"

Galliöm sighed. "Our immediate target is Ibromaliöm. We must convince the Seer to quest for the Cup, before Ibromaliöm manages to get his hands on it. We must do so with the greatest of care."

"Well, there is a simple way, Master," said Dariöm imperturbably. "The Candelabrum."

"Give him the Candelabrum you say?" replied Galliöm raising an eyebrow. "How clever, my dear Dariöm, we know the Candelabrum and the Cup are mysteriously connected. One will lead to the other. We give him the Candelabrum, and send him after the Cup. Once he finds it, we recover the Candelabrum, and acquire the Cup. Very well, Dariöm. Take six massrifuun, the Arayatian guardians of the central Tajéruun vault, and guide the Seer to the Cup, then use these." Galliöm opened the sixth drawer in front of him, took three medallions as thin as a serpent's skin, and slid them across the table.

"Vanishing medallions. You wish to send him to the Vanishing Land?"

"In case he proves to be recalcitrant," Galliöm explained.

"But his mind may not survive."

"Better a fool in the Vanishing Land than a free Seer in full possession of the Letters."

"We have never allowed the massrifuun outside of the vault before."

"How else do you propose to capture an Urkuun Slayer?"

"Consider it done."

Captain Zédrigue was already regretting his decision to take the tall man aboard his ship, the *Élégantine*. *Fifty golden diegans are hard to resist*, he reflected. The normal fare from Marsala in Togofalk, to Gilgal of Zemor, was five silver ferrovians, a fraction of a gold diegan.

They had left port only the day before, and already three of his men were dead. The rest of the crew threatened mutiny if he did not lock the mysterious passenger in the ship's jail. Reluctantly, the captain agreed, thinking he may have to return the money back to the traveler. Zédrigue shivered. When the men shackled Ibromaliöm and led him to the jail, the captive gazed at the captain with the eyes of a murderous madman. As he passed him he whispered, "The taste of blood is so sweet and I will have yours and that of your fleet." He chortled a bloodcurdling laugh and began to sing in a chilling tone:

> "To the Kingdom of Marada, to a wonderful Cup,
> A Cup of great delight to feast and sup,
> A Cup to ease the pain of my gnarly bones,
> To turn the heart of men to sand and stones.
> The heart of greedy men who steel my gold,
> And leave me to rot in a prison dark and cold,
> The heart of men who do not know they are fodders
> Soon to lie dead and rotting over their rudders.
> O sweet, sweet book of my delight,
> Together we shall soon take flight
> To the Kingdom of Marada to a wonderful Cup."

The captain shivered. *The sooner we reach Gilgal the better.* He felt the fifty gold diegans nestled in his breast pocket and pressed them against his quickly beating heart.

Wrath of the Urkuun – Departure

Captain Dostron of the *Baal Malaage*, a fast tri-masted military vessel, slammed his cabin door in frustration.

"What is wrong with these priests?" he boomed. "Getting a massive ship such as the Baal Malaage out of port in under two hours is not simple. It cost me the lives of five slaves. I've had to flog twenty of my High Riders for arriving late and now I have to deal with these malcontents. They can't make fools of us like this. I can't wait until Nebo takes control of the Temple and trains some discipline into them."

He paced in angry frustration. This proud Mycenaean could not stomach the humiliation he had just endured. He had intercepted the *Terion*, a commercial ship slower than a drunken slug, and caused its captain to hyperventilate. The High Riders searched the vessel but did not find the Silent they were supposed to lure.

"Inconceivable," eructed Dostron. "I protest!"

➢ ⁕⁕⁕ ➣

"So, the princess has died then?"

"Yes, boss," replied Perit. "Noraldeen died during the Battle of the Urkuun. She tried to stop the monster and he killed her."

Ashod heaved a deep, sad sigh. Perit could see how distressed the former priest was as he peered into the large orb.

"What are your orders, boss?"

"Are you on your way to Byblos?"

"As we speak. We are aboard the Terion. Good ship, good food, though I had a bit of a scare this morning. A fast High Rider's sail accosted us. They were searching for you know who, and the captain was outraged when he didn't find him. Anyway, we will reach Byblos long before you know who shows up."

"Anything else?"

"Yeah, the kid has got a thing to say."

"I'm not a kid," snapped Sheheluth. Perit moved away from the orb.

"He knows Hoda is alive," she added.

"Does he now?"

"Yes. The priestess' daughter told him."

"And you think they should meet?"

"Imperative," replied Sheheluth. "He won't make it otherwise."

"I see," replied Ashod. "Anything else?"

"Yes. Two things. First, someone helped him during the fight."

Ashod tensed. "Are you certain?"

"He is sooo inexperienced, it's painful to watch." she chided. "You were right when you asked me to shadow him. I thought he knew what he was doing, but he has no experience whatsoever in the magical realm. He didn't know how to use the golden tile. Someone helped him to release the energy he needed to defeat his enemy. I dare not say anymore, but I thought you should know."

"This is helpful. What is the second point?"

"I'll continue to shadow him." She locked eyes with Ashod, waiting for him to object or refuse.

"That is one dangerous game you are playing."

Sheheluth smiled a dreamy smile. "We need her. *You* need her." Who she was referring to, she did not say. Ashod did not answer immediately.

Ashod capitulated. "Fine," he said at last. "Perit, you know what to do when you arrive in Byblos?"

"Don't you worry boss, the stew is cookin' as it ought."

"Very well. Sheheluth, stay out of sight and … be careful. I am counting on the both of you."

The orb went dark. Sheheluth went back to the tiny bed and flopped on it. "I was hoping to get properly trained as a Silent and now I'm a fugitive," she said yawning. "Oh well."

Perit chuckled. "As if we have ever been anything but fugitives."

She looked at him with a shrewd smile, closed her eyes and fell asleep.

Wrath of the Urkuun – Departure

➢ ⦁⦁⦁⦁ ≺

Long after the Terion had disappeared over the horizon, after the last ferry between Tanniin and Mycene had moored, a shadow emerged silently from the sea. And like a giant bat, it flew over the Mycenaean shore, landing in a heavily wooded area. Ahiram carefully stowed away the wings, belt, mask, and shoes, and changed into a set of dry Mycenaean clothing he had brought with him. Slowly, he removed a cloth-covered, odd-looking long package from his bag. He unfurled the cloth, revealing an oily leather skin, which he also removed. Three cylindrical pieces of wood fell to the ground. Ahiram grabbed the one that terminated with an iron peg. He unscrewed a leather cover from the other end, revealing a grooved cavity. He slid the sword of El-Windiir between the grooves, hiding two-thirds of the scabbard. He took the second piece of wood, screwed it on top of the sheath into the first.

"Now the sword," he muttered. He slid his blade into the second piece, then took the last section and screwed it on top of the hilt. It locked in place and the three pieces of wood looked like a seamless staff with the sword's elaborate guard resembling a pair of small wings.

"Your swording sword will be visibly visible," Orwutt had told him.

The twin brothers had presented him with this ingenious devise to hide his sword within a staff.

"But that's not a simple staff," objected Ahiram. "It will attract attention, and I don't want any."

"Not by Mycenaean standards," Orwutt had retorted in the common tongue. "Mycene has a thriving community of shepherds and they take great pride in their staffs. You will see."

Shortly thereafter, a young Mycenaean man walked onto the main road linking Hopp to Ezoi, the central port in Mycene. His plan was simple: Head south. He would let the events of the day direct his actions.

"If you need helping help, call on the dwarfs," Orwutt had told him before he left. "They will help you in any way they can. Remember, all the dwarfish resources are at your disposal."

Ahiram smiled. *Spend a diegan to make two diegans. There must be a reason why the dwarfs are being so generous. Still, it's good to know I have allies along the way.*

⊱◈◈◈⊰

Two hundred and fifty miles south, in Parithen, the capital of Mycene, Dariöm and the six giant massrifuuns emerged from the Arayat into the tajéruun's hideout. The tajèr gave the giant creatures a box of medallions.

"Get to work," Dariöm ordered the creatures. "Find him before the agents of Baal do. Galliöm wants this Seer so badly he will go to war with the Temple to capture him. War is profitable only when using someone else's funds, not our own." Covering his head under a thick cloak, he opened the main door. "I'll have a chat with our local spies."

⊱◈◈◈⊰

A thousand miles due east, four cloaked figures crept into the desert. Silent as death, the khoblyss moved like slithering shadows of mist.

"To Mycene we go," whispered one of them.

"His scent is strong," added a second.

Soon they were gone from view, leaving behind a soft trail of decay.

⊱◈◈◈⊰

Farther southwest, a group of Sowasian assassins thundered across the western tundra of the Kingdom of Edfu. Their leader, Jade, had never failed to kill his target. His companions were all experienced assassins, and as their lightning steeds began eating away the distance, a dangerous smile slit his burnished face. *For ten thousand gold diegans, I am ready to kill every person I meet on the road. Ahiram, I am coming for you!*

The hunt for the Seer had just begun.

To Be Continued in

Epic of Ahiram

ಸಿಂಡಿ

Book Three

The Wretched Race

Glossary

Dates in the manuscript follow the American convention of month, day, year. For instance, Tébêt 7, 1197. The majority of the kingdoms used the Babylonian Calendar instituted by the Temple of Baal. A year was three hundred and sixty days in length, subdivided into twelve lunar months of thirty days each. A month had four weeks of seven days named after the seven abodes of the gods the Babylonian magi had seen. The first day of the week was Sin. Tébêt was the tenth month of the year. When adjusted to our solar calendar, Tébêt 7, 1197 fell on Sunday, August 10, 1181, of the Age of the Temple.

Most names have been transliterated from the Common Tongue of the Age of the Temple into English. There are marked differences in pronunciations, indicated below. Two of these bear further explanations. As a rule, the Common Tongue places the emphasis on the last syllable. For instance, an English reader will stress the first 'A' in the name A-hi-ram, but in the Common Tongue, the stress is on the last syllable, "am," a-hee-RAM.

Nouns in the Common Tongue are gendered. A month is masculine, a mountain is feminine, the moon is feminine, and the sun is masculine, etc. I have occulted these differences in the English to avoid unnecessary distractions except in dwarfish speech and in proper names.

The gender of a name in the Common Tongue is embedded in the last syllable and I have striven to preserve this in English, particularly with names whose last syllable contains "ii," "ee," "uu" and "oo." A double "e" and a double "i" are both pronounced like the double *ee* in words such as *sheet* or *meet*. The double "e" is used in feminine names as in Noraldeen and Layaleen, whereas the "ii" is used in masculine names as in "Tanniin" and "Jamiir."

Both "uu" and "oo" should be pronounced as in *moon*, the former in masculine names, such as Urkuun and Aramuun, and the latter in feminine names, such as Foosh and meyroon.

The double "aa" is an exception. The Common Tongue uses it to represent both feminine and masculine names. I have chosen, somewhat arbitrarily, to reserve the "aa" for masculine names, such as Arfaad, and used the accented "â," for feminine names such as Silbarâd. There is no difference in pronunciation between the double "a" and the accented "a."

In certain names of Empyrean, Togofalkian, or Zemorian origins, the "i," "o," or "y" modify the pronunciation of a preceding vowel. In those cases, I have represented these letters with an umlaut because the phonetic transliteration is too unwieldy. For instance, the name of the Empyrean Empress Gaëla Meïr Pen would have been approximately written as "Gahyela Mehyeer Pen."

a	In the table of pronunciation and the glossary, whenever an "a" is pronounced "ah" as in "apple," it will be spelled ă. When it is pronounced as "James" or "May," it will be written ā. For instance, the name *Arfaad* will be phonetically notated as Ărfăăd.
aa, â	Pronounced as a stressed "aah."
ai	Pronounced as in "bray" or "fray."

Wrath of the Urkuun – Glossary

an	Unless otherwise indicated, "an" in the middle of a proper name is pronounced as in "ant," or the French word "enfant," and not as in "Anna" or "Anne."
e	In almost all cases, it is pronounced as in the French article "le" or as the "u" in "burger."
ë	Appears after a vowel only. Pronounced "yeh" as in "yellow" where the "y" is stressed.
ei	Pronounced as in "vein" or "main."
g	Pronounced in all cases as in "group."
gh	No English equivalent. The best we can do is to pronounce it as in the word "ghoul."
h	The "h" is always soft as in "hello."
i	Pronounced as in "he" or "she" and not as in the personal pronoun "I."
ï	Appears after a vowel only. Pronounced as "yee" where the y is stressed.
ii	Stressed "ee" sound.
j	Pronounced as the "s" in "treasure" and not as in "just." In what follows, we use "ĵ" to remind the reader of this alternate pronunciation.
kh	No equivalent in English. It is a harder version of the "gh" in "ghoul."
ö	Appears after a vowel only. Pronounced as "yoh" where the y is stressed.
on	Pronounced as in "monsoon" or "monsieur."
oo	Pronounced as in "cool" or "pool." (Appears in feminine names.)

u	Pronounced as in "pure."
uu	Pronounced as the "oo" in "moon" or "soon." (Appears in masculine names.)

A

Adorant [Ah-do-**rant**] A special order of priestesses of the Temple of Baal whose voices can drive man to madness, despair, or slavery and become puppets in the hands of the priestesses.

Ahiram [Ah-hee-**raam**] Son of Jabbar and Hayat from the town of Baher-Ghafé. A member of the Silent.

Alendiir [Ah-len-**deer**] Nickname Sondra gave to Ahiram. It means 'blazing fire'.

Alkiniöm [Ah-l-**kee**-nee-yom] A famed minstrel who lived toward the end of the Troubled Peace, some fifteen hundred years before the birth of Ahiram.

Allelia [Ah-**lle**-lia] A female Silent and close friend of Sondra.

Alviad [Ah-l-vee-**yad**] A Silent and a close friend of Banimelek.

Amalein [Ah-mah-lein] Lantern of Hope; the name of a star.

Amalseer [Ah-mal-**seer**] Undying Hope; the name of a star.

Amaréya [Ah-ma-réya] Daughter of King Domin of Gordion, heiress to the throne, wife of Corintus and mother of Aquilina.

Amsheet [Ah-m-**sheet**] The city fortress of Tanniin guarding the northeastern boundary.

Andaxil [An-dah-**xeel**] The legendary cave of the southern dwarfish realm, where the greatest treasures of the seven southern tribes are buried. Lost during a major war. Cursed by Sureï.

Aquilina [Akey-**lee**-nah] Daughter of Corintus and Amaréya.

Aramuun [Ah-rah-**moon**] One of the highest peaks of the eastern Tangorian range in Tanniin. The Aramuun soars above nineteen thousand feet. Although 'mountain' is feminine in the Common Tongue, a 'peak' is actually masculine.

Arfaad [Ar-**faad**] Was a captain of the High Riders in the Temple of Baalbek. Promoted as oversee of Tirkalanzibar.

Ashod [Ash-od] Former High Priest of the Temple of Baal. Leader of the Black Robes.

Aylul [Eye-**lool**] The first name of the Empyrean Empress, Aylul Meïr Pen. Aylul can

Wrath of the Urkuun – Glossary

be translated as youthful fall, indicating someone who is young yet wise.

B

Baal Adiir [Baal Ah-**deer**] Highlights the power and omnipotence of Baal.
Baal Adonaï [Baal Ah-do-**nigh**] Baal, my lord.
Baal Essaru [Baal Eh-ss-ah-ru] Baal, Lord of the Dead.
Baal Majaar [Baal Mah-**jaar**] Baal, Lord of the Plenty.
Baal Shamaïm [Baal sh-ah-may-ee-m] Baal, Lord of the Seas.
Baalat Jubeil [Baal-ah-t j-u-b-eil] Lady of Byblos. A deity worshiped in Finikia.
Baher-Ghafé [Bah-hair Gh-**ah**-ff-eh] Coastal village of Finikia. Ahiram's birthplace.
Bahiya [**B**ah-hee-**y**-ah] High Priestess of the Temple of Baalbek. The name means 'comely' and 'beautiful'.
Balid [Bah-**leed**] Carpet merchant. Husband of Foosh, friend of Kwadil. His name means 'slow moving'.
Banimelek [Bah-**nee**-meh-leck] Silent. Friend of Ahiram. His name means 'son of king'.
Bayrul [Bai-**rule**] Great judge of the Games of the Mines who established the modern rules regulating the Games when Ahiram participated.
Beit-Windiir [Bey-t when-**deer**] 'The House of Windiir'. Southern coastal city of Tanniin.
Béghôm [Bay-Gom] Creature of the Arayat.
Bragafâr [Brah-gah-**faar**] Coastal city along the northwestern tip of the southern kingdom of Indolan. Famous for its strange frozen whale.
Byblos [Bee-**bloss**] Finikian coastal city. Closest port to Baher-Ghafé.

C

Cahloon [Ka-h-**loon**] Owner of the most expansive and permanent tent in Tirkalanzibar.
Chesbân [Ch-eh-s-**ban**] Second month of the year. Corresponds roughly to the month of May.
Corialynn [Cor-yah-**leen**] A female Silent.
Corintus [Co-rin-tus] A Solitary. Husband of Amaréya and father of Aquilina.

E

Eleeje [El-**ee**-ĵ] Hidden fountain of Silbarâd located inside Tessarah, the Unseen Tower. Reputed to heal and be a source of life.

Enryl [En-ril] Foremost captain at the service of Orgond, Lord of Amsheet.

F

Faernor [Faey-**nor**] Nickname given to Banimelek by Sondra. It means 'wolf-bear'.
Finikia [Fee-**nee**-kee-ah] Land of Finikia, from where Ahiram hails.
Foosh [F-**oo**-sh] Wife of Balid. Her name means 'to overflow'.
Frajil [Frah- ĵ-**ee**-l] A giant of a man. Warrior. Soloron's brother.

G

Gaëla Meïr Pen [Gah-**yell**-ah Mey-**yeer** Pen] Daughter of the Empyrean Empress. Heir to the throne.
Galliöm [Gah-lee-yom] Head of the Tajéruun.
Garu [**Gah**-roo] Principal judge of the Games.
Gordion [Gor-dion] Capital of the Kingdom of Teshub. Major commercial center.

H

Habael [Hah-bah-el] Gardner at Taniir-The-Strong.
Hardeen [Har-**deen**] Northwestern fortress of Tanniin. Protects the Kingdom against Empyrean incursions.
Haialeen [Hah-yah-**leen**] Primordial pool of life filled with Water of Blessing.
Hawâl [Ha-**waal**] The heart of the Pit where the Lords of the Deep are locked.
Hayat [Ha-**yah**-tt] Ahiram's mother. Her name means 'life'.
Hiyam [Hee-**yam**] Daughter of Bahiya, leader of the team of Baal during the Games of the Mines. Her name means "lost in love."
Hoda [Ho-dah] Ahiram's sister. Her name means 'she who shows the way'.
Hylâz [He-**laa**-z] Judge of the Games of the Mines. His name means 'Pensive'.

I

Ibromaliöm [Ee-bro-**mah**-lium] A judge for the Games of the Mines. Former Tajèr. His name means 'The one who buries poverty'.
Iliand [Eel-yand] Name of the vast northern plain in Tanniin, located between the western fortress of Amsheet and the eastern fortress of Hardeen.
Ithyl Shimea [Ee-thee-l She-meh-yah] A book of power the Temple cannot control.

Wrath of the Urkuun – Glossary

J

Jabbar [Ĵ-ah-bb-**aar**] Ahiram's father. His name means 'mighty'.
Jamiir [Ĵ-ah-**meer**] King of Tanniin. His name means 'burning coal'.
Jedarc [Ĵ-eh-dark] A silent and a friend of Ahiram.

K

Kalibaal [Kah-lee-**baal**] Priest of Baal. Member of the Inner Circle in Babylon. Sharr's right hand man.
Kanmar [Cahn-**maar**] The Lord of the Deep in Indolan. He is Yem, the god of the sea according to the Temple of Baal.
Karadon [Ka-ra-don] Member of the Black Robes. Husband to Hoda, Ahiram's sister.
Karangalatad [Ka-run-gala-tad] The dwarfish grand retelling of the history of the world since the beginning of time.
Kerta [Keir-Tah] Priestly order of the Temple of Baal. Kerta priests provide the Temple with the magical energy required to power the orbs and concentrators.
Khoblyss [kobl-**eess**] Creature of the Arayat. Amplifies the power of a Kerta priest.
Kwadil [Kwah-**deel**] Dwarf. Wealthy merchant. Friend of Balid. Sold Ahiram as a slave to Commander Tanios.

L

Lanudonis [lanu-donis] Capital of Bar-Tanic.
Layaléa [Laya-le-yah] Corintus' wife's full name is Layaléa Amaréya Vermaleen Noor, but she usually goes by the simpler name of Amaréya. Layaléa means 'lovely night'.
Layaleen [Lah-yah-**leen**] The wife of the El-Windiir. Her name means 'starry night'.
Laymeer [Ley-meer] Forest opposite Magdala along the Middle Road in Tanniin. The name means 'gentle refuge.'

M

Magdala [Mag-dala] The forbidden forest opposite Laymeer across the Middle Road in the Temple of Tanniin.
Malikuun [**Mah**-lee-**kuun**] Plural of Malku. The Lords of Light.
Marada [Ma-ra-dah] Plural form of Mâred, which means giant. Marada is the name

of their kingdom and is also the common word used to designate 'giants'.

Massrifuun [Mass-ree-**fuun**] Plural form of Masref, a creature of the Arayat that serves primarily as guardian of the central Tajéruun's vault.

Methodical [Methodical] One of the orders in the Temple of Baal to which Bahiya belongs.

Meyroon [Mey-**roon**] Metal lighter than a feather, harder than the hardest steel, and cannot be cursed nor melted by fire or shattered by the coldest ice.

N

Nebo [neh-beau] A high ranking officer of the High Riders and older brother to Olothe.

Noraldeen [No-rah-l-**deen**] Silent. Friend of Ahiram. Her name means 'shining light.'

O

Olothe [Olo-th] Prince of the dreaded house of Lurca and participant in the Games of Mines.

Ophir [O-feer] Powerful kingdom of the far south and one of the few kingdoms outside the control of the Temple of Baal.

Orgond [Or-gond] Lord of the fortress of Amsheet and father to Noraldeen.

Orwutt [Or-wutt] Dwarf, twin brother to Zurwott and nephew of Kwadil.

R

Raayiil [Raa-**yeel**] A creature of the spell world. It appears as a composite of a dream, a vision and a prophecy, and takes complete control of the human mind.

Ramany [Rah-**mah**-nee] A judge for the Games of the Mines.

Ramel [Rah-mel] Queen of Tanniin. Sharr's niece.

Rastoop [Rass-toop] Wealthy capital of the kingdom of Mitani.

S W

Sarand [Sar-und] The Soloist, leader of the dreaded order of the Adorants; an order of singers in the Temple of Baal whose magic lies in their voices.

Sharr [Sh-ar] High Priest of the Temple of Babylon and the ultimate authority of the entire Temple order of Baal. His name means 'fire'.

Sheheluth [Sheh-he-luth] A young female Silent.

Shogol [Sho-goal] A priestly order of Baal. Shogols are herders of spells. They are responsible for the care and feed of the spells and curses the Temple grows in the Arayat.

Slippery-Slued [Slippery sluud] A thief well known for his daring operations. He is wanted by the Temple and the Tajéruun for several high profile thefts.

Soloron [Saul-oron] The leader of the Undergrounder and the older brother to Frajil.

Sondra [Son-drah] A Silent.

Sureï [Su-ray] The greatest sorcerer the Temple has known.

T

Tajèr [**Tah-ĵ**-eh-r] The name of the first Zakiir, who thought to profit from the accumulated knowledge. His name came to mean 'merchant'.

Tajéruun [Tah-ĵ-eh-**ruun**] Plural of Tajèr.

Tamri [Tah-mry] An Adorant and a friend to Bahiya.

Taniir [Ta-**neer**] The name of the legendary castle in Tanniin built by El-Windiir (Taniir-On-High) and the name of the city where, currently, King Jamiir reigns. The name means 'To light'.

Tanios [Ta-nios] Commander of the Silent

Tanniin Ashod [Ta-neen **Ah**-shod] The greatest of all dragons, known as Daron Ashod among the dwarfs and as Black Dragon by the Empyreans.

Tébêt [**Teh**-bet] Lunar month corresponding roughly to the month of January.

Thermodon [ther-mo-don] A Kingdom of loosely federated tribes located north of Tanniin

Théleos [Teh-leh-os] God-crusher, which is what Sheheluth calls Ahiram.

Tinantel [Tea-nan-tell] A nickname Sondra gave to Jedarc. Tinantel means 'light foot.'

Tirkalanzibar [Tirka-lan-zee-bar] City of Tent. Located in the kingdom of Uratu, at the edge of the Great Desert, this city serves as a caravans' hub.

Tyrulan [Tea-rule-lan] An Empyrean child's game and the name Aquilina gave to the strange world she alone visits.

U

Urkuun [Ur-**kuun**] Creature of the spell world of incredible power. Cannot be defeated by natural means.

Uziguzi Aor Jar [Uzee-guzee Awor- ĵar] Councilor to the Empyrean Empress Aylul Meïr Pen.

Z

Zakiir [Zah-**keer**] A man whose sole purpose in life is to consign to memory the secrets of others.

Zakiruun [**Zah**-kee-**ruun**] Plural of Zakiir.

Zaril Andali [Zah-**reel** An-dah-lee] A mythical bird in Tanniin whose blue wings are the source of blue skies. Its feast is celebrated at the winter equinox to ward off the bad spirits of the night.

About the Author

Michael Joseph Murano is the author's pen name. Michael began writing at the age of sixteen and never stopped since. The curious fact that he delayed the publication of his first novel until now is a story too long to tell. Suffice it to say that Michael has written the ten books of the Epic of Ahiram over a period of fourteen years, with the initial intention to enchant his seven children by reading to them evening after evening.

Michael has written, in French and English, numerous plays, children's books, a collection of poems for his wife, and a series of audio stories he continues to record for his two youngest daughters.

Michael's blog, www.epicofahiram.com is a portal unto the rich world of Ahiram. He invites you to join him there and discover the epic of the slave, born to be a hero.

Made in the USA
Charleston, SC
19 October 2015